Praise for
The Mammoth Book of Vampire Stories by Women

Nominated for the 2002 World Fantasy Award
Nominated for the 2002 British Fantasy Award
Nominated for the 2001 International Horror Guild Award

"British horror maven Jones has assembled an impressive volume packed with period classics and fresh takes before and after the 21st century . . . this is a robust anthology sure to satisfy even the most jaded blood thirst."
—*Publishers Weekly* (Starred Review)

"Broad in scope and very lively . . . Fun, ghoulish stuff."
—*Booklist*

"Jones, King of the Horror Editors, opens the lid on the first-ever collection of vampire stories by women."
—*Kirkus*

"If there could be like, a King of Anthology Editors, it would be Stephen Jones . . . no one knows how to put together a great combination of short literature like Jones. He's like a really good DJ, except of stories, not music."
—*Vampires.com*

"Jones performs his usual exemplary job in this massive volume."
—*Starlog (UK)*

"This is a superb collection of vampire stories."
—*Bite Me*

T0072705

THE MAMMOTH BOOK OF VAMPIRE STORIES BY WOMEN

EDITED BY
STEPHEN JONES
INTRODUCTION BY INGRID PITT

Skyhorse Publishing
A Herman Graf Book

Library of Congress Cataloging-in-Publication Data is available on file.

Cover design by Erin Seaward-Hiatt
Cover photo credit: iStockphoto

Print ISBN: 978-1-5107-2383-2
Ebook ISBN: 978-1-5107-2384-9

Printed in the United States of America

Contents

In memory of all the wonderful women
who contributed to this anthology
who are no longer among us.

Introduction: My Life Among the Undead

Ingrid Pitt

THE SNOW WAS streaming horizontally along London's Wardour Street as I quit the taxi and cautiously picked my way across the deep slush on the pavement. I had spent quite a lot of time deciding to make the trip and, even now, standing in the shelter of the doorway of Hammer House, I was not sure that the choice had been right.

After all, I had just made a major epic with MGM and it seemed like a step backward to be considering a cheapo film in the horror genre. I was sure that neither Richard Burton nor Clint Eastwood, with whom I had appeared in *Where Eagles Dare*, would have considered it for a moment.

I shrugged off the snow and pushed open the door. Who was I trying to kid? Okay, so *Where Eagles Dare* was great; but since wrapping on that—zilch. It was time to move on. Capitalize on the great publicity I was getting and do something positive.

I ran up the short flight of stairs to the inner door and went through.

The previous evening I had been at an after-premiere party for *Alfred the Great* and had sat beside Sir James Carreras, the head of Hammer Productions. He told me he was looking for an actress to play the lead in a new vampire film he was making, and asked me if I was interested. I decided to drop the cool pose and looked interested.

And that was why I had braved the snowstorm and was now standing outside his office, dressed to kill and still wondering if I was doing the right thing.

Jimmy was great. He made it sound as if I would be doing him a favor if I took the job. I dimpled prettily and said I would speak to my agent, but we both knew that I was well and truly hooked.

The film was called *The Vampire Lovers*, and it was scripted by Tudor Gates from J. Sheridan Le Fanu's century-old story "Carmilla."

It was one of the happiest productions I have ever worked on. Hammer Films were well known for the sense of camaraderie they fostered, and *The Vampire Lovers* was no exception.

However, at times it did get a little out of hand.

The two producers, Harry Fine and Michael Style, always made sure that they were around when an "interesting" scene was about to be shot. Madeleine Smith and I shared a bedroom scene that could be uncomfortable if it was not approached in the right frame of mind. Neither of us had ever been photographed in the nude before, so we asked Jimmy to call Harry and Michael up to London on some pretext.

I was walking along a corridor at Elstree Studios, wearing only a dressing gown for the scene, when I saw the producers approaching. They looked so unhappy that I could not resist the urge to cheer them up. As we drew level, I threw open the robe! Their step was definitely lighter as they walked on.

One of the best scenes I have ever seen in a vampire film occurs toward the end of *The Vampire Lovers*. Carmilla, now exposed for what she is and hunted by the avenging vampire hunter General von Spielsdorf (Peter Cushing), hurries back to her graveyard tomb. The gravestones stand out as black monoliths in a moonlit miasma. Carmilla, dressed in a diaphanous white shift, floats through the cemetery no more substantial than the mist that surrounds her.

The atmosphere, at times, was very spooky. But with six young women on the set, it got a little frenetic. It was easy to get a fit of the giggles and hold up shooting. Roy Ward Baker, the director, was marvelous. He would wait patiently until everyone had control of themselves, then carry on as if nobody had been rolling around on the floor hooting with laughter.

One particular scene took a lot of work to get "in the can." I was supposed to bite Kate O'Mara. Kate is usually in control, but once she goes— she goes. Although my fangs had been specially fitted by a dentist, they did not fit as well as they might have. I had this big struggle with Kate, and my incisors decided to desert my mouth for the more enticing depths of Kate's cleavage. Of course, all the men on set gallantly jumped forward to retrieve them! Kate started to go. I was too concerned with my wayward teeth to be affected at first.

We tried the scene again. My teeth headed for Kate's cleavage like a rabbit down a hole. Kate "corpsed." Everybody tried to keep their cool. Kate managed to simmer down. And, would you believe it, those rotten teeth headed for their new home yet again. This time Kate freaked out with everybody else on the set.

All I got was mad. I noticed one of the grips chewing gum. I called him over, took his gum, and jammed the fangs back into my mouth using the gum as a suction-pad. Success. But Kate and the rest of the crew were hooting away even more frenetically by then. That finished work for the day. By that time, even I was rolling around in fits of hysteria.

The next day I made sure that my teeth were secure. And everybody made sure that they did not make eye contact with anyone else. That way led to disaster.

Overall, though, it was a wonderful introduction to the world of the vampire and Gothic overkill.

As we were finishing *The Vampire Lovers*, I heard that Hammer was setting up another film, called *Countess Dracula*. It was going to be a big, lavish production and the lead character seemed to be right up my street: a 16th-century serial killer called Countess Erzsebet Bathory.

I had also heard that Diana Rigg was up for the part. I could not have that, so I cornered Jimmy Carreras and made him promise to give me a chance.

There were also a couple of other vampire films in the early stages of development at Hammer: *Lust for a Vampire* and *Twins of Evil*. I read the first-draft scripts. The Carmilla character had another outing, but the part was a tag-on rather than the central role, and that made me even more determined to get the part of Erzsebet Bathory.

I do not know what happened, but one day Jimmy called me into his office and told me that I was to play Bathory.

Unfortunately, *Countess Dracula* was not quite the happiness factory that *The Vampire Lovers* had been. For one thing, the management had come to the conclusion that Hammer was in a battle for survival that it would be hard to win. To try and counter this, they had bought up the sets and many of the costumes from the historical film *Anne of the Thousand Days*. This was to give the production an unaccustomed gloss.

The director, Peter Sasdy, was not at all happy with the title. It was exploitative, and he was not making a vampire film. He wanted a title with more resonance. This caused big arguments on set with the producer, Alexander Paal.

However, there were still the odd moments of light relief. When Sandor Elès, my co-star, was building up to have his wicked way with me in the hay, I looked at his face and shouted, "*Cut!*" This did not go down well with the frazzle-nerved Sasdy, and he shouted at me that he was the one who said when to say "cut." I did not care, because I was having a fit of the giggles. I pointed to Sandor's face. Half of his false mustache was missing.

A thorough search was made, but it seems that it is as hard to find half a mustache in a haystack as a needle. I went off to my dressing room and levered myself out of the heavy skirt I was wearing. Then in the mirror I noticed something obscene crawling out of my navel. I gave a high-pitched scream, whacked at it with my corset, and leapt onto the bunk.

My dresser came running. I explained that I had been invested with something Satanic and pointed hysterically to where I had seen the alien item disappear. She bent down and held the hairy object up to the light. It was the missing half of Sandor's mustache!

The Vampire Lovers and *Countess Dracula* have since become classics of the genre, and I am glad that I braved that cold December morning to meet with Jimmy Carreras.

I did one more outing as a vampire. This was in the Amicus film *The House That Dripped Blood* with Jon Pertwee. Originally it was going to be a straight horror film, but Jon just worked on director Peter Duffell until he rejigged the script (by horror writer Robert Bloch) and made it into a comedy. I think the film benefited from it.

Although 'The Cloak' episode in which I appeared was a comedy, it was played out against a background that was surprisingly real. The coffin in the cellar, where my character Carla was supposed to pass the daylight hours, was the real McCoy. We were shooting a scene when a break for lunch was called. I was lying in the coffin, waiting for the scene where I reared up, fangs exposed, and frightened the life and juice out of a nasty police inspector. The crew thought it would be a splendid wheeze to leave me there.

After a while I cottoned on to the fact that I had been in the coffin a long time and there was no sound of movement getting through to me. I tried pushing the lid up. No go. I tried banging on the sides. Still no reaction.

It is amazing the thoughts that go through your mind at a time like that. The scenario I was looking at was some sort of catastrophe had overtaken the crew and they were all lying around the set in various dramatic attitudes of death. For a moment I panicked, scrabbled at the lid. Then reason cut in and I guessed what had happened. A typical film set prank.

But I was not having that. I settled down to wait. A couple of times the death scenario tried to kick in, but I still was not having any of it. When I at last heard some movement beyond the confining walls of my coffin, I pretended to be asleep. As the lid was lifted, I opened my eyes, gave an exaggerated yawn, and innocently asked what was happening! I think I pulled it off.

On a recent visit to the homeland of that old rogue Dracula, I had a disturbing experience. I thought that the inhabitants of Transylvania would be thrilled that their top export had been acknowledged as one of the most familiar icons of the cinema.

Not only was I wrong, but some of the denizens of darkest Sighișoara (the birthplace of Vlad the Impaler, also known as Dracula—son of Dracul) were positively hostile to the notion that their heroic Vlad had anything to do with the incarnation of the fictional Dracula. Why they are so opposed to the idea that Bram Stoker's version of the vampire is something to be ashamed of is hard to nail down. In many ways, the nattily-dressed and be-cloaked film star has much to offer a country still tethered by their communist past to a lifestyle not so different from that described by Stoker.

The vampire, of course, was not a creature conjured up in the 19th century. Before it was spruced up and introduced into the British drawing room it had ranged through history in a number of gruesome disguises, but always with its trademark calling card—the drinking of the victim's blood or essence. The vampires of Anne Rice hark back to the days of the Pharaohs, and maybe beyond. They are sophisticated beings who have found themselves a steady food source and live out their tainted existence accordingly.

Until recently, I thought that vampires had been thought up to suit the predilections of the top-hatted, child-molesting, wife-beating, power-crazed males of the 1800s. I was surprised to discover that nearly every country and culture had a variation on the theme of the vampire.

As the vampire became a literary property, its creator was acknowledged as the mad-bad Lord Byron. He only wrote a fragment of a story, but his physician-come-drug pusher, John Polidori, after an acrimonious bust-up with the fractious peer, left his employ, taking the document with him. Polidori himself took up the Gothic theme and substantially rewrote his former employer's story into what was to become the first classic vampire tale. *The Vampyre: A Tale* was issued in 1819 by London publisher Sherwood, Neely, and Jones who originally—and incorrectly—attributed the story to Byron. But Byron's involvement with the genesis of Polidori's story ensured that the vampire stepped straight out of the tomb and into society.

Now I am delighted to find myself introducing this new collection of superior vampire stories, written by talented women from diverse cultures and backgrounds. However, fashions change, and the urbane vampire created by Byron and cemented in place by Stoker has had to move on.

There are now New Age vampires aplenty, waiting in the shadows, just out of sight, ready to slither forth and seek new victims.

Are you, like me, ready for the new dusk . . . ?

—Ingrid Pitt
London, England

THE MASTER OF RAMPLING GATE

Anne Rice

For many years, Anne O'Brien Rice was the horror genre's female equivalent to Stephen King. A publishing phenomenon in her own right, having sold around one hundred million copies, she began her acclaimed Vampire Chronicles series in 1976 with the novel *Interview with the Vampire*. Responsible for creating a huge resurgence in the popularity of the undead, the book introduced readers to her sexually powerful bloodsucker, Lestat de Lioncourt.

Described as "the undisputed queen of vampire literature," she followed it with a string of best-selling sequels and spin-offs, including *The Vampire Lestat*, *The Queen of the Damned*, *The Tale of the Body Thief*, *Memnoch the Devil*, *Pandora*, *The Vampire Armand*, *Vittorio the Vampire*, *Merrick*, *Blood and Gold*, *Blackwood Farm*, *Blood Caticle*, and *Prince Lestat*.

Her other genre novels include the Lives of the Mayfair Witches trilogy (*The Witching Hour*, *Lasher* and *Taltos*), The Wolf Gift Chronicles (*The Wolf Gift* and *The Wolves of Midwinter*), *The Mummy or Ramses the Damned*, *Servant of the Bones*, and *Violin*. More recently, her Songs of the Seraphim series has so far included *Angel Time* and *Of Love and Evil*. She has also published a number of erotic novels under the pseudonyms "Anne Rampling" and "A.N. Roquelaure."

As with King, a mini-industry of nonfiction books has grown up around her work. Among the most prolific is Katherine Ramsland, whose biography of the author, *Prism of the Night*, appeared in 1991. She has since followed it with such titles as *The Vampire Companion*, *The Witches' Companion*, *The Anne Rice Trivia Book*, and *The Anne Rice Reader*. Rice's life before she became a writer was profiled in the 1993 BBC-TV documentary, *Bookmark: The Vampire's Life*, and the following year she was awarded the World Horror Convention's Grand Master Award.

Interview with the Vampire: The Vampire Chronicles was filmed in 1994 by Neil Jordan with an all-star cast that included Brad Pitt, Antonio Banderas, Christian Slater, and Tom Cruise as Lestat. It was followed by *Queen of the Damned* (2002), featuring Stuart Townsend as the undead antihero. The character has also turned up in a 2006 Broadway stage musical with music by Elton John and Bernie Taupin, and various comic-book series.

"You know, I was not a person who was obsessed with vampires," reveals Rice, "or who had pictures of them around the house. I hadn't seen any vampire movies in recent years, so it didn't grow out of any active obsession with them. It just happened that when I started to write through that image, everything came together for me. I was suddenly able to talk about reality by using fantasy."

The following tale is the author's only vampire short story, originally published in *Redbook* in 1984 and adapted into graphic format as a one-shot publication by Innovation Comics in 1991 . . .

SPRING 1888.

Rampling Gate. It was so real to us in the old pictures, rising like a fairy-tale castle out of its own dark wood. A wilderness of gables and chimneys between those two immense towers, gray stone walls mantled in ivy, mullioned windows reflecting the drifting clouds.

But why had Father never taken us there? And why, on his deathbed, had he told my brother that Rampling Gate must be torn down, stone by stone? "I should have done it, Richard," he said. "But I was born in that house, as my father was, and his father before him. You must do it now, Richard. It has no claim on you. Tear it down."

Was it any wonder that not two months after Father's passing, Richard and I were on the noon train headed south for the mysterious mansion that had stood upon the rise above the village of Rampling for four hundred years? Surely Father would have understood. How could we destroy the old place when we had never seen it?

But, as the train moved slowly through the outskirts of London I can't say we were very sure of ourselves, no matter how curious and excited we were.

Richard had just finished four years at Oxford. Two whirlwind social seasons in London had proved me something of a shy success. I still preferred scribbling poems and stories in my room to dancing the night away, but I'd kept that a good secret. And though we had lost our mother when we were little, Father had given us the best of everything. Now the carefree years were ended. We had to be independent and wise.

The evening before, we had pored over all the old pictures of Rampling Gate, recalling in hushed, tentative voices the night Father had taken those pictures down from the walls.

I couldn't have been more than six and Richard eight when it happened, yet we remembered well the strange incident in Victoria Station that had precipitated Father's uncharacteristic rage. We had gone there after supper to say farewell to a school friend of Richard's, and Father had caught a glimpse, quite unexpectedly, of a young man at the lighted window of an incoming train. I could remember the young man's face clearly to this day: remarkably handsome, with a head of lustrous brown hair, his large black eyes regarding Father with the saddest expression as Father drew back. "Unspeakable horror!" Father had whispered. Richard and I had been too amazed to speak a word.

Later that night, Father and Mother quarreled, and we crept out of our rooms to listen on the stairs.

"That he should dare to come to London!" Father said over and over. "Is it not enough for him to be the undisputed master of Rampling Gate?"

How we puzzled over it as little ones! Who was this stranger, and how could he be master of a house that belonged to our father, a house that had been left in the care of an old, blind housekeeper for years?

But now after looking at the pictures again, it was too dreadful to think of Father's exhortation. And too exhilarating to think of the house itself. I'd packed my manuscripts, for—who knew?—maybe in that melancholy and exquisite setting I'd find exactly the inspiration I needed for the story I'd been writing in my head.

Yet there was something almost illicit about the excitement I felt. I saw in my mind's eye the pale young man again, with his black greatcoat and red woolen cravat.

Like bone china, his complexion had been. Strange to remember so vividly. And I realized now that in those few remarkable moments, he had created for me an ideal of masculine beauty that I had never questioned since. But Father had been so angry. I felt an unmistakable pang of guilt.

It was late afternoon when the old trap carried us up the gentle slope from the little railway station and we had our first real look at the house. The sky had paled to a deep rose hue beyond a bank of softly gilded clouds, and the last rays of the sun struck the uppermost panes of the leaded windows and filled them with solid gold.

"Oh, but it's too majestic," I whispered, "too like a great cathedral, and to think that it belongs to us!"

Richard gave me the smallest kiss on the cheek.

I wanted with all my heart to jump down from the trap and draw near on foot, letting those towers slowly grow larger and larger above me, but our old horse was gaining speed.

When we reached the massive front door Richard and I were spirited into the great hall by the tiny figure of the blind housekeeper Mrs. Blessington, our footfalls echoing loudly on the marble tile, and our eyes dazzled by the dusty shafts of light that fell on the long oak table and its heavily carved chairs, on the somber tapestries that stirred ever so slightly against the soaring walls.

"Richard, it is an enchanted place!" I cried, unable to contain myself.

Mrs. Blessington laughed gaily, her dry hand closing tightly on mine.

We found our bedchambers well aired, with snow-white linen on the beds and fires blazing cozily on the hearths. The small, diamond-paned windows opened on a glorious view of the lake and the oaks that enclosed it and the few scattered lights that marked the village beyond.

That night we laughed like children as we supped at the great oak table, our candles giving only a feeble light. And afterward we had a fierce battle of pocket billiards in the games room and a little too much brandy, I fear.

It was just before I went to bed that I asked Mrs. Blessington if there had been anyone in this house since my father left it, years before.

"No, my dear," she said quickly, fluffing the feather pillows. "When your father went away to Oxford, he never came back."

"There was never a young intruder after that . . .?" I pressed her, though in truth I had little appetite for anything that would disturb the happiness I felt. How I loved the Spartan cleanliness of this bedchamber, the walls bare of paper and ornament, the high luster of the walnut-paneled bed.

"A young intruder?" With an unerring certainty about her surroundings, she lifted the poker and stirred the fire. "No, dear. Whatever made you think there was?"

"Are there no ghost stories, Mrs. Blessington?" I asked suddenly, startling myself. *Unspeakable horror.* But what was I thinking—that that young man had not been real?

"Oh, no, darling," she said, smiling. "No ghost would ever dare to trouble Rampling Gate."

Nothing, in fact, troubled the serenity of the days that followed—long walks through the overgrown gardens, trips in the little skiff to and fro across the lake, tea under the hot glass of the empty conservatory. Early evening found us reading and writing by the library fire.

All our inquiries in the village met with the same answers: the villagers cherished the house. There was not a single disquieting legend or tale.

How were we going to tell them of Father's edict? How were we going to remind ourselves?

Richard was finding a wealth of classical material on the library shelves and I had the desk in the corner entirely to myself.

Never had I known such quiet. It seemed the atmosphere of Rampling Gate permeated my simplest written descriptions and wove its way richly into the plots and characters I created. The Monday after our arrival I finished my first real short story, and after copying out a fresh draft, I went off to the village on foot to post it boldly to the editors of *Blackwood's* magazine.

It was a warm afternoon, and I took my time as I came back. What had disturbed our father so about this lovely corner of England? What had so darkened his last hours that he laid his curse upon this spot? My heart opened to this unearthly stillness, to an indisputable magnificence that caused me utterly to forget myself. There were times here when I felt I was a disembodied intellect drifting through a fathomless silence, up and down garden paths and stone corridors that had witnessed too much to take cognizance of one small and fragile young woman who in random moments actually talked aloud to the suits of armor around her, to the broken statues in the garden, the fountain cherubs who had had no water to pour from their conches for years and years.

But was there in this loveliness some malignant force that was eluding us still, some untold story? *Unspeakable horror* . . . Even in the flood of brilliant sunlight, those words gave me a chill.

As I came slowly up the slope I saw Richard walking lazily along the uneven shore of the lake. Now and then he glanced up at the distant battlements, his expression dreamy, almost blissfully contented.

Rampling Gate had him. And I understood perfectly because it also had me.

With a new sense of determination I went to him and placed my hand gently on his arm.

For a moment he looked at me as if he did not even know me, and then he said softly, "How will I ever do it, Julie? And one way or the other, it will be on my conscience all my life."

"It's time to seek advice, Richard," I said. "Write to our lawyers in London. Write to Father's clergyman, Doctor Matthews. Explain everything. We cannot do this alone."

It was three o'clock in the morning when I opened my eyes. But I had been awake for a long time. And I felt not fear, lying there alone, but something else—some vague and relentless agitation, some sense of emptiness and need that caused me finally to rise from my bed. What was this house, really? A place, or merely a state of mind? What was it doing to my soul?

I felt overwhelmed, yet shut out of some great and dazzling secret. Driven by an unbearable restlessness, I pulled on my woolen wrapper and my slippers and went into the hall.

The moonlight fell full on the oak stairway, and the vestibule far below. Maybe I could write of the confusion I suffered now, put on paper the inexplicable longing I felt. Certainly it was worth the effort, and I made my way soundlessly down the steps.

The great hall gaped before me, the moonlight here and there touching upon a pair of crossed swords or a mounted shield. But far beyond, in the alcove just outside the library, I saw the uneven glow of the fire. So Richard was there. A sense of well-being pervaded me and quieted me. At the same time, the distance between us seemed endless and I became desperate to cross it, hurrying past the long supper table and finally into the alcove before the library doors.

The fire blazed beneath the stone mantelpiece and a figure sat in the leather chair before it, bent over a loose collection of pages that he held in his slender hands. He was reading the pages eagerly, and the fire suffused his face with a warm, golden light.

But it was not Richard. It was the same young man I had seen on the train in Victoria Station fifteen years ago. And not a single aspect of that taut young face had changed. There was the very same hair, thick and lustrous and only carelessly combed as it hung to the collar of his black coat, and those dark eyes that looked up suddenly and fixed me with a most curious expression as I almost screamed.

We stared at each other across that shadowy room, I stranded in the doorway, he visibly and undeniably shaken that I had caught him unawares. My heart stopped.

And in a split second he rose and moved toward me, closing the gap between us, reaching out with those slender white hands.

"Julie!" he whispered, in a voice so low that it seemed my own thoughts were speaking to me. But this was no dream. He was holding me and the scream had broken loose from me, deafening, uncontrollable and echoing from the four walls.

I was alone. Clutching at the doorframe, I staggered forward, and then in a moment of perfect clarity I saw the young stranger again, saw him standing in the open door to the garden, looking back over his shoulder; then he was gone.

I could not stop screaming. I could not stop even as I heard Richard's voice calling me, heard his feet pound down that broad, hollow staircase and through the great hall. I could not stop even as he shook me, pleaded with me, settled me in a chair.

Finally I managed to describe what I had seen.

"But you know who it was!" I said almost hysterically. "It was he—the young man from the train!"

"Now, wait," Richard said. "He had his back to the fire, Julie. And you could not see his face clearly—"

"Richard, it was he! Don't you understand? He touched me. He called me Julie," I whispered. "Good God, Richard, look at the fire. I didn't light it—he did. He was here!"

All but pushing Richard out of the way, I went to the heap of papers that lay strewn on the carpet before the hearth. "My story . . ." I whispered, snatching up the pages. "He's been reading my story, Richard. And—dear God—he's read your letters, the letters to Mr. Partridge and Dr. Matthews, about tearing down the house!"

"Surely you don't believe it was the same man, Julie, after all these years . . .?"

"But he has not changed, Richard, not in the smallest detail. There is no mistake, I tell you. It was the very same man!"

The next day was the most trying since we had come. Together we commenced a search of the house. Darkness found us only half-finished, frustrated everywhere by locked doors we could not open and old staircases that were not safe.

And it was also quite clear by suppertime that Richard did not believe I had seen anyone in the study at all. As for the fire—well, he had failed to put it out properly before going to bed; and the pages—well, one of us had put them there and forgotten them, of course . . .

But I knew what I had seen.

And what obsessed me more than anything else was the gentle countenance of the mysterious man I had glimpsed, the innocent eyes that had fixed on me for one moment before I screamed.

"You would be wise to do one very important thing before you retire," I said crossly. "Leave out a note to the effect that you do not intend to tear down the house."

"Julie, you have created an impossible dilemma," Richard declared, the color rising in his face. "You insist we reassure this apparition that the house will not be destroyed, when in fact you verify the existence of the very creature that drove our father to say what he did."

"Oh, I wish I had never come here!" I burst out suddenly.

"Then we should go, and decide this matter at home."

"No—that's just it. I could never go without knowing. I could never go on living with knowing now!"

Anger must be an excellent antidote to fear, for surely something worked to alleviate my natural alarm. I did not undress that night, but rather sat in the darkened bedroom, gazing at the small square of diamond-paned window until I heard the house fall quiet. When the grandfather clock in the great hall chimed the hour of eleven, Rampling Gate was, as usual, fast asleep.

I felt a dark exultation as I imagined myself going out of the room and down the stairs. But I knew I should wait one more hour. I should let the night reach its peak. My heart was beating too fast, and dreamily I recollected the face I had seen, the voice that had said my name.

Why did it seem in retrospect so intimate, that we had known each other before, spoken together a thousand times? Was it because he had read my story, those words that came from my very soul?

"Who are you?" I believe I whispered aloud. "Where are you at this moment?" I uttered the word, "Come."

The door opened without a sound and he was standing there. He was dressed exactly as he had been the night before and his dark eyes were riveted on me with that same obvious curiosity, his mouth just a little slack, like that of a boy.

I sat forward, and he raised his finger as if to reassure me and gave a little nod.

"Ah, it is you!" I whispered.

"Yes," he said in a soft, unobtrusive voice.

"And you are not a spirit!" I looked at his mud-splattered boots, at the faintest smear of dust on that perfect white cheek.

"A spirit?" he asked almost mournfully. "Would that I were that."

Dazed, I watched him come toward me; the room darkened and I felt his cool, silken hands on my face. I had risen. I was standing before him, and I looked up into his eyes.

I heard my own heartbeat. I heard it as I had the night before, right at the moment I had screamed. Dear God, I was talking to him! He was in my room and I was talking to him! And then suddenly I was in his arms.

"Real, absolutely real!" I whispered, and a low, zinging sensation coursed through me so that I had to steady myself.

He was peering at me as if trying to comprehend something terribly important. His lips had a ruddy look to them, a soft look for all his handsomeness, as if he had never been kissed. A slight dizziness came over me, a slight confusion in which I was not at all sure that he was even there.

"Oh, but I am," he said, as if I had spoken my doubt. I felt his breath against my cheek, and it was almost sweet. "I am here, and I have watched you ever since you came."

"Yes . . ."

My eyes were closing. In a dim flash, as of a match being struck, I saw my father, heard his voice. *No, Julie . . .* But that was surely a dream.

"Only a little kiss," said the voice of the one who was really here. I felt his lips against my neck. "I would never harm you. No harm ever for the children of this house. Just the little kiss, Julie, and the understanding that it imparts, that you cannot destroy Rampling Gate, Julie—that you can never, never drive me away."

The core of my being, that secret place where all desires and all commandments are nurtured, opened to him without a struggle or a sound. I would have fallen if he had not held me. My arms closed about him, my hands slipping into the soft, silken mass of his hair.

I was floating, and there was, as there had always been at Rampling Gate, an endless peace. It was Rampling Gate I felt enclosing me; it was that timeless and impenetrable secret that had opened itself at last . . . *A power within me of enormous ken . . . To see as a god sees, and take the depth of things as nimbly as the outward eyes can size and shape pervade* . . . Yes, those very words from Keats, which I had quoted in the pages of my story that he had read.

But in a violent instant he had released me. "Too innocent," he whispered.

I went reeling across the bedroom floor and caught hold of the frame of the window. I rested my forehead against the stone wall.

There was a tingling pain in my throat where his lips had touched me that was almost pleasurable, a delicious throbbing that would not stop. I knew what he was!

I turned and saw all the room clearly—the bed, the fireplace, the chair. And he stood still exactly as I'd left him and there was the most appalling anguish in his face.

"Something of menace, unspeakable menace," I whispered, backing away.

"Something ancient, something that defies understanding," he pleaded. "Something that can and will go on." But he was shaken and he would not look into my eyes.

I touched that pulsing pain with the tips of my fingers and, looking down at them, saw the blood. "Vampire!" I gasped. "And yet you suffer so, and it is as if you can love!"

"Love? I have loved you since you came. I loved you when I read your secret thoughts and had not yet seen your face."

He drew me to him ever so gently, and slipping his arm around me, guided me to the door.

I tried for one desperate moment to resist him. And as any gentleman might, he stepped back respectfully and took my hand.

Through the long upstairs corridor we passed, and through a small wooden doorway to a screw stair that I had not seen before. I soon realized we were ascending in the north tower, a ruined portion of the structure that had been sealed off years before.

Through one tiny window after another I saw the gently rolling landscape and the small cluster of dim lights that marked the village of Rampling and the pale streak of white that was the London road.

Up and up we climbed, until we reached the topmost chamber, and this he opened with an iron key. He held back the door for me to enter and I found myself in a spacious room whose high, narrow windows contained no glass. A flood of moonlight revealed the most curious mixture of furnishings and objects—a writing table, a great shelf of books, soft leather chairs, and scores of maps and framed pictures affixed to the walls. Candles all about had dripped their wax on every surface, and in the very midst of this chaos lay my poems, my old sketches—early writings that I had brought with me and never even unpacked.

I saw a black silk top hat and a walking stick, and a bouquet of withered flowers, dry as straw, and daguerreotypes and tintypes in their little velvet cases, and London newspapers and opened books.

There was no place for sleeping in this room.

And when I thought of that, where he must lie when he went to rest, a shudder passed over me and I felt, quite palpably, his lips touching my throat again, and I had the sudden urge to cry.

But he was holding me in his arms; he was kissing my cheeks and my lips ever so softly.

"My father knew what you were!" I whispered.

"Yes," he answered, "and his father before him. And all of them in an unbroken chain over the years. Out of loneliness or rage, I know not which, I always told them. I always made them acknowledge, accept."

I backed away and he didn't try to stop me. He lighted the candles about us one by one.

I was stunned by the sight of him in the light, the gleam in his large black eyes and the gloss of his hair. Not even in the railway station had I seen him so clearly as I did now, amid the radiance of the candles. He broke my heart.

And yet he looked at me as though I were a feast for his eyes, and he said my name again and I felt the blood rush to my face. But there seemed a great break suddenly in the passage of time. What had I been thinking! *Yes, never tell, never disturb . . . something ancient, something greater than good and evil . . .* But no! I felt dizzy again. I heard Father's voice: *Tear it down, Richard, stone by stone.*

He had drawn me to the window. And as the lights of Rampling were subtracted from the darkness below, a great wood stretched out in all directions, far older and denser than the forest of Rampling Gate. I was afraid suddenly, as if I were slipping into a maelstrom of visions from which I could never, of my own will, return.

There was that sense of our talking together, talking and talking in low, agitated voices, and I was saying that I should not give in.

"Bear witness—that is all I ask of you, Julie."

And there was in me some dim certainty that by these visions alone I would be fatally changed.

But the very room was losing its substance, as if a soundless wind of terrific force were blowing it apart. The vision had already begun . . .

We were riding horseback through a forest, he and I. And the trees were so high and so thick that scarcely any sun at all broke through to the fragrant, leaf-strewn ground.

Yet we had no time to linger in this magical place. We had come to the fresh-tilled earth that surrounded a village I somehow knew was called Knorwood, with its gabled roofs and its tiny, crooked streets. We saw the monastery of Knorwood and the little church with the bell chiming vespers under the lowering sky. A great, bustling life resided in Knorwood, a thousand voices rising in common prayer.

Far beyond, on the rise above the forest, stood the round tower of a truly ancient castle; and to that ruined castle—no more than a shell of itself anymore—as darkness fell in earnest we rode. Through its empty chambers we roamed, impetuous children, the horses and the road quite forgotten, and to the lord of the castle, a gaunt and white-skinned creature standing before the roaring fire of the roofless hall, we came. He turned and fixed us with his narrow and glittering eyes. A dead thing he was, I understood, but he carried within himself a priceless magic. And my companion, my innocent young man, stepped forward into the lord's arms.

I saw the kiss. I saw the young man grow pale and struggle and turn away, and the lord retreated with the wisest, saddest smile.

I understood. I knew. But the castle was dissolving as surely as anything in this dream might dissolve, and we were in some damp and close place.

The stench was unbearable to me; it was that most terrible of all stenches, the stench of death. And I heard my steps on the cobblestones and I reached out to steady myself against a wall. The tiny marketplace was deserted; the doors and windows gaped open to the vagrant wind. Up one side and down the other of the crooked street I saw the marks on the houses. And I knew what the marks meant. The Black Death had come to the village of Knorwood. The Black Death had laid it waste. And in a moment of suffocating horror I realized that no one, not a single person, was left alive.

But this was not quite true. There was a young man walking in fits and starts up the narrow alleyway. He was staggering, almost falling, as he pushed in one door after another, and at last came to a hot, reeking place where a child screamed on the floor. Mother and father lay dead in the bed. And the sleek fat cat of the household, unharmed, played with the screaming infant, whose eyes bulged in its tiny, sunken face.

"Stop it!" I heard myself gasp. I was holding my head with both hands. "Stop it—stop it, please!" I was screaming, and my screams would surely pierce the vision and this crude little dwelling would collapse around me and I would rouse the household of Rampling Gate, but I did not. The young man turned and stared at me, and in the close, stinking room I could not see his face.

But I knew it was he, my companion, and I could smell his fever and his sickness, and the stink of the dying infant, and see the gleaming body of the cat as it pawed at the child's outstretched hand.

"Stop it, you've lost control of it!" I screamed, surely with all my strength, but the infant screamed louder. "Make it stop."

"I cannot," he whispered. "It goes on forever! It will never stop!"

And with a great shriek I kicked at the cat and sent it flying out of the filthy room, overturning the milk pail as it went.

Death in all the houses of Knorwood. Death in the cloister, death in the open fields. It seemed the Judgment of God—I was sobbing, begging to be released—it seemed the very end of Creation itself.

But as night came down over the dead village he was alive still, stumbling up the slopes, through the forest, towards that tower where the lord stood at the broken arch of the window, waiting for him to come.

"Don't go!" I begged him. I ran alongside him, crying, but he didn't hear.

The lord turned and smiled with infinite sadness as the young man on his knees begged for salvation, when it was damnation this lord offered, when it was only damnation that the lord would give.

"Yes, damned, then, but living, breathing!" the young man cried, and the lord opened his arms.

The kiss again, the lethal kiss, the blood drawn out of his dying body, and then the lord lifting the heavy head of the young man so the youth could take the blood back again from the body of the lord himself.

I screamed, "Do not—do not drink!"

He turned, and his face was now so perfectly the visage of death that I couldn't believe there was animation left in him; yet he asked: "What would you do? Would you go back to Knorwood, would you open those doors one after another, would you ring the bell in the empty church— and if you did, who would hear?"

He didn't wait for my answer. And I had none now to give. He locked his innocent mouth to the vein that pulsed with every semblance of life beneath the lord's cold and translucent flesh. And the blood jetted into the young body, vanquishing in one great burst the fever and the sickness that had racked it, driving it out along with the mortal life.

He stood now in the hall of the lord alone. Immortality was his, and the bloodthirst he would need to sustain it, and that thirst I could feel with my whole soul.

And each and every thing was transfigured in his vision—to the exquisite essence of itself. A wordless voice spoke from the starry veil of Heaven; it sang in the wind that rushed through the broken timbers; it sighed in the flames that ate at the sooted stones of the hearth. It was the eternal rhythm of the universe that played beneath every surface as the last living creature in the village—that tiny child—fell silent in the maw of time.

A soft wind sifted and scattered the soil from the newly-turned furrows in the empty fields. The rain fell from the black and endless sky.

Years and years passed. And all that had been Knorwood melted into the earth. The forest sent out its silent sentinels, and mighty trunks rose where there had been huts and houses, where there had been monastery walls. And it seemed the horror beyond all horrors that no one should know any more of those who had lived and died in that small and insignificant village, that not anywhere in the great archives in which all history is recorded should a mention of Knorwood exist.

Yet one remained who knew, one who had witnessed, one who had seen the Ramplings come in the years that followed, seen them raise their house upon the very slope where the ancient castle had once stood, one who saw a new village collect itself slowly upon the unmarked grave of the old.

And all through the walls of Rampling Gate were the stones of that old castle, the stones of the forgotten monastery, the stones of that little church.

We were once again back in the tower.

"It is my shrine," he whispered. "My sanctuary. It is the only thing that endures as I endure. And you love it as I love it, Julie. You have written it . . . You love its grandeur. And its gloom."

"Yes, yes . . . as it's always been . . ." I was crying, though I didn't move my lips.

He had turned to me from the window, and I could feel his endless craving with all my heart.

"What else do you want from me!" I pleaded. "What else can I give?"

A torrent of images answered me. It was beginning again. I was once again relinquishing myself, yet in a great rush of lights and noise I was enlivened and made whole as I had been when we rode together through the forest, but it was into the world of now, this hour, that we passed.

We were flying through the rural darkness along the railway towards London, where the nighttime city burst like an enormous bubble in a shower of laughter and motion and glaring light. He was walking with me under the gas lamps, his face all but shimmering with that same dark innocence, that same irresistible warmth. It seemed we were holding tight to each other in the very midst of a crowd. And the crowd was a living thing, a writhing thing, and everywhere there came a dark, rich aroma from it, the aroma of fresh blood. Women in white fur and gentlemen in opera capes swept through the brightly-lit doors of the theater; the blare of the music hall inundated us and then faded away. Only a thin soprano voice was left, singing a high, plaintive song. I was in his arms and his lips were covering mine, and there came that dull, zinging sensation again, that great, uncontrollable opening within myself. Thirst, and the promise of satiation measured only by the intensity of that thirst. Up back staircases we fled together, into high-ceilinged bedrooms papered in red damask, where the loveliest women reclined on brass beds, and the aroma was so strong now that I could not bear it and he said: "Drink. They are your victims! They will give you eternity—you must drink." And I felt the warmth filling me, charging me, blurring my vision until we broke free again, light and invisible, it seemed, as we moved over the rooftops and down again through rain-drenched streets. But the rain did not touch us; the falling snow did not chill us; we had within ourselves a great and indissoluble heat. And together in the carriage we talked to each other in low, exuberant rushes of language; we were lovers; we were constant; we were immortal. We were as enduring as Rampling Gate.

Oh, don't let it stop! I felt his arms around me and I knew we were in the tower room together, and the visions had worked their fatal alchemy.

"Do you understand what I am offering you? To your ancestors I revealed myself, yes; I subjugated them. But I would make you my bride, Julie. I would share with you my power. Come with me. I will not take you against your will, but can you turn away?"

Again I heard my own scream. My hands were on his cool white skin, and his lips were gentle yet hungry, his eyes yielding and ever young. Father's angry countenance blazed before me as if I, too, had the power to conjure. *Unspeakable horror.* I covered my face.

He stood against the backdrop of the window, against the distant drift of pale clouds. The candlelight glimmered in his eyes. Immense and sad and wise, they seemed—and oh, yes, innocent, as I have said again and again. "You are their fairest flower, Julie. To them I gave my protection always. To you I give my love. Come to me, dearest, and Rampling Gate will truly be yours, and it will finally, truly be mine."

—

Nights of argument, but finally Richard had come round. He would sign over Rampling Gate to me and I should absolutely refuse to allow the place to be torn down. There would be nothing he could do then to obey Father's command. I had given him the legal impediment he needed, and of course I told him I would leave the house to his male heirs. It should always be in Rampling hands.

A clever solution, it seemed to me, since Father had not told me to destroy the place. I had no scruples in the matter now at all.

And what remained was for him to take me to the little railway station and see me off for London, and not worry about my going home to Mayfair on my own.

"You stay here as long as you wish and do not worry," I said. I felt more tenderly toward him than I could ever express. "You knew as soon as you set foot in the place that Father was quite wrong."

The great black locomotive was chugging past us, the passenger cars slowing to a stop.

"Must go now, darling—kiss me," I said.

"But what came over you, Julie—what convinced you so quickly—?"

"We've been through all that, Richard," I said. "What matters is that Rampling Gate is safe and we are both happy, my dear."

I waved until I couldn't see him anymore. The flickering lamps of the town were lost in the deep lavender light of the early evening, and the dark hulk of Rampling Gate appeared for one uncertain moment like the ghost of itself on the nearby rise.

I sat back and closed my eyes. Then I opened them slowly, savoring this moment for which I had waited so long.

He was smiling, seated in the far corner of the leather seat opposite, as he had been all along, and now he rose with a swift, almost delicate movement and sat beside me and enfolded me in his arms.

"It's five hours to London," he whispered.

"I can wait," I said, feeling the thirst like a fever as I held tight to him, feeling his lips against my eyelids and my hair. "I want to hunt the London streets tonight," I confessed a little shyly, but I saw only approbation in his eyes.

"Beautiful Julie, my Julie . . ." he whispered.

"You'll love the house in Mayfair," I said.

"Yes . . ." he said.

"And when Richard finally tires of Rampling Gate, we shall go home."

HOMEWRECKER

Poppy Z. Brite

Before announcing his "retirement," for almost twenty years Billy Martin wrote a string of acclaimed and successful horror novels and short stories under the name "Poppy Z. Brite."

As Brite he published the novels *Lost Souls, Drawing Blood, Exquisite Corpse*, and *The Crow: The Lazarus Heart*, along with the story collections *Swamp Foetus* (aka *Wormwood*), *Are You Loathesome Tonight?* (aka *Self-Made Man*), *Wrong Things* (with Caitlín R. Kiernan), *The Devil You Know*, and *Antediluvian Tales*. He also edited the vampire anthologies *Love in Vein* and *Twice Bitten (Love in Vein II)*.

In 1999 he published *Courtney Love: The Real Story*, a semi-official biography of the singer, and he subsequently wrote a series of novels set in the restaurant world of New Orleans.

His short story "The Sixth Sentinel" was filmed in 1999 (under the title "The Dream Sentinel") for the Showtime TV series *The Hunger*.

"The vampire is the easiest horror trope to turn into a cliché," says the author, "and yet a great many writers try their hands at a vampire tale sooner or later, maybe because the familiar canvas shows off one's individual flourishes . . . To write about a creature that lives off the human life-force requires the ability to plumb one's own darkness."

MY UNCLE EDNA killed hogs. He came home from the slaughter-house every day smelling of shit and pig blood, and if I didn't have his bath drawn with plenty of perfume and bubble stuff, he'd whup my ass until I felt his hard-on poking me in the leg.

Like I said, he killed hogs. At night, though, you'd never have known it to see him in his satin gown. He swished around the old farmhouse like some kind of fairy godmother, swigging from a bottle of JD and cussing the bitch who stole his man. "Homewrecker!" he'd shriek, pounding his fist on the table and rattling the stack of rhinestone bracelets he wore on his skinny arm. "How could he want her when he had me? How could he do it, boy?"

And you had to wonder, because even with his lipstick smeared and his chest hair poking out of his gown, there was a certain tired glamour to Uncle Edna. Thing was, the bitch hadn't even *wanted* his man. Uncle Jude, who'd been with Uncle Edna since he was just plain old Ed Slopes, had all of a sudden turned hetero and gone slobbering off after a henna-headed barfly who called herself Verna. What Verna considered a night's amusement, Uncle Jude decided was the grand passion of his life. And that was the last we saw of him. We never could understand it.

Uncle Edna was thirty-six when Uncle Jude left. The years and the whiskey rode him hard after that, but the man knew how to do his makeup, and I thought Uncle Jude would fall back in love with him if they could just see each other again.

I couldn't do anything about it though, and back then I was more interested in catching frogs and snakes than in the affairs of grown-ups' hearts. But a few years later, I heard Verna was back in town.

I knew I couldn't let Uncle Edna find out. He'd want to get out his shotgun and go after her, and then he'd get cornholed to death in jail and who'd take care of me? So I talked to a certain kid at school. He made me suck his dick out behind the cafeteria, but I came home with four Xanax. I ground them up and put them in Uncle Edna's bottle of JD that same night. Pretty soon he was snoring like a chainsaw and drooling on his party dress. I went out to look for Verna. I didn't especially want to see her, but I thought maybe I could find out where she'd last seen Uncle Jude.

I parked my bike across the street from the only bar in town, the Silky Q. Inside, the men stood or danced in pairs. A few wore drag, but most were in jeans and flannels; this was a working man's town.

Then I saw her. She'd slid her meaty ass into a booth and was cuddled up to one of the men in it. The other man sat glaring at her, nearly in tears. I recognized them as Bob and Jim Frenchette, a couple who'd been married as long as I could remember. Verna's red-nailed hand was on Bob's thigh, stroking the worn denim.

I walked up to the table.

Jim and Bob were too far gone to pay me any mind. Verna didn't seem to recognize me. I'd been a little kid when she saw me last, and she'd hardly noticed me then, bent as she was on sucking Uncle Jude's neck. I stared into her eyes. Her lashes were clumped with black mascara, her lids frosted with turquoise shadow. Her mouth was a lipstick wound. Her lips twitched in a scornful smile, then parted.

"What you want, little boy?"

I couldn't think of anything to say. I didn't know what I had meant to do. I stumbled away from the table. My hands were trembling and my cheeks flaming. I was outside, unchaining my bike from the lamppost, when Verna came out of the bar.

She crossed the deserted street, pinning me where I stood with those wolf-pale eyes. I wanted to jump on my bike and speed away, or just run, but I couldn't. I wanted to look away from those slippery red lips that glistened like hog grease. But I couldn't.

"Your uncle . . ." she whispered. "Jules, wasn't it?"

I shook my head, but Verna kept smiling and bending closer until her lips were right against my ear.

"He was a lousy fuck," she said.

Her sharp red nails bit into my shoulder. She pushed me back against the lamppost and sank to her knees in front of me. I felt hot bile rising in my throat, but I couldn't move, even when her other hand undid my pants.

I tried to keep my dick from getting hard, I truly did. But it was like her mouth sucked the blood into it, right to the surface of the skin. I thought she might tear it out by the roots. Her tongue slithered over my balls, into my pee-hole. There came a sharp stinging at the base of my dick, unlike anything I'd felt when other boys sucked it. Then I was shooting my jizz into her mouth, much as I didn't want to, and she was swallowing it like she'd been starved.

Verna wiped her mouth and laughed. Then she stood, turned, and walked back to the bar like I wasn't even there. The door closed behind her, and I fell to my knees and puked until my throat was raw. But even as the rancid taste of half-digested food filled my mouth and nose, I could feel my dick getting hard again.

I had to whack off before I could get on my bike. As I came on the sidewalk, I imagined those fat shiny lips closing around me again, and I started to cry. I couldn't get the nasty thoughts out of my head, things I'd never thought about before: the smell of dank sea coves and fish markets, the soft squish of a body encased in a layer of fat, with big floppy globes of it stuck on the chest and rear like cancers. And the thoughts were like a cancer in me.

As fast as my feet could pedal, I rode home to Uncle Edna. But I had a feeling I could never really go home again.

WHEN GRETCHEN WAS HUMAN

Mary A. Turzillo

Mary A. Turzillo won the Nebula Award in 2000 for Best Science Fiction Novelette for her story "Mars is No Place for Children." A former professor at Kent State University, her critical books include *Reader's Guides* to the work of Anne McCaffrey and Philip José Farmer under the byline "Mary T. Brizzi."

She has published short stories in *Interzone, Analog, The Magazine of Fantasy & Science Fiction*, and *Science Fiction Age*, and her work has been included in such anthologies as *Nebula Awards Showcase 2001*, edited by Robert Silverberg, and *Tales of Wonder and Imagination*, edited by Ellen Datlow. Her collection *Bonsai Babies* appeared from Omnium Gatherum in 2016, and she has published four collections of poetry (two in collaboration with Marge Simon) and a novel, *Mars Girls*, from Apex in 2017.

"Not everyone has a victim or a vampire inside them," explains Turzillo, "but even those whose vampire-self is weak understand that the inner monster is lonely and craves love, while also fearing it. The passion that the vampire seeks and that the victim wants to give is an appalling and consecrated gift. Is it a metaphor for the love between the tyrant and willingly oppressed, or between the child and the parent who bleeds for the child's anguish?

"It is more. It is the deep core of ardor. We are afraid, and we desire."

"YOU'RE ONLY HUMAN," said Nick Scuroforno, fanning the pages of a tattered first edition of *Image of the Beast*. The conversation had degenerated from half-hearted sales pitch, Gretchen trying to sell Nick Scuroforno an early Pangborn imprint. Now they sat cross-legged on the scarred wooden floor of Miss Trilby's Tomes, watching dust motes dance in the August four o'clock sun. Gretchen was wallowing in self-disclosure and voluptuous self-pity.

"Sometimes I don't even feel human." Gretchen settled her back against the soft, dusty-smelling spines of a leather-bound 1910 imprint *Book of Knowledge*.

"I can identify."

"And given the choice, who'd really want to be?" asked Gretchen, tracing the grain of the wooden floor with chapped fingers.

"You have a choice?" asked Scuroforno.

"See, after Ashley was diagnosed, my ex got custody of her. Just as well." She rummaged her smock for a tissue. "I didn't have hospitalization after we split. And his would cover her, but only if she goes to a hospital way off in Seattle." Unbidden, a memory rose: Ashley's warm little body, wriggly as a puppy's, settling in her lap, opening *Where the Wild Things Are*, striking the page with her tiny pink index finger. *Mommy, read!*

Scuroforno nodded. "But can't they cure leukemia now?"

"Sometimes. She's in remission at the moment. But how long will that last?" Gretchen kept sneaking looks at Scuroforno. Amazingly, she found him attractive. She thought depression had killed the sexual impulse in her. He was a big man, chunky but not actually fat, with evasive amber eyes and shaggy hair. Not bad looking, but not handsome either, in gray sweatpants, a brown T-shirt, and beach sandals. He had a habit of twisting the band of his watch, revealing a strip of pale skin from which the fine hairs of his wrist had been worn.

"And yet cancer itself is immortal," he mused. "Why can't it make its host immortal too?"

"Cancer is immortal?" But of course cancer would be immortal. It was the ultimate predator. Why shouldn't it hold all the high cards?

"The cells are. There's some pancreatic cancer cells that have been growing in a lab fifty years since the man with the cancer died. And yet, cancer cells are not even as intelligent as a virus. A virus knows not to kill its host."

"But viruses do kill!"

He smiled. "That's true, lots do kill. Bacteria, too. But there are bacteria that millennia ago decided to infect every cell in our bodies. Turned into—let me think of the word. Organelles? Like the mitochondrion."

"What's a mitochondrion?"

He shrugged, slyly basking in his superior knowledge. "It's an energy-converting organ in animal cells. Different DNA from the host. You'd think you could design a mitochondrion that would make the host live forever."

She stared at him. "No. I certainly wouldn't think that. "

"Why not?"

"It would be horrible. A zombie. A vampire."

He was silent, a smile playing around his eyes.

She shuddered. "You get these ideas from Miss Trilby's Tomes?"

"The wisdom of the ages." He gestured at the high shelves, then stood. "And of course the Internet. Here comes Madame Trilby herself. Does she like you lounging on the floor with customers?"

Gretchen flushed. "Oh, she never minds anything. My grandpa was friends with her father, and I've worked here off and on since I was little." She took Scuroforno's proffered hand and pulled herself to her feet.

Miss Trilby, frail and spry, wafting a fragrance of face powder and moldy paper, lugged in a milk crate of pamphlets. She frowned at Gretchen. Strange, thought Gretchen. Yesterday she said I should find a new man, but now she's glaring at me. For sitting on the floor? I sit on the floor to do paperwork all the time. There's no room for chairs. It has to be for schmoozing with a male customer.

Miss Trilby dumped the mail on the counter and swept into the back room.

"Cheerful today, hmm?" said Scuroforno.

"Really, she's so good to me. She lends me money to go to Seattle and see my daughter. She's just nervous today."

"Ah. By the way, before I leave, do you have a cold, or were you crying?"

Gretchen reddened. "I have a chronic sinus infection." She suddenly saw herself objectively: stringy hair, bad posture, skinny. How could she be flirting with this man?

He touched her wrist. "Take care." And he strode through the door into the street.

"Him you don't need," said Miss Trilby, bustling back in and firing up the shop's ancient Kaypro computer.

"Did I say I did?"

"Your face says you think you do. Did he buy anything?"

"I'm sorry. I can never predict what he'll be interested in."

"I'll die in the poorhouse. Sell him antique medical texts. Or detective novels. He stands reading historical novels right off the shelf and laughs. Pretends to be an expert, finds all the mistakes."

"What have you got against him, besides reading and not buying?"

"Oh, he buys. But Gretchen, lambkin, a man like that you don't need. Loner. Crazy."

"But he listens. He's so understanding."

"Like the butcher with the calf. What's this immortal cancer stuff he's feeding you?"

"Nothing. We were talking about Ashley."

"Sorry, lambkin. Life hasn't been kind to you. But be a little wise. This man has delusions he's a vampire."

Gretchen smoothed the dust jacket of *Euryanthe and Oberon at Covent Garden.* "Maybe he is."

Miss Trilby rounded her lips in mock horror. "Perhaps! Doesn't look much like Frank Langella, though, does he?"

No, he didn't, thought Gretchen, as she sorted orders for reprints of Kadensho's *Book of the Flowery Tradition* and de Honnecourt's *Fervor of Buenos Aires.*

But there was something appealing about Nick Scuroforno, something besides his empathy for a homely divorcée with a terminally ill child. His spare, dark humor; maybe that was it. Miss Trilby did not understand everything.

Why not make a play for him?

Even to herself, her efforts seemed pathetic. She got Keesha, the single mother across the hall in her apartment, to help her frost her hair. She bought a cheap cardigan trimmed with Angora and dug out an old padded bra.

"Lambkin," said Miss Trilby dryly one afternoon when Gretchen came in dolled up in her desperate finery, "the man is not exactly a fashion plate himself."

But Scuroforno seemed flattered, if not impressed, by Gretchen's efforts, and took her out for coffee, then a late dinner. Mostly, however, he came into the bookstore an hour before closing and let her pretend to sell him some white elephant like the Reverend Wood's *Trespassers: How Inhabitants of Earth, Air, and Water Are Enabled to Trespass on Domains Not Their Own*. She would fiddle with the silver chain on her neck, and they would slide to the floor where she would pour out her troubles to him. Other customers seldom came in so late.

"You trust him with private details of your life," said Miss Trilby, "but what do you know of his?"

He did talk. He did. Philosophy, history, details of Gretchen's daughter's illness. One day, she asked, "What do you do?"

"I steal souls. Photographer."

Oh.

"Can't make much money on that artsy stuff," Miss Trilby commented when she heard this. "Rumor says he's got a private source of income."

"Illegal, you mean?"

"What a romantic you are, Gretchen. Ask him."

Gambling luck and investments, he told her.

One day, leaving for the shop, Gretchen opened her mail and found a letter—not even a phone call—that Ashley's remission was over. Her little girl was in the hospital again.

The grief was surreal, physical. She was afraid to go back into her apartment. She had bought a copy of Jan Pieńkowski's *Haunted House*, full of diabolically funny pop-ups, for Ashley's birthday. She couldn't bear to look at it now, waiting like a poisoned bait on the counter.

She went straight to the shop, began alphabetizing the new stock. Nothing made sense, she couldn't remember if O came after N. Miss Trilby had to drag her away, make her stop.

"What's wrong? Is it Ashley?"

Gretchen handed her the letter.

Miss Trilby read it through her thick lorgnette. Then, "Look at yourself. Your cheeks are flushed. Eyes bright. Disaster becomes you. Or is it the nearness of death bids us breed, like romance in a concentration camp?"

Gretchen shuddered. "Maybe my body is tricking me into reproducing again."

"To replace Ashley. Not funny, lambkin. But possibly true. I ask again, why this man? Doesn't madness frighten you?"

Next day, Gretchen followed him to his car. It seemed natural to get in, uninvited, ride home with him, follow him up two flights of stairs covered with cracked treads.

He let her perch on a stool in his kitchen darkroom while he printed peculiar old architectural photographs. The room smelled of chemicals, vinegary. An old Commodore 64 propped the pantry door open. She had seen a new computer in his living room, running a screensaver of Giger babies holding grenades, and wraiths dancing an agony-dance.

"I never eat here," he said. "As a kitchen, it's useless."

He emptied trays, washed solutions down the drain, rinsed. Her heart beat hard under the sleazy Angora. His body, sleek as a lion's, gave off a male scent, faintly predatory.

While his back was turned, she undid her cardigan. The buttons too easily slipped out of the cheap fuzzy fabric, conspiring with lust.

She slipped it off as he turned around. And felt the draft of the cold kitchen and the surprise of his gaze on her inadequate chest.

He turned away, dried his hands on the kitchen towel. "Don't fall in love with me."

"Not at all arrogant, are you?" She wouldn't, wouldn't fall in love. No. That wasn't quite it.

"Not arrogance. A warning. I'm territorial; predators have to be. For a while, yes, I'd keep you around. But sooner or later, you'd interfere with my hunting. I'd kill you or drive you away to prevent myself from killing you."

"I won't fall in love with you." Level. Convincing.

"All right." He threw the towel into the sink, came to her. Covered her mouth with his.

She responded clumsily, overreacting after the long dry spell, clawing his back.

The kiss ended. He stroked her hair. "Don't worry. I won't draw blood. I can control the impulse."

She half-pretended to play along with him. Half of her did believe. "It doesn't matter. I want to be like you." A joke?

He sat on the kitchen chair, pulled her to him and put his cheek against her breasts. "It doesn't work that way. You have to have the right genes to be susceptible."

"It really is an infection?" Still half-pretending to believe, still almost joking.

"A virus that gives you cancer. All I know is that of all the thousands I've preyed upon, only a few have gotten the fever and lived to become— like me."

"Vampire?"

"As good a word as any. One who I infected and who lived on was my son. He got the fever and turned. That's why I think it's genetic." He pulled her nearer, as if for warmth.

"What happens if the prey doesn't have the genes?"

"Nothing. Nothing happens. I never take enough to kill. I haven't killed a human in over a hundred years. You're safe."

She slid to her knees, wrapping her arms around his waist. He held her head to him, stroking her bare arms and shoulders. "Silk," he said finally, pulling her up, touching her breast. She had nursed Ashley, but it hadn't stopped her from getting leukemia. Fire and ice sizzled across her breasts, as if her milk were letting down.

"Are you lonely?"

"God, yes. That's the only reason I was even tempted to let you do this. You know, I have the instincts of a predator, it does that. But I was born human."

"How did you infect your son?"

"Accident. I was infected soon after I was married. Pietra, my wife, is long dead."

"Pietra. Strange name."

"Not so strange in thirteenth-century Florence. I turned shortly after I was married. I was very ill. I knew I needed blood, but no knowledge of why or how to control my thirst. I took blood from a priest who came to give me last rites. My thirst was so voracious, I killed him. Not murder, Gretchen. I was no more guilty than a baby suckling at breast. The first thirst is overpowering. I took too much, and when I saw that he was dead, I put on my clothes and ran away."

"Leaving your wife—"

"Never saw her again. But years later, I encountered this young man at a gambling table. Pretended to befriend him. Overpowered him in a narrow dark street. Drank to slake my thirst. Later I encountered him, changed. As a rival for the blood of the neighborhood. I had infected him, he had gotten the fever, developed into—what I am. Later I put the pieces together; I had left Pietra pregnant, this was our son, you see. He had the right genes. If he hadn't, he would have never even noticed that modest blood loss." His hand stroked her naked shoulder.

"Where is he now?"

"I often wonder. I drove him off soon after he finished the change. Vampires can't stand one another. They interfere with each other's hunting."

"Why have you chosen to tell me this?" She tried to control her voice, but heard it thicken.

"I tell people all the time what I am. Nobody ever believes it." He stood, pulling her to her feet, kissed her again, pressing his hips to her body. She ran her hands over his shoulders and loosened his shirt. "You don't believe me, either."

And then she smiled. "I want to believe you. I told you once, I don't want to be human."

He raised his eyebrows and smiled down at her. "I doubt you have the right genes to be anything else."

His bedroom was neat, sparsely furnished. She recognized books from Miss Trilby's Tomes, *Red Dragon, Confessions of an English Opium Eater*, on a low shelf near the bed. Unexpectedly, he lifted her off her feet and laid her on the quilt. They kissed again, a long, complicated kiss. He took her slowly. He didn't close the door, and from the bed she could see his computer screen in the living room. The Giger wraiths in his screensaver danced slowly to their passion. And then she closed her eyes, and the wraiths danced behind her lids.

When they were finished, she knew that she had lied; if she did not feel love, then it was something as strong and as dangerous.

She traced a vein on the back of his hand. "You were born in Italy?"

He kissed the hand with which she had been tracing his veins. "Hundreds of years ago, yes. Before my flesh became numb."

"Then why don't you speak with an accent?"

He rolled onto his back, hands behind his head, and grinned. "I've been an American longer than you have. I made it a point to get rid of my accent. Aren't you going to ask me about the sun and garlic and silver bullets?"

"All just superstition?"

"It would seem." He smiled wryly. "But there is the gradual loss of feeling."

"You say you can't love."

He groped in the bedside table for a pen. He drove the tip into his arm. "You see?" Blood welled up slowly.

"Stop! My God, must you hurt yourself?"

"Just demonstrating. The flesh has been consumed by the—by the cancer, if that's what it is. It starts in the coldest parts of the body. No nerves. I don't *feel*. It has nothing to do with emotion."

"And because you are territorial—"

"Yes. But the emotions don't die, exactly. There's this horrible conflict. And physically, the metastasis continues, very slowly. I heard of a very old vampire whose brain had turned. He was worse than a shark, a feeding machine—"

She pulled the sheets around her. The room seemed cold now that they were no longer entwined. "You seemed human enough, when you—"

"You didn't feel it when I kissed you?"

"Feel—"

He guided her index finger into his mouth, under the tongue. A bony little organ there, tiny spikes, retracted under the root of the tongue.

She jerked her hand away, suddenly afraid. He caught it and kissed it again, almost mockingly.

She shuddered, tenderness confounded with terror, and buried her face in the pillow. But wasn't this what she had secretly imagined, hoped for?

"Next time," she said, turning her face up to him, like a daisy to the sun, "draw blood, do."

The wraiths in his screensaver danced.

The idea of a bus trip to Seattle filled her with dread, and she put it off, as if somehow by staying in Warren she could stop the progress of reality. But a second letter, this from her ex-sister-in-law Miriam, forced her to face facts. The chemotherapy, Miriam wrote, was not working this time. Ashley was "fading."

"Fading"!

The same mail brought a postcard from Scuroforno. *Out of town on business, seeing to investments. Be well, human,* he wrote.

She told Miss Trilby she needed time off to see Ashley.

"Lambkin, you look awful. Don't go on the bus. I'll lend you money for the plane, and you can pay me back when you marry some rich lawyer."

"No, Miss Trilby. I have a cold, that's all." Her skin itched, her throat and mouth were sore, her head throbbed.

They dusted books that afternoon. When Gretchen came down from the stepladder, she was so exhausted she curled up on the settee in the back room with a copy of *As You Desire*. The words swam before her eyes, but they might stop her from thinking, thinking about Ashley, about cancer, immortal cells killing their mortal host. Thinking, *immortal*. It might have worked. A diffcrent cancer. And then she stopped thinking.

And awoke in All Soul's Hospital, in pain and confusion.

"Drink. You're dehydrated," the nurse said. The room smelled of bleach and dead flowers.

Who had brought her in?

"I don't know. Your employer? An elderly woman. Doctor will be in to talk to you. Try to drink at least a glass every hour."

In lucid moments, Gretchen rejoiced. It was the change, surely it was the change. If she lived, she would be released from all the degrading baggage that being human hung upon her.

The tests showed nothing. Of course, the virus would not culture in agar, Gretchen thought. If it was a virus.

She awoke nights thinking of human blood. She whimpered when they took away her roommate, an anorexic widow, nearly dry, but an alluring source of a few delicious drops, if only she could get to her while the nurses were away.

Miss Trilby visited, and only by iron will did Gretchen avoid leaping upon her. Gretchen screamed, "Get away from me! I'll kill you!" The doctors, unable to identify her illness, must have worried about her outburst; she didn't get another roommate. And they didn't release her, though she had no insurance.

Miss Trilby did not come back.

They never thought of cancer. Cancer does not bring a fever and thirst, and bright, bright eyes, and a numbness in the fingers.

Finally, she realized she had waited too long. The few moments of each day that delirium left her, she was too weak to overpower anybody.

Scuroforno came in when she was almost gone. She was awake, floating, relishing death's sweet breath, the smell of disinfectants.

"I'm under quarantine," she whispered. This was not true, but nobody had come to see her since she had turned on Miss Trilby.

He waved that aside and unwrapped a large syringe. "What you need is blood. They wouldn't think of that, though."

"Where did you get that?" Blood was so beautiful. She wanted to press Scuroforno's wrists against the delicate itching structure under her tongue, to faint in the heat from his veins.

"You're too weak to drink. Ideally, you should have several quarts of human blood. But mine will do."

She watched, sick with hunger, as he tourniqueted his arm, slipped the needle into the vein inside his elbow and drew blood.

She reached for the syringe. He held it away from her. She lunged with death-strength. He put the syringe on the table behind him, caught her wrists, held them together.

"You're stronger than I expected." He squeezed until the distant pain quelled her. She pretended to relax, still fixated on the sip of blood, so near. She darted at his throat, but he held her easily.

"Stop it! There isn't enough blood in the syringe to help you if you drink it! If I inject it, you'll get some relief. But my blood is forbidden."

Yes, she would have killed him, anybody, for blood. She sank back, shaking with desire. The needle entered her vein and she never felt the prick. She shuddered with pleasure as the blood trickled in. She could taste it. Old blood, sour with a hunger of its own, but the echo of satiety radiated from her arm.

"Here are some clothes. You should be just strong enough to walk to the car. I'll carry you from there."

She fumbled for his wrists. "No. Any more vampire blood would kill you. Or," he laughed grimly, "you might be strong enough to kill me. On your feet." He lifted her like a child.

In his apartment, he carried her to the bedroom and laid her on the bed. She smelled blood. Next to her was an unconscious girl, perhaps twenty, very blonde, dressed in white suede jeans, boots, a black lace bra.

Ineptly, she went for the girl's jugular. The girl was wearing strong jasmine perfume, a cheap knock-off scent insistent and sexy.

"Wait. Don't slash her and waste it all. Be neat." He leaned over, pressed his mouth to the girl's neck.

Gretchen lunged.

She thrilled to sink her new blood-sucking organ into the girl's neck, but discovered it was at the wrong place. Hissing with anger, she broke away and tried a third time. Salty, thick comfort seeped into her body like hot whiskey.

In an instant, Gretchen felt Scuroforno slip his finger into her mouth, breaking the suction. She came away giddy with frustration. Scuroforno held her arms, hurting her. The pain was in another universe. She tried to twist away.

"You're going to kill her," he warned.

"Who is she?" She shook herself into self-control, gazed longingly at the girl, who seemed comatose.

"Nobody. A girl. I take her out now and then. I never take enough blood to harm her. I don't actually enjoy hurting people."

"She's drugged?"

"No, no. I—we have immunity to bacteria and so on, but drugs are bad. I hypnotized her."

"You hypnotized—she sleeps through all this?"

"She thinks she's dead drunk. Here, help me get her sweater back on."

"She thinks you made love to her?"

Scuroforno smiled.

"You did make love to her?"

He busied himself with adjusting the girl's clothes.

Gretchen lay back against the headboard. "I need more, God, I need more."

"I know. But you'll have to find your own from now on."

"How do I get them to submit?"

Scuroforno yawned. "That's your problem. Rescuing you was hard work. Now you'll have to find your own way. You're cleverer and stronger than humans now. Did you notice your sinus infection is gone?"

"Nick, help."

He did not look at her. "It would be better if you left town now."

"But you saved me."

"You're my competitor now. Leave before the rage for blood takes you, before we go after the same prey."

She held the hunger down inside her, remembering human emotions. "It makes no difference that I love you?" And suddenly, she did love him.

"Tomorrow you'll know what hate is, too."

On the way out, she noticed he had a new screensaver: red blood cells floating on black, swelling, bursting apart.

On the bus to Seattle, she wept. Yes, she had loved him, and she had learned what hate was, too. She played with a sewing needle, stabbed her fingers. Numb. But her feelings were not numb, not yet. Would that happen? Was Nick emotionally dead?

Would the physical numbness spread? If her body was immortal, why would she need nerves, pain, to warn of danger?

Maybe she would regret the bargain she had made.

The numbness did spread. Her fingers and hands were immune to pain, but she still felt thirst. The cancer metastasized into her tongue and nerves, wanted to be fed.

Her seatmate was a Mormon missionary, separated from his partner because the bus was crowded. In Chicago, he asked her to change seats, so he could sit with his partner. But she refused. It didn't fit her plan.

She stroked his cheek, held the back of his neck in a vice grip, all the while smiling, catlike. Scarcely feeling her own skin, but vividly feeling the nourishment under his. He tried to repel her, laughing uneasily, taking it for an erotic game. A forward, sluttish gentile woman. Then he was fighting, uselessly. He twisted her thumb back, childish self-defense. She felt no pain. Then he was weeping, softening, falling into a trance. She kissed his throat with her open mouth. Drank from him. Drank again and again. Had he fought, she could have broken his neck. She was completely changed.

In Seattle, the floor nurse in Pediatrics challenged her. Sniffing phenol and the sweet, sick urine that could never quite be cleaned up, Gretchen glanced at her reflection in a dead computer screen behind the nurse. She did look predatory now. Like a wax manikin, but also like a cougar. Powerful. Not like anybody's mother. Two other nurses drifted up, as if sensing trouble.

She showed the nurse her driver's license. They almost believed her, then. Let her go down the hall, to room 409. But still the nurses' eyes followed her. She had changed.

She opened the door. The floor nurse drifted in behind her.

This balding, emaciated tyke, tangled in tubing, could not be her Ashley.

Ashley had changed, too. From a less benign cancer.

The nurse sniffed. "I'm sorry. She's gone downhill a lot in the last few weeks." The nurse clearly did not approve of noncustodial mothers. Maybe still did not believe this quiet, strong woman was the mother.

When Gretchen had been human, she would have been humiliated, would have tried to explain that Ashley had been taken from her by legal tricks. Now, she considered the nurse simply as a convenient beverage container from which, under suitable conditions, she might sip. She smiled, a cat smile, and the nurse could not hold her gaze.

"Ashley," said Gretchen, when they were alone. She had brought the Jan Pieńkowski book, wrapped in red velvet paper with black cats on it. Ashley liked cats. She would love the scary haunted house pop-ups. They would read them together. Gretchen put the gift on the chair, because first she must tend to more important things. "Ashley, it's Mommy. Wake up, darling."

But the little girl only opened her eyes, huge and bruised in the pinched face, and sobbed feebly.

Gretchen lowered the rail on the bed and slid her arm under Ashley. The child was frighteningly light.

Gretchen felt the warmth of her feverish child, smelled the antiseptic of the room, the sweet girl-smell of her daughter's skin. But those were all at a distance. Gretchen was being subsumed by something immortal.

We are very territorial. Isn't that what Nick had said? *It's not an emotional numbness; it's physical.* And the memory of him jabbing the pen into his arm, the needle into his vein, her own numb fingers, how everything, even her daughter's warmth and the smell of the child and the room were all receding, distant. Immortal. Numb. Strong beyond human strength. Alone.

She touched her new, predatory mouth to her child's throat. Would Ashley thank her for this?

Now she must decide.

THE VENGEFUL SPIRIT OF LAKE NEPEAKEA

Tanya Huff

Canada's Tanya Huff has written such fantasy and science fiction novels as the Wizard Crystal, Quarters, Keepers Chronicles, Valor Confederation, and Enchantment Emporium series, along with a handful of stand-alone novels and four short story collections.

However, her most popular series is the Blood books featuring former police detective Victoria ("Vicki") Nelson, her sometimes-lover Detective Mike Celluci, and centuries-old vampire and romance writer Henry Fitzroy solving mysteries together. The series began in 1991 with *Blood Price*, which was followed by *Blood Trail*, *Blood Lines*, *Blood Pact*, *Blood Debt*, and the short story collection *Blood Bank*. A further spin-off trilogy of Smoke books (*Smoke and Shadows*, *Smoke and Mirrors*, and *Smoke and Ashes*) features Henry's friend Tony Foster, who works on a TV show about a vampire detective.

The Blood books became the basis of the 2007 Lifetime Television series *Blood Ties*, starring Christina Cox as Vicki, Dylan Neal as Mike, and Kyle Schmid as Henry. It ran for twenty-two episodes.

"I have no idea why vampires have been so incredibly popular for the last few decades," says the author. "Perhaps it's our fascination with perpetual adolescence. As the poster-line for the 1987 Warner Bros. movie *The Lost Boys* says: 'Sleep all day. Party all night. Never grow old. Never die. It's fun to be a vampire.'

"Perhaps in those cultures that have removed themselves from any connection with a natural cycle of life it's another way to deny the inevitable. An easy immortality as it were. Perhaps it's because there's something innately tragic about a vampire, hero or villain—the fragility underlying the strength. Or perhaps there's just a lot of good people writing vampire fiction these days and readers are going where the quality is."

Huff reveals that she got the idea for "The Vengeful Spirit of Lake Nepeaka" while visiting a time-share resort down in Florida: "In this time of political correctness, it gets harder and harder to find a satisfactory villain, but after spending two hours with a high-pressure, smarmy time-share salesman, I realized I'd found a villain that pretty much everyone would be quite happy to see get what was coming to them.

"The tale grew in telling as I began to research the weird and wonderful possibilities in deepwater lakes. If any of you want to know what's really going on here, pick up a copy of Michael Bradley's fascinating book, *More Than a Myth: The Search for the Monster of Muskrat Lake*. It's certainly changed my mind about swimming after dark . . ."

"CAMPING?"

"Why sound so amazed?" Dragging the old turquoise cooler behind her, Vicki Nelson, once one of Toronto's finest and currently the city's most successful paranormal investigator, backed out of Mike Celluci's crawl space.

"Why? Maybe because you've never been camping in your life. Maybe because your idea of roughing it is a hotel without room service. Maybe . . ."— he moved just far enough for Vicki to get by then followed her out into the rec room—". . . because you're a . . ."

"A?" Setting the cooler down beside two sleeping bags and a pair of ancient swim fins, she turned to face him. "A *what*, Mike?" Gray eyes silvered.

"Stop it."

Grinning, she turned her attention back to the cooler. "Besides, I won't be on vacation, I'll be working. You'll be the one enjoying the great outdoors."

"Vicki, my idea of the great outdoors is going to the Skydome for a Jay's game."

"No one's forcing you to come." Setting the lid to one side, she curled her nose at the smell coming out of the cooler's depths. "When was the last time you used this thing?"

"Police picnic, 1992. Why?"

She turned it up on its end. The desiccated body of a mouse rolled out, bounced twice and came to rest with its sightless little eyes staring up at Celluci. "I think you need to buy a new cooler."

"I think I need a better explanation than *I've got a great way for you to use up your long weekend*," he sighed, kicking the tiny corpse under the rec room couch.

"So this developer from Toronto, Stuart Gordon, bought an old lodge on the shores of Lake Nepeakea and he wants to build a rustic, time-share resort so junior executives can relax in the woods. Unfortunately, one of the surveyors disappeared and local opinion seems to be that he's pissed off the lake's protective spirit . . ."

"The what?"

Vicki pulled out to pass a transport and deftly reinserted the van back into her own lane before replying. "The protective spirit. You know, the sort of thing that rises out of the lake to vanquish evil." A quick glance toward the passenger seat brought her brows in. "Mike, are you all right? You're going to leave permanent finger marks in the dashboard."

He shook his head. The truckload of logs coming down from Northern Ontario had missed them by inches. Feet at the very most. *All right, maybe meters but not very many of them.* When they'd left the city, just after sunset, it had seemed logical that Vicki, with her better night sight, should drive. He was regretting that logic now but, realizing he didn't have a hope in hell of gaining control of the vehicle, he tried to force himself to relax. "The speed limit isn't just a good idea," he growled through clenched teeth, "it's the law."

She grinned, her teeth very white in the darkness. "You didn't used to be this nervous."

"I didn't used to have cause." His fingers wouldn't release their grip so he left them where they were. "So this missing surveyor, what did he . . ."

"She."

". . . she do to piss off the protective spirit?"

"Nothing much. She was just working for Stuart Gordon."

"The same Stuart Gordon you're working for."

"The very one."

Right. Celluci stared out at the trees and tried not to think about how fast they were passing. *Vicki Nelson against the protective spirit of Lake Nepeakea. That's one for pay-per-view . . .*

"This is the place."

"No. In order for this to be 'the place' there'd have to be something here. It has to be '*a place*' before it can be '*the place*'."

"I hate to admit it," Vicki muttered, leaning forward and peering over the arc of the steering wheel, "but you've got a point." They'd gone through the village of Dulvie, turned right at the ruined barn and followed the faded signs to THE LODGE. The road, if the rutted lanes of the last few kilometers could be called a road, had ended, as per the directions she'd received, in a small gravel parking lot—or more specifically in a hard-packed rectangular area that could now be called a parking lot because she'd stopped her van on it. "He said you could see the lodge from here."

Celluci snorted. "Maybe *you* can."

"No. I can't. All I can see are trees." At least she assumed they were trees, the high contrast between the area her headlights covered and the total darkness beyond made it difficult to tell for sure. Silently calling herself several kinds of fool, she switched off the lights. The shadows separated into half a dozen large evergreens and the silhouette of a roof steeply angled to shed snow.

Since it seemed they'd arrived, Vicki shut off the engine. After a heartbeat's silence, the night exploded into a cacophony of discordant noise. Hands over sensitive ears, she sank back into the seat. "What the hell is that?"

"Horny frogs."

"How do you know?" she demanded.

He gave her a superior smile. "PBS."

"Oh." They sat there for a moment, listening to the frogs. "The creatures of the night," Vicki sighed, "what music they make." Snorting derisively, she got out of the van. "Somehow, I expected the middle of nowhere to be a lot quieter."

Stuart Gordon had sent Vicki the key to the lodge's back door and once she switched on the main breaker, they found themselves in a modern, stainless steel kitchen that wouldn't have looked out of place in any small, trendy restaurant back in Toronto. The sudden hum of the refrigerator turning on momentarily drowned out the frogs and both Vicki and Celluci relaxed.

"So now what?" he asked.

"Now we unpack your food from the cooler, we find you a room, and we make the most of the short time we have until dawn."

"And when does Mr. Gordon arrive?"

"Tomorrow evening. Don't worry, I'll be up."

"And I'm supposed to do what, tomorrow in the daytime?"

"I'll leave my notes out. I'm sure something'll occur to you."

"I thought I was on vacation?"

"Then do what you usually do on vacation."

"Your foot work." He folded his arms. "And on my last vacation—which was also your idea—I almost lost a kidney."

Closing the refrigerator door, Vicki crossed the room between one heartbeat and the next. Leaning into him, their bodies touching between ankle and chest, she smiled into his eyes and pushed the long curl of hair back off his forehead. "Don't worry, I'll protect you from the spirit of the lake. I have no intention of sharing you with another legendary being."

"Legendary?" He couldn't stop a smile. "Think highly of yourself, don't you?"

"Are you sure you'll be safe in the van?"

"Stop fussing. You know I'll be fine." Pulling her jeans up over her hips, she stared out the window and shook her head. "There's a whole lot of nothing out there."

From the bed, Celluci could see a patch of stars and the top of one of the evergreens. "True enough."

"And I really don't like it."

"Then why are we here?"

"Stuart Gordon just kept talking. I don't even remember saying yes but the next thing I knew, I'd agreed to do the job."

"He pressured *you*?" Celluci's emphasis on the final pronoun made it quite clear that he hadn't believed such a thing was possible.

"Not pressured, no. Convinced with extreme prejudice."

"He sounds like a prince."

"Yeah? Well, so was Machiavelli." Dressed, she leaned over the bed and kissed him lightly. "Want to hear something romantic? When the day claims me, yours will be the only life I'll be able to feel."

"Romantic?" His breathing quickened as she licked at the tiny puncture wounds on his wrist. "I feel like a box luuu . . . ouch! All right. It's romantic."

Although she'd tried to keep her voice light when she'd mentioned it to Celluci, Vicki really *didn't* like the great outdoors. Maybe it was because she understood the wilderness of glass and concrete and needed the anonymity of three million lives packed tightly around hers. Standing by the van, she swept her gaze from the first hints of dawn to the last lingering shadows of night and couldn't help feeling excluded, that there was something beyond what she could see that she wasn't a part of. She doubted Stuart Gordon's junior executives would feel a part of it either and wondered why anyone would want to build a resort in the midst of such otherness.

The frogs had stopped trying to get laid and the silence seemed to be waiting for something.

Waiting . . .

Vicki glanced toward Lake Nepeakea. It lay like a silver mirror down at the bottom of a rocky slope. Not a ripple broke the surface. Barely a mile away, a perfect reflection brought the opposite shore closer still.

Waiting . . .

Whipper-will!

Vicki winced at the sudden, piercing sound and got into the van. After locking both outer and inner doors, she stripped quickly—if she were found during the day, naked would be the least of her problems—laid down between the high, padded sides of the narrow bed and waited for the dawn. The bird call, repeated with Chinese water torture frequency, cut its way through special seals and interior walls.

"Man, that's annoying," she muttered, linking her fingers over her stomach. "I wonder if Celluci can sleep through . . ."

As soon as he heard the van door close, Celluci fell into a dreamless sleep that lasted until just past noon. When he woke, he stared up at the inside of the roof and wondered where he was. The rough lumber looked like it'd been coated in creosote in the far distant past.

"No insulation, hate to be here in the winter . . ."

Then he remembered where *here* was and came fully awake.

Vicki had dragged him out to a wilderness lodge, north of Georgian Bay, to hunt for the local and apparently homicidal protective lake spirit.

A few moments later, his sleeping bag neatly rolled on the end of the old iron bed, he was in the kitchen making a pot of coffee. That kind of a realization upon waking needed caffeine.

On the counter next to the coffee maker, right where he'd be certain to find it first thing, he found a file labeled LAKE NEPEAKEA in Vicki's unmistakable handwriting. The first few pages of glossy card stock had been clearly sent by Stuart Gordon along with the key. An artist's conception of the time-share resort, they showed a large L-shaped building where the lodge now stood and three dozen "cottages" scattered through the woods, front doors linked by broad gravel paths. Apparently, the guests would commute out to their personal chalets by golf cart.

"Which they can also use on . . ." Celluci turned the page and shook his head in disbelief. ". . . the nine-hole golf course." Clearly, a large part of Mr. Gordon's building plan involved bulldozers. And right after the bulldozes would come the cappuccino. He shuddered.

The next few pages were clipped together and turned out to be photocopies of newspaper articles covering the disappearance of the surveyor. She'd been working with her partner in the late evening, trying to finish up a particularly marshy bit of shore destined to be filled in and paved over for tennis courts, when, according to her partner, she'd stepped back into the mud, announced something had moved under her foot, lost her balance, fell, screamed, and disappeared. The OPP, aided by local volunteers, had set up an extensive search but she hadn't been found. Since the area was usually avoided because of the sinkholes, sinkholes a distraught Stuart Gordon swore he knew nothing about—"Probably distraught about having to move his tennis courts," Celluci muttered—the official verdict allowed that she'd probably stepped in one and been sucked under the mud.

The headline on the next page declared DEVELOPER ANGERS SPIRIT, and in slightly smaller type, SURVEYOR PAYS THE PRICE. The picture showed an elderly woman with long, gray braids and a hawklike profile staring enigmatically out over the water. First impressions suggested a First Nations elder. In actually reading the text, however, Celluci discovered that Mary Joseph had moved out to Dulvie from Toronto in 1995 and had become, in the years since, the self-proclaimed keeper of local myth. According to Ms. Joseph, although there had been many sightings over the years, there had been only two other occasions when the spirit of the Lake had felt threatened enough to kill. "*It protects the lake,*" she was quoted as saying, "*from those who would disturb its peace.*"

"Two weeks ago," Celluci noted, checking the date. "Tragic, but hardly a reason for Stuart Gordon to go to the effort of convincing Vicki to leave the city."

The final photocopy included a close-up of a car door that looked like it had been splashed with acid. SPIRIT ATTACKS DEVELOPER'S VEHICLE. During the night of May 13th, the protector of Lake Nepeakea had crawled up into the parking lot of the lodge and secreted something corrosive and distinctly fishy against Stuart Gordon's brand-new Isuzu trooper. *A trail of dead bracken, a little over a foot wide and smelling strongly of rotting fish, lead back to the lake.* Mary Joseph seemed convinced it was a manifestation of the spirit, the local police were looking for anyone who might have information about the vandalism, and Stuart Gordon announced he was bringing in a special investigator from Toronto to settle it once and for all.

It was entirely probable that the surveyor had stepped into a mud hole and that local vandals were using the legends of the spirit against an unpopular developer. Entirely probable. But living with Vicki had forced Mike Celluci to deal with half a dozen improbable things every morning before breakfast, so, mug in hand, he headed outside to investigate the crime scene.

Because of the screen of evergreens—although given their size, "barricade" was probably the more descriptive word—the parking lot couldn't be seen from the lodge. Considering the impenetrable appearance of the overlapping branches, Celluci was willing to bet that not even light would get through. The spirit could have done anything it wanted to, up to and including changing the oil, in perfect secrecy.

Brushing one or two small insects away from his face, Celluci found the path they'd used the night before and followed it. By the time he reached the van, the one or two insects had become twenty-nine or thirty and he felt the first bite on the back of his neck. When he slapped the spot, his fingers came away dotted with blood.

"Vicki's not going to be happy about that," he grinned, wiping it off on his jeans. By the second and third bites, he'd stopped grinning. By the fourth and fifth, he really didn't give a damn what Vicki thought. By the time he'd stopped counting, he was running for the lake, hoping that the breeze he could see stirring its surface would be enough to blow the little bastards away.

The faint but unmistakable scent of rotting fish rose from the dead bracken crushed under his pounding feet and he realized that he was using the path made by the manifestation. It was about two feet wide and lead down an uncomfortably steep slope from the parking lot to the lake. But not exactly all the way to the lake. The path ended about three feet above the water on a granite ledge.

Swearing, mostly at Vicki, Celluci threw himself backward, somehow managing to save both his coffee and himself from taking an unexpected swim. The following cloud of insects effortlessly matched the move. A quick glance through the bugs showed the ledge tapering off to the right. He bounded down it to the water's edge and found himself standing on a small, man-made beach staring at a floating dock that stretched out maybe fifteen feet into the lake. Proximity to the water *had* seemed to discourage the swarm, so he headed for the dock hoping that the breeze would be stronger fifteen feet out.

It was. Flicking a few bodies out of his coffee, Celluci took a long, grateful drink and turned to look back up at the lodge. Studying the path he'd taken, he was amazed he hadn't broken an ankle and had to admit a certain appreciation for who or what had created it. A graying staircase made of split logs offered a more conventional way to the water and the tiny patch of gritty sand, held in place by a stone wall. Stuart Gordon's plans had included a much larger beach and had replaced the old wooden dock with three concrete piers.

"One for papa bear, one for mama bear, and one for baby bear," Celluci mused, shuffling around on the gently rocking platform until he faced the water. Not so far away, the far shore was an unbroken wall of trees. He didn't know if there *were* bears in this part of the province but there were certainly bathroom facilities for any number of them. Letting the breeze push his hair back off his face, he took another swallow of rapidly cooling coffee and listened to the silence. It was unnerving.

The sudden roar of a motor boat came as a welcome relief. Watching it bounce its way up the lake, he considered how far the sound carried and made a mental note to close the window should Vicki spend any significant portion of the night with him.

The moment distance allowed, the boat's driver waved over the edge of the cracked windshield and, in a great, banked turn that sprayed a huge fantail of water out behind him, headed toward the exact spot where Celluci stood. Celluci's fingers tightened around the handle of the mug but he held his ground. Still turning, the driver cut his engines and drifted the last few meters to the dock. As empty bleach bottles slowly crumpled under the gentle impact, he jumped out and tied off his bowline.

"Frank Patton," he said, straightening from the cleat and holding out a callused hand. "You must be the guy that developer's brought in from the city to capture the spirit of the lake."

"Detective Sergeant Mike Celluci." His own age or a little younger, Frank Patton had a working man's grip that was just a little too forceful. Celluci returned pressure for pressure. "And I'm just spending a long weekend in the woods."

Patton's dark brows drew down. "But I thought . . ."

"You thought I was some weirdo psychic you could impress by crushing his fingers." The other man looked down at their joined hands and had the grace to flush. As he released his hold, so did Celluci. He'd played this game too often to lose at it. "I suggest, if you get the chance to meet the actual investigator, you don't come on quite so strong. She's liable to feed you your preconceptions."

"She's . . ."

"Asleep right now. We got in late and she's likely to be up . . . investigating tonight."

"Yeah. Right." Flexing his fingers, Patton stared down at the toes of his work boots. "It's just, you know, we heard that, well . . ." Sucking in a deep breath, he looked up and grinned. "Oh hell, talk about getting off on the wrong foot. Can I get you a beer, Detective?"

Celluci glanced over at the Styrofoam cooler in the back of the boat and was tempted for a moment. As sweat rolled painfully into the bug bites on the back of his neck, he remembered just how good a cold beer could taste. "No, thanks," he sighed with a disgusted glare into his mug. "I've, uh, still got coffee."

To his surprise, Patton nodded and asked, "How long've you been dry? My brother-in-law gets that exact same look when some damn fool offers him a drink on a hot almost-summer afternoon," he explained as Celluci stared at him in astonishment. "Goes to AA meetings in Bigwood twice a week."

Remembering all the bottles he'd climbed into during those long months Vicki had been gone, Celluci shrugged. "About two years now—give or take."

"I got generic cola . . ."

Celluci dumped the dregs of cold bug-infested coffee into the lake. The Ministry of Natural Resources could kiss his ass. "Love one," he said.

"So essentially everyone in town and everyone who owns property around the lake and everyone in a hundred-kilometer radius has reason to want Stuart Gordon gone."

"Essentially," Celluci agreed, tossing a gnawed chicken-bone aside and pulling another piece out of the bucket. He'd waited to eat until Vicki got up, maintaining the illusion that it was a ritual they continued to share. "According to Frank Patton, he hasn't endeared himself to his new neighbors. This place used to belong to an Anne Kellough who . . . What?"

Vicki frowned and leaned toward him. "You're covered in bites."

"Tell me about it." The reminder brought his hand up to scratch at the back of his neck. "You know what Nepeakea means? It's an old Indian word that translates as 'I'm fucking sick of being eaten alive by black flies; let's get the hell out of here'."

"Those old Indians could get a lot of mileage out of a word."

Celluci snorted. "Tell me about it."

"Anne Kellough?"

"What, not even one 'poor sweet baby'?"

Stretching out her leg under the table, she ran her foot up the inseam of his jeans. "Poor sweet baby."

"That'd be a lot more effective if you weren't wearing hiking boots."

Her laugh was one of the things that hadn't changed when she had. Her smile was too white and too sharp and it made too many new promises, but her laugh remained fully human.

He waited until she finished, chewing, swallowing, congratulating himself for evoking it, then said, "Anne Kellough ran this place as sort of a therapy camp. Last summer, after ignoring her for thirteen years, the Ministry of Health people came down on her kitchen. Renovations cost more than she thought, the bank foreclosed, and Stuart Gordon bought it twenty minutes later."

"That explains why she wants him gone—what about everyone else?"

"Lifestyle."

"They think he's gay?"

"Not his, theirs. The people who live out here, down in the village and around the lake—while not adverse to taking the occasional tourist for everything they can get—like the quiet, they like the solitude and, god help them, they even like the woods. The boys who run the hunting and fishing camp at the west-end of the lake . . ."

"Boys?"

"I'm quoting here. *The boys*," he repeated, with emphasis, "say Gordon's development will kill the fish and scare off the game. He nearly got his ass kicked by one of them, Pete Wegler, down at the local gas station and then got tossed out on said ass by the owner when he called the place 'quaint'."

"In the sort of tone that adds, 'and a Starbucks would be a big improvement'?" When Celluci raised a brow, she shrugged. "I've spoken to him, it's not that much of an extrapolation."

"Yeah, exactly that sort of tone. Frank also told me that people with kids are concerned about the increase in traffic right through the center of the village."

"Afraid they'll start losing children and pets under expensive sport utes?"

"That, and they're worried about an increase in taxes to maintain the road with all the extra traffic." Pushing away from the table, he started closing plastic containers and carrying them to the fridge. "Apparently, Stuart Gordon, ever so diplomatically, told one of the village women that this was no place to raise kids."

"What happened?"

"Frank says they got them apart before it went much beyond name calling."

Wondering how far "much beyond name calling" went, Vicki watched Mike clean up the remains of his meal. "Are you sure he's pissed off more than just these few people? Even if this was already a resort and he didn't have to rezone, local council must've agreed to his building permit."

"Yeah, and local opinion would feed local council to the spirit right alongside Mr. Gordon. Rumor has it, they've been bought off."

Tipping her chair back against the wall, she smiled up at him. "Can I assume from your busy day that you've come down on the mud hole/vandals side of the argument?"

"It does seem the most likely." He turned and scratched at the back of his neck again. When his fingertips came away damp, he heard her quick intake of breath. When he looked up, she was crossing the kitchen. Cool fingers wrapped around the side of his face.

"You didn't shave."

It took him a moment to find his voice. "I'm on vacation."

Her breath lapped against him, then her tongue.

The lines between likely and unlikely blurred.

Then the sound of an approaching engine jerked him out of her embrace.

Vicki licked her lips and sighed. "Six cylinder, sport utility, four-wheel drive, *all* the extras, black with gold trim."

Celluci tucked his shirt back in. "Stuart Gordon told you what he drives."

"Unless you think I can tell all that from the sound of the engine."

"Not likely."

"A detective sergeant? I'm impressed." Pale hands in the pockets of his tweed blazer, Stuart Gordon leaned conspiratorially in toward Celluci, too many teeth showing in too broad a grin. "I don't suppose you could fix a few parking tickets."

"No."

Thin lips pursed in exaggerated reaction to the blunt monosyllable. "Then what do you *do*, Detective Sergeant?"

"Violent crimes."

Thinking that sounded a little too much like a suggestion, Vicki intervened. "Detective Celluci has agreed to assist me this weekend. Between us, we'll be able to keep a twenty-four-hour watch."

"Twenty-four hours?" The developer's brows drew in. "I'm not paying more for that."

"I'm not asking you to."

"Good." Stepping up onto the raised hearth as though it were a stage, he smiled with all the sincerity of a television infomercial. "Then I'm glad to have you aboard Detective, Mike—can I call you Mike?" He continued without waiting for an answer. "Call me Stuart. Together we'll make this a safe place for the weary masses able to pay a premium price for a premium week in the woods." A heartbeat later, his smile grew strained. "Don't you two have detecting to do?"

"Call me Stuart?" Shaking his head, Celluci followed Vicki's dark on dark silhouette out to the parking lot. "Why is he here?"

"He's bait."

"Bait? The man's a certified asshole, sure, but we are *not* using him to attract an angry lake spirit."

She turned and walked backward so she could study his face. Sometimes he forgot how well she could see in the dark and forgot to mask his expressions. "Mike, you don't believe that call-me-Stuart has actually pissed off some kind of vengeful spirit protecting Lake Nepeakea?"

"You're the one who said 'bait' . . ."

"Because we're not going to catch the person, or persons, who threw acid on his car unless we catch them in the act. He understands that."

"Oh. Right."

Feeling the bulk of the van behind her, she stopped. "You didn't answer my question."

He sighed and folded his arms, wishing he could see her as well as she could see him. "Vicki, in the last four years I have been attacked by demons, mummies, zombies, werewolves . . ."

"That wasn't an attack, that was a misunderstanding."

"He went for my throat, I count it as an attack. I've offered my blood to the bastard son of Henry VIIII, and I've spent two years watching you hide from the day. There isn't anything much I don't believe in anymore."

"But . . ."

"I believe in you," he interrupted, "and from there, it's not that big a step to just about anywhere. Are you going to speak with Mary Joseph tonight?"

His tone suggested the discussion was over.

"No, I was going to check means and opportunity on that list of names you gave me." She glanced down toward the lake then up at him, not entirely certain what she was looking for in either instance. "Are you going to be all right out here on your own?"

"Why the hell wouldn't I be?"

"No reason." She kissed him, got into the van, and leaned out the open window to add, "Try and remember, Sigmund, that sometimes a cigar is just a cigar."

Celluci watched Vicki drive away and then turned on his flashlight and played the beam over the side of Stuart's car. Although it would have been more helpful to have seen the damage, he had to admit that the body shop had done a good job. And to give the man credit, however reluctantly, developing a wilderness property did provide more of an excuse than most of his kind had for the four-wheel drive.

Making his way over to an outcropping of rock where he could see both the parking lot and the lake but not be seen, Celluci sat down and turned off his light. According to Frank Patton, the black flies only fed during the day and the water was still too cold for mosquitoes. He wasn't entirely convinced, but since nothing had bitten him so far the information seemed accurate. "I wonder if Stuart knows his little paradise is crawling with blood-suckers." Right thumb stroking the puncture wound on his left wrist, he turned toward the lodge.

His eyes widened.

Behind the evergreens, the lodge blazed with light. Inside lights. Outside lights. Every light in the place. The harsh yellow-white illumination washed out the stars up above and threw everything below into such sharp relief that even the lush, spring growth seemed manufactured. The shadows under the distant trees were now solid, impenetrable sheets of darkness.

"Well at least Ontario Hydro's glad he's here." Shaking his head in disbelief, Celluci returned to his surveillance.

Too far away for the light to reach it, the lake threw up shimmering reflections of the stars and lapped gently against the shore.

Finally back on the paved road, Vicki unclenched her teeth and followed the southern edge of the lake toward the village. With nothing between the passenger side of the van and the water but a whitewashed guardrail and a few tumbled rocks, it was easy enough to look out the window and pretend she was driving on the lake itself. When the shoulder widened into a small parking area and a boat ramp, she pulled over and shut off the van.

The water moved inside its narrow channel like liquid darkness, opaque and mysterious. The part of the night that belonged to her, ended at the water's edge.

"Not the way it's supposed to work," she muttered, getting out of the van and walking down the boat ramp. Up close, she could see through four or five inches of liquid to a stony bottom and the broken shells of freshwater clams but beyond that, it was hard not to believe she couldn't just walk across to the other side.

The ubiquitous spring chorus of frogs suddenly fell silent, drawing Vicki's attention around to a marshy cove off to her right. The silence was so complete she thought she could hear half a hundred tiny amphibian hearts beating. One. Two . . .

"Hey, there."

She'd spun around and taken a step out into the lake before her brain caught up with her reaction. The feel of cold water filling her hiking boots brought her back to herself and she damped the hunter in her eyes before the man in the canoe had time to realize his danger.

Paddle in the water, holding the canoe in place, he nodded down at Vicki's feet. "You don't want to be doing that."

"Doing what?"

"Wading at night. You're going to want to see where you're going, old Nepeakea drops off fast." He jerked his head back toward the silvered darkness. "Even the ministry boys couldn't tell you how deep she is in the middle. She's got so much loose mud on the bottom it kept throwing back their sonar readings."

"Then what are you doing here?"

"Well, I'm not wading, that's for sure."

"Or answering my question," Vicki muttered stepping back out on the shore. Wet feet making her less than happy, she half-hoped for another smart-ass comment.

"I often canoe at night. I like the quiet." He grinned at her, clearly believing he was too far away and there was too little light for her to see the appraisal that went with it. "You must be that investigator from Toronto. I saw your van when I was up at the lodge today."

"You must be Frank Patton. You've changed your boat."

"Can't be quiet in a fifty-horsepower Evinrude, can I? You going in to see Mary Joseph?"

"No. I was going in to see Anne Kellough."

"Second house past the stop sign on the right. Little yellow bungalow with a carport." He slid backward so quietly even Vicki wouldn't have known he was moving had she not been watching him. He handled the big aluminum canoe with practiced ease. "I'd offer you a lift but I'm sure you're in a hurry."

Vicki smiled. "Thanks anyway." Her eyes silvered. "Maybe another time."

She was still smiling as she got into the van. Out on the lake, Frank Patton splashed about trying to retrieve the canoe paddle that had dropped from nerveless fingers.

"Frankly, I hate the little bastard, but there's no law against that." Anne Kellough pulled her sweater tighter and leaned back against the porch railing. "He's the one who set the health department on me, you know."

"I didn't."

"Oh yeah. He came up here about three months before it happened looking for land and he wanted mine. I wouldn't sell it to him so he figured out a way to take it." Anger quickened her breathing and flared her nostrils. "He as much as told me, after it was all over, with that big shit-eating grin and his, 'Rough luck, Ms. Kellough, too bad the banks can't be more forgiving.' The patronizing asshole." Eyes narrowed, she glared at Vicki. "And you know what really pisses me off? I used to rent the lodge out to people who needed a little silence in their lives; you know, so they could maybe hear what was going on inside their heads. If Stuart Gordon has his way, there won't *be* any silence and the place'll be awash in brand names and expensive dental work."

"If Stuart Gordon has his way?" Vicki repeated, brows rising.

"Well, it's not built yet, is it?"

"He has all the paperwork filed; what's going to stop him?"

The other woman picked at a flake of paint, her whole attention focused on lifting it from the railing. Just when Vicki felt she'd have to ask again, Anne looked up and out toward the dark waters of the lake. "That's the question, isn't it," she said softly, brushing her hair back off her face.

The lake seemed no different to Vicki than it ever had. About to suggest that the question acquire an answer, she suddenly frowned. "What happened to your hand? That looks like an acid burn."

"It is." Anne turned her arm so that the burn was more clearly visible to them both. "Thanks to Stuart fucking Gordon, I couldn't afford to take my car in to the garage and I had to change the battery myself. I thought I was being careful . . ." She shrugged.

"A new battery, eh? Afraid I can't help you, miss." Ken, owner of Ken's Garage and Auto Body, pressed one knee against the side of the van and leaned, letting it take his weight as he filled the tank. "But if you're not in a hurry I can go into Bigwood tomorrow and get you one." Before Vicki could speak, he went on. "No wait, tomorrow's Sunday, place'll be closed. Closed Monday too seeing as how it's Victoria Day." He shrugged and smiled. "I'll be open, but that won't get you a battery."

"It doesn't have to be a new one. I just want to make sure that when I turn her off on the way home I can get her started again." Leaning back against the closed driver's side door, she gestured into the work bay where a small pile of old batteries had been more or less stacked against the back wall. "What about one of them?"

Ken turned, peered, and shook his head. "Damn but you've got good eyes, miss. It's dark as bloody pitch in there."

"Thank you."

"None of them batteries will do you any good though, 'cause I drained them all a couple of days ago. They're just too dangerous, eh? You know, if kids get poking around?" He glanced over at the gas pump and carefully squirted the total up to an even thirty-two dollars. "You're that investigator working up at the lodge, aren't you?" he asked as he pushed the bills she handed him into a greasy pocket and counted out three loonies in change. "Trying to lay the spirit?"

"Trying to catch whoever vandalized Stuart Gordon's car."

"He, uh, get that fixed then?"

"Good as new." Vicki opened the van door and paused, one foot up on the running board. "I take it he didn't get it fixed here?"

"Here?" The slightly worried expression on Ken's broad face vanished to be replaced by a curled lip and narrowed eyes. "My gas isn't good enough for that pissant. He's planning to put his own tanks in if he gets that god-damned yuppie resort built."

"If?"

Much as Anne Kellough had, he glanced toward the lake. "If."

About to swing up into the van, two five-gallon glass jars sitting outside the office caught her eye. The lids were off and it looked very much as though they were airing out. "I haven't seen jars like that in years," she said, pointing. "I don't suppose you want to sell them?"

Ken turned to follow her finger. "Can't. They belong to my cousin. I just borrowed them, eh? Her kids were supposed to come and get them but, hey, you know kids."

According to call-me-Stuart, the village was no place to raise kids.

Glass jars would be handy for transporting acid mixed with fish bits.

And where would they have gotten the fish, she wondered, pulling carefully out of the gas station. *Maybe from one of the boys who runs the hunting and fishing camp.*

Pete Wegler stood in the door of his trailer, a slightly confused look on his face. "Do I know you?"

Vicki smiled. "Not yet. Aren't you going to invite me in?"

Ten to twelve. The lights were still on at the lodge. Celluci stood, stretched, and wondered how much longer Vicki was going to be. *Surely everyone in Dulvie's asleep by now.*

Maybe she stopped for a bite to eat.

The second thought followed the first too quickly for him to prevent it, so he ignored it instead. Turning his back on the lodge, he sat down and stared out at the lake. Water looked almost secretive at night, he decided as his eyes readjusted to the darkness.

In his business, secretive meant guilty.

"And if Stuart Gordon has gotten a protective spirit pissed off enough to kill, what then?" he wondered aloud, glancing down at his watch.

Midnight.

Which meant absolutely nothing to that ever-expanding catalogue of things that went bump in the night. Experience had taught him that the so-called supernatural was just about as likely to attack at two in the afternoon as at midnight, but he couldn't not react to the knowledge that he was as far from the dubious safety of daylight as he was able to get.

Even the night seemed effected.

Waiting . . .

A breeze blew in off the lake and the hair lifted on both his arms.

Waiting for *something* to happen.

About fifteen feet from shore, a fish broke through the surface of the water like Alice going the wrong way through the Looking Glass. It leapt up, up, and was suddenly grabbed by the end of a glistening, gray tube as big around as his biceps. Teeth, or claws, or something back inside the tube's opening sank into the fish and together they finished the arch of the leap. A hump, the same glistening gray, slid up and back into the water, followed by what could only have been the propelling beat of a flat tail. From teeth to tail the whole thing had to be at least nine feet long.

"Jesus H. Christ." He took a deep breath and added, "On crutches."

"I'm telling you, Vicki, I saw the spirit of the lake manifest."

"You saw something eat a fish." Vicki stared out at the water but saw only the reflection of a thousand stars. "You probably saw a bigger fish eat a fish. A long, narrow pike leaping up after a nice fat bass."

About to deny he'd seen any such thing, Celluci suddenly frowned. "How do you know so much about fish?"

"I had a little talk with Pete Wegler tonight. He provided the fish for the acid bath, provided by Ken the garage-man, in glass jars provided by Ken's cousin, Kathy Boomhower—the mother who went much beyond name-calling with our boy Stuart. Anne Kellough did the deed—she's convinced Gordon called in the Health Department to get his hands on the property—having been transported quietly to the site in Frank Patton's canoe." She grinned. "I feel like Hercule Perot on the Orient Express."

"Yeah? Well, I'm feeling a lot more Stephen King than Agatha Christie."

Sobering, Vicki laid her hand on the barricade of his crossed arms and studied his face. "You're really freaked by this, aren't you?"

"I don't know exactly what I saw, but I didn't see a fish get eaten by another fish."

The muscles under her hand were rigid and he was staring past her, out at the lake. "Mike, what is it?"

"I told you, Vicki. I don't know exactly what I saw." In spite of everything, he still liked his world defined. Reluctantly transferring his gaze to the pale oval of her upturned face, he sighed. "How much, if any, of this do you want me to tell Mr. Gordon tomorrow?"

"How about none? I'll tell him myself after sunset."

"Fine. It's late, I'm turning in. I assume you'll be staking out the parking lot for the rest of the night."

"What for? I guarantee the vengeful spirit won't be back." Her voice suggested that in a direct, one-on-one confrontation, a vengeful spirit wouldn't stand a chance. Celluci remembered the thing that rose up out of the lake and wasn't so sure.

"That doesn't matter, you promised twenty-four-hour protection."

"Yeah, but . . ." His expression told her that if she wasn't going to stay, he would. "Fine, I'll watch the car. Happy?"

"That you're doing what you said you were going to do? Ecstatic." Celluci unfolded his arms, pulled her close enough to kiss the frown lines between her brows, and headed for the lodge. *She had a little talk with Pete Wegler, my ass.* He knew Vicki had to feed off others, but he didn't have to like it.

Should never have mentioned Pete Wegler. She settled down on the rock still warm from Celluci's body heat and tried unsuccessfully to penetrate the darkness of the lake. When something rustled in the underbrush bordering the parking lot, she hissed without turning her head. The rustling moved away with considerably more speed than it had used to arrive. The secrets of the lake continued to elude her.

"This isn't mysterious, it's irritating."

As Celluci wandered around the lodge, turning off lights, he could hear Stuart snoring through the door of one of the two main-floor bedrooms. In the few hours he'd been outside, the other man had managed to leave a trail of debris from one end of the place to the other. On top of that, he'd used up the last of the toilet paper on the roll and hadn't replaced it; he'd put the almost empty coffee pot back on the coffee maker with the machine still on so that the dregs had baked onto the glass, and he'd eaten a piece of Celluci's chicken, tossing the gnawed bone back into the bucket. Celluci didn't mind him eating the piece of chicken, but the last thing he wanted was Stuart Gordon's spit over the rest of the bird.

Dropping the bone into the garbage, he noticed a crumpled piece of paper and fished it out. Apparently the resort was destined to grow beyond its current boundaries. Destined to grow all the way around the lake, devouring Dulvie as it went.

"Which would put Stuart Gordon's spit all over the rest of the area."

Bored with watching the lake and frightening off the local wildlife, Vicki pressed her nose against the window of the sports ute and clicked her tongue at the dashboard full of electronic displays, willing to bet that call-me-Stuart didn't have the slightest idea of what most of them meant.

"Probably has a trouble light if his air freshener needs . . . hello."

Tucked under the passenger seat was the unmistakable edge of a laptop.

"And how much do you want to bet this thing'll scream bloody blue murder if I try and jimmy the door . . ." Turning toward the now dark lodge, she listened to the sound of two heartbeats. To the slow, regular sound that told her both men were deeply asleep.

Stuart slept on his back with one hand flung over his head and a slight smile on his thin face. Vicki watched the pulse beat in his throat for a moment. She'd been assured that, if necessary, she could feed off lower life-forms—pigeons, rats, developers—but she was just as glad she'd taken the edge off the Hunger down in the village. Scooping up his car keys, she went out of the room as silently as she'd come in.

Celluci woke to a decent voice belting out a Beatles tune and came downstairs just as Stuart came out of the bathroom finger-combing damp hair.

"Good morning, Mike. Can I assume no vengeful spirits of Lake Nepeakea trashed my car in the night?"

"You can."

"Good. Good. Oh, by the way . . ." His smile could have sold attitude to Americans. ". . . I've used all the hot water."

"I guess it's true what they say about so many of our boys in blue."

"And what's that?" Celluci growled, fortified by two cups of coffee made only slightly bitter by the burned carafe.

"Well you know, Mike." Grinning broadly, the developer mimed tipping a bottle to his lips. "I mean, if you can drink that vile brew, you've certainly got a drinking problem." Laughing at his own joke, he headed for the door.

To begin with, they're not your boys in blue and then, you can just fucking well drop dead. You try dealing with the world we deal with for a while asshole, it'll chew you up and spit you out. But although his fist closed around his mug tightly enough for it to creak, all he said was, "Where are you going?"

"Didn't I tell you? I've got to see a lawyer in Bigwood today. Yes, I know what you're going to say Mike, it's Sunday. But since this is the last time I'll be out here for a few weeks, the local legal beagle can see me when I'm available. Just a few loose ends about that nasty business with the surveyor." He paused, with his hand on the door, voice and manner stripped of all pretensions. "I told them to be sure and finish that part of the shoreline before they quit for the day—I know I'm not, but I feel responsible for that poor woman's death, and I only wish there was something I could do to make up for it. You can't make up for someone dying though, can you, Mike?"

Celluci growled something noncommittal. Right at the moment, the last thing he wanted was to think of Stuart Gordon as a decent human being.

"I might not be back until after dark but hey, that's when the spirit's likely to appear so you won't need me until then. Right, Mike?" Turning toward the screen where the black flies had settled, waiting for their breakfast to emerge, he shook his head. "The first thing I'm going to do when all this is settled is drain every stream these little bloodsuckers breed in."

The water levels in the swamp had dropped in the two weeks since the death of the surveyor. Drenched in the bug spray he'd found under the sink, Celluci followed the path made by the searchers, treading carefully on the higher hummocks no matter how solid the ground looked. When he reached the remains of the police tape, he squatted and peered down into the water. He didn't expect to find anything, but after Stuart's confession, he felt he had to come.

About two inches deep, it was surprisingly clear.

"No reason for it to be muddy now, there's nothing stirring it . . ."

Something metallic glinted in the mud.

Gripping the marsh grass on his hummock with one hand, he reached out with the other and managed to get thumb and forefinger around the protruding piece of . . .

"Stainless steel measuring tape?"

It was probably a remnant of the dead surveyor's equipment. One end of the six-inch piece had been cleanly broken but the other end, the end that had been down in the mud, looked as though it had been dissolved.

When Anne Kellough had thrown the acid on Stuart's car, they'd been imitating the spirit of Lake Nepeakea.

Celluci inhaled deeply and spit a mouthful of suicidal black flies out into the swamp. "I think it's time to talk to Mary Joseph."

"Can't you feel it?"

Enjoying the first decent cup of coffee he'd had in days, Celluci walked to the edge of the porch and stared out at the lake. Unlike most of Dulvie, separated from the water by the road, Mary Joseph's house was right on the shore. "I can feel *something*," he admitted.

"You can feel the spirit of the lake, angered by this man from the city. Another cookie?"

"No, thank you." He'd had one and it was without question the worst cookie he'd ever eaten. "Tell me about the spirit of the lake, Ms. Joseph. Have you seen it?"

"Oh yes. Well, not exactly it, but I've seen the wake of its passing." She gestured out toward the water but, at the moment, the lake was perfectly calm. "Most water has a protective spirit, you know. Wells and springs, lakes and rivers, it's why we throw coins into fountains, so that the spirits will exchange them for luck. Kelpies, selkies, mermaids, Jenny Greenteeth, Peg Powler, the Fideal . . . all water spirits."

"And one of them, is that what's out there?" Somehow he couldn't reconcile mermaids to that toothed trunk snaking out of the water.

"Oh no, our water spirit is a new-world water spirit. The Cree called it a *mantouche*—surely you recognize the similarity to the word Manitou or Great Spirit? Only the deepest lakes with the best fishing had them. They protected the lakes and the area around the lakes and, in return . . ."

"Were revered?"

"Well, no actually. They were left strictly alone."

"You told the paper that the spirit had manifested twice before?"

"Twice that we know of," she corrected. "The first recorded manifestation occurred in 1762 and was included in the notes on native spirituality that one of the exploring Jesuits sent back to France."

Product of a Catholic school education, Celluci wasn't entirely certain the involvement of the Jesuits added credibility. "What happened?"

"It was spring. A pair of white trappers had been at the lake all winter, slaughtering the animals around it. Animals under the lake's protection. According to the surviving trapper, his partner was coming out of high-water marshes, just after sunset, when his canoe suddenly upended and he disappeared. When the remaining man retrieved the canoe he found that bits had been burned away without flame, and it carried the mark of all the dead they'd stolen from the lake."

"The mark of the dead?"

"The record says it stank, Detective. Like offal." About to eat another cookie, she paused. "You do know what offal is?"

"Yes, ma'am. Did the survivor see anything?"

"Well, he said he saw what he thought was a giant snake except that it had two stubby wings at the upper end. And you know what that is."

. . . a glistening, gray tube as big around as his biceps. "No."

"A wyvern. One of the ancient dragons."

"There's a dragon in the lake?"

"No, of course not. The spirit of the lake can take many forms. When it's angry, those who face its anger see a great and terrifying beast. To the trapper, who no doubt had northern European roots, it appeared as a wyvern. The natives would have probably seen a giant serpent. There are many so-called serpent mounds around deep lakes."

"But it couldn't just *be* a giant serpent?"

"Detective Celluci, don't you think that if there was a giant serpent living in this lake that someone would have gotten a good look at it by now? Besides, after the second death the lake was searched extensively with modern equipment—and once or twice since then as well—and nothing has ever been found. That trapper was killed by the spirit of the lake and so was Thomas Stebbing."

"Thomas Stebbing?"

"The recorded death in 1937. I have newspaper clippings . . ."

In the spring of 1937, four young men from the University of Toronto came to Lake Nepeakea on a wilderness vacation. Out canoeing with a friend at dusk, Thomas Stebbing saw what he thought was a burned log on the shore and they paddled in to investigate. As his friend watched in horror, the log "attacked" Stebbing, left him burned and dead and "undulated into the lake" on a trail of dead vegetation.

The investigation turned up nothing at all and the eyewitness account of a "kind of big worm thing" was summarily dismissed. The final, official verdict was that the victim had indeed disturbed a partially burnt log and, as it rolled over him, was burned by the embers and died. The log then rolled into the lake, burning a path as it rolled, and sank. The stench was dismissed as the smell of roasting flesh and the insistence by the friend that the burns were acid burns was completely ignored—in spite of the fact he was a chemistry student and should therefore know what he was talking about.

"The spirit of the *lake* came up on *land*, Ms. Joseph?"

She nodded, apparently unconcerned with the contradiction. "There were a lot of fires being lit around the lake that year. Between the wars this area got popular for a while and fires were the easiest way to clear land for summer homes. The spirit of the lake couldn't allow that, hence its appearance as a burned log."

"And Thomas Stebbing had done what to disturb its peace?"

"Nothing specifically. I think the poor boy was just in the wrong place at the wrong time. It is a vengeful spirit, you understand."

Only a few short years earlier, he'd have understood that Mary Joseph was a total nutcase. But that was before he'd willing thrown himself into the darkness that lurked behind a pair of silvered eyes. He sighed and stood, the afternoon had nearly ended. It wouldn't be long now until sunset.

"Thank you for your help, Ms. Joesph. I . . . what?"

She was staring at him, nodding. "You've seen it, haven't you? You have that look."

"I've seen something," he admitted reluctantly and turned toward the water. "I've seen a lot thi . . ."

A pair of jet skis roared around the point and drowned him out. As they passed the house, blanketing it in noise, one of the adolescent operators waved a cheery hello.

Never a vengeful lake spirit around when you really need one, he thought.

"He knew about the sinkholes in the marsh and he sent those surveyors out anyway." Vicki tossed a pebble off the end of the dock and watched it disappear into the liquid darkness.

"You're sure?"

"The information was all there on his laptop and the file was dated back in March. Now, although evidence that I just happened to have found in his computer will be inadmissible in court, I can go to the Department of Lands and Forests and get the dates he requested the geological surveys."

Celluci shook his head. "You're not going to be able to get him charged with anything. Sure, he should've told them, but they were both professionals, they should've been more careful." He thought of the crocodile tears Stuart had cried that morning over the death, and his hands formed fists by his side. Being an irresponsible asshole was one thing, being a manipulative, irresponsible asshole was on another level entirely. "It's an ethical failure," he growled, "not a legal one."

"Maybe I should take care of him myself then." The second pebble hit the water with considerably more force.

"He's your client, Vicki. You're supposed to be working for him, not against him."

She snorted. "So I'll wait until his check clears."

"He's planning on acquiring the rest of the land around the lake." Pulling the paper he'd retrieved from the garbage out of his pocket, Celluci handed it over.

"The rest of the land around the lake isn't for sale."

"Neither was this lodge until he decided he wanted it."

Crushing the paper in one hand, Vicki's eyes silvered. "There's got to be something we can . . . Shit!" Tossing the paper aside, she grabbed Celluci's arm as the end of the dock bucked up into the air and leapt back one section, dragging him with her. "What the fuck was that?" she demanded as they turned to watch the place they'd just been standing rock violently back and forth. The paper she'd dropped into the water was nowhere to be seen.

"Wave from a passing boat?"

"There hasn't been a boat past here in hours."

"Sometimes these long narrow lakes build up a standing wave. It's called a *seiche*."

"A *seiche*?" When he nodded, she rolled her eyes. "I've got to start watching more PBS. In the meantime . . ."

The sound of an approaching car drew their attention up to the lodge in time to see Stuart slowly and carefully pull into the parking lot, barely disturbing the gravel.

"Are you going to tell him who vandalized his car?" Celluci asked as they started up the hill.

"Who? Probably not. I can't prove it after all, but I will tell him it wasn't some vengeful spirit and it definitely won't happen again." At least not if Pete Wegler had anything to say about it. The spirit of the lake might be hypothetical, but she wasn't.

"A group of villagers, Vicki? You're sure?"

"Positive."

"They actually thought I'd believe it was an angry spirit manifesting all over the side of my vehicle?"

"Apparently." Actually, they hadn't cared if he believed it or not. They were all just so angry they needed to do something and since the spirit was handy . . . She offered none of that to call-me-Stuart.

"I want their names, Vicki." His tone made it an ultimatum.

Vicki had never responded well to ultimatums. Celluci watched her masks begin to fall and wondered just how far his dislike of the developer would let her go. He could stop her with a word, he just wondered if he'd say it. Or when.

To his surprise, she regained control. "Check the census lists then. You haven't exactly endeared yourself to your neighbors."

For a moment, it seemed that Stuart realized how close he'd just come to seeing the definition of his own mortality but then he smiled and said, "You're right, Vicki, I haven't endeared myself to my neighbors. And do you know what; I'm going to do something about that. Tomorrow's Victoria Day, I'll invite them all to a big picnic supper with great food and fireworks out over the lake. We'll kiss and make up."

"It's Sunday evening and tomorrow's a holiday. Where are you going to find food and fireworks?"

"Not a problem, Mike. I'll e-mail my caterers in Toronto. I'm sure they can be here by tomorrow afternoon. I'll pay through the nose but hey, developing a good relationship with the locals is worth it. You two will stay, of course."

Vicki's lips drew back off her teeth, but Celluci answered for them both. "Of course."

"He's up to something," he explained later, "and I want to know what that is."

"He's going to confront the villagers with what he knows, see who reacts and make their lives a living hell. He'll find a way to make them the first part of his expansion."

"You're probably right."

"I'm always right." Head pillowed on his shoulder, she stirred his chest hair with one finger. "He's an unethical, immoral, unscrupulous little asshole."

"You missed annoying, irritating, and just generally unlikable."

"I could convince him he was a combination of Mother Theresa and Lady Di. I could rip his mind out, use it for unnatural purposes, and stuff it back into his skull in any shape I damn well chose, but I can't."

Once you start down the dark side, forever will it dominate your destiny? But he didn't say it aloud because he didn't want to know how far down the dark side she'd been. He was grateful that she'd drawn any personal boundaries at all, that she'd chosen to remain someone who couldn't use terror for the sake of terror. "So what are we going to do about him?"

"I can't think of a damned thing. You?"

Suddenly he smiled. "Could you convince him that *you* were the spirit of the lake and that he'd better haul his ass back to Toronto unless he wants it dissolved off?"

She was off the bed in one fluid movement. "I knew there was a reason I dragged you out here this weekend." She turned on one bare heel then turned again and was suddenly back in the bed. "But I think I'll wait until tomorrow night. He hasn't paid me yet."

"Morning, Mike. Where's Vicki?"

"Sleeping."

"Well, since you're up, why don't you help out by carrying the barbecue down to the beach. I may be willing to make amends but I'm not sure they are, and since they've already damaged my car, I'd just as soon keep them away from anything valuable. Particularly when in combination with propane and open flames."

"Isn't Vicki joining us for lunch, Mike?"

"She says she isn't hungry. She went for a walk in the woods."

"Must be how she keeps her girlish figure. I've got to hand it to you, Mike, there aren't many men your age who could hold on to such a woman. I mean, she's really got that independent thing going, doesn't she?" He accepted a tuna sandwich with effusive thanks, took a bite and winced. "Not light mayo?"

"No."

"Never mind, Mike. I'm sure you meant well. Now, then, as it's just the two of us, have you ever considered investing in a time share . . ."

Mike Celluci had never been so glad to see anyone as he was to see a van full of bleary-eyed and stiff caterers arrive at four that afternoon. As Vicki had discovered during that initial phone call, Stuart Gordon was not a man who took "no" for an answer. He might have accepted "Fuck off and die!" followed by a fast exit, but since Vicki expected to wake up on the shores of Lake Nepeakea, Celluci held his tongue. Besides, it would be a little difficult for her to chase the developer away if they were halfway back to Toronto.

Sunset.

Vicki could feel maybe two dozen lives around her when she woke, and she laid there for a moment reveling in them. The last two evenings she'd had to fight the urge to climb into the driver's seat and speed toward civilization.

"Fast food."

She snickered, dressed, and stepped out into the parking lot.

Celluci was down on the beach talking to Frank Patton. She made her way over to them, the crowd opening to let her pass without really being aware she was there at all. Both men nodded as she approached, and Patton gestured toward the barbecue.

"Burger?"

"No thanks, I'm not hungry." She glanced around. "No one seems to have brought their kids."

"No one wants to expose their kids to Stuart Gordon."

"Afraid they'll catch something," Celluci added.

"Mike here says you've solved your case and you're just waiting for Mr. Congeniality over there to pay you."

Wondering what Mike had been up to, Vicki nodded.

"He also says you didn't mention any names. Thank you." He sighed. "We didn't really expect the spirit of the lake thing to work but . . ."

Vicki raised both hands. "Hey, you never know. He could be suppressing."

"Yeah, right. The only thing that clown suppresses is everyone around him. If you'll excuse me, I'd better go rescue Anne before she rips out his tongue and strangles him with it."

"I'm surprised she came," Vicki admitted.

"She thinks he's up to something and she wants to know what it is."

"Don't we all," Celluci murmured as he walked away.

The combined smell of cooked meat and fresh blood making her a little light-headed, Vicki started Mike moving toward the floating dock. "Have I missed anything?"

"No, I think you're just in time."

As Frank Patton approached, Stuart broke off the conversation he'd been having with Anne Kellough—or more precisely, Vicki amended, *at* Anne Kellough—and walked out to the end of the dock where a number of large rockets had been set up.

"He's got a permit for the damned things," Celluci muttered. "The son of a bitch knows how to cover his ass."

"But not his id." Vicki's fingers curved cool around Mike's forearm. "He'll get his, don't worry."

The first rocket went up, exploding red over the lake, the colors muted against the evening gray of sky and water. The developer turned toward the shore and raised both hands above his head. "Now that I've got your attention, there's a few things I'd like to share with you all before the festivities continue. First of all, I've decided not to press charges concerning the damage to my vehicle although I'm aware that . . ."

The dock began to rock. Behind him, one of the rockets fell into the water.

"Mr. Gordon." The voice was Mary Joseph's. "Get to shore, now."

Pointing a finger toward her, he shook his head. "Oh no, old woman, I'm Stuart Gordon . . ."

Not *call-me-Stuart*, tonight, Celluci noted.

". . . and you don't tell me what to do, I tell . . ."

Arms windmilling, he stepped back, once, twice, and hit the water. Arms and legs stretched out, he looked as though he was sitting on something just below the surface. "I have had enough of this," he began . . .

. . . and disappeared.

Vicki reached the end of the dock in time to see the pale oval of his face engulfed by dark water. To her astonishment, he seemed to have gotten his cell phone out of his pocket and all she could think of was that old movie cut line, *Who you gonna call?*

One heartbeat, two. She thought about going in after him. The fingertips on her reaching hand were actually damp when Celluci grabbed her shoulder and pulled her back. She wouldn't have done it, but it was nice that he thought she would.

Back on the shore, two dozen identical wide-eyed stares were locked on the flat, black surface of the lake, too astounded by what had happened to their mutual enemy, Vicki realized, to notice how fast she'd made it to the end of the dock.

Mary Joseph broke the silence first. "Thus acts the vengeful spirit of Lake Nepeakea," she declared. Then as heads began to nod, she added dryly, "Can't say I didn't warn him."

Mike looked over at Vicki, who shrugged.

"Works for me," she said.

La Diente

Nancy Kilpatrick

Nancy Kilpatrick has been described by *Fangoria* as "Canada's answer to Anne Rice." Best known for her vampire-themed fiction, she is the award-winning author of nineteen novels, more than two hundred short stories, six collections, and one nonfiction book. She has also edited fifteen anthologies, including *Danse Macabre: Close Encounters with the Reaper, Expiration Date,* and *nEvermore! Tales of Murder, Mystery and the Macabre.* Her most recent novel is *Revenge of the Vampire King,* the first in the six-volume Thrones of Blood cycle, while under her "Amarantha Knight" pseudonym she wrote the erotic novels *Dracula* and *Carmilla* in The Darker Passions series.

"I met a man from Ecuador who showed me four of his baby teeth," recalls the author, "which his mother had made into jewelry—a custom in his homeland. The vampire is very popular with Spanish-speaking people, and they have their own variation, *el Chupa-cabra.*

"Combining these images inspired 'La Diente.'"

SUDDENLY, THE VAMPIRE appeared in the doorway! Tall, cadaverous, eyes glowing with the fires of Hell. His fingers curled around the doorframe, spider-like.

Remedios trembled. Her heart beat wildly, as if it wanted to explode inside her chest.

He inched forward, movements ratlike. He focused on his victim, his prey.

She clutched the wooden arm of the chair and squeezed her body into a tighter ball. "*Diosito! Mio Diosito!* Protect me Santa Marianita de Jesus!" she cried, but he kept coming.

"Submit to me!" he insisted, his voice low and seductive, the tone not one that could be argued with. "I am stronger. I will have what I want!"

"No!" She shook her head. Her sweaty hand slipped off the chair arm where she had gripped it so tightly.

His face came close, ungodly close, and then his blood-red lips turned upward into a sinister smile. A smile that split apart to reveal two long, sharp teeth. Teeth that glistened with saliva. Teeth that wanted her neck.

Demanded the vein, plumped with her life's blood, pulsing in terror. Teeth that would bite and rend and take what they needed in order to survive.

A loud, harsh buzzer caused Remedios to jolt.

She leapt from the chair and hurried into the kitchen to turn off the oven timer. Quickly she opened the door and lifted the lid of the clay pot—the meat looked and smelled delicious, just the way the Richviews liked it—rare. It had taken her almost three months to be able to prepare it the way her employers preferred. She wanted to please them, but something about that red color when she cut into it, all the blood, made her feel nauseous, and she found herself frequently overcooking. Remedios had never eaten rare meat. At home in Ecuador, everyone overcooked meat, to be safe. She preferred it well done, so that it did not resemble anymore the poor helpless animal that it had been.

With a deft hand, she switched the oven knob to WARM, and turned on the element under the pot on the stovetop that would steam the summer squash. The salad and dessert had been prepared in advance, the table set, all was well. She headed back to the living room for the end of the movie, only to find a commercial on the TV for feminine hygiene products, as they liked to call them in North America. It had taken her most of the six months she had been in San Diego to make sense of this new language, but finally she was beginning to feel as if she had mastered at least the basics. Now she could shop and take the bus without incident, mostly, and the Richviews seemed more comfortable around her. At least as comfortable as they could be.

Just as the commercial finished and the movie resumed, she heard a car pull into the driveway. Well, that was that. She switched off the television and returned to the kitchen. She would never know how the movie ended, but of course the vampire would be staked. He always was, or at least most of the time. She preferred movies where the vampire was destroyed. The ones where he escaped caused her nightmares.

It was a peculiar thing, that she watched these movies so fervently. Even back in San Francisco de Quito where she was born, vampire movies were her favorite films, even though they terrified her. She hated the vampire, always taking advantage of those weaker than himself for his own satisfaction, yet she could not stop watching. Her mother—may the saints intercede with the Holy Father on behalf of her eternal soul!—preferred the soaps, and in Ecuador there were many. "Why do you want to watch those awful movies? Why frighten yourself? Turn them off!" her mother had said so often when she was alive. "My soap operas are much better, like real life."

"Yes," Remedios answered, "always the same. A family as poor as us, with as many problems as we have, worrying. About money, about health, the arguments because one does not get along with the other . . . It is like every day! And they always come to the same conclusion—you must accept your lot in life."

"This is not a bad way to be," her mother said. "Life is full of trouble. When you have family, you are better off than those who do not. And when you accept what God decrees as your life, you are better off. Remedios, you were always the strange one. I knew this from the moment you were born, at midnight. That is why I named you God's remedy."

And now Remedios thought that yes, her mother had been wise. Life is much simpler when one accepts what is one's role. And her own destiny had not been such a bad one. Coming from the poverty of de Quito to the opulence of California to work as a domestic—not many were able to do that. The Richviews were decent people, they gave her four days off each month, did not make exceptional demands most of the time, and she had been able to send money home to support her sisters and brothers. She knew she had no right to complain. Many of the domestics—mostly girls from Mexico she had met at the shops—told of terrible conditions, where they were forced to work long hours at low wages, and sometimes they could not get paid. It was difficult to do anything about the conditions because they were all in the United States on a working visa, and the minute they ceased to be employed, they were deported.

Remedios told herself often that she was lucky. Her conditions were good, and far better than in her homeland. There, everyone lived in poverty except government officials and landowners. From the President down to the *policia municipal*, extortion was the rule. Even out of the money she sent home, almost half went to the corrupt local government, and another quarter went to her Uncle Antonio, her mother's brother-in-law, who had arranged with the Richviews for Remedios to work for them.

Mr. Richview told her if she saved the money in an American bank account where it would gather compound interest, rather than send it home and have most of it eaten away before it even reached her family, she could be almost a millionaire in twenty years. But she could not do that—her sisters and brothers had to eat, and she was now the head of the family.

The front door opened and Mrs. Richview rushed in. Remedios heard the children, Jessica and Robert—Mrs. Richview drove them to and from school. Jess ran into the kitchen, all flying yellow hair and sky-blue eyes. Immediately she hugged Remedios. "Guess what we did at school today? We made buttermilk! The teacher put milk into a churn and we all took turns pushing this big thing down into the milk and then we had buttermilk and we all drank some!"

Remedios laughed and smoothed back Jessica's hair. So large for a six year old—just a year younger than her youngest sister Dolores. Dolores was not in school, since the family could not afford to send her. Remedios had not seen Dolores in half a year and missed the baby of the family. She missed all of her family: Juan, and the twins José-Luis and María, and even her sister Esperanza, whom she did not get along well with. And her grandmother, of course, who took care of all of them.

"Wash up," Mrs. Richview was telling Robert, "and I don't want to keep saying that. Your father will be home any minute, and you know he likes to eat right away on Wednesdays so he can get to the homeowners meeting."

"I'm not hungry," the boy complained, as he did most nights.

"Well, then don't eat very much. You can have a snack later."

"But I want to go to the games store with Brad."

"On a school night? I don't think so."

"But, Mom, his brother is driving us and you said last week—"

"Oh, there's your father's car. Hurry up so we can eat."

"But I want to go with Brad. You said—"

"God, Robert, stop reminding me of things I've said! Look, eat something, so we can have our weekly family dinner, then you can go . . ."

And so it went with the Richviews, always busy, always going someplace, living their lives so quickly, and so separately. So different than in Ecuador. Her family had spent most of their time together. And no one went out after dark—the streets were just not safe. They said on the news that it was not safe in California. Remedios had only been to Los Angeles when the Richviews flew her here. She had never been to East Los Angeles, or to The Barrio. Still, she could not believe there were gangs like in de Quito—young boys, some no older than five years, roaming the streets and alleyways all night, carrying knives, ready to cut the throat of anyone they encountered to obtain food, or money to buy food . . . No, California was nothing like home.

Remedios placed the bread and butter on the table as Mr. Richview came through the door. Jess ran to him, and he lifted her high in his arms. Remedios looked on, wondering what that would feel like. Her own father had died when she was young, just after the birth of Dolores—perhaps he had lifted her that way, but she could not remember him being healthy and strong. Her grandmother said her father's death had caused her mother's death, because it was not long after when her mother became very, very ill. Remedios could still remember the blood flowing from her, and how pale she became at the end, because of the pain. They had no money for a doctor. There was nothing to do but watch her mother die slowly over the next two years. She was weak; it was God's will, her grandmother said.

Mr. Richview headed for his small office at the back of the house, beside the garden. Remedios knew it was not a good time, but she had been trying to find him alone for a week, and there never did seem to be the right moment.

She stood in the doorway, watching him taking papers from his briefcase. "Mr. Richview. May I speak with you a moment?"

He did not look up, and she wondered if her voice had been too low for him to hear her.

But after another few heartbeats, he seemed to notice her standing there. "Yes? What is it?" He spoke with his "office" voice, the one she heard him speak with on the telephone when he was discussing the stock market.

"Mr. Richview, I . . . I would like to have a raise. Ten dollars a month."

He stared at her for a moment blankly, then went back to sorting through his papers, saying, "You've only been with us six months. We'll discuss it in another six months."

There was nothing to do but return to the kitchen and bring in the platter of meat.

The Richviews sat around the table, all talking at once. "This is very good, Remy," Mrs. Richview said about the meat, and Remedios blushed. It was Mrs. Richview who had taken to calling her Remy because the children could not easily pronounce her name. Now they all called her that. Remedios did not mind. She was just grateful to be working for such a good family.

Robert pecked at his food like a bird. Then, when the horn blared outside and Mr. Richview snapped, "Tell him not to use the horn, it disturbs the neighbors," and Mrs. Richview said, "When did people stop coming to the door?" Robert jumped up, grabbed his jacket from the coat tree by the door and left.

Mr. Richview was the next to leave. He ate quickly, then went upstairs to change his clothes for the meeting with the other homeowners who lived in this area. Mrs. Richview took Jess upstairs as well, to help her with her homework, and to ". . . have a sauna. I've got my cell with me. Please tell any callers on the house phone I'll get back to them," she told Remedios. Mr. Richview hurried out the door. And Remedios was left alone to clear away the partially-eaten plates of food.

As always, she felt guilty as she scraped the remains into the garbage disposal. With just what was left on these plates, she could feed her entire family for one day. Early on she had eaten the leftover food from their plates, but Mrs. Richview caught her and insisted it was not "sanitary" and that Remedios must throw it away.

Remedios carved off a piece of meat from the outside of the roast, avoiding as much of the red part as possible, and made her own plate, with a small piece of squash, and a little bowl of salad. All her life she had eaten the largest meal in the middle of the day, and something light before bed; she could not get used to having so much food in her stomach at night. Before she sat down to eat, she wrapped the rest of the meat in clear plastic, stored the salad and squash in airtight containers, and placed everything in the refrigerator already bulging with food. The children had eaten their desserts. Mr. Richview ate some. Mrs. Richview's pudding went untouched, as always—she never ate dessert. Remedios placed the pudding next to her plate. Finally she sat down to eat.

She missed the food she had been raised on. Rice, and rich red and black beans, heavily spiced, sometimes with a little meat, if the family could afford a *cui*. And the flatbread! There was nothing like it here. She had made a traditional Ecuadorean meal when she first arrived. Mr. and Mrs. Richview ate a little, but the children would not even try. Mrs. Richview said that it might be best if she told Remedios exactly what foods to cook every week, and how to cook them.

Just as she was about to take a bite of the meat, Mrs. Richview said from the hallway, "Remy," and she jumped to her feet.

"Yes, Mrs. Richview?"

"I forgot. This package came for you, to the postal box."

Remedios met Mrs. Richview at the doorway and took from her a small brown parcel. Even before she saw the address, she knew it was from home. The oily dark paper, and the hemp cord holding it together. The parcel had gone through two postal systems, and was damaged.

"Thank you," she said, and waited until Mrs. Richview was halfway up the stairs before returning to the kitchen table.

She opened the package. First she found a piece of newspaper, *el Comercio*, with an article about the *les Chupa-cabras*. Now there were sightings in Ecuador! She read the article about the vampirelike creature, the "sheep-sucker" that attacked not only sheep, but horses, cows, even dogs and cats, biting into them, draining their blood. The article said eyewitnesses had seen *el Chupa-cabra*, and described it as four or five feet tall, having the body of a bat, with large wings, and scales along the back of the neck, a cat's face, and the teeth! Remedios shivered just reading about it.

Next, she found a note, from her grandmother. Or, from Uncle Antonio, the only one in the family besides herself who could write in Spanish. Her grandmother had told him what to say, of course.

Remedios, my dearest one. You are blessed by the Holy Virginsita, and God has seen to it that you were born strong, and must help your family. You are the one we rely on.

The letter went on with news of the family. Grandmother suffered pains in her arms and legs, and felt very tired. The twins had both been sick, coughing a lot, but were now well again. Dolores, who had been born with a clubfoot, was having difficulty walking. The neighbor examined the foot and said it was turning more inward—was it possible there could be money for a doctor . . .? Esperanza was pregnant. This did not surprise Remedios—her sister had always been pretty, and always liked to flirt with the boys. But it meant one more mouth to feed! News of Juan was the most troubling. He had begun to go out at nights, and grandmother suspected he was using cocaine and traveling with the packs of boys that murdered.

Remedios lowered the piece of paper, shaken. Tears sprang from her eyes. What could she do? She was not there. If she went home to try to make Juan behave, they would have no food. And he was now thirteen. Even before she had left home, he had been nearly impossible to control. Esperanza had never listened to her, and that would not change. Could she find money for a doctor? Already she sent everything home but for ten dollars a month, and that was only for little things she might need for herself—the Richviews gave her food, clothing, bus fare—she did not need much.

Perhaps she could send half of that home every month and then in three or four months there would be enough for a doctor, and Dolores could be taken to one . . . But half of the ten dollars would go to the government, and Uncle Antonio . . . Home. If she were there, Grandmother would not have to look after everyone. But then who would earn the money? There was no work in de Quito. Or in most of Ecuador. All of her thoughts seemed to end in impossibilities, and she could do nothing but cry silent tears.

Eventually, the ringing telephone forced her to pull herself together. She wiped her eyes with her sleeve and wrote down the message for Mr. Richview, then returned to the kitchen. Her plate of food looked very unappetizing; she scraped the uneaten meal into the garbage disposal.

With all of the troublesome news, she had forgotten about the parcel itself. Perhaps she should have opened it before reading the letter, before becoming upset.

Inside she found a small cardboard box, and inside that a little black leather pouch, very worn, tied shut with a black leather thong, a pouch she had never seen before. She opened it to find a rosary. There, the gold crucifix at the end. And the *Virginsita*. And ... *Diosito! Mio Diosito!* What was this? There were no beads that formed this rosary, but *los dientes!* Small teeth. She picked it up to examine it in the light, and at the same time reached for the letter.

At the bottom, her grandmother had added, *This belonged to my mother. The rosary is made from a baby tooth from each of her children, grandchildren, and great-grandchildren, including you. I gave it to your mother, and she wanted you to have it, when it was time. You are to give it to your eldest daughter. Maybe you will now see how special you are, Remedios. Your family needs you.*

Remedios looked closely at the rosary. All these baby teeth! It was true, her mother had sisters and brothers, and her grandmother too. So many teeth, all coated to keep them from turning too brown. There were back teeth, and front, from every area of the mouth. Some had come from her sisters and brothers, a tooth from her mother was here, her grandmother, but she did not know which belonged to who. She looked at the familiar pattern of the rosary: one, three, one from the crucifix to the connector. Then: one, ten, one, ten, one, ten, one, ten, one, ten. Sixty all together. And all similar. All but one. One she now noticed, and how had she missed it before?

A tooth like no other on this chain. Longer than the rest. One of the two they call the "eye" teeth. Pointed, sharp, not like a human tooth at all, more like the fang of an animal. Like the tooth of a vampire.

Remedios gasped, and the rosary slipped between her hands and hit the tile floor below.

Stupid girl! she chided herself, bending instantly to retrieve this precious gift from her mother. *Thank the Saints, may none of the teeth have broken.*

She examined them all, one by one. Yes, none had broken or chipped. Oh, how lucky! And then she stared in horror at the long incisor. Gingerly she touched her fingertip to the point. Sharp! Like a knife.

Unnerved by this gift, by the letter, Remedios returned the rosary to the pouch. She stacked the dishwasher quickly, cleaned up the kitchen, then took the parcel to her room. She found the rosary and the letter so upsetting she placed the entire package in the bottom dresser drawer, under her T-shirts. Suddenly, she felt exhausted. Without undressing, just removing her shoes, she lay on the bed and closed her eyes with the lights still on.

Remedios awoke with a start from a deep and disturbing dream she could not remember. Her bedroom at the Richview's looked strange, unfamiliar, with shadows moving in the corners, concealing ... what? *El Chupa-cabra!*

She bolted upright and stared hard at the shadows, examining them from the safety of her bed, listening—the house seemed unnaturally quiet, as if she were the only living breathing soul under the roof. Outside her partially-opened window there were no sounds in the dark night air, not even crickets. As if pulled by an invisible force, her eyes became focused on the dresser, and what she knew lay in the bottom drawer, hidden, but not. The awareness caused her heart to race, and her lungs felt compressed, as if there was no room for air, or not enough air to fill them. Her stomach cramped.

She got up from the bed and wandered into the hallway, listening. No sounds came from the upstairs. She padded barefoot to the kitchen, the familiar place where she spent so much time. She plugged in the electric kettle, and that simple, everyday act calmed her.

The undercurrent of terror she felt began to dissipate and she was left with a gnawing in her stomach she understood to be hunger. She opened the refrigerator, took out the plate with the roast, and reached for a carving knife from the rack. Hardly aware of what she was doing, Remedios cut deep into the flesh, to the bloodiest part, pulling out the reddest bits with her hands and stuffing them into her mouth, licking the blood from her fingers.

She looked at her hands, stained crimson with the meat juice, the blood, and suddenly remembered this: in the days between seasons, when the weather begins to turn even cooler at night, when she had been a child, very young—had Esperanza been born yet?—she had tasted blood!

Her mother, her father—he looked tired always—her grandmother before her hair had turned all white . . . She stood with them, her mother's hands on her shoulders, in the square of the village. The square, with the church at one end, was crowded with friends and neighbors, other relatives. "It is a feast day," her grandmother said that morning, "*el Día de los Muertos*, the day when the people pray to all of the Saints for all the dead."

How can you pray to all of the Saints, Remedios wondered, *because there are so many?* Her grandmother said the day would be filled with prayers. The Mass had been long, with all the names of the dead read out by the padre, many together for the poor families, and individual Masses for the families that could pay more. The procession from the church where they had just attended the tiring Masses was underway, moving around and around the square, the prayers chantlike, led by the padre, with the people echoing and responding to his words. The pungent scent of burning *incienso* filled the air, and the altar boys rang bells as they followed slowly behind the priest, while others sprinkled dark purple flower petals before the procession.

Remedios sucked on the *guagua de pan* that came from the basket of *Día de los Muertos* bread her grandmother had baked that week—the little bread men and women representing the dead. This one had red sugar eyes and bright green hair and lips, and she wore a colorful dress. "Esperanza," her grandmother called this one—Remedios's mother's dead sister, Esperanza, the one *her* own sister would be been named for.

"Her name means 'hope,'" her grandmother said. She stuffed little Esperanza into her pocket to later place on the altar in their home, an altar that held the large picture of Sainte Marianita de Jesus, and many, many candles. It would also hold some of the flowers they brought back home from the cemetery.

Remedios felt hungry, and wondered when they could return home and eat the good, thick *locro* soup, and drink the hot purple jellylike *colada morada* that her mother only made for the Day of the Dead feast.

The colorful pageant lasted a long time, with large wreaths carried back and forth through the square, with little *stampas* of the Saints, and prayer cards for the dead affixed to the red-and-yellow flowers. The padre held a big banner with a picture of the *Virginsita*, and two other priests carried an enormous one of Santa Marianita de Jesus, who gave her life to save the city from earthquakes, both images decorated with glitter and sea shells and many flowers.

Remedios felt sleepy and sat on the hard ground, leaning against her grandmother's legs. And then, when she opened her eyes, the light had faded from the sky and the night descended over them like a dark figure swooping across the heavens to stifle all life . . . She realized they were now in the cemetery.

Here, the home of the dead. Stacked in cement drawers, one atop the other, four and five high. Many dead but little space, her mother said. She stayed seated on the ground before the graves of their ancestors while the adults placed beautiful white death lilies, and floral wreaths against the graves and behind the marble plaques that bore the names of the departed. The air became thick with the scent of flowers, and alive with the hum of chanting, and Remedios felt drowsy.

"Bring them!" the padre called. Suddenly, the night had become black, with only the light of the stars overhead. Dogs! So many! Where had they all come from? Hardly any of their neighbors could afford a dog. These animals roamed the streets, wild, in packs, competing with the people for food. How had they been lured here? It was the food scraps—Remedios had never seen so many dogs in one place, nor so much food handed over to them.

Much time passed with heated discussions as the men observed the dogs and argued in a friendly way—which animal was strongest, which the weakest? Would the large one be more determined than the second largest? And this little white one, it showed aggression—perhaps he would grow to become the dominant male that mated! Finally, finally, one was selected. A she-dog not so small, with brown fur, but she seemed to lack energy. The weakest, her grandmother said. "*Someter*," her uncle said, telling the dog to submit.

Remedios stood rooted to the earth as Uncle Antonio sliced the throat from side to side. The animal reared, gnashed her teeth, howled—a haunting sound. She dropped to the earth, first on her front knees, then her side. Before she stopped twitching, the women rushed to the corpse and collected the spilled blood into basins—Remedios's mother among them. Each family gathered as much of the precious lifeblood as they could, struggling to keep it from seeping into the earth.

Then, another dog was captured and brought snarling to the front, and Remedios tensed, tears still stinging her eyes. He was strong, this one, filled with life, not as large as the biggest animal, but his spirit felt enormous, and all could sense that. "The one best suited to survive," Uncle Antonio said, and Remedios watched her uncle feed that dog the blood of his slain sister. And then she watched her uncle sip of the blood himself.

"Here, Remedios, drink this," her mother said. "It will make you strong. You are the strongest, you must survive."

Obediently, she placed her lips against the cool metal basin and drank the steaming thick blood down, as if it were milk. "The weak feed the strong," her grandmother had said as she drank. "Sometimes the strong ones escape the herd and become wild, because once they have tasted it, they can only feed on blood. It has always been this way and will be this way again. The strong must be encouraged to survive, or all die."

Remedios stared at her blood-covered hands. Why did they not repulse her as before? She sucked the sweet juice and could almost feel it charging her body with energy, just as she now remembered the blood of the weak dog sparking through every inch of her being.

She put the roast away and returned to her bedroom, to the dresser. Carefully she removed the rosary from the leather pouch and held it under the night table light.

So many teeth! Some looked so fragile they might crumble to dust if she touched them too much. Others seemed larger, stronger, more capable to cutting, chewing, taking in and transforming the food that would nourish and sustain. And then the one so unlike the others. One designed by nature for survival. A fierce tooth. It could defend and protect, or destroy. She lifted the rosary over her head and placed it around her neck, letting it drop under her T-shirt. She felt the cool teeth rest against her skin. The point of one tooth pressed slightly between her breasts.

Remedios did not even need to ask herself the question she had been avoiding, for she knew in her heart the answer. The vampire tooth had come from her own mouth. A tooth unlike the others. The tooth of the strongest. The one who could live and survive in a place not like her homeland. The one who could look after an entire family, and make certain they were provided for. The one who had the strength to prey on the weak in order to survive, for survival was crucial. Her grandmother had said this; this is why they fed her the blood of the weak dog. Why her mother had named her God's remedy—her mother was wise. She knew Remedios was born to remedy the wrongs that had been her legacy.

And now, images came to Remedios of the vampire, and of *el Chupacabra*, and she no longer felt threatened.

As the sky grew lighter, the knowledge that Remedios had unearthed with the rosary did not fade, but solidified within her, melding worries and insecurities, leaving behind a certainty from which to act.

The house lay shrouded in quiet, still as the dead. Remedios passed the rooms where Jess and Robert slept without pausing. She continued along the second floor hallway, watching her shadow creep over the walls. Finally, she reached the master bedroom and opened the door quietly.

Inside the room the air smelled of sweat mixed with the fragrance of Mrs. Richview's perfumes. Remedios stared at the couple for a moment, making her decision. Her employers lay sleeping soundly, Mrs. Richview with plugs in her ears and a mask over her eyes. Mr. Richview sprawled close to the edge, on his back, snoring loudly. Remedios made her way to his side of the bed. She crouched beside him and reached out to gingerly touch the bulging blue in his neck. His breath caught for a moment. He opened his eyes and stared fearfully at her. She placed her finger to her lips and quietly whispered, "*Someter*." His eyelids lowered as if he longed to return to his dreams. He turned his head, the vein an offering.

Remedios pierced it easily, quickly, naturally, like any strong animal that had learned somewhere in its life to love the taste of blood.

Remedios sat at the kitchen table, feeling refreshed. She signed her name at the bottom of the letter to her Uncle Antonio, telling him that he must use a portion of the money he took from the family as his "fee" to provide medical care to little Dolores, whose name, she reminded him, meant "pain." The pain of his failing to comply, she assured him, would not be only for Dolores, but it would become his pain as well. She would cease sending home money until he did this. And if he refused? Yes, her family would suffer. Dolores would suffer more. But he would suffer most—she would personally see to it.

She folded the letter and placed it into an envelope, sealing all of their fates.

Just then, Mr. Richview walked into the kitchen. "Good morning, Remedios. How are you today?" He looked tired. Bewildered.

"I am very well, Mr. Richview. May I speak with you?"

"Yes, of course. About what?"

"I ask of you three things. First, I would like to visit my family for two weeks. I will need a plane ticket."

He rubbed his neck for a moment, an absent look on his face. "That can be arranged."

"Next, I must have an increase. I would like to be paid an additional one hundred dollars each month."

Rather than scowling, or being even more annoyed then he had been the evening before, now Mr. Richview nodded, a dreamy expression filling his face. He spoke to her respectfully, as to an equal; to Remedios, a strong person, who knew what she wanted, what was fair. "All right. I think we can find an extra hundred dollars for you each month."

"And for the last," she said, "I would like for you to deposit this new money into a bank account, like the one you told me of, that will make me a millionaire in twenty years."

She was only mildly astonished to see him nod approval. "Well, I can't promise you'll be a millionaire, but if you don't touch it, I can promise you'll have quite a bit of money. That's a wise decision, Remedios. I'll stop at the bank today and pick up the forms for you to sign so you can open an account—my accountant will make the deposits automatically, and you can go in any time and update your passbook. Once the principle increases, we can invest it in a high-yield fund. You need to be brave, take a few risks. Nothing ventured, nothing gained. It's a tough world, dog eat dog. Only the strongest survive."

"The strongest and the smartest," she said, thinking how much more sense it makes to live off the strong rather than the weak.

Miss Massingberd and the Vampire

Tina Rath

Author and actress Tina Rath gained her doctorate from London University with a thesis on "The Vampire in Popular Fiction" and her MA with a dissertation on "The Vampire in the Theatre."

She has lectured on vampires for various groups and universities and has been widely interviewed about the subject on radio and television.

She sold her first dark fantasy story to *Catholic Fireside* in 1974, and since then her short fiction has appeared in such periodicals as *The Velvet Vampyre*, *All Hallows*, *Ghosts and Scholars*, *Supernatural Tales*, *Amazing*, *The Magazine of Fantasy & Science Fiction*, and *Weird Tales*, along with the anthologies *The 19th Fontana Book of Great Ghost Stories*, *The 17th Fontana Book of Great Horror Stories*, *Midnight Never Comes*, and *The Year's Best Horror Stories XV*.

She is currently Poet in Residence at the Dracula Society.

"While I was finishing my thesis on 'The Vampire in Popular Fiction,'" explains Dr. Rath, "I came to the conclusion that the vampire's cloak is an extraordinarily versatile costume: it can be worn by men or women; it can conceal and disguise, but paradoxically it can also be used for display; it can suggest the cowled monk, or the sophisticated opera-goer; it can itself be concealed, rolled up and carried unobtrusively, but as soon as it is put on it transforms the wearer.

"The vampire, which is both male and female, terrifying and alluring, similarly offers the ultimate disguise, fancy-dress, fantasy—a persona which we can slip on either to hide or parade; a unisex, one-size fits all masquerade. The cloak is an ink-blot test, in which we can see our obsessions, not only our fears but also our desires—for sexual potency, freedom from the restraints of gender, morality, and the entire material world.

"And of course, it's not real, so when we have enjoyed our fantasy we can discard the cloak and be human again. It is hardly surprising that the vampire has an immortal appeal."

About the following story, the author explains: "I wrote this particular story because I live near a very beautiful, ivy-covered churchyard, which actually does have a path running through it. It was crying out for a vampire, so I gave it one."

MISS MASSINGBERD FIRST heard about the vampire from her fifth-formers. They were quite the silliest girls in the school, and she paid very little attention to them. Of course, she delivered her little lecture about going straight home from school, and walking in a brisk and ladylike way.

"And then no one will bother you. Human or vampire," she concluded, and confiscated all the pieces of garlic and crosses made from broken rulers and Sellotape that seemed to have found their way into most desks in the classroom.

Now Miss Massingberd's own quickest route to school and back lay through St. Elphege's churchyard. In the mornings there was no problem, but sometimes, at night, when she had been kept late by a parents' meeting, or a committee, or rehearsals for the school play, she might go the long way round. However, she was a strong-minded woman, and scorned superstitious fears. You did not, she told herself, become Head of English at the biggest comprehensive school in her area of London by allowing yourself to be easily frightened.

So on that luminous autumn evening when she met the vampire herself she was taking her shortcut. And she was not walking briskly either, but loitering like the silliest of her fifth-formers, breathing in the scent of burning leaves from a hidden bonfire and enjoying that strange nostalgia for a past she had never actually experienced that she always felt in autumn, when she saw the dark cloaked figure standing among the headstones.

At first she naturally supposed it was the vicar, and she was passing him with a polite "Good evening," when he turned to look at her. He was quite unmistakably a vampire. The points of his canine teeth were just visible on his lower lip. And he was tall, and dark, and heartbreakingly handsome. Miss Massingberd looked at him and fell helplessly in love.

She was so taken aback by the sensation (she had never even thought of such a thing before in her life) that she stood quite still, gazing into the vampire's dark and haunted eyes. And the vampire gazed back at Miss Massingberd. It is difficult to know what might have happened if the real vicar had not ridden past them on his bicycle, calling a cheerful greeting.

The vampire's eyes flashed ruby red in the light of the bicycle lamp, and he vanished into the dusk. Miss Massingberd was left, shocked and shivering, and feeling as if she had suddenly awakened out of a deep sleep.

But she could not say if she had been roused from a dream or a nightmare.

The vicar, seeing her standing looking so lost in the dusk, wheeled his bicycle around with a swish of gravel and asked her to come in for a cup of tea. He was new in the parish, and unmarried, so he was always glad to see visitors, and he knew Miss Massingberd well by sight, as vicars and schoolmistresses often sit on the same committees.

Miss Massingberd was too flustered by her encounter with the vampire to refuse, and she followed him into his horrible late Victorian vicarage, which seemed to have been designed for a polygamist with an unusually large extended family.

"I call it the barracks," the vicar shouted cheerfully across the echoing spaces of the entrance hall.

It was paved with tiles depicting the sacrifice of Jephtha's daughter, Miss Massingberd noticed, averting her eyes hastily.

"Just chuck your coat on the hall-stand."

He led her into a parlor so large that the corners of the high ceiling were lost in the dimness beyond the power of a single sixty-watt bulb to dispel. The vicar lit the gas fire and recommended Miss Massingberd to sit close to it.

"It's always freezing in here," he said, "and it's worse upstairs. If you don't mind hanging on here for a moment, I'll go and rustle up some tea."

Miss Massingberd sat, staring into the dark corners of the room, wondering how she came to be having tea with the vicar, instead of going home to do her marking. It was the vampire's fault, of course, but she could not blame him. Her thoughts drifted away, to moonlight, and ruined towers, and fiery eyes, becoming more and more unsuitable for a schoolmistress every moment.

When the vicar came back with his tray, he was surprised to see how flushed and pretty she looked in the dim light.

"Only Indian tea, I'm afraid," he said, wishing suddenly that he had something more exotic to offer her, "but there's some rather good cake."

Miss Massingberd withdrew her gaze from the darkness and smiled at the vicar. She thought she was giving him her bright, efficient, friendly, committee smile. She had no way of knowing that it was now the rapt, mysterious smile of a woman who has fallen in love with a vampire, and the vicar was taken aback. He had never realized, in all those committee meetings, how blue Miss Massingberd's eyes were, and how bright her hair.

He smiled too, and fought a ridiculous and unclerical impulse to put a finger very lightly on one of those tiny coils of hair at the nape of her neck, which had sprung from her severely-rolled French pleat. Instead he concentrated on cutting her a piece of cake.

He started to talk sensibly about their committee, and asked Miss Massingberd her feelings on the Christmas bazaar, but Miss Massingberd simply crumbled the cake on her plate and smiled like Mona Lisa.

It was not really very long before his stream of cheerful commonplace things to say began to run dry and he said, almost accusingly, "You're not eating your cake."

Miss Massingberd murmured that she was not very hungry. So the vicar, always a polite host, stood up to take the plate out of her way. Miss Massingberd, recalled to her proper social role, stood up too and smiled again, and the vicar, lost and drowning in her blue eyes, kissed her.

And Miss Massingberd, having learned the trick of it, fell in love all over again.

She and the vicar were married, of course. They turned the dreadful, echoing barracks of a vicarage into a hostel for homeless families. And what with that, and the Youth Club, and the Brownies, and all the other parish duties, they never seemed to have a moment even to think.

Only sometimes, in the long green dusks of spring, or the short red twilights of autumn, Miss Massingberd would walk alone in the church-yard for a while. She would come back looking greatly refreshed, if a little pale, and wind a silk scarf around her throat before going to the Youth Club, or the Brownie meeting, or the Parish Council. And her husband would sigh a little, and remind her to take her iron tonic.

THE RAVEN BOUND

Freda Warrington

Freda Warrington began writing her first stories at the age of five. Inspired by such fantasy writers as C.S. Lewis, J.R.R. Tolkien, Tanith Lee, Michael Moorcock, Joy Chant, Ursula LeGuin, Anne McCaffrey, and J. Sheridan Le Fanu, her first novel, *A Blackbird in Silver*, was published in 1986.

Since then she has published more than twenty more, including *A Blackbird in Darkness*, *A Blackbird in Amber*, *A Blackbird in Twilight*, *A Taste of Blood Wine*, *A Dance in Blood Velvet*, *The Dark Blood of Poppies*, *The Dark Arts of Blood*, *Dark Cathedral*, *Pagan Moon*, *Dracula the Undead* (winner of the Dracula Society Award for Best Gothic Novel), *The Court of the Midnight King*, *Elfland* (the Romantic Times 2009 Award for Best Fantasy Novel), *Midsummer Night*, and *Grail of the Summer Stars*. Her latest book is a short story collection, *Nights of Blood Wine*.

"I love the paradox of vampires," reveals Warrington. "They personify things we dread, such as death or (horrors!) the dead coming back from the grave; yet also attributes we may covet, such as eternal youth, power over others, guilt-free sensuality. The possibilities offered by vampire characters are endless. Away with cardboard heroes chasing cardboard monsters! In *A Taste of Blood Wine* and its sequels, my characters Karl, Charlotte, Violette, and their friends took me down many fascinating dark labyrinths exploring themes of love, pain, jealousy, psychology, philosophy, religion, sex . . . I found no limit.

"'The Raven Bound' came about when a French editor, Lea Silhol, asked me to write a story for her vampire anthology, *De Sang et d'Encre*. She hinted strongly that she would like to see an appearance of her favorite characters from the books, Karl and Charlotte. I had an idea all worked out—until I actually put pen to paper, when something entirely unplanned came out instead! I don't know where Antoine came from, but I think he would smile at a quote in my desk diary by the writer Susan Ertz, which turned up in apposite fashion shortly after I'd written his story: 'Millions long for immortality who don't know what to do with themselves on a rainy Sunday afternoon . . .'"

I WALK A tightrope above an abyss. The silver line of wire is all that keeps me from a thousand feet of darkness yet I feel no fear. I flit across the rooftops of London like a cat, I lie flat on top of underground trains as they roar through sooty tunnels. I climb the ironwork of the Eiffel Tower and I dance upon the girders at its pinnacle, daring gravity to take me. And all of this is so dull.

Dull, because I can do it.

I move with the lightness and balance of a bird. I never fall, unless I throw myself wantonly at the ground. Then I may break bones, but my bones heal fast. It is not difficult. It will not kill me. All of these wild feats bore me for they hold no challenge, no excitement.

What is a vampire to do?

I see him in a nightclub. He could be my twin—a brooding young man with a lean and handsome face, dark hair hanging in his eyes, his eyes lovely miserable pools of shadow. How alone he looks, sitting there oblivious to the crush of bodies, the women glittering with beads and pearls. He is hunched over a glass of whiskey and he raises a long, gaunt hand to his mouth, sucking hard on a cigarette stub. Dragging out its last hot rush of poisons.

"May I join you?" I say.

"If you must." His voice is a bored, English upper-class drawl. I love that.

"There is no free table." I wave to emphasize the obvious; the club is crowded, a sepia scene in a fog of smoke. "My name is Antoine Matisse."

"Rupert Wyndham-Hayes." He shakes my hand half-heartedly. His cigarette is finished so I offer him another, a slim French one from a silver case. He accepts. I light it for him—an intimate gesture—and he sits back, blowing smoke in sulky pleasure. "Over from Paris, one assumes? First visit?"

"I have been here before," I reply. "London always draws me back."

He makes a sneering sound. "I should prefer to be in Paris. Funny how we always want what we haven't got."

"What is preventing you from going to Paris, Rupert?"

I look into his eyes. He doesn't seem to notice that I am not smoking. He sees something special in me, a kindred soul, someone who will understand him.

He calls the waiter and orders drinks, although I tip mine into his while he isn't looking. Presently his story comes tumbling out. A family seat in the country, a father who is proud and wealthy and mean. Mother long dead. Rupert the only son, the only child, with a vast freight of expectations on his shoulders. But he has disappointed his father in everything.

"All the things he wanted me to be—I can't do it. I was to be a scholar, an officer, a cabinet minister. Worthy of him. Married to some earl's daughter. That's how he saw me. But I let him down. I tried and failed; gods, how I tried! Finally something snapped, and I refused to dance to his tune any longer. Now he hates me. Because what I truly am is an artist. The only thing I can do, the only thing I've ever wanted to do, is to paint!"

He takes a fierce drag on his cigarette. His eyes burn with resentment. "Isn't your father proud that you have this talent?"

"Proud?" he spits. "He despises me for it! Says I'll end up in the gutter."

"Why don't you leave?" I speak softly, and I am paying more attention to the movement of his tender throat than to his words. "Go to Montmartre, be an artist. Prove the old man wrong."

"It's not that easy. There's this girl, Meg . . ."

"Take her with you."

"That's just it. I can't. She's the gardener's daughter. My father employs her as a maid. D'you see? Not content with being a failure at everything else, I go and fall in love with a common servant. So now the old man tells me that if I don't give her up and toe the line, he'll disinherit me! And Meg's refusing to see me. Says she's afraid of my father. Damn him!"

I have not been a vampire so very long. I still recall how hopeless such dilemmas seem to humans. "That's terrible."

"Vindictive old swine! I'll lose her and I'll be penniless! He can't do this to me!"

"What will you do about it, Rupert?"

He glares down into his whiskey. How alluring he looks in his wretchedness. "I wish the old bastard would die tomorrow. That would solve all my problems. I'd like to kill him!"

"Will you?"

He sighs. "If only I had the guts! But I haven't."

So I smile. I rest my hand on his, and he is too numb with whiskey to feel the coldness of my fingertips. I have thought of something more interesting to do than just take him outside and drain him.

"I'll do it for you."

"What?" His eyes grow huge.

I should explain, I am poor. It seems so cheap to go through the pockets of my victims like a petty thief. I do it anyway, but it yields little reward. The wealth I crave, in order to live in the style a vampire deserves, is harder to come by.

"Give me a share of your inheritance and I'll kill him for you. No one will ever link the crime to you. Natural causes, they'll say."

His breathing quickens. His hands shake. Does he know what I am? Yes and no. Look into our eyes and a veil lifts in your mind and you step into a dream where anything is possible. "My God," he says, over and over. "My God." And at last, with a wild light in his eyes, "Yes. Quickly, Antoine, before he has a chance to change his will. Do it!"

I am standing in the garden, looking up at the house.

It's an impressive pile, but ugly. Gray-brown stone, stained and pitted by the weather, squatting in a large, bleak estate. A sweep of gravel leads to a crumbling portico. No flowerbeds to soften the walls, only prickly shrubs. It's tidy enough but no love, no imagination and no money have been lavished upon it for many a cold year.

In the autumn twilight I traverse the lawns to the rear of the house. The gardens, too, are austere and formal, with clipped hedges standing like soldiers on flat stretches of grass. But there are chestnut and elm and beech trees to add somber grandeur to the landscape. Brown leaves are scattered on the ground. The gardener has raked them into piles and I smell that English autumn scent of bonfires and wet grass.

Somewhere behind the windows of the house sits the father, the rat in his lair, Daniel Wyndham-Hayes.

It's growing dark. Rooks are gathering in the treetops. I am taking my time, savoring the experience, when a figure in a long black overcoat steps out of the blue darkness and comes toward me.

"Antoine, what are you doing?"

It is another vampire. His name is Karl. Perhaps you know him, but if not I shall tell you that Karl is far older than me and thinks he knows everything. Imagine the face of an angel, one who felt as much bliss as guilt when he fell, and still does, every time he strikes. Amber eyes that eat you. Hair the color of burgundy, which fascinates me, the way it looks black in shadow then turns to crimson fire in the light. That's Karl. He's like a deadly ghost, always warning me not to make the same mistakes he made.

"I am thinking that this house and garden are the manifestation of the owner's soul," I reply archly. "Will they change, when he is dead?"

"Don't do this," Karl says, shaking his head. "If you single out humans and make something special of them, you'll drive yourself mad."

"Why should it matter to you, if I am driven mad?"

He puts his hand on my shoulder, and although I have always desired him, I am too irritated with him to respond. "Because you are young, and you'll only find out for yourself when it is too late. Don't become involved with humans. Keep yourself apart from them."

"Why?"

"Otherwise they will break your heart," says Karl.

They think they know it all, the older ones, but they will each tell you something different. You can't listen to them. Give them no encouragement, or they will never shut up.

We stand like a pair of ravens on the grass. Then I am stepping away from him, turning lightly as a dancer to look back at him as I head for the house. "Go to hell, Karl. I'll do what I like."

—

I am inside the house. The corridors are draughty and need a coat of paint. Yet old masters hang on the walls and I finger the gilt frames with excitement. Riches. This seems ironic, that Daniel should collect these grimy old oils for their value and yet consider his own son's potential work valueless.

Following Rupert's instructions, I find the white paneled door of the bedroom, and I go in.

The father is not as I expect.

I stand beside the bed staring down at him. With one hand I press back the bed-curtain. I am as still as a snake; if he wakes he will think someone has played a dreadful joke on him, placed a mannequin with glittering eyes and waxen skin there to frighten him. But he sleeps on, alone in this big austere room. Dying embers in the grate give the walls a demonic glow. Like the rest of the house it is clean but threadbare. Daniel is hoarding his wealth. Perhaps he thinks that if he disinherits Rupert, he can take it with him.

Why did I assume he would be old? Rupert is only twenty-three and this man is barely fifty, if that. And he is handsome. He has a strong face like an actor, thick chestnut and silver hair flowing back from a high forehead. His arms are muscular, the hands well-shaped on the bedcover. Even in sleep his face is taut and intelligent. I stand here admiring the aquiline sweep of his nose and the long curves of his eyelids, each with a little fan of wrinkles at the corner.

He will not be easy to kill. I expected a frail old goat in a nightcap. Not this magnificent creature, who is so full of blood and strength, a lion.

I bend over the bed. I am salivating. I touch my tongue to his neck and taste the salt of his skin, the creamy remnant of shaving soap, such a masculine perfume . . . I am shaking with desire as I press him down with my hands, and bite.

He wakes up and roars.

I try to silence him with my hand in his mouth, and he bites me in return! His teeth are lodged there in the fleshy part of my hand but I endure the pain, I don't care about it, all is swept away by the ecstasy of feeding. We lie there, biting each other. His body arches up under mine.

A scratching noise at the door.

We both freeze, like lovers caught in the act. I stop swallowing. Slowly I withdraw my fangs from the wounds. Daniel gives only a faint gasp, though the pain must be excruciating. We look at each other; the door opens; an apparition floats in.

She's wearing a thick white nightgown and she carries a candle that reflects in her eyes. "Daniel?" she whispers. "It's midnight . . ."

I can tell from her manner that she hasn't come in response to his cry. I doubt she even heard it. No, she comes in like a thief and it's obvious that she is here by appointment. I am partly hidden by the bed curtain so I have a good look at her before she sees me.

She is lovely. Dark brown hair flowing loose over the white gown. Ah, such colors in it, the lovely strands of bronze and red. She has the sweetest face. Dark eyes and brows, a red, surprised bud of a mouth.

She's coming toward the bed. Daniel rasps, "Meg, no!" and then she sees us, sees the blood on his neck and on my mouth.

The candle falls to the carpet, her hands fly to her face. She is backing toward the door crying, "Oh God, no! Help! Murder!"

I have to stop her. I launch myself at her, pinning her to the door before she's taken two steps. I'm in a frenzy now, I must have her, I can't stop. I savor his blood still in my mouth as I bite down, and then he is swept away by the taste of Meg flooding over my tongue. Ripe and red and salty and . . .

Her head falls back. She clings to me. It is so exquisite that I slow down and draw delicately on her until she presses her body along the whole length of me and I feel her heart pounding and the breath coming out of her in little staccato cries of amazement.

For some reason I can't kill her. My fangs slip out of the wounds they have made and I hold her close as she sighs. I haven't the energy or will to finish it. No, I like her alive. I love the heavy warmth of her body slumping against mine, and her hair soft against my wet red mouth.

We stand like that for a few minutes. Then I feel Daniel touching my shoulder. He has staggered from his bed. "Who are you?" he whispers. His big hand wanders over my arm, my shoulder blade, my spine. It slides in between me and the woman and lies warm against my ribs. He's resting against my back. The three of us, pressed together.

Well, this is cozy.

I am in the garden again when she finds me. I am pacing back and forth on the grass beneath the cold windows of the mansion with the moon staring down at me; and suddenly there is Charlotte. She steps from the shadow of a hedge to walk at my side.

"It's difficult to leave, isn't it?" she says, slipping her cool hand into mine. "What are they like, your family?"

"Interesting," I say. "Rupert, the son, is in love with the delicious housemaid, Meg. How am I to tell him that Meg slips in regularly to service the father? No wonder Daniel has forbidden Rupert to see her."

Charlotte utters a soft, sensuous laugh. "Oh, Antoine, hasn't Karl told you what a mistake it is to ask their names, to become involved in their lives? You know you shouldn't, yet you can't stop. That's always my downfall, too."

Ah now, Charlotte. She is Karl's lover and her presence is all it takes to reveal the folly of Karl's advice. Don't get involved with humans, he tells me? Hypocrite. For he took Charlotte when she was human, couldn't stop himself, couldn't leave her alone. And who could blame him? There is something of the ice-queen and something of the English rose about her. She is the perfect gold-and-porcelain doll with a heart of darkness. She's like a princess who ran away with the gypsies, all tawny silk and bronze lace. But ask which of them is the more dangerous, the more truly a vampire—it is Charlotte.

She is the seducer. She is the lethal one. You will never see Karl coming; he takes you swiftly and is gone before you know what happened, no promises, no apologies. But Charlotte will worship you from afar, and bring you flowers, and run away from you and come back to you, until you are so mad with love for her that you don't know which way to turn. Oh, and then she'll turn on you and take you down, our lady viper, and soak your broken body with her tears.

Not that I was her victim, you understand. But I have watched her in complete admiration.

"Why must it be a downfall?" I ask, annoyed.

"Humans are so alluring, aren't they? You can't go only for one taste. You can't be like Karl—just strike and never look back. You're like me, Antoine. You want to play with them, to get to know them, to love them. Is the pleasure worth the pain? I never quite know. You have to do it again and again, to see if it will be different this time."

"It's only a game to me. I don't care about them. I'm doing it for money, that's all."

"Really?" she says. "Then why couldn't you kill them? Why are you still here?"

Charlotte stands on tiptoe and presses her rosy mouth to mine; and she's gone, in a whisper of silk and lilac.

Behind this hedge I find a kitchen garden, where Meg's father lovingly grows vegetables to feed the household. Ah, now I see. He is a man who despises flowers and prettiness, loves prosaic potatoes and beans—just like his employer. The air is thick with the rot of Brussels sprouts, the scent of wet churned soil and compost.

Through a gap I see the cold shine of the greenhouse, and—where the garden meets the servants' area of the house—the tantalizing glint of glass in the kitchen door.

When Rupert discovers that I have not killed his father, he is volcanic with rage.

We meet beneath a line of elm trees. The rooks squawk and squabble in the bare branches above us.

"You liar!" Rupert screams. "You traitor!"

He flies at me, arms going like windmills, but I hold him off. He's useless at fighting, as he is at everything. Perhaps he is a useless artist too, merely in love with the idea of brooding and suffering and being misunderstood.

"Why didn't you finish the old devil off? You only wounded him!"

"I was interrupted."

"What the hell do you mean—'interrupted'?"

So I tell him. Rupert rages. He paces, he punches trees, he weeps. Finally he turns to me like a man in the grip of a fatal illness, his face white and frail as the skin of a mushroom.

"This is a disaster!" he cries. "If Meg and my father are lovers, then I have nothing left to live for. They'll have a child, and I shall have no inheritance, no house, no wife—nothing!"

He flings himself at me, grabbing the lapels of my coat. I am really enjoying this.

"Kill me," he begs, tears running from his beautiful, anguished eyes. "Kill me instead."

Oh, my pleasure.

Only I can't do it.

I hold Rupert close and we are the same height so he looks into my eyes for an instant before my head goes down to his throat. He is tense, desperate for oblivion. But then the inevitable happens. He softens in my arms and clasps my head. He sighs. He forgets what he was angry about.

We are locked together, his blood running sweetly into my open mouth, his groin pressed hard against mine. And it happens. I fall in love with him.

And I'm satiated so I stop drinking; I just want to hold him against me. But I haven't taken nearly enough to kill him and he knows it.

"You bastard," he says weakly. "You liar."

He faints. I let him go. I leave him lying there, slumped on the roots of a tree, and I run.

I don't go far. There is an ancient rose arbor halfway across the grounds, with a dry fountain and some sad-looking, mossy statues. Here I hesitate, undecided, my mind full of Rupert and Meg and Daniel. I want them so badly. I am in anguish.

Karl startles me. I am not looking where I'm going and I don't see him there in the shadow of a rose trellis. I almost step on him. He's like a statue coming to life, with fire for eyes, and if I had been human I believe I should have died of fear. He's still following me, watching me, warning me—just for the hell of it, I swear.

"Are you simply going to leave him?" He grips my arms, forcing me to meet his gaze. "You have a choice, Antoine. Go back and finish them all—or leave now, and never come back. Make a decision or this will destroy you!"

"Why don't you leave me the hell alone!" I growl, pulling free of him.

"I shall," he says coldly. "But I have seen so many of our kind sabotage their own existence through their obsession with mortals. I have even known them to kill themselves."

"Kill themselves?" The idea is shocking to me. Abhorrent. What's the use of becoming immortal, only to waste it?

"As soon as I am sure that you understand—then I shall leave you to your folly."

I laugh. "Karl, do you really not see? How boring do you want our existence to be? Oh yes, I have tried all the things that new-made vampires think will thrill them. And it does thrill, for a little while. I have climbed mountains where the cold and the lack of air would kill humans. I have swum deep in the ocean. I have thrown myself like a bird off the Eiffel Tower and walked away with a broken wrist."

"And have you not found wonder in any of this?"

"The thing is that when such feats come so easily to us, there is no point in doing them. No challenge." My voice is throaty and I hate myself for being sincere and fervent in front of Karl, but there it is. "All that's left, the only challenge, the only chance of passion . . ." I point across the garden at the gray-brown hulk of stone, ". . . lies in that house."

"I disagree," says Karl, but his eyes betray him.

"If you disagree, my friend, why are you pestering me? There is no reason under the moon for you to be haunting me, except that you get some *frisson* of excitement from it."

Karl can find no reply to that. I dance away, quite pleased to have silenced him for once.

I am back at the house again. Moth to the flame. Of course.

I'm outside the parlor window and they are inside, sitting there by the light of an open fire and gas-lamps. A brown scene, with little touches of green, red and gold. To my surprise, Rupert and his father are sitting in armchairs on opposite sides of the grate. They are not speaking but, my

God! At least they are in the same room! They are sipping brandy from balloon glasses and the liquor shines like rubies in the fire-glow.

Meg is perched on a couch, sewing. She wears a simple skirt and cardigan—not the maid's uniform I expected—and her hair is coiled on her head, beautifully disheveled. They are listening to music on the wireless—such a big box to produce such small, tinny, jaunty sounds! But this is not a scene of happy domesticity.

There is a dreadful tension between them. Even through the glass I feel it.

They're waiting for me, thinking of me. I can feel the heat of their dreams and desires. For me they would forget their quarrels, even forget their relationships to each other, just to feel my lips on them again and my fangs driving into them . . . to lose themselves in bliss. I long to go to them. I want to feel their arms around me, and their bodies pliant under mine, and their genitals stiffening and opening like exotic flowers and their blood leaping into me, God, yes, their blood . . .

The woman pricks herself with the needle. I watch the blood-bead swell on her finger. Then her lips close on the wound, and my desires throb like pain.

My hand is on the window . . .

Meg looks up with her finger still pressed to the moist bud of her mouth, and sees me. I grip the frame of the sash window and push it upward. The warmth of the room rushes to meet me and I hear her gasp, "He's here!"

The men jump to their feet. Their faces are rapt, eyes feverish, lips parted. All three of them are coming towards me and I long to stroke their hair, to feel the heat of their bodies through their clothes and taste their skin. Brooding Rupert and leonine Daniel and sensual Meg. Three golden figures in a cave of fire. "There you are," they whisper. "Come in, Antoine, come in to us."

I reach out to them, as they are reaching out to me. Our fingertips touch . . .

Someone slams down the window between us. A hand grips my arm.

"They will suck you in," says Charlotte into my ear. "They will be your slaves and you will be theirs."

Now if it had been Karl who shut the window I should have been furious. But I can never be angry with Charlotte; not for long, anyway. In a flash I am detached and ironic. "That sounds quite appealing."

Their faces are pressed against the cold pane, staring into the twilight. Charlotte pulls me aside so they can't see us. I yield, and we walk slowly along the back of the house, with grit and soil and the debris of autumn accumulating on our shoes. A graveyard scent. I'm looking for another way in. I feel like a revenant, scratching at windows, rattling door handles.

This path leads us into the kitchen garden again. In the gloom there are rooks on the furrows, pecking at the delicious morsels Meg's father has turned up with his digging. Will he know what his daughter does with Daniel, and with Rupert, and with me? Will he join us? An old man, smelling of sweat and earth, creating green life from the ground . . . I should like to taste his essence.

"If you go in, they won't let you go," says Charlotte. "You won't be able to leave."

I pull her to me and kiss her neck. "I shouldn't want to leave. I love them. And you sound thrilled at the idea yourself."

She laughs. "Wasn't I right, Antoine? Yes . . . this is excitement. This is ecstasy. Shall I tell you why Karl is so cold? Not because he's different to us. No, it's because he's the same, he can't leave humans alone. Only he hates the consequences. Oh, I always plunge in headfirst, I can't help myself, I always think it will be different this time. But Karl . . . he's the realist."

And Karl is there, as if he stepped out of thin air in the shadows. He has been waiting for us. Now he's strolling on the other side of me, his hand so affectionate upon my arm. They are guiding me away from the house, along the grassy path towards the hedge at the top of the garden and the bare trees beyond, away, towards redemption. Every step is agony.

"The trouble is, there's a price to pay," Karl tells me. "You can say 'yes' to them and you can let yourself fall—but you can't have them and keep them. They're dying, Antoine. The more you love them, the more you kill them."

"Don't think it won't hurt you, when they die," says Charlotte. "Don't imagine the pain of it won't claw your heart to pieces!"

"But if I . . ." My voice is weak.

Charlotte knows what I'm thinking. "Yes, you could make them into vampires," she says crisply. "With a great amount of energy and will and strength, you could do that. But it won't be the same. Then you will have three cold-eyed predators, vying with you, resenting you, perhaps hating you. But your warm, moist, blood-filled lovers will be gone."

"So leave," says Karl. "Leave them now!"

We have reached the gap in the hedge. I stand there despairingly. I raise my arms in anguish and the flapping of my overcoat makes a dozen rooks rise in alarm. But one remains. It hops in circles on the grass, trailing a damaged wing. It cannot escape the earth.

I break away from Karl and Charlotte. I run back to the house and stand outside, breathing hard.

My lovers are inside, waiting for me. I can hear the blood thundering through their hearts, their red tongues moistening their lips in anticipation. I only have to turn away and they will remain like that forever . . . aching for me, waiting, their lust turning to fevered agony . . . but alive.

Grief will, I think, be interesting.

I press my fingers to the cold glass of the kitchen door, and I go in.

VAMPIRE KING OF THE GOTH CHICKS

From the journals of Sonja Blue

Nancy A. Collins

Nancy A. Collins currently makes her home in Atlanta, Georgia. She is the author of several novels and numerous short stories, as well as having served a two-year stint as the writer of DC Comics' *Swamp Thing*. The recipient of the HWA's Bram Stoker, British Fantasy Society's Icarus, and the Deathrealm Awards, her books include *Sunglasses After Dark*, *Lynch: A Gothik Western*, *Knuckles & Tales*, a Southern Neo-Gothic collection, and the Golgotham urban fantasy series.

Her newest works include a thirteen-issue run as the first woman to write the Vampirella comic, the *Red Sonja: Vultures Circle* mini-series, and the *Army of Darkness: Furious Road* limited series, as well as a hardcover release of the *Sunglasses After Dark* graphic novel.

"'Vampire King of the Goth Chicks' originally started out as the first comic book appearance of Sonja Blue," explains Collins. "Entitled 'The Real Thing,' the script was commissioned by Joe R. Lansdale for *Weird Business*, a hefty hardback comic 'book' he was coediting for Mojo Press back in 1995.

"Although I was not overly thrilled with the art that ended up being used, I always liked the story, and after a couple of years I decided to translate the story into prose—making it the first Sonja Blue short story. The transition from comic book to prose story wasn't particularly hard for me to accomplish, since the original script for the comic story was extremely detailed."

THE RED RAVEN is a real scum-pit. The only thing marking it as a bar is the vintage Old Crow ad in the front window and a stuttering neon sign that says LOUNGE. The Johns are always backing up and the place perpetually stinks of piss.

During the week it's just another neighborhood dive, serving truck drivers and barflies. Not a Bukowski among them. But, since the drinks are cheap and the bartenders never check ID, the Red Raven undergoes a sea change come Friday night. The bar's clientele changes radically; growing younger and stranger, at least in physical appearance. The usual

suspects that occupy the Red Raven's booths and barstools are replaced
by young men and women tricked out in black leather and so many facial
piercings they resemble walking tackle boxes. Still not a Bukowski among
them.

This Friday night's no different from any others. A knot of Goth kids
are already gathered outside on the curb as I arrive, plastic go-cups full
of piss-warm Rolling Rock clutched in their hands as they talk among
themselves. Amid all the bad Cure haircuts, heavy mascara, dead-white
face powder and black lipstick, I hardly warrant a second look.

Normally I don't bother with joints like this, but I've been hearing this
persistent rumor that there's a blood cult operating out of the Red Raven.
I make it my business to check out such rumors for myself. Most of the
time it turns out to be nothing, but occasionally there's something far
more sinister at the heart of urban legends.

The interior of the Red Raven is crowded with young men and
women, all of whom look far stranger and more menacing than myself.
What with my black motorcycle jacket, ratty jeans, and equally tattered
New York Dolls T-shirt, I'm somewhat on the conservative end of the
dress code.

I wave down the bartender, who doesn't seem to consider it odd I'm
sporting sunglasses after dark, and order a beer. It doesn't bother me that
the glass he hands me bears visible greasy fingerprints and a smear of lipstick on the rim. After all, it's not like I'm going to drink it.

Now that I have the necessary prop, I settle in and wait. Finding out
the lowdown in places like this isn't that hard, really. All I've got to do
is be patient and keep my ears open. Over the years I've developed a
method for listening to dozens of conversations at once—sifting the
meaningless ones aside without even being conscious of it most of the
time, until I find the one I'm looking for. I suspect it's not unlike how a
shark can pick out the frenzied splashing of a wounded fish from miles
away.

"*. . . told him he could kiss my ass goodbye . . .*"

"*. . . really liked their last album . . .*"

"*. . . bitch acted like I'd done something . . .*"

"*. . . —until next payday? I promise you'll get it right back . . .*"

"*. . . the undead. He's the real thing . . .*"

There. That one.

I angle my head in the direction of the voice I've zeroed in on, trying
not to look at them directly. There are three of them—one male and two
female—apparently in earnest conversation with a young woman. The
two females are archetypal Goth chicks. They look to be in their late

teens, early twenties, dressed in a mixture of black leather and lingerie and wearing way too much eye makeup. One is tall and willowy, her heavily applied makeup doing little to mask the bloom of acne on her cheeks. Judging from the roots of her boot-black hair, she's probably a natural dishwater blonde.

Her companion is considerably shorter and a little too pudgy for the black satin bustier she's shoehorned into. Her face is painted clown white with an ornate tattoo at the corner of her eye, which I've been told is more in imitation of a popular comic book character than as tribute to the Egyptian gods. She's wearing a man's riding derby draped in a length of black lace that makes her look taller than she really is.

The male member of the group is tall and skinny, outfitted in a pair of leather pants held up by a monstrously ornate silver belt buckle, and a leather jacket. He isn't wearing a shirt, his bare breastbone hairless and a tad sunken. He's roughly the same age as the girls, perhaps younger, constantly nodding in agreement with whatever they say, nervously flipping his lank, burgundy-colored hair out of his face. It doesn't take me long to discern that the tall girl is called Sable, the short one in the hat Tanith, and that the boy is Serge. The girl they are talking to has close-cropped Raggedy Ann–red hair and a nose ring. She is Shawna.

Out of habit, I drop my vision into the Pretender spectrum and scan them for sign of inhuman taint. All four check out clean. Oddly, this piques my interest. I move a little closer to where they are standing huddled, so I can filter out the Marilyn Manson blaring out of the nearby jukebox.

Shawna shakes her head and smiles nervously, uncertain as to whether she's being goofed on or not. "C'mon—a *real* vampire?"

"We told him about you, Shawna, didn't we, Serge?" Tanith looks to the gawky youth hovering at her elbow. Serge nods his head eagerly, which necessitates his flipping his hair out of his face yet again.

"His name is Rhymer. Lord Rhymer. He's three hundred years old," Sable adds breathlessly, "and he said he wanted to meet you!"

Despite her attempts at post-modern death-chic, Shawna looks like a flattered schoolgirl.

"*Really?*"

I can tell she's hooked as clean as a six-pound trout and that it won't take much more work on the trio's part to land their catch. The quartet of black-leather-clad young rebels quickly leave the Red Raven, scurrying off as fast as their Doc Martens can take them. I give it a couple of beats then set out after them.

As I shadow them from a distance, I can't shake the nagging feeling that something is wrong. Although I seem to have found what I've come looking for, something's not quite right about it, but I'll be damned (I know—I'm being redundant) if I can say what.

In my experience, vampires avoid Goths like daylight. While their adolescent fascination with death and decadence might, at first, seem to make them natural choices as servitors, their extravagant fashion sense calls far too much attention to them. Vampires prefer their servants far more nondescript and discreet. But perhaps this Lord Rhymer, whoever he may be, is of a more modern temperament than those I've encountered in the past.

I don't know what to make of this trio who seem to be acting as his Judas goats. Judging by their evident enthusiasm, perhaps "converts" is a far more accurate description than servitors. They don't seem to have the predator's gleam in their eyes, nor is there anything resembling a killer's caution in their walk or mannerisms. As they stroll down the darkened streets their chatter is more like that of mischievous children out on a lark—say, TPing the superintendent's front lawn or soaping the gym teacher's windows. They certainly aren't aware of the extra shadow that attached itself to them the moment they left the Red Raven with their fresh pickup.

After a ten-minute walk they arrive at their destination: an abandoned church. Of course. It's hardly Carfax Abbey, but I suppose it will do. The church is a two-story wooden structure boasting an old-fashioned spire, stabbing a symbolic finger in the direction of Heaven.

The feeling of ill ease rises in me again. Vampires dislike such obvious lairs. Hell, these aren't the Middle Ages. They don't have to hang out in ruined monasteries and family mausoleums anymore—not that there are any to be found in the US, anyhow. No, contemporary bloodsuckers prefer to dwell within warehouse lofts or abandoned industrial complexes, even condos. I tracked one dead boy to ground in an inner-city hospital that had been shut down during the Reagan administration and left to rot. I suspect I'll have to start investigating the various military bases scheduled for shutdown for signs of infestation within a year or two.

As I watch the little group troop inside the church, there is only one thing I know for certain: if I want to know what's going down here, I better get inside. I circle around the building, keeping to the darkest shadows, my senses alert for signs of the usual sentinels that guard a vampire's lair, such as ogres and renfields. Normally vampires prefer to keep their bases covered. Ogres for physical protection, renfields—warped psychics—to protect them against psionic attacks from rival bloodsuckers.

I reach out with my mind as I climb up the side of the church, trying to pick up the garbled snarl of ogre-thought or the telltale dead space of shielded minds that accompany renfields, but all my sonar picks up is the excited heat of the foursome I trailed from the Red Raven and a slightly more complex signal from deeper inside the church. Curiouser and curiouser.

The spire doesn't house a bell, just a rusting Korean War–era public address system dangling from frayed wires. As it is, there is barely enough room for a man to stand, much less ring, but at least the trapdoor isn't locked. It opens with a tight squeal of disused hinges, but nothing stirs in the shadows at the foot of the ladder below. Within seconds I find myself with the best seat in the house, crouched in the rafters spanning the nave.

The interior of the church looks appropriately atmospheric. What pews remain are in disarray, the hymnals tumbled from their racks and spilled across the floor. Saints, apostles and prophets stare down from the windows, gesturing with upraised shepherd's crooks or hands bent into the sign of benediction. I lift my own mirrored gaze to the mullion window located above and behind the pulpit. It depicts a snowy lamb kneeling on a field of green and framed against a cloudless sky, in which a shining disc is suspended. The large brass cross just below the sheep-window has been inverted, in keeping with the desecration motif.

The only light is provided by a pair of heavy cathedral-style candelabra, each bristling with over a hundred dripping red and black candles, flanking either side of the pulpit. The Goth kids from the Red Raven gather at the chancel rail, their faces turned toward the pulpit situated above the black-velvet-draped altar.

"Where is he?" whispers Shawna, her voice surprisingly loud in the empty church.

"Don't worry," Tanith assures her. "He'll be here."

As if on cue, there is the smell of ozone and a gout of purplish smoke arises from behind the pulpit. Shawna gives a little squeal of surprise despite herself and takes an involuntary step backward, only to find her way blocked by the others.

A deep, highly cultured masculine voice booms forth. "Good evening, my children. I bid you welcome to my abode, and that you enter gladly and of your own free will."

The smoke clears, revealing a tall man dressed in tight-fitting black satin pants, a black silk poet's shirt, black leather English riding boots, and a long black opera cape with a red silk lining. His hair is long and dark, pulled back into a loose ponytail by a red satin ribbon. His skin is as white as milk in a saucer, his eyes reflecting red in the dim candlelight. Lord Rhymer has finally elected to make his appearance.

Serge smiles nervously at his demon lord and steps forward, gesturing to Shawna as Tanith and Sable watch expectantly. "W-we did as you asked, master. We brought you the girl."

Lord Rhymer smiles slightly, his eyes narrowing at the sight of her. "Ah, *yesss.* The new girl."

Shawna stands there gaping up at the vampire lord as if he were Jim Morrison, Robert Smith, and Danzig rolled into one. She starts, gasping more in surprise than fright, as Rhymer addresses her directly.

"Your name is Shawna, is it not?"

"Y-yes." Her voice is so tiny it makes her sound like a little girl. But there is nothing childlike in the lust dancing in her eyes.

Lord Rhymer holds out a pale hand to the trembling young woman. His fingernails are long and pointed and lacquered black. He smiles reassuringly, his voice calm and strong, designed to sway those of weaker nature.

"Come to me, Shawna. Come to me, so that I might kiss you."

A touch of apprehension crosses the girl's face. She hesitates, glancing at the others, who close in about her even tighter than before.

"I . . . I don't know."

Rhymer narrows his blood-red eyes, intensifying his stare. His voice grows sterner, revealing its cold edge. "*Come* to me, Shawna."

All the tension in her seems to drain away and Shawna's eyes grow even more vacant than before, if possible. She moves forward, slowly mounting the stairs to the pulpit. Rhymer holds his arms out to greet her.

"That's it, my dear. Come to me as you have dreamed, so many times before . . ." Rhymer steps forward to meet her, the cape outstretched between his arms like the wings of a giant bat. His smile widens and his mouth opens, exposing pearly white fangs dripping saliva. His voice has been made husky by lust.

"Come to me, my bride . . ."

Shawna grimaces in pain and pleasure as Rhymer's fangs penetrate her throat. Even from my shadowy perch above it all I can smell the sharp tang of blood, and feel a dark stirring at the base of my brain, which I quickly push aside. I don't need that kind of trouble—not now. Still, I find it hard to look away from the tableau below me.

Rhymer holds Shawna tight against him. She whimpers as if on the verge of orgasm. The blood rolling down her throat and dripping into the pale swell of her cleavage is as sticky and dark as spilled molasses.

Rhymer draws back, smiling smugly as he wipes the blood off his chin. "It is done. You are now bound to me by blood and the strength of my immortal will."

Shawna's lids flutter and she seems to have a little trouble focusing her eyes. She touches her bloodied neck and stares at her red-stained finger for a long moment. "Wow . . ." She steps back, a dazed, post-orgasmic look on her face. She staggers slightly as she moves to rejoin the others, one hand still clamped over her bruised and bleeding throat. Tanith and Sable eagerly step forward to help their new sister, their hands quickly disappearing up her skirt as they steady her, cooing encouragement in soothing voices.

"Welcome to the family, Shawna," Sable whispers, kissing first her cheek, then tonguing her ear lobe.

"You're one of us, now and forever," Tanith purrs, giving Shawna a probing kiss while scooping her breasts free of her blouse. Sable presses even closer, licking at the blood smearing Shawna's neck. Serge stands off to one side, nervously chewing a thumbnail and occasionally brushing his forelock out of his face. Every few seconds his eyes flicker from the girls to Lord Rhymer, who stands in the pulpit, smiling and nodding his approval. After a few more moments of groping and gasping, the three women begin undressing one another in earnest, their moans soon mixed with nervous giggles. Black leather and lace drop away, revealing black fishnet stockings and garter belts and crotchless underwear. At the sight of Shawna's pubic thatch—mousy brown, as opposed to her fluorescent red locks—Serge's eyes widen and his nostrils flare. He looks to Rhymer, who nods and gestures languidly with one taloned hand that the boy has his permission to join the orgy.

Serge fumbles with his ornate silver belt buckle, which hits the wooden floor with a solid *clunk!* I lift an eyebrow in surprise. While Serge is thin to the point of emaciation, I must admit the boy's hung like a stallion. Sable mutters something into Serge's ear that makes him laugh just before he plants his lips against her own blood-smeared mouth. Tanith, her eyes heavy-lidded and her lips pulled into a lascivious grin, reaches around from behind to stroke him to full erection.

Serge breaks free of his embrace with Sable and turns to lift Shawna in his arms, carrying her to the black-draped altar, the other girls quickly joining in. There is much biting and raking of exposed flesh with finger-nails. Soon they are a mass of writhing naked flesh, giggling and moaning and grunting, the slap of flesh against flesh filling the silent church. And overseeing it all from his place of power is Lord Rhymer, his crimson eyes twinkling in the candlelight as he watches his followers cavorting below him. To his credit, Serge proves himself tireless, energetically rutting with all three girls in various combinations for hours on end.

It isn't until the stained-glass windows of the church begin to lighten with the coming dawn that it finally comes to an end. The moment Rhymer notices the light coming through one of the windows the smile disappears from his face.

"*Enough!*" he thunders, causing the others to halt in midlick. "The sun will soon be upon me! It is time for you to leave, my children!"

The Goths pull themselves off and out of each other without a word of complaint and begin to struggle back into their clothes. Once they're dressed they waste no time hurrying off, taking pains not to look one another in the eye. It is all I can do to suppress a groan of relief as the last of the blood cultists lurches out of the building. I thought those losers were *never* going to leave!

I check my own watch against the shadows sliding across the floor below me. Now would be a good time to pay a social call on their so-called "master." I hope he's in the mood for a little chat before beddy-bye.

Lord Rhymer yawns as he makes his way down the basement stairs. What with the candelabra he's holding and the flowing a cloak, I'm reminded of Lugosi's Dracula. But then, Bela Lugosi is dead.

The basement runs the length of the building above it, with a poured concrete floor. Stacks of old hymnals, folding chairs and moldering choir robes have been pushed into the corners. A rosewood casket with a maroon velvet lining rests atop a pair of sawhorses in the middle of the room. An old-fashioned steamer stands on end nearby.

I watch the vampire lord set the candelabra down and, still yawning, unhook his cape and carefully drape it atop the trunk. If he senses my presence, here in the shadows, he gives no evidence of it in his manner. Smiling crookedly, I deliberately scrape my boot heel against the concrete floor. My smile becomes a grin when he spins around, eyes bugging in fear.

"What—? Who's there?"

He blinks, genuinely surprised to see me standing to one side of the open casket balanced atop the sawhorse. I'd already caught the telltale smell of it when I first entered the basement, but a quick glance into the casket confirms what I already knew: it's lined with earth. I reach inside and lift a handful of dirt, allowing it to spill between my splayed fingers. I look up and meet Rhymer's scarlet gaze.

"Okay, buddy, what the hell are you trying to pull here?"

Rhymer squares his shoulders and pulls himself up to his full height, hissing and exposing his fangs, hooking his fingers into talons. His red eyes glint in the dim light like those of a cornered animal.

I am not impressed.

"Can the Christopher Lee act, asshole! I'm not some Goth chick tripping her brains out! You're not fooling me for one moment!" I kick the
sawhorses out from under the casket, sending it tumbling to the floor,
spilling its layer of soil. Rhymer gasps, his eyes darting from the ruined
coffin to me and back and again. "Only humans think vampires need to
sleep on a layer of their home soil!"

Rhymer tries to regain the momentum by pointing a trembling finger
at me, doing his best to sound menacing. "You have defiled the resting
place of Rhymer, Lord of the Undead! And for that, woman, you will pay
with your life!"

"Oh yeah?" I sneer. "Buddy, I knew Dracula—and, believe me, you ain't him!"

I move on him so fast it's like blinking. One moment I'm halfway
across the room, the next I'm standing over him, his blood dripping from
my knuckles. Rhymer's lying on the basement floor, dazed and wiping at
his gushing mouth and nose. A set of dentures, complete with fangs, lies
on the floor beside him. I nudge the upper plate with the toe of my boot,
shaking my head in disgust.

"Just what I thought: fake fangs! And the eyes are contact lenses, right?
I bet the nails are theatrical quality press-ons, too . . ."

Rhymer tries to scuttle away from me like a crab, but he's much too
slow. I grab him by the ruff of his poet's shirt, pulling him to his feet with
one quick motion that causes him to yelp in alarm.

"What the fuck are you playing at here? Are you running some kind of
scam on these Goth kids?"

Rhymer opens his mouth, and although his lips are moving here's no
sound coming out. At first I think he's so scared he's not able to speak—
then I realize he's a serious stutterer when he's not a vampire.

"I'm n-not a con m-man, if that's what y-you're thinking. I'm n-not
doing it for m-money!"

"If it's not for money, then why?" Not that I haven't known his motiva-
tion from the moment I first laid eyes on him. But I want to hear it from
his own lips before I make my decision.

"All m-my life I've been an outsider. N-no one ever p-paid any attention to m-me. N-not even m-my own p-parents. N-no one ever took me
seriously. I was a j-joke and everyone k-knew. The only p-place where I
could escape from being m-me was the m-movies. I really admired the
v-vampires in the m-movies. They were d-different, too. But n-no one
m-made fun of them or ignored them. They were p-powerful and p-people re afraid of them. They c-could m-make w-women do whatever they
w-wanted.

"W-when my p-parents died a c-couple of years ago, they left m-me a lot of m-money. So m-much I'd n-never have to work again. An hour after their funeral I w-went to a dentist and had I m-my upper teeth removed and the dentures m-made.

"I always w-wanted to be a v-vampire—and now I had the c-chance to live m-my d-dreams. So I b-bought this old church and s-started hanging out at the Red Raven, looking for the right type of g-girls.

"T-Tanith was the first. Then came S-sable. The rest w-was easy. They w-wanted m-me to b-be real so b-badly, I didn't even have to p-pretend that m-much. B-but then things started to g-get out of hand. They w-wanted m-me t-to—you know—p-ut my thing in them. B-but m-my thing c-can't get hard. N-ot with other p-people. I told them it w-was because I w-was dead. So we f-found S-serge. I-I like to w-watch."

Rhymer fixes one of his rapidly blackening eyes on me. His fear is beginning to give way to curiosity. "B-but w-what difference is any of this to y-you? Are y-you a family m-member? One of S-serge's ex g-girlfriends?"

I can't help but laugh as I let go of him, careful to place myself between Rhymer and the exit. He staggers backward and quickly, if inelegantly, puts distance between us. He flinches at the sound of my laughter as if it were a physical blow.

"I knew there was something fishy going on when I spotted the belt buckle on the Goth studmuffin. No self-respecting dead boy in his right mind would let that chunk of silver within a half-mile of his person! And all that hocus-pocus with the smoke and the Black Sabbat folderol! All of it a rank amateur's impression of what vampires and vampirism is all about, cobbled together from Hammer films and Anton Levy paperbacks! You really are a pathetic little twisted piece of crap, Rhymer—or whatever the hell your real name is! You surround yourself with the icons of darkness and play at damnation; but you don't recognize the real thing even when it steps forward and bloodies your fuckin' nose!"

Rhymer stands there for a long moment, then his eyes suddenly widen and he gasps aloud, like a man who has walked into a room and seen someone he has believed long dead. Clearly overcome, he drops to his feet before me, his bloodstained lips quivering uncontrollably.

"*You're real!*"

"Get up," I growl, flashing a glimpse of fang.

Instead of inspiring fear in Rhymer, all this does is cause him to cry out even louder than before. He is now actually groveling, pawing at my boots as he blubbers.

"At last! I k-knew if I w-waited long enough, one of y-you w-would finally come!"

"I said *get up*, you little toad-eater!" I kick him away, but it does no good. Rhymer crawls back on his belly, as fast as a lizard on a hot rock. I was afraid something like this would happen.

"I'll do anything you w-want—give you anything you n-need!" He grabs the cuffs of my jeans, tugging insistently. "B-bite me! Drink my b-blood! *Pleeease!* M-make me like you!"

As I look down at this wretched human who has lived a life so stunted, his one driving passion is to become a walking dead man, I feel my memory slide back across the years, to the night a foolish young girl, made giddy by the excitement that comes with the pursuit of forbidden pleasures and made stupid by the romance of danger, allowed herself to be lured away from the safety of the herd. I remember how she found herself alone with a blood-eyed monster that hid behind the face of a handsome, booth-talking stranger. I remember how her nude, blood-smeared body was hurled from the speeding car and tossed in the gutter and left for dead. I remember how she was far from dead. I remember how she was me.

I can feel myself trembling like I've got a high fever. My disgust has become anger, and I've never been very good at controlling my anger. And part of me—a dark, dangerous part—has no desire ever to learn.

I try hard to keep a grip on myself, but it's not easy. In the past when I've been overwhelmed by my anger I've tried to make sure I only vent it at those I consider worthy of such murderous rage. Such as vampires. Real ones, that is. Like myself. But sometimes . . . well, sometimes I lose it. Like now.

"You want to be like *me*?"

I kick the groveling little turd so hard that ribs splinter as he flies across the basement floor and collides with the wall. He cries out, but it doesn't exactly sound like pain.

"You stupid bastard! *I* don't even want to be like *me!*"

I tear the mirrored sunglasses away, and Rhymer's eyes widen as he sees my own. They look nothing like his scarlet-tinted contact lenses. There is no white, no corona—merely seas of solid blood boasting vertical slits that open and close, like those of a snake, depending on the strength of the light. The church basement is very gloomy, so my pupils are dilated wide—like those of a shark rising from the sunless depths to savage a luckless swimmer.

Rhymer lifts a hand to block out the sight of me as I advance on him, his trembling delight now replaced by genuine, 100 percent monkey-brain fear. For the first time he seems to realize that he is in the presence of a monster.

"Please don't hurt me, mistress! Forgive me!"

I don't know what else he might have said to try and avoid his fate because his head comes off in my hands right about then.

For a brief second Rhymer's hands still flutter in their futile attempt to beg my favor, then there is a spurt of scarlet from the neck-stump, not unlike that from a spitting fountain, as his still-beating heart sends a stream of blood to where the brain would normally be. I quickly side-step the gruesome spray without letting go of my trophy.

Turning away from Rhymer's still-twitching corpse, I step over the ruins of the antique coffin and its payload. No doubt the dirt had been imported from the Balkans—perhaps Moldavia or even Transylvania. I shake my head in amazement that such old wives' tales are still in circulation and given validity by so many.

As I head up the stairs, Rhymer's head tucked under my arm, I pause one last time to survey what is left of the would-be vampire king of the Goth chicks. Man, what a mess. Glad I'm not the one who has to clean it up.

This isn't the first vampire-wannabe I've run into, but I've got to admit he had the best scam. The Goth chicks wanted the real thing and he gave them what they thought they wanted, even down to retro-fitting the church with theatrical trapdoors and magician's flash-pots. And they bought into the bullshit because it made them feel special, it made them feel real, and, most importantly, it made them feel *alive*. Poor, stupid bastards. To them it's all black leather, lovebites, and tacky chrome jewelry; where everyone is eternally young and beautiful and no one can ever hurt you ever again.

Like hell.

As for Rhymer, he wanted the real thing as badly as the Goths. Perhaps even more so. He'd spent his entire life aspiring to monstrosity; hoping that, given time, his heartfelt mimicry of the damned would either turn him into what he longed to be thorough sympathetic magic, or that his actions would eventually draw the attention of the creatures of the night he worshipped so ardently. As, indeed, it had. I was the real thing all right; big as life and twice as ugly.

But I was hardly the bloodsucking seductress Rhymer had been dreaming of all those years. There was no way he could know that his little trick would lure forth not just a vampire—but a vampire-slayer as well.

You see, my unique and unwanted predicament has denied me many things: the ability to age, to love, to feel life quicken within me. And in retaliation against this unwished-for transformation, I've spent decades denying the monster inside me; trying—however futilely—to turn my back on the horror that is the Other who dwells in the dark side of my soul. However, there is one pleasure, and one alone, I allow myself to indulge, and that is killing vampires . . .

And those that would become them.

Dawn is well under way by the time I reenter the nave. The white-washed walls are dappled with light dyed blue, green and red by the stained glass. I take a couple of steps backward, then drop-kick Rhymer's head right through the Lamb-of-God window.

The birds are chirping happily away in the trees, greeting the coming day with their morning songs, as I push open the wide double doors of the church. A stray dog with matted fur and slats for ribs is already sniffing Rhymer's ruined noggin where it has landed in the high weeds. The cur lifts its muzzle and automatically growls, but as I draw closer it flattens its ears and tucks its tail between its legs and quickly scurries off. Dogs are smart. They know what is and isn't of the natural world—even if humans don't.

Last night was a bust, as far as I'm concerned. When I go out hunting I prefer bringing down actual game, not *faux* predators. Still, I wish I could hang around and see the look on the faces of Rhymer's groupies when they find out what's happened to their "master." That'd be good for a chuckle or two.

No one can say I don't have a sense of humor about these things.

Just His Type

Storm Constantine

Storm Constantine is the creator of the Wraeththu Mythos, the first trilogy of which was published in the 1980s. She has written more than thirty books, including full-length novels (such as *Hermetech* and *Burying the Shadow*), novellas, short story collections, and nonfiction titles, such as *Sekhem Heka*.

She is currently working on a new novel and several short stories. Storm is the founder of the independent publishing imprint, Immanion Press. She lives in the Midlands of the UK with her husband and four cats.

"When I was researching my novel *Stalking Tender Prey*," she recalls, "which was primarily about the legends of fallen angels, it seemed clear to me that the vampire myths might also have stemmed from the same origins.

"The Biblical rendition of the fallen angels derived from earlier myths from the ancient Mesopotamian civilization of Sumer, which perhaps came from times earlier than that. The old stories seem tantalizingly to suggest that the image of winged beings grew from memories of a real race of flesh and blood, who were vulture shamans. The idea of them having wings could derive from the fact that in their rituals they wore the wings of griffin vultures around their shoulders. (Ancient remains of these wings have been found in caves in the Middle East, along with bones and other evidence of ritual.) Drinking the blood of both animals and humans is something the fallen angels were accused of doing, and this may well have been part of their shamanic rites.

"It wasn't really appropriate to include this aspect of the myth in *Stalking Tender Prey*, so I was glad to be given the opportunity to explore it in the story for this anthology."

THE TROUBLE WAS she was just his type. Sitting at the back of the stuffy pub function room, her eyes fixed upon him, she commanded his attention, apparently without effort. He could tell she was tall, because her head was the highest on the row. Her hands were clasped in her lap and she was dressed in black.

She had come to watch the famous historical investigator and author, Noah Johnson, deliver a lecture. He found he was playing to her alone throughout the evening. He knew the talk, "Vampires in Myth and History," by heart, having delivered it countless times before. He updated it constantly, but essentially, it was the same old stuff: colorful but careful. He was selective about what he gave the punters. He knew how to please a mixed crowd.

The regular meetings, "Enigmas of History," were going well. He ran them once a fortnight in the upstairs room of his local pub, The Gun and Duck, and now had a regular attendance of around fifty people. Sometimes, he had to turn some away. More than fifty and the front row started fainting. He'd started it to augment his writing income, for the periods when funds were slack—a downside of any writer's life. But it was going so well, he had planned more events; outdoors, now that summer was coming. Sarah would have loved all this. But he mustn't think about her now. She was no longer part of his life.

Noah's friend and assistant, Gary, dimmed the lights in preparation for the slide-show. Some of the audience were fanning themselves with the handouts Gary's girlfriend, Abby, had placed on every seat prior to the meeting. The windows were open, but did little to improve the air quality in the room.

One by one, the slides slipped across the screen: illustrations copied from ancient texts, photographs Noah had taken himself while investigating in far corners of obscure eastern European countries. Some of them had been reproduced in Noah's bestselling book, *The Search for Nosferatu.* The subject no longer captivated him: he'd done it and it was over, but the public was always hungry for it. Noah had moved on to other things and was currently researching his next book, which was concerned with the mythical landscape of the remote Scottish islands, and how the strange ancient structures there might have come to be built.

When the lights came back on, Noah's eyes were drawn immediately to the girl in the back row. He half-expected to see that she'd left. That would be just his luck, but no, there she was, sitting straight and demure, gazing at him from beneath downcast lashes, a slight smile on her lips.

He began to answer questions from the audience, but was anxious to keep it short tonight. If people wanted to air their opinions, which most of them did, especially the regulars, they could continue in the bar downstairs. He interrupted a woman as she was speaking. "Hey, it's too hot up here. Shall we move down?"

Most of them would go home, but the ones who saw themselves as the core of his group would remain until closing time. It was only nine o'clock.

People started getting out of their seats, apparently as eager as he was to escape the hot function room. The woman who'd been interrupted looked crestfallen, somewhat confused.

Gary and Abby began clearing up, gathering the dropped leaflets, packing away the slide equipment. "Good turnout," Gary said.

"You could hire a bigger place," Abby suggested. "You'd still pack it."

Noah was looking at the crowd shuffling out. He saw that the girl in black had remained in her seat. He smiled at her and she stood up. He went toward her.

"Excuse me, Mr. Johnson, would you mind if I asked you something?"

"Of course not," he said. "Come down to the bar. We usually stay on for a few drinks."

"Thank you."

He put his arm behind her proprietarily to guide her to the door.

"Thanks, Noah!" Abby called behind him. "We'll just finish off, shall we?"

He grinned back at her and she shook her head in mock disapproval. Abby was used to him and he knew how much he could get away with.

Downstairs, punters insisted on buying Noah drinks, but he bought one for the girl himself. "I haven't seen you here before," he said, leaning on the bar.

She pulled a face. Her features were delicate, mobile. "No, I've only just moved here. It was great to discover this group, especially that it's run by you. I've got all your books."

He laughed. "Thanks." In his mind, he could hear Abby's warning cry of: *"Noah! She's a fan, okay? For God's sake, be careful."*

The girl brushed strands of dark hair from her eyes. Her well-shaped lips were painted perfectly in a dark purple. Her dress was of black lace and velvet, down to the floor. She was virtually the same height he was. "I'm Lara, by the way. Lara Hoskins."

Noah handed her a vodka and tonic. When she took it from him, he saw that her lace cuffs came right down to her fingers. The nails were painted black. "So, what did you want to ask me?" He was conscious of the eyes of his "core group" upon him, their resentment at a newcomer monopolizing him. Normally, this was the time for Noah to hold court.

"Well, I have to admit it was the subject of the talk tonight that most attracted me," Lara said. She laughed nervously. "Not that I wouldn't have come anyway, of course . . ."

"And?"

"Why don't you talk about the origins of the vampire myth?"

"I do. You heard it."

She was silent for a moment. "I think we both know there's more to it than that."

"Essentially, it's European, although there are parallels in Mesopotamian and Judaic mythology."

"But where do *those* myths come from?"

"There are recurrent themes in every mythology. People the world over have the same fears, the same desires. There's no reason to think the vampire myth comes from a single root source."

"But in *Nosferatu*, you implied differently."

"What are you getting at?" Noah said, grinning. "Don't tell me you're a vampire searching for your roots!"

A vampire would certainly not color up the way she did then. "I have a serious interest in the subject," she said. "I'd hoped you'd take me seriously too."

"Look," he said. "If you want the truth, I think people can become obsessed with certain myths, especially the vampire ones. It's dangerous."

"How?" She looked hungry.

"Any obsession is dangerous. I don't like to encourage it." He was thinking of Sarah. Her face was before his eyes, sad and despairing.

"What happened?" Lara asked in a low voice. It was as if she knew already.

He could tell her easily. She could be his confessor. "I knew someone," he began. Then a hand slapped his back.

"Hey!" It was Abby. "Don't tell me you haven't got drinks in for us!" She smiled at Lara. "He treats us like lackeys!"

"Sorry," Noah said. He turned to attract the attention of the barman.

For the rest of the evening Abby refused to leave Noah's side. He knew why. Abby knew him too well. She was good company and gave no indication to Lara that she was suspicious of her, but Noah was well aware of his friend's feelings.

After last orders, when the group was breaking up, Noah said to Lara, "There's an event next Sunday. We're going on a tour of local ancient sites, churches, springs and so on. Should be quite a convoy. Would you like to come?"

"Well . . ." Lara put her empty glass down on the bar. "Might be difficult. I don't have transport."

"I could pick you up," said Noah.

"Great!" Lara opened her bag and rummaged in it. "I'll give you my address. What time?"

"Oh, about midday."

"It'll cost a tenner," said Abby, somewhat darkly.

"Good value," Lara said, taking the lid off a fountain pen.

Outside, in the car park, Abby started on Noah. "What are you up to?" she demanded. "I thought you'd decided to leave punters well alone."

"What do you mean?" Noah countered, fiddling with his keys.

"I mean that you fancy her. It's obvious. But you've been down this road many times before. You know where it leads."

"She's just coming to the event," Noah said. "What's wrong with that? Lots of other people are going and they're all punters as well."

Abby folded her arms belligerently across her chest. "I'm not stupid!"

"Give him a break, will you," Gary snapped.

Abby was not to be deterred. "She's a fan, Gary, and she's got her sights set. There's something a bit odd about her. I can just feel it."

"He's a grown man," Gary said in a tired voice. "For Christ's sake, Ab, you sound like his bloody mother."

"I'm the nearest he has to that," Abby said, getting into the front passenger seat of Noah's car.

For the next few days, Noah couldn't stop thinking about Lara Hoskins. Abby was wrong to be so suspicious. Of course, he *had* met Sarah at a lecture, long before he'd begun the regular meetings, and perhaps this was why Abby was so scared for him. He'd dated lots of girls since, some of them plucked from the "Enigmas of History" group, and he was the first to admit that none of them had worked out particularly well, but he was sure this was different. Lara was bright and had an inquiring mind. There were no warning signs. Her hands had been steady on her glass all evening. She'd been open and sociable.

By Sunday morning, he was buzzing with anticipation, and spent more time than usual on his appearance. Lara was probably about ten years younger than him, in her midtwenties by the look of her, but that didn't matter. He looked young for his age. All his life, women had flocked to him.

When he drew up outside her house, she came through the front door before he'd even turned off the engine. She was dressed in black jeans and T-shirt, with a black hooded fleece tied around her waist, presumably in case it got cold later. Her long black hair was caught up in a severe ponytail but swished provocatively around her head and shoulders as she ran down the short drive to the road. She was as slim as a boy and looked athletic. Noah's heart turned over. She was gorgeous.

"Hi!" she said breathlessly as she virtually threw herself into the car. She smelled strongly of an oriental yet floral scent.

"Hi," Noah echoed. "I like a woman who's ready on time."

Lara laughed. It was a bright, free sound, devoid of artifice. Of course, she'd been ready for hours.

When they arrived at the meeting point, Noah was pleased to see there was a good turnout—about seven packed cars. Abby was going round collecting money and distributing maps.

At each site they visited, Noah had the group sit down and meditate to see if they could pick up any information from the past, such as what the site might have been used for in ancient times. He never did this at the indoor meetings. This was his select group, with whom he was prepared to try more "weird stuff," as some referred to it. During the meditation, Lara saw a great deal of detailed and pertinent imagery. "I think you're psychic," Noah told her privately.

"Oh, I know *that*," she said.

"You couldn't be more perfect," Noah said.

Lara smiled. "When can we continue our conversation?"

"Later. How about dinner?"

"Sounds great."

Noah had to lose Abby and Gary for the evening, which was not easy. He didn't want Abby to know he was taking Lara out, sure that she would insist that she and Gary went with him. Fortunately, they'd brought their own car that day, so at the last site Noah whisked Lara off quickly, virtually without saying goodbye to anybody. He knew he'd have to pay for it later and could anticipate Abby's terse message that would be waiting on his answerphone when he got home. But for the time being, he didn't give a damn. Both he and Lara were giggling as his car skidded away in a cloud of dust and gravel.

"Why do I get the feeling we're playing truant?" Lara asked.

"Sometimes, I want a bit of privacy, that's all," Noah answered. "The trouble with these events is that people want it to carry on till all hours. Sometimes, that's fine, but tonight . . ." He glanced at her and she smiled.

He took her to a Thai restaurant he'd never visited before, secure in the knowledge that none of the group would track him there. The food was rather lackluster, but it didn't matter, because Lara was sitting opposite him and her smile seemed to enfold him in a hazy golden mist. They were both high on the sense of being secret conspirators. They were high on the potential of what might happen later.

Lara seemed content to listen to Noah talk about his new book, and it wasn't until the coffee arrived that she broached the subject she'd brought up after the meeting last Tuesday. "Why did you react so badly to my question?"

"I don't think I did. Some things I just steer clear of."

"So what's the story behind it?" She took a sip of coffee, smiled disarmingly. "Or is it a secret?"

Noah leaned back in his chair. "It's no secret. If you become part of the core group—and I'm sure you will—anyone would tell you about it.

Basically, while I was writing *Nosferatu*, I was involved in more than the obvious method of research. The problem came from that."

Lara put her head to one side. "What do you mean?"

"You saw what we did today. People are keen on the psychic stuff. On one level, it's harmless, and most people never go beyond that. But on another, it isn't. Sitting outside an old church and trying to visualize images of the past can't hurt anyone, because it's dead and gone. It's nothing more than a psychic photograph. But other things, well, they're more alive, still around, so to speak."

Lara laughed, lit a cigarette. "Are you trying to tell me that you contacted a vampire psychically?"

Noah hesitated for a moment. Part of him didn't want to say more, but Lara's wide eyes were fixed upon him with a bright, intelligent gaze. He felt safe with her. "I worked with a girl called Sarah. People don't realize it, but a lot of the information in my books comes from what I call 'inspired' sources, from psychics. Most of what I find out can't be used in a serious book, because it can't be checked out and verified as fact, but it gives me a feel for and understanding of the subject. Sarah was my assistant and also my partner. She was very psychic."

"*Was*," Lara said, her chin resting on her hands. Smoke curled around her in slow tendrils. "That sounds ominous."

"Let's just say that I was interested in the origin of the vampire myth, like you are. I'd investigated all the legends of blood-drinking demons, from medieval Europe right back to Sumerian times. Somewhere along the way, the flavor of the subject changed." He gestured with both hands. "It's difficult to describe, but the idea of the vampire as unfortunate undead—perhaps a victim of their circumstances—mutated into the idea that the original vampires were very much alive and that their vampirism was by choice, a necessary facet of their belief system."

Lara nodded enthusiastically. "That's my thought also."

"It all seemed very academic to us. We called them the vulture people, a shamanic tribe who indulged in blood drinking and sacrifice. Sarah picked up some interesting stuff that pointed us in the direction of certain ancient sites in Turkey. The imagery she saw could be verified. These places existed and there was archaeological evidence that a shamanic culture existed there, who had worshipped vultures. They believed that drinking blood gave them superhuman abilities. Whether that was true or not, we thought that other tribes would probably have regarded them as supernatural, as demons, even, because of their bloodthirsty habits. We believed that there was a diaspora and that factions of this tribe might have moved gradually into Europe, eventually giving rise to the vampire legend.

"Every evening, I'd have Sarah go into a kind of trance, guiding her further and further back into the past, seeking the true story. It seemed we were meant to discover all this, to make the link. The vulture people became more real for us: powerful shamans, who used the rites of blood to change their world. As time went on, Sarah started to get jumpy about it. She said she sensed little dark things that scuttled in the folds of these creatures' vulture wing robes, that they had begun to touch her. She wanted to stop, but I persuaded her otherwise. I thought we were getting close to something that would prove my theory incontrovertibly. We had to continue. But then, one night, Sarah brought something back with her."

There was a silence, while Lara took a long, meditative draw on her cigarette. Then she said, "And Sarah couldn't cope?"

Noah pressed the fingers of one hand briefly against his eyes. He could hear her screams even now. "It was too overwhelming, too *alien*. We always did these sessions by the light of one candle, so we couldn't see much, but it was as if the night just surged into the room. We were surrounded by a presence, not evil exactly, but beyond good and evil. It was amoral, and we were *nothing* to it. Even I could sense it, and I'm no great psychic. In moments, I realized how we'd been playing with something inconceivably huge and beyond us, something immeasurably powerful. We'd pulled at its skirts too insistently and now it had noticed us."

"What happened?"

"Well, once Sarah started screaming, I just leapt up and put the lights on. If something really had been there, it disappeared." He finished off the warm lager left in his glass and shook his head. "Sarah was writhing on the floor. I didn't know what to do. The noises were hideous. In the end, I slapped her. It's what you're supposed to do, isn't it? And she kind of came out of it. But even if the thing had gone, it left a taint behind."

"Did it kill her?" Lara asked bluntly.

Noah detected a faint note of scorn in her voice. "No, no. Of course not. Sarah was an experienced psychic, but she was damaged by what she'd felt and seen. It changed her and there was nothing I could do about it. Nothing. She became paranoid, jealous, and afraid. It destroyed us."

"It wasn't your fault," Lara said, reaching out to touch one of Noah's hands.

He laughed cynically. "They all said that, but it's not true. I was so eager to discover the truth, I didn't think about the dangers. I just kept pushing and pushing. After we split up, Sarah lost her job. She just lost it, big time. The last I heard she'd admitted herself to hospital. She dropped all her old friends."

"It wasn't your fault," Lara insisted. "Sarah just wasn't strong enough."

"She was," Noah said. "*It* was stronger than both of us."

"I don't believe that."

"You weren't there. Even as a writer, I don't have the words to describe to you how terrible that night was, how real the entity that came to us. This wasn't Christopher Lee in a silk cape, Lara. This wasn't a nice, safe little meditation like all those we did today. This was the most raw and primeval energy; it could snuff you out like that!" He snapped his fingers before her face, but she did not flinch.

"I want it," she said.

He laughed shakily. "What?"

"It's what I want. I need to know the truth. I'm not afraid."

Noah raised his hands and shook his head emphatically. "No. You don't know what you're asking for. The vampires you're so enamored of, they're just fashion accessories, a romantic myth. You don't want the truth of it, believe me."

"How dare you!" Lara snapped. "You make me sound like some stupid little girl who's just into looking weird. I'm not enamored by anything." She thumped her chest with a closed fist. "I've lived with this stuff all my life, felt it tugging at the corners of my mind, trying to make itself known to me. Their carrion smell has always been strong to my senses. When I read *Nosferatu*, I thought I'd found someone who would understand, who wouldn't think I was mad." She put her hands against her head, scraped them through her sleek, confined hair, pulling strands of it free. "If you really are so against it, why did you put all those coy clues in the book?"

Noah thought she now looked demented, with her hair beginning to fall over her face, a hectic flush along her cheekbones and those wild, wide eyes. But she was breathtakingly beautiful and, in those moments, he could believe she was as strong as she claimed to be. "You'd better tell me what you mean by saying you've lived with it," he said.

Lara ducked her head in assent and then summoned a waiter to order more drinks.

"No," Noah said. "I'm driving. Let's get the bill. We can talk at my place."

They were silent in the car on the drive home. Lara sat with her hands folded in her lap, staring through the windscreen. Noah wondered what he was doing. He guessed what would come. In was as inexorable as a tidal wave, and he could already see it massing on the horizon. He could stop it now, take her home.

They passed the turnoff that would lead to her road. His hands tightened on the steering wheel. In ten minutes, he was parking the car outside his house.

Inside, Lara wandered around the living room, touching lightly the ancient artifacts that clustered on every available surface. Sarah had collected most of them, but hadn't wanted to take them with her when she left. She hadn't taken anything, or exercised her rights to have half of the house. She'd just wanted out, to cast off any vestige of her life with Noah, desperate to live in the here and now, in safe mundaneity. But it was denied her. No one else should go to the place where Sarah was. No one.

Noah made coffee in the vast silent kitchen, where modern appliances gleamed on the spotless work surfaces. Sarah had had the kitchen installed, paid for it herself. The cutlery and crockery Noah had used for his lunch still lay in the sink, but generally he kept the house tidy out of respect for her, as if she was still around in an etheric kind of way, and might disapprove of clutter and mess. On the way back to the living room, he took a bottle of brandy and two huge globe glasses out of his liquor cupboard and placed them onto the tray next to the *cafetière* and mugs.

Lara was curled up in the big leather armchair by the hearth and had lit the log effect gas fire. She had also managed to find the tiny ashtray that Noah kept reluctantly for guests. "You're so lucky," she said, as Noah came into the room. "This place is great. Tons of books and things. How many bedrooms has it got?"

"Five," Noah answered.

"I'm in the wrong job!" Lara said, laughing. She seemed just like an ordinary girl now, gamine and flirtatious.

Noah set down the tray on the coffee table and set about pouring drinks. "We got this place for a song," he said, rather apologetically. "It was a dump. Sarah did it up." He looked around the room. "It's worth a bit now, of course, but all I'd need is a couple of bad years and I'd have to sell it. Writing is not the millionaire's game it's made out to be, you know."

"I'm surprised to hear you say that," Lara said.

"Most people are. They think we all live like Jackie Collins."

"No, I meant that you know how to change fate, how to make things happen. Why don't you use it for yourself, so that you don't get any of those 'bad years'?"

"You've lost me," Noah said, pushing a glass of brandy and a coffee across the table toward her. "I'm a writer, a researcher, not a bloody magician!"

Lara smiled, turning in her fingers a lock of hair that hung beside her face. "Oh, come on! What about the 'weird stuff'?"

"If I knew how to meditate money into existence, I'd be rich. But I don't. I just use the 'weird stuff' to delve into the past."

"But the vulture people knew how to change their world. You said so."

"Strangely enough, I have no compelling desire to drink blood and murder people." He was enjoying their exchange, sure that the undercurrent was sexual.

Lara picked up the brandy globe. "You've contacted them," she said. "How many people have done that? If you weren't scared shitless, you could use that energy for yourself." Slowly, sensuously, she drained her glass.

Noah knelt back on his heels, his hands braced against his thighs. "I think you are a dangerous young woman," he said.

"You wouldn't have to kill anybody," she said, holding out her glass for more brandy. "I'm sure the smallest of blood sacrifices would do."

Noah poured out a generous measure of the golden liquor. "I'm not going back there, Lara. I got burned and sensibly pay attention to what hurts. You don't put your hand in the fire twice."

"When people have no fear, they can walk across red-hot coals," Lara said. "I'm scared of madmen with knives, and perverts hiding in alleys. I'm scared of people, because they're shit. But etheric entities don't frighten me. They don't have hands of flesh and blood. They can't fire a gun. The only way they can hurt you is through fear, your own mind. You must know that."

Noah hesitated. He could feel the conviction pulsing from Lara's body. "You are a witch," he said and took a long drink of his brandy. It burned his throat, felt good.

Her eyes were hooded now. "Take me there, Noah. I'm not afraid to go alone and I won't freak you out by having the screaming heeby-jeebies. Just take me there."

"Why?" he said.

"Because they want you to," she said. "I've heard their voices whispering in my dreams since I was a child. I've seen their shadows in the curtains of my bedroom every night. I've felt their carrion breath on my face in the dark. I'm one of them, Noah. Not in this life perhaps, but I *know* them. I want to go home."

The silence in the room was absolute and the atmosphere had become still and watchful, like vulture shamans. It was as if Lara had already conjured something into being through the passion of her words. There was no way he could disbelieve her. She looked remarkably sane, but driven. He could not speak.

"I'm not some sick cow who wants to drink blood," Lara said in a conversational tone. "I don't have a black bedroom or collect horror films. I don't want to be a vampire in the traditional sense. I just need to know what it is that has been trying to get through to me, that's all." She smiled. "God, I must sound mad. What else do I have to say to convince you I'm not?"

He stared at her, wrestling with himself, thinking of Sarah.

"I'm a bloody good psychic," she said mischievously, cocking her head to the side. "You can always use one of those, can't you?"

"Then why do you need me? If you're that good, do it yourself."

"You have the map," she said. "You are the guide. It's that simple." She adopted a mock serious tone. "I'll look after you, Noah, don't worry. You'll be *perfectly* safe."

His meditation room was at the back of the house on the second floor, overlooking fields and a small wood. As he'd always done with Sarah, he kept the curtains open and lit a single candle. His heart was beating fast, but not through fear. He was not sure exactly what he felt. As he prepared to light some loose incense, to help conjure the right atmosphere, Lara said, "Have you got a pin?"

"What?"

"To prick our fingers. We should put our blood into the incense."

"Lara . . ."

"*Noah . . . !*" She was laughing at him.

It took some minutes to find a pin, by which time Lara had consumed another globe of brandy. Noah himself was beginning to feel the effects of the alcohol. Perhaps it was numbing his sense of apprehension. He let Lara prick his thumb and squeeze a bright droplet of blood from the wound, which she shook into the incense. Then she put his thumb into her warm mouth and sucked it. "Scared?" she said.

"Horrified."

She pricked her own thumb, but didn't offer to let him taste her blood. It was a slight disappointment.

Lara lay down on the rug before the cold hearth, while Noah sat crossed-legged beside her, and took her gently into a light trance. The words were soporific. His own eyelids began to droop. He led her back through time, made her watch the centuries fall away, until he told her to visualize herself standing at the mouth of a cave amid high, wind-sculpted crags. Beyond the threshold, all was dark.

"This is the Shanidar Cave," he murmured. "Home of the vulture people. Walk into it."

He paused, listening to her light breathing. "Tell me what you see," he said.

"Darkness," she replied. Her brow had creased into a frown. "But I can smell . . ."

She would say *blood*, he thought.

"Flowers," she said faintly. "Everywhere, flowers. They've placed them over the bones. I see them. So many bones. There are wings . . ."

"Is anyone there with you?"

"Yes." Her voice was like that of a child, young and tremulous.

"Do you want to leave?" Noah said. "You can leave at any time."

"No. He knows me. He wants to give me something."

"What?"

"The talking bone . . ."

"What does he look like?"

Suddenly, Lara gasped, her eyes flew open and she sat bolt upright. Noah reached out to steady her. "It's okay," he said.

She turned her head slowly and when she spoke, her voice was deep and rasping. "Keep me not from her, son of Lamech. Her laughter filled the mountains and bowed the heads of the wild beasts. Shame took her from me. Shame!"

Noah could smell carrion, the reek of her breath.

Abruptly, Lara sighed and fell back gracefully onto the floor.

"Lara," Noah breathed, leaning over her. "Lara. Are you all right?"

She laughed and wriggled her body on the rug. "Oh *yes*." Without opening her eyes, she reached up for him, dragged him down. When he kissed her, he tasted brandy, the flame of it.

"Thank you," she murmured, between kisses. "Thank you."

Her skin was hot beneath his hand, exuding the last warmth of her perfume. He made love to her where she lay, wondering if she was fully in this world or not. It didn't matter. She was a dream come to life, a woman who could walk alone into the dark and come back laughing and smelling of flowers.

Afterward, she lay naked beside him, smoking a cigarette. "What the hell was there to be scared of?" she said. "Have I brought anything back with me? No. And believe me, I willed it."

Noah lay on his side, stroking her taut belly. "What did it—he—look like?"

She grimaced. "Pretty much how you'd think. At first, he was crouched down, wrapped in this immense cloak of black feathers. It looked like it had been made from the whole wings of a single vulture. I could just see the slits of his eyes peering over the top. He looked like a vulture himself . . . like a vampire! Although he was crouched down, I could tell he was a giant; magnificent, wise and savage."

"That's pretty powerful imagery," Noah said.

"Then he stood up and opened his cloak of wings. Beneath it, he was dressed in animal skins. His body was covered in some kind of paint, but it wasn't blood. There were patterns in it like primitive cave paintings. He did have bones in his hair and wore a necklace of bones. Bird bones, I think. You'll be pleased to know he had pointy teeth. All of them."

"Filed down?"

"Probably." She took a fierce draw off her cigarette. "Oh, I don't know. Maybe I saw what I wanted to see, or was influenced by what you said earlier."

"What about what he said through you?"

"I don't know. It was as if he'd known me before, obviously. He seemed to know you too, in a way. Lamech was the father of Noah in biblical myth, wasn't he?"

Noah nodded, uncomfortable with the idea that the entity might be aware of him.

"If the whole thing wasn't subjective," Lara said, "maybe I lived in his time once. Maybe we were lovers. I certainly felt really horny when I came out of it."

"He doesn't sound very attractive!"

Lara stubbed out her cigarette and reached for Noah's crotch. "Oh, but he was! Beautiful, in fact. His eyes were amazing, this deep piercing blue. Christ, I wanted him to possess me. Utterly. It was the archetypal thing." She laughed huskily. "I'd have been quite happy for him to sink his teeth into me."

Noah leaned over and nipped the skin of her throat. "Come on, let's go to bed. It's getting cold in here."

They made love several more times. Noah felt euphoric, hardly daring to believe a woman such as this could come into his life. She was full of humor and warmth, serious about her ability yet amusingly irreverent. She was uninhibited, open, mysterious, and fey. A witch woman. A priestess.

"Where have you been all my life?" Noah said.

"I bet you say that to all the girls," she replied, and they giggled like children at the stupid clichés for several minutes.

About four o'clock, Lara said she was tired and turned onto her side in the bed. Noah studied her for some time, drinking in each detail of her smooth contours, the spill of dark hair upon the pillow. He passed his hand in the air above her body, and she squirmed and made a sound of pleasure as if she felt him stroking her aura.

"Beauty," he whispered. "Love." He lay down to sleep, closing his eyes with the afterimage of her white flesh burning in his mind.

Waking came with a shock in the gray of predawn twilight.

He was aware at once of cold, and saw that the bed beside him was empty. A terrified pang of loss coursed through him, then he saw her clothes still draped on the pale wicker chair by the window and told himself she had gone to the bathroom, or else to get herself a drink.

He lay on his back and pulled the duvet over his chilled torso. A hiss in the corner of the room made him start.

"Lara?"

He sat up. Most of the room was still in shadow, but he thought he could make out a dark shape hunched in the corner near his clothes rail. "Lara . . ."

He reached to turn on the bedside lamp, but the switch did not respond. The bulb must have gone.

Again, a hiss, low and sibilant.

Something moved in the shadows, sidled forward. He saw the eyes clearly first: a deep piercing blue. She was naked and had covered herself in what looked like dark paint, which was possible because there were a few tins left in the garage. Her hair was wild and strawlike, filled with a sticky substance. Her tongue protruded unnaturally from her mouth, like that of the destroyer goddess, Kali. Her teeth could not possibly be pointed. There were no tools in his house she could have used to do that. She hissed and stamped with one foot.

"Lara."

He got out of bed slowly. This was so different to the time before with Sarah. Lara wasn't screaming. She wasn't raving or weeping.

Her eyes followed him as he skirted the room.

He held out his hands in the universal gesture of peace. "Lara, wake up. You're dreaming. It's not real. Lara."

She made a threatening lunge toward him, growled and stamped both feet. He jumped back. It was unreal. He couldn't feel anything, because it was so unreal.

The night had come into the room. Not darkness, but the essence of night, the absence of light. The cold of the Earth before the first dawn rose.

"Lara . . ."

She came for him then, scuttling with crablike speed across the room. She grabbed him by the shoulders and he felt the sharp prick of her fingernails. She stank of rotten meat and there was a crust around her lips. She was bleeding from the mouth. Her teeth were filed away to ragged points.

What pain she must be in. What pain . . .

He fought back. This wasn't Lara. This was the darkness he had hidden from for so long. Perhaps it had always been here, lurking in the shadows of his house, in his memories.

She was so strong, like a tigress. She pushed him back onto the bed and straddled him. Her breasts looked heavier than they had been earlier, scored with the marks of her own fingernails. She uttered a shriek and lunged for his neck.

He should be afraid, shouldn't he? This *thing*, this monstrous abomination dredged from the primal soup, was feasting on him, tearing at his flesh, kneading his skin with its claws, sucking the life from him. It stank of Hell. Yet he was aroused by it. He wanted her and she let him do it, her body bucking in frenzy.

And he saw it then, the tunnel into history. The rivers of blood that carried the memories of humanity. It is within all of us, he thought. We have tamed it and dressed it up in a silk suit. We have made it dead. We have contained it in books and films and lascivious dreams. We have contained it in nightmares. But ultimately, it is within us all the time. And it is alive, pulsing, warm and wet, stinking of musk and spoiled meat.

Lara wasn't stronger than Sarah. The opposite was true. Because Sarah had rejected this. It was what she had seen and felt and had never spoken of. The search for Nosferatu didn't begin in the grave, but in the reptile brain, the primordial remnant of beast within every human mind. It was demonic. It was divine.

In the late morning, with bright sunshine coming into the kitchen, they were politely formal with each other. She said she had badly chipped a tooth falling over in the dark. They didn't talk about how she'd decorated her body. The mess in the kitchen had been cleaned up by the time he had come downstairs and she was freshly showered, smelling of his patchouli body wash. She joked about her loathing of dentists as she carefully drank hot coffee. He made toast, then apologized and offered something softer: scrambled eggs perhaps? She wasn't hungry, she said.

He rubbed his neck. "Ah well . . ."

She had to go to work at two. Worked part-time in a local shop. Perhaps she could get an emergency dental appointment before she went in.

He had work to do too. The book would be late to his publishers otherwise. Nice day, though.

Yes, nice day.

At the door, she pecked his cheek in a brief kiss. "We must do this again," she said.

"Must we?" Many words hung unspoken between them.

She smiled. She looked very tired and there were purple rings beneath her eyes. "I think I got what I wanted. Didn't you?"

"Lara . . ."

"You can call me. Or not," she said. "I don't need you now, Noah, but I kind of like you."

He watched her run down the path to the road. She had rejected a lift. He leaned his forehead on the doorframe. Once your eyes are open, you can never close them. Sarah knew this.

He shouldn't see Lara again. He should attempt to forget all that had occurred. They'd been drunk. She'd broken one tooth, that's all. It had been less than he'd imagined. As if to remind him otherwise, his neck twinged painfully. He felt light-headed, sick, suddenly able to imagine the future, the long, slow, agonizing stretch of it, the descent into realms he dared not think about.

He shouldn't see her again. But she was just his type, wasn't she? Just his type.

Prince of Flowers

Elizabeth Hand

Elizabeth Hand is the author of many genre-spanning novels and collections of short fiction, as well as a longtime reviewer and critic for a number of publications.

Her acclaimed novels include *Winterlong, Aestival Tide, Icarus Descending, Waking the Moon, Glimmering, Black Light, Mortal Love, Illyria, Radiant Days, Mortal Love, Generation Loss, Available Dark,* and its recent sequel, *Hard Light,* along with the movie tie-ins *The Bride of Frankenstein: Pandora's Bride, 12 Monkeys, Catwoman,* and a series of Boba Fett Star Wars books for middle-grade children. PS recently published her novella, *Wylding Hall,* and some of the author's stories are collected in *Last Summer at Mars Hill, Bibliomancy, Saffron and Brimstone: Strange Stories,* and *Errantry.* With Paul Witcover, Hand also created the cult comic series *Anima* for DC in the early 1990s. She is a multiple winner of the World Fantasy Award, the Nebula Award, the Shirley Jackson Award, and the International Horror Guild Award, along with the Mythopoeic Award and the James Tiptree, Jr. Award.

"This was my first published story," reveals the author, "bought by Tappan King for *The Twilight Zone Magazine* in 1987; it appeared early in 1988. In a phone conversation, Tappan said that I would be a good writer for the 1990s, because my work had 'heart and also sharp little teeth.'

"At the time I was living in Washington, DC, and working at the Smithsonian. The demonic puppet of the title was something I bought on my lunch hour one afternoon, walking from the Mall to a dim little shop called The Artifactory. I fell in love with the puppet and paid fifty dollars for it, a huge chunk of my meager paycheck; but when I brought it back to my cubicle at the National Air and Space Museum I announced that it would bring me luck. It did: shortly thereafter I wrote the story, and even though it took a year or so, I finally sold it."

HELEN'S FIRST ASSIGNMENT on the inventory project was to the Department of Worms. For two weeks she paced the narrow alleys between immense tiers of glass cabinets, opening endless drawers of freeze-dried invertebrates and tagging each with an acquisition number. Occasionally she glimpsed other figures, drab as herself in government-issue smocks, gray shadows stalking through the murky corridors. They waved at her but seldom spoke, except to ask directions; everyone got lost in the museum.

Helen loved the hours lost in wandering the labyrinthine storage rooms, research labs, chilly vaults crammed with effigies of Yanomaño Indians and stuffed jaguars. Soon she could identify each department by its smell: acrid dust from the feathered pelts in Ornithology; the cloying reek of fenugreek and syrup in Mammalogy's roach traps; fish and formaldehyde in Icthyology. Her favorite was Paleontology, an annex where the air smelled damp and clean, as though beneath the marble floors trickled hidden water, undiscovered caves, mammoth bones to match those stored above. When her two weeks in Worms ended she was sent to Paleo, where she delighted in skeletons strewn atop cabinets like forgotten toys, disembodied skulls glaring from behind wastebaskets and bookshelves. She found a fabrosaurus ischium wrapped in brown paper and labeled in crayon; beside it a huge hand-hewn crate dated 1886 and marked WYOMING MEGOSAUR. It had never been opened. Some mornings she sat with a small mound of fossils before her, fitting the pieces together with the aid of a Victorian monograph. Hours passed in total silence, weeks when she only saw three or four people, curators slouching in and out of their research cubicles. On Fridays, when she dropped off her inventory sheets, they smiled. Occasionally even remembered her name. But mostly she was left alone, sorting cartons of bone and shale, prying apart frail skeletons of extinct fish as though they were stacks of newsprint.

Once, almost without thinking, she slipped a fossil fish into the pocket of her smock. The fossil was the length of her hand, as perfectly formed as a fresh beech leaf. All day she fingered it, tracing the imprint of bone and scale. In the bathroom later she wrapped it in paper towels and hid it in her purse to bring home. After that she started taking things.

At a downtown hobby shop she bought little brass and Lucite stands to display them in her apartment. No one else ever saw them. She simply liked to look at them alone.

Her next transfer was to Mineralogy, where she counted misshapen meteorites and uncut gems. Gems bored her, although she took a chunk of petrified wood and a handful of unpolished amethysts and put them in her bathroom. A month later she was permanently assigned to Anthropology.

The Anthropology Department was in the most remote corner of the museum; its proximity to the boiler room made it warmer than the Natural Sciences wing, the air redolent of spice woods and exotic unguents used to polish arrowheads and axe-shafts. The ceiling reared so high overhead that the rickety lamps swayed slightly in draughts that Helen longed to feel. The constant subtle motion of the lamps sent flickering waves of light across the floor. Raised arms of Balinese statues seemed to undulate, and points of light winked behind the empty eyeholes of feathered masks.

Everywhere loomed shelves stacked with smooth ivory and gaudily beaded bracelets and neck-rings. Helen crouched in corners loading her arms with bangles until her wrists ached from their weight. She unearthed dusty, lurid figures of temple demons and cleaned them, polished hollow cheeks and lapis eyes before stapling a number to each figure. A corner piled with tipi poles hid an abandoned desk that she claimed and decorated with mummy photographs and a ceramic coffee mug. In the top drawer she stored her cassette tapes and, beneath her handbag, a number of obsidian arrowheads. While it was never officially designated as her desk, she was annoyed one morning to find a young man tilted backward in the chair, shuffling through her tapes.

"Hello," he greeted her cheerfully. Helen winced and nodded coolly. "These your tapes? I'll borrow this one some day, haven't got the album yet. Leo Bryant—"

"Helen," she replied bluntly. "I think there's an empty desk down by the slit-gongs."

"Thanks, I just started. You a curator?"

Helen shook her head, rearranging the cassettes on the desk. "No. Inventory project." Pointedly she moved his knapsack to the floor.

"Me, too. Maybe we can work together sometime."

She glanced at his earnest face and smiled. "I like to work alone, thanks." He looked hurt, and she added, "Nothing personal—I just like it that way. I'm sure we'll run into each other. Nice to meet you, Leo." She grabbed a stack of inventory sheets and walked away down the corridor.

They met for coffee one morning. After a few weeks they met almost every morning, sometimes even for lunch outside on the Mall. During the day Leo wandered over from his cubicle in Ethnology to pass on departmental gossip. Sometimes they had a drink after work, but never often enough to invite gossip themselves. Helen was happy with this arrangement, the curators delighted to have such a worker—quiet, without ambition, punctual. Everyone except Leo left her to herself.

Late one afternoon Helen turned at the wrong corner and found herself in a small cul-de-sac between stacks of crates that cut off light and air. She yawned, breathing the faint must of cinnamon bark as she traced her path on a crumpled inventory map. This narrow alley was unmarked; the adjoining corridors contained Malaysian artifacts, batik tools, long teak boxes of gongs. Fallen crates, clumsily hewn cartons overflowing with straw were scattered on the floor. Splintered panels snagged her sleeves as she edged her way down the aisle. A sweet musk hung about these cartons, the languorous essence of unknown blossoms.

At the end of the cul-de-sac an entire row of crates had toppled, as though the weight of time had finally pitched them to the floor. Helen squatted and chose a box at random, a broad flat package like a portfolio. She pried the lid off to find a stack of leather cutouts curling with age, like desiccated cloth. She drew one carefully from the pile, frowning as its edges disintegrated at her touch. A shadow puppet, so fantastically elaborate that she couldn't tell if it was male or female; it scarcely looked human. Light glimmered through the grotesque lattice-work as Helen jerked it back and forth, its pale shadow dancing across the wall. Then the puppet split and crumbled into brittle curlicues that formed strange hieroglyphics on the black marble floor. Swearing softly, Helen replaced the lid, then jammed the box back into the shadows. Her fingers brushed another crate of smooth polished mahogany. It had a comfortable heft as she pulled it into her lap. Each corner of the narrow lid was fixed with a large, square-headed nail. Helen yanked these out and set each upright in a row.

As she opened the box, dried flowers, seeds and wood shavings cascaded into her lap. She inhaled, closing her eyes, imagined blue water and firelight, sweet-smelling seeds exploding in the embers. She sneezed and opened her eyes to a cloud of dust wafting from the crate like smoke. Very carefully she worked her fingers into the fragrant excelsior, kneading the petals gently until she grasped something brittle and solid. She drew this out in a flurry of dead flowers.

It was a puppet: not a toy, but a gorgeously costumed figure, spindly arms clattering with glass and bone circlets, batik robes heavy with embroidery and beadwork. Long whittled pegs formed its torso and arms and the rods that swiveled it back and forth, so that its robes rippled tremulously, like a swallowtail's wings. Held at arm's length it gazed scornfully down at Helen, its face glinting with gilt paint. Sinuous vines twisted around each jointed arm. Flowers glowed within the rich threads of its robe, orchids blossoming in the folds of indigo cloth.

Loveliest of all was its face, the curve of cheeks and chin so carefully arched it might have been cast in gold rather than coaxed from wood. Helen brushed it with a finger: the glossy white paint gleamed as though still wet. She touched the carmine bow that formed its mouth, traced the jet-black lashes stippled across its brow, like a regiment of ants. The smooth wood felt warm to her touch as she stroked it with her fingertips. A courtesan might have perfected its sphinx's smile; but in the tide of petals Helen discovered a slip of paper covered with spidery characters. Beneath the straggling script another hand had shaped clumsy block letters spelling out the name PRINCE OF FLOWERS.

Once, perhaps, an imperial concubine had entertained herself with its fey posturing, and so passed the wet silences of a long green season. For the rest of the afternoon it was Helen's toy.

She posed it and sent its robes dancing in the twilit room, the frail arms and tiny wrists twitching in a marionette's waltz.

Behind her a voice called, "Helen?"

"Leo," she murmured. "Look what I found."

He hunched beside her to peer at the figure. "Beautiful. Is that what you're on now? Balinese artifacts?"

She shrugged. "Is that what it is? I didn't know." She glanced down the dark rows of cabinets and sighed. "I probably shouldn't be here. It's just so hot . . ." She stretched and yawned as Leo slid the puppet from her hands.

"Can I see it?" He twisted it until its head spun and the stiff arms flittered. "Wild. Like one of those dancers in *The King and I*." He played with it absently, hypnotized by the swirling robes. When he stopped, the puppet jerked abruptly upright, its blank eyes staring at Helen.

"Be careful," she warned, kneading her smock between her thumbs. "It's got to be a hundred years old." She held out her hands and Leo returned it, bemused.

"It's wild, whatever it is." He stood and stretched. "I'm going to get a soda. Want to come?"

"I better get back to what I was working on. I'm supposed to finish the Burmese section this week." Casually she set the puppet in its box, brushed the dried flowers from her lap and stood.

"Sure you don't want a soda or something?" Leo hedged plaintively, snapping his ID badge against his chest. "You said you were hot."

"No thanks," Helen smiled wanly. "I'll take a raincheck. Tomorrow."

Peeved, Leo muttered and stalked off. When his silhouette faded away she turned and quickly pulled the box into a corner. There she emptied her handbag and arranged puppet at its bottom, wrapping Kleenex about its arms and face. Hairbrush, wallet, lipstick: all thrown back into her purse, hiding the puppet beneath their clutter. She repacked the crate with its sad array of blossoms, hammering the lid back with her shoe. Then she scrabbled in the corner on her knees until she located a space between stacks of cartons. With a resounding crack the empty box struck the wall, and Helen grinned as she kicked more boxes to fill the gap. Years from now another inventory technician would discover it and wonder, as she had countless times, what had once been inside the empty carton.

When she crowded into the elevator that afternoon the leather handle of her purse stuck to her palm like wet rope. She shifted the bag casually as more people stepped on at each floor, heart pounding as she called goodbye to the curator for Indo-Asian Studies passing in the lobby. Imaginary prison gates loomed and crumbled behind Helen as she strode through the columned doors and into the summer street.

All the way home she smiled triumphantly, clutching her handbag to her chest. As she fumbled at the front door for her keys a fresh burst of scent rose from the recesses of her purse. Inside, another scent over-powered this faint perfume—the thick reek of creosote, rotting fruit, unwashed clothes. Musty and hot and dark as the museum's dreariest basement, the only two windows faced on to the street. Traffic ground past, piping bluish exhaust through the screens. A grimy mirror reflected shabby chairs, an end table with lopsided lamp: furniture filched from college dormitories or reclaimed from the corner dumpster. No paintings graced the pocked walls, blotched with the crushed remains of roaches and silverfish.

But beautiful things shone here, gleaming from windowsills and cracked Formica counters: the limp frond of a fossil fern, etched in obsidian glossy as wet tar; a whorled nautilus like a tiny whirlpool impaled upon a brass stand. In the center of a splintered coffee table was the imprint of a foot-long dragonfly's wing embedded in limestone, its filigreed scales a shat-tered prism.

Corners heaped with lemur skulls and slabs of petrified wood. The exquisite cone shells of poisonous molluscs. Mounds of green and golden iridescent beetles, like the coinage of a distant country. Patches of lino-leum scattered with shark's teeth and arrowheads; a tiny skull anchoring a handful of emerald plumes that waved in the breeze like a sea-fan. Helen surveyed it all critically, noting with mild surprise a luminous pink geode; she'd forgotten that one. Then she set to work.

In a few minutes she'd removed everything from her bag and rolled the geode under a chair. She unwrapped the puppet on the table, peeling tissue from its brittle arms and finally twisting the long strand of white paper from its head, until she stood ankle-deep in a drift of tissue. The puppet's supporting rod slid neatly into the mouth of an empty beer bot-tle, and she arranged it so that the glass was hidden by its robes and the imperious face tilted upward, staring at the bug-flecked ceiling.

Helen squinted appraisingly, rearranged the feathers about the puppet, shoring them up with the carapaces of scarab beetles: still it looked all wrong. Beside the small proud figure, the fossils were muddy remains, the nautilus a bit of sea wrack. A breeze shifted the puppet's robes, knocking the scarabs to the floor, and before she knew it Helen had crushed them, the little emerald shells splintering to gray dust beneath her heel. She sighed in exasperation: all her pretty things suddenly looked so mean.

She moved the puppet to the windowsill, to another table, and finally into her bedroom. No corner of the flat could hold it without seeming even grimier than before. Helen swiped at cobwebs above the doorway before setting the puppet on her bedstand and collapsing with a sigh onto her mattress.

In the half-light of the windowless bedroom the figure was not so resplendent. Disappointed, Helen straightened its robes yet again. As she tugged the cloth into place, two violet petals, each the size of her pinky nail, slipped between her fingers. She rolled the tiny blossoms between her palms, surprised at how damp and fresh they felt, how they breathed a scent like ozone, or seawater. Thoughtfully she rubbed the violets until only a gritty pellet remained between her fingers.

Flowers, she thought, and recalled the name on the paper she'd found. The haughty figure wanted flowers.

Grabbing her key and a rusty pair of scissors, she ran outside. Thirty minutes later she returned, laden with blossoms: torn branches of crepe myrtle frothing pink and white, drooping tongues of honeysuckle, over-blown white roses snipped from a neighbor's yard; chicory fading like a handful of blue stars. She dropped them all at the foot of the bed and then searched the kitchen until she found a dusty wine carafe and some empty jars. Once these were rinsed and filled with water she made a number of unruly bouquets, then placed them all around the puppet, so that its pale head nodded amid a cloud of white and mauve and frail green.

Helen slumped back on the bed, grinning with approval. Bottles trapped the wavering pools of light and cast shimmering reflections across the walls. The crepe myrtle sent the palest mauve cloud onto the ceiling, blurring the jungle shadows of the honeysuckle.

Helen's head blurred, as well. She yawned, drowsy from the thick scents of roses, cloying honeysuckle, all the languor of summer nodding in an afternoon. She fell quickly asleep, lulled by the breeze in the stolen garden and the dozy burr of a lost bumblebee.

Once, her sleep broke. A breath of motion against her shoulder—mosquito? spider? centipede?—then a tiny lancing pain, the touch of invisible legs or wings, and it was gone. Helen grimaced, scratched, staggered up and into the bathroom. Her bleary reflection showed a swollen bite on her shoulder. It tingled, and a drop of blood pearled at her touch. She put on a nightshirt, checked her bed for spiders, then tumbled back to sleep.

Much later she woke to a sound: once, twice, like the resonant *plank* of a stone tossed into a well. Then a slow melancholy note: another well, a larger stone striking its dark surface. Helen moaned, turning onto her side. Fainter echoes joined these first sounds, plangent tones sweet as rain in the mouth. Her ears rang with this steady pulse, until suddenly she clenched her hands and stiffened, concentrating on the noise.

From wall to ceiling to floor the thrumming echo bounced; grew louder, diminished, droned to a whisper. It did not stop. Helen sat up, bracing herself against the wall, the last shards of sleep fallen from her. Her hand slipped and very slowly she drew it toward her face. It was wet. Between her fingers glistened a web of water, looping like silver twine down her wrist until it was lost in the blue-veined valley of her elbow. Helen shook her head in disbelief and stared up at the ceiling. From one end of the room to the other stretched a filament of water, like a hairline fracture. As she watched, the filament snapped and a single warm drop splashed her temple. Helen swore and slid to the edge of the mattress, then stopped.

At first she thought the vases had fallen to the floor, strewing flowers everywhere. But the bottles remained on the bedstand, their blossoms casting ragged silhouettes in the dark. More flowers were scattered about the bottles: violets, crimson roses, a tendril rampant with tiny fluted petals. Flowers cascaded to the floor, nestled amid folds of dirty clothes. Helen plucked an orchid from the linoleum, blinking in amazement. Like a wavering pink flame it glowed, the feathery pistils staining her fingertips bright yellow. Absently Helen brushed the pollen on to her thigh, scraping her leg with a hangnail.

That small pain jarred her awake. She dropped the orchid. For the first time it didn't feel like a dream. The room was hot, humid as though moist towels pressed against her face. As she stared at her thigh the bright fingerprint, yellow as a crocus, melted and dissolved as sweat broke on her skin. She stepped forward, the orchid bursting beneath her heel like a ripe grape. A sickly smell rose from the broken flower. Each breath she took was heavy, as with rain, and she choked. The rims of her nostrils were wet. She sneezed, inhaling warm water. Water streamed down her cheeks and she drew her hand slowly upward, to brush the water from her eyes. She could move it no further than her lap. She looked down, silently mouthing bewilderment as she shook her head.

Another hand grasped her wrist, a hand delicate and limp as a cut iris wand, so small that she scarcely felt its touch open her pulse. Inside her skull the blood thrummed counterpoint to the *gamelan*, gongs echoing the throb and beat of her heart. The little hand disappeared. Helen staggered backward on to the bed, frantically scrambling for the light switch. In the darkness, something crept across the rippling bedsheets.

When she screamed her mouth was stuffed with roses, orchids, the corner of her pillowcase. Tiny hands pinched her nostrils shut and forced more flowers between her lips until she lay still, gagging on aromatic petals. From the rumpled bedclothes reared a shadow, child-size, grinning. Livid shoots of green and yellow encircled its spindly arms and the sheets whispered like rain as it crawled toward her. Like a great mantis it dragged itself forward on its long arms, the rough cloth of its robe catching between her knees, its white teeth glittering. She clawed through the sheets, trying to dash it against the wall. But she could not move. Flowers spilled from her mouth when she tried to scream, soft fingers of orchids sliding down her throat as she flailed at the bedclothes.

And the clanging of the gongs did not cease: not when the tiny hands pattered over her breasts; not when the tiny mouth hissed in her ear. Needle teeth pierced her shoulder as a long tongue unfurled and lapped there, flicking blood onto the blossoms wreathed about her neck. Only when the slender shadow withdrew and the terrible, terrible dreams began did the *gamelans* grow silent.

Nine-thirty came, long after Helen usually met Leo in the cafeteria. He waited, drinking an entire pot of coffee before he gave up and wandered downstairs, piqued that she hadn't shown up for breakfast.

In the same narrow hallway behind the Malaysian artifacts he discovered her, crouched over a pair of tapered wooden crates. For a long moment he watched her, and almost turned back without saying anything. Her hair was dirty, twisted into a sloppy bun, and the hunch of her shoulders hinted at exhaustion. But before he could leave, she turned to face him, clutching the boxes to her chest.

"Rough night?" croaked Leo. A scarf tied around her neck didn't hide the bruises there. Her mouth was swollen, her eyes soft and shadowed with sleeplessness. He knew she must see people, men, boyfriends. But she had never mentioned anyone, never spoke of weekend trips or vacations. Suddenly he felt betrayed, and spun away to leave.

"Leo," murmured Helen, absently stroking the crate. "I can't talk right now. I got in so late. I'm kind of busy."

"I guess so." He laughed uncertainly, but stopped before turning the corner to see her pry open the lid of the box, head bent so that he could not tell what it was she found inside.

A week passed. Leo refused to call her. He timed his forays to the cafeteria to avoid meeting her there. He left work late so he wouldn't see her in the elevator. Every day he expected to see her at his desk, find a telephone message scrawled on his memo pad. But she never appeared.

Another week went by. Leo ran into the curator for Indo-Asian Studies by the elevator.

"Have you seen Helen this week?" she asked, and Leo actually blushed at mention of her name.

"No," he mumbled. "Not for a while, really."

"Guess she's sick." The curator shrugged and stepped on to elevator. Leo rode all the way down to the basement and roamed the corridors for an hour, dropping by the Anthropology office. No Helen, no messages from her at the desk.

He wandered back down the hall, pausing in the corridor where he had last seen her. A row of boxes had collapsed and he kicked at the cartons, idly knelt and read the names on the packing crates as if they held a clue to Helen's sudden change. Labels in Sanskrit, Vietnamese, Chinese, English, crumbling beside baggage labels and exotic postage stamps and scrawled descriptions of contents, WAJANG GOLEH, he read. Beneath was scribbled PUPPETS. He squatted on the floor, staring at the bank of crates, then half-heartedly started to read each label. Maybe she'd find him there. Perhaps she'd been sick, had a doctor's appointment. She might be late again.

A long box rattled when he shifted it. KRIS, read the label, and he peeked inside to find an ornate sword. A heavier box bore the legend SANGHYANG: SPIRIT PUPPET. And another that seemed to be empty, embellished with a flowing script: SEKAR MAS, and the clumsy translation PRINCE OF FLOWERS.

He slammed the last box against the wall and heard the dull creak of splintering wood. She would not be in today. She hadn't been in for two weeks.

That night he called her.

"Hello?"

Helen's voice; at least a man hadn't answered.

"Helen. How you doing? It's Leo."

"Leo." She coughed and he heard someone in the background. "It's you."

"Right," he said dryly, then waited for an apology, her embarrassed laugh, another cough that would be followed by an invented catalogue of hay fever, colds, flu. But she said nothing. He listened carefully and realized it wasn't a voice he had heard in the background but a constant stir of sound, like a fan, or running water. "Helen? You okay?"

A long pause. "Sure. Sure I'm okay." Her voice faded and he heard a high, piping note.

"You got a bird, Helen?"

"What?"

He shifted the phone to his other ear, shoving it closer to his head so he could hear better. "A bird. There's this funny voice, it sounds like you got a bird or something."

"No," replied Helen slowly. "I don't have a bird. There's nothing wrong with my phone." He could hear her moving around her apartment, the background noises rising and falling but never silent. "Leo, I can't talk now. I'll see you tomorrow, okay?"

"Tomorrow?" he exploded. "I haven't seen you in two weeks!"

She coughed and said, "Well, I'm sorry. I've been busy. I'll see you tomorrow. Bye."

He started to argue, but the phone was already dead.

She didn't come in the next day. At three o'clock he went to the Anthropology Department and asked the secretary if Helen had been in that morning.

"No," she answered, shaking her head. "And they've got her down as AWOL. She hasn't been in all week." She hesitated before whispering. "Leo, she hasn't looked very good lately, think maybe . . ." Her voice died and she shrugged, "Who knows," and turned to answer the phone.

He left work early, walking his bicycle up the garage ramp and wheeling it to the right, toward Helen's neighborhood. He was fuming, but a sliver of fear had worked its way through his anger. He had almost gone to her supervisor; almost phoned Helen first. Instead, he pedaled quickly down Pennsylvania Avenue, skirting the first lanes of rush-hour traffic. Union Station loomed a few blocks ahead. He recalled an article in yesterday's *Post*: vandals had destroyed the rose garden in front of the station. He detoured through the bus lane that circled the building and skimmed around the desecrated garden, shaking his head and staring back in dismay. All the roses: gone. Someone had lopped each bloom from its stem. In spots the cobblestones were littered with mounds of blossoms, brown with decay. Here and there dead flowers still dangled from hacked stems. Swearing in disgust, Leo made a final loop, nearly skidding into a bus as he looked back at the plundered garden. Then he headed toward Helen's apartment building a few blocks north.

Her windows were dark. Even from the street the curtains looked filthy, as though dirt and exhaust had matted them to the glass. Leo stood on the curb and stared at the blank eyes of each apartment window gaping in the stark concrete façade.

Who would want to live here? he thought, ashamed. He should have come sooner. Shame froze into apprehension and the faintest icy sheath of fear. Hurriedly he locked his bike to a parking meter and approached her window, standing on tiptoe to peer inside. Nothing. The discolored curtains hid the rooms from him like clouds of ivory smoke. He tapped once, tentatively; then, emboldened by silence, rapped for several minutes, squinting to see any movement inside.

Still nothing. Leo swore out loud and shoved his hands into his pockets, wondering lamely what to do. *Call the police? Next of kin?* He winced at the thought: as if she couldn't do that herself. Helen had always made it clear that she enjoyed being on her own. But the broken glass beneath his sneakers, wind-blown newspapers tugging at the bottom steps; the whole unkempt neighborhood denied that. *Why here?* he thought angrily; and then he was taking the steps two at a time, kicking bottles and burger wrappers out of his path.

He waited by the door for five minutes before a teenage boy ran out. Leo barely caught the door before it slammed behind him. Inside, a fluorescent light hung askew from the ceiling, buzzing like a wasp. Helen's was the first door to the right. Circulars from convenience stores drifted on the floor, and on the far wall was a bank of mailboxes. One was ajar, stuffed with unclaimed bills and magazines. More envelopes piled on the steps. Each bore Helen's name.

His knocking went unanswered; but he thought he heard someone moving inside.

"Helen," he called softly. "It's Leo. You okay?"

He knocked harder, called her name, finally pounded with both fists. Still nothing. He should leave; he should call the police. Better still, forget ever coming here. But he was here now; the police would question him no matter what; the curator for Indo-Asian Studies would look at him askance. Leo bit his lip and tested the doorknob. Locked; but the wood gave way slightly as he leaned against it. He rattled the knob and braced himself to kick the door in.

He didn't have to. In his hand the knob twisted and the door swung inward, so abruptly that he fell inside. The door banged shut behind him. He glanced across the room, looking for her; but all he saw was gray light, the gauzy shadows cast by gritty curtains. Then he breathed in, gagging, and pulled his sleeve to his mouth until he gasped through the cotton. He backed toward the door, slipping on something dank, like piles of wet clothing. He glanced at his feet and grunted in disgust.

Roses. They were everywhere: heaps of rotting flowers, broken branches, leaves stripped from bushes, an entire small ficus tree tossed into the corner. He forgot Helen, turned to grab the doorknob and tripped on an uprooted azalea. He fell, clawing at the wall to balance himself. His palms splayed against the plaster and slid as though the surface was still wet. Then, staring upward he saw that it *was* wet. Water streamed from the ceiling, flowing down the wall to soak his shirt-cuffs. Leo moaned. His knees buckled as he sank, arms flailing, into the mass of decaying blossoms. Their stench suffocated him; his eyes watered as he retched and tried to stagger back to his feet.

Then he heard something, like a bell, or a telephone; then another faint sound, like an animal scratching overhead. Carefully he twisted to stare upward, trying not to betray himself by moving too fast. Something skittered across the ceiling, and Leo's stomach turned dizzily. *What could be up there?* A second blur dashed to join the first; golden eyes stared down at him, unblinking.

Geckos, he thought frantically. *She had pet geckos. She* has *pet geckos. Jesus.*

She couldn't be here. It was too hot, the stench horrible: putrid water, decaying plants, water everywhere. His trousers were soaked from where he had fallen, his knees ached from kneeling in a trough of water pooling against the wall. The floor had warped and more flowers protruded from cracks between the linoleum, brown fronds of iris and rotting honeysuckle. From another room trickled the sound of water dripping steadily, as though a tap were running.

He had to get out. He'd leave the door open—police, a landlord. Someone would call for help. But he couldn't reach the door. He couldn't stand. His feet skated across the slick tiles as his hands tore uselessly through wads of petals. It grew darker. Golden bands rippled across the floor as sunlight filtered through the gray curtains. Leo dragged himself through rotting leaves, his clothes sopping, tugging aside mats of greenery and broken branches. His leg ached where he'd fallen on it and his hands stung, pricked by unseen thorns.

Something brushed against his fingers and he forced himself to look down, shuddering. A shattered nautilus left a thin red line across his hand, the sharp fragments gilded by the dying light. As he looked around he noticed other things, myriad small objects caught in the morass of rotting flowers like a nightmarish ebb tide on the linoleum floor. Agates and feathered masks; bird of paradise plumes encrusted with mud; cracked skulls and bones and cloth of gold. He recognized the carved puppet Helen had been playing with that afternoon in the Indonesian corridor, its headdress glittering in the twilight. About its neck was strung a plait of flowers, amber and cerulean blossoms glowing like phosphorescence among the ruins.

Through the room echoed a dull clang. Leo jerked to his knees, relieved. Surely someone had knocked? But the sound came from somewhere behind him, and was echoed in another, harsher, note. As this second bell died he heard the geckos' feet pattering as they fled across the ceiling. A louder note rang out, the windowpanes vibrating to the sound as though wind-battered. In the corner the leaves of the ficus turned as if to welcome rain, and the rosebushes stirred.

Leo heard something else, then: a small sound like a cat stretching to wakefulness. Now both of his legs ached, and he had to pull himself forward on his hands and elbows, striving to reach the front door. The clanging grew louder, more resonant. A higher tone echoed it monotonously, like the echo of rain in a well. Leo glanced over his shoulder to the empty doorway that led to the kitchen, the dark mouth of the hallway to Helen's bedroom. Something moved there.

At his elbow moved something else and he struck at it feebly, knocking the puppet across the floor. Uncomprehending, he stared after it, then cowered as he watched the ceiling, wondering if one of the geckos had crept down beside him.

There was no gecko. When Leo glanced back at the puppet it was moving across the floor toward him, pulling itself forward on its long slender arms.

The gongs thundered now. A shape humped across the room, something large enough to blot out the empty doorway behind it. Before he was blinded by petals, Leo saw that it was a shrunken figure, a woman whose elongated arms clutched broken branches to propel herself, legs dragging uselessly through the tangled leaves. About her swayed a host of brilliant figures no bigger than dolls. They had roped her neck and hands with wreaths of flowers and scattered blossoms on to the floor about them. Like a flock of chattering butterflies the surged toward him, tiny hands outstretched, their long tongues unfurling like crimson pistils, and the gongs rang like golden bells as they gathered about him to feed.

Services Rendered

Louise Cooper

British writer Louise Cooper (1952–2009) began writing stories when she was old enough to control a pencil. Her first novel, *The Book of Paradox*, was published when she was twenty-one, and she worked in publishing before becoming a full-time writer in 1977. Her more than eighty books for both adults and children included the Time Master trilogy (*The Initiate*, *The Outcast*, and *The Master*), the Indigo sequence (*Nemesis*, *Inferno*, *Infanta*, *Nocturne*, *Troika*, *Avatar*, *Revenant*, and *The Aisling*), the Daughter of Storms trilogy (*Daughter of Storms*, *The Dark Caller*, and *Keepers of the Light*), and the Mirror, Mirror trilogy (*Breaking Through*, *Running Free*, and *Testing Limits*), along with the novels *Storm Ghost*, *The Summer Witch*, *Hunter's Moon*, *The Bad Seed*, and *Doctor Who: Rip Tide*.

"I haven't the faintest notion how this story came into my head," the author admitted. "It just did. One moment I was racking my brain for a plot that would make for a slightly different twist on the vampire theme; the next, the complete idea was sitting grinning in my mind. That's unusual for me.

"The theme of 'Services Rendered' came from a question that I find endlessly fascinating: how an ordinary, down-to-earth human being reacts when faced with the apparently impossible, especially so when that 'impossibility' combines something terrifying (possibly), repellent (probably), and dangerous (potentially) with the lure of a 'dream come true' scenario.

"As for vampires . . . I've yet to encounter one of the classical kind outside of a movie screen, and I sincerely hope it stays that way. But there are individuals whose effect on those around them has something in common with the vampire of legend: who seem to attach themselves to others and take nourishment from their energies. I saw Carmine as one of these individuals, in addition to her more 'traditional' qualities. Even vampires, if they exist, must surely have their hopes and fears and dreams, like any ordinary person.

"However you define that . . ."

THE CULTURED FEMALE voice at the other end of the phone line said, "I saw your advertisement in *Alternatives*. It's possible that I might be able to help."

The sick lurch of hope had become all too familiar over the last few months, and Penny tried to ignore it and keep her mind neutral. "I see. What . . . uh . . . exactly would you be suggesting?"

There was a slight pause. Then: "I'd guess from your tone that you've had other calls, yes? But nothing worthwhile came of them?"

"You could say that." Hope turned sour as she recalled them: two fringe herbalists, a crystal healer, a woman trying to sell her a "magic luck talisman" complete with a *Your Personal Love Rhythms* chart. Oh, and the crank who had banged on about Jesus and the wages of sin, until she had sworn at him and slammed the receiver down. The magazine had advised her, when she placed the advert, not to include her home number. Desperate needs, though, called for desperate measures.

"Look," Penny said, "if you're marketing some new miracle cure, then—"

"Oh, no. It's nothing like that, I assure you; what I could offer is entirely practical, and entirely effective. The only caveat is that the patient must be prepared to accept certain side effects."

Hope began to creep back. Words such as "patient" and "side effects" were reassuring; they had a ring of orthodoxy.

"May I ask you a question?" said the woman.

Penny snapped back from the tangent her thoughts had abruptly taken. "Yes; yes, please do."

"You obviously couldn't go into detail in the advertisement. It's your husband who's ill?"

"Yes."

"And the doctors say that . . . well, that there's nothing more they can do?"

"Yes." The GP; tests; the specialist; more tests; that *loathsome* hospital . . . Penny breathed deeply and carefully to knock the tremor out of her voice. "It's incurable, and it's progressive. Over the last two years we've tried everything, but it didn't . . . And now—now, he might have a couple of months, but the doctors say that . . ." Something caught in her throat; she turned her head aside from the receiver and tried to clear it.

"That there's no hope," the woman gently finished the sentence for her. "I understand. I'm so sorry."

"Thank you," Penny said tightly.

"So, then. I think I *can* help you, if you want me to. But I'd prefer to talk about it face-to-face."

Penny's cynicism had begun to come back in a reaction to the last few moments, and she demanded, "Why? That's the sort of thing the

evangelists do: worm an invitation, then start on their conversion technique. Only last week I answered the doorbell and there were some
bloody—"

"Please. I promise you, I am *not* an evangelist in any shape or form. Far
from it. But what I . . . need to explain really does need a personal meeting."

Penny looked down the length of the hall. The thin February daylight
made everything look bleak and depressing; the stairs were deeply shadowed, and David was lying up there in their bedroom, drugged to the
eyeballs with painkillers, hardly knowing her, hardly knowing anything.

"All right," she said on an outward rush of breath. "When, and where?"

"It's best if I come to your house, I think. Would this evening be convenient?"

"Yes." *Face the thing quickly. If it's yet another disappointment, better to
have it over with.* Feeling that the situation wasn't quite real, Penny gave
her address and agreed on 7:00 p.m.

"I don't know your name," she added.

"Oh, of course. It's Smith. Carmine Smith."

Penny didn't believe that, and she didn't believe that the woman could
be of any use at all. But what did it matter? There was nothing left to lose.

Carmine Smith was probably in her early forties, elegant in classically
understated dark clothes and expensive black silk coat. Her hair, too, was
dark, cut in a young, gamine style that suited her perfectly. Her eyes were
subtly made-up, but she wore no lipstick.

"Thank you," she said, taking the coffee (black, no sugar) that Penny
handed to her. She looked around the room, assessing it, her expression
inscrutable. Then she asked, "Is your husband at home?"

Penny nodded. "They said there was no point his staying in the hospital. They need the beds, and there's nothing . . ."

"Of course. Could I see him?"

Penny became defensive. "He's probably asleep. He sleeps a lot, and
even when he's awake he's vague. He couldn't tell you much."

"All the same, if I could just look in?" Carmine's eyes were very intense.

Penny hesitated, then shrugged.

They climbed the stairs. Carmine walked noiselessly, which Penny
found faintly unsettling. She fancied that if she were to turn her head she
would find nobody at all behind her, and that this whole encounter was
a delusion.

David, as she had predicted, was asleep. Carmine moved to the bed
and stood gazing down at him by the soft light of the bedside lamp, while

Penny, who no longer liked to look at her husband too often, hovered by the window.

At length Carmine said quietly, "He's very handsome."

"Yes." *Or was, before he couldn't eat properly anymore and started to waste away.*

"How old is he?"

"Forty-six." Penny moved restlessly. "Look, I don't want to wake him. You've seen him now; if we're going to talk, I'd prefer to do it downstairs."

"Of course." Carmine led the way out with a confidence that she hadn't exhibited before, as if in the space of a few seconds she had observed, considered and come to a decision. Back in the sitting room she sat in what had always been David's favorite chair, sipped her coffee, then set the cup down and looked directly at Penny.

"I can bring him back to you," she said.

A crawling, electrical sensation went through Penny's entire body and she stared, disbelieving. "How?"

Carmine studied her own hands where they lay in her lap. "This is the hard part, Mrs. Blythe. The part you're going to find difficult to accept."

"You mentioned side effects—"

"Yes, yes; but I'm not talking about those, not yet." She inhaled deeply. "Perhaps it's best if I put it bluntly, rather than beating about the bush. I can restore your husband to you, whole and healthy, stronger than he has ever been before. Because I can make him immortal."

There was a brief, lacerating silence: then Penny stood up.

"Get out of my house," she said. "Now."

"Mrs. Blythe—"

"*Now*," Penny repeated ferociously. "People like you—you're *sick*. I suppose you find it funny, do you, playing your jokes, having your laughs at someone else's expense? Some kind of turn-on, is it?" She strode to the door, wrenched it open. "Get out!"

Carmine was also on her feet now, but she didn't leave. "Mrs. Blythe, I'm serious!" She sounded almost angry, and Penny turned, thumping a clenched fist against the edge of the door.

"Oh, she's *serious*! So it's not a sick joke; she really believes it! God give me *strength*!" She swung round again. "What kind of moron do you take me for? And what kind of moron are you? *Immortality*, she says! You're in some cult, right? Well, I'll tell you right now, Ms. Smith, or whatever your real name is, *you* have been brainwashed, and *I'm* not listening to another moment of this crap!"

"*Mrs. Blythe*," said Carmine, and something in her voice made Penny stop. "Mrs. Blythe, I do *not* belong to any cult or other organization. But I am immortal, and I am offering your husband the chance to be the same, because it's the only alternative he has to dying. You see, I'm a vampire."

Penny pressed her forehead against the doorframe and started to laugh. The laughter became hysterical, then turned into gulping, hiccuping sobs; then she threw anything movable within her reach at Carmine, screaming abuse. Carmine avoided the missiles and waited calmly for the worst of the storm to pass. When it did, and Penny was slumped on her haunches against the wall with both hands covering her face, she asked, "Have you got a mirror?"

Penny raised her head and stared, but she didn't speak. Looking past her through the open door, Carmine saw an oval mirror hanging in the hall. She fetched it, and crouched down at Penny's side.

"Look in the glass," she said.

Too drained to argue, Penny looked. She saw her own red-eyed, disheveled reflection, decided that she resembled an unhealthy pig and even in extremity felt shamed. Then her brain caught up as she took in Carmine's image beside hers. In the mirror, Carmine had no face. She was nothing more than a vague, gray blur, as if an isolated patch of fog had floated in and settled at Penny's shoulder. The fog dimly suggested a humanlike shape, and there might have been a fading hint of features shrouded somewhere in it, but that was all.

"The superstition that we're invisible in mirrors isn't *quite* accurate," said Carmine mildly, "but it's close enough." She stood up, saving the glass as Penny's numb fingers lost their grip on it, and stepped back a pace or two, to show that she meant no threat. "What else can I do to convince you?"

Very slowly, Penny's head came up. She looked shocked, confused, and there was a witless, corpselike grin on her face. "Garlic," she said. "Vampires can't stand garlic. And they turn to dust if sunlight touches them." She flung a swift glance toward the window, but the curtains were closed. It was dark outside. She had forgotten that.

"Not true," Carmine told her. "Personally I adore garlic. And sunlight . . . well, we find it debilitating, and our skin tends to burn more easily than most people's, but it doesn't do any lasting damage."

Penny persisted. "Coffins, then. They sleep in *coffins*."

"Again, not true. I did try it once, when I was a child, but one night was enough to make me see sense. Beds are far more comfortable." Carmine smiled wryly. "It's Chinese Whispers, isn't it? Stories become exaggerated and distorted as they're passed from one person to another, until you end up with a mixture of fact and fiction. That's how the folklore about us grew up over the centuries."

"Centuries . . ." Penny repeated dully, then uttered a peculiar little bark of a laugh. "How old are you?"

"Far older than any woman wants to admit to. In my case the condition's hereditary. It's another myth, by the way, that vampires can only be made, not born—either is possible. Which brings us back to David—"

"*No*," said Penny.

"Mrs. Blythe—"

"*No*. Anyway, I don't believe any of this."

"You mean, you don't want to believe it. Look at me. Please. Just so that I can show you something."

Her teeth, of course. The canines *were* abnormally long; not outright Dracula fangs, but certainly very pronounced. They looked sharp, too.

Penny giggled stupidly, and Carmine said, "If you still won't believe, then there's only one other way I can prove my *bona fides*."

The giggling stopped and Penny eyed her suspiciously. "What's that?"

"Begin the treatment." Carmine raised her gaze meaningfully upward, in the direction of the bedroom. "And before you shout at me again, consider: I can't do anything to damage him, because he's already terminally damaged. So what have you got to lose?"

Penny's rational self—what was left of it—said: *this is completely insane. I'm talking to a woman who claims to be a vampire, and claims she can give David his life back by turning him into one, too. And part of me wants that ludicrous impossibility to be true, because anything's better than losing him, and so here I stand on the verge of saying, yes, go ahead, then; let's see if you really can do it!*

She heard herself say aloud: "Go ahead, then. Let's see if you really can do it." She turned away from Carmine and stared at the wall. "As you said, what have I got to lose? The most likely scenario is that you're barking mad, and you'll jump around and shout mumbo-jumbo, and nothing will happen. But okay. Why not? I wouldn't have put that ad in pleading for a cure if I hadn't been ready to try just about anything." She stopped then, and frowned. "What will you actually do?"

"Bite him," said Carmine levelly. "That part of the myth is accurate. The first session won't do much—he'll need several—but it will sct the ball rolling, so to speak. You might even find his health starts to improve straight away."

"Sure." Penny waved a hand. *Unreal. Maybe I've flipped, and it isn't happening at all. What the hell?* "Go on, then. Yes. Go on."

Carmine wouldn't let Penny accompany her upstairs. They argued about that, but in the end Penny gave way. Instead she paced the hall, listening but hearing nothing, until footsteps moved overhead to the bathroom. There was a splashing of water, then Carmine came back down the staircase.

"Is that it?" Penny asked. She had half-expected to see some change in the woman. But apart from the fact that her cheeks looked a little less pale than before, there was nothing discernible.

"For the time being," Carmine told her. "I'll go now. See how he is over the next forty-eight hours."

She took her coat from the hook and started to put it on. "Wait," Penny said. "Yes?"

"Why are you doing this? I mean—if what you claim is true, and you are a . . . a . . ." She couldn't quite bring herself to utter the word. ". . . there's got to be something in it for you."

"There is," said Carmine. "Money."

It was the last answer Penny had expected, and she blinked, thrown. "What?"

Carmine shrugged. "Everyone has to earn a living. If your husband improves, and you decide to go on with the treatment, then I'll expect you to pay me a fee."

"What sort of a fee?"

"I usually charge ten thousand. That's assuming the treatment is completed; if you decide to stop at any stage, we'll work out a percentage."

"Ten . . . *thousand* . . .?"

"I don't wish to be rude," said Carmine, "but what price would you put on your husband's future?"

When one thought about it, it was, of course, a perfectly reasonable business deal. The car had cost twice that, and the market value of the house was in a different league altogether. As Carmine pointed out, what price for David's future? Nonetheless, in her naïvety Penny had assumed that Carmine must be motivated by some unspecified altruism, and to find out that she was as hard-nosed as any showroom salesman or estate agent was something of a shock.

"It's—" She laughed, choked, collected herself. "It's not exactly the NHS rate, is it?"

"No," Carmine agreed. The outer edges of her mouth twitched faintly. "Strictly private, I'm afraid."

The car could go. It must still be worth at least eight thousand. Two more wouldn't be impossible to find.

"All right," Penny said. "*If* it works." She pressed her knuckles to her brow. "I don't believe I'm *doing* this."

Carmine produced a silver-edged business card. "My office number's on it," she said. "Call me the day after tomorrow, and we'll take it from there."

Penny looked at the card. "'Carmine Smith, Consultant' . . . That's what you call yourself, is it?"

"It's a useful word. Covers a multitude of sins." The hint of a smile increased and became faintly wicked. "Good night, Penny. I may call you Penny now? We'll speak soon."

She saw herself out.

David Blythe did not wake that evening, but slept through the night, as peacefully as a child, without the aid of drugs. With movies in mind, Penny examined his neck for puncture marks. She found nothing, and went to bed in the adjoining room, where she had long periods of uneasy wakefulness with bouts of bad dreams between them.

David woke shortly after seven, and told her that he was feeling very little pain. The smallest hint of color alleviated the gray of illness in his face. He slept again through the morning. At lunchtime he ate half a bowl of soup, and didn't vomit it back. Then he slept again, ate a little more, and had a second peaceful night.

By the following morning Penny had forgotten the forty-eight-hour agreement and at 10:00 a.m. she was dialing the number on Carmine Smith's card.

"He's better," she said in a tiny, frightened voice. "I don't understand, and I almost daren't believe it, but he's so much *better!*"

"Yes," said Carmine, with a certain satisfaction. "Ten thousand, then?"

"Ten thousand," Penny repeated. "Oh God, *yes.*"

She came to the house four more times. On each occasion the routine was the same: coffee first, then the walk upstairs leaving Penny nervously pacing, then the bathroom, then goodbye. Once she did accept a glass of Burgundy after her visit to the bedroom, but that was all. As yet she had asked for no payment, and when Penny tentatively raised the subject she only shook her head and said that she preferred to take her fee on completion. Either she was trusting, Penny decided, or her clients would be too frightened to try to renege on the agreement.

At Carmine's insistence, David knew nothing of what was going on. Though his health was rapidly improving he still slept a great deal, so the visits were timed accordingly. Penny eased her conscience by telling herself that, had he been consulted, David would have gladly chosen anything as an alternative to death.

Then one evening, as they sipped their ritual coffee, Carmine said that tonight's visit would be her last.

Penny's hand and cup stopped midway to her mouth. "Why? What's wrong?"

"Nothing's wrong." Carmine set her own cup down. "It's simply that the initial stage of the cure is complete. It's time for the second and final stage."

She was gazing steadily at Penny, and with an inner curling sensation Penny realized that she had not prepared herself for this. Carmine had explained—or tried to—the nature and the consequences of what would eventually happen to David. The way he would live. The way he would eat. The heightened energy; the fact that he would not age but remain as he was for . . . well, in theory forever. Penny had pretended to listen, but in fact Carmine's words had flowed through her and past her without taking hold in her mind. She hadn't wanted to know the details; all that had mattered to her was that David was slowly but surely gaining his life back.

Now, though, the reality of the situation hit her with a jolt that made her feel sick. Tonight, if Carmine had her way, David would become what she was. A vampire. Penny believed in vampires now. Carmine claimed to be such a creature, and in the light of the miracle that had been wrought, how could she doubt anything that Carmine said?

Vampire. "I . . ." Then, finding the pronoun utterly pointless, she fell silent. Carmine did not drink any more coffee; she merely waited, and at last Penny found a semblance of a question.

"What . . . will you do?"

"What I've done before." Carmine's voice was quiet, soothing; irrationally, the tone of it reassured. "But to a greater degree. I'd rather not tell you the details; they might upset you, and there are some things that we . . . find uncomfortable to expose to those who aren't of our kind."

David. Vampire. "Will you hurt him?"

"Not at all. I guarantee it."

My husband. Then Penny faced the question she really wanted to ask; the only one that mattered. "Will he . . . die . . . ?"

She thought Carmine might fudge that one, possibly out of delicacy or kindness, or for more obscure reasons. She didn't. She said, as casually as if referring to the workings of a car engine, "Technically, yes. He'll be out—that is, not breathing—for something like twelve hours; then he'll wake and—" She spread her hands. "That's it."

It. My husband, undead. A vampire . . .

"Oh, one warning," Carmine added. "Twelve hours is a long time to wait; it'll probably feel more like twelve days to you. You could easily panic and think that something's gone wrong, but you must *not* be tempted to act on that fear. If you call a doctor, an ambulance, anything like that, the consequences will be disastrous, and I am *not* exaggerating." One hand, resting on the arm of her chair, clenched, as though an unpleasant memory had risen. "Imagine it, Penny. A dead man who suddenly and inexplicably returns to life. Believe me, you do *not* want to condemn David, and yourself, to facing the results of that!"

Penny nodded. She was feeling worse with every moment, and suddenly she found herself on the verge of changing her mind, ordering Carmine out of the house as she had done at their first encounter.

"I'm afraid," Carmine said softly, "that it's a little late for that."

Penny stared. "How do you—"

"Know what you're thinking? Don't worry, I'm not telepathic. It's simply all there in your face—cold feet, the last-minute doubts; it's always the same. But you can't turn back. He's already too far down the line, and if it stops now, he'll die sooner and more unkindly than he would have done if this had never begun." She stood up. "So, with your permission . . ."

Penny's face was a frozen sculpture. She nodded, once, barely perceptibly, and Carmine silently left the room.

She was gone longer than usual, and when she returned Penny had not been pacing but still sat motionless in her chair.

"Twelve hours," Carmine said. Her cheeks were flushed and there was an excited, faintly feverish look in her eyes. "For his sake and yours, please remember what I said and don't panic."

Penny didn't look at her but fumbled for her handbag on the floor near her feet. "I'd better . . ." She swallowed. The car was sold, the money was in the bank. She wanted rid of it. "Will you take a check . . .?"

"Of course." While Penny wrote, her hand shaking, Carmine put her coat on. "Thank you," she said. The check disappeared into a small black leather wallet. "Oh, and if you need me again, just phone. It's inclusive; no extra charge."

"Need you?" Penny demanded sharply. "For what?"

"Well . . . you may already have worked out how to do it, in which case there's no problem," said Carmine. "But if you haven't . . ." Her shoulders lifted in an eloquent but slightly self-effacing way. "You might want some help when you have to break the news of what we've done to David."

Penny sat beside her husband's bed, her gaze fixed glassily on his face, her body and mind numb. David wasn't breathing, and she had gotten through nearly half a bottle of vodka, and if Carmine's calculation was right there were still nine more hours to endure before his chest would move and his eyes would open and look at her, and she would have to tell him the truth. She didn't know how she would do it, and she wished that she had the barefaced gall to pray for guidance. But she didn't, and so waiting the hours away with the help of the vodka bottle seemed the only viable option.

At midnight she was asleep, slumped forward with her face on the bed, in a posture that would give her a diabolical backache by morning. At 7:45 a.m. a sound and a movement disturbed her, and she raised her head blearily. Her eyes wouldn't focus properly at first, but after a second or two David's face registered.

He was awake. He was sitting up. And he was *hungry*.

"Champagne." Carmine produced a bag with a refinedly understated logo and presented it to Penny. "To mark the occasion and celebrate a happy outcome."

The champagne was expensive and already chilled to the perfect temperature, both of which made Penny feel faintly inadequate. She said thank you too gushingly, but before she could make any move to open the bottle David took it from her. "Let me, darling. You know what you're like; you'll struggle with it and then it'll go off bang and we'll lose half the contents before we even start."

The remark stung, but Penny didn't want to show it. She returned a stiff smile, fetched glasses, watched as the cork came out with nothing more than a soft hiss and the champagne bubbled into the bowls. Carmine was given the first glass (naturally enough; she was a guest), Penny the second.

"Well, then." David raised the third glass. "To all of us." But he was looking at Carmine as he said it.

Carmine smiled warmly. They drank, then a constrained silence crept in.

Penny said, "I'll see how the food's coming along . . ."

All right, she told herself in the kitchen. *This is still very new to him and she's been more than helpful; in fact I very much doubt if we could have coped without her. So stop resenting her, and stop being paranoid.* Lecture over. If she repeated it often enough, the message would get through eventually. There was no cause to be suspicious.

She started to prepare the food, trying to concentrate on the filleted sole she had prepared for herself and not dwell too much on what David and Carmine were to eat. Only a desire not to alienate David had stopped her from staggering mealtimes so that they no longer sat together at the dinner table. She frankly couldn't bear to watch him; she had always been squeamish about red meat, and in the past their meals had majored on fish, chicken, or vegetarian dishes. All that had changed now, and if David's diet wasn't as grotesque as legend, it was still bad enough. And the *way* he ate; the speed, the relish of it . . . Meat, and especially beef or veal, either totally raw or so rare that the blood still ran and congealed on his plate, and fish only in the form of sushi. He enjoyed jugged hare, if the local butcher could provide one complete with blood. (When the butcher did, Penny had put her foot down and told David that he must cook it himself.) No vegetables whatsoever; no fruit or cereals or grains. Oh, and the daily breakfast of raw eggs and black pudding, of course. Alcohol wasn't a problem, though he had a marked preference for the heavier red wines, and he did not get drunk no matter how much he put away.

Tonight, with two of David's kind to cater for, Penny had forced herself to provide fillet steak (cooking omitted), with a creamy and plentiful pepper sauce that she could pour on before serving, to mask the look and the smell. Vegetables would also be served, but only she herself would touch them; ditto the tiramisu she had prepared for dessert.

She was not looking forward to this evening. During the early, difficult stage (she smiled humorlessly at that piece of *litotes*) Carmine had been a rock to her, a mediator and ally in the painful process of getting David through the initial shock and enabling him to come to terms with what he had become. That nightmare was over now, though, and the idea that Carmine should come to dinner on a purely social basis—thus shifting the relationship between the three of them from the professional to the personal—dismayed Penny. She did not want Carmine as a friend. The woman unnerved her (understandably), and now that she was no longer needed, Penny would have vastly preferred never to set eyes on her again.

David, though, had argued that one invitation was the very least they could do to thank Carmine. Anything less would be downright rude, he had said, and considering that without her intervention Penny would now be a widow, he found her attitude hard to understand, and more than a little disappointing. He had expected better of her. Feeling like a petty-minded schoolgirl, Penny had flushed and capitulated and spent the rest of the day torn between feelings of shame and guilt, and fervent hopes that Carmine would decline the invitation. But Carmine had not declined, so the motions must be gone through, and David would be pleased; and when it was over she could, with luck, bid Carmine a final *adieu*.

The meal progressed in decorous, civilized style, only marred for Penny (if one overlooked the actual content of the food) by the amount of wine that David and Carmine drank. It wasn't that she *really* minded, Penny told herself. It wasn't as if either of them became drunk or obnoxious. But Carmine's contribution was only the one bottle of champagne; they had paid for the rest, and considering that ten thousand pounds of their money was now sitting in her bank account . . .

She pushed the thought away. The matter of the money was niggling at her too often for comfort, and she reminded herself that, as Carmine had said at the time, what price for her husband's future? David had been a v . . . had been what he was for four months now, and even in her meanest moments Penny had to acknowledge that the condition had its advantages. Take the sex, for instance. Through their married life he had never had a high sex drive; it had been a bone of contention at times, and once his illness set in, any question of conjugal rights had gone straight out of the window. Penny had never complained, naturally, but she had suffered a lot of frustration. Not so now. Now, David was *tireless*. Inventive, too, and so keen that in fact his demands were starting to become exhausting and just a little tedious. *Ice cream is delectable, but too much makes you sick . . .*

Penny pushed that thought away, too, and tried to shake her mind out of its bout of self-pity. What did the money matter, or the small irritations? David was alive (*well . . . but no; don't go down that path*), strong, and guaranteed to remain that way for—

The word hit her suddenly and hard. *Forever*. David wasn't going to age. As years passed, he would remain exactly as he was tonight, while she—

"Penny?" Carmine's voice snapped the chain of the horror rising in her. "Is anything wrong?"

Oh, no; of course nothing's wrong. Only that I'm such a cretin that I've only just started to consider the implications of immortality! "No," Penny said, in such a peculiarly strangled voice that she gave the complete lie to the statement. "No, I—something stuck in my throat, I think."

She might have imagined it, but Penny thought Carmine and David exchanged a very private look. "Not a fishbone, I hope?" Carmine said solicitously. "They can be dangerous. Can I—"

"No!" She swallowed. "Thank you. It's gone now." She took a large and unladylike swig from her wineglass, and this time distinctly saw David raise an eyebrow.

"More, darling?" No trace of disapproval in his voice; but he was good at hiding things. Always had been, now she thought about it.

"Yes. Thanks." Defiantly she emptied the refilled glass in one, challenging him to make any comment. He didn't.

"It was a lovely meal, Penny," Carmine said, possibly to ease the sudden sharp change in the atmosphere.

"Absolutely," David concurred before Penny could think of a reply. "We must do it again, mustn't we?"

Penny opened her mouth to snap "Must we?", but had the wit to close it again before anything came out. David offered Carmine coffee, and when Penny showed no sign of volunteering to make it, he headed to the kitchen to do it himself. Penny watched him go (tall, slim; that old tendency to put on weight had quite gone, and he looked extremely hand-some these days) and as he disappeared, a question sprang into her mind. It was a spin-off from the immortality thing (she was feeling calmer about that, though doubtless it would come back and hit her again later), and suddenly she wanted, extremely badly, to know the answer.

She turned to Carmine. "May I ask you something?"

"Of course." Carmine inclined her head in a way that made Penny wonder if she was being patronized. *Third thought to push away.*

"It's about children."

"Ah." Carmine's expression grew wary. "I've been wondering if that would come up."

Penny bristled, though not visibly. "I think it's a natural enough con-cern. Whatever David might—"

"You didn't have children before. Was that choice, or . . .?"

"Choice, of course." Her hackles were rising by the moment and she wished she had not begun this conversation. Too late for regret, though, and with determination she collected herself. "It's a perfectly straightfor-ward question. Can we?"

Carmine said, "No."

Penny's bravado and aggression collapsed. "Why not?"

Carmine's eyes held a world of sympathy, even if Penny was unwilling to acknowledge it. "It's a harsh fact of his—our—condition," she said. "A vampire can procreate—naturally, or our kind would have died out in the earliest days; maybe never even have evolved in the first place when you think about it logically. Chickens and eggs, you know . . ." She saw Penny's face become very tight, and quickly let the metaphor drop. "I was born what I am, and I could make a child with any man, mortal or oth-erwise. David, though, was not born what he is, and when the condition isn't hereditary, the rules are different. He could only father a child on a woman who was vampire-born. But with you, it isn't possible."

Penny's mind spun off into space, and her lungs seemed to be clogging up with something murky and angry and bitter. "So," she said, "*you* could have a child with my husband, but I can't."

What did that pause signify? Anything? Nothing? At length Carmine did answer. "Yes. Theoretically."

Theoretically. Penny asked, "Have you had any children?"

Carmine broke eye contact and looked away. It was the first time Penny had ever known her to do that. "Yes."

Penny's bitterness was growing, and with it a desperate desire to strike out, to *hurt*, because *she* was hurting and she wanted Carmine to suffer along with her. "Where are they now?" she demanded.

The second pause was longer than the first. Then: "One," Carmine said, apparently without emotion, "is in New York. Or was, the last time I heard anything of him. He's a heroin addict, and he wants to die of it, but he can't, because of . . . what he is. The other . . ." her voice caught momentarily, ". . . did die, though she was the one who didn't want to. Ironic, yes? But it was a long time ago, and a long way east of here, and people believed in us then, so when she made a serious tactical mistake they . . ." She coughed. "Well, you know how the legend runs. The method of killing us is one of the facts that hasn't been distorted."

Penny stared, fascination creeping in despite herself. "A stake through the heart?" she prompted softly.

Carmine nodded. Her face had tightened, taking on the look of a fixed clay mask. "It doesn't . . . actually have to be a stake," she said. "Anything will do, as long as it . . . pierces far enough. In her case—"

"Your daughter?"

Carmine swallowed. "My daughter, yes. In her case it was a—a kitchen knife. Just a kitchen knife."

David came back then. "Coffee's brewing," he began cheerfully, then saw Carmine's tension, the expression on Penny's face. "What is it?" His tone became sharp. "What's happened?"

Penny mouthed "*tell you later*" but he didn't see it; his attention was on Carmine. She, however, straightened her shoulders and smiled up at him. "Nothing to concern you," she said lightly. "Women's talk, that's all. David, when we've had coffee I really must go. It's been a lovely evening, but I have to be up tomorrow; I've got an early appointment."

Penny wanted to say bitchily, "Another ten grand in the bank?" but held her tongue. This wasn't the moment for scoring points; in a few minutes more Carmine would be out of here. She disciplined herself to make polite and superficially pleasant small talk while the coffee was enjoyed and they all had a cognac, then David fetched Carmine's coat and walked her to her car. Penny watched covertly from the window, but it was too dark to see what sort of car she had. Something expensive, no doubt. She could afford it, couldn't she? And why was a simple farewell taking so long? What were they *doing*?

When David did return (six minutes: Penny had counted) she was washing up with a pointed amount of noise and splashing. Before his illness, he had promised to buy her a dishwasher. Out of the question now, of course. They couldn't afford it. As she slammed another plate into the rack he came up behind her and slid his hands around her waist.

"Leave that. I'll do it in the morning." His lips touched the back of her neck. "Come to bed."

Oh God, not again. "I'm tired," she said. "Let's give it a miss tonight, shall we?"

He laughed. "No way. I want you. Come on, darling; I'm not taking no for an answer."

You never do, do you? Penny pulled a face that he couldn't see, and sighed. No point in arguing; she would waste more time and energy that way than by giving him what he wanted, yet again. She pulled off her rubber gloves, dumped them on the draining board and went with him up the stairs.

David always fell soundly asleep after sex, and when she was certain of not disturbing him Penny got up and went into the bathroom. Switching on the small vanity light she faced her reflection in the mirror above the washbasin. On first impression she was pretty good for forty-three, but she wasn't in a mood to be optimistic, and she studied herself more closely and critically. Proto-crow's feet at the borders of her eyes. Lines developing at the corners of her mouth. Chin starting to sag; barely noticeable yet, but *she* could see it. She wasn't a natural blonde, so couldn't tell if there were any traces of gray in her hair yet. Gray was distinguishing in a man, aging in a woman. Carmine wasn't gray, was she?

Carmine could have his child. I can't.

It wasn't that she wanted children. Never had, really; she wasn't the maternal type. But the principle of the thing was different, and the thought that Carmine and David were capable of doing what she and David weren't made her very, very angry. It also led, quite naturally from the perspective of this dissatisfied moment, to the conclusion that if they *could*, they just *might*. That tonight, she had possibly witnessed the opening gambits of a sexual affair. Or even if she hadn't, that the potential was there.

Potential—or inevitability? Penny leaned closer still to the mirror, dissecting her image now. Even if lines and gray hair weren't yet worth worrying about, that would change soon enough. *Think forward three years; five; ten.* In ten years she would be fifty-three. In fifteen, sixty would be looming on her horizon, but David would still be exactly as he was tonight; youthful, energetic, handsome. What would he want with a sixty-year-old wife? She would be a turn-off, an embarrassment, and that would be the end of it, marriage over, goodbye.

David was no fool; he must have considered the long-term future. Maybe he had even discussed it with Carmine, in some private conversation that Penny knew nothing about? Penny's stomach churned at the thought of him talking to Carmine, possibly meeting Carmine, when she was not present to play chaperone. *Or gooseberry. Remember how he kept looking at her tonight. Are they already having an affair? Are they?*

Suddenly she felt tainted, and with the feeling came an overwhelming urge to walk back into the bedroom, shake David forcibly awake and confront him with her suspicions. Or to go to the phone, key Carmine's number and demand the truth from her. Yes: that was the better option. Because if there was an affair David would lie about it, and she was too vulnerable to his charm not to be taken in. If Carmine lied, Penny would not be fooled. Yes. The better option. In the morning, when David had left for work, she would do it.

Penny did not make the planned phone call. For by morning, she had thought of a new idea; so radical that at first it shocked her and she mentally hid from it, finding a hundred reasons why it was utterly out of the question. Through the first half of the day, though, the reasons seemed somehow to break down of their own accord, until by midafternoon they were gone, leaving in their place the same kind of queasy, heart-racing excitement that young children feel on the night before Christmas when nothing can persuade them to sleep.

With an hour to go before David came home, she summoned the courage to ring Carmine.

Carmine said: "No. I'm sorry, Penny, but I just won't do it."

With her world collapsing around her Penny screamed down the phone. "Why *not*, damn you? You were eager enough to do it for David; what's the bloody difference all of a sudden?' She sucked in a huge, painful breath. "I know it's all business to you, but I can find the money, I'll—"

"Penny, listen to me! Have you talked to David about this?"

"No, I haven't!"

"Then I think you should. And I also think I know what he'll say."

Penny saw red. "David's not my bloody owner—I make my own decisions! And how the hell would you know what he'd say? Telepathic, are you? Or are you so cozy with my husband these days that you know him better than I do?"

"I'm not saying that. I'm only saying—"

"*What* are you saying? Tell me the truth, for once!"

"I'm trying to. The circumstances aren't the *same*, Penny. David was terminally ill, and what I did for him was the only alternative to death. It isn't like that with you. You're healthy and with a long, normal life ahead of you. It isn't—it wouldn't be *right* to turn you into—"

"But I *want* it!" Then with a great effort Penny brought herself under control. *Keep your temper. Reason with her.* "Look. I've thought it through, I have no doubts, and I can get the money. Don't you want another ten thousand?"

Carmine gave a strange little laugh. "Money doesn't come into it. You could offer me half a million and I'd turn it down. The plain fact is, I will not do this for any living soul unless there is a very, very good reason indeed."

"And my reason isn't good enough."

"No. Frankly, it isn't."

"I see. So you're happy to give David your gift, but you won't consider giving it to me."

"It isn't like that, Penny."

"No, I'm sure it isn't." Then something dawned, and Penny wondered why on earth she hadn't thought of it before. "Well, I won't bother you again, then. I'll ask my husband to do it for me instead. He is *my husband*, after all. Which is something you seem to conveniently forget when it suits you."

There was a sharp pause. "What's that supposed to mean?"

"Work it out, Carmine. You're intelligent enough." Penny was completely calm now. *Yes, David can do it. Fool I am: I needn't even have made this call.* Coolly, she added, "I won't take up any more of your time. Oh, one last thing. You're not welcome in this house from now on."

She didn't hang up immediately; she wanted to hear and savor Carmine's reaction. There was a short silence. Then Carmine said:

"Message understood. But before you go, it's only fair to tell you that David can't help you. Even if he agreed to it—which I frankly doubt—he doesn't possess the ability. Only those who are born to the club, as you might say, can initiate new members. Goodbye, Penny. I think I feel rather sorry for you."

Carmine was the one to break the connection.

Penny did not tell David about the phone call, and she did not ask him to do what she wanted. Instead, she kept the memory of the conversation locked privately in her mind, picking over every detail until it festered like a sore that wouldn't heal. *David can't.* Was that true, or had Carmine lied for her own purposes? *I doubt if he would agree.* How did she know what David would or wouldn't agree to? Discussed it, had they? How often? How intimately? *Your reason isn't good enough.* Carmine Smith, aka God. Well, the motive was obvious, wasn't it? Wives get in the way of affairs, and the last thing Carmine and David would want was Penny joining the club, as Carmine had put it. Penny would cramp their style. Penny would be a damned nuisance. So she must be prevented from joining, mustn't she? Provided Penny stayed in the ranks of ordinary mortals, Carmine and David need only wait a few years—nothing, to them—until Penny began seriously to age, then faded, withered and finally dropped out of the picture altogether. Problem solved: until then they could simply carry on their liaison behind her back.

The dark thoughts hung on Penny like a shroud all evening. David must have been aware of it but he made no comment, which to her only compounded his guilt. She refused sex that night (unusually, he didn't try too hard to persuade her), slept badly and, when it was time for him to get up, lay still and silent, pretending that the alarm clock hadn't woken her. It fooled David; he dressed silently, then went downstairs to make his own breakfast, as she had begun to insist he should do.

Then the phone rang. It was unusually early for anyone to call, and Penny raised her head from the pillow. David answered it on the kitchen extension, and the kitchen was directly below their bedroom, so his side of the conversation carried clearly.

"David Blythe . . . Oh—hi. This is a surprise . . . No, no; it's all right . . . What? When? . . . Well, I don't . . . Ah. Well, yes, perhaps we should . . . Okay; 12:45 suit you? . . . Right. I'll meet you there." *Click.* End of call.

When he had eaten and came back upstairs, Penny yawned and stretched and put on a sleepy voice. "Who was that on the phone?"

David had his back to her and was putting on his tie. He didn't use a mirror; there was no point. "I told you about that new client, didn't I?"

"No."

"Oh. Well, it was his secretary; just changing the time of a meeting. Bloody nuisance; I've got a lot of other things scheduled today." He turned and glanced at her. "You all right?"

"Fine." *Go on, go away. I've got something to find out, and I don't want you around while I do it.*

He left a few minutes later. Penny listened to the sounds of the troublesome car eventually starting (an old banger: *we all know what happened to the decent one, don't we?*) and as soon as he drove away she picked up the phone and keyed "recall," to see who had *really* phoned.

The number given was local, but not familiar. Could be the supposed client's secretary. However . . . Penny entered the code that would stop her own call being traced, then punched the number in. A ringing tone began.

Click. "Carmine Smith."

Penny hung up. Carmine. Not at her office but, obviously, at home. Well, now she had all her answers. New client. Oh, *sure.*

"You bastard. You two-faced, lying, cheating, cold-blooded *bastard*!"

And that, although she didn't realize it until quite some time afterwards, was the moment when everything was set in motion.

She watched. Oh, she watched, and she listened, and at every opportunity she searched through David's clothes, David's wallet, anything that David was unsuspecting enough to leave lying around for her. For six days she found nothing. Then on the seventh evening, while he was in the bath, the incriminating evidence finally appeared.

Penny did not know whether to feel triumphant or sick as she read the scribbled note at the back of David's diary. It said simply: *Carmine, The Scream—Friday 12:30.* Not last Friday, because she'd looked in the diary more recently than that. Today was Thursday. Tomorrow, then. The Scream was a new minimalist café; Penny had suggested to David that they go there, but he had poo-poohed the idea, dismissing it as an overpriced trap for fashion victims. Now she knew why. Not exactly sensible to take one's wife to the same place where one met one's mistress . . .

Noises from the bathroom announced David emerging, and hastily Penny replaced the diary in the inner pocket of his jacket. Twelve-thirty tomorrow. Good. It would be the final proof.

The rain gave her the advantage of anonymity. It was easy to loiter next door to the café, hiding under a plain black umbrella and pretending to window-shop. Sheer good fortune staged the meeting as if it had been scripted: David arrived on foot, and as he reached the doorway a taxi drew up and Carmine got out. Heart thudding painfully, Penny watched sidelong as they moved towards each other, and saw Carmine reach up to kiss her husband. It was not a sisterly kiss, and Penny waited no longer but turned and, quietly and unnoticed, walked away.

She therefore didn't see David's reaction to the kiss; didn't see him lay his hands on Carmine's upper arms and push her gently away. Carmine hesitated, searching his face, and what she saw there changed her expression. A small smile, a regretful and half-apologetic shrug. Then they went into the café together.

"I'm sorry." Carmine stirred her coffee but showed no inclination to drink it. "Yes, I confess I did hope that maybe something might . . . develop between us. I'd be a liar if I didn't admit to finding you very attractive, and as we're both . . . Well, it seemed logical somehow."

David thought the morality of that was dubious, but didn't comment. "Apology accepted," he said. "And maybe under different circumstances—"

"Thank you for being so tactful about it. But I overstepped the mark. I simply didn't realize how strongly you feel about Penny."

"I love her," he said. "And I don't want to lose her. When you called the first time, and told me what she'd asked you to do, it shocked me. I hadn't faced it before; hadn't thought through the implications of what I've become and what it'll mean to us in the future. Now, though . . ."

"You want me to do it." She looked down at the table.

"Yes. So that Penny and I can stay together." His fingers moved restlessly. "I know it's a great deal to ask, Carmine; especially when you . . . well, when I've disappointed you." He shook his head quickly. "Christ, that sounds so arrogant; I didn't mean—"

"Forget it. I haven't lived as long as I have without developing a very thick skin. Yes, it is a great deal to ask. But you're asking it out of love, and I'd have a hard time coping with my conscience if I used love as an excuse for refusing."

David's eyes lit. "Then—"

"I'll do it. Not for money; I won't accept payment this time." She raised her head, seemed to force herself to meet his gaze, and smiled. "Call it my love token to you."

There was a brief silence, then David let out a long breath and relaxed in his chair. "Thank you. I don't know how to tell you what this means to me."

"Then don't try." One of her hands, under the table, clenched until the fingernails dug painfully into her flesh. "I could begin this evening," she added after a few moments. "Sooner the better, yes? Then I'll be out of your hair for good."

"I don't know what to say, Carmine."

"You're making a habit of these 'don't knows.'" She manufactured a laugh to show that that was a joke. "I'll come to your house at eight o'clock, then?"

"Eight o'clock. Yes. *Thank* you."

Carmine stood up to leave, her coffee still untouched. "It might be better if you don't tell Penny before I arrive. She . . . isn't very well disposed towards me at the moment."

"That'll change."

"Ah. My consolation, and reward for services rendered." Her mouth twitched with a sad drollery. "I'll see you this evening. Oh, and a glass or two of a decent Bordeaux or Burgundy would be welcome afterward. Goodbye, David."

He hadn't intended to say a word to Penny about it, but when he walked into the house and saw her tight face and tense posture, he wanted to cheer her into a happier mood. So he kissed her (she responded stiffly) and said, "I've got a surprise for you."

"Oh?" Penny eyed him uncertainly, wishing she could hate him for what he was doing to her.

"Mmm. You'll find out what it is at eight o'clock. When Carmine arrives."

"Carmine?" She stared at him, her eyes glaring disbelief and outrage, but David was already on his way upstairs and didn't see the change. "That's right. No need to worry about food: she won't be eating with us. But I've bought some wine; if you open it now, it can breathe for an hour or two. Just going to have a quick shower and get changed."

His voice diminished up the stairs and Penny stood motionless in the living room doorway. She hadn't taken in his exact words; hadn't listened to them. One word, one name, was all that had registered. All afternoon she had been preparing herself for the great confrontation, when she would hurl down what she had seen today like a gauntlet and challenge him to deny it. Now all her plans were thrown into chaos; he had pre-empted her and snatched the advantage. Carmine was coming *here*. He had *invited* her, as if there was nothing between them, nothing to hide, nothing going on. What "surprise" had they cooked up between them to mollify her, put her off the scent? They must think she was a fool, a *moron*, to be taken in by their games!

Upstairs in the bedroom David was singing as he stripped off. He had a good baritone voice, but now it grated hatefully on Penny's ears. *Fool. Dupe. Taken for granted, used*, mocked . . . A huge and uncontrollable rage was rising inside her like a storm-tide, and though a small part of her brain warned her it was a kind of madness, another part welcomed it because it was better, so much better, than the pain of enduring betrayal and making no effort to counter it.

Counter it. Penny moved at last. Down the hall, into the kitchen. Foot-falls overhead; David was in the bathroom now. Faint sound of the shower running. *He's stopped singing. I don't ever want to hear him sing again.*

She opened one of the kitchen drawers at random, looked inside, closed it. Her mind wasn't functioning properly: it was the rage that was doing it, blocking logic, blocking efficient reasoning and leaving her only with a robotic level of half-conscious reflex to drive her. Second drawer. No, not in there. Third.

Ah . . .

It doesn't actually have to be a stake. Anything will do, as long as it pierces far enough. Carmine's own words. Her daughter had died that way, caught out by—how had Carmine phrased it? "A tactical mistake," that was it.

Found out, unmasked for what she was, and summarily executed without a judge, jury or lawyer in sight. It must have happened a long time ago, of course. A century, two centuries: Carmine was coy about her age, so she hadn't put a date on the event. Attitudes were different then. This was the modern world, a rational age. People didn't do such things. Did they?

As long as it pierces far enough.

Penny took the cook's knife with the eight-inch blade out of its plastic sheath in the drawer, and started to weigh and balance it gently in her palm.

Carmine was fifteen minutes late, but that didn't matter. Penny heard a car approach and slow down, and settled herself more comfortably in her cross-legged position on the hall floor. It would take Carmine a minute or so to park; spaces were always tight in the evenings as more and more people arrived home and squeezed into diminishing slots. *Yes; there she goes. Rev, rev. Sounds as if she doesn't know the length of her own car. I don't think I'll go outside and help her. I don't think that would be a good idea.*

The stain on the carpet was spreading. Her hands and arms still dripped, probably from when she had punched her clenched fists into his chest afterwards, to make absolutely sure. Funny; she was so squeamish about red meat, but tonight she hadn't felt sick. Still didn't, despite the fact that the whole thing had been much more spectacular than she had anticipated. Penny giggled. Moviemakers didn't know the half of it. The marks might come out of the stairs and hall carpet, but there wasn't a chance of eradicating the mess upstairs. Bathroom, bedroom—she hadn't quite struck cleanly (*Ha! Joke!*) the first time, so David had managed to get to the bedroom before shock and pain keeled him over and she had been able to finish it all properly. *The heart really is an efficient pump, isn't it? I hadn't realized it would go on for so long.*

The revving outside stopped at last. Footsteps now, click of elegant heels approaching the front gate. Penny giggled again, and this time had a degree of trouble making it stop. *Silly woman. Control yourself. It's no laughing matter.*

At that thought she covered her mouth with a stained hand and snorted like a horse. Her face was smeared when she finally sobered and took the hand away, but she wasn't aware of it and wouldn't have minded in the least anyway. Come on, *footsteps. I can hear you. Up the path. Hello, Carmine. Come in. I've been expecting you and I'm all ready.*

A shape loomed dimly through the frosted glass panel in the door, and the bell rang, just once, demurely.

Bitch. Two-timer. Cheat. Betrayer. Made my husband immortal, did you? Well, he isn't immortal anymore. Maybe I'll let you see him. But I think it's better if I don't. Safer. I don't want to lose the element of surprise, after all.

Penny stood up and started to smile. The hall mirror, as she passed it, reflected a demonic vision of gory red and deathly white, with eyes that burned and laughed and burned. Her hands felt as if they were burning, too, but it didn't matter, any more than Carmine's lateness mattered. The smile on her face was fixed now, as if nothing could ever erase it, and her right hand closed more firmly on the hilt of the scarlet knife behind her back, as with her left she reached out to open the front door.

Aftermath

Janet Berliner

South African–born American author Janet Berliner (1939–2012) served as president of the Horror Writers Association from 1997 to 1998. Her novels include The Madagascar Manifesto series (with George Guthridge), *Execution Exchange* (with Woody Greer), *Rite of the Dragon* (as Janet Gluckman), and *Artifact* (with Kevin J. Anderson, F. Paul Wilson, and Matthew J. Costello), while her short fiction appeared in *Shayol, The Magazine of Fantasy & Science Fiction* and various anthologies. As an anthologist herself, she edited *Peter S. Beagle's Immortal Unicorn, David Copperfield's Tales of the Impossible*, and *David Copperfield's Beyond Imagination*. Berliner won the Bram Stoker Award in 1997 (with Guthridge) for the story "Children of the Dusk."

"At the risk of being branded a traitor, I admit to the fact that, excepting the original, I was never much into vampires of the traditional blood-sucking variety," the author admitted. "Or so I believed, until I had an epiphany at a party in Las Vegas.

"Living in such an environment, running into Elvis or Marilyn at a party or the crap tables is commonplace, so it didn't seem all that peculiar to me when I met a tall, handsome man who called himself Vlad, spoke with a strong Balkan accent, and claimed to be from Transylvania.

"Immediately Vlad found out that I was a writer, he asked me if I had ever written any vampire stories. I hadn't. Then, as fate would have it, the very next day I was asked to write a vampire story, set in Jerusalem in or around the year 1197.

"There it was. The challenge I needed. I could continue to write about the human condition, and the next time I met Vlad I could tell him honestly that I had now written a true vampire tale . . ."

IN CANAAN, WHICH was also known as the land of Israel, in the spring of the year Christians called 1197, Moslems prayed openly but with a sense of unease. Jews, for whom the spring coincided with the celebration of Passover, called the year 4957. They prayed, too, in secret and with no less nervousness. Moslems and Jews alike were people whose families had endured and survived the injustices and cruelties of three Crusades. They knew, to a man and to a woman, that this brief respite from war would not last; a fourth Crusade would follow the third as surely as camels carried their own water across the desert.

The first three Crusades had been devastating. Entire Moslem families had been decimated; Jews, falsely accused of engaging in blood rites too horrific to contemplate, refused to convert to Christianity, to deny *ha-rachamim*, their Merciful Father, and laid down their lives for the sanctification of His name.

The Crusades denied fathers the pleasure of seeing their sons grow up; they denuded both communities of single men who could marry their daughters, so that they could no longer obey the Lord's or Allah's instruction to go forth and multiply.

And so it was that Meyer ben Joseph and Hamid el Faisir, who were the leaders of their communities and knew that they all needed protection against the evil to come, befriended each other. "If we are destroyed, it will not matter to the few survivors which God we worshipped," Meyer said.

Hamid assented.

On the first night of Passover, in the same spirit of cooperation, Hamid agreed to be present at the religious meal which his new friend Meyer called the Seder. "In this way," Hamid told his people, "I shall be an eye-witness to their rituals. If they do not drink of the blood of Christian children, as has been reported, then we shall defend our City together against the soldiers when they come."

And so it came to be that Hamid and his family joined Meyer, his wife Rose, and their only surviving child, Devora, on the first night of Passover. They reclined and listened with respect as Meyer told the story of his people's journey across the desert in search of the Promised Land, they enjoyed the melodic songs, and they bowed their heads respectfully during the prayers.

"Pour the last of the wine, Meyer," Rose said, finally. "I sense that our guests are growing hungry."

Meyer poured a small amount of prayer wine for each person, though he knew that his Moslem guests did not drink. He was emptying the last of the carafe into a large goblet set aside for the Prophet Elijah when there came a knock at the door. Meyer's hand jerked in surprise and a few drops missed the large goblet and landed on his wife's handwoven table-cloth. He grimaced; there was little more where that had come from. The extra glass of wine they poured each year—the extra place setting at the table—was a tradition he would never have ignored. But for a stranger to know the exact moment in the Seder bordered on miraculous.

"Timing is everything," he said, thinking, *the Prophet has a good nose.*

"Go, Devora. Open the door for our visitor," he said, addressing his sixteen-year-old daughter.

She was not surprised, for each year at Passover her father had not so subtly knocked under the table and instructed her youngest brother to open the door and welcome the Prophet Elijah. Of course, there had never been anyone there, though her father said that Elijah's spirit entered.

Not so this time.

Standing at the door in the darkness was a robed stranger, a tall man whose handsome face spoke of unbearable weariness. Slightly behind him stood a second man whose appearance and bearing cast him in the role of manservant.

"Welcome to our home," Meyer said, beckoning the strangers to the table and thinking that Rose would have to set yet another place. "It may not be much, but it is one of the best in Mea Shearim."

Gesturing first to his manservant in such a manner that it was apparent he would remain outside, the Stranger entered Meyer's house. He did not remove his robe, nor did he look into the eyes of his host.

"Will you pray with us over the wine?" Meyer asked, thinking that he must remember later to have Devora take food and wine outside to the manservant.

The man sat but did not speak, neither did he eat or drink, even after the prayers were done. He was dark and swarthy, but did not seem to be of Jerusalem.

"What road have you traveled, Stranger?" Meyer asked, wondering if the man had been sent to observe the blood rites of which the Jews were accused. If so, he would leave disappointed.

"I travel the Road of Humanitatis," the man said.

Those were all the words he spoke.

When the meal was over, there was one more tradition to be observed before the final song could be sung. Earlier, Devora—the oldest and the youngest—had hidden a piece of unleavened bread known as the *Afikomen*. Now she was sent to retrieve it.

"Let our daughter also take food and wine to the man who is outside in the moonlight," Meyer said to Rose. "She will be rewarded for returning the *Afikomen* to the table," Meyer explained to his guests, "for without it the Seder cannot be completed. It will not take long for her to find it. Rose and I watched her hide it in the garden."

After a few moments, when Devora had not returned, the Stranger stood as if to leave. Meyer bade him Godspeed and glanced at the family of Hamid el Faisir, wishing they too would depart. Despite his best efforts it had been a strained night; he wanted it to be over.

When their daughter still did not return with the *Afikomen*, which fairly translated meant Aftermath, Rose said, "I am worried about our daughter. It is that time of the month for her. She should not be outside alone and in the dark for so long."

Meyer excused himself and went to find Devora.

He found her in the small arbor which stood permanently in the garden, ready to be decorated each autumn in thanks for God's bounty. She held the *Afikomen* in her hand. Silently, she gave it to her father.

Silently, he took it.

"We have been waiting for you," Meyer said. "All but the Stranger, who came out of the night and has returned to it."

"I have been with him," Devora responded. "And I have fed his manservant."

Devora, daughter of Rose and of Meyer ben Joseph, never spoke again of the two men or even of the child of the manservant, conceived that Passover during her time of bleeding and growing in her womb. More and more, she became morose. Each time she passed a mirror, it was spotted with droplets of blood and she was shamed before her father, the remaining man of her family. Soon she ceased to be obedient to him or to any man. As if she wished to die in childbirth, she baked *challahs* and deliberately neglected to take from the dough and give what she had taken to a priest in tithing.

Meyer did not like his daughter's behaviors but he accepted them as part of the changes wrought by childbearing, a process he did not pretend to understand. Rose was more frightened than angered. Though it was the word of God and of Allah that Their followers go forth and multiply, it was also His word that no child be conceived during *niddah*—menstruation—and for good reason.

She feared for the life of her daughter and trembled for her daughter's child, lest that child—conceived in blood—be claimed by the demon queen, Lilith.

The child, a girl, grew strong inside the womb of her mother, Devora. Like all embryos growing into the fullness of their heritage, this one saw the history of her people by the light of a candle which burned in the womb, a white glow which allowed her to see the beginning and the end of the universe.

Inside the womb, an angel kept watch over her, teaching her the *Torah*; outside the womb, Lilith—overpowered by the remembrance of her own childless and unhappy marriage—watched the angel and seethed with jealousy of Devora's motherhood. She bided her time, smiling evilly as Rose constructed an amulet from the *Sefer Raziel* to protect the mother and child after birth and hung amulets aplenty around the walls and on the birth-bed to discourage the demonic queen from claiming the child.

Just before birth, when—as it was written—the angel readied itself to touch the child lightly on her top lip so that the cleavage on her upper lip could be formed and she could forget all she had learned, Lilith interfered. Dousing the light in the womb, she pushed the infant into the birth canal.

In that moment, Devora's soul took leave of its earthly body. In that moment, Marisa was born. She emerged from her mother's womb with a collective consciousness and with an arrogance which, in combination with her facial flaw, set her apart from the other children in Mea Shearim.

Of the 613 Laws of the *Torah*, *Rekhilut*—the first, though the least prohibitive, law against bad-of-mouth gossip—was the most frequently disobeyed in the quarter where Marisa was born. In the case of this girl-child, the gossip derived more from fear than from any intent to do harm. It was no secret that she had been conceived during *niddah*, nor could it be kept secret that the child had no cleavage on her upper lip. Since her mother had died in childbirth, it was logical to assume that she had been claimed as the daughter and servant of Lilith. But the greatest fear was the one spoken in whispers, that because of the circumstances of her conception and birth, Marisa could be infected with the most dreaded of all diseases, leprosy.

Meyer and Rose showered all of their love upon their granddaughter, whom they called Marisa Devora and who was the last of their living kin. Unfortunately, no amount of their goodwill could change the nervousness of a community which had been so badly hurt by the passage of the years that they feared anything which might bring more trouble into their midst.

Again, Hamid el Faisir, who had reported favorably on the household ben Joseph, came together with Meyer. This time they joined forces to try to protect Marisa from those who, driven by unreasoned anxiety, threatened harm to the fatherless child.

The strength of the two proved to be sadly insufficient against the many. One evening, when it was almost sundown, Marisa was wrest from them and taken into the desert. There, a dried water-hole had been filled with the blood of several lambs and a meager shelter had been built to shield the child from the last rays of the desert sun.

As if she were being baptized in blood, the little girl was submerged and held there until nightfall. Being barely six years old, she could certainly not fight her way out of the grasp of strong adults. She could have cried out, but she did not even do that and appeared, instead, to submit herself to the wishes of the good people of Jerusalem.

In the house in the district of Mea Shearim, Hamid said in an anguished voice, "Surely they intend to dry her off and carry her home at the rise of the moon."

"Surely they do," Meyer agreed, his eyes filled with tears for his granddaughter. "What do you say, Rose?"

Rose said nothing. She left the house and walked into the desert. Even had she wanted to speak, her anger and foreboding would have prevented the words from forming on her tongue. As the rim of the moon appeared on the horizon, she came upon the child.

She stood at a distance, her gaze was riveted upon the little girl.

The child had never looked more contented. She dabbled happily in the red pond, drinking from her cupped hand with an eagerness she had never shown for her grandmother's chicken soup.

Looking up, Rose saw the Stranger, tall and hooded, riding a camel led by his manservant. "No," she cried out, as the townsfolk stepped aside and he laid claim to Marisa Devora.

The child raised her arms and the manservant lifted her up. The Stranger took her, seated her astride the camel with him, and rode away.

Rose wept, but she did nothing to try to stop him.

At dawn, the people of Jerusalem returned to their daily business and to gossiping of other things. Only then did Rose cease her weeping and make her report to Meyer ben Joseph and Hamid el Faisir. She did not tell them that she had heard a female voice, calling the man and the child to join her. She did not say that Lilith had taken the man and the child to her bosom.

Meyer and his friend Hamid embraced each other. Now it was their turn to weep. Then they dried their tears and waited as the message of Marisa Devora and the dark stranger traveled to Cyprus and reached the ears of Amalric; "Beware," the messenger said. "In the land of Canaan, there is a daughter of Lilith who is loved by man and God and Allah and marked by the Devil. Do not cause her to be angry, for her anger could devour you all."

One Among Millions

Yvonne Navarro

Yvonne Navarro lives in southern Arizona with her husband, writer Weston Ochse, and a menagerie of animals. She has published more than twenty novels, ranging from vampires (*AfterAge*) to the end of the world (*Final Impact* and *Red Shadows*). Other titles include *deadrush*, *DeadTimes*, *That's Not My Name*, *Mirror Me*, *Highborn*, and *Concrete Savior*. She is also the author of a number of tie-ins and spin-offs, including the movie novelizations *Ultraviolet*, *Elektra*, *Species*, *Species II*, *Hellboy*, and *Aliens: Music of the Spheres*, and seven novels in TV's *Buffy the Vampire Slayer* "Buffyverse." Her work has won the HWA's Bram Stoker Award, plus a number of other writing awards.

"'One Among Millions' evolved from a pretty run-of-the-mill 'what if' question," explains the author, "namely, *What if you were being stalked by someone?* From there it grew to the stalker being a vampire, but why would a vampire do such a thing to an ordinary woman . . . unless the woman were anything but ordinary.

"So many people think vampire stories are used up, out of vogue, or all the same; I think they couldn't be more wrong. Yes, vampirism is about stealing, but it isn't just about blood. It's about the theft, or loss, of life, of self, of everything that you are or could have ever been, the evolution of that thing that you once were into something you might or might not be able to control.

"There's so much potential in it, and there always will be. Those who turn up their noses and declare vampires are extinct should remember their own mortality. New generations of readers are born every day, and they are always hungry.

"Just like vampires."

SONDRA KNEW EXACTLY when the vampire started stalking her and the babies.

She called the police and they came out to the house, two dutiful small-town, small-minded men with beer bellies and the smell of grease and old cigarettes on their clothes. The twins, their cherubic blue-eyed faces achingly beautiful beneath wispy, platinum curls, cooed and giggled from the playpen in their room, oblivious to the terror on their mother's face and the tense conversation a room away.

"Listen," Sondra said, "I've seen it following us—"

"It?" The older of the two cops wore a nametag that said MᴄSʜᴀᴡ and sent his partner a meaningful look. He jotted something quickly on the form attached to his clipboard.

"Him, I mean." Her face was calm but inside she slapped herself for the verbal slip. Fear was a nasty, constant companion and could cause all kinds of mistakes, make a person tell the truth when that was the last thing in the world she wanted to do. She couldn't afford the truth here, not when the price was Mallory and Meleena's safety. "I've seen *him*."

"Okay." The other lawman was younger but headed the way of his chunky partner; too many donuts and sitting on his ass in the patrol car, wheeling around town and thinking he looked so smart in his blue uniform and spitshined shoes, the carefully oiled .38 snug in its leather holster. Galena was far enough from Chicago to leave the murders and brutality to the city folk; little occupied these men during the day besides petty theft and speeding teenagers, maybe a few alcohol and drug situations. His revolver had probably never been fired at anything but a paper target—what did this man know of blood and terror? "So you saw someone following you in Fox Valley Mall," he repeated. "And you say he walked behind you and your children nearly all the way to your car—"

"Yes."

"—then disappeared when you turned to confront him in the presence of another couple."

Sondra finally saw his nameplate, slightly askew on his shirt pocket. "Exactly, Officer Walters." She sat back.

McShaw grimaced. "Fox Valley is a big place, Ms. Underwood." He peered at her over the rim of his glasses, brown eyes full of skepticism. "Isn't it conceivable that this man's car could have been parked close to yours? That it was nothing but a coincidence?"

"I'm telling you he was following us," Sondra said, too loudly.

The twins made a noise from the other room and she glanced anxiously toward the doorway, then lowered her voice. "He . . ."

Her voice trailed away and she rubbed at her neck absently. These two placid cops . . . how could she explain the panic she'd felt when the man with the familiar razored teeth fastened his gaze on hers in front of the Toys 'R' Us store? She was only window-shopping with the babies, of course—she had no money for anything other than the essentials—but Sondra had forgotten all about the silly mechanical dog that yapped happily from behind the plate glass. The wide, brightly-lit corridors and garish lights of the mall had done an odd sort of spin and fade, until nothing remained in the world but her, and *him* . . . and the twins, of course. Their little arms waving in the air as they began to cry for him, as mesmerized as her by his dark presence amid the shine and hustle.

"He what?" prompted McShaw. Pen poised above his clipboard, another three dozen boxes to be filled and checked-off before he could leave for his next coffee-shop appointment.

Sondra swallowed. Careful now, she warned herself. Be very, *very* careful. "I've seen him following us before."

The younger policeman's attention picked up. "How many times?"

"Twice," she said. "Once when I took the children to the clinic, and once when we were out for a walk."

"So he knows where you live?"

Walters's voice had sharpened, but instead of feeling vindicated, Sondra had the urge to slap him. Why should she have to lie to get them to protect her? Because being stalked once or twice was okay, but the magical number *three* was not. "I'm afraid to go out anymore."

"Tell us about the other two times," McShaw said.

Abruptly, Sondra stood. "Would you . . . like some coffee?" she asked shakily. "I'm going to pour myself a cup."

"If it's no trouble." The older policeman looked at her speculatively.

"None at all." She walked to the door of the nursery and checked inside before pulling it shut. Mallory and Meleena were settling down for a nap within the netted confines of the playpen, their soft, chubby bodies curled around each other like well fed kittens. The door firmly closed, she turned back to the men waiting on the couch. "Sugar? Cream?"

"Black is fine," Walters said. "For both of us."

Sondra nodded and hurried to the kitchen, fumbling out mismatched mugs from one of the cabinets and making sure none of the nasty cockroach egg casings were stuck to the bottom. The insects in this place were a terrible problem and she didn't want to be embarrassed, but what could she expect from a place of hiding, a place of exile?

The coffee was too strong from sitting on the burner since this morning, and she didn't really want any, but she needed time to gather her thoughts so she didn't screw up the story. Her claim of seeing the man who hunted her and her babies by the clinic had been a lie, but Sondra could gloss that over by saying she'd only had a glimpse of him then; they might write that sighting off, but they might not. Saying he knew where they lived was the truth, as was telling that he trailed after them every time she stepped out of the house, a specter of living hunger that was impossible to deny.

Her knees went suddenly weak and she leaned against the counter for support. Would any of this do any good? Perhaps she would have to run again, flee in an endless, exhausting effort to give her babies a normal life. Dear God, would he never let them be?

Without warning his mocking, cruel chuckle filled her mind and the memory of his frigid hands sliding over her skin made her flush—

"Open your legs."

"No!"

His eyes were black, his gaze oddly sprinkled with yellow glitter, like a reflection of a midnight sky swollen with stars. His fingers, tipped with nails sharp enough to split her skin, scraped along the insides of her thighs. His touch made her veins throb with need.

"Bear my children."

"Let me go!" she cried. She cursed him, then damned her own body as her thin knees began to spread. Lying against the black sheets, her limbs were like the petals of a pale lily unfolding to float upon an onyx ocean.

"I will fill you with blood and fire," he whispered in her ear as his body weighed her down and pierced her with exquisite ice. Her insides pulsed around him in involuntary response and he moaned against her neck as he rocked, a wolf's growl of pleasure as the sharp edges of his teeth rubbed along her throat, so very close to the one thing he had yet to steal from her. Everything else was gone; her pride, her self-esteem, her virginity. She was his harlot and his slave, and soon she would carry the ultimate proof that he had used her. Surely he would allow her to keep the final, fragile bit of her humanity that pumped within her arteries. Surely—

The sugar jar jittered dangerously in her grasp and she slammed it on the counter and decided to do without rather than risk spilling it. *He* had sent the cockroaches to this place to torment her, to try and make her leave, and she'd be damned if she'd do anything to feed them. Turning to the sink, Sondra rinsed her hands and face in cool water, then used a paper towel to pat her skin dry. Easy does it, she told herself. Ten more seconds and her hands were steady enough to fish a battered rectangular cake pan from the drawer by the oven and use it as a makeshift serving tray to hold the mugs. She nearly dropped it when she turned from the counter and found the younger of the cops standing directly behind her. His eyes met hers and she felt trapped for an instant, came perilously close to telling him everything, the whole corrupt story burning at the edges of her lips. On the battered aluminum surface, the mugs rattled against each other.

"I'll take that for you," Walters said. He reached for the pan and his fingers, cold like hers, brushed her arm. His face was unreadable but his touch left her oddly weak, disoriented. Standing before him in the small kitchen, Sondra saw that she'd been wrong about his build; he wasn't overweight at all. In fact, his entire body seemed to have elongated somehow and become lean, like a dog that looks soft and warm and sleepy until it stands up and stretches. Fear bubbled into Sondra's throat, but he only took her elbow with his free hand and guided her toward the living room and his waiting partner, his flesh burning against her own like dry ice.

McShaw looked up from scribbling on his form and dropped his pen onto the coffee table, reaching eagerly for one of the mugs. Sondra sank onto the worn love seat with a feeling of relief that shattered when Walters settled loosely next to her instead of returning to his place on the old rocking chair across the coffee table. Everything about the apartment was small: the rooms, the windows and the meager amount of sunlight they permitted inside, the furniture; his thigh, bunched with muscle beneath the fabric of his slacks, pressed coolly against hers, but there was nowhere for her to move to get away. Was she suffocating here or was the pulse hammering in her throat simply getting in the way of the air trying to flow into her lungs?

"Okay," McShaw said after a moment. He made no move to pick up the clipboard he'd set on the table next to his pen. "Tell us about the other two times."

"I thought I saw him when I took the babies to the pediatrician at the free clinic last Tuesday," Sondra said hoarsely. She was proud of the way she kept her voice from shaking, from giving away her petty deception. "Following us again. But it was too crowded there and when we got out it was rush hour. He was gone."

"You thought?"

Sondra nodded but didn't elaborate. Let them discount this one if they wanted; it was a lie anyway, mere icing on an already poisoned cake.

"And when was the other time?"

"Last . . . night. I took the babies up to the park for the fall festival. He wwas there, and he followed us home."

McShaw leaned forward. "Ms. Underwood, if he followed you home last night, why did you wait until this morning to call us?"

Sondra looked at her hands, the knuckles red from scrubbing furiously at the filth of this place, the fingernails strangely white under the edges from baby powder. "II don't know," she whispered. "I guess I was hoping he would just go away, but when I got up this morning and I thought about it, I realized that's probably not going to happen."

"Has he ever tried to make contact? Threatened you?" Walters's voice was smooth and vaguely . . . *sweet*, like one of those expensive frozen drinks the upscale restaurants served. She thought she heard all kinds of innuendo in it, as rich and varied as the variety of liquors dumped into the exotic glasses edged with garnishes made of fruit and plastic sticks.

Sondra's gaze found his unwillingly and she lost herself for a single, panicked moment, snapped back in time to answer before McShaw noticed her lag. "No." With a dying feeling, she realized how lame all of this must sound and she had to force the answer past her stiff lips. She had called too soon, they would never believe her; she was alone in her efforts to protect Mallory and Meleena, as she had been from the moment of their birth—

"We're going to have to call a doctor," the midwife said grimly. Sondra lifted her head and saw the woman's heavy, black face peering back at her through the inverted triangle of her spread legs and over the spasming mound of her bloated stomach. Apprehension made her south side accent run the words together. "You're bleeding too much and you've been in labor way too long."

"No doctor," Sondra hissed. The refusal ended in a scream as agony rippled through her uterus, as if the child inside were trying to tear its way through the prison of tissue and mother's blood. Had it heard the midwife's words and realized the danger of prolonging her agony? "It's coming now!" she screamed and pushed, bore down as she had never done before to expel the thing within her body that was trying to kill her.

"I see it—push again!" The midwife's hands were warm and wet with Sondra's blood and they pried at her ravaged flesh for a moment, then locked around something huge and painful. "I've got the head. Come on, Sondra—if you don't keep pushing you'll kill it and yourself besides!"

Sondra screamed again and dug into the sides of the mattress with her fingernails, felt the decrepit fabric tear at the same time as the child shot from her body with a wave of pain that nearly made her lose consciousness. Dear God, she thought disjointedly as she fought to find her breath, why hadn't the mound of her stomach grown smaller? Was it afterbirth—could the fruits of her coupling have filled her with that much dark debris?

She was still panting from Mallory's birth when deep within her belly the fire began anew, making her writhe on the soaked sheets and open her mouth in a scream too huge to be heard. The midwife was there in an instant, her large, slick hands working at Sondra's belly, kneading and pressing—

"Twins!" she declared. "Hold on, girl—there's another one coming!"

Sondra's wail found substance as a second child forced its way free. Something deep inside her relaxed and let her breathe, disregarded the short, puny cramps that followed as the midwife worked her stomach to get Sondra's body to eject the bloody afterbirth. "What . . .?" Sondra finally managed, sucking in welcome air as she fought to sit up. "W—what are they?"

"Girls," the midwife said, turning back to the changing table. "Just as healthy as can be, too. A little over six and a half pounds each—big for twins." Despite her assurances, the black woman's voice was reserved, puzzled. Exhausted,

Sondra listened to the splash of water from the basin as the midwife expertly sponged down the infants, then wrapped them in receiving blankets.

"Can I see?"

"Here you go. One for each arm."

Warmth settled on either side of her and Sondra tucked her chin to her chest for a glimpse of her babies. Sleeping already, come into the world without so much as a whimper; tiny fingers bunched into loose fists, delicate lips still bluish-purple but pinkening by the second. Their heads were crowned with thick, wet hair above perfect eyebrows and petite, tilted noses; as she gazed at them, the second one—Meleena—spread her heart-shaped mouth in a barely discernible yawn.

Sondra jerked and both babies opened their eyes and regarded her solemnly. "What was that?" she asked. Her voice was shaking.

For a moment the midwife said nothing, then the big woman folded her hands in front of her as though she were trying to pray unobtrusively. "Something I've never seen on a newborn," she said at last. "Teeth."

—and now Sondra faced a new danger: Walters. There was something about him that reminded her of the twins' father, an elusive call to forbidden sexuality that she'd thought only one man, one creature, possessed.

"Open your legs."

"No!"

"Bear my children."

She gasped when someone touched her arm, then realized it was McShaw. "Are you all right, Ms. Underwood? You don't look like you feel very well."

"I'm ffine," Sondra stammered. "Tired, that's all. It's hard to get a good night's sleep with two crying babies." She clamped her lips shut, abruptly afraid she was whining. It was another lie anyway; the twins never cried. Her sleep was broken by the stealthy creaking of the stairs in the hallway outside the apartment, a thousand phantom shadows in the corners of the dark rooms, the hushed rasp of steel fingernails along the bottom of the too-flimsy front door.

Walters nodded sympathetically and for a moment she had the absurd notion that he could read her mind. "Of course," he said. "We understand."

Sondra bit back a sharp remark and they both stood, as if some invisible puppet master had pulled the "up" strings simultaneously. She found herself watching the subtle movement of muscles beneath the taut fabric of Walters's uniform, then flushed when her gaze traveled to his face and she realized he was watching her watch him. For the first time she noticed that his eyes were a strange yellowish color unlike anything she'd ever seen, the stare of a lion surveying its prey.

"If you see him again, you call 911," McShaw said. "Plus we'll put your building down for a few extra drive-bys every shift, try to make the squad cars more visible. Until you give us something more concrete, that's about all we can do. I'm sorry." The chunkier cop looked down at his clipboard and frowned. "It doesn't seem like he's ever gotten close enough for you to get a solid description."

Sondra opened her mouth, then shut it again when Walters ran his catcolored gaze across her. She'd been about to say *He looks like* him, and point to Officer Walters; horrified, she put a trembling hand to her mouth and prayed McShaw wouldn't see her shivering. Was there that much of a resemblance? No, of course not.

Of course not.

Open your legs.

Walters was the last of the two to go out the front door. She didn't know why the tense words came, but when he looked back at her, all she could say was, "He wants the twins."

He nodded. "I know." Before she could close the door, he reached back through the opening and placed his fingers lightly on her wrist—a speed search for the hot pulse of life just below the skin?—then glanced surreptitiously toward his partner's retreating back, as though he were her colleague in some great and secret conspiracy. "I'll be in touch," he whispered.

I will fill you with blood and fire.

Sondra slammed the front door and stood trembling with anticipation and terror.

The babies were bathed and fed and put down for the night. They lay crowded against each other in the playpen—she couldn't afford a crib—content and quiet, like two halves of a whole. Sondra watched them for a while, knowing they wouldn't close their eyes for hours, wondering what they'd be like when they grew up. Right now they were small for their age, but would they catch up later? Go through one of those amazing growth spurts that parents were always crowing about and pediatricians predicted with nauseating regularity? She wished she could think of a way to keep them small and safe forever, by her side and without the sweet, dangerous offering of the rest of the world.

After a while she went into the bathroom and stared at herself in the mirror. Her image was shell-shocked and pale, a thin face with prominent cheekbones and a nondescript nose, hazel eyes undercut with purple shadows of exhaustion. Budget shopping and constant worrying had made her gaunt and graceless, left her mouth an oversize flesh-colored slash across the bottom part of her face. Even her brown hair was nothing special—cut to shoulder length, then falling into a stupid wave that made the ends go in all directions. What was it about her that drew them? Why *her?*

"*Because you are one among millions, Sondra.*"

She spun with a slow motion movement that felt like she was trying to turn underwater. "You!"

Officer Walters gave her a handsome smile. "I told you I'd . . . be in touch."

Sondra took a step backward, felt the sharp edge of the cheap drawer-pull dig into her spine. For a moment she thought it was teeth and her knees tried to buckle; she locked her muscles and felt behind her for reas-surance—an old, bent brass handle, that's all. "How—how did you get in?"

"The door was unlocked."

"That's impossible," she said hotly. "I didn't—"

He was standing in front of her before she had time to form her next word, the width of the room no more than a blink between them. What-ever she was going to say broke off when his hand, cool and white and alarmingly powerful, reached up to cup her jaw. His thumb skated deli-cately along the line of bone, then skipped up to trace her lips. "I think you left it open for me—"

"No!"

"—didn't you?" Walters leaned over her, his face only an inch away. His breath was thick and meaty but not unpleasant, a cool, unnatural draft against her cheeks. He looked different than he had earlier, as if the chunky, donutplied town-cop were only a costume he donned to give ste-reotypical service to the public job and complement his partner's rotund figure. The basic features were still there, but now he looked like a preda-tor, something long and sleek and dark; a panther, slipping through the night that was her life and ready to ambush its quarry.

"Please," she heard herself say. She wanted to cry, but her eyes were as dry as her mouth. "Don't touch me."

"You don't mean that," Walters murmured against her neck as he grasped her upper arms and pulled her from the bathroom and into the cramped kitchen. Sondra tried to turn her head and made the monu-mental mistake of locking gazes with him. Immediately she felt like she was dropping through space, an exhilarating dive from a hundred-story building and no concern about the unyielding earth rushing up to crash into her; she would have tilted sideways except that he was pressed fully against her now, holding her, the temperature of his skin bleeding through both his clothes and hers.

"Open yourself to me, Sondra."

His voice had deepened and twisted and sounded so much like the other's that a moan of dread made it past her lips. Shivering violently, she could be lying facedown on a blanket of finished leather for all the heat she felt from his muscular chest, the hard plane of his stomach, the firm pressure of his thighs. Her heart was slamming in her chest long before his fingers hooked around the collar of her blouse and tore it open.

"You can do this for me, make a miracle. Let me be inside you—"

"I am not a fucking breeding farm!" Sondra wailed. "Get away from me!" She tried to beat at him but she was pinned against the wall, the refrigerator, against *something* that made it impossible to escape. When his hands slid over her breasts and cupped them, then began to massage away the chill of his own touch, she wanted to screech as she unwillingly pressed her hips against his and her fingers tangled in the heavy locks of his hair to yank him closer.

"I can make you warm again, my sweet. I can fulfill you. With blood—"

His teeth, so sharp and wet, scratched along the line of her neck and sent a spike of pleasure into the deepest pit of her stomach.

"—and fire."

In response, damning herself the entire time, she started tearing at his clothes, desperate to feel his wintry flesh against her heat, shuddering with the need to cool the fire he'd started inside her. Sondra screamed as he took her standing against a kitchen cabinet, then screamed again when she came and remembered she didn't even know his first name.

"Nicholas will come for you," Sondra said woodenly. It was the first time she'd spoken the other's name aloud since the night sixteen months before when he had first possessed her mind and body in a basement bedroom more than five hundred miles away. Perhaps she deserved all of this for letting him bewitch her so easily back then, allowing him to pick her up in a bar and enchant her into following him docilely into his loft apartment with the huge windows and blacksheeted, oversize bed. But how well she had suffered for her weakness! She should have been stronger then; she should have been stronger tonight. But she was nothing to Nicholas, or to Walters, a poorly used and ragged feather, blown crazily about by the wind of their cravings. "He might even kill you."

Her words were slurred with cold, her legs still sticky with the testimony of their mating. The dull tiles of the kitchen floor beneath her bare skin were freezing, the unseasonable cold outside seeping through the concrete foundation and crawling up her limbs and lower back. She wanted to move, get up and huddle within something warm until she could feel her blood pulse once again in her veins, but Walters had wrapped his legs and arms around her from behind like a giant spider sucking the essence out of its juiciest kill. Even the cockroaches had gone, fled from this oh-so-superior hunter.

"Nicholas only wants to see his children," Walters said against her hair. His lips nuzzled the strands, tongue flicking out now and then to taste. "If you allow him a meager visit every so often, everyone will be happier. His mind is . . . younger, more fickle. His life has lacked experience and the babies will prove overwhelming—I doubt he'll even stay. Instead you run from place to place like a terrified jackrabbit with her offspring, forcing him to follow and calling the police every time he comes too close. But I am not so foolish or irresponsible as brother Nicholas, my love."

"What do you mean, *brother*? What are you talking about?" Panicked by the realization that he knew their pursuer was actually the twins' father, Sondra tried to twist out of Walters's grasp and face him, but the arm across her rib cage was like a tight steel band. She started kicking at his feet in frustration and his free hand dipped between her legs and stroked; behind her spine he began to harden again and he ground his hipbones against her and started to rock. Gasping with shame and pleasure, her hands gripped his knees as her legs parted and she arched to meet his fingers. She forgot the icy kitchen floor and the disappearing cockroaches and most of everything else as Walters probed and readied her, finally raised her whole body effortlessly and settled it on his. Beyond the orgasm pounding through her senses, Sondra still managed her strangled question. "What did you *mean*?"

"*I thought it was clear*," Walters said. His voice had deepened to the familiar sexual growl and he rolled forward with her, still joined, until Sondra was on her knees beneath him. One of his large hands slipped beneath her left arm and encircled her throat; he didn't squeeze—never that—simply held tight enough to feel the hot rush of her pulse through the artery so close to his killing fingers. The feel of her blood excited him more and he drove deeper into her, making her cry out in surprise and spiraling ecstasy. His other arm snaked across her hipbones and lifted until her knees were clear of the floor and she dangled from his body with only her fisted hands to keep her face from banging against the tiles. Flopping loosely in the air while he fucked her like she was some kind of whore doll, Sondra would have been furious except for the tenderness in his dark voice and the convulsions of rapture that were enveloping her. The words in her ear were like icecrusted velvet as his mouth grazed the soft juncture of her throat and shoulder and left another barely bloody scratch for him to suckle like an infant.

"*Remember what I said, Sondra? You're one among millions, able to do something which should be treasured. And I will do just that. I will exalt you and place you above all else, forever.*"

Sondra didn't know if it was his next words and the way his hand moved from her throat to caress her waiting belly, her rippling, final orgasm, or her sanity giving way that made her begin to shriek as he came and filled her with a blazing, bloodstreaked icy liquid and passion.

"*Unlike my twin brother Nicholas, I will be with you at every moment as you carry my precious sons and bear them into this world.*"

Luella Miller

Mary E. Wilkins-Freeman

Mary Eleanor Wilkins (1852–1930) was born in Randolph, Massachusetts. Her husband, Dr. Charles Manning Freeman, was an alcoholic who was committed to the state hospital for the insane in 1920, where he died three years later.

Having made her literary debut in 1881 with a ballad for children, her poems and fiction appeared in a number of publications. A member of the regionalist "local color" movement of American fiction, she wrote twelve novels, including *Jane Field* (1892), *The Shoulders of Atlas* (1908), and *The Butterfly House* (1912), and some of her more than two hundred short stories are collected in *A Humble Romance and Other Stories* (1887), *A New England Nun and Other Stories* (1891), and *The Best Stories of Mary E. Wilkins* (1927). In April 1926, the author received the William Dean Howells Gold Medal for Fiction from the American Academy of Letters.

During her lifetime, only six of the author's supernatural stories were collected between hardcovers, in *The Wind in the Rose-Bush and Other Stories of the Supernatural* (1903). The 1974 Arkham House volume, *Collected Ghost Stories*, added five more.

One of her most famous tales was adapted for the 1970 episode "Certain Shadows on the Wall" of the TV series *Rod Serling's Night Gallery*. It is a pity that nobody has yet attempted to film the classic vampire tale that follows . . .

CLOSE TO THE village street stood the one-story house in which Luella Miller, who had an evil name in the village, had dwelt. She had been dead for years, yet there were those in the village who, in spite of the clearer light which comes on a vantage-point from a long-past danger, half-believed in the tale which they had heard from their childhood. In their hearts, although they scarcely would have owned it, was a survival of the wild horror and frenzied fear of their ancestors who had dwelt in the same age with Luella Miller. Young people even would stare with a shudder at the old house as they passed, and children never played around it as was their wont around an untenanted building. Not a window in the old Miller house was broken: the panes reflected the morning sunlight in patches of emerald and blue, and the latch of the sagging front door was never lifted, although no bolt secured it. Since Luella Miller had been carried out of it, the house had had no tenant except one friendless old soul who had no choice between that and the far-off shelter of the open sky. This old woman, who had survived her kindred and friends, lived in the house one week, then one morning no smoke came out of the chimney, and a body of neighbors, a score strong, entered and found her dead in her bed. There were dark whispers as to the cause of her death, and there were those who testified to an expression of fear so exalted that it showed forth the state of the departing soul upon the dead face. The old woman had been hale and hearty when she entered the house, and in seven days she was dead; it seemed that she had fallen a victim to some uncanny power. The minister talked in the pulpit with covert severity against the sin of superstition; still the belief prevailed. Not a soul in the village but would have chosen the almshouse rather than that dwelling. No vagrant, if he heard the tale, would seek shelter beneath that old roof, unhallowed by nearly half a century of superstitious fear.

There was only one person in the village who had actually known Luella Miller. That person was a woman well over eighty, but a marvel of vitality and unextinct youth. Straight as an arrow, with the spring of one recently let loose from the bow of life, she moved about the streets, and she always went to church, rain or shine. She had never married, and had lived alone for years in a house across the road from Luella Miller's.

This woman had none of the garrulousness of age, but never in all her life had she ever held her tongue for any will save her own, and she never spared the truth when she essayed to present it. She it was who bore testimony to the life, evil, though possibly wittingly or designedly so, of Luella Miller, and to her personal appearance. When this old woman spoke— and she had the gift of description, although her thoughts were clothed in the rude vernacular of her native village—one could seem to see Luella Miller as she had really looked. According to this woman, Lydia Anderson by name, Luella Miller had been a beauty of a type rather unusual in New England. She had been a slight, pliant sort of creature, as ready with a strong yielding to fate and as unbreakable as a willow. She had glimmering lengths of straight, fair hair, which she wore softly looped round a long, lovely face. She had blue eyes full of soft pleading, little slender, clinging hands, and a wonderful grace of motion and attitude.

"Luella Miller used to sit in a way nobody else could if they sat up and studied a week of Sundays," said Lydia Anderson, "and it was a sight to see her walk. If one of them willows over there on the edge of the brook could start up and get its roots free of the ground, and move off, it would go just the way Luella Miller used to. She had a green shot silk she used to wear, too, and a hat with green ribbon streamers, and a lace veil blowing across her face and out sideways, and a green ribbon flyin' from her waist. That was what she came out bride in when she married Erastus Miller. Her name before she was married was Hill. There was always a sight of 'l's' in her name, married or single. Erastus Miller was good lookin', too, better lookin' than Luella. Sometimes I used to think that Luella wa'n't so handsome after all. Erastus just about worshiped her. I used to know him pretty well. He lived next door to me, and we went to school together. Folks used to say he was waitin' on me, but he wa'n't. I never thought he was except once or twice when he said things that some girls might have suspected meant somethin'. That was before Luella came here to teach the district school. It was funny how she came to get it, for folks said she hadn't any education, and that one of the big girls, Lottie Henderson, used to do all the teachin' for her, while she sat back and did embroidery work on a cambric pocket-handkerchief. Lottie Henderson was a real smart girl, a splendid scholar, and she just set her eyes by Luella, as all the girls did. Lottie would have made a real smart woman, but she died when Luella had been here about a year—just faded away and died: nobody knew what ailed her. She dragged herself to that schoolhouse and helped Luella teach till the very last minute. The committee all knew how Luella didn't do much of the work herself, but they winked at it. It wa'n't long after Lottie died that Erastus married her. I always thought he hurried it up because she wa'n't fit to teach. One of the big boys used to help her after Lottie died, but he hadn't much government, and the school didn't do very well, and Luella might have had to give it up, for the committee couldn't have shut their eyes to things much longer. The boy that helped her was a real honest, innocent sort of fellow, and he was a good scholar, too. Folks said he over-studied, and that was the reason he was took crazy the year after Luella married, but I don't know. And I don't know what made Erastus Miller go into consumption of the blood the year after he was married: consumption wa'n't in his family. He just grew weaker and weaker, and went almost bent double when he tried to wait on Luella, and he spoke feeble, like an old man. He worked terrible hard till the last try-ing to save up a little to leave Luella. I've seen him out in the worst storms on a wood-sled—he used to cut and sell wood—and he was hunched up on top lookin' more dead than alive. Once I couldn't stand it: I went over and helped him pitch some wood on the cart—I was always strong in my arms. I wouldn't stop for all he told me to, and I guess he was glad enough for the help. That was only a week before he died. He fell on the kitchen floor while he was gettin' breakfast. He always got the breakfast and let Luella lay abed. He did all the sweepin' and the washin' and the ironin' and most of the cookin'. He couldn't bear to have Luella lift her finger, and she let him do for her. She lived like a queen for all the work she did. She didn't even do her sewin'. She said it made her shoulder ache to sew, and poor Erastus's sister Lily used to do all her sewin'. She wa'n't able to, either; she was never strong in her back, but she did it beautifully. She had to, to suit Luella, she was so dreadful particular. I never saw anythin' like the fagottin' and hemstitchin' that Lily Miller did for Luella. She made all Luella's weddin' outfit, and that green silk dress, after Maria Babbit cut it. Maria she cut it for nothin', and she did a lot more cuttin' and fittin' for nothin' for Luella, too. Lily Miller went to live with Luella after Erastus died. She gave up her home, though she was real attached to it and wa'n't a mite afraid to stay alone. She rented it and she went to live with Luella right away after the funeral."

Then this old woman, Lydia Anderson, who remembered Luella Miller, would go on to relate the story of Lily Miller. It seemed that on the removal of Lily Miller to the house of her dead brother, to live with his widow, the village people first began to talk. This Lily Miller had been hardly past her first youth, and a most robust and blooming woman, rosy-cheeked, with curls of strong, black hair overshadowing round, candid temples and bright dark eyes. It was not six months after she had taken up her residence with her sister-in-law that her rosy color faded and her pretty curves became wan hollows. White shadows began to show in the black rings of her hair, and the light died out of her eyes, her features sharpened, and there were pathetic lines at her mouth, which yet wore always an expression of utter sweetness and even happiness. She was devoted to her sister; there was no doubt that she loved her with her whole heart, and was perfectly content in her service. It was her sole anxiety lest she should die and leave her alone.

"The way Lily Miller used to talk about Luella was enough to make you mad and enough to make you cry," said Lydia Anderson. "I've been in there sometimes toward the last when she was too feeble to cook and carried her some blancmange or custard—somethin' I thought she might relish, and she'd thank me, and when I asked her how she was, say she felt better than she did yesterday, and asked me if I didn't think she looked better, dreadful pitiful, and say poor Luella had an awful time takin' care of her and doin' the work—she wa'n't strong enough to do anythin'—when all the time Luella wa'n't liftin' her finger and poor Lily didn't get any care except what the neighbors gave her, and Luella eat up everythin' that was carried in for Lily. I had it real straight that she did. Luella used to just sit and cry and do nothin'. She did act real fond of Lily, and she pined away considerable, too. There was those that thought she'd go into a decline herself. But after Lily died, her Aunt Abby Mixter came, and then Luella picked up and grew as fat and rosy as ever. But poor Aunt Abby begun to droop just the way Lily had, and I guess somebody wrote to her married daughter, Mrs. Sam Abbot, who lived in Barre, for she wrote her mother that she must leave right away and come and make her a visit, but Aunt Abby wouldn't go. I can see her now. She was a real good-lookin' woman, tall and large, with a big, square face and a high forehead that looked of itself kind of benevolent and good. She just tended out on Luella as if she had been a baby, and when her married daughter sent for her she wouldn't stir one inch. She'd always thought a lot of her daughter, too, but she said Luella needed her and her married daughter didn't. Her daughter kept writin' and writin', but it didn't do any good. Finally she came, and when she saw how bad her mother looked, she broke down and cried and all but went on her knees to have her come away. She spoke her mind out to Luella, too. She told her that she'd killed her husband and everybody that had anythin' to do with her, and she'd thank her to leave her mother alone. Luella went into hysterics, and Aunt Abby was so frightened that she called me after her daughter went. Mrs. Sam Abbot she went away fairly cryin' out loud in the buggy, the neighbors heard her, and well she might, for she never saw her mother again alive. I went in that night when Aunt Abby called for me, standin' in the door with her little green-checked shawl over her head. I can see her now. 'Do come over here, Miss Anderson,' she sung out, kind of gasping for breath. I didn't stop for anythin'. I put over as fast as I could, and when I got there, there was Luella laughin' and cryin' all together, and Aunt Abby trying to hush her, and all the time she herself was white as a sheet and shakin' so she could hardly stand. 'For the land sakes, Mrs. Mixter,' says I, 'you look worse than she does. You ain't fit to be up out of your bed.'

"'Oh, there ain't anythin' the matter with me,' says she. Then she went on talkin' to Luella. 'There, there, don't, don't, poor little lamb,' says she. 'Aunt Abby is here. She ain't goin' away and leave you. Don't, poor little lamb.'

"'Do leave her with me, Mrs. Mixter, and you get back to bed,' says I, for Aunt Abby had been layin' down considerable lately, though somehow she contrived to do the work.

"'I'm well enough,' says she. 'Don't you think she had better have the doctor, Miss Anderson?'

"'The doctor,' says I, 'I think you had better have the doctor. I think you need him much worse than some folks I could mention.' And I looked right straight at Luella Miller laughin' and cryin' and goin' on as if she was the center of all creation. All the time she was actin' so—seemed as if she was too sick to sense anythin'—she was keepin' a sharp lookout as to how we took it out of the corner of one eye. I see her. You could never cheat me about Luella Miller. Finally I got real mad and I run home and I got a bottle of valerian I had, and I poured some boilin' hot water on a handful of catnip, and I mixed up that catnip tea with most half a wine-glass of valerian, and I went with it over to Luella's. I marched right up to Luella, a-holdin' out that cup, all smokin'. 'Now,' says I, 'Luella Miller, *you swallar this!*'

"'What is—what is it, oh, what is it?' she sort of screeches out. Then she goes off a-laughin' enough to kill.

"'Poor lamb, poor little lamb,' says Aunt Abby, standin' over her, all kind of tottery, and tryin' to bathe her head with camphor.

"'*You swaller this right down*,' says I. And I didn't waste any ceremony. I just took hold of Luella Miller's chin and I tipped her head back, and I caught her mouth open with laughin', and I clapped that cup to her lips, and I fairly hollered at her: 'Swaller, swaller, swaller!' and she gulped it right down. She had to, and I guess it did her good. Anyhow, she stopped cryin' and laughin' and let me put her to bed, and she went to sleep like a baby inside of half an hour. That was more than poor Aunt Abby did. She lay awake all that night and I stayed with her, though she tried not to have me; said she wa'n't sick enough for watchers. But I stayed, and I made some good cornmeal gruel and I fed her a teaspoon every little while all night long. It seemed to me as if she was jest dyin' from bein' all wore out. In the mornin' as soon as it was light I run over to the Bisbees and sent Johnny Bisbee for the doctor. I told him to tell the doctor to hurry, and he come pretty quick. Poor Aunt Abby didn't seem to know much of anythin' when he got there. You couldn't hardly tell she breathed, she was so used up. When the doctor had gone, Luella came into the room lookin' like a baby in her ruffled nightgown. I can see her now. Her eyes were as blue and her face all pink and white like a blossom, and she looked at Aunt Abby in the bed sort of innocent and surprised. 'Why,' says she, 'Aunt Abby ain't got up yet?'

"'No, she ain't,' says I, pretty short.

"'I thought I didn't smell the coffee,' says Luella.

"'Coffee,' says I. 'I guess if you have coffee this mornin' you'll make it yourself.'

"'I never made the coffee in all my life,' says she, dreadful astonished. 'Erastus always made the coffee as long as he lived, and then Lily she made it, and then Aunt Abby made it. I don't believe I *can* make the coffee, Miss Anderson.'

"'You can make it or go without, jest as you please,' says I.

"'Ain't Aunt Abby goin' to get up?' says she.

"'I guess she won't get up,' says I, 'sick as she is.' I was gettin' madder and madder. There was somethin' about that little pink-and-white thing standin' there and talkin' about coffee, when she had killed so many better folks than she was, and had jest killed another, that made me feel 'most as if I wished somebody would up and kill her before she had a chance to do any more harm.

"'Is Aunt Abby sick?' says Luella, as if she was sort of aggrieved and injured.

"'Yes,' says I, 'she's sick, and she's goin' to die, and then you'll be left alone, and you'll have to do for yourself and wait on yourself, or do without things.' I don't know but I was sort of hard, but it was the truth, and if I was any harder than Luella Miller had been I'll give up. I ain't never been sorry that I said it. Well, Luella, she up and had hysterics again at that, and I jest let her have 'em. All I did was to bundle her into the room on the other side of the entry where Aunt Abby couldn't hear her, if she wa'n't past it—I don't know but she was—and set her down hard in a chair and told her not to come back into the other room, and she minded. She had her hysterics in there till she got tired. When she found out that nobody was comin' to coddle her and do for her she stopped. At least I suppose she did. I had all I could do with poor Aunt Abby tryin' to keep the breath of life in her. The doctor had told me that she was dreadful low, and give me some very strong medicine to give to her in drops real often, and told me real particular about the nourishment. Well, I did as he told me real faithful till she wa'n't able to swaller any longer. Then I had her daughter sent for. I had begun to realize that she wouldn't last any time at all. I hadn't realized it before, though I spoke to Luella the way I did. The doctor he came, and Mrs. Sam Abbot, but when she got there it was too late; her mother was dead. Aunt Abby's daughter just give one look at her mother layin' there, then she turned sort of sharp and sudden and looked at me.

"'Where is she?' says she, and I knew she meant Luella.

"'She's out in the kitchen,' says I. 'She's too nervous to see folks die. She's afraid it will make her sick.'

"The doctor he speaks up then. He was a young man. Old Doctor Park had died the year before, and this was a young fellow just out of college. 'Mrs. Miller is not strong,' says he, kind of severe, 'and she is quite right in not agitating herself.'

"*You are another, young man; she's got her pretty claw on you*, thinks I, but I didn't say anythin' to him. I just said over to Mrs. Sam Abbot that Luella was in the kitchen, and Mrs. Sam Abbot she went out there, and I went, too, and I never heard anythin' like the way she talked to Luella

Miller. I felt pretty hard to Luella myself, but this was more than I ever would have dared to say. Luella she was too scared to go into hysterics. She jest flopped. She seemed to jest shrink away to nothin' in that kitchen chair, with Mrs. Sam Abbot standin' over her and talkin' and tellin' her the truth. I guess the truth was most too much for her and no mistake, because Luella presently actually did faint away, and there wa'n't any sham about it, the way I always suspected there was about them hysterics. She fainted dead away and we had to lay her flat on the floor, and the Doctor he came runnin' out and he said somethin' about a weak heart dreadful fierce to Mrs. Sam Abbot, but she wa'n't a mite scared. She faced him jest as white as even Luella was layin' there lookin' like death and the Doctor feelin' of her pulse.

"'Weak heart,' says she, 'weak heart; weak fiddlesticks! There ain't nothin' weak about that woman. She's got strength enough to hang onto other folks till she kills 'em. Weak? It was my poor mother that was weak: this woman killed her as sure as if she had taken a knife to her.'

"But the doctor he didn't pay much attention. He was bendin' over Luella layin' there with her yellow hair all streamin' and her pretty pink-and-white face all pale, and her blue eyes like stars gone out, and he was holdin' onto her hand and smoothin' her forehead, and tellin' me to get the brandy in Aunt Abby's room, and I was sure as I wanted to be that Luella had got somebody else to hang onto, now Aunt Abby was gone, and I thought of poor Erastus Miller, and I sort of pitied the poor young doctor, led away by a pretty face, and I made up my mind I'd see what I could do.

"I waited till Aunt Abby had been dead and buried about a month, and the doctor was goin' to see Luella steady and folks were beginnin' to talk; then one evenin', when I knew the doctor had been called out of town and wouldn't be round, I went over to Luella's. I found her all dressed up in a blue muslin with white polka dots on it, and her hair curled jest as pretty, and there wa'n't a young girl in the place could compare with her. There was somethin' about Luella Miller seemed to draw the heart right out of you, but she didn't draw it out of *me*. She was settin' rocking in the chair by her sittin'-room window, and Maria Brown had gone home. Maria Brown had been in to help her, or rather to do the work, for Luella wa'n't helped when she didn't do anythin'. Maria Brown was real capable and she didn't have any ties; she wa'n't married, and lived alone, so she'd offered. I couldn't see why she should do the work any more than Luella; she wa'n't any too strong; but she seemed to think she could and Luella seemed to think so, too, so she went over and did all the work—washed, and ironed, and baked, while Luella sat and rocked. Maria didn't live long afterward. She began to fade away just the same fashion the others had. Well, she was warned, but she acted real mad when folks said anythin': said Luella was a poor, abused woman, too delicate to help herself, and they'd ought to be ashamed, and if she died helpin' them that couldn't help themselves she would—and she did.

"'I s'pose Maria has gone home,' says I to Luella, when I had gone in and sat down opposite her.

"'Yes, Maria went half an hour ago, after she had got supper and washed the dishes,' says Luella, in her pretty way.

"'I suppose she has got a lot of work to do in her own house tonight,' says I, kind of bitter, but that was all thrown away on Luella Miller. It seemed to her right that other folks that wa'n't any better able than she was herself should wait on her, and she couldn't get it through her head that anybody should think it *wa'n't* right.

"'Yes,' says Luella, real sweet and pretty, 'yes, she said she had to do her washin' tonight. She has let it go for a fortnight along of comin' over here.'

"'Why don't she stay home and do her washin' instead of comin' over here and doin' *your* work, when you are just as well able, and enough sight more so, than she is to do it?' says I.

"Then Luella she looked at me like a baby who has a rattle shook at it. She sort of laughed as innocent as you please. 'Oh, I can't do the work myself, Miss Anderson,' says she. 'I never did. Maria *has* to do it.'

"Then I spoke out: 'Has to do it!' says I. 'Has to do it!' She don't have to do it, either. Maria Brown has her own home and enough to live on.. She ain't beholden to you to come over here and slave for you and kill herself.'

"Luella she jest set and stared at me for all the world like a doll-baby that was so abused that it was comin' to life.

"'Yes,' says I, 'she's killin' herself. She's goin' to die just the way Erastus did, and Lily, and your Aunt Abby. You're killin' her jest as you did them. I don't know what there is about you, but you seem to bring a curse,' says I. 'You kill everybody that is fool enough to care anythin' about you and do for you.'

"She stared at me and she was pretty pale.

"'And Maria ain't the only one you're goin' to kill,' says I. 'You're goin' to kill Doctor Malcom before you're done with him.'

"Then a red color came flamin' all over her face. 'I ain't goin' to kill him, either,' says she, and she begun to cry.

"'Yes, you *be*!' says I. Then I spoke as I had never spoke before. You see, I felt it on account of Erastus. I told her that she hadn't any business to think of another man after she'd been married to one that had died for her: that she was a dreadful woman; and she was, that's true enough, but sometimes

I have wondered lately if she knew it—if she wa'n't like a baby with scissors in its hand cuttin' everybody without knowin' what it was doin'.

"Luella she kept gettin' paler and paler, and she never took her eyes off my face. There was somethin' awful about the way she looked at me and never spoke one word. After awhile I quit talkin' and I went home. I watched that night, but her lamp went out before nine o'clock, and when Doctor Malcom came drivin' past and sort of slowed up he see there wa'n't any light and he drove along. I saw her sort of shy out of meetin' the next Sunday, too, so he shouldn't go home with her, and I begun to think mebbe she did have some conscience after all. It was only a week after that that Maria Brown died—sort of sudden at the last, though everybody had seen it was comin'. Well, then there was a good deal of fee-lin' and pretty dark whispers. Folks said the days of witchcraft had come again, and they were pretty shy of Luella. She acted sort of offish to the Doctor and he didn't go there, and there wa'n't anybody to do anythin' for her. I don't know how she *did* get along. I wouldn't go in there and offer to help her—not because I was afraid of dyin' like the rest, but I thought she was just as well able to do her own work as I was to do it for her, and I thought it was about time that she did it and stopped killin' other folks. But it wa'n't very long before folks began to say that Luella herself was goin' into a decline jest the way her husband, and Lily, and Aunt Abby and the others had, and I saw myself that she looked pretty bad. I used to see her goin' past from the store with a bundle as if she could hardly crawl, but I remembered how Erastus used to wait and 'tend when he couldn't hardly put one foot before the other, and I didn't go out to help her.

"But at last one afternoon I saw the doctor come drivin' up like mad with his medicine chest, and Mrs. Babbit came in after supper and said that Luella was real sick.

"'I'd offer to go in and nurse her,' says she, 'but I've got my children to consider, and mebbe it ain't true what they say, but it's queer how many folks that have done for her have died.'

"I didn't say anythin', but I considered how she had been Erastus's wife and how he had set his eyes by her, and I made up my mind to go in the next mornin', unless she was better, and see what I could do; but the next mornin' I see her at the window, and pretty soon she came steppin' out as spry as you please, and a little while afterward Mrs. Babbit came in and told me that the doctor had got a girl from out of town, a Sarah Jones, to come there, and she said she was pretty sure that the doctor was goin' to marry Luella.

"I saw him kiss her in the door that night myself, and I knew it was true. The woman came that afternoon, and the way she flew around was a caution. I don't believe Luella had swept since Maria died. She swept and dusted, and washed and ironed; wet clothes and dusters and carpets were flyin' over there all day, and every time Luella set her foot out when the doctor wa'n't there there was that Sarah Jones helpin' of her up and down the steps, as if she hadn't learned to walk.

"Well, everybody knew that Luella and the doctor were goin' to be married, but it wa'n't long before they began to talk about his lookin' so poorly, jest as they had about the others; and they talked about Sarah Jones, too.

"Well, the doctor did die, and he wanted to be married first, so as to leave what little he had to Luella, but he died before the minister could get there, and Sarah Jones died a week afterward.

"Well, that wound up everything for Luella Miller. Not another soul in the whole town would lift a finger for her. There got to be a sort of panic. Then she began to droop in good earnest. She used to have to go to the store herself, for Mrs. Babbit was afraid to let Tommy go for her, and I've seen her goin' past and stoppin' every two or three steps to rest. Well, I stood it as long as I could, but one day I see her comin' with her arms full and stoppin' to lean against the Babbit fence, and I run out and took her bundles and carried them to her house. Then I went home and never spoke one word to her though she called after me dreadful kind of pitiful. Well, that night I was taken sick with a chill, and I was sick as I wanted to be for two weeks. Mrs. Babbit had seen me run out to help Luella and she came in and told me I was goin' to die on account of it. I didn't know whether I was or not, but I considered I had done right by Erastus's wife.

"That last two weeks Luella she had a dreadful hard time, I guess. She was pretty sick, and as near as I could make out nobody dared go near her. I don't know as she was really needin' anythin' very much, for there was enough to eat in her house and it was warm weather, and she made out to cook a little flour gruel every day, I know, but I guess she had a hard time, she that had been so petted and done for all her life.

"When I got so I could go out, I went over there one morning. Mrs. Babbit had just come in to say she hadn't seen any smoke and she didn't know but it was somebody's duty to go in, but she couldn't help thinkin' of her children, and I got right up, though I hadn't been out of the house for two weeks, and I went in there, and Luella she was layin' on the bed, and she was dyin'.

"She lasted all that day and into the night. But I sat there after the new doctor had gone away. Nobody else dared to go there. It was about midnight that I left her for a minute to run home and get some medicine I had been takin', for I begun to feel rather bad.

"It was a full moon that night, and just as I started out of my door to cross the street back to Luella's, I stopped short, for I saw something."

Lydia Anderson at this juncture always said with a certain defiance that she did not expect to be believed, and then proceeded in a hushed voice:

"I saw what I saw, and I know I saw it, and I will swear on my death bed that I saw it. I saw Luella Miller and Erastus Miller, and Lily, and Aunt Abby, and Maria, and the doctor, and Sarah, all goin' out of her door, and all but Luella shone white in the moonlight, and they were all helpin' her along till she seemed to fairly fly in the midst of them. Then it all disappeared. I stood a minute with my heart poundin', then I went over there. I thought of goin' for Mrs. Babbit, but I thought she'd be afraid. So I went alone, though I knew what had happened. Luella was layin' real peaceful, dead on her bed."

This was the story that the old woman, Lydia Anderson, told, but the sequel was told by the people who survived her, and this is the tale which has become folklore in the village.

Lydia Anderson died when she was eighty-seven. She had continued wonderfully hale and hearty for one of her years until about two weeks before her death.

One bright moonlight evening she was sitting beside a window in her parlor when she made a sudden exclamation, and was out of the house and across the street before the neighbor who was taking care of her could stop her. She followed as fast as possible and found Lydia Anderson stretched on the ground before the door of Luella Miller's deserted house, and she was quite dead.

The next night there was a red gleam of fire athwart the moonlight and the old house of Luella Miller was burned to the ground. Nothing is now left of it except a few old cellar stones and a lilac bush, and in summer a helpless trail of morning glories among the weeds, which might be considered emblematic of Luella herself.

Sangre

Lisa Tuttle

Lisa Tuttle was born in Texas but has lived in the United Kingdom for nearly four decades. Her novels include *Windhaven* (with George R. R. Martin), *Familiar Spirit*, *Gabriel*, *Lost Futures*, *The Pillow Friend*, *The Silver Bough*, *The Mysteries*, and the first in the Jesperson and Lane series, *The Curious Affair of the Somnambulist & the Psychic Thief*.

The author of numerous short stories, including the International Horror Guild Award-winning "Closet Dreams," her fiction has been collected in *A Spaceship Built of Stone and Other Stories*, *A Nest of Nightmares*, *Memories of the Body: Tales of Desire and Transformation*, *My Pathology*, and *Stranger in the House*. She has also edited the anthologies *Skin of the Soul* and *Crossing the Border: Tales of Erotic Ambiguity*.

"Although I've often used the vampire theme metaphorically," says the author, "I think 'Sangre' is the only time I've written about a traditional, blood-drinking vampire . . ."

GLENDA STEPPED OUT of the shower and stopped before the mirror. Her hair looped up and confined beneath a shower cap left her long neck bare and made her eyes look larger and darker.

"You look Spanish," Steve said.

She didn't turn, but continued staring at herself in the mirror, her beautiful face impassive.

He put his hands on her wet shoulders, bent his head to kiss her neck.

"Dry me," she said.

He picked up a towel and patted her reverently, tenderly dry. She reached up and pulled off the cap and let her hair tumble, a flow of honey and brown, to her waist. He caught his breath.

"When is checkout?" she asked.

"Noon."

Now she turned to face him. "And then what? After we leave an hour from now, then what?"

"Anything you want. I'll take you to lunch anywhere you say, and then we'll have time to do a little shopping before you have to be at the airport. Anything you want." His eyes pleaded with her.

"Anything you want," she mimicked. Her face contorted in anger; she gave the towel he still held a jerk and wrapped it around herself. "How can you?"

"Glenda—"

"I'm not talking about today! I'm talking about what after today? When I come back, do we just pretend it never happened? Do we just forget about us? How can you take me out and screw me, and then go tripping home to my mother? And what is this trip to Spain thing? Can't you handle it anymore? Mother getting suspicious?"

"Darling, don't. Of course I don't want you out of the way. I love you. And I love your mother. Believe me, this is as hard for me—"

"Oh, sure it is. Just tell me this—why should I be the one to lose? What happens to me after you marry my mother?"

"Sweetheart, try to understand . . ."

"Oh, yes, I'm the one who has to understand, and Mother's the one who doesn't suspect. Just how long do you think that's going to last?"

"In time," he said, straining for patience, for the sound of wisdom in his voice, "in time I hope we . . . the three of us . . . can work something out. But this is very difficult. You, you're young, while people like your mother and myself are very much shackled by the old morality; you can accept relationships that are . . . more free . . . and in time, maybe after your mother and I are married, the three of us can . . ." he faltered and stopped. Her expression mocked him.

"I never lied to you," he said, suddenly defensive, suddenly angrily sure that he was making a fool of himself. "You knew what you were getting into; you knew who I was when you became my mistress—"

"Mistress." She said the word with loathing, and he caught the steely glint of hatred in her eyes. He tried to recoup but before he could speak she shook her head impatiently and let the towel drop.

"Well," she said. "We've still got an hour."

Debbie opened her mouth and desperately forced a yawn as the plane began to take off. As the air pressure stabilized she turned to Glenda and said approvingly, "Your stepfather is good-looking."

"Steve's not my stepfather."

"Well, whatever. They're getting married soon, aren't they?"

"July. Right after I come back from Spain." Glenda laid her cheek against the window and shut her eyes.

"He looks awfully young."

Glenda shrugged. "A couple of years younger than my mother."

Debbie bent her dark head over her copy of *The Sun Also Rises* when it became obvious that Glenda was in no mood for conversation. The two had played together as children and remained friends into the same college in an undemanding, almost superficial fashion.

Glenda chewed her lip. "Look what he gave me," she said suddenly, holding out her hand. "Steve, I mean." It was a silver ring, very simple, the ends bent into a curving "S" design. It had been made for her while she watched in the narrow dark handcrafts shop, clutching Steve's hand with emotion she didn't show on her calm face.

Debbie nodded. "Pretty. He's paying for this trip, isn't he?"

"He insisted. And Mother—well, she's so hung up on him that whatever he says is fine with her."

"I think it's great," Debbie said. "Your mother getting married again. And you like him so much, too."

"Oh, we're great friends."

Their room in Sevilla had two beds, a red-brick floor and a balcony from which could be seen La Giralda, the Moorish tower. Glenda stood on the balcony in the evening, the heat of the day already fading from the air, and watched the swallows dip and soar around the tower, pink-auraed from the setting sun.

Glenda had not known why, but coming to Sevilla after the noise and cars of gray Madrid had felt like coming home. She had led Debbie (plump Debbie panting a little under her backpack) through the winding streets as if guided by something, coming upon the little hotel and finding it perfect without feeling surprise. But at the same time she felt giddy, her stomach clenched with excitement, the way she always felt on those rare occasions when she was to be alone with Steve. With evening the feeling of something impending had become stronger and Glenda felt reality slipping away from her as if it were a dream.

She put a hand to her cheek and found it unnaturally hot. She turned back into the room where Debbie was putting on a skirt.

"It's nearly eight," Debbie said. "I think it's legal to go out to dinner now."

Glenda felt herself drifting as they sat at dinner, and blamed it on the wine when Debbie commented on her inattentiveness. Things were slipping away from her. Everything seemed unnaturally bright and unreal as if she watched it on a screen in a dark, muffled room.

Once back, Glenda went straight to bed while Debbie wrote a letter to her parents.

"Sure the light won't bother you?"

"I'm sure." It was an effort to say the words. The room went spinning away from her, telescoping into another world, and Glenda slept.

She woke, her mouth dry. Debbie was a dark lump in the next bed. The shutters were open and moonlight sliced into the room. Glenda felt ragingly hot. With part of her mind she noted that fact and it registered that perhaps she was sick, with a fever. Her own body began to seem as remote to her as everything else around her.

There was someone on the balcony. Now he blocked the light, now he moved and it illuminated him. There was the tightness of terror in her throat, but her mind clicked observations into her consciousness as unemotionally as a typewriter.

He wore a cloak, and some sort of slouch-brimmed hat. Polished boots gleamed in the moonlight, and was that a sword hung at his side? *Don Juan?* noted a coolly amused voice within her. *Come to seduce this Andalusian cutie?*

Oh, really?

He made no move to enter the room and she gained some measure of courage from that, enough to raise herself on her elbows and stare at him. If he noticed her movement he made no sign. She sat up then and swung her legs over the side of the bed. The room receded and advanced dizzyingly before it settled into its detached and unreal, but at least stable, form.

He was waiting for her on the balcony. She opened her mouth to speak, to end the joke, to let him know she was awake and that, perhaps, he had come to the wrong window. But to speak seemed a desecration, a monumental undertaking of which she was not capable. He opened his arms to her, that cloaked figure, his face masked by shadow, and waited for her to step into them. She saw herself as if from a distance, a somnambulant figure in a long white gown, long hair flowing, face pale and innocent from sleep, and she watched this figure move into the waiting arms.

She looked up, he moved his head and the moonlight spilled fully across his features. She realized then that it was not Don Juan at all, but another legend entirely; the pasty face, the oddly peaked eyebrows, the parted red lips over which pointed teeth gleamed . . . Her head fell back against his arm, her eyes closed and her sacrificial neck gleamed white and pure.

"Glenda?"

A rush of nausea hit her; she opened her eyes, stumbled, and caught herself at the railing.

"Glen, are you all right?"

Glenda turned her head and saw Debbie—no one else, only Debbie, solid and comforting in pink nylon.

"I was hot," she said, and had to clear her throat and say it again. She was hot, and very thirsty. "Is there anything to drink?"

"Part of that liter of Coke from the train. Are you sure you're okay?"

"Yes, yes . . . only thirsty." She gulped the Coke desperately but it burned her throat. She choked and felt sick. "G'night." She crawled back into bed and would say nothing more to Debbie, who finally sighed and went back to sleep herself.

"I hate to leave you alone," Debbie said, hovering uncertainly at the door. "How do you feel?"

Glenda lay in bed. "Really, it's nothing. I just don't feel up to anything today. But I'm not so sick that I can't make it down three flights to get the manager or his wife if I need something. You go out sightseeing with that nice Canadian and don't worry about me. I'll get some sleep. Best thing."

"You're sure? You wouldn't rather move to a bigger hotel? So we'd have our own bathroom?"

"Of course not. I like it here."

"Well . . . Shall I bring you anything?"

"Something to drink. A bottle of wine. I'm so thirsty."

"I don't think wine . . . well, I'll get you something."

And finally Debbie was gone. Glenda relaxed her stranglehold on a reality that had become more strange and tenuous with every passing second. She fell.

She was on the street called Death, one of the narrow, cobbled streets bound on each side by houses painted a blinding white. The name of the street was painted in blue on a tile set into one of the houses: MUERTE.

The girl had been crying. She was dirty and her face was sticky with tears and dirt. It was *siesta* and she was alone on the quiet street but she knew that she would not be alone for long. And they must not find her. She knew that she must leave the city for safety, but the thought of wandering alone through the countryside frightened her as much as did the thought of remaining, and so she was at an impasse, incapable of action.

If they found her, they would take their vengeance on her although she had done nothing, was innocently involved. She thought of the past month, of the widespread sickness throughout the town, of the deaths—bodies found in the street, pale and dead with the unmistakable marks upon their necks—and of the fear, the growing terror.

Her mother had taken to staying out all night, returning pale and exhausted at dawn to fall into a heavy sleep. But as she slept she smiled, and the girl, standing by the pillow and smoothing her mother's tangled hair, found the words of the townspeople creeping, unwanted, into her mind. Was it true, what they said, that she consorted with the devil? That her mother with her lover swooped through the night in the form of bats, seeking out unwary night travelers, to waylay them and drink their blood? She began to be frightened of her mother, while still loving her, and watched through half-closed eyes as she crept out every night. And finally one night had ended without bringing her mother home and the girl had been alone ever since.

She wandered, not knowing where to go, hungry and thirsty but too frightened to knock on a door and ask for wine and shelter. It grew later, and as it grew dark doors began to close and people went hurriedly in twos and threes. Once the streets had been as filled with lanterns as a summer meadow is filled with fireflies, but now there was a monster abroad.

The moon came up and gave her light and finally she came to a small plaza with a fountain in the center. But the fountain was dead and dry and she leaned against it, crying with frustration until she was too tired to cry anymore.

Something made her look up, some feeling of danger. The moon was high. A man stood in one of the four entrances to the plaza, a man draped in the folds of an all-encompassing cloak. The toes of his boots gleamed as did his eyes, two points of light beneath his slouch hat.

She kept still, hoping he had not noticed her in the shadows.

"Daughter," he said, in a voice like dry leaves in the wind.

An involuntary twitch.

"My darling daughter." He took a step forward.

She was running, never looking back, sobbing deep in her throat and running down one street and then another, perilously afraid that she would run a circle and re-enter the plaza to find him there . . . She ran. Then down a street she should not have taken, a cul-de-sac. She turned to escape and found him there, in her way.

She was rigid. The dry leaves rustled in his throat as be came toward her. He raised his arms and his cloak as if they were joined, as if he were draped in huge wings which he would fold around the two of them. His lips parted; she could hear his breathing, could see the gleam of his teeth. She fell.

Glenda woke, trembling violently.

"Did I wake you up? Honey, are you all right? You look pale as a ghost. We're going for lunch, do you want—"

Glenda shook her head. "Uh, I'm not feeling too great." The words felt torn from her raw throat. She was thirsty. "Did you get me something to drink?"

"Oh, I'm sorry! I forgot. What would you like? I'll run get it for you. And something to eat?"

Glenda shook her head again. "No. Just a drink." It was hard to concentrate, harder still to focus.

Debbie came to the bed and reached toward Glenda, who pulled away violently.

"Glen, I just want to see if you have a fever. Hmmm . . . you are pretty hot. My God, what'd you do to your neck?"

Glenda caressed the twin shallow wounds with her fingertips and shook her head.

"I think we should get you to a hospital."

"No. I'll be . . . I'll take some aspirin . . . I'll stay . . . I'll be all right . . ."

Debbie's face was blurring and clearing like something seen from underwater. She fell.

The moon was down and the sky beginning to lighten when she opened her eyes. She was sprawled on the cobblestones of a short narrow street, and got painfully to her feet. She was ragingly thirsty. Her mouth felt gummy, her tongue too large. She pushed her hair back, away from her face, with both hands and felt the trace of something sticky. She returned her hand for a lingering exploration and remembered the marks on the necks of certain townspeople, and remembered their eventual deaths.

She traveled twisting streets until she came within sight of La Giralda. The rising sun illuminated it and she saw a single bat hanging like a curled leaf in the tower.

The people of Sevilla, in the form of two drunken men, had at one time attempted to keep the devil (who was reputed to inhabit the Moorish tower in the form of a bat) in his resting place and out of the streets of Sevilla by boarding up the door. But it was pointed out to them that, even assuming wooden slats could keep the devil prisoner, bats did not need to fly through doorways when the tower had so many windows, and they abandoned their project half-finished.

She climbed over the uncompleted barricade, scratching her leg as she did so. She watched the tiny beads of blood appear in a curving line and then looked away. And now, up? To the bell tower where bells hung which never rang? And then she saw a door to one side, a wooden door free of spiderwebs, as if it were often used. She went to it and pushed it open, revealing steps which led down into darkness. She left the door open behind her, for the little light its being open provided, and descended the steps. They were shallow steps, but there were a great many of them. Her legs began to ache from the seemingly endless descent.

At the bottom was a huge chamber, she could not tell how large, poorly lit by torches burning smokily in wall niches. She saw the coffin at once, and went to it. It was open and inside, his slouch hat discarded but still clothed in cape and boots, was the man she had run from in the night; the man her mother had loved, or served.

A bat flew at her head, silent and deadly. She ducked, but felt the edge of its leathery wings across her cheek. She turned and ran for the stairs; the bat did not pursue her. Upstairs, in the daylight, she rested and thought of what she had seen. She thought of his cruel face, and of his bloodred lips. Slowly she licked her own dry lips and, unconsciously, her hand went toward her throat. Was he the devil, or something else? The devil could not be killed, but something else . . .

Her hands were covered with tiny cuts and full of splinters when she was done, but she had her weapon: a large, sharply pointed piece of wood. Outside there was a pile of rubble and she found a brick. An old woman in black, an early riser, glared at her suspiciously as she passed, but said nothing.

When she entered the chamber again the bat swooped at her and flew around her head. She ducked to keep it from her eyes, but did not let it deter her. She put the brick down to grasp the wooden stake with both dirty, bloody hands and plunge it into the man's heart. She was blinded by her hair, and then by her own blood as the bat bit and tore at her head, but finally the stake was anchored and she was rewarded with a low moan from her victim. The bat chittered once, a screech of defeat, and flapped away. She raised the brick and brought it down with all her might on the stake.

There was a scream, which seemed to come from the walls around her, and then a fountain of blood spattered her chest, arms and head. She kept pounding, unwilling or unable to stop, until the stake must have been driven entirely through him, and then, triumphant, she threw the brick away and stood, panting, watching the still-bubbling blood. It was very quiet. And then the thirst assailed her, sweeping away all pains and triumphs with its intensity. She sank to her knees, laid her face to his chest, and drank and drank until she was sated.

Glenda opened her eyes. The room was empty and sunlight lay warm on the red bricks and white walls of the room. Everything was hard and clear to her now; the fever must have passed. Things had a diamond edge on them, with textures and solidity she had never noticed before.

Debbie came in, from off the balcony, looking startled to see Glenda sitting up. "Well! How do you feel? You really had us worried."

"'Us?'"

"Roger, the Canadian from down the hall. He's gone for a doctor."

"I don't need a doctor. Didn't I tell you?"

"Yeah, right before you fainted. Lie down, will you? Take it easy. How do you feel?"

"Fine. Excellent. Never better."

"Well, just stay in bed. Do you want something to drink?"

"No thanks." She lay back.

The doctor found nothing wrong with Glenda although he was puzzled by the marks on her neck. When his inquisition began to annoy her she pretended not to understand his actually quite adequate English, and pulled the sheet over her head, complaining that the light hurt her eyes and that she was very tired.

Glenda was very determined and very persuasive and came at last to be seated on a 747 headed for New York. Debbie—poor, confused Debbie—remained in Spain, traveling now with her Canadian and his friends.

"You ought at least to cable your Mom, then," Debbie had said, but Glenda had shaken her head, smiling. "I'll surprise her—take a cab in." Steve would be with her mother, she knew. It would be early morning when she arrived and they would not be awake yet, but sweetly sleeping. They would be asleep in each other's arms, not expecting her.

Glenda smiled at the blackness beyond her window and touched her silver ring. She pulled it off and toyed with it, tracing the "S" with her finger. S for Steve, she thought. And S for Spain. She suddenly caught the ring between her fingers and pulled at it, distorting the S shape and forcing it finally into a design like twin curved horns. Then she held it and clenched it tightly until the blood came.

A Question of Patronage

A Saint-Germain Story

Chelsea Quinn Yarbro

Chelsea Quinn Yarbro is an author and professional Tarot reader whose first story was published in 1969 in *If* magazine. A full-time writer since the following year, she has sold more than seventy novels and numerous short stories in various genres.

Her books include the werewolf volumes *The Godforsaken* and *Beastnights*; the quasi-fictional occult series *Messages from Michael, More Messages from Michael, Michael's People,* and *Michael for the Milennium*; and the movie novelizations *Dead & Buried* and *Nomads*. Yarbro's Sisters of the Night trilogy (*Kelene: The Angry Angel, Fenice: The Soul of an Angel,* and *Zhameni: The Angel of Death*) is about Dracula's three undead wives. Unfortunately, the last volume remains unpublished, with the rights being retained by the packager.

She is best known for her series of historical horror novels featuring the Byronic vampire Le Comte de Saint-Germain, loosely inspired by the real-life eighteenth-century aristocrat of the same name. The first book in the cycle, *Hotel Transylvania: A Novel of Forbidden Love*, appeared in 1978. To date it has been followed by nearly twenty sequels. A spin-off sequence featuring Saint-Germain's lover Atta Olivia Clemens comprises *A Flame in Byzantium, Crusader's Torch,* and *A Candle for D'Artagnan*, while *Out of the House of Life* and *In the Face of Death* feature Saint-Germain's immortal beloved Madeline de Montalia.

The author's short fiction has been collected in *Cautionary Tales, Signs & Portents, The Vampire Stories of Chelsea Quinn Yarbro,* and *Apprehensions Other Delusions*, and she has coedited the anthologies *Two Views of Wonder* (with Thomas N. Scortia) and *Strangers in the Night* (with Anne Stuart and Maggie Shayne).

"When a publisher approached me about doing a limited-edition collection of my vampire short stories, he asked if I would do a story for that specific volume," recalls Yarbro. "He said he would like it to be a Saint-Germain story and, if possible, have some reference to *Dracula*. At the time, I said yes to the Saint-Germain part, but told him I doubted I could manage *Dracula* as well, since the two vampire concepts were so very different as to have almost nothing but Transylvania in common.

"Toying with the possibilities, I finally hit upon Henry Irving, Bram Stoker's boss. I had a look at a few references about him, hoping to find a time I could slip Saint-Germain into his life. The beginning of his career seemed more attractive to me than when he was well-established, as well as giving an indirect link to Stoker, making Saint-Germain someone Stoker might hear about but never meet.

"This story was the result . . ."

OUTSIDE IT WAS dank and clammy; inside it was stuffy and over-warm. The clerks in the merchants' emporium office yawned as the afternoon ran quickly down to the early falling November night.

"Do lock the door, John Henry," said the oldest of the clerks to the youngest, exercising his privilege. "No one will come at this hour."

John Henry Brodribb got off his stool and bowed to the senior clerk with a flourish that amused and annoyed the other clerks; John Henry was known for his lavish, theatrical manner. He pitched his voice to carry. "Whatever you desire, Mr. Tubbs, it is my honor to perform for you." His accent was curious mix of London public school flavored with a broadness that might be Devon or Cornwall. He was long-headed and lanky with the last remnants of youth; he was three months shy of his eighteenth birthday.

Before he could reach the door, it opened suddenly and a man in a black, hooded cloak stepped into the office, looking like a visitor from another age; a monk from the Middle Ages perhaps, or an apparition of a Plantagenet in disfavor with his cousins. "Good afternoon. Is Mr. Lamkin available?" he asked in a pleasant, foreign voice, taking John Henry's startled surprise in his stride. There was a suggestion of a glint in dark eyes within the shadow of the hood.

"Is he expecting you?" asked John Henry, recovering himself adroitly, and doing his best to match the style of the man.

"Yes, but not necessarily at this time," said the stranger. "I have only just arrived in London, you see." He threw back his hood, revealing an attractive, irregular countenance, fine-browed and mobile if unfashionably clean-shaven; his hair was dark and waved enough to make up for his lack of mutton-chop whiskers or mustache. Although he was somewhat less than average height, he had a presence that was commanding no matter how amiable his demeanor; it originated in his dark, compelling eyes.

"Mr. Lamkin has left for the day," said John Henry, glancing toward the door of the office of the man who handled the firm's overseas business. "He will not be back until Thursday next. He is bound for South-ampton, to inspect the arrival of a cargo of muslin."

"From Egypt or America?" asked the foreigner with enough curiosity to require an answer.

"From Amer—" John Henry began only to be interrupted.

Mr. Tubbs, the senior clerk, intervened, shoving himself off his stool and hastening toward the newcomer, prepared to take charge of the unknown gentleman. "I am Parvia Tubbs, the senior clerk; good afternoon. May I, possibly assist you, Mr. . . .?" He waited for the stranger to give his name.

"Ragoczy," he answered. "Count Ferenc Ragoczy, of Sain—"

John Henry cut him short with enthusiasm. "Ragoczy! Of almost everywhere." His eyes lit and he flung out one hand. "I've been copying your accounts, sir, and let me say you are far the most traveled gentleman of all those buying from us abroad. You have holdings in Bavaria, in Saint Petersburg, in Christiania, in Holland, in Italy, in Prague, in—"

Mr. Tubbs stopped this catalogue. "I am certain Mr. Ragoczy does not wish his affairs bruited about, John Henry."

The youngest clerk lowered his eyes and stifled himself. "No, Mr. Tubbs," he said.

Ragoczy took pity on him. "It is good to know that at least one of your staff has my interests in hand." His smile was quick and one-sided, and held John Henry's attention as Ragoczy turned towards him, encouraging him. "Where else do I have property: can you tell me?"

Now John Henry faltered, upset by Mr. Tubbs's covert glare. "In . . . in Hungary." He steadied himself and went on. "There are two addresses in Hungary, now I think of it; one in Buda and one in a remote area of the eastern sector. In the Carpathians. That place is in Hungary, isn't it?"

"Technically, yes, at present it is," he replied, and glanced up as the office clock struck the half-hour. "Although it is closer to Bucharest than to Buda-Pest. Saint-Germain is on the current border of Hungary and Romania, but that has not always been the case. It is a very ancient estate." Ragoczy fell silent.

After an awkward pause, Mr. Tubbs said, "Is that all you can tell Mr. Ragoczy, John Henry? You are the one who has his ledger to copy. Show him you are not a laggard."

Stung by this reprimand, John Henry squared his angular shoulders and continued. "You have holdings, Count, in Moscow, in Egypt, in Crete, in Persia, in Morocco, in Spain, in Poland, in Armenia, in Canada, and in South America: Peru, as I recall."

"Yes, and in Mexico, as well." He nodded his approval.

"You also have transferred goods to China and India, according to our records, during the last thirty years. I have not seen any entries before that time. The ledger begins thirty-one years ago." This last was John Henry's most determined bid to show his grasp of what he had recorded.

"You keep excellent records," Ragoczy said.

"It is necessary for merchants to do that, or they will not last long in business," said Mr. Tubbs officiously.

They had the attention of the other four clerks now, and John Henry made the most of it. "If you would like to inspect the account books, Count, it would be my pleasure to show them to you."

Mr. Tubbs looked askance. "John Henry!" he admonished the youngest clerk. "That is for Mr. Lamkin to do."

"Well, but he is away, isn't he?" countered John Henry with a show of deference. "I have the records on my desk. I've been copying them for Mr. Lamkin, at his request, of course. So long as Count Ragoczy is here, it would be practical to show him what our records show instead of requiring him to return when Mr. Lamkin gets back."

"It is a late hour; Mr. Ragoczy would have to come back in the morning, in any case, or at another, more suitable time." Mr. Tubbs regarded the youngest clerk in consternation, then turned on Ragoczy with an obsequious gesture. "It is unfortunate that you came at this hour. We do not wish to offend, but we will be closing business for the day shortly."

John Henry's expression brightened. "I don't mind staying late if that will make matters easier for you, Count." He made a point of emphasizing Ragoczy's title, as much for his own satisfaction as for the discomfort it gave Mr. Tubbs. "If would be convenient?"

"A very generous offer, I'm sure, John Henry," said Mr. Tubbs, his jowls becoming mottled with color and his manner more stiff and overbearing. "But such a man as Mr. Ragoczy must have other claims upon his time. He will inform us of when he wishes to review the accounts."

Ragoczy favored the two clerks with an affable look. "I have no plans for this evening until much later. I am bidden to . . . dine at ten."

"Then it's settled," said John Henry before Mr. Tubbs could speak. He indicated his desk. "Yours is the oldest of the account books there." His gaze was speculative. "Your family must have a long tradition of enterprise."

"Um," said Ragoczy, a suggestion of amusement in his fathomless eyes.

Mr. Tubbs, aware that he had been outmaneuvered by the most junior clerk, began to dither. "It is not acceptable, John Henry. You have not worked here long enough to be entitled to lock the door." He cringed as he looked towards Ragoczy. "I am afraid that we will have to arrange another time, Mr. Ragoczy."

Before John Henry could voice his objection, Ragoczy said smoothly, "You would not be averse to entrusting a key to me, would you? I have done business with this firm for longer than I you have been employed here. Surely that makes me trustworthy, Mr. Tubbs. I will return it tomorrow, if that is satisfactory to you?" He said it politely enough, but it was apparent he would not be refused. "I appreciate your concern and precaution, of course."

This was more opposition than Mr. Tubbs was prepared to fight. He ducked his head. "It would be most acceptable; I will provide you with a key at once, Mr. Ragoczy," he said, and moved away, casting a single, angry look back toward John Henry and the black-cloaked stranger.

John Henry paid no notice of his superior's disapproval; he motioned to Ragoczy to come with him, and hastened back to his desk, his face radiant with anticipation.

"I don't understand it," said John Henry, shaking his head at what he read in the old ledger. "There should be another two hundred pounds in this transfer. How can it have been overlooked? They can't have made such an error in arithmetic, can they?" The office was quite dark now, and the rumble in the streets had died to an irregular echo of hooves and wheels; the oil lamp on John Henry's desk and the lume of the dying fire in the hearth provided the only light. It was no longer hot in the office, but it remained stuffy in spite of the chill.

"They did not," said Ragoczy with a sigh of annoyance. He had shed his cloak and was revealed in a black woolen jacket cut in the latest French fashion. His shirt was silken broadcloth and immaculately white. He wore his cravat in the Russian mode: it was silk, patterned in red and black. His trousers were also of black wool, expertly tailored so that the fullness never became baggy. Indeed, the only note that John Henry could find in the foreigner's ensemble to criticize was the thickness of the soles of Rogoczy's neat black boots.

John Henry's eyes widened. "But, Count, that would mean . . . that someone has . . . has . . ."

"Been stealing," Ragoczy supplied gently; he tapped the open ledger with the end of his pencil. "Yes, it would seem so."

"But . . . why?"

"For gain, I would suppose," said Ragoczy, making a worn attempt at a philosophical smile. "That is the usual reason people steal; for gain of one sort or another."

"Gain," repeated John Henry, as if the notion was unfamiliar to him. "In this firm?"

"Probably there are two of them: one here and one outside England." He hefted the old ledger. "It will take time to find out who has done it, and for how long." He put the ledger down and pulled a watch from his waistcoat pocket. "Look at the hour."

John Henry glanced up at the clock over the desks. "It is coming nine," he said, astonished that so much time should have passed. "I ought not to have kept you so very late, Count."

"I supposed I had kept you." Ragoczy held out his hand to John Henry. "I have to thank you for giving me so much of your time, Mr. Brodribb. I am grateful to you for the attention you have shown me."

"It is my pleasure," said John Henry, flushing as they shook hands.

Ragoczy's expression remained friendly, but he said, "I doubt it." And in response to John Henry's startled look, went on. "No doubt a young man like you has things he would rather do of an evening than assist in discovering a pattern of errors in a ledger."

"Most evenings, I study," said John Henry, for once not very forthcoming.

"Ah," said Ragoczy. "Then perhaps you will let me impose upon you a bit more. If you would be willing to continue this examination for another evening, I would be willing to pay for your time. Provided you do not feel you are compromised by helping me."

"Why would I feel that?" asked John Henry. "They are the ones who are taking from you. You are entitled to recover all that has been pilfered. I would be a poor employee indeed if I countenanced wrongdoing by my employer."

"Quite so. And all the more reason for you to accept money for your aid. I would have required much more time if you had not been willing to help me." Ragoczy looked pleased.

"Oh, that is hardly necessary." John Henry directed his gaze toward the dying fire. "Mr. Tubbs allowed me to stay because I am the most junior of the clerks. He did not think I could uncover anything of significance."

"You assume he knows there is something to uncover," said Ragoczy, his expression remaining kindly but with a keenness in his eyes that was unnerving to John Henry.

"I doubt he would have let me remain if he feared you would learn . . . what you have learned." He lifted his hands. "And you could have managed without me. I have done very little to earn—"

"Nevertheless, you will permit me to compensate you for the time you have lost." Beneath the elegant manner there was something unyielding; John Henry sensed it and nodded.

"Thank you, Count," he said. "I will stay tomorrow night, if that is suitable."

"Eminently," said Ragoczy, and reached out for his cloak even while he slipped his hand into one of his inner jacket pockets. He drew out a five-pound note and handed the flimsy to John Henry, who stared at it, for it represented more than a month's wages. "For your service. At this hour, I should take a cab home if I were you, Mr. Brodribb."

"But five pounds . . ." John Henry could not find the words to go on.

"Considering the magnitude of the theft you have helped me to uncover this evening, it is a very poor commission. Had I retained someone to perform this task, he should have cost me much more. And who knows what success we would have? You are familiar with the ledger entries, which another might not be." Ragoczy's swift smile lit his face again. "And he would have been much less entertaining."

John Henry looked up from the money in his hand and stared at Ragoczy. "That's very kind, Count."

"Do you think so." Ragoczy slipped his cloak on with a style John Henry swore to himself he would one day master.

"Tomorrow night, then," said John Henry as he watched Ragoczy go to the door while he folded up his five pound note to a size small enough to slip into his waistcoat pocket.

"You had better come with me," said Ragoczy in amusement. "I have the key."

"Oh. Yes." Hurriedly John Henry grabbed his greatcoat, thinking it was sadly shabby next to Ragoczy's splendid cloak. He extinguished the lamp, stirred the embers of the dying fire with the poker, and hurried out of the door and watched while the Count set the locks.

"Please inform Mr. Tubbs that I will keep the key another evening," he said, then reconsidered. "No. That will not do." He nodded decisively once. "I will send a note around in the afternoon, informing him that I will need the key one night longer. I will request you remain to assist me again. He will not have time to ask me to change plans."

"Do you think he would?" John Henry asked, shocked at the implication of Ragoczy's instructions.

"I think it is possible," said Ragoczy as he raised his hood. "Come. At the next corner we should find cabs about, no matter how late it is."

For an instant the five pound note in this waistcoat pocket seemed to emit a brilliant light; John Henry realized that such an extravagance would truly be a sensible, prudent act when he had so much money. "Right you are, Count," he said, and tagged after the black-cloaked foreigner.

"This is really most inconsiderate," complained Mr. Tubbs as he lingered at the door the following evening, glaring balefully at the thickening Thames fog. "Imagine! Putting you out this way twice! It is outside of enough, and so I will tell Mr. Lamkin when he returns. What right does he think he has, making these demands?" He modified his indignation. "Well, foreigners never do know what is proper behavior."

John Henry professed surprise that Ragoczy had not yet arrived, though he had anticipated the excitement when the Count's note, written in a fine, small, sloping hand on cream-laid stationery, had been delivered a few minutes after four by an austere man of middle years and steadfast demeanor.

Mr. Tubbs,

I find I cannot get away for another hour at least. Would you be kind enough to ask Mr. Brodribb to wait for me? I realize this is an inconvenience for you and for him, and I regret the necessity of making this request of you. Believe me all contrition; the press of circumstances are such that my time will not be my own for a while.

Accept my thanks and the enclosed for any inconvenience I may have caused you.

Ferenc Ragoczy
Count Saint-Germain
(his seal, the eclipse)

Three shillings had accompanied the note; Mr. Tubbs pocketed them with alacrity.

"I'll use the time to study," said John Henry. "It's no matter to me if I do it here or elsewhere."

"That's generous of you," said Mr. Tubbs. "You are aware, are you not, that if Ragoczy fails to arrive, you will have to spend the night here? I cannot yet entrust a key to you, or I would do it." This last was patently false and both of them knew it.

"I will manage," said John Henry, going to draw the shades. "Hurry on, Mr. Tubbs. You'll miss your tea."

Reluctantly Mr. Tubbs backed into the street, his coat collar raised and his hat set low against the mizzle. After he pulled the door to behind him, he made a point of testing the lock when he had set it.

John Henry listened to Mr. Tubbs's footsteps fade into the rest of the noise from the street. He finished the last of a cold, bitter cup of tea that stood on his desk, and then, with caution, he removed a small book from the locked lower drawer of his desk. He could not help grinning at the well-thumbed pages: *The Tragedy of Romeo and Juliet* by William Shakespeare.

He moved the chairs and made himself a small rehearsal area in the middle of the room, then set about his ongoing memorization of Romeo.

Then plainly know my heart's dear love is set
On the fair daughter of rich Capulet:
As mine on hers, so hers is set on mine;

And all combined, save what thou must combine
By holy marriage: when, and where, and how,
We met, we woo'd and made exchange of vow
I'll tell thee as we pass; but this I pray,
That thou consent to marry us today.

Henry was so caught up in his performance that the spoken answer rattled him the more for being the words he spoke in his mind.

"Holy Saint Francis, what a change is here!" said Ragoczy. He was standing just inside the door, his cloak blending with the shadows.

Looking around as if he feared he had a larger audience, John Henry said, "I didn't hear you knock."

Ragoczy held up the key.

"Of course," said John Henry, his manner now crestfallen. "You came in very quietly."

"You were preoccupied," said Ragoczy, indicating the script John Henry held.

"This." He sighed. "You know my secret, then. I suppose you'll tell Mr. Tubbs."

"Why should I?" asked Ragoczy, taking off his cloak and revealing formal evening dress, including a glistening red silken sash over his shoulder with the diamond-studded Order of Saint Stephen of Hungary blazing on it. "What has Shakespeare to do with your work here?"

"They would turn me off if they knew that I am studying to be an actor," said John Henry with a direct candor that was as unexpected to him as it was to Ragoczy.

"Why?" Ragoczy chose one of the pulled-back chairs, turned it to face John Henry, and sat down. "What reason would they have to turn you off?"

"Acting is not a very . . . honorable profession," said John Henry quietly.

"It was good enough for Shakespeare, and he ended up a baronet." Ragoczy looked slightly amused. "But the Elizabethans were not so squeamish as you modern English are."

"Influence makes a difference," said John Henry, with a sigh. "And a clerk at a merchant's emporium has little to hope for in regard to advancement of that sort."

"They say Shakespeare himself began in the butcher's trade, in Warwickshire." He shook his head once. "He made his own advancement, and you can, as well. What do you want to do, Mr. Brodribb?" asked Ragoczy as he made himself more comfortable. "You may tell me without fear. I will keep your confidence."

"Finish up tonight, if we can," said John Henry at once.

"No," Ragoczy responded. "In regard to your acting: what do you want to do?"

John Henry stared at Ragoczy, thinking the answer was obvious. "Why, be an actor, of course. To perform Shakespeare well for appreciative audiences. To introduce new plays of merit." There was much more to it, but he hesitated to voice these intentions, for that might jinx them.

"Is that all?" asked Ragoczy blandly.

"No," John Henry admitted.

"Would you be willing to tell me of your aspirations?" He asked so casually but with a look of acceptance that broke through John Henry's reserve.

"You must not tell anyone," he cautioned Ragoczy, his nerve all but deserting him.

"Of course," said Ragoczy gravely. He gave John Henry a measuring look. "And how would you set about being an actor? Have you planned?"

As this very subject had taken up most of John Henry's dreams since he came to London, eight years before, he had an answer; over that time he had arrived at a plan that he was sure would succeed if only he could get the funds to put it into operation. "First," he said, launching into his scheme with gusto, "first I would arrange to act with a good amateur company, one where I can gain the basic experience, and meet those who know others in the profession. If I could afford to pay to play a leading role, that would be the best—"

"Pay to play a leading role?" Ragoczy interrupted. "Is that usual?"

"It is," said John Henry, thrown off his stride. "It would be better to pay for a whole production, but that is wishing for the stars." He paused and regained his inner momentum. "I would train myself and take lessons in fencing and other skills. Once I had some favorable reviews, and a few introductions, I would find a touring company, probably in the north or the Midlands, and sign on to do small parts. That way I would master my craft and have the advantage of experience in the process. Eventually, I would want to come back to London. And one day, I would like to have my own company." This last came out in a rush.

Ragoczy studied him, then said, "And you are learning Romeo as a starting point?"

"Yes. I have learned Brutus and Henry V already, and I am working on Angelo. Eventually I will learn Macbeth. Not that I would be ready to play them yet, at my age." He laughed self-consciously. "I can make myself up to appear older, but I haven't the training to carry it off, yet. When I try, I do too much and the results are laughable."

"Hence Romeo, since you are a young man," said Ragoczy.

"Oh, yes," said John Henry, his eyes bright. "But I have been studying people, trying to learn their characteristics so that I may use them at some future time." He strode across the floor in the ponderous roll Mr. Tubbs affected. "That is but one example."

"Very well done," said Ragoczy. "You have caught his obsequious pomposity."

John Henry lowered his eyes. "Thank you."

Ragoczy continued to watch him in silence. Then he got to his feet. "Well, shall we give our attention to the ledger? The sooner we are finished here, the sooner you will be able to return to Romeo." He went to John Henry's desk and glanced at the page John Henry had set out earlier. "How bad do you think it is?"

Difficult though it was, John Henry set his own ambitions aside and gave his attention to the figures on the page. "I would have to say, Count, that in the last decade alone, more than two thousand pounds have been . . . siphoned off your accounts. Between that and what appears to be a consistent pattern of overcharging, you are at a considerable disadvantage." He found himself wondering what it must be like to have more than three thousand pounds to lose.

"And you have no doubt that the pattern you have discovered is deliberate?" Ragoczy's voice was light but firm and John Henry knew that one day he would duplicate it on the stage.

"I wish I did have doubts," he admitted. "But today I have gone over all the records of the accounts in the ledger, not just the current ones but those going back some time. What disturbs me is that the same theft has been continuing for thirty years, or so I have come to suspect. I'll show you," he went on, proffering two large, neat pages of numbers. "This is what I was able to find today."

"What a great deal of work you have done on my behalf," said Ragoczy, looking down at the neat entries.

"It is as much for myself as for you," said John Henry. "I want the name of the firm restored, and it cannot be without these records."

"No one has exposed the firm yet," Ragoczy reminded him.

"It is enough that I know," said John Henry, standing straighter.

"And have you determined which of the London partners is the culprit on this end?" Ragoczy glanced swiftly at John Henry, all the while studying the pages.

"I . . . I cannot be certain, though Mr. Lamkin is in the best position to do it," he said. "If the trouble comes from that part of the firm."

"So I think, as well," agreed Ragoczy, then perused the figures John Henry had supplied him a third time. "How is it," he mused aloud, "that this can have gone on for so long without someone catching the errors? Do you know?"

John Henry had an answer for him. "I've been thinking about that, and I suppose it is because your ledger has not been copied until now. You are not often in London, and when you are, you rarely call here. The entries have been made with great correctness and regularity, and by a senior member of the firm, and so here would be no occasion to doubt what had been done, unless you were suspicious from the first. And since the errors could not be easily seen without extensive comparisons, I would imagine it would be surprising to have them found."

Ragoczy nodded. "But what possessed them to give you the ledger to copy, do you suppose?"

"It is an old ledger. Your family has long done business with us, or so I would suppose." He lowered his eyes. "The account has been here for a very long time. More than thirty years from the entries in the ledger, for there are figures that have been carried forward from earlier entries in what would have to be an older record-book."

"It is a reasonable assumption, Mr. Brodribb," said Ragoczy. "And you doubt that I was signing documents thirty years ago?"

"Possibly not," said John Henry. "For you are not much more than forty, judging by your appearance." He wanted to say more, but could not bring himself to go on.

"What is it?" Ragoczy prompted in a neutral voice.

This time John Henry found it difficult to answer. "It is only . . . that I observe people closely. It is what I must do if I am to be a good actor." He collected himself and said in a rush, "I have noticed something about your eyes. They are not as other eyes I have seen, except, occasionally, in the very old, who have kept their strength and their wits."

Ragoczy nodded. "I am older than I appear," he said without obvious emotion. "Those of my blood do not show their years."

John Henry made a nervous gesture, his burst of confidence deserting him. "I thought it might be . . . something like that. There is a world-weariness that . . . Foreigners are not as easily . . ." He began to flounder in a number of half-finished words.

"Let us return to these records," suggested Ragoczy. "There is much to finish, and I want it accomplished tonight, if that is possible."

"But you must—" John Henry broke off, indicating Ragoczy's finery.

Ragoczy smiled and shook his head. "I have come from a reception; there is a banquet in progress even now."

John Henry was more startled than ever. "I would have thought you would prefer to attend the banquet than look over figures. It is an honor to be invited to such an event." He managed a quick, quirky smile. "Surely the fare at . . . so elegant a function is better than what you can purchase from the local publican, and that is likely to be your lot if we work much later."

"It is certainly more elaborate, and my needs, in that regard, are simple," said Ragoczy.

"Oh," said John Henry, hoping to imply he understood what Ragoczy meant, though he knew he did not.

"How inconsiderate of me. I ask you to forgive my rudeness. Are you hungry?" Ragoczy inquired suddenly. "If you are, I will wait while you purchase something to eat."

"No," said John Henry quickly. "I made a good collation for tea, and it will suit me well enough. I want to continue with your records."

"Let us look at the records from Greece," Ragoczy recommended, opening the page in question. "As you have indicated, the entries there begin in 1828," he added as he ran his finger down the second page of the ledger. "It would appear that the first few years were without incident. All the entries tally, by the look of them. Would you agree?"

"Your family has traded in spices for a long time, haven't they, Count? The indication here is that your account with the spice traders in Arabia is an old one. And the entries from Egypt are of long standing," commented John Henry as he allowed himself to be drawn back into the haven of numbers.

"Yes," said Ragoczy. He inspected the pages closely and in silence for several minutes, and then looked over at John Henry. "I gather that the senior clerk was a Mr. Boulton for many years."

"I've heard that," said John Henry, cautiously.

"And Mr. Boulton was a relative of sorts of the founder?" asked Ragoczy.

"Yes, that is my understanding," said John Henry, his confidence again increasing. "He died more than twenty years ago; at least that's what I've been told."

"Yes," said Ragoczy. "And the uncle of Mr. Tubbs took his place. A Mr. Harbridge. This looks to be the place where the trouble starts."

"So you think that Mr. Tubbs is aware of what is going on?" asked John Henry, doing his best not to be shocked by this suspicion.

"It is possible. He certainly was not eager to have me review these accounts, as you will recall, which, under the circumstances, is significant," said Ragoczy. "How long has he been senior clerk?"

"Mr. Tubbs? About four years, I think. Four or five." He looked around the office as if he expected to be overheard. "He was given quick advancement through the graces of his uncle, or so two of the clerks say." He cleared his throat, and continued. "He was already the senior when I was taken on here."

"Perhaps the partners expected him to protect their interests, and perhaps his uncle advanced him in order to conceal his thefts," said Ragoczy, his face growing somber. "Whatever the case, I will have to put a stop to this, I fear."

"Certainly you must," said John Henry, astonished that Ragoczy could sound so reluctant to protect himself from theft. "It cannot be overlooked or allowed to continue. If they have stolen from you, it may be that there are others who have been so lamentably—"

"Yes," said Ragoczy, cutting him short. "No doubt you are right." He looked at the figures one last time. "Would you be willing to make a copy of these two pages for me? I will send my manservant to get them from you tomorrow, if that would suit you. He will also return the key to Mr. Tubbs, with my apology for keeping it so long." There was a quality to his words that disturbed John Henry.

"I will do as you like, Count," he said, a chill tracing itself up his spine.

"That is very good of you," said Ragoczy. "All in all, it has been most interesting to meet you, Mr. Brodribb."

"Thank you," John Henry said, and suppressed a shudder. Then, before he could master himself, he blurted out, "Are you Doctor Faustus?" Beginning to realize he had actually spoken his apprehension aloud, he stepped back, the enormity of what he had done coming over him; he could think of nothing to say that would be a sufficient apology.

Ragoczy looked faintly amused. "No, Mr. Brodribb, I am not. Nor am I 'going to and fro in the earth and walking up in down in it,' as Mephistopheles is said to do." He looked John Henry over carefully. "You will probably succeed very well at your chosen profession; you have a keen eye and an insightful nature, which should take you far."

"I did not mean . . . it was . . ." John Henry faltered.

"Do not fear," said Ragoczy with an ironic chuckle. "In my time I have heard worse."

"How old are you?" John Henry demanded, convinced that he was in too deep to attempt to escape now.

"If I told you," said Ragoczy at his most urbane, "you would not believe me."

"Oh, I would," said John Henry, too caught up to be frightened. He knew the terror would come later, when he was safe in bed and his imagination would have free rein.

"I think not," said Ragoczy, closing the subject.

"Are you going to demand anything of me now? Order me to silence or face a terrible fate?"

Ragoczy cocked his head. "This is not a performance. You are not playing a role now, Mr. Brodribb. I rely on your discretion and good sense to keep your various speculation to yourself."

"Or I will suffer for it?" John Henry knew he had gone too far again, and for a second time could not arrive at an adequate apology.

"No," said Ragoczy quietly but beyond any dispute. "You have nothing to fear from me: my word on it." He walked away from John Henry toward the fire, then stopped and turned back to him, asking in a different voice, "Tell me: how much would you need to put your acting plans into motion? Have you arrived at a figure for that in all your calculations?"

This change of subject jolted John Henry, but he did his best to answer. "Well, I would need wigs and beards and paint, and all the rest of that; and swords and costumes, too." He did not need to consult the pages of the notebook he kept in his waistcoat pocket. "That would cost between forty and fifty pounds, all told. And then there would be the payment for the leading part. That would be another fifty pounds, if I am to do Romeo." He brightened as he said this, but his enthusiasm waned as he listened to himself, thinking that it would be impossible for him to earn enough to achieve his dreams.

Ragoczy tapped his small, well-shaped hands together, fingertips to fingertips. "Suppose," he said, "I should settle a portion of what I recover from this firm upon you for the service you have rendered me? From what you have discovered, the amount might be considerable."

Chagrined, John Henry shook his head. "It would appear that I have been bribed to show things in your favor, at least that could be claimed by the partners to the court. And the other clerks would probably believe the worst of me, because I am the newest of them. The partners might well have a claim against me, one that the courts would uphold."

"A legacy, then," said Ragoczy, undaunted by John Henry's protestation. "You must have a relative somewhere who might leave you an inheritance."

John Henry sighed. "Why should any of my family do that? Not that most of them have ten shillings to spare for anyone. And coming immediately after I have helped you, it would not be a useful ruse, in any case. Someone here would be bound to question how I came by it."

"Listen to me," said Ragoczy firmly. "Suppose that six months from now a distant . . . shall we say uncle? . . . of yours leaves you a hundred pounds. The money would be handled by a solicitor in the north, and there would be no question of compromising you, no matter what the courts might or might not do to the partners here. Could you then afford to start on your theatrical career?"

Little as he wanted to admit it, John Henry's pulse raced at the thought. He calculated what it would mean to him to have the money, and he set his prudence aside. "It might work, saying it was left to me, if it happened later." His excitement was building and he could not contain the satisfaction he felt.

"Six months, then. My London solicitors should have made all the necessary arrangements for recovering what is owed me by that time." Ragoczy watched John Henry with interest.

"Will things be unpleasant for you here when my claim against the firm has been filed? There could be police involvement, you understand."

"It is possible they could hold me to blame," said John Henry. "It is no secret that I have been copying your ledger. They will have to assume you had your information from me."

"But they need not know you discovered the theft," Ragoczy said persuasively. "I could charge my London solicitors to review the ledgers; I could require a full disclosure of the state of my account. That would spare you the brunt of the partners' displeasure. I do not like to think you would be punished for being an honest man, Mr. Brodribb."

"When I leave the company, it will not matter," said John Henry.

"You think it will not, but it will, you know," said Ragoczy. "You do not want whispers following you, saying that you have abused the trust of your employer. Not even the theater excuses such things, Mr. Brodribb. Rumors are constant in the world of players, and you do not want to begin with a reputation that is tainted. Believe this."

John Henry could not help but agree. He realized that Ragoczy was not only generous but more knowledgeable than he had suspected. "All right. A distant relative could be invented. An uncle. In the north."

"You would do well to mention that you have heard the fellow is ailing, and dismiss any suggestion that you might benefit from his death," Ragoczy recommended. "That way when you express your amazement at the legacy, none of clerks will link your good fortune to the assistance you have given me."

As he slapped his hand on his thigh, John Henry burst out, "By all that's famous! You've hit on the very means to make this happen." He laughed aloud. "You are a canny man, Count, a complete hand; a 'peevy cove,' as the lower orders would say."

"A peevy cove. What a delightful expression," said Ragoczy sardonically, his fine brows lifting. "Still, I have been called worse." For an instant a bleakness came over him; seeing it, John Henry was chilled.

He started to speak, coughed, and tried again. "I suppose you've learned, over the years, to guard yourself. That's why you're so quick to make the suggestions you have."

"There is some truth to that, yes," said Ragoczy, his dark, enigmatic eyes haunted. With a gesture he dismissed the gloom that threatened to overcome him. "But you will think you've been caught in one of Mrs. Radcliffe's dismal romances if I say much more, or that farrago of Maturin's."

"Melmoth the Wanderer?" asked John Henry, a little taken aback that Ragoczy should know the work.

Ragoczy did not answer. He glanced at the ledger one last time. "Tomorrow a clerk from my solicitor will visit Mr. Tubbs. He will say that I have asked to have my business here reviewed. Oh, never fear. I will demand the same of the other merchants with whom I have done business. I will not single this firm out for the solicitors' attention." He took a rapid turn around the room; the lamplight danced and sparkled in the jewels on his Order. "I will do everything I can to make it appear that this is not an unusual request. Since I am a foreigner, I am certain that Mr. Tubbs will be willing to think the worst of me for that."

John Henry colored. "He is one of those who thinks Jesus Christ spoke in English."

"He has that look to him," Ragoczy agreed. He halted in front of John Henry and held out his hand. "It's settled then."

"Yes, all right," said John Henry as his large hand closed over Ragoczy's small one. "It's settled."

In the private parlor of the pub, the company of actors were still exhilarated by the great success they had had with their new production of Romeo and Juliet. At the head of the long table, the young man who had paid for the Royal Soho Theatre production and for the privilege of playing Romeo, was still holding court, flushed with a heady combination of port and applause.

"You were quite wonderful, Henry," said the woman beside him, a cozy matron who had played Lady Capulet. "You'll go far, you mark my words."

Henry was willing to be convinced. "Ah, Meg, Meg. It's such a good play, that's what makes the difference." He frowned a little, wishing his family had been willing to come, but they were such strict Christians that they rarely ventured out to public entertainments of any sort.

The director, who had also played Mercutio, was more than half-drunk, and he swung around to face Henry, lifting his glass.

"So you think you'll . . . take the London stage by storm, do you?"

"One day I hope to," said Henry, already hungry for the time it would happen.

"That's what they all do," the director muttered, sounding bitter.

"You leave off baiting him," Meg ordered the director. "Just because he's a better player than you—"

"Better player!" scoffed the director, taking another long draught of dark ale. "Why, he's as green as . . . as . . ." He lost the direction of his thought.

"Yes, he's green," said Meg with some heat. "But he's got it in him. You can tell by what he does. He's got the touch." She beamed at Henry, her smile not as motherly as it had been. "You'll all see. I know Henry's going to go far."

Henry basked in her approval and watched as the rest of the company caroused themselves into fatigue, and then began to drift off into the night. Henry was one of the last to leave, pausing to tip the landlord for allowing them to hire the private parlor for the later hours.

As he stepped into the street, he paused, realizing it was very late; the windows were dark in the buildings that faced the road. No traffic moved over the cobbles. Only the skitter of rats attracted his attention as he pulled his coat about him and started toward his home.

Then he heard a soft, crisp footfall, and with a cry of alarm he turned, expecting to see one of the desperate street thieves who preyed upon the unwary. He brought up his arm. "I have a pistol," he warned.

The answer out of the dense shadows was amused. "Do you really, Mr. Brodribb." A moment later, Ferenc Ragoczy stepped out of the darkness. He was wearing his hooded cloak, as he had been the first time John Henry had seen him. As he walked up to the young actor, he said, "Congratulations. That was a very impressive debut."

"You saw it?" asked John Henry.

"Yes." Ragoczy smiled, the pallid light from the distant streetlamp casting a sharply angled shadow over his features. "I am pleased your . . . inheritance was so well spent."

John Henry felt suddenly very callow. "I should have thanked you, I know, but with the trial and all, I didn't think it would—"

"What reason do you have to thank me? The legacy was from our uncle, wasn't it?" He started to walk toward the main road, motioning to John Henry to walk with him. "If anything I should thank you for the six thousand pounds my solicitors recovered from Mr. Tubbs and Mr. Lamkin."

"Everyone believed it," said John Henry, still marveling at how easily the clerks had been convinced that so distant and unknown an uncle would leave a sizable amount to his nephew. "I never thought they would."

"People believe things they want to think happen. What clerk would not like a distant relative to make them a beneficiary of his estate? So they are willing to think it has happened to you." He went a few steps, in silence. "Tell me, was there some specific reason for taking the name Irving?"

"Yes," said John Henry. "There was. My mother used to read me the sermons of Edward Irving. He was a Scottish evangelist, and a powerful orator. And I admire the American author Washington Irving."

"And why Henry instead of John?" asked Ragoczy. They were nearing Charing Cross Road and could see a few heavily laden wagons making their way along the almost deserted thoroughfare, and one or two cabs out to pick up what few shillings they might from late-night stragglers.

"It sounds more distinguished," said John Henry at once; he had given the matter much thought and was prepared to defend his choice if questioned.

But Ragoczy, it seemed, was satisfied. "Then the best of good fortune to you, Henry Irving." He nodded to an elegant coach waiting at the corner. "This is where we part company, I think."

John Henry accepted this with a surge of embarrassment. "You should have come into the pub. We could have had a drink. They have decent port at the pub." He hated to see Ragoczy walk away. "I want to thank you. To drink your health."

Ragoczy paused, and bowed, and said in a voice John Henry would never forget, "You are very kind, Mr. Irving, but I do not drink wine."

Hisako San

Ingrid Pitt

Polish-born actress and author Ingrid Pitt (Ingoushka Petrov, 1937–2010) was best known to film fans as Hammer Film's Queen of Horror. In the early 1970s she became a horror icon when the British studio starred her in *The Vampire Lovers* (based on J. Sheridan Le Fanu's "Carmilla") and *Countess Dracula*.

Her other film credits include the Spanish *Sound of Horror*, *The Omegans*, *The House That Dripped Blood* (in a segment based on Robert Bloch's story "The Cloak"), *The Wicker Man* (1973), *Artemis 81*, *The House*, *Underworld* (aka *Transmutations*, based on a story by Clive Barker), *The Asylum*, the short *Green Fingers*, *Minotaur*, Hammer's *Beyond the Rave*, and *Sea of Dust*. She also appeared on TV in episodes of the BBC's *Doctor Who* ("The Time Monster" and "Warriors of the Deep"), Brian Clemens's *Thriller* ("Ilse"), and *Urban Gothic* ("Vampirology").

The actress wrote the nonfiction studies *The Ingrid Pitt Bedside Companion for Vampire Lovers*, *The Ingrid Pitt Bedside Companion for Ghosthunters*, and *The Ingrid Pitt Book of Murder, Torture & Depravity*, as well as contributing regular columns to such magazines as *Shivers*, *Femme Fatales*, *Bite Me*, *It's Alive*, and *The Cricketer*.

Her 1999 autobiography, entitled *Life's a Scream*, detailed the harrowing experiences of her early life in a Nazi Concentration camp, her search throughout the European Red Cross Refugee Camps for her father, and her escape from East Berlin one step ahead of the *Volkpolitzei*.

About her various appearances as an undead *femme fatale*, the actress once revealed: "They are always roles you can get your teeth into."

DETECTIVE SERGEANT JANET Cooper picked up a photograph from the Shinto altar and studied it. It was black and white and slightly faded, but it gave a good likeness of the man and woman dressed in traditional Japanese kimonos and proudly holding a newborn baby. Janet carefully put the picture back and fingered the other mementos on the small makeshift altar. A couple of spent candles in saucers, a battered watch with Japanese characters on the dial, and a string of beads. She looked around the room but found nothing else of interest.

She went back into the sitting room. It was sparely but expensively furnished. The door was open, and the caretaker of the block stood just inside the door watching them suspiciously. Detective Inspector Tom Brasher turned away from the window and raised an inquisitive eyebrow. Janet shook her head.

"Nothing there," she reported.

Brasher took a colorful folder off the table and handed it to her.

"What d'you think of that?" he asked.

The folder was from a Japanese shipping line. Inside were a number of newspaper clippings. They were all from London papers and the subject was the same in each. Senator Osram Manhelm. Janet skimmed through a couple of articles and learned that the Senator was in London with a trade mission. He was due to meet his Japanese counterparts and sign a Nippon/US agreement that evening. But first there was some socializing to do. Janet handed the folder back to Brasher.

"What does that tell us?"

Brasher shrugged. "For one thing this Hisako woman seems to have a special interest in the Senator," he said and turned to the caretaker.

"When did Miss Hisako arrive?"

The caretaker was determined to be unhelpful. "It's in the book," he said coldly.

Brasher smiled brightly. "Right. How about you fetch the book and we go down to the station and my sergeant gives it a nice long once-over?"

The smile unsettled the caretaker.

"Three days ago," he mumbled.

"Where from?" Janet encouraged.

The caretaker shrugged. "It's a private booking. Try the estate agents."

Brasher and Janet walked back to their car parked outside the flats. Brasher leaned on the bonnet.

"You go round to the estate agents, see what you can pick up there. I'll take a taxi back to the station and check on immigration," he said as he pushed away from the car and opened the door for Janet in one smooth move.

Janet got in behind the wheel and wound down the window.

"What d'you think this Hisako woman's got to do with those blokes falling to pieces in the hospital?" she queried.

Brasher gave her a bland, humorless smile. "Nothing probably, but she is interesting," he told her.

Brasher stood and watched the car disappear into the traffic. Janet was right of course. Twelve young, fit men cut down in their prime took a lot of swallowing. And just because the Japanese woman had been seen to kiss them shortly before they became walking cesspits didn't necessarily mean that she had anything to do with it. Brasher wasn't keen on coincidences. He couldn't see how the two disparate facts knitted together, but visceral prompting told him the connection was there. He was lucky with a taxi and was back at the station within ten minutes.

A DC called to him as he opened his office door. "Hi, Guv. You're on this rowing club thing, aren't you?" he asked.

Brasher nodded.

"Two more," the DC said cryptically.

"Two more?" Brasher echoed.

"Two more . . . er . . . suspicious deaths."

He placed a couple of sheets of paper in front of the Inspector. Brasher scanned them and looked up in surprise.

"Why wasn't I told about this before?" he asked, a note of threat in his voice.

"They were just separate incidents. No follow-up for us." The DC shrugged off responsibility adroitly.

"Okay. Get onto the Japanese Embassy. Ask them what they know about a woman called Hisako. Probably just arrived in London. Maybe with the Japanese trade delegation."

The DC nodded and left. Brasher thought for a moment and was about to follow when the phone rang.

"Brasher." He listened, nodded. "Fine. Meet me at St. George's Dock. We've got two more . . . nothing to do with the rowing club as far as I can see."

The large wooden crate stood isolated by a cordon of POLICE KEEP OUT tape. Brasher walked slowly around the box. The front of the crate was slightly open. He pulled the lid wider and examined the interior. There wasn't much to examine. Just a crudely padded plank at sitting height and straps screwed to the wall. Janet was talking to one of the security men. Brasher called her over.

"See if you can get in there," he said.

Janet couldn't come near to wedging her five-foot, nine-inch frame into the space provided.

"I'd need to shed two stone and saw my legs off at the knees," she volunteered.

Brasher helped her out of the case.

"What did you get from the guard?" he asked.

"Doesn't know anything," she said as she straightened up. "Jim Bailey has worked here for about twenty years. Retiring at the end of the year." She thought and carefully corrected herself. "Was."

"And the seaman?"

Janet took out her notebook.

"Taki Takamura, twenty-eight-years old, from Soma. Taken ill yesterday evening and died this morning," she read.

"Anything else?" he asked in a negative tone.

Janet shook her head. Brasher's cell rang and he hooked it out of his pocket.

"Brasher." He listened intently without interrupting. "You're sure of this . . .? Right, put out a bulletin and let me know if we get a break." Brasher pocketed his telephone.

"We've had feedback from the Japanese Embassy," he said. "Hisako is not a member of the trade delegation and there is no report of anyone with her name or fitting her description entering the country in the last ten days." He thought through his next words carefully before continuing.

"There is, however, a report about a Hisako who went missing from a military hospital in Soma. Her description fits and it could be her—except for one thing. She has a rare lymphatic disease and has been living in an isolation bubble since shortly after she was born. The doctors insist that she would be dead by now. And you know what caused the disease?"

Brasher sucked in his breath and answered his own question. "Fallout from the hydrogen bomb the Yanks dropped on Nagasaki."

Janet frowned and walked to the edge of the jetty and stared out over the gently heaving water.

"She can't be that old," she said slowly.

Brasher nodded agreement.

"She's not. It was her parents who were affected. They showed no ill-effects but passed on the disorder to their daughter."

He thought for a minute. "Any ideas?" he asked.

Janet turned to face him. "Those clippings in the folder. There was one that gave some background on Senator Manhelm. He was a part of the team that dropped the bomb."

The party at the American embassy in Grosvenor Square was in full swing when Brasher and Janet arrived. The embassy staff had flatly refused to give them security status and insisted that they were there only as guests.

The invitation had said 8:00 p.m. to 10:30 p.m. It was 9:45 p.m. and Brasher was beginning to think they had overreacted, seen too many Arnie Schwarzenegger films. When you thought it through rationally, in a detached manner, the whole theory was ridiculous. How could a young woman with a deadly disease come all the way to London, leave a trail of hideous death behind her and still move around with every appearance of good health?

He was about to suggest to Janet that they picked up their coats and left when there was a ripple of comment that cut across the hubbub of sound. Brasher glanced around. Everyone was looking toward the main entrance.

Nothing had prepared Brasher for the sheer beauty of the exquisite woman who stood in the doorway. She was small but beautifully proportioned. Her midnight-black hair was piled high on her head and secured with brightly-lacquered combs. The light blue silk kimono she was wearing covered her from throat to toe, but the thin material did nothing to disguise the body beneath.

"That's got to be her," Janet stated unnecessarily.

The Senator was the first to snap out of it. He put on a wide Texas grin and bore down on the diminutive woman like an avalanche in early spring.

Janet tapped Brasher on the arm and claimed his attention. "What now?" she asked simply but to the point.

Brasher physically shook himself and refocussed on the job in hand. "Just keep an eye on her."

The Senator was busy introducing Hisako to the other guests. He was obviously smitten and he was oblivious to the venomous looks his wife shot at him as he pranced around in a flawed attempt to shed fifty years. Half an hour later the guests were beginning to drift away. Brasher beckoned to Janet and stationed himself by the door. Janet joined him.

"When she leaves, identify yourself and ask her to come down to the station. If you get any trouble, arrest her," he instructed.

Janet winced. "What are the charges?"

"Being a danger to the health of aging Senators, for a start. We'll think of something. Just don't lose her," Brasher told her.

He looked around. There was no sign of either the Senator or Hisako.

"Damn. Where'd they go? Watch the door," Brasher ordered.

He placed the empty glass he had been nursing on the windowsill and walked purposefully toward the spot where he had last seen the Senator and his lovely guest.

The door to the terrace was open and he eased into a position where he could see outside. As his eyes adjusted to the dark, he could just make out two figures standing by the balustrade. He didn't now what to do. He felt like a Peeping Tom. Hisako moved closer to the Senator and took off the long gloves she was wearing. There was something menacing about the way she unveiled her hands and it was not lost on Brasher. He still had no clear idea what he was going to do. He coughed and stepped out onto the terrace. The Senator saw him and swayed back, putting a little distance between himself and temptation. But he wasn't pleased.

"Yes?" he barked.

Before Brasher could think of something to say, Hisako reached up and took the Senator's face in her hands and gave the old man a passionate kiss on the lips. Hisako stepped back and gave a deep bow. A faint, amused smile lurked around her lips, taunting the policeman to do something. With a movement that Gypsy Rose Lee would have envied, Hisako ripped off her silk kimono and dropped it to the floor. Underneath she was wearing a tight-fitting catsuit that revealed every curve and dimple of her perfect body. The Senator was beginning to recover his equilibrium.

"What's going on here?" he asked loudly, but nobody bothered to answer. Still with her eyes fixed mesmerically on Brasher's face, Hisako tossed aside the highly-lacquered hairpiece she was wearing. Beneath it her skull was hairless. But even this didn't diminish her ravishing beauty. Brasher managed to pump some air through his vocal chords.

"Detective Inspector Brasher. I wonder if you would mind accompanying me to the station. I would like to ask . . ." He trailed to a halt, feeling inept.

Hisako walked slowly toward him.

"I don't think so, Inspector. I have other plans," she said softly.

Before Brasher had a chance to move, her hand shot out and crashed into his throat. Brasher staggered back, knocking over a stand with a huge pot plant. The sound of the crash brought two of the guards running, pistols in hand. Hisako was already on the move. As the first guard came through the door he was met with a flying *mata-geri* which crashed him into the wall. The second guard decided it was one of those times when you shoot first and ask questions later.

Hisako did a back flip and her arched foot thudded into his neck. His gun went off but missed Hisako. Other guards came running. They were no match for their daintily lethal opponent.

Janet arrived on the scene in time to see one of the eighteen-stone bodyguards tossed over the balustrade. If the trained American guards with their guns weren't getting anywhere she was hardly likely to make a difference with her telescopic night-stick.

Janet hastily hid behind the thick wooden door leading to the entrance hall. She saw Hisako break away and run toward where she was hiding. The policewoman threw her weight at the heavy door. There was a satisfying crash as Hisako, taken completely off guard, ran into the swinging portal. The force propelled her across the room.

Janet didn't hang about. The dazed Japanese woman was already recovering, almost on her feet. Janet snatched up a bronze statuette of John Wayne and dived forward. The heavy ornament smashed into the side of Hisako's head with the full weight of the policewoman and the impetus of her dive behind it. The *thud* as it crunched into Hisako's bald head echoed around the room.

Exhausted by the effort, Janet slumped to the floor and stared at the hideous wound she had opened in Hisako's naked skull.

She let the guards take care of the unconscious woman and eventually went looking for Brasher. She found him crouched over the Senator. He looked up.

"Get an ambulance," he told her. "The Senator's been shot."

Hisako was proving to be a medical miracle. The wound in her head was healing at a phenomenal rate. It was only four hours since Janet had laid her out, but already the gash had closed and left only a jagged red scar to mark its passing.

The Senator hadn't fared so well. He had begun to develop the symptoms that were becoming so well known to Brasher and Janet.

The doctors had no answers to their questions. The best they could come up with was that Hisako's body was basically *different*, it had become more efficient and, they reluctantly added, improved. The interesting thing about her immune system seemed to be that it was externalized through her lymph glands. This explained the deaths of those unfortunate enough to come into physical contact with her.

Shortly before midnight the Senator died an agonizing death, virtually rotting alive. The doctors were having a field day. Already they were calling the disease, which totally destroyed the victim's immune system, "The Hisako Syndrome," and vying for the honor of giving it a Latin label. Hisako was locked up in an isolation cell until a secure and germ-free environment could be made available to her at the hospital.

Janet finished reading through her report on the incidents of the day. She felt a certain sympathy toward the captured woman. It must have been terrible for her. All her life she had been kept in an airtight bubble. Treated like a guinea pig. Somehow she had been touched by another human being. Only to see him or her die, rot and shrivel before her eyes. Janet could imagine the rage that welled inside her.

Her records showed that she was way above average intelligence. She spoke several languages and had a score of PhDs. Her intelligence and isolation had fed her mind, but she had no idea about the simple things of life. And it was all down to the bomb the Americans had dropped on her hometown.

Somehow Senator Manhelm had become responsible for all her problems and she had set out to destroy him. The rowing club and the others had just been unfortunate to get in her way.

Janet locked the report in her drawer and was preparing to leave when the telephone rang. Hisako had become ill and was asking to see her. Janet hesitated. Although sympathetic, she didn't want to get too close to the captured woman. Then she shrugged. What harm could it do?

When Janet entered the cell she gagged on the smell of putrefaction which even penetrated the surgical mask she was wearing. Hisako was strapped in a straitjacket, lying on her side facing the wall. Her bald head was already mottled and had developed nauseating, pus-dribbling, boils. Hisako rolled over so that she was facing Janet. The policewoman was shocked at the change to the delicate features of the beautiful woman. Hisako's face had blown up into a scarlet pumpkin. Her eyes, which had been so fine and clear a few hours earlier, were now milky cataracts that flickered feverishly. Her perfect mouth a deformed crater of festering ulcers. Slowly Hisako pushed herself to her feet. Effortlessly, she flexed her muscles and the straitjacket ripped and fell in a heap on the floor.

Janet wanted to call out, alert the guard to what was happening, but she couldn't move.

Hisako limped painfully towards the mesmerized policewoman and reached out her nightmarish hands.

Janet felt her mind slipping away as the ghoulish entity ripped aside her shirt and jacket and gently touched ulcerated lips to her bare breast. As consciousness fled, Janet felt Hisako's feverish breath suck the vitality from her body.

When Janet regained consciousness, Hisako was sitting on the floor by the side of the door. She was still naked, but her skin was as clear and unblemished as it had been defiled and corrupt a few minutes earlier.

Janet knew with a terrible certainty what that meant. She calmed the panic the thought provoked in her mind and looked at Hisako. She was no longer afraid of the woman.

The beautiful killer grabbed the front of Janet's tattered shirt and hauled her to her feet so that she was standing facing the entrance. With the flat of her hand she pounded on the cell door. There was a flutter at the spy-hole, a rattle of the key in the lock and before Janet could shout a warning the door began to open.

Hisako gave Janet a sweet smile as she wrenched open the door. The policeman on guard didn't stand a chance. Hisako's daggerlike hand pierced the wall of his stomach and drove up into his heart. Janet lunged forward but the deranged woman brushed her, almost gently, aside. It was as if she didn't want to harm her. Just leave her to die the horrendous death that was her ultimate legacy.

Brasher was on his way to check out the condition of the prisoner for himself. He heard the scream as Hisako ripped open the PC's body. He was just in time to see Hisako smash through the door which led into the reception area of the station. He ran after her, but by the time he reached the outer office she had overpowered the officers who attempted to restrain her and left by the front door.

A couple of police constables walking toward the building stopped in surprise as the naked woman burst out of the front door. Brasher shouted to them to stop her. There was a ten-foot wall along the side of the road. Without decreasing her speed, Hisako leapt onto a parked car and without apparent effort cleared the obstacle.

Brasher ran to his car. As he began to pull away from the curb, Janet leaped into the road and stopped him. She jumped into the front passenger seat.

"What happened?" he asked as he accelerated away in the direction taken by Hisako. "You all right?"

Janet ignored the question and pointed off to the right. "There she is."

Hisako had made it to the Embankment and was running along the parapet at a fantastic speed. Brasher tried to cut across the traffic to the opposite side of the road, but the after-theater rush-hour was heavy and he lost valuable seconds before he managed it. By this time Hisako had disappeared.

"Where the hell has she got to?" Brasher demanded.

Janet opened the car door. "She's making for Lambeth Bridge. It'll be quicker on foot."

Brasher nodded agreement and pulled out his radio.

"Control—Brasher here. Get someone to block off the south side of Lambeth Bridge. I'm in pursuit on foot with DS Cooper, north of the Embankment. We need back-up. Fast!"

Brasher stowed his radio away and set off at a jog behind Janet. As they turned onto the bridge they saw a police car pull across the road at the far end. Janet slowed to a walk and Brasher caught her up.

"Can you see her?" he panted as he bent over and sucked air into his heaving lungs.

Janet shook her head. "She must be on the bridge. She didn't have time to get completely across."

A police car pulled up beside them and the driver leaned out of the window.

"What you want me to do, Guv?" he asked.

Janet answered. "One of you stay here and divert the traffic. The other clear the bridge. Now!" she ordered.

The driver swung the car sideways, effectively blocking off that end of the bridge. Brasher and Janet took opposite sides of the road and walked slowly toward the patrol cars at the far end. Brasher was the first to spot the hunted woman. She was leaning elegantly against one of the suspension struts of the antique viaduct, the suspicion of a smile on her lips.

"Okay, Miss," Brasher said reassuringly. "Just come down off there and let's talk. I'm sure we can sort something out."

Hisako swung around one of the stanchions and landed on the side wall with a peal of laughter, as if it was all a game.

"Of course we can, Inspector. You'll find me a nice warm isolation cell where I can become a clinical curiosity for every half-baked doctor with a theory and a fascination with Jekyll and Hyde. Thanks but no thanks, Inspector."

Hisako hunched down on her knees so that her head was almost at the same level as Brasher's. Her eyes appeared to have become enormous. The Inspector had an overwhelming desire to let himself float down into their dark depths.

"Come on, Inspector. Come to me," Hisako whispered.

Brasher's reason told him to keep a safe distance between them, but his will was not strong enough. He took a faltering step toward the woman.

"That's right, don't fight it, you know you want me. Quick, give me your hand." Her voice was a soft erotic caress. Brasher was a spectator as his hand reached out to the beautiful temptress crouched naked on the parapet. Their fingers were almost touching. Brasher made one last supreme effort to control his action, but Hisako's will was too strong.

He heard Janet's voice call out to him to stop, but it meant nothing. He had to be with Hisako.

Suddenly there was a pounding of feet and he was thrown violently aside.

Hisako saw Janet coming and tried to move into a more secure position on the narrow parapet. The policewoman had nothing left to lose. She knew with a terrible certainty that within hours she would fall victim to all the ills that Hisako was able to release and that knowledge drove her on.

She hurled herself at the ogress on the parapet, wrapped her arms around the other woman's legs.

Hisako tried to brace herself, but the force of the impact of Janet's hurtling body was too much for even her superior strength to withstand. For a moment they teetered on the edge of the bridge and then, almost in slow motion, they toppled backward.

Brasher snapped out of the trance he was in and ran to the bridge, too late to save either woman.

He could only stand and watch as they plunged down into the dark, swirling waters of the River Thames below.

The police searched the river and its banks for days, but they never recovered the bodies of either Janet Cooper or the mysterious Hisako San.

Butternut and Blood

Kathryn Ptacek

Kathryn Ptacek's novels include *Gila!*, *Shadoweyes*, *Kachina*, *The Phoenix Bells*, *The Black Jade Road*, *The Willow Garden*, *Ghost Dance*, and *The Hunted*, under her own name and other bylines. She edited two volumes of the *Women in Darkness* anthologies, and her short fiction was collected by Wildside Press in *Looking Backward in Darkness: Tales of Fantasy and Horror*. She also edits *The Gila Queen's Guide to Markets*, a market newsletter that goes to writers, artists, editors, and agents throughout the world.

Ptacek was married to author and editor Charles L. Grant from 1982 until his death in 2006.

"Vampires in the American Civil War?" asks the author. "A natural, if you ask me. The War Between the States proved one of the bloodiest conflicts known to man, and what better place to find a lamia who preys upon young men?

"My novel, *Blood Autumn*, marked the first appearance of a lamia sister (there are many in this lethal family), and then she and another sister played instrumental roles in the prequel, *In Silence Sealed* (the true story of what happened to Byron, Keats, and Shelley). Different sisters have also surfaced in numerous short stories, and I'm sure other historical tales of their deadly deeds will be unearthed from time to time."

HE FIRST SAW her on the autumn night when the temperature plunged toward freezing, and the stink of smoke combined with that of dying leaves and dying men.

John Francis Foster had himself been wounded just three days ago in battle, and after laying a full day and a chill rainy night on the blood-soaked field—there were not enough able-bodied men to collect the wounded and dying—he had finally been located and brought in.

The first evening there in the relative comfort of the hospital tent Foster had done nothing but sleep and occasionally moan. The second night he had slept less heavily, and once he woke, fell back to sleep quickly, hardly aware of his injuries, for the moment.

The third night he was fully awake, fully aware of the pain in his side where the Minié ball had puckered his flesh, and where a fall had broken his arm in two places; and it was then he saw the woman.

She stood at the far end of the tent talking to one of the patients there, a young dark-haired man whose left leg had been shattered by shot, and then later amputated. The man's condition was fair because he was young and in good health overall, and he was expected to leave the hospital in a week or so. The man was far luckier than many other of his comrades here, Foster thought.

A woman in this hellish place was an odd sight, Foster realized, for all the nurses, save one, were male, mostly marines assigned to this duty. Perhaps this woman was one of the civilians from a nearby farm or town, come to visit the wounded, come with gifts of food, come to cheer them up.

He shifted his head slightly, closed his eyes when the nausea hit him, then once he was all right, looked to his right. A boy, surely no older than fourteen, lay curled on the cot. A smell of pus and urine came from him. Foster, too long accustomed to the sharp smells of battlefield and hospital now, scarcely noticed the stench. On the far side of the boy—Foster thought the lad's name was Willy—slept an overweight man with a reddened countenance.

A drinker, Foster thought, and envied the man his liquid escape. Now, though, the drinker snored heavily, spittle bubbling on his plump lips. Foster didn't know what was wrong with the drinker, but he'd been there the longest of any of the patients, and he did not seem likely to leave any time soon.

To Foster's left lay an old sergeant; the man must have been all of fifty or so, but he looked elderly now. His skin was gray, and hung in folds upon his body where he had lost so much weight. Since Foster had been there, the sergeant had not opened his eyes; his breathing, scarcely audible, never varied. Across the narrow walkway between rows of cots Foster could see others similar to him—men with bandages on heads, across their eyes, around stumps of arms, and legs, swathing torsos.

During the day some of them talked—those in less pain—but at night it was bad. While some slept, oblivious to their pain and the anguish of those around them, most of the wounded suffered more through the long dark hours. Few spoke at all, but Foster heard much groaning and sobbing and cursing and whimpering, while others wordlessly tossed in their fevered states; occasionally a plaintive voice prayed to die.

At the end of the tent, just a few feet away from the woman, stood a tall moveable screen. It had once been white cloth, but now was spotted with red and yellow and black, from all the patients who had faced the surgeon's desperate ministrations behind it. A sturdy table upon which operations were conducted sat behind that barrier, and one modest cabinet which stored the surgeon's meager supply of drugs and tools.

The woman glanced up now and saw Foster watching, and she smiled, and he thought how beautiful she was, quite the loveliest he had seen in a long time. Her waist-length hair, caught at the nape of her slender neck, appeared to be a reddish gold, or so it seemed in the dim light. He could not see the color of her eyes though they seemed dark. Her lips were red and full, her skin pale, but that was the way of many of our Southern ladies, he reflected. She wore a gown of good cloth, a sober gray in color, much like the uniforms of Foster's army.

Or the uniforms that we once had, he thought, as he noted the appearance of each of the patients. Some still wore the remnants of their uniforms—the gray with butternut trim, but most had only discolored rags, and even those with nearly whole uniforms had added a color; the men wore gray and butternut and blood.

The woman was bending over the young amputee now, holding his hand. Foster looked away. Perhaps she was a sister or the man's fiancée.

He fell asleep soon after that, and when he woke again, the woman was gone.

The next day the young man died.

The doctors came by that afternoon and examined each man. They told Foster that he must rest more and spooned down some awful-tasting medicine. His meals that day were several mouthfuls of a thin gruel over which a chicken had been passed for flavor, or so he suspected, and in which floated a few wild onions. It was all that his stomach could tolerate.

That night he felt much worse than he had the night before, the pain radiating out from his side, coursing down his legs until he thought his limbs were on fire; his arm throbbed each time he took a breath. He forced himself not to think about his condition, forced his mind to other matters, such as his family.

His family waited for him at home in eastern Tennessee and, God willing, he would be with them soon. He wished he could get a letter home to his wife, but no one had come by, asking if he wanted to write letters, no one in the tent had pencil or paper for him to use. So he wrote the letters to Sarah, and to his parents, in his mind. Each night he revised the letter from the previous night; he concentrated on each word, each phrase. He thought it was the only way to keep the pain at bay.

He was not always successful.

That night he slept fitfully, and once he woke—or perhaps it was simply a dream—he saw the titian-haired woman again, and this time she was at the second cot from the door, and she had somehow *crawled* up onto the body of the sleeping soldier there, and she seemed to be leaning over his chest and whispering to him. Her hair hung in long burnished folds, and all Foster could see through that curtain was the tips of her breasts pushing at the confines of her gown. He blinked, his vision blurred, and when he awoke, the man in the second cot—an Irishman with flaming red hair—lay alone.

The next day as Foster struggled to sit upright he thought of his dream the night before. How curious it had been. He'd never dreamt anything like that before; never. And what did this most peculiar dream mean?

Perhaps it meant, he thought with what passed for a grin, he had been too long without a woman.

He saw that a man across from him was awake and spooning down the gruel the nurses brought them, and he decided that he would visit a little.

"John Francis Foster," he said when he had caught the other man's attention.

"Webster Long," the other said.

They exchanged information on their individual companies and their fighting experiences real and exaggerated, and that last battle which had sent them to the hospital. Long, a private who'd volunteered as had Foster, had lost an eye to a bayonet and his head was nearly encased with dressings so that Foster couldn't tell what color the man's hair was. Long had a fair mustache, though, and pale blue eyes. Foster shifted slightly, wincing at the jab of pain.

"Did you see something odd here last night?" he asked when he'd settled himself more comfortably.

"Odd?" Long paused, a piece of corn bread in his hand.

"What do you mean by that?"

"A woman was here. I saw her last night and one night before."

Long shook his head. "Didn't see no woman. You must be dreaming." He smiled. "Wisht I had those dreams."

Foster grinned back. "No, brother, I tell you; I saw a woman. Down there." He pointed with his chin where the red-haired Irishman lay.

"No; didn't see it." Long popped the last of the corn bread in his mouth, then brushed the crumbs from his mustache. "Was she purty?"

"Beautiful."

"Tell me," Long said as he leaned back against the wall.

Foster proceeded to describe the woman in great detail; it was true that after a moment or so he began to embellish the description. It was the look in Long's remaining eye that made him do it. Long wanted something out of the ordinary, something to keep him from thinking of his condition, and Foster decided he would give it to the other man.

"An angel," Long breathed.

"I would think so," Foster said. It was true he had never seen a woman as lovely as this one. His Sarah was right comely, but not the way this other woman was. Sarah, too, worked the farm with him and she had red roughened hands and skin darkened by the sun. She was just as lovely, he thought, as the day he'd first married her three years before.

At that moment one of the nurses, a husky man—they had to be, Foster knew, strapping and strong so that they could hold down the screaming men whose arms or legs were being sawn off without the benefit of anesthesia—entered the tent. He was here to check each convalescing man; he began at Foster's and Long's end, and then when he reached the other end he shouted for another nurse, who rushed in.

"This man's dead," and the first nurse pointed at the red-haired Irishman.

Foster had thought the man was simply sleeping.

The two nurses managed to take the corpse out; Foster and Long looked at one another, but said nothing. An hour later another man, freshly injured in the fighting that continued, had claimed the vacant cot.

Foster spoke a little more with Long and several others who were that day more alert; and when nightfall came, and their last meal was being served, he knew he was ready to sleep.

Still, it puzzled him that Long hadn't seen the woman; and neither had the two other men Foster questioned. He could see that Long might not have seen her because of the bandages across that side of his face. Still . . .

Foster ate his corn bread, slightly greasy but still tasting the best he'd ever had, and quickly slurped up his broth and called for more. It was the first time he'd ever wanted more than the one bowlful.

After using the chamber pot held by one of the nurses, a great ugly fellow who looked as if he much preferred to kill each one of the wounded men rather than wait upon them, Foster eased himself down onto his cot, pulled up the coarse sheet. The sun had long ago set and a light chill had set in. From outside he could smell newly mown hay, the last of the year, and he wondered if the hospital lay close to a farm still being worked. There were so few left intact since the war had begun.

He missed his own farm and wondered how it fared. He had men to work it, but had they left for the war as he had? What had his wife done, left with only her old infirm father and the handful of slaves they owned?

He caught a scent of something else now, a smell almost of spice, some exotic fragrance that seemed to have no place in this hell that reeked of urine and loosened bowels and unwashed bodies, and he opened his eyes and saw that the woman had returned. She was sitting primly in a chair alongside the bed of Patrick DeLance, a lieutenant in Foster's own company. DeLance had been injured a day or two before Foster, but his wounds were healing rather nicely. DeLance was talking intently with the woman, his eyes never once straying from her face. Their voices were low, so Foster couldn't make out too many words, but once he thought he heard the name "Ariadne."

Foster was a man of some education, having gone two years to college before returning home to the farm where he was needed, and he knew the name was classical in origin. The daughter of King Minos, as he recalled, the woman who had loved Theseus and had helped him find his way out of the labyrinth.

Ariadne. A beautiful name. He murmured it aloud. It set right on his tongue and lips.

Ariadne. It fit her. A beautiful name for a beautiful woman. He glanced once more at her, and like that one other time she seemed to have crawled atop the other man. He blinked; surely he could not be seeing what he saw, and yet even though the light in the tent was dim, he could make out the outline of the woman straddling the prone DeLance, the skirts of her gown spread out. She rocked back and forth, and murmured all the while, and he could hear DeLance groan.

Embarrassed, Foster still watched; he couldn't look away. DeLance cried out in release, and the woman whispered, and bent down over DeLance's lips and kissed him long.

Foster felt a warmth suffusing through his body and he closed his eyes tightly and thought of Sarah, good-hearted Sarah. Sarah who was just a little too thin because of their hard times; not with a voluptuous body like this woman . . . this Ariadne . . . here in the tent.

A woman in the hospital. Impossible, he told himself, and he looked once more, and Ariadne was rising from DeLance, straightening her skirts. Foster watched as she ran a hand down DeLance's chest to his groin, and DeLance shuddered.

He glanced across at Long, but the man was asleep. Foster looked up and down the double rows and saw that of the other men he was the only one awake, the only one to see . . . what he had seen. But what was that?

The woman—Ariadne—had done something to DeLance. She had climbed atop—no, Foster decided, climbed wasn't quite the proper word. Slithered? No.

She had seduced . . . no, that wasn't the right word. Nothing was right, he decided, nothing tonight.

He closed his eyes and willed sleep to come, but stubbornly it refused.

The following day it rained, and the dampness seeped through the canvas walls and into the bones of the men, chilling them to their very souls. Foster felt the worst he had since coming to the hospital. The flap to the tent had been left open, and he could see the grayness outside, the dripping leaves, the subdued colors, and remembered what autumn was like at home.

He and the other farmers in the area would be done with their harvesting, and the wives and mothers and sisters would have been cooking all day long, and then toward sundown would come the dances in someone's barn. Some man would bring out a fiddle and maybe a mouth harp, then maybe a bucket or two or even some old jugs—they didn't much care what they used as musical instruments as long it made noise—and William, Foster's oldest slave, a man who'd worked for his father, would bring out his banjo. They'd all dance, too, the slaves and their owners in their own separate circles. The barn would smell of drying apples and old manure, of new hay and dust which rose under the stamping of their feet on the dirt floor. A cow, somewhere down the line in a crib, would low in response, a bird in the eaves might flutter briefly, and in the flickering yellow light of the lanterns they would sing and laugh and drink homemade brew and celebrate the good harvest.

Only the past two years there'd been no good harvest; times had gotten rougher, and there'd been no dances. There'd been setbacks in the planting, he'd lost a crop or two, and several times army companies had marched through the farmland and taken what food they wanted. They'd also hurt Nell, William's granddaughter, and William had grabbed a pitchfork before Foster could stop him and had run after the retreating soldiers. He'd been shot in the head and he'd simply sunk to his knees, lifeless already, and when Foster had finally reached the old man, his skin was already cooling.

Sarah had cried when Foster and Tom and George, William's sons, buried the old man out on the hill behind the house.

And for a long time after that Foster had sat upon the porch thinking. It had been Confederate troops who had come through his farm, who had hurt Nell, killed poor old William.

His own kind, Foster kept saying. His own kind did this. But it was war, one part of him said. That doesn't excuse it, another argued. And he knew then that if the Southern troops would do such awful things, what could he—and Sarah and the others—expect if the Yankees were to come down here, to come through these bountiful farms? What sort of horrors could they expect at these Northerners' hands? What would these Yankees who hated them so much do?

And so the next day he'd kissed his wife goodbye, taken his best hat and best rifle and a pouch full of shot, and had left the farm to volunteer. He would fight, and he would keep the Yankees and the others away from his family. It was the only thing he could do.

But that had been a year ago, and he didn't see that the Yankees were being pushed back. Sometimes the Union forces won a battle, sometimes his people did. And even when they did, there didn't seem to be an advantage. More men got killed and injured, some lay in the fields for days, some were never found. And the officers didn't seem to care for their men, as he thought they would. They weren't the ones at the beginning of the charges. It was the young men like him, some men hardly more than boys, or the old men who should have been at home being waited on by their sons and daughters. It was these men who died, and whose bodies the horses of the mounted officers picked their way over.

Foster rubbed a hand across his face, felt the dampness at the corners of his eyes. A year of fighting, of eating off the land and mostly that meant not eating, of being either too hot or too cold, and mostly too wet, had soured him on the army—Northern or Southern.

He knew now that he should have stayed home, should have laid in as much food as possible, as many supplies as he could find, should have barricaded the house, and kept Sarah and the others together, and maybe they could have fought off anyone who approached.

Maybe it wasn't too late now, though; he had to believe that. As soon as he got out of here he was going home. The doctors might say he was fit to go to the front lines again, but he wasn't. He was going back to Sarah. He would worry about the Yankees when and if they came.

He had no appetite that day. He knew his fever was returning, and nothing tasted good. He laid on the cot, never opening his eyes, hardly moving.

All he could think of was his family, and he wondered if he would ever see them again.

That night Ariadne returned. She was closer now to Foster, and he could see the darkness of her lovely eyes; they looked almost as if they'd been lined with something black; Sarah had called it kohl and said all the fancy ladies wore it. Ariadne's bodice was lower than he'd seen before, and her breasts were full and pale in the dimness.

She murmured to the young man three beds down from Foster, and he responded lethargically. She kissed the man, caressed the back of his hands with her curling eyelashes, and Foster once more felt the stirrings inside him.

He turned his head, though, so he wouldn't watch, but he couldn't escape the sounds of the couple's passion. Illicit passion, he told himself, but those were empty words. What did illicit mean anyway when he'd seen men blown to bits by cannon, horses that screamed in their death agonies?

Once more Foster smelled the scent of Ariadne. Some spice almost like cloves or perhaps cinnamon mixed with musk, and he licked his lips. That strange perfume almost overcame the stench of blood and pus and sweat that pervaded the tent.

When he looked back, she was gone.

The next day when the doctor came, Foster asked when he could leave the hospital. The doctor seemed preoccupied and merely said soon. Still, those few words heartened Foster because before then the doctor had refused to say.

The nurses came in and carried out the body of the young man he had seen the night before.

Foster looked across at Long, who was sitting up once more. "Another one."

"Yeah," Long said. He was chewing a wad and leaned over his bed and spat into the chamberpot.

"She's getting closer," Foster said, his voice low.

"What's that?"

"The woman I saw."

"You on that agin? Long shook his head. "You need a woman, boy; I can see it plain and simple."

Foster nodded, slightly distracted, then said, "But there was one. I saw her. She was at the sides of those three men—one of 'em that Irishman—and now they're all dead."

"Plenty o' men here are dead, and there ain't been no woman with 'em."

"Not this time."

Long shook his head again and pushed himself down and rolled over, and Foster knew their conversation was over.

That night the woman brought with her the scent of woodsmoke and spices, and she knelt beside the red-faced man.

In the morning he was dead. And when the nurses hauled him out, Foster could see that the drinker was no longer red-faced. The dead man was pale, paler than he should have been even in death, and he seemed to have shrunk down upon himself, as if something—his blood, his soul—had been . . . sucked . . . out of him.

Foster looked at Long. "She's coming down this way."

"You're crazy, you know. Crazy." Long concentrated on drinking his broth.

Foster pushed back the sheet and swung his legs over the side. Momentarily he felt light-headed, and his arm pained him. He tried to push up from the cot to stand, trembled, and fell back. He couldn't escape, not even if he wanted to. He managed to get under the covers again, and saw that Long was watching him.

"You could help me," Foster said. He hated to ask for help—it wasn't his way—but there was no other choice.

"Help you?"

Foster nodded. "To escape."

"You're here to heal, boy, and that's good enough for me. I'll be out in a day or two, or so the docs say. You need to stay a little longer and rest up."

"You don't understand," Foster said bitterly.

"No, I guess not."

Two nights went by and the woman didn't appear. Then on the third night she was across from Foster, by Long's bed.

"No," Foster said, struggling to sit up, but his limbs were entangled in the sheets, and they dragged him down. His head was spinning, and he couldn't hardly keep his eyes open, and yet he saw the woman, so beautiful, *slithering* atop Long, who was staring wide-eyed at her. She caressed and kissed the one-eyed man, and delicately nipped at the skin on his chest. Foster watched as her mouth slid lower and lower, and suddenly Long moaned, a loud, sensual sound.

She spread her skirts around them, and rode Long like he was a horse being broke, and Foster could hear Long's cry of lust, the cry that was almost a scream.

Foster struggled once more to sit up; he had to help Long. But he couldn't manage, and every time he moved his arm throbbed so fiercely he himself momentarily blacked out. He could only lay back and watch helplessly.

When it was over, Ariadne smoothed her skirts, kissed Long upon the lips and left.

In the dimness Foster stared at Long. The man was pale, too pale.

"Long?" he called.

No response.

And when morning came, the nurses took Long away.

"I don't understand it," Foster called to them. "He was getting better. He was going to be out in a day or two. He didn't have no killing disease."

The burliest of the two nurses shrugged. "It happens sometimes. They seem all right and then just up and die."

"No, no, not Long. He was all right, I tell you." Foster labored to sit. "That woman came for him. I warned him, I did, but he wouldn't listen. No one would." He looked around the ward, but most of the patients were sleeping or had slipped into their own private hells. "Long didn't listen to me—he didn't believe—and now look at him."

"Calm down," one of the nurses said, and he glanced across at the other. They called for a third nurse, and between the three of them they restrained him and tied him down with ropes to the cot.

He fought and screamed and shouted at them, but they told him it was for his own good, that he was too violent to be left on his own.

He tried to undo his bonds, but couldn't, and after a while, he stopped fighting. He closed his eyes. Some time later one of the nurses came back and fed him some broth, this time with a little bit of potato and onion in it. He tasted nothing.

He simply lay there, his eyes shut, and waited. He felt the coolness of the air when the sun went down. And when he smelled the spices, he opened his eyes.

Ariadne stood at the foot of his cot.

She was smiling at him.

She whispered his name, and he realized then what that strange odor about her was.

It was the smell of death.

SLEEPING CITIES

Wendy Webb

Wendy Webb is an author and playwright. Her short stories have appeared in such anthologies as *Shadows 10*, *Women of Darkness*, *When the Black Lotus Blooms*, *The SeaHarp Hotel*, *Final Shadows*, *Dark Love*, *In the Shadow of the Gargoyle*, and *Confederacy of the Dead*.

She has published three Beluga Stein mysteries: *Last Resort*, *Bee Movie*, and *Mean Cuisine*, and has coedited the anthologies *Phobias: Stories of Your Deepest Fears*, *More Phobias: Stories of Unparalleled Paranoia!* (with Richard Gilliam, Edward E. Kramer and Martin Greenberg), and *Gothic Ghosts* (with Charles L. Grant).

"In 1989, I found myself standing in Beijing's Tiananmen Square a few months after the conflict witnessed around the world," reveals the author. "Activity in the square had returned to the honorable duty of jobs, family, and order and tradition—all under what seemed watchful eyes.

"During that trip there seemed a consistency among the people in something unspoken and elusive, even though they were always kind to me. An outsider who does not belong, and never will, might speculate that such behavior was rooted in culture or genetics, or perhaps directed by those watchful eyes. I don't know.

"In 'Sleeping Cities' I wondered what would happen to an otherwise honorable man who chose to be different from the vast population above ground, as well as those interred below."

WITH SHOVELS AND picks they attacked the hard earth, breaking it into jagged pieces to exhume what lay below. Men and women, working shoulder to shoulder, sweated with the effort, but continued without complaint, without a spoken word to break the cadence. Last week their priority was the land and growing food for the masses, an honorable duty. It was necessary work for survival.

This week it was different. This week what lay below the land was more important in this time-honoring and slow-paced society.

Delicate instruments replaced destructive equipment. With tiny probes they scraped dirt away from row after row of heads that erupted from the floor of the earthen pit. By removing soil with soft brushes they revealed tiny scraps of silk, red lacquered boxes bound with metal belts, and splinters of wood that once had been limbs.

These were more than mere artifacts, Liu knew. Much more.

He walked the site as an archaeologist in these times. In times past he had been many other things. As a member of a special group, he, too, had chosen to hide in plain sight. His goal, and that of other respected elders, was the same: freedom, finally, from vast darkness.

But, unlike the others, those goals weren't enough for him anymore.

This then, was the beginning of a new time. The cycle would once again be renewed.

A small, old man silently appeared at Liu's side. As was his duty, he wore the common man's black pants, thin sweater and sandals, and pressed a tall mug of warm green tea in his boss's hands. Liu accepted the assistant's offering without comment or thanks. As everyone else on these sites, Hsu had a job to do. His compensation came from pride in working with someone as notable and important as the archaeologist. That was more than ample to meet an assistant's minimal needs.

Liu dismissed his assistant with a short wave of his hand, then stroked the surface of the medallion that clung to his chest. He looked around at the black-haired workers, his fellow scientists, and to the rudimentary scaffolding and handmade ladders that dipped into the newly excavated pits. His own dark eyes rose to scan the rural landscape that stretched out all around him. Prepared for planting, the topography was broken up in its monotony only by the occasional hills that would be ruthlessly farmed for what they could bear, barely concealing the tombs that lay below.

He added another stroke to the piece that hung from his neck and touched his chest. Here, in this place of all places, in this country, the dragon etched clockwise from its fire-breathing head to its curled tail on the medallion was more than just a symbol. It signified good fortune.

But the medallion was only part of what had come to him in recognition of his work and sacrifice. It was Liu's scientific skill, his honed abilities and intuitive gifts that brought him to stand on this hallowed ground in anticipation of that which lay below. These same virtues would prove him a great leader. Contrary to the respected elders, he deserved the ultimate honor. He was owed it.

Liu tapped his watch and looked with some concern to the afternoon sun. Now darkness was the new enemy. But much as he would like, Liu could not push the calendar. It was not the way of his people. Destiny could be controlled, but it could not be rushed.

They had waited, after all, for over two thousand years for this moment. He could wait a little longer. The time for complete exhumation would come at its own pace.

The first discovery took place in March of 1974. A work brigade of farmers drilling a well accidentally found a subterranean chamber. It had been the first.

There would be many more.

In 1974 Liu had watched from a distance for this finding. His calculations, countless hours of research, and intuition in the form of dreams had led him to this place. The call had been sounded and he had waited patiently for his colleagues to converge on this site near the now modern Chinese city of Xi'an.

They came. And they had worked. Hours turned to days, to months, then years, in the careful and painstaking exhumation of Qin Shi Huang Di's terracotta army. The funerary compound had revealed archaeological treasures that cheered country and sent ripples of excitement around the world

For Liu it had been much more than that. The past had now become the future. His future. And he was more than willing to accept the honor this find bestowed upon him. He was owed, after all. It was his right, if not his honor-bound duty, to see it through.

Walking the underground chambers, he had considered his choice carefully. The moment he had waited for would not be until the armies were fully exhumed. But enough had been carefully dusted and touched with delicate instruments that he would know if his intuition had guided him correctly.

The pottery bodyguard faced east and was poised for battle. Life-sized figures, once brightly painted with mineral colors, were grouped into specific military formation.

He had paused, considered, then made his selection. The chamber of 1,400 figures held a sixty-eight-member elite command unit. They would be the first. Staring into the individual faces, no two of which were alike, he knew the theory was true. These figures, all of them, had been created from life. And somewhere deep in the terracotta, life was ready to resume itself. Liu would be the catalyst in this resurrection, then their leader.

Digging deep into a pack slung across his shoulder, he had pulled out four small purple candles to set in front of the figures. Arranging them in a star-like pattern, he touched match to wick and watched them blaze to life. Liu stepped back, took a long deep breath and held it. He gestured to the four directions that they should bring wholeness back to these terracotta people.

Then he waited.

The breath that had been held too long in his chest began to burn.

Had the figures been the victims of an opposing ceremony? Or, perhaps, they were never touched to begin with.

His lungs ached. Fighting hard against release, he found he could hold his breath no longer. His eyes went from figure to figure for a last-minute sign.

Sadly, it was not to be.

Breath escaped him in a long, singular and disappointed burst.

The first fully exposed soldier, then the second, fifth and tenth, stood tall and immovable. Their individual expressions stayed fixed and rigid as they had for thousands of years and would for thousands more.

The calculations had been wrong. His intuition had been reduced to nothing more than dreams of a common man, among far too many, hoping for something better.

Eyeing the dusty crossbows that had at one time been mechanically triggered to shoot intruders, he had walked from this chamber and would never return. There was no need. Bitterness burned his throat. Disappointment lodged in his stomach and gnawed his insides.

The medallion of the clockwise-etched dragon that clung to his chest swung back and forth with each heavy step as he left this place to the others. There was nothing more for him here. Good fortune would have to wait for another time.

Then, in March of 1990, workers building a highway noticed a strange condition in the soil. A new team of scientists arrived to dig in the fields.

Another special place had been discovered.

And another opportunity had arrived for the archaeologist to test his theory.

Liu removed the top to the porcelain mug Hsu had pressed into his hands, and sipped the warm green tea. Pushing his pack further up his shoulder, he stared at the late afternoon sun, then rubbed his face as if worry could be erased so easily. Turning, he scanned the horizon east of the city of Xi'an.

Over there was where the first emperor of China had chosen to place his terracotta army of 10,000 soldiers in preparation for death. Qin Shi Huang Di had built the Great Wall to protect the lives of his people, but had constructed the twenty-square-mile compound for his own protection after his life ended. He needn't have bothered.

But here, at the starting point of the Silk Road, south-west of Xi'an, was the place of Jing Di. And perhaps this time good fortune would arise from the dark and seek the light.

The assistant, Hsu, ran up to him and spoke in rapid staccato tones. The small, old man in black pants, thin sweater and sandals gestured close and animated. "Come quick and see. Quick. It is just finished." He pointed, then stepped behind the archaeologist to watch for a response.

Liu offered a barely perceptible nod and walked to where the old man indicated. Ducking under a makeshift roof held up by wooden scraps used for studs, he gauged his steps in the loose earth. Careful not to disrupt the ledge, he approached the new finding excavated from the tunnel wall. A skeleton, pulled tight as if in a defensive posture, lay face to the wall. Liu knelt beside it with caution and restrained interest.

The skull was broken into jagged pieces. Nearby was a brick.

The old man resumed his quick gestures and rapid discourse with explanation of this event. "An intruder, I think. Someone most unwelcome. Or an accident. Maybe an accident. Maybe it is not. He was not careful. He wished for more than he should have."

"Quiet." Liu spoke harshly. "Your theories are of no interest to me." He dismissed the assistant with a wave of his hand.

Hsu stepped quietly back into the shadow.

Perhaps it was, indeed, an accident. Liu looked about the room and the brush-stroked row of heads that bloomed there. Or perhaps this unwelcome intruder had found more than he had bargained for.

The calendar could not be pushed.

The cycle would soon begin.

This victim had not been the first done in by greed, curiosity, or even vengeance. Grave robbing, it was speculated, had started as far back as the first century, and still continued today. Few had been successful. Far more had lost their lives. Many had even lost their souls.

The philosophy of the elders, and one that had followed since, held that human contact was motivated by self-interest. Here now lay proof of that thinking. Liu stood slowly. He paused, then kicked dust over the intruder.

This week what lay below the land was of more importance than what grew from it. It was a necessary work for survival. An honorable work. But the day was drawing to a close and the farmers would be forced to return to their more meaningful labor.

Liu held back growing impatience that filled his chest and made his head ache. Impatience was unacceptable in this time, in this culture. Urge it away, he told himself, for it cannot win. There is no other way but to let things be as they must.

He could not push the calendar.

Could not . . . could not.

Sighing deeply, he looked out over the edge of the pit.

The sun had dropped. Bright light from the day now became muted and thick. A hint of pink and orange touched the horizon. A short distance away a small airplane taxied down the runway and took to the air. The roar of a modest engine followed seconds later.

Early model Russian cars sparsely dotted the highway that ran near this place. Wheezing engines coughed and sputtered black exhaust. A rare bus passed, filled with passengers. The crowd of people bulged from open windows, others barely clung to handrails that lined the steps to the open door.

Nearby a baby cooed.

He turned his attention to a slender young woman making notes on a clipboard some feet away from the edge of the pit. Her foot gently rocked the tightly bound baby, but her work continued. She never made a sound.

The child was a boy. A son.

He was a son of a long line of sons that had created this place. And he was bound. Swaddled in tight cloth for warmth and safety on this day, he was also enclosed by culture and necessity for a lifetime.

It was a legacy of the ages to be enclosed, walled off by others. Qin Shi Huang Di was the first, having built the Great Wall. Now he rested with his army. There had been another in history who built a line of walls and fortresses for protection. But unlike the creator of the Great Wall, this leader and his followers coveted the dark. Until now.

Liu turned back to glance into the pit.

While the army of Qin Shi Huang Di forever rested, perhaps the figures of Jing Di only slept.

He stroked the medallion.

There, in the shadow of the waning day, were the first few. Liu spied row after row of heads led now by a few tiny exposed figures . . .

Good fortune.

. . . and walked the narrow path to them.

They were small, much smaller than the terracotta army, and stood only two feet tall. Unlike the sculpted and painted clothes on the armies of Qin Shi Huang Di, these smaller figures had worn garments of silk and other fine materials.

Liu stroked the cold face of a small soldier. Its eyes revealed compassion, the mouth remained upturned ever so slightly in an embarrassed smile. And that one. Here the cheekbones were high, the eyes direct, mouth set. This one was a fighter, determined in a personal goal. Each face was different in their beauty and their varied range of human emotion. There was pride, innocence, high-spiritedness, and there was something else.

Youth.

Liu gasped in recognition and sudden joy.

They were children.

Children. All of them. Offspring. And more important, if he were right, they were descendants. Fathered in mission by Jing Di, these were the minions Liu and the others sought.

The children had waited. Waited for over two thousand years to come out of the dark.

Liu licked his dry lips and swallowed hard. He had to know if his intuition had steered him correctly this time. The discovery in this pit was far from complete, so if these children slept, they did not sleep alone.

Individually, and collectively—only when they were completely exhumed, brushed free from dirt, and the tiny instruments put away—would they awaken to take their place. Then they would join the vast population of this continent, and the world, to hide in plain sight. And he would be their new leader.

He had to know.

Now.

Reaching into his pack, he produced the four purple candles, arranged them in the star-like shape, then lit them. He pulled a deep breath, stepped back, and called once again upon the four directions to bring these figures to wholeness.

Nothing.

He kept his breath, and whispered soundless hope.

A stirring came then.

An exhalation like muted wind arrived from a distance, but ever so close that he could feel it brush against his cheek.

Far away the howling began. From the four directions a keening traveled close, closer, then converged on a point between the candles. The flames flickered, then went out. Small tendrils of candle-smoke rose and spiraled to the roof of the pit. The sound echoed through the excavated site, then died.

The new cycle had begun.

Liu tempered the small smile on his lips, but in his heart was exaltation. This time he had been right. Still, there was work to be done.

Slowly, ever so slowly, he reached deep into a pocket for a knife. It glittered with the captured lowering rays of sun that would bring about dusk. Closing his eyes, and breathing deep the musky scent of the tombs and newly extinguished candles, he slashed the knife across his open palm. Like the statues void of but one fixed emotion, he clenched his fist, dropped the blade, and approached the figure of the child fighter.

A drop of blood touched the fighter's lips. Then, a second. He moved to the compassionate child, repeated the act, then waited.

His gaze darted from one child to the next.

Unacceptable as the emotion was, he could no longer fight the impatience that grew deep within him. And then he saw it.

The fighter, of course. It pleased Liu the fighter would be first.

Orange-brown hues in the small terracotta face lightened to gray, then to warmer shades. A hint of blue surrounded the set mouth. The direct eyes turned dark and clear.

Liu touched the young face and felt cold, hard clay begin to warm. The start of a renewed life burned deep within this one.

The compassionate child figure's eyes twinkled with a suggestion of light. New color touched the upturned smile and spoke of animation as well.

The archaeologist clasped his hands together in reserved delight. The calculations were correct. His dreams, this time, had been accurate and unflinching. The children were awakening from the dark to see the light of his authority. He would lead them to greatness as he deserved. As it was owed to him.

A faint movement in the shadow. Quick. Decided.

The brick crashed down on his head. He crumpled and fell into a tight defensive posture, face to the wall, then looked up his attacker.

Hsu, the assistant, held the brick high for a second assault if one were needed, then slowly lowered the old weapon. Reaching under his sweater, he pulled out a medallion of a dragon. This one was etched counterclockwise. He spoke in quiet tones. "It is too soon. The exhumation is not complete."

Liu tried to move, to protest, but his body was unwilling. He stared horrified as Hsu pulled candles out of a satchel, placed them in a single line, then set them ablaze.

The assistant beckoned something unseen, then, palms out, held it back by offering Liu as a companion on its travels.

Liu mouthed the word "no," but the wind had already started. Soon it would touch him. And when the dark came it would take his soul. He would not be the leader of these children as he deserved, as he was owed. The small ceremony performed by the assistant had reduced him to the vulnerabilities of nothing more than a common man among far too many.

"It is finished." Hsu blew out the candles and looked at Liu with pity. "Maybe an accident. Maybe it is not. You wished for more than you should have. It was not the way." The small, old man in black pants, thin sweater and sandals bowed slightly, then kicked dust over the new intruder. He turned and walked from the pit.

The sun dipped behind a hill. Colors on the horizon brightened, then turned dull. Dusk had settled and brought the end of day and a temporary halt to the subterranean work in progress. It was necessary. It was honorable. But it would have to wait.

Growing food for the masses was, for now, more important.

Liu watched through foggy eyes as the little light waned, disappeared, then turned to inky black. Walled in by culture and necessity, he took a final breath.

The calendar could not be pushed. But soon enough, there would be freedom from the darkness. Then, with another more worthy, his child army would awaken.

The trenches were quickly filled in. The pit was covered by sod.

On the surface farmers had begun to sow seed.

The Haunted House

E. Nesbit

Edith Nesbit (1858–1924) is today best remembered for her classic children's books *Five Children and It* (1902), *The Phoenix and the Carpet* (1904), and *The Railway Children* (1906). However, she also wrote a number of short horror stories, often hiding her gender beneath the byline "E. Nesbit" or, following her marriage in 1880, "E. Bland" or "Mrs. Hubert Bland."

The best of these stories are collected in *Grim Tales* (1893), *Something Wrong* (1893), *Fear* (1910), and *In the Dark: Tales of Terror by E. Nesbit* (1988), the latter selected and introduced by Hugh Lamb and expanded by a further seven stories for Ash-Tree Press in 2000.

Her other books include the fantasies *The Story of the Amulet* (1906), *The Enchanted Castle* (1907), *The House of Arden* (1908), *Harding's Luck* (1909), *The Magic City* (1910), and *Dormant* (1911), plus the collections *The Book of Dragons* (1899) and *Nine Unlikely Tales for Children* (1901).

The following story was originally published in *The Strand Magazine* for December 1913 under the author's "E. Bland" pseudonym . . .

IT WAS BY the merest accident that Desmond ever went to the Haunted House. He had been away from England for six years, and the nine months' leave taught him how easily one drops out of one's place.

He had taken rooms at the Greyhound before he found that there was no reason why he should stay in Elmstead rather than in any other of London's dismal outposts. He wrote to all the friends whose addresses he could remember, and settled himself to await their answers.

He wanted someone to talk to, and there was no one. Meantime he lounged on the horsehair sofa with the advertisements, and his pleasant gray eyes followed line after line with intolerable boredom. Then, suddenly, "Halloa!" he said, and sat up. This is what he read:

A HAUNTED HOUSE.—Advertiser is anxious to have phenomena investigated. Any properly accredited investigator will be given full facilities. Address, by letter only, Wildon Prior, 237 Museum Street, London.

"That's rum!" he said. Wildon Prior had been the best wicket-keeper in his club. It wasn't a common name. Anyway, it was worth trying, so he sent off a telegram.

WILDON PRIOR, 237, MUSEUM STREET, LONDON. MAY I COME TO YOU FOR A DAY OR TWO AND SEE THE GHOST?—WILLIAM DESMOND

On returning next day from a stroll there was an orange envelope on the wide Pembroke table in his parlor.

DELIGHTED—EXPECT YOU TODAY. BOOK TO CRITTENDEN FROM CHARING CROSS. WIRE TRAIN.—WILDON PRIOR, ORMEHURST RECTORY, KENT.

"So that's all right," said Desmond, and went off to pack his bag and ask in the bar for a timetable. "Good old Wildon; it will be ripping, seeing him again."

A curious little omnibus, rather like a bathing-machine, was waiting outside Crittenden Station, and its driver, a swarthy, blunt-faced little man, with liquid eyes, said, "You a friend of Mr. Prior, sir?" shut him up in the bathing-machine, and banged the door on him. It was a very long drive, and less pleasant than it would have been in an open carriage.

The last part of the journey was through a wood; then came a church-yard and a church, and the bathing-machine turned in at a gate under heavy trees and drew up in front of a white house with bare, gaunt windows.

"Cheerful place, upon my soul!" Desmond told himself, as he tumbled out of the back of the bathing-machine.

The driver set his bag on the discolored doorstep and drove off. Desmond pulled a rusty chain, and a big-throated bell jangled above his head.

Nobody came to the door, and he rang again. Still nobody came, but he heard a window thrown open above the porch. He stepped back on to the gravel and looked up.

A young man with rough hair and pale eyes was looking out. Not Wildon, nothing like Wildon. He did not speak, but he seemed to be making signs; and the signs seemed to mean, *Go away!*

"I came to see Mr. Prior," said Desmond. Instantly and softly the window closed.

"Is it a lunatic asylum I've come to by chance?" Desmond asked himself, and pulled again at the rusty chain.

Steps sounded inside the house, the sound of boots on stone. Bolts were shot back, the door opened, and Desmond, rather hot and a little annoyed, found himself looking into a pair of very dark, friendly eyes, and a very pleasant voice said:

"Mr. Desmond, I presume? Do come in and let me apologize."

The speaker shook him warmly by the hand, and he found himself following down a flagged passage a man of more than mature age, well-dressed, handsome, with an air of competence and alertness which we associate with what is called "a man of the world." He opened a door and led the way into a shabby, bookish, leathery room.

"Do sit down, Mr. Desmond."

This must be the uncle, I suppose, Desmond thought, as he fitted himself into the shabby, perfect curves of the armchair. "How's Wildon?" he asked, aloud. "All right, I hope?"

The other looked at him. "I beg your pardon," he said, doubtfully.

"I was asking how Wildon is?"

"I am quite well, I thank you," said the other man, with some formality.

"I beg your pardon"—it was now Desmond's turn to say it—"I did not realize that your name might be Wildon, too. I meant Wildon Prior."

"I am Wildon Prior," said the other, "and you, I presume, are the expert from the Psychical Society?"

"Good Lord, no!" said Desmond. "I'm Wildon Prior's friend, and, of course, there must be two Wildon Priors."

"You sent the telegram? You are Mr. Desmond? The Psychical Society were to send an expert, and I thought—"

"I see," said Desmond; "and I thought you were Wildon Prior, an old friend of mine—a young man," he said, and half rose.

"Now, don't," said Wildon Prior. "No doubt it is my nephew who is your friend. Did he know you were coming? But of course he didn't. I am wandering. But I'm exceedingly glad to see you. You will stay, will you not? If you can endure to be the guest of an old man. And I will write to Will tonight and ask him to join us."

"That's most awfully good of you," Desmond assured him. "I shall be glad to stay. I was awfully pleased when I saw Wildon's name in the paper, because—" And out came the tale of Elmstead, its loneliness and disappointment.

Mr. Prior listened with the kindest interest.

"And you have not found your friends? How sad! But they will write to you. Of course, you left your address?"

"I didn't, by Jove!" said Desmond. "But I can write. Can I catch the post?"

"Easily," the elder man assured him. "Write your letters now. My man shall take them to the post, and then we will have dinner, and I will tell you about the ghost."

Desmond wrote his letters quickly, Mr. Prior just then reappearing. "Now I'll take you to your room," he said, gathering the letters in long, white hands. "You'll like a rest. Dinner at eight."

The bed-chamber, like the parlor, had a pleasant air of worn luxury and accustomed comfort. "I hope you will be comfortable," the host said, with courteous solicitude. And Desmond was quite sure that he would.

Three covers were laid, the swarthy man who had driven Desmond from the station stood behind the host's chair, and a figure came toward Desmond and his host from the shadows beyond the yellow circles of the silver-sticked candles.

"My assistant, Mr. Verney," said the host, and Desmond surrendered his hand to the limp, damp touch of the man who had seemed to say to him, from the window above the porch, *Go away!* Was Mr. Prior perhaps a doctor who received "paying guests," persons who were, in Desmond's phrase, "a bit barmy"? But he had said "assistant."

"I thought," said Desmond, hastily, "you would be a clergyman. The Rectory, you know—I thought Wildon, my friend Wildon, was staying with an uncle who was a clergyman."

"Oh, no," said Mr. Prior. "I rent the Rectory. The rector thinks it is damp. The church is disused, too. It is not considered safe, and they can't afford to restore it. Claret to Mr. Desmond, Lopez." And the swarthy, blunt-faced man filled his glass.

"I find this place very convenient for my experiments. I dabble a little in chemistry, Mr. Desmond, and Verney here assists me."

Verney murmured something that sounded like "only too proud," and subsided.

"We all have our hobbies, and chemistry is mine," Mr. Prior went on. "Fortunately, I have a little income which enables me to indulge it. Wildon, my nephew, you know, laughs at me, and calls it the science of smells. But it's absorbing, very absorbing."

After dinner Verney faded away, and Desmond and his host stretched their feet to what Mr. Prior called a "handful of fire," for the evening had grown chill.

"And now," Desmond said, "won't you tell me the ghost story?"

The other glanced round the room. "There isn't really a ghost story at all. It's only that—well, it's never happened to me personally, but it happened to Verney, poor lad, and he's never been quite his own self since."

Desmond flattered himself on his insight. "Is mine the haunted room?" he asked.

"It doesn't come to any particular room," said the other, slowly, "nor to any particular person."

"Anyone may happen to see it?"

"No one sees it. It isn't the kind of ghost that's seen or heard."

"I'm afraid I'm rather stupid, but I don't understand," said Desmond, roundly. "How can it be a ghost, if you neither hear it nor see it?"

"I did not say it was a ghost," Mr. Prior corrected. "I only say that there is something about this house which is not ordinary. Several of my assistants have had to leave; the thing got on their nerves."

"What became of the assistants?" asked Desmond.

"Oh, they left, you know; they left," Prior answered, vaguely. "One couldn't expect them to sacrifice their health. I sometimes think—village gossip is a deadly thing, Mr. Desmond—that perhaps they were prepared to be frightened; that they fancy things. I hope the Psychical Society's expert won't be a neurotic. But even without being a neurotic one might—but you don't believe in ghosts, Mr. Desmond. Your Anglo-Saxon common sense forbids it."

"I'm afraid I'm not exactly Anglo-Saxon," said Desmond. "On my father's side I'm pure Celt; though I know I don't do credit to the race."

"And on your mother's side?" Mr. Prior asked, with extraordinary eagerness; an eagerness so sudden and disproportioned to the question that Desmond stared. A faint touch of resentment as suddenly stirred in him, the first spark of antagonism to his host.

"Oh," he said, lightly, "I think I must have Chinese blood, I get on so well with the natives in Shanghai, and they tell me I owe my nose to a Red Indian great grandmother."

"No Negro blood, I suppose?" the host asked, with almost discourteous insistence.

"Oh, I wouldn't say that," Desmond answered. He meant to say it laughing, but he didn't. "My hair, you know—it's a very stiff curl it's got, and my mother's people were in the West Indies a few generations ago. You're interested in distinctions of race, I take it?"

"Not at all, not at all," Mr. Prior surprisingly assured him; "but, of course, any details of your family are necessarily interesting to me. I feel," he added, with another of his winning smiles, "that you and I are already friends."

Desmond could not have reasoningly defended the faint quality of dislike that had begun to tinge his first pleasant sense of being welcomed and wished for as a guest.

"You're very kind," he said; "it's jolly of you to take in a stranger like this."

Mr. Prior smiled, handed the cigar-box, mixed whisky and soda, and began to talk about the history of the house.

"The foundations are almost certainly thirteenth century. It was a priory, you know. There's a curious tale, by the way, about the man Henry gave it to when he smashed up the monasteries. There was a curse; there seems always to have been a curse—"

The gentle, pleasant, high-bred voice went on. Desmond thought he was listening, but presently he roused himself and dragged his attention back to the words that were being spoken.

"—that made the fifth death . . . There is one every hundred years, and always in the same mysterious way."

Then he found himself on his feet, incredibly sleepy, and heard himself say: "These old stories are tremendously interesting. Thank you very much. I hope you won't think me very uncivil, but I think I'd rather like to turn in; I feel a bit tired, somehow."

"But of course, my dear chap."

Mr. Prior saw Desmond to his room.

"Got everything you want? Right. Lock the door if you should feel nervous. Of course, a lock can't keep ghosts out, but I always feel as if it could," and with another of those pleasant, friendly laughs he was gone.

William Desmond went to bed a strong young man, sleepy indeed beyond his experience of sleepiness, but well and comfortable. He awoke faint and trembling, lying deep in the billows of the feather bed; and lukewarm waves of exhaustion swept through him. Where was he? What had happened? His brain, dizzy and weak at first, refused him any answer. When he remembered, the abrupt spasm of repulsion which he had felt so suddenly and unreasonably the night before came back to him in a hot, breathless flush. He had been drugged, he had been poisoned!

"I must get out of this," he told himself, and blundered out of bed toward the silken bell-pull that he had noticed the night before hanging near the door.

As he pulled it, the bed and the wardrobe and the room rose up round him and fell on him, and he fainted.

When he next knew anything someone was putting brandy to his lips. He saw Prior, the kindest concern in his face. The assistant, pale and watery-eyed. The swarthy manservant, stolid, silent, and expressionless. He heard Verney say to Prior: "You see it was too much—I told you—"

"Hush," said Prior, "he's coming to."

—

Four days later Desmond, lying on a wicker chair on the lawn, was a little disinclined for exertion, but no longer ill. Nourishing foods and drinks, beef-tea, stimulants, and constant care—these had brought him back to something like his normal state. He wondered at the vague suspicions, vaguely remembered, of that first night; they had all been proved absurd by the unwavering care and kindness of everyone in the Haunted House.

"But what caused it?" he asked his host, for the fiftieth time. "What made me make such a fool of myself?" And this time Mr. Prior did not put him off, as he had always done before by begging him to wait till he was stronger.

"I am afraid, you know," he said, "that the ghost really did come to you. I am inclined to revise my opinion of the ghost."

"But why didn't it come again?"

"I have been with you every night, you know," his host reminded him. And, indeed, the sufferer had never been left alone since the ringing of his bell on that terrible first morning.

"And now," Mr. Prior went on, "if you will not think me inhospitable, I think you will be better away from here. You ought to go to the seaside."

"There haven't been any letters for me, I suppose?" Desmond said, a little wistfully.

"Not one. I suppose you gave the right address? Ormehurst Rectory, Crittenden, Kent?"

"I don't think I put Crittenden," said Desmond. "I copied the address from your telegram." He pulled the pink paper from his pocket.

"Ah, that would account," said the other.

"You've been most awfully kind all through," said Desmond, abruptly.

"Nonsense, my boy," said the elder man, benevolently. "I only wish Willie had been able to come. He's never written, the rascal! Nothing but the telegram to say he could not come and was writing."

"I suppose he's having a jolly time somewhere," said Desmond, enviously; "but look here—do tell me about the ghost, if there's anything to tell. I'm almost quite well now, and I should like to know what it was that made a fool of me like that."

"Well"—Mr. Prior looked round him at the gold and red of dahlias and sunflowers, gay in the September sunshine—"here, and now, I don't know that it could do any harm. You remember that story of the man who got this place from Henry VIII, and the curse? That man's wife is buried in a vault under the church. Well, there were legends, and I confess I was curious to see her tomb. There are iron gates to the vault. Locked, they were. I opened them with an old key—and I couldn't get them to shut again."

"Yes?" Desmond said.

"You think I might have sent for a locksmith; but the fact is, there is a small crypt to the church, and I have used that crypt as a supplementary laboratory. If I had called anyone in to see to the lock they would have gossiped. I should have been turned out of my laboratory—perhaps out of my house."

"I see."

"Now, the curious thing is," Mr. Prior went on, lowering his voice, "that it is only since that grating was opened that this house has been what they call 'haunted.' It is since then that all the things have happened."

"What things?"

"People staying here, suddenly ill—just as you were. And the attacks always seem to indicate loss of blood. And . . ." He hesitated a moment. "That wound in your throat. I told you you had hurt yourself falling when you rang the bell. But that was not true. What is true is that you had on your throat just the same little white wound that all the others have had. I wish"—he frowned— "that I could get that vault gate shut again. The key won't turn."

"I wonder if I could do anything?" Desmond asked, secretly convinced that he had hurt his throat in falling, and that his host's story was, as he put it, "all moonshine." Still, to put a lock right was but a slight return for all the care and kindness. "I'm an engineer, you know," he added, awkwardly, and rose. "Probably a little oil. Let's have a look at this same lock."

He followed Mr. Prior through the house to the church. A bright, smooth old key turned readily, and they passed into the building, musty and damp, where ivy crawled through the broken windows, and the blue sky seemed to be laid close against the holes in the roof. Another key clicked in the lock of a low door beside what had once been the Lady Chapel, a thick oak door grated back, and Mr. Prior stopped a moment to light a candle that waited in its rough iron candlestick on a ledge of the stonework. Then down narrow stairs, chipped a little at the edges and soft with dust. The crypt was Norman, very simply beautiful. At the end of it was a recess, masked with a grating of rusty ironwork.

"They used to think," said Mr. Prior, "that iron kept off witchcraft. This is the lock," he went on, holding the candle against the gate, which was ajar.

They went through the gate, because the lock was on the other side. Desmond worked a minute or two with the oil and feather that he had brought. Then with a little wrench the key turned and re-turned.

"I think that's all right," he said, looking up, kneeling on one knee, with the key still in the lock and his hand on it.

"May I try it?"

Mr. Prior took Desmond's place, turned the key, pulled it out, and stood up. Then the key and the candlestick fell rattling on the stone floor, and the old man sprang upon Desmond.

"Now I've got you," he growled, in the darkness, and Desmond says that his spring and his clutch and his voice were like the spring and the clutch and the growl of a strong savage beast.

Desmond's little strength snapped like a twig at his first bracing of it to resistance. The old man held him as a vice holds. He had got a rope from somewhere. He was tying Desmond's arms.

Desmond hates to know that there in the dark he screamed like a caught hare. Then he remembered that he was a man, and shouted, "Help! Here! Help!"

But a hand was on his mouth, and now a handkerchief was being knotted at the back of his head. He was on the floor, leaning against something. Prior's hands had left him.

"Now," said Prior's voice, a little breathless, and the match he struck showed Desmond the stone shelves with long things on them—coffins, he supposed. "Now, I'm sorry I had to do it, but science before friendship, my dear Desmond," he went on, quite courteous and friendly. "I will explain to you, and you will see that a man of honor could not act otherwise. Of course, you having no friends who know where you are is most convenient. I saw that from the first. Now I'll explain. I didn't expect you to understand by instinct. But no matter. I am, I say it without vanity, the greatest discoverer since Newton. I know how to modify men's natures. I can make men what I choose. It's all done by transfusion of blood. Lopez—you know, my man Lopez—I've pumped the blood of dogs into his veins, and he's my slave—like a dog. Verney, he's my slave, too—part dog's blood and partly the blood of people who've come from time to time to investigate the ghost, and partly my own, because I wanted him to be clever enough to help me. And there's a bigger thing behind all this. You'll understand me when I say"—here he became very technical indeed, and used many words that meant nothing to Desmond, whose thoughts dwelt more and more on his small chance of escape.

To die like a rat in a hole, a rat in a hole! If he could only loosen the handkerchief and shout again!

"Attend, can't you?" said Prior, savagely, and kicked him. "I beg your pardon, my dear chap," he went on, suavely, "but this is important. So you see the elixir of life is really the blood. The blood is the life, you know, and my great discovery is that to make a man immortal, and restore his youth, one only needs blood from the veins of a man who unites in himself blood of the four great races—the four colors, black, white, red, and yellow. Your blood unites these four. I took as much as I dared from you that night. I was the vampire, you know." He laughed pleasantly. "But your blood didn't act. The drug I had to give you to induce sleep probably destroyed the vital germs. And, besides, there wasn't enough of it. Now there is going to be enough!"

Desmond had been working his head against the thing behind him, easing the knot of the handkerchief down till it slipped from head to neck. Now he got his mouth free, and said, quickly: "That was not true what I said about the Chinamen and that. I was joking. My mother's people were all Devon."

"I don't blame you in the least," said Prior, quietly. "I should lie myself in your place."

And he put back the handkerchief. The candle was now burning clearly from the place where it stood—on a stone coffin. Desmond could see that the long things on the shelves were coffins, not all of stone. He wondered what this madman would do with his body when everything was over. The little wound in his throat had broken out again. He could feel the slow trickle of warmth on his neck. He wondered whether he would faint. It felt like it.

"I wish I'd brought you here the first day—it was Verney's doing, my tinkering about with pints and half-pints. Sheer waste—sheer wanton waste!"

Prior stopped and stood looking at him.

Desmond, despairingly conscious of growing physical weakness, caught himself in a real wonder as to whether this might not be a dream—a horrible, insane dream—and he could not wholly dismiss the wonder, because incredible things seemed to be adding themselves to the real horrors of the situation, just as they do in dreams. There seemed to be something stirring in the place—something that wasn't Prior. No—nor Prior's shadow, either. That was black and sprawled big across the arched roof. This was white, and very small and thin. But it stirred, it grew—now it was no longer just a line of white, but a long, narrow, white wedge—and it showed between the coffin on the shelf opposite him and that coffin's lid.

And still Prior stood very still looking down on his prey. All emotion but a dull wonder was now dead in Desmond's weakened senses. In dreams—if one called out, one awoke—but he could not call out. Perhaps if one moved . . . But before he could bring his enfeebled will to the decision of movement—something else moved. The black lid of the coffin opposite rose slowly—and then suddenly fell, clattering and echoing, and from the coffin rose a form, horribly white and shrouded, and fell on Prior and rolled with him on the floor of the vault in a silent, whirling struggle. The last thing Desmond heard before he fainted in good earnest was the scream Prior uttered as he turned at the crash and saw the white-shrouded body leaping toward him.

"It's all right," he heard next. And Verney was bending over him with brandy. "You're quite safe. He's tied up and locked in the laboratory. No. That's all right, too." For Desmond's eyes had turned towards the lidless coffin. "That was only me. It was the only way I could think of, to save you. Can you walk now? Let me help you, so. I've opened the grating. Come."

Desmond blinked in the sunlight he had never thought to see again. Here he was, back in his wicker chair. He looked at the sundial on the house. The whole thing had taken less than fifty minutes.

"Tell me," said he. And Verney told him in short sentences with pauses between.

"I tried to warn you," he said, "you remember, in the window. I really believed in his experiments at first—and—he'd found out something about me—and not told. It was when I was very young. God knows I've paid for it. And when you came I'd only just found out what really had happened to the other chaps. That beast Lopez let it out when he was drunk. Inhuman brute! And I had a row with Prior that first night, and he promised me he wouldn't touch you. And then he did."

"You might have told me."

"You were in a nice state to be told anything, weren't you? He promised me he'd send you off as soon as you were well enough. And he had been good to me. But when I heard him begin about the grating and the key I knew—so I just got a sheet and—"

"But why didn't you come out before?"

"I didn't dare. He could have tackled me easily if he had known what he was tackling. He kept moving about. It had to be done suddenly. I counted on just that moment of weakness when he really thought a dead body had come to life to defend you. Now I'm going to harness the horse and drive you to the police station at Crittenden. And they'll send and lock him up. Everyone knew he was as mad as a hatter, but somebody had to be nearly killed before anyone would lock him up. The law's like that, you know."

"But you—the police—won't they—"

"It's quite safe," said Verney, dully. "Nobody knows but the old man, and now nobody will believe anything he says. No, he never posted your letters, of course, and he never wrote to your friend, and he put off the Psychical man. No, I can't find Lopez; he must know that something's up. He's bolted."

But he had not. They found him, stubbornly dumb, but moaning a little, crouched against the locked grating of the vault when they came, a prudent half-dozen of them, to take the old man away from the Haunted House. The master was dumb as the man. He would not speak. He has never spoken since.

Turkish Delight

Roberta Lannes

Roberta Lannes has been publishing in the science fiction, dark fantasy, and horror genres since 1985, including her acclaimed collection of short stories, *The Mirror of Night*, from Silver Salamander Press. Her work has been translated into numerous languages, and South African filmmaker Aryan Kaganof's 1994 movie *Ten Monologues from the Lives of the Serial Killers* included an adaptation her short story "Goodbye, Dark Love."

Her digital artwork has appeared in *Cemetery Dance* magazine, and her photographs in *JPG Magazine*, and she has exhibited in galleries and designed iPhone App splash screens, CD covers, calendars, and greeting cards. More recently, she collaborated with author Christopher Conlon as illustrator for his epic zombie poem *When They Came Back*, contributing over fifty horror photographs to the book.

"Traditional vampire stories only intrigue me in one way," reveals the author, "that being the seduction. Nowadays, even that has been superseded by the impulsive, compulsive vampires who attack, drink, and run. I wanted to write something more subtle, more about the vampires we meet in our everyday lives. Those that take something vital to ourselves against our will, yet by seduction or manipulation, are far more real and frightening than the bloodsuckers.

"In the following tale, Andrew has something of value to himself and to those whose lives are empty of that which keeps us delighted and full of wonder. I liken Andrew to a Turkish Delight—merely a chocolate sweet without its prized aromatic, succulent rose jelly inside. And so a vampire story was born . . ."

THE WALK HOME from school took Andrew up Long Row to Green Street where he lived with his mother and Aunt Molly. Two doors down from Andrew's house was an old nailer's cottage. Tourists sometimes stopped to look into its dusty windows and see the old tools and furnishings of the eighteenth century nail-maker's shop. It had little historical interest to tourists, what with the famous mill in the same town, but once in a while someone other than the schoolchildren who'd learned of it in school stopped by.

Today, as Andrew trudged up the cobbled road, he saw an unfamiliar old man and a boy about his own age staring into the cottage window.

They had the look of tourists with cameras slung around their necks, small clean backpacks and hiking boots that still looked new, stiff, and uncomfortable. When they heard Andrew's footsteps, they turned.

The boy was pretty, Andrew thought, almost like a girl. His dark hair was cut scraggily so that it fell over his eyes and ears in a fashionable way. His eyes were large, round, and luminous on his pale face. He didn't smile. The man had small eyes, very light in color, almost like pale aquamarine quartz, and large fuzzy eyebrows just like Andrew's Granddad. He was tall and thin, with a long flat nose and around very thin lips, the skin wrinkled in vertical ravines, reminding Andrew of a cartoon skull.

"Do you live around here, son?" The man spoke as the boy turned his stare back into the cottage. He had an accent. German or Danish. Andrew wasn't good at telling one accent from another unless it was American, Spanish or French.

Andrew frowned at the man and continued walking. It didn't occur to Andrew to walk past his house that day and turn onto another street, but later he would think about how different things would have been if he had. He walked right up to the door, eyes still on the tourists, turned the doorknob, and went in.

"That must be Andy. Guess what your Aunt Molly made?" The air was full of the aroma of butter, flour and currents.

"You made scones, Auntie, I could smell them outside." Andrew set down his book bag and took off his blazer and cap.

"Go up and change your clothes, Andy, then come down and have one before they cool down."

There wasn't much better than warm Molly scones and a cup of cocoa. He hurried upstairs and changed into a sweatshirt and jeans. As he put his school shoes on the chair by the window, he looked down at the nailer's cottage. The old man had stepped away from the building into the street and was staring right up at Andrew's window. At Andrew. He thought of the scones, the hot cocoa, of his Aunt waiting downstairs, but somehow he found the stranger's curious stare compelling. Then the man smiled. His teeth were very straight, large, and white. Like Chiclets, Andrew thought, like dice without the dots.

"What's taking you, Andy? The scones are cooling!"

His Aunt was at his door, her graying yellow apron smeared with the by-products of baking. He spun around, startled.

"Oh, Auntie, I didn't hear you coming up the stairs."

"What's out there so interesting you reckon it's worth more than a warm scone or two?" She came up beside him and looked out the window. Andrew looked as well. Nothing. No one was there, the street was deserted.

"I saw some tourists looking in the cottage and the old one tried to talk to me."

"You didn't speak with him, did you? You know what your mum says. *One doesn't speak to strangers, look what happened to Wally Burdock and Gwen Shafford.* They talked to strangers and both of them ended up d-e-a-d, dead."

Well, Andrew thought, that wasn't quite true. Wally, who was seventeen and in trouble with local thugs all the time, was beaten with a bat until he had terrible brain damage and his folks let the hospital take him off life-support, then he died. And Gwen was raped by her stepbrother and went crazy. She was in some asylum or hospital somewhere. Still, he knew what his mum meant. She'd stopped to talk with a stranger once and the next thing she knew after three weeks of romance, bingo, bango, no more stranger. Andrew was the result of that fiasco.

"I know. I know. I gave a good frown and came right in." He sniffed at the air. "I must have smelled them scones anyway, 'cause nothing ever stops me from coming in when you're baking."

His Aunt grinned. "Well, then, let's have one, and I'll make you a cup of cocoa. It's getting cold outside."

Andrew followed her down the narrow stairs to the tiny kitchen. He sat down to wait. Aunt Molly had her set ways of doing things, and there would be no impatient grabbing or rushing her. She busied herself with canisters, spoons, and a pan of milk.

"Tell me what you did today."

"Maths. We worked on problems. Lucky for me they're really easy."

"They are, well then, give me one and see if I can do it. It's been thirty years since I did any maths, but I'm still pretty smart for an old lady."

"You're not old, Auntie. Mum is older than you and she's still young. She says so all the time." His mouth watered at the smell of the cocoa stirred in the hot milk. His Aunt set the cup before him, then went to the counter for a scone. He watched as she broke open the dusty cream-colored mass and steam rolled out into the warm kitchen.

"Give me a problem, then, Andy. See if I can do it." She sat across from him, eager for his usual reaction to her scones.

A bit annoyed at having to speak when he wanted to eat, he licked his lips and stared at his scone. "All right, Auntie. If a train travels at 50 mph, and it took the train four hours and ten minutes to get from London to Newcastle, what is the distance from London to Newcastle?"

"Oh, my, that is a tough one. Let me think . . ." She scratched her head and wrinkled her mouth in concentration. "Do you know the answer?"

Andrew nodded. "Do you?" He bit into the scone. It was almost too good. He swooned.

"Well, 218 miles give or take few miles. Yes?"

"It's got a decimal figure in it, but you're close. That's really good, Auntie."

They heard a key in the lock. "That'll be your mum. We should ask her to solve one of your problems."

Andrew's mother came in with her arms full of groceries. "Come help."

"Mum, my scone's getting cold."

His aunt put her hands on his shoulders. "You stay here, Andy, I'll get them."

He grinned up at his aunt then took a sip of the cocoa. She always made it a bit too rich, just the way he liked it.

While his mum and aunt put away groceries, Andrew thought about the pretty boy and old man he'd seen. He wondered why the man had spoken to him, why the boy seemed so sad. Why would he want to know if Andrew lived nearby? What could he have wanted?

"There was just an accident at the triangle. I heard in Safeway. Young boy crossing with his Granddad got hit by a lorry."

Andrew spun around in his chair. "Just now?"

"Just a few minutes ago. Didn't you hear the siren? I was going to go have a look, but I have frozen puddings in my bags. What, you think you know who it might have been?"

"May I go look? Please? I might know him. I might."

His mother looked to his aunt and back to him. His aunt was the lenient one, over-feeding and over-loving him, while his mother was bitter and restrictive. His aunt gave his mum a pleading look. Sometimes it worked, and sometimes it didn't.

"Finish the scone and cocoa, then you and your Aunt Molly can go take a look while I start supper."

"Me? You want me to go with him. Bernadette, I look like I've been in all day cleaning, which I have. Can't he go on his own?"

"It's almost dark."

"Please, Mum, I just want to take a look. I won't stay. Really, I promise."

"You'll wear a coat?"

"Yeah, yeah, I will. Promise."

"Go, then, but don't dawdle."

Andrew grabbed the unfinished scone and ran upstairs to get a jacket. He knew it was the pretty boy. Just knew. It could be any one of the boys he knew, but there was more of a reason for a stranger to be hit. The triangle confused tourists. They often got caught out in the traffic. He hoped that the boy wasn't hurt too badly.

He shouted goodbye to his mum and aunt as he raced out the front door. He ran down Green Street to Bridge Street until he reached the triangle. There were two police cars and a casualty van. The crowd was large and traffic backed up Bridge Street as far as he could see in both directions. Frank Delaney rushed over when he saw Andrew at the edge of the crowd.

"Did you see it happen?" Frank shivered in just a football jersey.

"You mean the accident. No, my mum just told me about it. She heard about it in Safeway. Did you see?"

"No, dammit. I was doing my report for Ol' Noddy Bennett. Who d'you think it was?"

Andrew rose up on his toes as the attendants lifted the stretcher into the van. The body was entirely covered by a sheet. "Dunno. He's dead. Can't see his face." His throat was tight and his eyes burned to cry.

As he surveyed the crowd, Andrew saw the old man with a police officer, his bony hand over his face, hiding his tears, shaking his head. When he took his hand away from his face to get a handkerchief, he turned to look right at Andrew, as if he knew the boy was there. His eyes lingered on him until Andrew felt his stomach clench. Then the old man turned back to the police officer and blew his nose.

"I hate missing all the blood and guts." Frank complained. "Bet it's someone from school. Probably that big baby, Tim Broadbank. His mum won't let him cross the street without holding her hand *still*. He's a year ahead of us, you know."

"Tim? No. Don't think so. I saw a boy with his Granddad an hour ago up by my house. They were standing at the nailer's cottage. The Granddad is right over there with the police crying his bloody eyes out. It had to be his grandson."

"D'you know them?" Frank rubbed his hands together.

Andrew shook his head. "Tourists. They had the look."

"Just think. You go on a trip with your Granddad and end up going home in a coffin. That's a sodding awful vacation if I ever heard . . ."

Andrew couldn't take his eyes off the old man. Frank went on talking but he didn't really hear. The old man didn't look at him again, but Andrew watched for his eyes to wash over him again. He shivered.

". . . so they stuck these big pins in his eyes."

"Pins?" He turned to see Frank going on. "Hey, Frank, I had better get on.

Supper'll be ready and my mum wasn't happy to let me come out here as it is."

"Yeah, well, all right. If I find anything out, I'll tell you Monday. See you."

"Right, see you." He gave the old man one more lingering glance, then walked away. Just as Andrew turned up Green Street thinking of his supper, the old man searched the crowd.

Andrew's legs felt leaden as he trudged up his street. He wanted to go to the old man, comfort him. Even as he felt it, he knew it was unreasonable. He didn't know this stranger about who everything seemed suspiciously odd. As he reached his door, he wondered if he had just spoken to the old man, kept them a few minutes more, the boy might not have been killed.

The next morning, Andrew grabbed up *The Belper News* from the doorstep. He was certain there would be a report of the accident. Not much qualified as news in town. This was front-page stuff. And there it was.

VISITOR ACCIDENT
by Rosalie Bishop

A man and his ten-year-old ward, traveling through England, stopped in Belper on their way to Matlock Baths. At approximately 5:00 p.m., they were crossing at the triangle near The Mill Park when a lorry, on its way to Derby, hit the boy who was killed on impact. The two visitors were unfamiliar with the traffic patterns in that area and the boy stepped out in front of the lorry. The driver was not at fault in this tragic accident. The boy's guardian plans to return to his native Turkey within the week. Local families have rallied to give the man a place to stay and meals until his plane departs from Heathrow on Thursday. Anyone interested in giving aid or expressing sympathies can contact Elizabeth Horner at The Methodist Chapel.

Andrew was now more curious than before. *Turkey.* He'd never much thought about people living there, though he'd heard of it in geography. What he did know was that he loved Turkish Delight. The rosy jelly center with the yummy chocolate all around made him think of the occasional bouts of happiness his mother had, when she bought them a bag of sweets, always with some Turkish Delight for Andrew. Did Turkish Delight originate in Turkey? Was the jelly part Turkish or the chocolate or both? For once, he couldn't wait for Monday. He'd go straight to the school library after class.

The library was a small room that had once been a supply cabinet and coat room. Books lined every wall and two half-sized bookcases divided the room. Paintings done by the infants covered the wall over the librarian's desk. Andrew loved the smell of the books and the ancient oiled tables where students could read. The library was empty except for Miss Eklund, a woman the kids called "the Swede." She was in her fifties, wore her hair clipped short, had funny little hairs on her chin and smelled of men's aftershave. The Swede was actually a wrestler, and Miss Eklund had a stocky build like a man, hence the moniker. She let the girls get away with murder and slapped the back of boy's heads if they spoke.

He had a book on Turkey when Frank appeared around the corner. He grabbed at Andrew's sleeve to see the book. He scanned it then looked over at Miss Eklund who was deep into stamping loan cards.

"Hey, you get in trouble when you got in Friday?"

"Naw. You?"

"Hell, no. Nobody comes home until late at my house. My dad goes straight to the pub from work and my mum . . . well, she's with her friends a lot. Nick's living with his girlfriend in Sheffield now, so it's just me."

"Did you see anything after I left?"

Frank took the book on Turkey from Andrew's hand. "Hey, did you know that the old guy is from Turkey? I was standing there while this lady was asking him about the kid."

Andrew put the book under his arm. "Yeah? Really? What'd you hear? I read the newspaper but it doesn't say much."

"He was staying at the Hollingshead Hotel. The kid wasn't his grandson, but a friend of the family. He was taking the kid to the baths because he had some kind of illness. Leukemia or something. Hell, the baths don't do anything and anybody who knows something knows that. It's just a tourist attraction. A joke, really."

"Wow. I saw the kid. He looked sad or sick. Weak like. Maybe he was going to die anyway." Andrew watched Frank's face grow more animated.

"Or maybe the old guy pushed the kid in front of the lorry to make sure he didn't suffer. Hey, that would be sinister, like when . . ."

Miss Eklund drifted over to the boys. "You two want to make conversation, do it outside. This is a library. We don't converse in the library."

Frank winked at Andrew and fled. Andrew checked the book out to take home.

Frank wasn't in school the next day. Andrew wanted to share his discoveries about Turkey with him, not that it was the kind of thing Frank would have wanted to know. Turkey was right near Russia. It had the Black Sea on one side and the Mediterranean on the other. The country had its own language, called Turkish. He hadn't gone far enough in the book to learn if Turkish Delight came from Turkey, though. He also read that they had bad earthquakes there. Maybe Frank would find all the deaths that came from their earthquakes interesting. That was the kind of thing he found fascinating.

On his way home, he stopped by Frank's. Mrs. Delaney answered the door.

"Is Frank at home?"

Her face screwed up and she leaned over to put her nose about an inch from Andrews's. She stunk of brandy. "Well, now, he's supposed to be with you, Mr. Andrew Crawford, so I should be asking you just that thing. He told me he was going to meet you on the tarmac and you were both going to the church to see about helping that old man."

"To the church . . ." Andrew tried to recall which church that might be. "Well, I must've got it wrong, Mrs. Delaney. I thought we were meeting here. I'd better get on to the church then, hadn't I?" He smiled sheepishly.

"You two aren't cooking something up together, are you?"

"No, Mrs. Delaney. We honestly want to make the man feel better. His kid was about our age and we just thought . . ."

"How nice. You had better get going, Andrew. It'll be dark soon." She shut the door before he could reply.

Why hadn't Frank told him he was going to the church? And which church? He couldn't recall. He walked down to the Catholic Church which was closest and looked for someone to help him. A washerwoman told him the old man was staying with a family up by Strutts School. The Methodist Chapel was where they were coordinating aid for the Turkish man. He thanked the woman and started off in the direction of Strutts. It occurred to him that his Aunt Molly would be sick with worry if he didn't stop home first. But then he risked being told he couldn't go at all.

It was a long walk down to Strutts. The only way to get there before dark would be to take a bus. He checked for change in his pocket and raced to the bus stop where a bus had just pulled up. It was the number 14 that stopped right across from The Methodist Chapel at the bus station. Just his luck.

Though the bus was crowded, he got a seat by the window behind the driver. He watched the people walking determinedly up and down the streets, the cars moving ever so slowly in the traffic of the A6. Another bus crawled along going in the opposite direction. They were across from each other at one point. Andrew stared into the other bus, scanning the faces. He stopped at the old man, the one he had seen by the cottage. He was sitting with his arm around another boy, smiling his dicey smile, and listening to the boy's animated chatter. Andrew felt a flurry of butterflies in his belly before he really looked at the boy, knowing anyway that it was Frank Delaney.

Andrew spun in his seat, hands to the windows, and shouted Frank's name. "Frank, Frank. Oh, no . . ." The bus driver asked Andrew to quiet down, but Andrew had already gone silent. He kept his eyes on the bus as it ambled on in the other direction. He wasn't certain, but he thought that for a second the old man looked right at him.

He got off at King Street and walked back up toward home. When he told his mum and auntie what was going on, they would understand why he was late. He hoped so. Nothing else had gone right that day.

"It's none of your business what that Frank Delaney does with his life, Andy. If he wants to run off with the Queen, he can, but you have your own life to live."

His mother started on him before dinner and it was now his bedtime. His auntie had listened carefully and said, "What a shame." But when his mum got home, Molly retold Andrew's story with unusual histrionics. She used expressions like "kidnapped" and "pedophile," working his mum into a frantic state.

"And if he was kidnapped, all the better then that you keep away from that boy. Frank finds trouble where there isn't any, isn't that right Molly?"

Aunt Molly was wringing her hands and nodding. "At least the authorities know who he is and where he's staying. That old man isn't going to get far."

Andrew's mum made moaning noises in her throat. "Let's call the police. It can't hurt. If it's innocent, then we'll just feel like fools, but if Frank was kidnapped, they'll be glad of our call."

As his mum and auntie got on the telephone, Andrew sneaked out the back door. He had to get over to Frank's. The bus had been going in the direction of his house. It could all have been innocent. Couldn't it?

This time, when Mrs. Delaney answered the door, a strange man barked from upstairs to get back to him. She looked disheveled in her bathrobe and her face flushed in the light of the foyer.

"What's it now? You get it wrong again? Were you supposed to meet up at school then?"

"You mean Frank's not here?"

She shuddered at his anxious tone. "No, Frank is not here. What is going on, Andrew Crawford?"

Andrew looked down at his feet. "I think he's gone off with someone. I saw him on the bus with the old man whose ward was killed at the triangle last week. I thought maybe they were coming here."

Though she looked a bit panicked, Mrs. Delaney held her robe shut at her throat and said, "Frankie does as he pleases. He's tough enough to take care of himself. I'll worry if he don't come home for days. He's like his brother that way." The man's voice came from upstairs again, more insistent this time. Mrs. Delaney lowered her voice to Andrew. "Don't you worry, Andrew Crawford. Frankie's all right. Go home." Then she shut the door on him, again.

He ran home, hoping his mum and auntie were consumed by the police and hadn't noticed he'd gone, but there they were, in the street, a police van pulled up to the house, two coppers talking to them.

"Where the hell did you go you stupid, stupid boy?" His mother grabbed his arm and yanked him into the house. "You knew you'd scare me to death, didn't you?" She was slapping at him. He kept his arms up as she flailed. "How dare you!"

His Aunt Molly came in with the police officers and shouted for her sister to stop. One of the police officers grabbed at his mum. His Aunt Molly swept him into her arms.

"Mrs, it's no good hitting the boy. Stop. Relax. We'll talk to him."

"Bernadette, go upstairs and wash your face in cold water. I'll talk with Andy and the police. Go on."

His mum ripped herself from the policeman's grasp and growled, foam at the corners of her mouth. "You'll do no such thing. He's *my* son. I'll deal with him."

The constable shook his head. "Mrs, do as your sister says. You take this into your own hands, you'll be leaving with *us*."

Andrew tried not to cry, but he couldn't stop himself. He was more afraid than he was sad, but tears came anyway.

"Look what you've done, Bernadette. Andrew's in tears. Go upstairs. Go, now."

His mother stomped upstairs, but he knew she wouldn't wash her face or anything else. She'd stew in her rage until she couldn't stand it any longer and come hit him again. His auntie tried to stop it, but she didn't have any place else to live, so she turned away when she failed. Andrew felt sorry for her, thankful that at least she tried.

One of the police officers sat down beside Andrew and asked him a hundred questions. Or so it seemed. It was past his bedtime and he was beginning to fall asleep. When the man decided he had enough information, he told Andrew they were going to go by the Delaney's house. Then the constable asked if Andrew felt safe enough to stay in his house. That they had somewhere else he could stay.

"It'll be all right. She gets upset easily. But she always cools down. Besides, I have my auntie." Aunt Molly grinned from across the room.

"Okay, then. But you call us if things get heated again. Don't be afraid." The police officer looked to Aunt Molly then back to Andrew. "We'll let you know what our investigation turns up."

"Yes, please," Andrew managed. His eyelids sagging, body limp.

Last thing he heard was his auntie opening the blanket chest to get him an extra bit of warmth.

When Andrew woke, he knew half the day had gone. Though it was gray out, he could tell by the angle of the light in his room. His mum was off at work, surely, and his auntie was probably cleaning someone's house, since it was Wednesday. He dressed in his school clothes and went down to the kitchen. His auntie was sitting at the table having lunch.

"Ah, well, look who finally got himself up. Did you sleep all right?"

"Yes, Aunt Molly. I don't remember going up to bed, though. Is Mum all right?"

"One of those nice policemen carried you up. You fell asleep before they reached the door, and I knew I'd never get you up those stairs alone."

"Is Mum okay?"

"What do you care? She beats you terribly and wails into the night about how awful you are to make her worry. She doesn't deserve you, Andy. She was too young to have a child alone in the first place. It should have been me. I'm a better mum to you than she is." She stopped, looking away from Andrew. "I'm sorry. I know you love your mum. Sometimes, I can't help myself. The truth slips out. Forgive me."

"I love you too, Aunt Molly. Don't be mad at Mum. She's unhappy."

His auntie smirked at him. "She and all the rest of us miserable old women."

"You're not old."

She looked Andrew over. "You think you can go to school now?"

He looked at the clock over the sink. It was nearly noon. "Four more classes after midday. Yeah. I'm okay, now. Are you cleaning today?"

Aunt Molly set a sack on the table. "Here's a sandwich, then. There's a note inside, but I'll telephone the school and let them know you're on your way. And yes, not a day goes by I don't have a house to clean. I got a cancellation today, that's all."

"Thanks, Auntie. You're the best!"

"Oh!" Andrew stopped at the door as his auntie spoke. "Your friend Frank is fine. You'll see him in school, I'd wager."

"Thanks!" Andrew closed the door too hard, but he hardly heard it. He ran to school, anxious to learn what had happened to Frank.

He caught up with Frank on his way to class. When he saw Andrew, his friend frowned.

"What? You mad at me?"

"You pissed off my mum, you stupid idiot. She told me to get lost after school 'cause she was entertaining her friends; so I told her I was meeting you at the church. She just guessed we was going to visit that old guy. You really ruined it for me. When the police showed up, she got even angrier. Don't you get it? Can't you be cool?"

Andrew was speechless. Wouldn't Frank have done the same for him if he'd seen Andrew on the bus with the old man? Wouldn't Frank have suspected something was up with the old man being friendly to another boy right after his ward died?

Frank walked off. Nothing bad had happened to Frank, and that was good, but couldn't he see that Andrew's concern was heartfelt and real? Couldn't he understand that? He hadn't meant to make Mrs. Delaney angry. Andrew did his best not to cry. He hung his head and shoulders as he went to class.

He was listless the rest of his day in school. He questioned everything from the moment he saw the old man at the nailer's cottage with his ward. Were all the strange things he saw and felt just his imagination? Didn't it seem odd that the old man stayed around Belper after the accident? That he seemed happy and chatty on the bus with Frank? It was creepy. Very creepy.

All the way home, Andrew kept his head down, watching his feet as he went. When he got there, his mother was remote, ashamed of her behavior, but unable or refusing to apologize and make it up to Andrew. His auntie was quiet, on edge that she'd set off her sister. He felt very alone.

Up in his room, after he did his homework, Andrew sat in his window staring down at the nailer's cottage. Growing up, he often sat there, wondering what the street looked like 200 years before when the nailer was busy making his nails and the smoke from his furnace curled upward, meeting the clouds. Were mothers and their sons walking by telling their boys about how their fathers worked in the building trade, and needed the nails? How the nailer had no competition, therefore had a grand house up on the hill near the Lutheran church? Did the sons grow up wanting to be a nailer and have grand houses? Was one of those boys the great-great-granddad to his own father, whom he'd never met? What did his father do now? Was he a builder, a sales clerk, or a doctor? His mother told Andrew little about him. Aunt Molly, well, she had told him all he knew now.

"Don't you dare tell your mum I've told you about him. She'd have a fit. You still want to know?"

"Yes, Auntie. Please." He was about six, or maybe he'd been five.

"Well, his name was William, but your mum called him Will. She didn't know when she met him that he was married, but he turned out to be the husband of a very wealthy woman on Jersey. Her parents were very very rich and they all lived in a palace of a house. Of course, Will told your mum he was miserable, no one in his wife's family respected him and expected that he continue the family business, which had him on the road five days a week. He'd once loved his wife a lot, but she wouldn't have children because it would ruin her figure. She was evidently very vain.

"Your mum was far prettier ten years ago than she is now, and Will fell deeply and quickly in love with her. I believe that. Your mum was cautious, only then because she knew he traveled a lot and she wanted someone closer. He did what he could to stay close to Belper for almost a month, but then his wife's family got suspicious and he disappeared. He wrote to me once. I was married to your Uncle Phillip, then. He asked me to tell Bernadette that he would never forget her. That she'd made him happier than he'd ever known, but he was married. He explained his entire situation to me, but I thought it best that it all remain a mystery. I told your mum I thought he was probably married and a cad and to leave it at that. A month later, she realized that you were on your way.

"She was extremely hurt by Will abandoning her. When your Uncle Phillip died suddenly and left me with huge debts, your mum and I found we needed each other too much to dwell on any one betrayal or loss. We agreed that you would be the one thing that made up for it all. And you have. One day, when you're all grown up, we'll see if we can find your father."

Andrew thought about that every time his mother beat him. It was with his father that she was truly angry. But he could never say that. That would betray his auntie's confidence. And that confidence had given him all there was of his father. It was too precious to let go.

The next day, it rained. The class stayed inside instead of going out to the playground. Frank did not attempt to talk to Andrew, nor did he acknowledge Andrew when he tried to speak with him. One of the girls who fancied Andrew, thrilled by the fact that there was no one to take

Andrew away, flirted with him, completely embarrassing him. Andrew's fleeting attempts at attracting attention, praying someone would save him, went unseen. When she told him she'd like to be his girlfriend, he mumbled something about his mother not allowing him to have girl-friends and bolted.

At the bottom of Green Street, he saw the tall, thin figure of a man, his face covered by an umbrella, standing across from his home. Andrew knew it was the old man even before he turned to look at him. He continued to walk up the street, then stopped a few feet away, suddenly taken by a thought.

Perhaps this was *his* granddad. He had found out that his son had sired a child and was looking for Andrew everywhere. Maybe, the boy with him had been his brother! What if his father had fled his unhappy marriage and moved to Turkey? And that was why the old man was friendly with Frank? To find out if he was the lost child he'd been looking for! Why hadn't he thought of this before?

The old man stepped close to Andrew. "Do you live around here?"

"Yes, there." Andrew pointed across the way. "You asked me that before, but then I didn't know it was you."

"You know who I am, then?" The stranger smiled, pleased.

"My father's father?" Andrew's heart was beating so fast, soaring with desperate hope.

"Yes!" The old man put his hand over his mouth. "My grandson! It *is* you!"

"Granddad?"

"Yes! It is I. What do they call you . . .?" He looked away a moment, which to Andrew felt like an eternity. "Andy, isn't it?"

"Yes, Granddad. Andy."

"I've come to take you home." The old man's face held such warmth and benevolence. Andrew was about to burst with joy.

"To my father?"

He nodded. "To your father. He will be so pleased to see you. The whole family will."

"I have a whole family? Oh, Granddad. Really?"

"Yes, I'll tell you all about them. But the airplane leaves from Heathrow tomorrow. We will have to leave now if we are going to make it. I have a hotel room near Paddington."

"But Mum. Auntie Molly." The lights were on in the kitchen and he knew his auntie was busy with supper.

"They've had you for ten years. It's time your father gets to know you, yes?"

The flicker of fear, the moment of hesitation melted into decision. He would go where a real family awaited him. The unknown, for which his mum and auntie had long prepared him to meet with trepidation and reluctance, was suddenly a welcome place.

"Yes, all right. But my clothes? I've got my school blazer and . . ."

"There is a suitcase full of clothes for you in the hotel. Have you ever been to London before?"

"Granddad, I've never even been in a taxi!"

"Then a taxi we shall take to Derby. Then a first class coach on the train just for you."

"I'll need a passport. Won't I need papers or something? On television, when they . . ."

"Yes! Yes, my son. You'll have all of that. I have taken care of everything." The old man squeezed Andrew's shoulder, grinning down at Andrew. "Everything."

Andrew grinned back. "Is my family rich then, Granddad?"

"We are an old and wealthy family, my son."

"Yes, Auntie told me. You don't mind if she told me, do you? She's kept the secret from Mum all of these years."

"Of course not. When you write to your mother and aunt, once you are settled, it will no longer be a secret. You can relax and be free."

Suddenly, Andrew realized that it was no longer raining and a taxi waited at the bottom of the street. It was dark, the streets glistened, his life was ahead of him and he was going to his father's home!

Of course, there was no father waiting, though there was a rich family on a huge estate in Turkey. Granddad told Andrew once he was on the airplane, strapped into a seat in First Class up 33,000 feet in the air, that he would one day help him find his father. For now though, there was an ancient and revered family waiting just for him in a home far grander than anything he could imagine, where he would never feel lonely again.

Andrew realized then, too late, that the words his mum and auntie had bantered about that evening two days ago, "kidnapped" and "pedophile" now related to him. He told Granddad this, but the old man denied it. Andrew had been *chosen*. He was special. No one would ever touch him in that way; he was a sacred vessel. Everything the old man said was full of vagaries and obfuscations. Andrew couldn't get a straight answer. The long limousine ride lulled Andrew into a series of naps, each time waking him into the nightmare. They finally slowed as they came to a towering wall of pale bricks covered with climbing vines. Two men without shirts on and fabric wrapped around their heads pulled on the iron gate in the wall until it was open wide enough for the limousine.

When Andrew saw the great mansion, he still hoped that his father really was inside and that Granddad had just been playing around with him. Within were many other boys and girls, some near his age, some younger and older. They spoke many languages and dressed in white, from neck to toes. They wandered about freely, but they all seemed sad like the boy who'd died on the triangle, their eyes empty.

Granddad sat on the chair beside the large bed that would be Andrew's. Andrew changed into a white shirt and trousers and white sandals. Granddad watched, but was not curious. His stare was benign. Disinterested.

Andrew shivered, though the room was warm. "Why did you choose me? You had Frank Delaney."

"Yes, the boy who came to me. Frank was his name?" Granddad looked out the window to the bleak, rust and gray sunset, musing. "Frank. A hard boy. Old in his soul. He lacked the most important attribute. The essence for which we travel the world. The pure emanation. It was you all the while, Andrew. The moment I saw you, I *knew*."

Andrew felt emboldened by pride in having been chosen. No one had really noticed Andrew before, at least not to pick him out from all the others. And never before Frank Delaney. Perhaps this gave him power. He could survive this!

"What happened to him? The boy you were with. Did you kill him?"

Granddad laughed dryly. "Oh, no. Why would I have done that? He was a great loss." The old man got up and went to the window. "No, I didn't kill him, but I was at fault in a way. I was to bring him here in full essence, but I was too hungry. I took from him and could not stop myself. He was exhausted from my feeding, not watching where he was going. I was deeply upset by his passing. My tears were real. Once he was gone, there was nothing for me to do but wait for you."

"Do you even know if I have a father somewhere?" Andrew was scared, angry, and hopeful all at once.

"Oh, yes. I'd know it if you had lost him. Boys like you, growing up with overprotective single mothers, absent fathers, sometimes grow into angry, hard young men. Just as Frank will, though his father is in the house. Then it is too late. These boys meet the 'old man,' as they inevitably call him, and hate him. Not you, young Andrew. You have kept the hope, a rich part of the essence. You will be prized." The Granddad walked to him and placed his hands on his shoulders. "But you must retain your essence until you meet the mistress, so I will leave you. I've said too much already."

"I don't understand any of this. Don't go. Please. I don't want to be alone in here." He began to cry.

"I don't dare stay, young Andrew. I'd be too tempted. You are my penance, my find to make up for the losses I was so foolishly unable to protect from myself." The old man saw the fear in Andrew, his confusion. "You are not a prisoner, son. Look around. Meet some of the others." He went to the door. "Are you hungry?"

Andrew nodded, though he was more afraid than hungry. His stomach was a tight fist in his belly.

"There is more food than you can dream of downstairs. Go find the dining room. Make friends. See all the toys and books and games available around the grounds. One day soon, you will wonder why you ever thought to leave." He waited a moment. "You are thinking you'd like to leave, aren't you?"

Again, Andrew nodded. There were no other thoughts in his head.

"And you're thinking of your mother, your aunt. What will become of them without you?"

Andrew looked away, his eyes aching, his face wet with tears.

"Soon you will not care. Find comfort in the knowledge that you will have *no* cares, and that you will be treasured far more than you ever were in that dingy mill town of yours."

Granddad left. Andrew found himself at the balcony with dry heaves, no food in his gut. He cried, wept until he ached all over. Then he crawled onto the bed and stared up at the canopy of gilded silk. He longed for the smells of home. The wet stone, moss, the musty cellar, a crackling fire of hickory and oak, and Aunt Molly's scones. Here, the dry air smelled of dust and peat, cinnamon and sage.

It was dark when the door opened and an old woman entered. She went to the bedside and sat down, stroking Andrew's hair. In the darkness, he whispered, "Mum?"

"I will be your mother, your father, your God, my son. And you will be my greatest joy. Lie still, remember all that has been your life, and feel the joy and pleasure that innocence brings. I will not cause you pain, or touch you. In turn, your fear will pass, your cares and longings will lessen."

Andrew tried to sit up. Her hand went softly to his chest. "No, Andrew. Trust me. This will be like a dream. Lie still."

He obeyed. The woman had a quality even more compelling than the Granddad. Her eyes shone in the dark, the same pale blue, her pupils sharp pinpoints floating in the center. She smelled of cedar wood and orange blossoms, though it was more like distant smoke from a smoldering fire than emanating from her. She put her hands over him, as if warming them on the heat that rose from him. He closed his eyes and the dream came.

Nightmares, really. First, he saw his mother, young and naïve, silly and carefree. She went to the pub to drink ale with her girlfriends, until a tall, handsome man came in and broke up the girls. He cornered Bernadette and filled her full of flattery. She kissed the man she hardly knew and let him paw her right there in the pub. His hand went under her skirt and she was wet with desire.

The man walked her to his car and proceeded to take her. They were like two naked organisms, undulating and folding into and out of each other. After he was done with her, he told her he loved her. She didn't believe him. She didn't dare. They kissed passionately, he promised he would call on her, and then he dropped her at her parent's flat.

The next night, she found another man, and the next night another. None of them ever called for her, and none of them was around when she found herself pregnant. So, she began sleeping with her sister's husband Phillip, who had always fancied her more than the plain Molly. She claimed Phillip was the father. He killed himself rather than face the shame, and Molly. Poor Molly.

Phillip had mortgaged the house to the limit, had gambling debts and expense accounts for presents to the lovely young Bernadette that were begging payment. Molly lost the house, destitute, on the dole, but when her sister came crawling for help with the brat, Molly swallowed her pride and went to live with Bernadette in their parent's house. In the end, Molly thought, the baby boy could not have been Phillip's. The timing was off by almost three months. Phillip had just been another one of Bernadette's fools.

Then there was poor Aunt Molly; stealing from the people she cleaned house for, taking a ring here, a watch there. Nothing they could prove Molly had taken, things they could have easily misplaced. In the dream, Andrew saw her standing at her wardrobe, a box of booty in her arms, thinking of the life she'd have when she hocked it all and bought herself a flat of her own. Her antipathies for her bitter sister were evident in her wish that all that was Bernadette's turn to dross. That Andrew was more her child than Bernadette's and one day she would tell Andrew the truth. That his mother was a whore, not a secretary at Babington Hospital. She laughed then, deeply, loudly, without remorse.

The nightmare ended. The woman swooned, sated, as he awoke. He looked up to her. She had an aura of light around her that twinkled and pulsed. She sat down on the chair beside the bed and wept. Andrew sat up. In his mind, he thought to go to her, comfort her. She sobbed on. But he could not seem to muster the concern to move. He watched her until she went quiet.

"What happened to you? Why do I feel like this?"

She seemed to wake from a reverie, and then fixed him with her bright eyes. "He did not tell you?"

"The Granddad? No, he just talked about essence and treasures. Was it me made you cry?"

The old woman rose up, took a few steps away. She thought a moment about what she might say, then said nothing. She opened the door.

"Please." Andrew said flatly.

"Oh, what's the harm." She returned to the bed. "You will know as soon as you talk with the other children." She sat down, leaned against the bedpost.

"My son, do you see some of the uglier truths of your life now? Do you feel the sorrow in that truth?" She waited but Andrew remained impassive, silent. "I have lifted the veil of ignorance you have relied on all of your ten years. Do you not feel different for the weight of your innocence now gone into me?"

Andrew looked within. It was as dark and wet as the night the Granddad had taken him, but there was no glistening.

"You are unlucky in that you are mine. I will always weep at your loss and the sweetness of my fullness. It confuses. In time, you will no longer be confused. You will just *be*." She laughed dryly, as the Granddad had. "And to think that some of the silly human race rather reveres that state . . . *be-ing*. They call it 'enlightenment' and spend a lifetime seeking to attain it." She rose again, chuckling, went to the door and smiled a smile like dice without dots. "Until tomorrow."

When the door shut behind her, Andrew looked at his hands, felt his face. They were the same as always. He had not changed, really. Tomorrow. Tomorrow, he would look and see if they had a library with any books on Turkey. He hadn't finished the one he'd left behind. Somewhere.

Venus Rising on Water

Tanith Lee

Tanith Lee (1947–2015) did not learn to read—she was dyslexic—until almost age eight, and then only because her father taught her. This opened the world of books to her, and by the following year she was writing stories. She worked in various jobs, including shop assistant, waitress, librarian and clerk, before Donald A. Wollheim's DAW Books issued her novel *The Birthgrave* in 1975.

The imprint went on to publish a further twenty-six of her novels and collections. Since then, she published more than a hundred novels and collections, including *Death's Master*, *The Silver Metal Lover*, *Red as Blood*, and the Arkham House volume *Dreams of Dark and Light*. She also scripted two episodes of the BBC series *Blakes 7*, and her story "Nunc Dimittis" was adapted as an episode of the TV series *The Hunger*.

She was a winner of the World Fantasy Award and the British Fantasy Award, and she received Life Achievement Awards from the World Horror Convention, the World Fantasy Convention, and the Horror Writers Association.

"I've written several novels about vampires," revealed the author, "or types of vampire, and quite a lot of short stories of various lengths. Vampirism, to me, is one of those themes where somehow another idea or twist is always making itself known to me. The subject seems limitless, perhaps because the vampire seems somehow to have woven itself among the human psyche.

"'Venus Rising on Water' came initially from a fascination with Venice. It's about the clash between the future and the past—although the denouement, however odd or apparently fortuitous, demonstrates the hold everyday Real Life can get on the strangest matters."

LIKE LONG HAIR, the weeds grew down the façades of the city, over ornate shutters and leaden doors, into the pale green silk of the lagoon. Ten hundred ancient mansions crumbled. Sometimes a flight of birds was exhaled from their crowded mass, or a thread of smoke was drawn up into the sky. Day long a mist bloomed on the water, out of which distant towers rose like snakes of deadly gold. Once in every month a boat passed, carving the lagoon that had seemed thickened beyond movement. Far less often, here and there, a shutter cracked open and the weed hair broke, a stream of plaster fell like a blue ray. Then, some faint face peered out, probably eclipsed by a mask. It was a place of veils. Visitors were occasional. They examined the decaying mosaics, loitered in the caves of arches, hunted phantoms through marble tunnels. And under the streets they took photographs: one bald flash scouring a century off the catacombs and sewers, the lacework coffins, the handful of albino rats perched up on them, caught in a second like ghosts of white hearts, mute, with waiting eyes.

The dawn star shone in the lagoon on a tail of jagged silver. The sun rose. There was an unsuitable noise—the boat was coming.

"There," said the girl on the deck of the boat, "stop there, please."

The boat sidled to a pavement and stood on the water, trembling and murmuring. The girl left it with a clumsy gracefulness, and poised at the edge of the city with her single bag, cheerful and undaunted before the lonely cliffs of masonry, and all time's indifference.

She was small, about twenty-five, with ornately short fair hair, clad in old-fashioned jeans and a shirt. Her skin was fresh, her eyes bright with intelligent foolishness. She looked about, and upward. Her interest clearly centered on a particular house, which overhung the water like a face above a mirror, its eyes closed.

Presently the boat pulled away and went off across the lagoon, and only the girl and the silence remained.

She picked up her bag and walked along the pavement to an archway with a shut, leaden door. Here she knocked boldly, as if too stupid to understand the new silence must not yet be tampered with.

Her knocking sent hard blobs of sound careering round the vault of greenish crystal space that was the city's morning. They seemed to strike peeling walls and stone pilasters five miles off. From the house itself came no response, not even the vague sense of something stirring like a serpent in sleep.

"Now this is too bad," said the girl to the silence, upbraiding it mildly. "They told me a caretaker would be here, in time for the boat."

She left her bag (subconscious acknowledgment of the emptiness and indifference) by the gate, and walked along under the leaning face of the house. From here she saw the floors of the balconies of flowered iron; she listened for a sudden snap of shutters. But only the water lapped under the pavement, component of silence. This house was called the Palace of the Planet. The girl knew all about it, and what she did not know she had come here to discover. She was writing a long essay that was necessary to her career of scholastic journalism. She was not afraid.

In the façade of the Palace of the Planet was another door, plated with green bronze. The weed had not choked it, and over its top leaned a marble woman with bare breasts and a dove in her hands. The girl reached out and rapped with a bronze knocker shaped like a fist. The house gave off a sound that after all succeeded in astonishing her. It must be a hollow shell, unfurnished, half its walls fallen . . .

These old cities were museums now, kept for their history, made available on request to anyone—not many—who wished to view. They had their dwellers also, but in scarcity. Destitutes and eccentrics lived in them, monitored by the state. The girl, whose name was Jonquil Hare, had seen the register of this place. In all, there were 174 names, some queried, where once had teemed thousands, crushing each other in the ambition to survive.

The hollow howling of her knock faded in the house. Jonquil said, "I'm coming in. I am." And marched back to her bag beneath the leaden gate. She surveyed the gate, and the knotted weed which had come down on it. Jonquil Hare tried the weed. It resisted her strongly. She took up her bag, in which there was nothing breakable, seasoned traveler as she was, and flung it over the arch. She took the weed in her small strong hands and hauled herself up in her clumsy, graceful way, up to the arch, and sat there, looking in at a morning-twilight garden of shrubs that had not been pruned in a hundred years, and trees that became each other. A blue fountain shone dimly. Jonquil smiled upon it, and swung herself over in the weed and slithered down, into the environ of the house.

By midday, Jonquil had gone busily over most of the Palace of the Planet. Its geography was fixed in her head, but partly, confusedly, for she liked the effect of a puzzle of rooms and corridors. Within the lower portion of the house a large hall gave on to a large enclosed inner courtyard, that in turn led to the garden. Above, chambers of the first story would have opened onto the court, but their doors were sealed by the blue-green weed, which had smothered the court itself and so turned it into a strange undersea grotto where columns protruded like yellow coral. Above the lower floor, two long staircases drew up into apparently uncountable annexes and cells, and to a great salon with tarnished mirrors, also broken like spiderwebs. The salon had tall windows that stared through their blind shutters at the lagoon.

There were carvings everywhere; lacking light, she did not study them now. And, as suspected, there was very little furniture—a pair of desks with hollow drawers, spindly chairs, a divan in rotted ivory silk. In one oblong room was a bedframe with vast tapering pillars like idle rockets. Cobwebby draperies shimmered from the canopy in a draught, while patches of bled emerald sunlight hovered on the floor.

Jonquil succeeded in opening a shutter in the salon. A block of afternoon fell in. Next door, in the adjacent chamber, she set up her inflatable mattress, her battery lamp and heater, some candles she had brought illegally in a padded tube. Sitting on her unrolled mat in the subaqueous light of a shuttered window which refused to give, she ate from her pack of food snacks and drank cola. Then she arranged some books and notepads, pens and pencils, a magnifier, camera and unit, and a miniature recorder on the unfolded table.

She spoke to the room, as from the start she had spoken consecutively to the house. "Well, here we are."

But she was restless. The caretaker must be due to arrive, and until this necessary procedure had taken place, interruption hung over her. Of course, the caretaker would enable Jonquil to gain possession of the house secrets, the holostetic displays of furnishings and earlier life that might have been indigenous here, the hidden walks and rooms that undoubtedly lay inside the walls.

Jonquil was tired. She had risen at 3:00 a.m. for the boat after an evening of hospitable farewells. She lay down on her inflatable bed with the pillow under her neck. Through half-closed eyes she saw the room breathing with pastel motes of sun, and heard the rustle of weed at the shutter.

She dreamed of climbing a staircase which, dreaming, seemed new to her. At the foot of the stair a marble pillar supported a globe of some aquamarine material, covered by small configurations of alien landmasses, isolate in seas. The globe was a whimsical and inaccurate eighteenth-century rendition of the planet Venus, to which the house was mysteriously affiliated. As she climbed the stairs, random sprinklings of light came and went. Jonquil sensed that someone was ascending with her, step for step, not on the actual stair, but inside the peeling wall at her left side. Near the top of the stair (which was lost in darkness) an arched window had been let into the wall, milky and unclear and further obscured by some drops of waxen stained glass. As she came level with the window, Jonquil glanced sidelong at it. A shadowy figure appeared, on the far side of the pane, perhaps a woman, but hardly to be seen.

Jonquil started awake at the sound of the caretaker's serviceable shoes clumping into the house.

The caretaker was a woman. She did not offer her name, and no explanation for her late arrival. She had brought the house manual, and advised Jonquil on how to operate the triggers in its panel—visions flickered annoyingly over the rooms and were gone. A large box contained facsimiles of things pertaining to the house and its history. Jonquil had seen most of these already.

"There are the upper rooms, the attics. Here's the master key."

The woman showed Jonquil a hidden stair that probed these upper reaches of the house. It was not the stairway from the dream, but narrow and winding as the steps of a belltower. There were no other concealed chambers.

"If there's anything else you find you require, you must go out to the booth in the square. Here is the code to give the machine."

The caretaker was middle-aged, stout and uncharming. She seemed not to know the house at all, only everything about it, and glanced around her disapprovingly. Doubtless she lived in one of the contemporary golden towers across the lagoon, which, in the lingering powder of mist, passed for something older and stranger that they were not.

"Who came here last?" asked Jonquil. "Did anyone?"

"There was a visitor in the spring of the last Centenary Year. He stayed only one day, to study the plaster, I believe."

Jonquil smiled, pleased and smug that the house was virtually all her own, for the city's last centenary had been twenty years ago, nearly her lifetime.

She was glad when the caretaker left, and the silence of the house did not occur to Jonquil as she went murmuring from room to room, able now to operate the shutters, bring in light and examine the carvings in corners, on cornices. Most of them showed earlier defacement, as expected. She switched on, too, scenes from the manual, of costumed, dining and conversing figures amid huge pieces of furniture and swags of brocade. No idea of ghosts was suggested by these holostets. Jonquil reserved a candlelit masked ball for a later, more fitting hour.

The greenish amber of afternoon slid into the plate of water. A chemical rose flooded the sky, like color processing for a photograph. Venus, the evening star, was visible beyond the garden.

Jonquil climbed up the belltower steps to the attics.

The key turned easily in an upper door. But the attics disappointed. They were high and dark—her flashlight penetrated like a sword—webbed with the woven dust, and thick with damp, and a sour cloacal smell that turned the stomach of the mind. Otherwise, there was an almost emptiness. From beams hung unidentified shreds. On one wall a tapestry on a frame, indecipherable, presumably not thought good enough for renovation. Jonquil moved reluctantly through the obscured space, telling it it was in a poor state, commiserating with it, until she came against a chest of cold black wood.

"Now what are you?" Jonquil inquired of the chest.

It was long and low, its lid carved over with a design that had begun to crumble . . . Curious fruits in a wreath.

The shape of the chest reminded her of something. She peered at the fruits. Were they elongate lemons, pomegranates? Perhaps they were meant to be Venusian fruits. The astrologer Johanus, who had lived in the Palace of the Planet, had played over the house his obsession and ignorance with, and of, Venus. He had claimed in his treatise closely to have studied the surface of the planet through his own telescope. There was an atmosphere of clouds, parting slowly; beneath, an underlake landscape, cratered and mountained, upon limitless waters. "The mirror of Venus is her sea," Johanus wrote. And he had painted her, but his daubs were lost, like most of his writing, reputedly burned. He had haunted the house alive, an old wild man, watching for star-rise, muttering. He had died in the charity hospital, penniless and mad. His servants had destroyed his work, frightened of it, and vandalized the decorations of the house.

Jonquil tried to raise the lid of the chest. It would not come up.

"Are you locked?"

But there was no lock. The lid was stuck or merely awkward. "I shall come back," said Jonquil.

She had herself concocted an essay on the astrologer, but rather as a good little girl writes once a year to her senile grandfather. She appreciated his involvement—that, but for him, none of this would be—but he did not interest her. It was the house which did that. There was a switch on the manual that would conjure acted reconstructions of the astrologer's life, even to the final days, and to the rampage of the vandals. But Jonquil did not bother with this record. It was to her as if the house had adorned itself, using the man only as an instrument. His paintings and notes were subsidiary, and she had not troubled much over their disappearance.

"Yes, I'll be back with a wrench, and you'd just better have something in there worth looking at," said Jonquil to the chest. Doubtless it was vacant.

Night on the lagoon, in the city. The towers in the distance offered no lights, being constructed to conceal them. In two far-off spots, a pale glow crept from a window to the water. The silence of night was not like the silence of day.

Jonquil sang as the travel-cook prepared her steak, and, drinking a glass of reconstituted wine, going out into the salon, she switched on the masked ball.

At once the room was over two hundred years younger. It was drenched in gilt, and candle-flames stood like flowers of golden diamond on their stems of wax, while the ceiling revealed dolphins and doves who escorted a goddess over a sea in a ship that was a shell. The windows were open to a revised night hung with diamanté lamps, to a lagoon of black ink where bright boats were passing to the sound of mandolins. The salon purred and thrummed with voices. It was impossible to decipher a word, yet laughter broke through, and clear notes of the music. No one danced as yet. Perhaps they never would, for they were creatures from another world indeed, every one clad in gold and silver, ebony and glacial white, with jewels on them like water-drops tossed up by a wave. They had no faces. Their heads were those of plumed herons and horned deer, black velvet cats and lions of the sun and moon lynxes, angels, demons, mer-things from out of the lagoon, and scarabs from the hollows of time. They moved and promenaded, paused with teardrops of glass holding bloodlike wine, fluttered their fans of peacocks and palm leaves.

Jonquil stayed at the edge of the salon. She could have walked straight through them, through their holostetic actors' bodies and their prop garments of silk, steel and chrysoprase, but she preferred to stay in the doorway, drinking her own wine, adapting her little song to the tune of the mandolins.

After the astrologer had gone, others had come, and passed, in the house. The rich lady, and the prince, with their masks and balls, suppers and recitals.

The travel-cook chimed, and Jonquil switched off two hundred elegantly acting persons, one thousand faked gems and lights, and went to eat her steak.

She wrote with her free hand: *Much too pretty. Tomorrow I must photograph the proper carvings.* And said this over aloud.

Jonquil dreamed she was in the attic. There was a vague light, perhaps the moon coming in at cracks in the shutters, or the dying walls. Below, a noise went on, the holostetic masked ball which she had forgotten to switch off. Jonquil looked at the chest of black wood. She had realized she did not have to open it herself. Downstairs, in the salon, an ormolu clock struck midnight, the hour of unmasking. There was a little click. In the revealing darkness, the lid of the chest began to lift. Jonquil knew what it had reminded her of. A shadow sat upright in the coffin of the chest. It had a slender but indefinite form, and yet it turned its head and Jonquil saw the two eyes looking at her, only the eyeballs gleaming, in two crescents, in the dark.

The lid fell over with a crash.

Jonquil woke up sitting on her inflatable bed, with her hands at her throat, her eyes raised toward the ceiling.

"A dream," announced Jonquil.

She turned on her battery lamp, and the small room appeared. There was no sound in the house. Beyond the closed door the salon rested. "Silly," said Jonquil.

She lay and read a book having nothing to do with the Palace of the Planet, until she fell asleep with the light on.

The square was a terrifying ruin. Hidden by the frontage of the city, it was nearly inconceivable. Upper stories had collapsed onto the paving, only the skeletons of architecture remained, with occasionally a statue, some of them shining green and vegetable (the dissolution of gold) piercing through. The paving was broken up, marked by the slough of birds. Here the booth arose, unable to decay.

"There's a chest in the attics. It won't open," Jonquil accused the receiver. "The manual lists it. It says, one sable-wood jester chest."

The reply came. "This is why you are unable to open it. A jester chest was just that, a deceiving or joke object, often solid. There is nothing inside."

"No," said Jonquil, "some jester chests do open. And this isn't solid."

"I am afraid you are wrong. The chest has been investigated, and contains nothing, neither is there any means to open it."

"An x-ray doesn't always show——" began Jonquil. But the machine had disconnected. "I won't have this," said Jonquil.

Three birds blew over the square. Beneath in the sewers, the colony of voiceless rats, white as moonlight, ran noiselessly under her feet. But she would not shudder. Jonquil strutted back to the house through alleys of black rot where windows were suspended like lingering cards of ice. Smashed glass lay underfoot. The awful smell of the sea was in the alleys, for the sea came in and in. It had drowned the city in psychic reality, and already lay far over the heads of all the buildings, calm, oily and still, reflecting the sun and the stars.

Jonquil got into the house by the gate-door the manual had made accessible, crossing the garden where the blue fountain was a girl crowned with myrtle. Jonquil went straight up over the floors to the attic stair, and climbed that. The attic door was ajar, as she believed she had left it.

"Here I am," said Jonquil. The morning light was much stronger in the attics and she did not need her torch. She found the chest and bent over it.

"You've got a secret. Maybe you're only warped shut, that would be the damp up here . . . There may be a lining that could baffle the x-ray."

She tried the wrench, specifically designed not to inflict any injury. But it slipped and slithered and did no good. Jonquil knelt down and began to feel all over the chest, searching for some spring or other mechanism. She was caressing the chest, going so cautiously and delicately over it. Its likeness to a coffin was very evident, but bones would have been seen. "Giving me dreams," she said. Something moved against her finger. It was very slight. It was as if the chest had wriggled under her tickling and testing like a sleeping child. Jonquil put back her hand—she had flinched, and reprimanded herself. At her touch the movement came again. She heard the clarity of the click she had heard before in the dream. And before she could stop herself, she jumped up, and stepped backward, one, two, three, until the wall stopped her.

The lid of the chest was coming up, gliding over, and slipping down without any noise but a mild slap. Nothing sat up in the chest. But Jonquil saw the edge of something lying there in it, in the shadow of it.

"Yes, it is," she said, and went forward. She leaned on the chest, familiarly now. Everything was explained, even the psycho-kinetic activity of the dream. "A painting."

Jonquil Hare leaned on the chest and stared in. Presently she took hold of the elaborate and gilded frame, and got the picture angled upward a short way, so it too leaned on the chest.

The painting was probably three centuries old. She could tell that from the pigments and disposition of the oils, but not from the artist. The artist was unknown. In size it was an upright oblong, about fifteen meters by one meter in width.

The work was a full-length portrait, rather well executed and proportioned, lacking only any vestige of life, or animation. It might have been the masterly likeness of a handsome doll—this was how the artist had given away his amateur status.

She looked like a woman of about Jonquil's age, which given the period meant of course that she would have been far younger, eighteen or nineteen years. Her skin was pale, and had a curious tint, as did in fact the entire scene, perhaps due to some corrosion of the paint—but even so it had not gone to the usual brown and mud tones, but rather to a sort of yellowish blue. Therefore the color scheme of clothing and hair might be misleading, for the long loose tresses were yellowish blonde, and the dress bluish gray. Like the hair, the dress was loose, a robe of a kind. And yet, naturally, both hair and robe were draped in a particular manner that dated them, as surely as if their owner had been gowned and coiffured at the apex of that day's fashion. She was slender but looked strong. There was no plumpness to her chin and throat, her hands were narrow. An unusually masculine woman, more suitable to Jonquil's century, where the sexes often blended, slim and lightly muscular—the woman in the painting was also like this. Her face was impervious, its eyes black. She was not beautiful or alluring. It was a flat animal face, tempered like the moon by its own chill light, and lacking sight or true expression because the artist had not understood how to intercept them.

Behind the woman was a vista that Jonquil took at first for the lagoon. But then she saw that between the fog-bank of blued-yellow cloud and the bluish-greenish water, a range of pocked and fissured mountains lurched like an unearthly aqueduct. It was the landscape of Johanus's Venus. The artist of the picture was the mad astrologer who had invested the house.

How could it be that the authorities had missed this find?

"My," said Jonquil to the painting. She was excited. What would this not be worth in tokens of fame?

She pulled on the painting again, more carefully than before. It was light for its size. She could manage it. She paused a moment, close to the woman on the canvas. The canvas was strange, the texture of it under the paint—but in those days three centuries before, they had sometimes used odd materials. Even some chemical or experimental potion could have been mixed with the paint, to give it now its uncanny tinge.

A name was written in a scroll at the bottom of the picture. Jonquil took it for a signature. But it was not the astrologer's name, though near enough it indicated some link. Johnina.

"Jo-*nine*-ah," said Jonquil, "we are going for a short walk, down to where I can take a proper look at you."

With enormous care now, she drew the picture of Johnina out of the attics, and down the narrow stair toward the salon.

Jonquil was at the masked ball. In her hand was a fan of long white feathers caught in a claw of zircons, her costume was of white satin streaked with silver veins, and her face was masked like a white-furred cat. She knew her hair was too short for the day and age, and this worried her by its inappropriateness. No one spoke to her, but all around they chattered to each other (incomprehensibly), and their curled powdered hair poured out of their masks like milk boiling over. Jonquil observed everything acutely, the man daintily taking snuff (an addict), the woman in the dress striped black and ivory peering through her ruby eyeglass. Out on the lagoon, the gleaming boats went by, trailing red roses in the water.

Jonquil was aware that no one took any notice of her, had anything to do with her, and she was peevish, because they must have invited her. Who was she supposed to be? A duke's daughter, or his mistress? Should she not be married at her age, and have borne children? She would have to pretend.

There was a man with rings on every finger, and beyond him a check-ered mandolin player, and beyond him, a woman stood in a gray gown different from the rest. Her mask covered all her face, it was the counte-nance of a globe, perhaps the moon, in silver, and about it hair like pale tarnished fleece, too long as Jonquil's was too short, was falling to her pelvis over the bodice of the gown.

A group of actors—yes, they were only acting, it was not real—inter-vened. The woman was hidden for a moment, and when the group had passed, she was gone.

She was an actress, too, which was why Jonquil had thought something about her recognizable.

Jonquil became annoyed that she should be here, among actors, for acting was nothing to do with her. She turned briskly, and went toward the door of the chamber that led off from the salon. Inside, the area was dark, yet everything there was visible, and Jonquil was surprised to see a huge bedframe from another room dominating the space. Surely Jonquil's professional impedimenta had been put here, and the inflatable sleeping couch she traveled with? As for this bed, she had seen it elsewhere, and it had been naked then, but now it was dressed. Silk curtains hung from the pillars, and a mattress, pillows, sheets and embroidered coverlet were on it. Rather than the pristine appearance of a model furnishing, the bed had a slightly rumpled, tumbled look, as if Jonquil had indeed used it. Jonquil closed the door of the room firmly on the ball outside, and all sound of it at once ceased.

To her relief, she found that she was actually undressed and in the thin shirt that was her night garment. She went to the bed, resigned, and got into it. She lay back on the pillows. The bed was wonderfully comfortable, lushly undisciplined.

Johanus's house was so silent—noiseless. Jonquil lay and listened to the total absence of sound, which was like a pressure, as if she had floated down beneath the sea. Her bones were coral, and pearls her eyes . . . Fish might swim in through the slats of a shutter, across the water of the air. But before that happened, the door would open again.

The door opened.

The doorway was lit with moonlight, and the salon beyond it, for the masked ball had gone. Only the woman with the silver planet face remained, and she came over the threshold. Behind her, in lunar twilight, Jonquil saw the lagoon lying across the salon, and the walls had evapo-rated, leaving a misty shore, and mountains that were tunneled through. The bed itself was adrift on water, and bobbed gently, but Johnina crossed without difficulty.

Her silver mask was incised, like the carvings in the house corners, the globes that were the planet Venus. The mask reflected in the water. Two silver discs, separated, drawing nearer.

Jonquil said sternly, "I must wake up."

And she dived upward from the bed, and tore through layers of cloud or water and came out into the actual room, rolling on the inflatable couch.

"I'm not frightened," stated Jonquil. "Why should I be?"

She turned on her battery lamp and angled the light to fall across the painting of Johnina, which she had leaned against the wall.

"What are you trying to tell me now? In the morning I'm going to call them up about you. Don't you want to be famous?"

The painting had no resonance. It looked poorly in the harsh glare of the lamp, a stilted figure and crackpot scenery, the brushwork disordered. The canvas was so smooth.

"Go to sleep," said Jonquil to Johnina, and shut off the light as if to be sensible with a tiresome child.

In the true dark, which had no moon, the silence of the house crept closer. Dispassionately, Jonquil visualized old Johanus padding about the floors in his broken soft shoes. He thought he had seen the surface of the planet Venus. He had painted the planet as an allegory that was a woman, just like the puns of Venus the goddess in marble over the door, and on the ceiling of the salon.

Jonquil began to see Johanus in his study, among the alchemical muddle, the primeval alchemical chaos from which all perfect creation evolved. But she regarded him offhandedly, the dust and grime and spillages, the blackened skulls and lembics growing moss.

Johanus wrote on parchment with a goose quill.

He wrote in Latin also, and although she had learned Latin in order to pursue her study, this was too idiosyncratic, too much of its era, for her to follow. Then the words began to sound, and she grasped them. Bored, Jonquil attended. She did not recall switching on this holostet, could not think why she had decided to play it.

"So, on the forty-third night, after an hour of watching, the cloud parted, and there was before me the face of the planet. I saw great seas, or one greater sea, with small masses of land, pitted like debased silver. And the mountains I saw. And all this in a yellow glow from the cloud . . ."

Jonquil wondered why she did not stop the holostet. She was not interested in this. But she could not remember where the manual was.

"For seven nights I applied myself to my telescope, and on each night, the clouds of the planet sensuously parted, allowing me a view of her bareness."

Jonquil thought she would have to leave the bed in order to switch off the manual. But the bed, with its tall draped posts, was warm and comfortable.

"On the eighth night it came to me. Even as I watched, I was watched in my turn. Some creature was there, some unseen intelligence, which, sensing my appraisal, reached out to seize me. I do not know how such a thing is possible. Where I see only a miniature of that world, it sees me exactly, where and what I am, every atom. At once I removed myself, left my perusal, and shut up the instrument. But I believe I was too late. Somehow it has come to me, here, in the world of men. It is with me, although I cannot hear it or behold it. It is the invisible air, it is the silence of the night. What shall I do?"

The holostet of Johanus was no longer operating. Jonquil lay in the four-poster bed in the room that led from the salon. The door was shut. Someone was in the room with her, beside the bed. Jonquil turned her head on the pillow, without hurry, to see.

A hand was stroking back her short hair; it was very pleasant; she was a cat that was being caressed. Jonquil smiled lazily. It was like the first day of the holidays, and her mother was standing by her bed, and they would talk. But no, not her mother. It was the wonderful-looking woman she had seen—where was that, now? Perhaps in the city, an eccentric who lived there, out walking in the turquoise of dusk or funeral orchid of dawning, when the star was on the lagoon. Very tall, a developed, lithe body, graceful, with the blue wrap tied loosely, and the amazing hair, so thick and blonde, falling over it, over her shoulders and the firm cupped line of the breasts, the flat belly, and into the mermaid V of the thighs.

"Hello," said Jonquil. And the woman gave the faintest shake of her lion's head in its mane. Jonquil was not to speak. They did not need words. But the woman smiled, too. It was such a sensational smile. So effortless, stimulating and calming. The dark, dark eyes rested on Jonquil with a tenderness that was also cruel. Jonquil had seen this look in the eyes of others, and a *frisson* of eagerness went over her, and she was ashamed; it was too soon to expect—but the woman was leaning over her now, the marvel of face blurred and the mane of hair trickling over Jonquil's skin. The mouth kissed, gently and unhesitatingly. "Oh, yes," said Jonquil, without any words.

The woman, who was called Johnina, was lying on her. She was heavy, her weight crushed and pinned, and Jonquil was helpless. It was the most desired thing, to be helpless like this, unable even to lift her own hands, as if she had no strength at all. And Johnina's hands were on her breasts somehow, between their two adhering bodies, finding out Jonquil's shape with slow smooth spiralings. And softly, without anything crude or urgent, the sea-blue thigh of Johnina rubbed against Jonquil until she ached and melted. She shut her eyes and could think only of the sweet unhurried journey of her body, of the hands that guided and stroked, and the mermaid tail that bore her up, and the sound of the sea in her ears. Johnina kissed and kissed, and Jonquil Hare felt herself dissolving into Johnina, into her body, and she could not even cry out. And then Jonquil was spread-eagled out into a tidal orgasm, where with every wave some further part of her was washed away. And when there was nothing left, she woke up in the pitch-black void of the silence, with something hard and cold, clammy, but nearly weightless, lying on her, an oblong in a gilded frame, the painting which had dropped over on top of her and covered her from breast to ankle.

She flung it off and it clattered down. She clutched at her body, thinking to discover herself clotted with a sort of glue or slime, but there was nothing like that.

She was weak and dizzy and her heart drummed noisily, so she could not hear the silence anymore.

"Let me speak to the house caretaker," snapped Jonquil at the obtuse machine. Outside the booth, the ruin of the great square seemed to sway on the wind, which was violent, ruffling the lagoon in flounces, whirling small scraps of colored substances that might have been paper, rags, or skin.

"The caretaker is not available. However, your request has been noted."

"But this picture is an important find—and I want it removed, today, to a place of safety."

The machine had disconnected.

Jonquil stood in the booth, as if inside a spacesuit, and watched the alien atmosphere of the city swirling with bits and colors.

"Don't be a fool," said Jonquil. She left the booth and cowered before the wind, which was not like any breeze felt in civilized places. "It's an old painting. A bad old painting. So, you're lonely, you had a dream. Get back to work."

Jonquil worked. She photographed all the carvings she had decided were relevant or unusually bizarre—Venus the goddess riding the crescent moon, a serpent coiled about a planet that maybe was simply an orb. She put these into the developer and later drew them out and arranged them in her room beside the salon. (She had already moved the painting of Johnina into the salon—she felt tired, and it seemed heavier than before—left it with its face to the wall, propped under the mirrors. It was now about twenty-five meters from her inflatable bed, and well outside the door.)

She went over the house again, measuring and recording comments. She opened shutters and regarded the once hive-like cliffs of the city, and the waters on the other side. The wind settled and a mist condensed. By midafternoon the towers of modernity were quite gone.

"The light always has a green tinge—blue and yellow mixed. When the sky pinkens at dawn or sunset the water is bottle green, an apothecary's bottle. And purple for the prose," Jonquil added.

In two hours it would be dusk, and then night.

This was ridiculous. She had to face up to herself, that she was nervous and apprehensive. But there was nothing to be afraid of, or even to look forward to.

She still felt depressed, exhausted, so she took some more vitamins. Something she had eaten, probably, before leaving for the city, had caught up with her. And that might even account for the dream. The dreams.

She did not go up into the attics. She spent some time out of doors, in the grotto of the courtyard, and in the garden, which the manual showed her with paved paths and carven box hedges, orange trees, and the fountain playing. She did not watch this holostet long. Her imagination was working too, and too hard, and she might start to see Johnina in a blue-gray gown going about between the trees.

What, anyway, was Johnina? Doubtless Jonquil's unconscious had based the Johanus part of the dream on scraps of the astrologer's writings she had seen, and that she had consciously forgotten. Johanus presumably believed some alien intelligence from the planet he observed had made use of the channel of his awareness. For him it was female (interesting women then were always witches, demons; he would be bound to think in that way) and when she suborned him, in his old man's obsession, he painted her approximately to a woman—just as he had approximated his vision of the planet to something identifiable, the pastorale of a cool Hell. And he gave his demoness a name birthed out of his own, a strange daughter.

Jonquil did not recollect, try as she would, reading anything so curious about Johanus, but she must have done.

He then concealed the painting of his malign inamorata in the trick chest, to protect it from the destructive fears of the servants.

Only another hour, and the sky would infuse like pale tea and rose petals. The sun would go, the star would visit the garden. Darkness.

"You're not as tough as you thought," said Jonquil. She disapproved of herself. "All right. We'll sit this one out. Stay awake tonight. And tomorrow I'll get hold of that damn caretaker lady if I have to swim there."

As soon as it was sunset, Jonquil went back to her chosen room. She had to pass through the salon, and had an urge to go up to the picture, turn it round, and scrutinize it. But that was stupid. She had seen all there was to see. She shut her inner door on the salon with a bang. Now she was separate from all the house.

She lit her lamp, and, pulling out her candles, lit those too. She primed the travel-cook for a special meal, chicken with a lemon sauce, creamed potatoes, and as the wing of night unfolded over the lagoon she closed the shutter and switched on a music tape. She sat drinking wine and writing up that day's notes on the house. After all, she had done almost all that was needed. Might she not see if she could leave tomorrow? To hire transport before the month was up and the regular boat arrived would be expensive, but then, she could get to work the quicker perhaps, away from the house . . . She had meant to explore the city, of course, but it was in fact less romantic than dejecting, and potentially dangerous. She might run into one of the insane inhabitants, and then what?

Jonquil thought, acutely visualizing the nocturnal mass of the city. No one was alive in it, surely. The few lights, the occasional smokes and whispers, were inaugurated by machines, to deceive. There were the birds, and their subterranean counterpart, the rats. Only she alone, Jonquil Hare, was here this night between masonry and water. She alone, and one other.

"Don't be silly," said Jonquil.

How loud her voice sounded, now the music had come to an end. The silence was gigantic, a fifth dimension.

It seemed wrong to put on another tape. The silence should not be angered. Let it lie, move quietly, and do not speak at all.

Johanus wrote quickly, as if he might be interrupted; his goose pen snapped, and he seized another ready cut. He spoke the words aloud as he wrote them, although his lips were closed.

"For days, and for nights when I could not sleep, I was aware of the presence of my invader. I told myself it was my fancy, but I could not be rid of the sensation of it. I listened for the sounds of breathing, I looked for a shadow—there were none of these. I felt no touch, and when I dozed fitfully in the dark, waking suddenly, no beast crouched on my breast. Yet, it was with me, it breathed, it brushed by me, it touched me without hands, and watched me with its unseen eyes.

"So passed five days and four nights. And on the evening of the fifth day, even as the silver planet stood above the garden, it grew bold, knowing by now it had little to fear from me in my terror, and took on a shape.

"Yes, it took on a sort of shape, but if this is its reality I cannot know, or only some semblance, all it can encompass here, or deigns to assume.

"It hung across the window, and faintly through it the light of dusk was ebbing. A membraneous thing, like a sail. It did not move, no pulse of life seemed in it, and yet it lived. I shut the door on it, but later I returned. In the candle's light I saw it had fallen, or lowered itself, to my table. It had kept its soft sheen of blue. I touched it, I could not help myself, and it had the texture of velum—that is, of skin. It lay before me, the length of the table, and under it dimly I could discern the outline of my books, my dish of powders, and other things. I cannot describe my state. My terror had sunk into a sort of blinded wonderment. I do not know how great a while I stood and looked at it, but at length I heard the girl with my food, and I went out and locked up the room again. What would it do while I was gone? Would it perhaps vanish again?

"That night I slept, stupefied, and in the morning opened my eyes and there the thing hung, above me, inside the canopy of the very bed. How long had it been there, watching me with its invisible organs of sight? Of course, its method had been simple: it had slid under the doors of my house—my house so long dressed for it, and named for its planet in the common vernacular.

"What now must I do? What is required of me? For clearly I shall become its slave. It seems to me I am supposed to be able to give it a more usual form, some camouflage, so that if may pass with men, but how is that possible? How render such a thing ordinary, and attractive?

"The means came to me in my sleep. Perhaps the being has influenced my brain. There is one sure way. It has noticed my canvases. Now I am to stretch this skin upon a frame, and put paint to it. What shall I figure there? No doubt, I shall be guided in what I do, as it has led me to the idea.

"I must obscure my actions from my servants. They are already ill at ease, and the man was very threatening this morning; he is a ruffian and capable of anything—it will be wise to destroy these papers, when all else is done."

Jonquil turned from Johanus, and saw a group of friends she had not communicated with in three years, gliding over the lagoon in a white boat. They waved and shouted, and Jonquil knew she had been rescued, she would escape, but running toward the boat she heard a metallic crash, and jumped inadvertently up out of the dream into the room, where her candles were burning low, fluttering, and the air quivered like a disturbed pond. The silence had been agitated after all. There had been some noise, like the noise in the dream which woke her.

She sat bolt upright in the lock of fear. She had never felt fear in this way in her life. She had meant to stay awake, but the meal, the wine . . .

And the dream of Johanus—absurd.

Outside, in the mirrored nighttime salon, there came a sharp screech-ing scrape.

Jonquil's mind shrieked, and she clamped her hand over her mouth. Don't be a fool. Listen! She listened. The silence. Had she imagined—

The noise came again, harsher and more absolute.

It was like the abrasion of a rusty chain dragged along the marble floor. And again—

Jonquil sprang up. In her life, where she had never before known such fear, the credo had been that fear, confronted, proved to be less than it had seemed. Always the maxim held true. It was this brainwashing of accred-ited experience which sent her to the door of the room, and caused her to dash it wide and to stare outward.

The guttering glim of the candles, so apposite to the house, gave a half-presence to the salon. But mostly it was black, thick and composite, black, watery and uncertain on the ruined faces of the mirrors. And out of this blackness came a low flicker of motion, catching the candlelight along its edge. And this motion made the sound she had heard and now heard again. Jonquil did not believe what she saw. She did not believe it. No. This was still the dream, and she must, she must wake up.

The picture of Johnina, painted by the astrologer on a piece of membra-neous bluish alien skin, had fallen over in its frame, and now the framed skin pulled itself along the floor, and, catching the light, Jonquil saw the little formless excrescences of the face-down canvas, little bluish-yellow paws, hauling the assemblage forward, the big balanced oblong shape with its rim of gilt vaguely shining. Machine-like, primeval, a mutated tortoise. It pulled itself on, and as the frame scraped along the floor it screamed, toward Jonquil in the doorway.

Jonquil slammed shut the door. She turned and caught up things—the inflatable bed, the table—and stuffed them up against the doorway. And the mechanical tortoise screamed twice more—and struck against the door, and the door shook.

Jonquil turned round and round in her trap as the thing outside thud-ded back and forth and her flimsy barricade trembled and tottered. There was no other exit but the window. She got it open and ran on to the balcony, which creaked and dipped. The weed was there, the blue-green

Venus weed which choked the whole city. Jonquil threw herself off into it. As she did so, the door of the room gave way.

She was half-climbing, half-rebounding and falling down the wall of the house. Everywhere was darkness, and below the sucking of the water at the pavement.

As she struggled in the ropes of weed, tangled, clawing, a shape reared up in the window above her.

Jonquil cried out. The painting was in the window. But something comically macabre had happened. In rearing, it had caught at an angle between the uprights of the shutters. It was stuck, could not move out or in.

Jonquil hung in the weed, staring up at Johnina in her frame of gilt and wood and plaster and night. How soulless she looked, how without life.

And then a convulsion went over the picture. Like a blue amoeba touched by venom it writhed and wrinkled. It tore itself free of the golden frame. It billowed out, still held by a few filaments and threads, like a sail, a veil, the belly of something swollen with the hunger of centuries . . .

And Jonquil fought, and dropped the last two meters from the weed, landing on the pavement hard, in the box of darkness that was the city.

She was not dreaming, but it was like a dream. It seemed to her she saw herself running. The engine of her heart drove her forward. She did not know where or through what she ran. There was no moon, there were no lights. A kind of luminescence filmed over the atmosphere, and constructions loomed suddenly at her, an arch, a flight of steps, a platform, a severed wall. She fell, and got up and ran on.

And behind her, that came. That which had ripped itself from an oblong of gilding. It had taken to the air. It flew through the city, between the pillars and under the porticos, along the ribbed arteries carrying night. It rolled and unrolled as it came, with a faint soft snapping. And then it sailed, wide open, catching some helpful draught, a huge pale bat.

Weed rushed over Jonquil and she thought the thing which had been called Johnina had settled on her lightly, coaxingly, and she screamed. The city filled with her scream like an empty gourd with water.

There were no lights, no figures huddled at smoldering fires, no guards or watchmen, no villains, no one here to save her, no one even to be the witness of what must come, when her young heart finally failed, her legs buckled, when the sailing softness came down and covered her, stroking and devouring, caressing and eating—its tongues and fingers and the whole porous mouth that it was—to drink her away and away.

Jonquil ran. She ran over streets that were cratered as if by meteorites, through vaulted passages, beside the still waters of night and death. It occurred to her (her stunned and now almost witless brain) to plunge into the lagoon, to swim toward the unseen towers. But on the face of the mirror, gentleness would drift down on her, and in the morning mist, not even a ripple . . .

The paving tipped. Jonquil stumbled, ran, downward now, hopeless and mindless, her heart burning a hole in her side. Down and down, cracked tiles spinning off from her feet, down into some underground place that must be a prison for her, perhaps a catacomb, to stagger among filigree coffins, where the water puddled like glass on the floor, no way out, down into despair, and yet, mockingly, there was more light. More light to see what she did not want to see. It was the phosphorus of the death already there, the mummies in their narrow homes. Yes, she saw the water pools now, as she splashed through them, she saw the peculiar shelves and cubbies, the stone statue of a saint barnacled by the sea-rot the water brought into a creature from another world. And she saw the wall also that rose peremptory before her, the dead-end that would end in death, and for which she had been waiting, to which she had run, and where now she collapsed, her body useless, run out.

She dropped against the wall, and, in the coffin-light, turned and looked back. And through the descending vault, a pale blue shadow floated, innocent and faithful, coming down to her like a kiss.

I don't believe this, Jonquil would have said, but now she did. And anyway she had no breath, no breath even to scream again or cry. She could only watch, could not take her eyes off the coming of the feaster. It had singled her out, allowed her to bring it from the chest. With others it had been more reticent, hiding itself. Perhaps it had eaten of Johanus, too, before he had been forced to secure it against the witch-hunting servants. Or maybe Johanus had not been to its taste. How ravenous it was, and how controlled was its need.

It alighted five meters from her, from Jonquil, as she lay against the death-end wall. She saw it down an aisle of coffins. Touching the water on the floor, it rolled together, and furled open, and skimmed over the surface onto the stone.

She was fascinated now. She wanted it to reach her. She wanted it to be over. She dug her hands into the dirt and a yellow bone crumbled under her fingers.

The painting of Johnina was crawling ably along the aisle. There was no impediment, no heavy frame to drag with it.

Sweat slipped into Jonquil's eyes and for a moment she saw a blue woman with ivory hair walking slowly between the coffins, but there was something catching at her robe, and she hesitated, to try to pluck the material away.

Jonquil blinked. She saw a second movement, behind the limpid roll of the Venus skin. A flicker, like a white handkerchief. And then another.

Something darted, and it was on the painting, on top of it, and then it flashed and was gone. And then two other white darts sewed through the blueness of the shadow, bundling it up into an ungainly lump, and two more, gathering and kneading.

The painting had vanished. It was buried under a pure white jostling. And there began to be a thin high note on the air, like a whistling in the ear, without any emotion or language. Ten white rats of the catacombs had settled on the painting, and with their teeth and busy paws they held it still and rent it in pieces, and they ate it. They ate the painted image of the Venus Johnina, and her background of mountains and sea, they ate the living shrieking membrane of the flesh. Their hunger too had been long unappeased.

Jonquil lay by the wall, watching, until the last crumb and shred had disappeared into dainty needled mouths. It did not take more than two or three minutes. Then there was only a space, nothing on it, no rats, no other thing.

"Get up," Jonquil said. There was a low singing in her head, but no other noise. She stood in stages, and went back along the aisle of dead. She was very cold, feeble and sluggish. She thought she felt old. She walked through the water pools. She had a dreadful intimation that everything had changed, that she would never be the same, that nothing ever would, that survival had sent her into an unknown and fearful world.

A rat sat on a coffin overseeing her departure, digesting in its belly blueness and alien dreams. The walls went on crumbling particle by particle. Silence flowed over the city like the approaching sea.

Year Zero

Gemma Files

Gemma Files was born in England and raised in Toronto, Canada. She has won a 1999 International Horror Guild Award for best short fiction with her story "The Emperor's Old Bones" and saw five of her stories adapted into episodes of *The Hunger*, an erotic horror anthology TV show produced by Tony and Ridley Scott.

Her first novel, *A Book of Tongues* (ChiZine Publications), won the 2010 Dark Scribe Magazine Black Quill Award for Best Small Press Chill; it was followed by two sequels, completing the Hexslinger Series.

She has also published two short fiction collections, two chapbooks of poetry, and a story cycle (*We Will All Go Down Together*, CZP). Her latest book, *Experimental Film*, won the Shirley Jackson Award for Best Novel of 2015.

"Vampires, as all my non-horror-friendly pals so often sneer, are a dead-end concept," explains Files; "the same tropes repeated without variation, over and over—dirty little sex fantasies masquerading as good, clean fear. But it only requires a few nights' cursory research to realize that even the oldest stories posit as many different types of vampires as there are different types of people for them to feed on (and not all of them drink blood, either).

"I think of vampires, therefore, as the dark literature world's equivalent of the Rorschach blot. If you're limited, your idea of what vampires are—or could be—will be similarly limited. And if you're not . . ."

About the following story, the author reveals: "When I was a kid, I remember being wonderfully impressed by the TV adaptation of *The Scarlet Pimpernel* starring Anthony Andrews, Ian McKellen, and Jane Seymour; of course, given my perverse nature and interests, I found myself identifying far more heavily with the embattled Agent Chauvelin and his fellow Revolutionaries than with that rather vicious fop Sir Percy. At any rate, it started me off on a lifelong French Revolution kick that cross-bred perfectly with my equally lifelong vampire fetish: blood, decapitation, a general violent upheaval of the nature order . . . ooh, yeah, baby.

"And since 'walking corpses who suck blood' has always seemed like a pretty good description of any given aristocracy to me, I guess this particular story could be read as nothing deeper than my chance to elaborate on that metaphor a tad—not to mention have quite a bit of good (albeit messy) fun doing so."

And when I passed by thee, and saw thee polluted in thine own blood, I said unto thee when thou wast in thy blood, Live; yea, I said unto thee when thou wast in thy blood, Live.

—*Ezekiel 6:16.*

AT THE VERY height of the French Revolution, after they killed the king and drank his blood, they started everything over: New calendar, new months, new history. Wind back the national clock and smash its guts to powder; wipe the slate clean, and crack it across your knee. A failed actor named Fabre d'Eglantine drew up the plans. He stretched each seven-day week to a ten-day decade, and recarved the months into a verdant litany of rural images: Fruit and flowers, wind and rain. The Guillotine's red flash, masked in a mist of blistering, lobster-baked heat.

The first year of this process was to be known as Year Zero. Everything that happened next would be counted from then on. And all that had happened *before* would be, very simply . . .

. . . gone.

Then: Paris, 1793. Thermidor, Year Three, just before the end of the Terror . . .

"Oh, la, Citizen. How you do blush."

I must wake up, Jean-Guy Sansterre thinks, slow and lax—the words losing shape even as he forms them, like water dripping through an open mental hand, fingers splayed and helpless. *Rouse myself. Act. Fight . . .*

But feeling, instead, how his whole body settles inexorably into some arcane variety of sleep—limbs loose and heavy, head lolling back on dark red satin upholstery. Falling spine-first into the close, dim interior of the Chevalier du Prendegrace's coach, a languorous haze of drawn velvet curtains against which Jean-Guy lies helpless as some microorganism trapped beneath the fringed, softly sloping convex lens of a partially lidded eye.

Outside, in the near distance, one can still hear the constant growl and retch of the Widow, the National Razor, the legendary Machine split the air from the Place De La Revolution—that excellent device patented by dapper Dr. Guillotin, to cure forever the pains and ills of headaches, hangovers, insomnia. The repetitive thud of body on board, head in basket. The jeers and jibes of the *tricoteuses* knitting under the gallows steps, their Phrygian caps nodding in time with the tread of the executioner's ritual path; self-elected keepers of the public conscience, these grim hags who have outlived their former oppressors again and again. These howling crowds of *sans-culottes*, the trouserless ones—all crying in unison for yet more injurious freedom, still more, ever more: A great, sanguinary river with neither source nor tide, let loose to flood the city streets with visible vengeance . . .

"Do you know what complex bodily mechanisms lie behind the workings of a simple blush, Citizen Sansterre?"

That slow voice, emerging—vaporous and languid as an audible curl of smoke—from the red half-darkness of the coach. Continuing, gently: "I have made a sometime study of such matters; strictly amateur in nature, of course, yet as thorough an inquiry as my poor resources may afford me."

In the Chevalier's coach, Jean-Guy feels himself bend and blur like melting waxwork beneath the weight of his own hypnotized exhaustion—fall open on every level, like his own strong but useless arms, his nerveless, cord-cut legs . . .

"The blush spreads as the blood rises, showing itself most markedly at the skin's sheerest points—a map of veins, eminently traceable. Almost . . . readable."

So imperative, this urge to fly, to fight. And so, utterly . . .

. . . impossible.

"See, here and there, where landmarks evince themselves: Those knots of veins and arteries, delicately entwined, which wreathe the undersides of your wrists. Two more great vessels, hidden at the tongue's root. A long, humped one, outlining the shaft of that other boneless—organ— whose proper name we may not quote in mixed company."

Sitting. Sprawling, limp. And thinking:

I—must . . .

"And that, stirring now? In that same . . . unmentionable . . . area?"

. . . *must*—wake . . .

"Blood as well, my friend. Blood, which—as the old adage goes—will always tell."

But: *This is all a dream,* Jean-Guy reminds himself, momentarily surprised by his own coherence. *I have somehow fallen asleep on duty, which is bad, though hardly unforgivable—and because I did so while thinking on the* ci-devant *Chevalier du Prendegrace, that traitor Dumouriez's master, I have spun out this strange fantasy.*

For Prendegrace cannot be here, after all; he will have fled before Jean-Guy's agents, like any other hunted lordling. And, knowing this . . .

Knowing this, I will wake soon, and fulfill the mission set me by the Committee For Public Safety: catch Dumouriez, air out this nest of silken vipers. And all will be as I remember.

At the same time, meanwhile, the Chevalier (or his phantom—for can he really actually *be* there, dream or no?) smiles down at Jean-Guy through the gathering crimson shade, all sharp—and tender—amusement. A slight, lithe figure, dressed likewise all in red, his hereditary elegance undercut by a distressingly plebian thread of more-than-usually poor hygiene: lurid velvet coat topped by an immaculately tied but obviously dingy cravat; silken stockings, offhandedly worn and faded, above the buckled shoes with their neat cork heels. Dark rims to his longish fingernails—dirt, or something else, so long-dried it's turned black.

His too-white skin has a stink, faintly charnel. Acrid in Jean-Guy's acquiescent, narrowed nostrils.

"You carry a surplus of blood, Citizen, by the skin-map's evidence," the Chevalier seems to say, gently. "And thus might, if only in the name of politeness, consider willing some small portion of that overflowing store . . . to me."

"Can't you ever speak clearly, you damnable aristo?" Jean-Guy demands, hoarsely.

And: "Perhaps not," comes the murmuring reply. "Though, now I think on it . . . I cannot say I've ever tried."

Bending down, dipping his sleek, powdered head, this living ghost of an exterminated generation; licking his thin white lips while Jean-Guy lies still beneath him, boneless, helpless. So soft, all over—in every place . . .

. . . but one.

So: Now, 1815. Paris again, late September—an old calendar for a brand-new Empire—in the Row of the Armed Man, near dusk . . .

. . . where the Giradoux family's lawyer meets Jean-Guy, key in hand, by the door of what was once Edouard Dumouriez's house.

Over the decade since Jean-Guy last walked this part of Paris, Napoleon's civil engineers have straightened out most of the overhanging tangle of back-alleys into a many-spoked wheel of pleasant, tree-lined boulevards and well-paved—if bleakly functional—streets. The Row of the Armed Man, however, still looks much the same as always: A narrow path of cracked flagstones held together with gravel and mortar, stinking of discarded offal and dried urine, bounded on either side by crooked doorways or smoke-darkened signs reading BUTCHER, CANDLE-MAKER, NOTARY PUBLIC. And in the midst of it all, Dumouriez's house, towering shadowy and slant above the rest—three shaky floors' worth of rooms left empty, in a city where unoccupied living space is fought over like a franc left lying in the mud.

"The rabble do avoid it," the lawyer agrees, readily. Adding, with a facile little shrug: "Rumor brands the place as . . . haunted."

And the unspoken addendum *to* said addendum, familiar as though Jean-Guy had formed the statement himself . . .

. . . though I, of course, do not ascribe to the same theory . . . being, as I am, a rational man living in this rational and enlightened state of Nouvelle France, an age without kings, without tyrants . . .

With Jean-Guy adding, mentally, in return: *For we were all such reasonable men, once upon a time. And the Revolution, our lovely daughter, sprung full-blown from that same reason—a bare-breasted Athena clawing her way up to daylight, through the bloody ruin of Zeus's shattered skull.*

The Giradoux lawyer wears a suit of black velvet, sober yet festive, and carries a small satin mask; his hair has been pulled back and powdered in the "antique fashion" of twelve scant years past. And at his throat, partially hidden in the fold of his cloak's collar, Jean-Guy can glimpse the sharp red edge of a scarlet satin ribbon knotted—oh so very neatly—just beneath his jugular vein.

"I see you've come dressed for some amusement, *m'sieu.*"

The lawyer colors slightly, as if caught unaware in some dubious action.

"Merely a social engagement," he replies. "A *Bal des Morts.* You've heard the term?"

"Not that I recall."

"Where the dead go to dance, *m'sieu* Sansterre."

Ah, indeed.

Back home in Martinique, where Jean-Guy has kept himself carefully hidden these ten years past and more, the "Thermidorean reaction" which attended news of the Terror's end—Jacobin arch-fiend Maximilien Robespierre first shot, then guillotined; his Committee for Public Safety disbanded; slavery reinstated, and all things thus restored to their natural rank and place—soon gave rise to a brief but intense period of public celebration on those vividly colored shores. There was dancing to all hours, Free Black and Creole French alike, with everything fashionable done temporarily *a la victime*—a thin white shift or cravatless blouse, suitable for making a sacrifice of oneself on the patriotic altar in style; the hair swept up, exposing the neck for maximum accessibility; a ribbon tied where the good Widow, were she still on hand to do so, might be expected to leave her red and silent, horizontal kiss . . .

At the *Bal des Morts*, participants' dance-cards were filled according to their own leftover notoriety; for who in their family might have actually gone to good Dr. Guillotin's Machine, or who their family might have had a hand in sending there. Aping executed and executioners alike, they dressed as corpses and preened like resurrected royalty, bobbing and spinning in a sluggish stream of old blood—trash caught in frenzied motion against the gutter's grate, at the end of a hard night's deluge.

The roll-call of the tumbrils: Aristocrats, collaborators, traitors and Tyrannists, even the merely argumentative or simply ignorant—one poor woman calling her children in to dinner, only to find herself arrested on suspicion of sedition because her son's name happened to be (like that of the deposed king) Louis. And in the opposing camp, Jean-Guy's fellow Revolutionaries: Girondists, Extremists, Dantonists, Jacobins, patriots of all possible stamps and stripes—many of whom, by the end of it all, had already begun to fall under fatal suspicion themselves.

And these, then, their inheritors and imitators . . . these remnants wrapped in party-going silk, spending their nights laying a thin skin of politeness, even enjoyment, over the unhealed temporal wounds of *la Mère France*.

Jean-Guy met the girl who would become his late wife at such an affair, and paid her bride-price a few scant weeks later. Chlöe, her name had been. An apricot-colored little thing, sweet-natured and shy, her eyes almost blue; far less obviously *du sang nègre* than he himself, even under the most—direct—scrutiny.

And it is only now, with her so long dead, that he can finally admit it was this difference of tone . . . rather than any true heart's affection . . . which was the primary motive of their union.

He glances down at a puddle near his boot, briefly considering how his own reflection sketches itself on the water's dim skin: A dark man in a dark frock-coat—older now, though no paler. Beneath his high, stiff silk hat, his light brown hair has been cropped almost to the skull to mask its obvious kink; under the hat-brim's shade, his French father's straight nose and hazel eyes seem awkwardly offset by the unexpected tint of his slave-born mother's teak-inflected complexion. His mixed-race parentage is writ large in every part of him, for those who care enough to look for it—the telltale detritus of colonization, met and matched in flesh and bone. His skin still faintly scarred, as it were, by the rucked sheets of their marriage-bed.

Not that any money ever changed hands to legalize that relationship, Jean-Guy thinks. *Maman having been old Sansterre's property, at the time.*

This is a tiring line of thought to maintain, however . . . not to mention over-familiar. And there will be much to be done, before the Paris sun rises again.

"I wish you the joy of your *Bal*, m'sieu," Jean-Guy tells the lawyer. "And so, if it please you—my key?"

Proffering his palm and smiling, pleasantly. To which the lawyer replies, coloring again . . .

"Certainly, *m'sieu*."

. . . and hands it over. Adding, as Jean-Guy mounts the steps behind him:

"But you may find very little as you remember it, from those days when *m'sieu* Dumouriez had the top floor."

Jean-Guy pauses at the building's door, favoring the lawyer with one brief, backward glance. And returns . . .

"That, one may only hope . . . *m'sieu*."

1793:

Jean-Guy wakes to twilight, to an empty street—that angry crowd which formerly assembled to rock and prison the Chevalier du Prende-grace's escaping coach apparently having passed on to some further, more distant business. He lies sprawled on a pile of trash behind the butcher's back door, head abuzz and stomach lurching; though whether the nausea in question results from his own physical weakness, the smell of the half-rotten mess of bones beneath him or the sound of the flies that cluster on their partially denuded surface, he truly cannot tell. But he wakes, also, to the voice of his best spy—the well-named La Hire—telling him he must open his eyes, lurch upright, rouse himself at last . . .

"May the Goddess of Reason herself strike me dead if we didn't think you lost forever, Citizen—murdered, maybe, or even arrested. Like all the other Committee members."

Much the same advice Jean-Guy remembers giving himself, not all so very long ago. Back when he lay enveloped in that dark red closeness between those drawn velvet curtains, caught and prone under the stale air's weight in damnably soft, firm grip of the Chevalier's upholstery.

But: "Citizen Sansterre!" A slap across the jaw, jerking his too-heavy head sharply to the left. "Are you tranced? I said, we couldn't *find* you."

Well . . . you've found me now, though. Haven't you . . .

. . . Citizen?

The Chevalier's murmuring voice, reduced to an echo in Jean-Guy's blood. His hidden stare, red-glass-masked, coming and going like heat lightning's horizon-flash behind Jean-Guy's aching eyes.

He shakes his head, still reeling from the sting of La Hire's hand. Forces himself to form words, repeating:

". . . the Committee."

"Gone, Citizen. Scattered to the winds."

"Citizen . . . Robespierre?"

"Arrested, shot, jaw held on with a bandage. He'll kiss the Widow tomorrow—as will we, if we don't fly this stinking city with the Devil's own haste."

Gaining a weak grip upon La Hire's arm, Jean-Guy uses it to lever himself—shakily—upward. His mouth feels swollen, lips and gums raw-abraded; new blood fresh and sticky at one corner, cud of old blood sour between his back teeth, at the painful root of his tongue. More blood pulls free as he rises, unsticking the left panel of his half-opened shirt from the nub of one nipple; as he takes a step forward, yet more blood still is found gluing him fast to his own breeches, stiff and brown, in that . . .

. . . *unmentionable area* . . .

And on one wrist, a light, crescent-shaped wound—bruised and inflamed, pink with half-healed infection. A painfully raised testimony to dream-dim memory: The Chevalier's rough little tongue pressed hard, cold as a dead cat's, against the thin skin above the uppermost vein.

I have set my mark upon you, Citizen.

Jean-Guy passes a hand across his brow, coughing, then brings it away wet—and red. Squints down, and finds himself inspecting a palm-full of blood-tinged sweat.

"Dumouriez," he asks La Hire, with difficulty. "Taken . . . also?"

"Hours ago."

"Show me . . . to his room."

And now, a momentary disclaimer: Let it be here stated, with as much clarity as possible, that Jean-Guy had never—hitherto—given much credence to those old wives' tales which held that aristos glutted their delicate hungers at the mob's expense, keeping themselves literally fat with infusions of carnal misery and poor men's meat. Pure rhetoric, surely; folktales turned metaphor, as quoted in Camille Desmoulins's incendiary pamphlets: *Church and nobility—vampires. Observe the color of their faces, and the pallor of your own.*

Not that the Chevalier du Prendgrace's face, so imperfectly recalled, had borne even the slightest hint *of* color . . . healthy, or otherwise.

Not long after his return to Martinique, Jean-Guy had held some brief discourse with an English doctor named Gabriel Keynes—a man famous for spending the last ten years of his own life trying to identify the causes of (and potential cures for) that swampy bronze plague known as yellow fever. Bolstered by a bottle or two of good claret and Keynes's personal promise of most complete discretion, Jean-Guy had unfolded to him the whole, distressing story of his encounter with the Chevalier: shown him the mark on his wrist, the marks . . .

. . . elsewhere.

Those enduring wounds which, even now, would—on occasion—break open and bleed anew, as though at some unrecognizable signal;

the invisible passage of their maker, perhaps, through the cracks between known and unknown areas of their mutual world's unwritten map?

As though we could really share the same world, ever, we two—such as I, and such as . . .

. . . he . . .

"What y'have here, monsewer Sansterre," Keynes observed—touching the blister's surface but delicately, yet leaving behind a dent, along with a lingering, sinister ache—"is a continual pocket of sequestered blood. 'Tis that what we sawbones name haematoma: From the Latin *haematomane*, or 'drinker of blood.'"

There was, the doctor explained, a species of bats in the Antipodes—even upon Jean-Guy's home island—whose very genus was labeled after the common term for those legendary undead monsters Desmoulins had once fixated upon. These bats possessed a saliva which, being composed mainly of anticoagulant elements, aided them in the pursuit of their filthy addiction: A mixture of chemicals which, when smeared against an open wound, prolong—and even increase—the force and frequency of its bleeding. Adding, however:

"But I own I have never known of such a reaction left behind by the spittle of any *man* . . . even one whose family, as your former Jacobin compatriots might term it, is—no doubt—long-accustomed to the consumption of blood."

Which concludes, as it ensues, the entire role of science in this narrative.

And now, the parallel approach to Dumouriez's former apartment—past and present blending neatly together as Jean-Guy scales the rickety staircase toward that last, long-locked door, its hinges stiff with rust . . .

Stepping, in 1815, into a cramped and low-hung attic space clogged with antique furniture: fine brocades, moth-eaten and dusty; sway-backed Louis Quatorze chairs with splintered legs. Splintered armoires and dun-smoked walls, festooned with cobweb and scribbled with foul words.

On one particular wall, a faint stain hangs like spreading damp. The shadow of some immense, submerged, half-crucified gray bat.

Jean-Guy traces its contours, wonderingly. Remembering, in 1793 . . .

. . . a blood-stained pallet piled high with pale-eyed corpses left to rot beneath this same wall, this same great watermark: its bright red darkness, splashed wet across fresh white plaster.

Oh, how Jean-Guy had stared at it—struck stupidly dumb with pure shock—while La Hire recounted the details his long day's sleep had stolen from him. Told him how, when the Committee's spies broke in at last,

Dumouriez had merely looked up from his work with a queasy smile, interrupted in the very midst of dumping yet another body on top of the last. How he'd held a trowel clutched, incongruously, in one hand—which he'd then raised, still smiling . . .

. . . and used, sharp edge turned inward—even as they screamed at him to halt—to cut his own throat.

Under the stain's splayed wing, Jean-Guy closes his eyes and casts his mind back even further—right back to the beginning, before Thermidor finally stemmed the Revolutionary river's flood; before the Chevalier's coach, later found stripped and abandoned at the lip of a pit stuffed with severed heads and lime; before Dumouriez's suicide, or Jean-Guy and La Hire's frantic flight to Calais, and beyond—back to Martinique, where La Hire would serve as plantation-master on Old Sansterre's lands 'til the hour and the day of his own, entirely natural, demise. The very, very beginning.

Or: Jean-Guy's—necessarily limited—version of it, at any rate.

1793, then, once more. Five o'clock on that long-gone "August" day, and the afternoon sun has already begun to slant down over the Row of the Armed Man's ruined roofs—dripping from their streaming gutters in a dazzle of water and light, along with the last of the previous night's rainfall. Jean-Guy and La Hire sit together at what passes for a table by the open window of a street-side café, their tricolor badges momentarily absent from sashes and hats; they sip their coffee, thus disguised, and listen to today's tumbrils grind by through the stinking mist. Keeping a careful tandem eye, also, upon the uppermost windows of Dumouriez's house—refuge of a suspected traitor, and previously listed (before its recent conversion into a many-roomed, half-empty "citizens' hotel") as part of the ancestral holdings of a certain M. le Chevalier du Prendegrace.

Jean-Guy to La Hire: "This Prendegrace—who is he?"

"A *ci-devant* aristo, what else? Like all the rest."

"Yes, to be sure; but besides."

La Hire shrugs. "Does it matter?"

Here, in that ill-fit building just across the way, other known aristocrats—men, women and children bearing papers forged expertly enough to permit them to walk the streets of Paris, if not exit through its gates—have often been observed to enter, though rarely been observed to leave. Perhaps attracted by Prendegrace's reputation as "one of their own", they place their trust in his creature Dumouriez's promises of sanctuary, refuge, escape—the very fact of their own absence, later on, seems to prove that trust has not been given in vain.

"The sewers," La Hire suggests. "They served *us* well enough during the old days, dodging royalist scum through the Cordelliers' quarter . . ."

Jean-Guy scoffs. "A secret entrance, perhaps, in the cellar? Down to the river with the rest of the garbage, then to the far shore on some subterranean boat?"

"It's possible."

"So the *dénoncé* Church used to claim, concerning Christ's resurrection."

A guffaw. "Ah, but there's no need to be so bitter about *that*, Citizen. Is there? Since they've already paid so well, after all—those fat-arsed priests—for spreading such pernicious lies."

And: *Ah, yes*, Jean-Guy remembers thinking, as he nods in smiling agreement. *Paid in full, on the Widow's lap . . . just like the King and his Austrian whore, before them.*

Across the street, meanwhile, a far less elevated lady of ill-repute comes edging up through the Row proper, having apparently just failed to drum up any significant business amongst the crowds which line the Widow's bridal path. Spotting them both, she hikes her skirt to show Jean-Guy first the hem of her scarlet petticoat, then the similarly red-dyed tangle of hair at her crotch. La Hire glances over, draws a toothless grin, and snickers in reply; Jean-Guy affects to ignore her, and receives a rude gesture for his *politesse*. Determined to avoid the embarrassment of letting his own sudden spurt of anger show, he looks away, eyes flicking back toward the attic's windows . . .

. . . where he sees, framed between its moth-worn curtains, another woman's face appear: a porcelain-smooth girl's mask peering out from the darkness behind the cracked glass, grub-pale in the shadows of this supposedly unoccupied apartment. It hangs there, pale and empty as a wax head from Citizen Curtuis's museum—that studio where images of decapitated friend and foe to France alike are modeled from casts taken by his "niece" Marie, the Grosholtz girl, who will one day abandon Curtuis to the mob he serves and marry another man for passage to England. Where she will set up her own museum, exhibiting the results of her skills under the fresh new name of Madame Tussaud.

That white face. Those dim-hued eyes. Features once contemptuously regal, now possessed of nothing but a dull and uncomplaining patience. The same wide stare which will meet Jean-Guy's, after the raid, from atop the grisly burden of Dumouriez's overcrowded pallet. That proud aristo, limbs flopped carelessly askew, her nude skin dappled—like that of every one of her fellow victims . . .

(like Jean-Guy's own brow now, in 1815, as he studies that invisible point on the wall where the stain of Dumouriez's escape once hung, dripping)

. . . with bloody sweat.

His "old complaint," he called it, during that brief evening's consultation with Dr. Keynes. A cyclic, tidal flux, regular as breath, unwelcome as nightmare—constantly calling and recalling a blush, or more, to his unwilling skin.

And he wonders, Jean-Guy, just as he wondered then: why look at all? Why bother to hide herself, if only to periodically brave the curtain and offer her unmistakable face to the hostile street outside?.

But . . .

"You aristos," he remembers muttering while the Chevalier listened, courteously expressionless. "All, so . . . arrogant."

"Yes, Citizen."

"Like . . . that girl. The one . . ."

"At Dumouriez's window? Oh, no doubt."

". . . but how . . ." Struggling manfully against his growing lassitude, determined to place the reference in context: "How . . . could you know . . .?"

And the Chevalier, giving his version of La Hire's shrug, all sleek muscle under fine scarlet velvet.

"But I simply *do*, Citizen Sansterre."

Adding, in a whisper—a hum? That same hum, so close and quiet against the down of Jean-Guy's paralyzed cheek, which seems to vibrate through every secret part of him at once whenever the blood still kept sequestered beneath his copper-ruddy mixed-race flesh begins to . . . flow . . .

For who do you think it was who told her to look out, in the first place?

In Martinique—with money and time at his disposal, and a safe distance put between himself and that Satanic, red-lined coach—Jean-Guy had eventually begun to make certain discreet inquiries into the long and secretive history of the family Prendegrace. Thus employed, he soon amassed a wealth of previously hidden information: facts impossible to locate during the Revolution, or even before.

Like picking at a half-healed scab, pain and relief in equal measure— and since, beyond obviously, he would never *be* fully healed, what did it matter just . . . what . . . Jean-Guy's inquiries managed to uncover?

Chevalier Joffroi d'Iver, first of his line, won his nobility on crusade under Richard Coeur-de-Lion, for services rendered during the massacre at Acre. An old story: reluctant to lose the glory of having captured three hundred infidels in battle—though aware that retaining them would prevent any further advancement toward his true prize, the holy city of

Jerusalem—the hot-blooded Plantagenet ordered each and every one of them decapitated on the spot. So scaffolds were built, burial pits dug, and heads and bodies sent tumbling in either direction for three whole days—while swords of d'Iver and his companions swung ceaselessly, and a stream of fresh victims slipped in turn on the filth their predecessors had left behind.

And after their task was done, eyewitnesses record, these good Christian knights filled the pits with Greek fire—leaving the bodies to burn, as they rode away.

Much as, during your own famous Days of September, a familiar voice seems to murmur at Jean-Guy's ear, *378 of those prisoners awaiting trial at the Conciergie were set upon by an angry horde of good patriots like yourself, and hacked limb from limb in the street.*

Eyes closed, Jean-Guy recalls a gaggle of women running by—red-handed, reeling drunk—with clusters of ears adorning their open, fichu-less bodices. Fellow citizens clapping and cheering from the drawn-up benches as a man wrings the Princess de Lamballe's still-beating heart dry over a goblet, then takes a long swig of the result, toasting the health of the Revolution in pale aristo blood. All those guiding lights of Liberty: ugly Georges Danton, passionate Camille Desmoulins . . .

. . . Maximilien Robespierre himself, in his Incorruptible's coat of sea-green silk, nearsighted cat's eyes narrowed against the world through spectacles with smoked-glass lenses; the kind one might wear, even today, to protect oneself while observing an eclipse.

Le Famille Prend-de-grace, moving to block out the sun; a barren new planet, passing restless through a dark new sky. And their arms, taken at the same time—an axe *argent et gules*, over a carrion field, *gules seulement.*

A blood-stained weapon, suspended—with no visible means of support—above a field red with severed heads.

We could not have been more suited to each other, you and I. Could we . . .

. . . Citizen?

1793:

Blood and filth, and the distant rumble of passing carts—the hot mist turns to sizzling rain, as new waves of stench eddy and shift around them. Dumouriez rounds the corner into the Row of the Armed Man, and La Hire and Jean-Guy exchange a telling glance: the plan of attack, as previously determined. La Hire will take the back way, past where the prostitute lurks, while Jean-Guy waits under a convenient awning—to keep his powder dry—until he hears their signal, using the time between to prime his pistol. They give Dumouriez a few minutes' lead, then rise as one.

Crimson-stained sweat, memories swarming like maggots in his brain. Yet more on the clan Prendegrace, a red-tinged stream of sinister trivia . . .

Their motto: *nus souvienz le tous.* "We remember everything."

Their hereditary post at court: attendant on the king's bedchamber, a function discontinued sometime during the reign of Henri de Navarre, for historically obscure reasons.

The rumor: that during the massacre of Saint Barthelme's Night, one—usually unnamed—Prendegrace was observed pledging then-King Charles IX's honor with a handful of Protestant flesh.

Prendegrace. "Those who have received God's grace."

Receive.

Or—is it—*take* God's grace . . .

. . . for themselves?

Jean-Guy feels himself start to reel, and rams his fist against the apartment wall for support. Then feels it lurch and pulse in answer under his knuckles, as though his own hammering heart were buried beneath that yellowed plaster.

Pistol thrust beneath his coat's lapel, Jean-Guy steps toward Dumouriez's door—only to find his way blocked by a sudden influx of armed and shouting fellow Citizens. Yet another protest whipped up from general dissatisfaction and street-corner demagoguery, bound for nowhere in particular, less concerned with destruction than with noise and display; routine "patriotic" magic transforming empty space into chaos-bent rabble, with no legerdemain or invocation required.

Across the way, he spots La Hire crushed up against the candle-maker's door, but makes sure to let his gaze slip by without a hint of recognition as the stinking human tide . . . none of them probably feeling particularly favorable, at this very moment, toward any representative of the Committee who—as they keep on chanting—have *stole our blood to make their bread . . .*

(a convenient bit of symbolic symmetry, that)

. . . sweeps him rapidly back past the whore, the garbage, the café, the Row itself, and out into the cobbled street beyond.

Jean-Guy feels his ankle turn as it meets the gutter; he stumbles, then rights himself. Calling out, above the crowd's din:

"Citizens, I . . ." No answer. Louder: "Listen, Citizens—I have no quarrel with you; I have business in there . . ." And, louder still: "Citzens! Let . . . me . . . *pass!*"

But: No answer, again, from any of the nearest mob-members—neither that huge, obviously drunken man with the pike, trailing tricolor streamers, or those two women trying to fill their aprons with loose stones while ignoring the screaming babies strapped to their backs. Not even from that dazed young man who seems to have once—however mistakenly—thought himself to be their leader, now dragged hither and yon at the violent behest of his "followers" with his pale eyes rolling in their sockets, his gangly limbs barely still attached to his shaking body . . .

The price of easy oratory, Jean-Guy thinks, sourly. *Cheap words, hasty actions; a whole desperate roster of very real ideals—and hungers—played on for the mere sake of a moment's notoriety, applause, power . . .*

. . . our Revolution's ruin, in a nutshell.

And then . . .

. . . a shadow falls over him, soft and dark as the merest night-borne whisper—but one which will lie paradoxically heavy across his unsuspecting shoulders, nevertheless, for long years afterward. His destiny approaching through the mud, on muffled wheels.

A red-hung coach, nudging at him—almost silently—from behind.

Perfect.

He shoulders past the pikeman, between the women, drawing curses and blows; gives back a few of his own, as he clambers onto the coach's running-board and hooks its nearest door open. Rummages in his pocket for his tricolor badge, and brandishes it in the face of the coach's sole occupant, growling . . .

"I commandeer this coach in the name of the Committee for Public Safety!"

Sliding quick into the seat opposite as the padded door shuts suddenly, yet soundlessly, beside him. And that indistinct figure across from him leans forward, equally sudden—a mere red-on-white-on-red silhouette, in the curtained windows' dull glare—to murmur:

"The Committee? Why, my coach is yours, then . . ."

. . . *Citizen.*

Jean-Guy looks up, dazzled. And notices, at last, the Prendegrace arms which hang just above him, embroidered on the curtains' underside—silver on red, *red* on red, outlined in fire by the sun which filters weakly through their thick, enshrouding velvet weave.

1815:

Jean-Guy feels new wetness trace its way down his arm, soaking the cuff of his sleeve red: His war-wound, broken open once more, in sympathetic proximity to . . . what? His own tattered scraps of memory, slipping and sliding like phlegm on glass? This foul, haunted house, where Dumouriez—like some Tropic trapdoor spider—traded on his master's aristocratic name to entice the easiest fresh prey he could find into his web, then fattened them up (however briefly) before using them to slake M. le Chevalier's deviant familial appetites?

Blood, from wrist to palm, printing the wall afresh; blood in his throat from his tongue's bleeding base, painting his spittle red as he hawks and coughs—all civility lost, in a moment's spasm of pure revulsion—onto the dusty floor.

Spatter of blood on dust, like a ripe scarlet hieroglyphic: liquid, horrid, infinitely malleable. Utterly . . . uninterpretable.

I have set my mark upon you, Citizen.

Blood at his collar, his nipple. His . . .

(. . . groin.)

My hook in your flesh. My winding reel.

Jean-Guy feels it tug him downward, into the maelstrom.

1793:

The coach. Prendegrace sits right in front of Jean-Guy, a mere hand's grasp away, slight and lithe and damnably languid in his rich, red velvet; his hair is drawn back and side-curled, powdered so well that Jean-Guy can't even tell its original color, let alone use its decided lack of contrast to help him decipher the similarly-pallid features of the face it frames. Except to note that, as though in mocking imitation of Citizen Robespierre, the Chevalier too affects a pair of spectacles with smoked glass lenses . . .

. . . though, instead of sea-green, these small, blank squares glint a dim—yet unmistakable—shade of scarlet.

Play for time, Jean-Guy's brain tells him, meanwhile—imparting its usually good advice with uncharacteristic softness, as though, if it were to speak any louder, the Chevalier might somehow overhear it. *Pretend not to have recognized him. Then work your pistol free, slowly; fire a warning shot, and summon the good citizens outside . . .*

. . . those same ones you slipped in here to avoid, in the first place . . .

. . . *to aid you in his arrest.*

Almost snorting aloud at the very idea, before he catches himself: as though an agent of Jean-Guy's enviable size and bulk actually need *fear* the feeble defenses of a *ci-devant* fop like this one, with his frilled wrists and his neat, red-heeled shoes, their tarnished buckles dull and smeared—on the nearest side, at least—with something which almost looks like . . .

. . . blood?

Surely not.

And yet . . .

"You would be Citizen Sansterre, I think," the Chevalier observes, abruptly.

Name of God.

Recovering, Jean-Guy gives a stiff nod. "And you—the traitor, Prende-grace."

"And that would be a pistol you reach for, under your collar."

"It would."

A punch, a kick, a cry for help, the drawing forth of some secret weapon of his own: Jean-Guy braces himself, a match-ready fuse, tensed to the point of near-pain against any of the aforementioned. But the Chevalier merely nods as well, undeterred in the face of Jean-Guy's honest aggression—his very passivity itself a form of arrogance, a cool and languid aristocratic challenge to the progressively more hot and bothered plebian world around him. Then leans just a bit forward, at almost the same time: a paralytic blink of virtual nonmovement, so subtle as to be hardly worth noting . . . for all that Jean-Guy now finds himself beginning—barely recognizing *what* he does, let alone why—to match it.

Leaning in, far too slow to stop himself, to arrest this fall in mid-plunge. Leaning in, as the Chevalier's red lenses dip, slipping inexorably downward to reveal a pale rim of brow, of lash, of eye-socket. And leaning in yet further, to see—below that . . .

. . . first one eye, then another: Pure but opaque, luridly empty. Eyes without whites (or irises, or pupils), the same blank scarlet tint—from lower lid to upper—as the spectacles which masked them.

Words in red darkness, pitched almost too low to hear; Jean-Guy must strain to catch them, leaning closer still. Places a trembling hand on the Chevalier's shoulder, to steady himself, and feels them thrum up through his palm, his arm, his chest, his wildly beating heart: a secret, interior embrace, intimate as plague, squeezing him between the ribs, between the thighs. And . . .

. . . deeper.

Before him, the Chevalier's own hand hovers, clean white palm turned patiently upward. Those long, black-rimmed nails. Those red words, tracing the myriad paths of blood. Suggesting, mildly . . .

Then you had best give it to me, Citizen—this pistol of yours. Had you not?

Because: That *would* be the right thing to do, really. All things considered.

Do you not think?

Yes.

For safety. For—safe-keeping.

. . . exactly that, yes.

Such sweet reason. Such deadly reasonable*ness.*

Jean-Guy feels his mouth drop open as though to protest, but hears only the faint, wet pop of his jaw-hinges relaxing in an idiot yawn;

watches, helpless, as he drops the pistol—butt-first—into the Chevalier's grip. Sees the Chevalier seem to blink, just slightly, in return: all-red no-stare blurred by only the most momentary flicker, milky and brief as some snake's nictitating membrane.

And . . .

"There, now," the Chevalier observes, aloud. "That . . . must suit us both . . . *so* much better."

Must it—not?

A half-formed heave, a last muffled attempt at a thrash, muscles knotted in on themselves like some mad stray cur's in the foam-flecked final stages of hydrophobia—and then, without warning, the Chevalier is on him. Their mouths seal together, parted lip to bared, bone-needle teeth: blood fills Jean-Guy's throat, greasing the way as the Chevalier locks fast to his fluttering tongue. His gums burn like ulcers. This is far less a kiss than a suddenly open wound, an artery slashed and left to spurt.

The pistol falls away, forgotten.

Venom spikes Jean-Guy's heart. He chokes down a numbing, stinging mouthful of cold that takes him to the brink of sleep and the edge of climax simultaneously as the Chevalier's astringent tongue rasps over the inflamed tissues of his mouth, harsh as a cat's. Finds himself grabbing this whippet-slim thing in his arms by the well-arranged hair, anchoring himself so it can grind them ever more firmly together, and feels a shower of loose powder fall around both their faces like dirty city snow; the Chevalier's ribbon has come undone, his neat-curled side-locks unraveling like kelp in an icy current. At the same instant, meanwhile, the nearest lapel of his lurid coat peels back—deft as some mountebank's trick—to reveal the cold white flesh beneath: No pulse visible beneath the one flat pectoral, nipple peak-hard but utterly colorless . . .

. . . oh yes, yes, yes . . .

Jean-Guy feels the Chevalier's hands—clawed now—scrabble at his fly's buttons, free him to slap upward in this awful red gloom. Then sees him give one quick double thumb-flick across the groove, the distended, weeping velvet knob, and send fresh scarlet welling up along the urethral fold faster than Jean-Guy can cry out in surprised, horrified pain.

Name of death and the Devil!

The Chevalier gives a thin grin of delight at the sight of it. His mouth opens wide as a cat's in flamen, tasting the slaughterhouse-scented air. Nearly drooling.

People, Revolution, Supreme Being, please . . .

Lips skinning back. Fangs extending. His sleek head dipping low, as though in profane prayer . . .

. . . oh God, oh Jesus, *no* . . .

. . . to sip at it.

More muffled words rippling up somehow through the femoral knot of Jean-Guy's groin, even as he gulps bile, his whole righteous world dimming to one pin-prick point of impossible pain, of unspeakable and unnatural ecstasy—as he starts to reel, come blood, black out:

Ah, Citizen—do not leave me just yet. Not when . . .

. . . we are . . . so close . . .

. . . to meeting each other, once more.

In 1815, meanwhile:

Jean-Guy looks up from the bloody smudge now spreading wide beneath his own splayed fingers to see—that same familiar swatch of wet and shining scarlet resurface, like a grotesque miracle, above his gaping face. Dumouriez's death-stain, grown somehow fresh again, as though the wall . . . the room, itself . . . were bleeding.

Plaster reddens, softens. Collapses inward, paradoxically, as the wall bulges outward. And Jean-Guy watches, frozen, as what lies beneath begins to extrude itself, at long last, through that vile, soaked ruin of chalk-dust, glue and hemoglobin alike—first one hand, then another, one shoulder, then its twin. The whole rest of the torso, still dressed in the same rotten velvet *equipage*, twisting its deft way out through the sodden, crumbling muck . . . grub-white neck rearing cobralike, poised to strike . . . grub-white profile turning outward—its lank mane still clotted with calcified powder, its red-glazed glasses hung carelessly askew—to once more cast empty eyes Jean-Guy's way . . .

This awful revenant version of M. the former Chevalier du Prende-grace shakes his half-mummified head, studying Jean-Guy from under dusty lashes. He opens his mouth, delicately—pauses—then coughs out a fine white curl, and frowns at the way his long-dormant lungs wheeze.

Fastening his blank red gaze on Jean-Guy's own. Observing:

"How terribly you've changed, Citizen." A pause. "But then—that *is* the inevitable fate of the impermanent."

"The Devil," Jean-Guy whispers, forgetting his once-vaunted atheism.

"La, sir. You do me entirely too much honor."

The Chevalier steps forward, bringing a curled and ragged lip of wall along with him; Jean-Guy hears it tear as it comes, like a scab. The sound rings in his ears. He puts up both palms, weakly, as though a simple ges-ture might really be enough to stave off the—living?—culmination of a half-lifetime's nightmare visions.

The Chevalier notices, and gives that sly half-smile: teeth still white, still intact, yet jutting now from his fever-pink gums at slight angles, like a shark's . . . but could there really be *more* of them, after all these years? Crop upon crop, stacked up and waiting to be shed after his next feeding, the one which never came?

They almost seem to glow, translucent as milky glass. Waiting . . .

. . . to be filled.

"Of course, one does hear things, especially inside the walls," the Chevalier continues, brushing plaster away with small, fastidious strokes. "For example: that—excepting certain instances of regicide—your vaunted Revolution came to naught, after all. And that, since a Corsican general now rules an empire in the monarchy's place, old Terrorists such as yourself must therefore count themselves in desperate need of new . . . positions."

Upraised palms, wet—and red; his "complaint" come back in force, worse than the discards in Dumouriez's long-ago corpse-pile. Jean-Guy stands immersed in it, head swirling, skin one whole slick of cold sweat and hot blood admixed—and far more blood than sweat, all told. So much so, he must swallow it in mouthfuls, just to speak. His voice comes out garbled, sludgy, *clotted*.

"You . . ." he says, with difficulty. "*You* . . . did this . . . to me . . ."

"But of course, Citizen Sansterre; sent the girl to the window, tempted you within my reach, and set my mark upon you, as you well know. As I . . ."

. . . *told you.*

Or . . . do you not recall?

Sluiced and veritably streaming with it, inside and out: palate, nipples, groin. That hematoma on his wrist's prickling underside, opening like a flower. The Chevalier's remembered kiss, licking his veins full of cold poison.

(If I can't stop this bleeding, it'll be my death.)

Numb-tongued: "As you did with Dumouriez."

"Exactly so."

Raising one clawed hand to touch Jean-Guy's face, just lightly—a glancing parody of comfort—and send Jean-Guy arching away, cursing, as the mere pressure of the Chevalier's fingers is enough to draw first a drip, then a gush, of fresh crimson.

"God damn your *ci-devant* eyes!"

"Yes, yes." Quieter: "But I can make this stop, you know."

I. And only I.

Seduction, then infection, then cure—for a price. Loyalty, 'till death . . .

. . . and—after?

How Prendegrace trapped Dumouriez, no doubt, once upon a long, long time past—or had Dumouriez simply offered himself up to worship at this thing's red-shod feet, without having to be enticed or duped into such an unequal Devil's bargain? Coming to Prendegrace's service gratefully, even gladly—as glad as he would be, eventually, to cut his own throat to save this creature's no-life, or spray fresh blood across a wet plaster wall to conceal the thing he'd hunted, pimped and died for, safely entombed within?

And for Jean-Guy, an equally limited range of choices: to bleed out all at once in a moment's sanguinary torrent, and die now, or live as a tool, the way Dumouriez did—and die *later*.

Minimally protected, perhaps even cherished; easily used, yet . . . just as easily . . .

. . . discarded.

"There can be benefits to such an arrangement," Prendegrace points out, softly.

"He sacrificed himself for you."

"As was required."

"As you demanded."

The Chevalier raises a delicate brow, sketched in discolored plaster. "I? I demand nothing, Citizen. Only accept—what's offered me."

"Because you aristos deign to do *nothing* for yourselves."

"Oh, no doubt. But then, that's why I chose you: For being so much more able than I, in every regard. Why I envied and coveted your strength, your vital idealism. Your . . ."

. . . life.

Jean-Guy feels the monster's gaze rove up and down, appraisingly—reading him, as it were, like . . .

Hoarse: "A . . . map."

The Chevalier sighs, and shakes his head.

"A pretty pastime, once. But your body no longer invites such pleasantries, more's the pity; you have grown somewhat more—opaque—with age, I think."

Taking one further step forward, as Jean-Guy recoils; watching Jean-Guy slip in his own blood, go down on one knee, hand scrabbling helplessly for purchase against that ragged hole where the wall once was.

"What *are* you?" He asks. Wincing, angrily, as he hears his own voice crack with an undignified mixture of hatred, fear . . .

(. . . longing?)

The Chevalier pauses, midstep. And replies, after a long moment:

"Ah. Yet this would be the one question we none of us may answer, Citizen Sansterre—not even myself, who knows only that I was born this way, whatever way that might be . . ."

Leaning closer still. Whispering. Words dimming to blood-thrum, and lower, as the sentence draws to its long-sought, inevitable close . . .

". . . just as you were born, like everyone else I meet in this terrible world of ours, to bear my mark . . ."

. . . *or be my prey.*

With Jean-Guy's sight narrowing to embrace nothing but those empty eyes, that mouth, those *teeth*: his disease made flesh, made terminal. His destiny, buried too deep to touch or think of, 'till it dug itself free once more.

But . . .

. . . *I am not just this, damn you, he thinks, as though in equally silent, desperate reply—not just your prey, your pawn, your tool. I was someone, grown and bred entirely apart from your influence: I had history, hopes, dreams. I loved my father, and hated his greed; loved my mother, and hated her enslavement. Loved and hated what I saw of them both in myself: my born freedom, my slave's skin. I allied myself with a Cause that talked of freedom, only to drown itself in blood. But I am more than that, more than anything that came out of that . . . more than just this one event, the worst—and most defining— moment of my life. This one encounter with . . .*

. . . you.

Stuck in the same yearning, dreadful moment through twelve whole years of *real* life—even when he was working his land, loving his wife, mourning her, mourning the children whose hope died with her. Running his father's plantation, adjudicating disputes, approving marriages, attending christenings; watching La Hire decline and fall, being drunk at his funeral, at the *Bal*, at his own wedding . . .

. . . only to be drawn back here, at last, like some recalcitrant cur to his hidden master's call. To be reclaimed, over near-incalculable distances of time and space, as though he were some piece of property, some tool, some merest creeping . . .

. . . slave.

Marked, as yours. By you. *For* you.

But—this was the entire point of "my" Revolution, Jean-Guy remembers, suddenly. *That all men were slaves, no matter their estate, so long as kings and their laws ruled unchecked. And that we should all, all of us, no matter how low or high—or mixed—our birth either rise up, take what was ours, live free . . .*

. . . or *die.*

Die quick. Die clean. Make your last stand now, Citizen, while you still have the strength to do it . . .

. . . or never.

"It occurs to me," the Chevalier says, slowly, "that . . . after all this . . . we still do not know each other's given name."

Whatever else, Jean-Guy promises himself, with one last coherent thought, *I will not allow myself to beg.*

A spark to oil, this last heart's flare: he turns for the door, lurching up, only to find the Chevalier upon him, bending him backward by the hair.

Ah, do not leave me, Citizen.

But: "I *will*," Jean-Guy snarls, liquid, in return. And hears the Chevalier's laugh ring in his ear through a fresh gout of blood, distant as some underwater glass bell. That voice replying aloud, as well as—otherwise . . .

"Ohhhh . . . I think not."

I have set my mark upon you.

My mark. Mine.

That voice in his ear, his blood. That smell. His traitor's body, opening wide to its sanguine, siren's song. That unforgettable red halo of silent lassitude settling over him like a bell jar once more, sealing them together: Predator, prey, potential codependents.

This fatal Widow's kiss he's waited for, in vain, for oh so very long— Prendegrace's familiar poison, seeping into Jean-Guy's veins, his heart. Stopping him in his tracks.

All this—blood . . .

Blood, for all that bloodshed. The Revolution's tide, finally stemmed with an offering made from his own body, his own—damned . . .

. . . soul.

Prendegrace raises red lips. He wipes them, pauses, coughs again— more wetly, this time. And asks, aloud:

"By your favor, Citizen . . . what year is this, exactly?"

"Year Zero," Jean-Guy whispers back.

And lets himself go.

Good Lady Ducayne

Mary Elizabeth Braddon

Mary Elizabeth Braddon (1835–1915) was one of the most sensationalist and best-selling Victorian authors. Although her best-known work is probably *Lady Audley's Secret* (1862), a melodramatic tale of madness and murder that led to the rise in popularity of "sensation fiction," and she also turned out dozens of novels and numerous short stories often anonymously or under various pseudonyms, in addition to editing two of her husband John Maxwell's publications: the monthly magazine for ladies, *Belgravia*, and the Christmas annual *The Miseltoe Bough*.

"If I could plot like Miss Braddon, I would be the greatest writer in the English language," wrote *Vanity Fair* author William Makepeace Thackeray, while Arnold Bennett described her in 1901 as, "Part of England."

Braddon's other books include a variation on the Faust legend, *The World, the Flesh and the Devil* (aka *Gerard*, 1891), and eighteen of her best supernatural stories were collected by editor Richard Dalby in *The Cold Embrace and Other Ghost Stories*, published in 2000 by Ash-Tree Press.

The following story originally appeared in *The Strand Magazine*, just a year before Bram Stoker published *Dracula*. It was one of the first tales to feature an unconventional incarnation of the undead, in which a nonsupernatural vampire exploits a dependent relationship with her victim. It also has some interesting things to say about the role of women in British society at that time . . .

I

BELLA ROLLESTON HAD made up her mind that her only chance of earning her bread and helping her mother to an occasional crust was by going out into the great unknown world as companion to a lady. She was willing to go to any lady rich enough to pay her a salary and so eccentric as to wish for a hired companion. Five shillings told off reluctantly from one of those sovereigns which were so rare with the mother and daughter, and which melted away so quickly, five solid shillings, had been handed to a smartly-dressed lady in an office in Harbeck Street, W., in the hope that this very Superior Person would find a situation and a salary for Miss Rolleston.

The Superior Person glanced at the two half-crowns as they lay on the table where Bella's hand had placed them, to make sure they were neither of them forms, before she wrote a description of Bella's qualifications and requirements in a formidable-looking ledger.

"Age?" she asked curtly.

"Eighteen, last July."

"Any accomplishments?"

"No; I am not at all accomplished. If I were I should want to be a governess—a companion seems the lowest stage."

"We have some highly accomplished ladies on our books as companions, or chaperon companions."

"Oh, I know!" babbled Bella, loquacious in her youthful candor. "But that is quite a different thing. Mother hasn't been able to afford a piano since I was twelve years old, so I'm afraid I've forgotten how to play. And I have had to help mother with her needlework, so there hasn't been much time to study."

"Please don't waste time upon explaining what you can't do, but kindly tell me anything you can do," said the Superior Person, crushingly, with her pen poised between delicate fingers waiting to write. "Can you read aloud for two or three hours at a stretch? Are you active and handy, an early riser, a good walker, sweet-tempered, and obliging?"

"I can say yes to all those questions except about the sweetness. I think I have a pretty good temper, and I should be anxious to oblige anybody who paid for my services. I should want them to feel that I was really earning my salary."

"The kind of ladies who come to me would not care for a talkative companion," said the Person, severely, having finished writing in her book. "My connection lies chiefly among the aristocracy, and in that class considerable deference is expected."

"Oh, of course," said Bella; "but it's quite different when I'm talking to you. I want to tell you all about myself once and forever."

"I am glad it is to be only once!" said the Person, with the edges of her lips.

The Person was of uncertain age, tightly laced in a black silk gown. She had a powdery complexion and a handsome clump of somebody else's hair on the top of her head. It may be that Bella's girlish freshness and vivacity had an irritating effect upon nerves weakened by an eight-hours day in that overheated second floor in Harbeck Street. To Bella the official

324 / Mary Elizabeth Braddon

apartment, with its Brussels carpet, velvet curtains and velvet chairs, and French clock, ticking loud on the marble chimney-piece, suggested the luxury of a palace, as compared with another second floor in Walworth where Mrs. Rolleston and her daughter had managed to exist for the last six years.

"Do you think you have anything on your books that would suit me?" faltered Bella, after a pause.

"Oh, dear, no; I have nothing in view at present," answered the Person, who had swept Bella's half-crowns into a drawer, absentmindedly, with the tips of her fingers. "You see, you are so very unformed—so much too young to be companion to a lady of position. It is a pity you have not enough education for a nursery governess; that would be more in your line."

"And do you think it will be very long before you can get me a situation?" asked Bella, doubtfully.

"I really cannot say. Have you any particular reason for being so impatient—not a love affair, I hope?"

"A love affair!" cried Bella, with flaming cheeks. "What utter nonsense. I want a situation because mother is poor, and I hate being a burden to her. I want a salary that I can share with her."

"There won't be much margin for sharing in the salary you are likely to get at your age, and with your—very—unformed manners," said the Person, who found Bella's peony cheeks, bright eyes, and unbridled vivacity more and more oppressive.

"Perhaps if you'd be kind enough to give me back the fee I could take it to an agency where the connection isn't quite so aristocratic," said Bella, who—as she told her mother in her recital of the interview—was determined not to be sat upon.

"You will find no agency that can do more for you than mine," replied the Person, whose harpy fingers never relinquished coin. "You will have to wait for your opportunity. Yours is an exceptional case: but I will bear you in mind, and if anything suitable offers I will write to you. I cannot say more than that."

The half-contemptuous bend of the stately head, weighted with borrowed hair, indicated the end of the interview. Bella went back to Walworth—tramped sturdily every inch of the way in the September afternoon—and "took off" the Superior Person for the amusement of her mother and the landlady, who lingered in the shabby little sitting-room after bringing in the tea-tray, to applaud Miss Rolleston's "taking off."

"Dear, dear, what a mimic she is!" said the landlady. "You ought to have let her go on the stage, mum. She might have made her fortune as a hactress."

ii

Bella waited and hoped, and listened for the postman's knocks which brought such store of letters for the parlors and the first floor, and so few for that humble second floor, where mother and daughter sat sewing with hand and with wheel and treadle, for the greater part of the day.

Mrs. Rolleston was a lady by birth and education; but it had been her bad fortune to marry a scoundrel; for the last half-dozen years she had been that worst of widows, a wife whose husband had deserted her. Happily, she was courageous, industrious, and a clever needlewoman; and she had been able just to earn a living for herself and her only child, by making mantles and cloaks for a West End house. It was not a luxurious living. Cheap lodgings in a shabby street off the Walworth Road, scanty dinners, homely food, well-worn raiment, had been the portion of mother and daughter; but they loved each other so dearly, and Nature had made them both so light-hearted, that they had contrived somehow to be happy.

But now this idea of going out into the world as companion to some fine lady had rooted itself into Bella's mind, and although she idolized her mother, and although the parting of mother and daughter must needs tear two loving hearts into shreds, the girl longed for enterprise and change and excitement, as the pages of old longed to be knights, and to start for the Holy Land to break a lance with the infidel.

She grew tired of racing downstairs every time the postman knocked, only to be told "nothing for you, miss," by the smudgy-faced drudge who picked up the letters from the passage floor.

"Nothing for you, miss," grinned the lodging-house drudge, till at last Bella took heart of grace and walked up to Harbeck Street, and asked the Superior Person how it was that no situation had been found for her.

"You are too young," said the Person, "and you want a salary."

"Of course I do," answered Bella; "don't other people want salaries?"

"Young ladies of your age generally want a comfortable home."

"I don't," snapped Bella; "I want to help Mother."

"You can call again this day week," said the Person; "or, if I hear of anything in the meantime, I will write to you."

No letter came from the Person, and in exactly a week Bella put on her neatest hat, the one that had been seldomest caught in the rain, and trudged off to Harbeck Street.

It was a dull October afternoon, and there was a grayness in the air which might turn to fog before night. The Walworth Road shops gleamed brightly through that gray atmosphere, and though to a young lady reared

in Mayfair or Belgravia such shop-windows would have been unworthy
of a glance, they were a snare and temptation for Bella. There were so
many things that she longed for, and would never be able to buy.

Harbeck Street is apt to be empty at this dead season of the year, a long,
long street, an endless perspective of eminently respectable houses. The
Person's office was at the further end, and Bella looked down that long,
gray vista almost despairingly, more tired than usual with the trudge from
Walworth. As she looked, a carriage passed her, an old-fashioned, yellow chariot, on cee springs, drawn by a pair of high gray horses, with the
stateliest of coachmen driving them, and a tall footman sitting by his side.

It looks like the fairy godmother's coach, thought Bella. *I shouldn't wonder
if it began by being a pumpkin.*

It was a surprise when she reached the Person's door to find the yellow
chariot standing before it, and the tall footman waiting near the doorstep.
She was almost afraid to go in and meet the owner of that splendid carriage. She had caught only a glimpse of its occupant as the chariot rolled
by, a plumed bonnet, a patch of ermine.

The Person's smart page ushered her upstairs and knocked at the official door. "Miss Rolleston," he announced, apologetically, while Bella
waited outside.

"Show her in," said the Person, quickly; and then Bella heard her murmuring something in a low voice to her client.

Bella went in fresh, blooming, a living image of youth and hope, and
before she looked at the Person her gaze was riveted by the owner of the
chariot.

Never had she seen anyone as old as the old lady sitting by the Person's
fire: a little old figure, wrapped from chin to feet in an ermine mantle; a
withered, old face under a plumed bonnet—a face so wasted by age that
it seemed only a pair of eyes and a peaked chin. The nose was peaked,
too, but between the sharply-pointed chin and the great, shining eyes, the
small, aquiline nose was hardly visible.

"This is Miss Rolleston, Lady Ducayne."

Claw-like fingers, flashing with jewels, lifted a double eyeglass to Lady
Ducayne's shining black eyes, and through the glasses Bella saw those
unnaturally bright eyes magnified to a gigantic size, and glaring at her
awfully.

"Miss Torpinter has told me all about you," said the old voice that belonged
to the eyes. "Have you good health? Are you strong and active, able to eat
well, sleep well, walk well, able to enjoy all that there is good in life?"

"I have never known what it is to be ill, or idle," answered Bella.

"Then I think you will do for me."

"Of course, in the event of references being perfectly satisfactory," put in the Person.

"I don't want references. The young woman looks frank and innocent. I'll take her on trust."

"So like you, dear Lady Ducayne," murmured Miss Torpinter.

"I want a strong young woman whose health will give me no trouble."

"You have been so unfortunate in that respect," cooed the Person, whose voice and manner were subdued to a melting sweetness by the old woman's presence.

"Yes, I've been rather unlucky," grunted Lady Ducayne.

"But I am sure Miss Rolleston will not disappoint you, though certainly after your unpleasant experience with Miss Tomson, who looked the picture of health—and Miss Blandy, who said she had never seen a doctor since she was vaccinated—"

"Lies, no doubt," muttered Lady Ducayne, and then turning to Bella, she asked, curtly, "You don't mind spending the winter in Italy, I suppose?"

In Italy! The very word was magical. Bella's fair young face flushed crimson.

"It has been the dream of my life to see Italy," she gasped.

From Walworth to Italy! How far, how impossible such a journey had seemed to that romantic dreamer.

"Well, your dream will be realized. Get yourself ready to leave Charing Cross by the train deluxe this day week at eleven. Be sure you are at the station a quarter before the hour. My people will look after you and your luggage."

Lady Ducayne rose from her chair, assisted by her crutch-stick, and Miss Torpinter escorted her to the door.

"And with regard to salary?" questioned the Person on the way.

"Salary, oh, the same as usual—and if the young woman wants a quarter's pay in advance you can write to me for a check," Lady Ducayne answered, carelessly.

Miss Torpinter went all the way downstairs with her client, and waited to see her seated in the yellow chariot. When she came upstairs again she was slightly out of breath, and she had resumed that superior manner which Bella had found so crushing.

"You may think yourself uncommonly lucky, Miss Rolleston," she said. "I have dozens of young ladies on my books whom I might have recommended for this situation—but I remembered having told you to call this afternoon—and I thought I would give you a chance. Old Lady Ducayne is one of the best people on my books. She gives her companion a hundred a year, and pays all travelling expenses. You will live in the lap of luxury."

"A hundred a year! How too lovely! Shall I have to dress very grandly? Does Lady Ducayne keep much company?"

"At her age! No, she lives in seclusion—in her own apartments—her French maid, her footman, her medical attendant, her courier."

"Why did those other companions leave her?" asked Bella.

"Their health broke down!"

"Poor things, and so they had to leave?"

"Yes, they had to leave. I suppose you would like a quarter's salary in advance?"

"Oh, yes, please. I shall have things to buy."

"Very well, I will write for Lady Ducayne's check, and I will send you the balance—after deducting my commission for the year."

"To be sure, I had forgotten the commission."

"You don't suppose I keep this office for pleasure."

"Of course not," murmured Bella, remembering the five shillings entrance fee; but nobody could expect a hundred a year and a winter in Italy for five shillings.

iii

From Miss Rolleston, at Cap Ferrino, to Mrs. Rolleston, in Beresford Street, Walworth.

How I wish you could see this place, dearest; the blue sky, the olive woods, the orange and lemon orchards between the cliffs and the sea—sheltering in the hollow of the great hills—and with summer waves dancing up to the narrow ridge of pebbles and weeds which is the Italian idea of a beach! Oh, how I wish you could see it all, mother dear, and bask in this sunshine, that makes it so difficult to believe the date at the head of this paper. November! The air is like an English June—the sun is so hot that I can't walk a few yards without an umbrella. And to think of you at Walworth while I am here! I could cry at the thought that perhaps you will never see this lovely coast, this wonderful sea, these summer flowers that bloom in winter. There is a hedge of pink geraniums under my window, mother—a thick, rank hedge, as if the flowers grew wild—and there are Dijon roses climbing over arches and palisades all along the terrace-a rose garden full of bloom in November! Just picture it all! You could never imagine the luxury of this hotel. It is nearly new, and has been built and decorated regardless of expense. Our rooms are upholstered in pale blue satin, which shows up Lady Ducayne's parchment complexion; but as she sits all day in a corner of the balcony basking in the sun, except when she is in her carriage, and all the evening in her armchair close to the fire, and never sees anyone but her own people, her complexion matters very little.

She has the handsomest suite of rooms in the hotel. My bedroom is inside hers, the sweetest room—all blue satin and white lace—white enameled furniture, looking-glasses on every wall, till I know my pert little profile as I never knew it before. The room was really meant for Lady Ducayne's dressing-room, but she ordered one of the blue satin couches to be arranged as a bed for me—the prettiest little bed, which I can wheel near the window on sunny mornings, as it is on castors and easily moved about. I feel as if Lady Ducayne were a funny old grandmother, who had suddenly appeared in my life, very, very rich, and very, very kind.

She is not at all exacting. I read aloud to her a good deal, and she dozes and nods while I read. Sometimes I hear her moaning in her sleep—as if she had troublesome dreams. When she is tired of my reading she orders Francine, her maid, to read a French novel to her, and I hear her chuckle and groan now and then, as if she were more interested in those books than in Dickens or Scott. My French is not good enough to follow Francine, who reads very quickly. I have a great deal of liberty, for Lady Ducayne often tells me to run away and amuse myself; I roam about the hills for hours. Everything is so lovely. I lose myself in olive woods, always climbing up and up towards the pine woods above—and above the pines there are the snow mountains that just show their white peaks above the dark hills. Oh, you poor dear, how can I ever make you understand what this place is like—you, whose poor, tired eyes have only the opposite side of Beresford Street? Sometimes I go no farther than the terrace in front of the hotel, which is a favorite lounging-place with everybody. The gardens lie below, and the tennis courts where I sometimes play with a very nice girl, the only person in the hotel with whom I have made friends. She is a year older than I, and has come to Cap Ferrino with her brother, a doctor—or a medical student, who is going to be a doctor. He passed his M.B. exam at Edinburgh just before they left home, Lotta told me. He came to Italy entirely on his sister's account. She had a troublesome chest attack last summer and was ordered to winter abroad. They are orphans, quite alone in the world, and so fond of each other. It is very nice for me to have such a friend as Lotta. She is so thoroughly respectable. I can't help using that word, for some of the girls in this hotel go on in a way that I know you would shudder at. Lotta was brought up by an aunt, deep down in the country, and knows hardly anything about life. Her brother won't allow her to read a novel, French or English, that he has not read and approved.

"He treats me like a child," she told me, "but I don't mind, for it's nice to know somebody loves me, and cares about what I do, and even about my thoughts."

Perhaps this is what makes some girls so eager to marry—the want of someone strong and brave and honest and true to care for them and order them about.

I want no one, mother darling, for I have you, and you are all the world to me. No husband could ever come between us two. If I ever were to marry he would have only the second place in my heart. But I don't suppose I ever shall marry, or even know what it is like to have an offer of marriage. No young man can afford to marry a penniless girl nowadays. Life is too expensive.

Mr. Stafford, Lotta's brother, is very clever, and very kind. He thinks it is rather hard for me to have to live with such an old woman as Lady Ducayne, but then he does not know how poor we are—you and I—and what a wonderful life this seems to me in this lovely place. I feel a selfish wretch for enjoying all my luxuries, while you, who want them so much more than I, have none of them—hardly know what they are like—do you, dearest?—for my scamp of a father began to go to the dogs soon after you were married, and since then life has been all trouble and care and struggle for you.

This letter was written when Bella had been less than a month at Cap Ferrino, before the novelty had worn off the landscape, and before the pleasure of luxurious surroundings had begun to cloy. She wrote to her mother every week, such long letters as girls who have lived in closest companionship with a mother alone can write; letters that are like a diary of heart and mind. She wrote gaily always; but when the new year began Mrs. Rolleston thought she detected a note of melancholy under all those lively details about the place and the people.

My poor girl is getting homesick, she thought. *Her heart is in Beresford Street.*

It might be that she missed her new friend and companion, Lotta Stafford, who had gone with her brother for a little tour to Genoa and Spezzia, and as far as Pisa. They were to return before February; but in the meantime Bella might naturally feel very solitary among all those strangers, whose manners and doings she described so well.

The mother's instinct had been true. Bella was not so happy as she had been in that first flush of wonder and delight which followed the change from Walworth to the Riviera. Somehow, she knew not how, lassitude had crept upon her. She no longer loved to climb the hills, no longer flourished her orange stick in sheer gladness of heart as her light feet skipped over the rough ground and the coarse grass on the mountain side. The odor of rosemary and thyme, the fresh breath of the sea, no longer filled her with rapture. She thought of Beresford Street and her mother's face with a sick longing. They were so far—so far away! And then she thought of Lady Ducayne, sitting by the heaped-up olive logs in the overheated salon—thought of that wizened-nutcracker profile, and those gleaming eyes, with an invincible horror.

Visitors at the hotel had told her that the air of Cap Ferrino was relaxing—better suited to age than to youth, to sickness than to health. No doubt it was so. She was not so well as she had been at Walworth; but she told herself that she was suffering only from the pain of separation from the dear companion of her girlhood, the mother who had been nurse, sister, friend, flatterer, all things in this world to her. She had shed many tears over that parting, had spent many a melancholy hour on the marble terrace with yearning eyes looking westward, and with her heart's desire a thousand miles away.

She was sitting in her favorite spot, an angle at the eastern end of the terrace, a quiet little nook sheltered by orange trees, when she heard a couple of Riviera habitués talking in the garden below. They were sitting on a bench against the terrace wall.

She had no idea of listening to their talk, till the sound of Lady Ducayne's name attracted her, and then she listened without any thought of wrong-doing. They were talking no secrets—just casually discussing a hotel acquaintance.

They were two elderly people whom Bella only knew by sight. An English clergyman who had wintered abroad for half his lifetime; a stout, comfortable, well-to-do spinster, whose chronic bronchitis obliged her to migrate annually.

"I have met her about Italy for the last ten years," said the lady; "but have never found out her real age."

"I put her down at a hundred—not a year less," replied the parson. "Her reminiscences all go back to the Regency. She was evidently then in her zenith; and I have heard her say things that showed she was in Parisian society when the First Empire was at its best—before Josephine was divorced."

"She doesn't talk much now."

"No; there's not much life left in her. She is wise in keeping herself secluded. I only wonder that wicked old quack, her Italian doctor, didn't finish her off years ago."

"I should think it must be the other way, and that he keeps her alive."

"My dear Miss Manders, do you think foreign quackery ever kept anybody alive?"

"Well, there she is—and she never goes anywhere without him. He certainly has an unpleasant countenance."

"Unpleasant," echoed the parson, "I don't believe the foul fiend himself can beat him in ugliness. I pity that poor young woman who has to live between old Lady Ducayne and Dr. Parravicini."

"But the old lady is very good to her companions."

"No doubt. She is very free with her cash; the servants call her good Lady Ducayne. She is a withered old female Croesus, and knows she'll never be able to get through her money, and doesn't relish the idea of other people enjoying it when she's in her coffin. People who live to be as old as she is become slavishly attached to life. I daresay she's generous to those poor girls—but she can't make them happy. They die in her service."

"Don't say they, Mr. Carton; I know that one poor girl died at Mentone last spring."

"Yes, and another poor girl died in Rome three years ago. I was there at the time. Good Lady Ducayne left her there in an English family. The girl had every comfort. The old woman was very liberal to her—but she died. I tell you, Miss Manders, it is not good for any young woman to live with two such horrors as Lady Ducayne and Parravicini."

They talked of other things—but Bella hardly heard them. She sat motionless, and a cold wind seemed to come down upon her from the mountains and to creep up to her from the sea, till she shivered as she sat there in the sunshine, in the shelter of the orange trees in the midst of all that beauty and brightness.

Yes, they were uncanny, certainly, the pair of them—she so like an aristocratic witch in her withered old age; he of no particular age, with a face that was more like a waxen mask than any human countenance Bella had ever seen. What did it matter? Old age is venerable, and worthy of all reverence; and Lady Ducayne had been very kind to her. Dr. Parravicini was a harmless, inoffensive student, who seldom looked up from the book he was reading. He had his private sitting-room, where he made experiments in chemistry and natural science—perhaps in alchemy. What could it matter to Bella? He had always been polite to her, in his far-off way. She could not be more happily placed than she was—in this palatial hotel, with this rich old lady.

No doubt she missed the young English girl who had been so friendly, and it might be that she missed the girl's brother, for Mr. Stafford had talked to her a good deal—had interested himself in the books she was reading, and her manner of amusing herself when she was not on duty.

"You must come to our little salon when you are 'off,' as the hospital nurses call it, and we can have some music. No doubt you play and sing?" Upon which Bella had to own with a blush of shame that she had forgotten how to play the piano ages ago.

"Mother and I used to sing duets sometimes between the lights, without accompaniment," she said, and the tears came into her eyes as she thought of the humble room, the half-hour's respite from work, the sewing-machine standing where a piano ought to have been, and her mother's plaintive voice, so sweet, so true, so dear.

Sometimes she found herself wondering whether she would ever see that beloved mother again. Strange forebodings came into her mind. She was angry with herself for giving way to melancholy thoughts.

One day she questioned Lady Ducayne's French maid about those two companions who had died within three years.

"They were poor, feeble creatures," Francine told her. "They looked fresh and bright enough when they came to Miladi; but they ate too much and they were lazy. They died of luxury and idleness. Miladi was too kind to them. They had nothing to do; and so they took to fancying things; fancying the air didn't suit them, that they couldn't sleep."

"I sleep well enough, but I have had a strange dream several times since I have been in Italy."

"Ah, you had better not begin to think about dreams, or you will be like those other girls. They were dreamers—and they dreamt themselves into the cemetery."

The dream troubled her a little, not because it was a ghastly or frightening dream, but on account of sensations which she had never felt before in sleep—a whirring of wheels that went round in her brain, a great noise like a whirlwind, but rhythmical like the ticking of a gigantic clock: and then in the midst of this uproar as of winds and waves she seemed to sink into a gulf of unconsciousness, out of sleep into far deeper sleep—total extinction. And then, after that blank interval, there had come the sound of voices, and then again the whirr of wheels, louder and louder—and again the blank—and then she knew no more till morning, when she awoke, feeling languid and oppressed.

She told Dr. Parravicini of her dream one day, on the only occasion when she wanted his professional advice. She had suffered rather severely from the mosquitoes before Christmas—and had been almost frightened at finding a wound upon her arm which she could only attribute to the venomous sting of one of these torturers. Parravicini put on his glasses, and scrutinized the angry mark on the round, white arm, as Bella stood before him and Lady Ducayne with her sleeve rolled up above her elbow.

"Yes, that's rather more than a joke," he said, "he has caught you on the top of a vein. What a vampire! But there's no harm done, *signorina*, nothing that a little dressing of mine won't heal.

"You must always show me any bite of this nature. It might be dangerous if neglected. These creatures feed on poison and disseminate it."

"And to think that such tiny creatures can bite like this," said Bella; "my arm looks as if it had been cut by a knife."

"If I were to show you a mosquito's sting under my microscope you wouldn't be surprised at that," replied Parravicini.

Bella had to put up with the mosquito bites, even when they came on the top of a vein, and produced that ugly wound. The wound recurred now and then at longish intervals, and Bella found Dr. Parravicini's dressing a speedy cure. If he were the quack his enemies called him, he had at least a light hand and a delicate touch in performing this small operation.

Bella Rolleston to Mrs. Rolleston—April 14th.

EVER DEAREST,

Behold the check for my second quarter's salary—five and twenty pounds. There is no one to pinch off a whole tenner for a year's commission as there was last time, so it is all for you, mother, dear. I have plenty of pocket-money in hand from the cash I brought away with me, when you insisted on my keeping more than I wanted. It isn't possible to spend money here—except on occasional tips to servants, or sous to beggars and children—unless one had lots to spend, for everything one would like to buy—tortoise-shell, coral, lace—is so ridiculously dear that only a millionaire ought to look at it. Italy is a dream of beauty: but for shopping, give me Newington Causeway.

You ask me so earnestly if I am quite well that I fear my letters must have been very dull lately. Yes, dear, I am well—but I am not quite so strong as I was when I used to trudge to the West End to buy half a pound of tea—just for a constitutional walk—or to Dulwich to look at the pictures. Italy is relaxing; and I feel what the people here call "slack." But I fancy I can see your dear face looking worried as you read this. Indeed, and indeed, I am not ill. I am only a little tired of this lovely scene—as I suppose one might get tired of looking at one of Turner's pictures if it hung on a wall that was always opposite one. I think of you every hour in every day—think of you and our homely little room—our dear little shabby parlor, with the armchairs from the wreck of your old home, and Dick singing in his cage over the sewing-machine. Dear, shrill, maddening Dick, who, we flattered ourselves, was so passionately fond of us. Do tell me in your next that he is well.

My friend Lotta and her brother never came back after all. They went from Pisa to Rome. Happy mortals! And they are to be on the Italian lakes in May; which lake was not decided when Lotta last wrote to me. She has been a charming correspondent, and has confided all her little flirtations to me. We are all to go to Bellaggio next week—by Genoa and Milan. Isn't that lovely? Lady Ducayne travels by the easiest stages—except when she is bottled up in the train deluxe. We shall stop two days at Genoa and one at Milan. What a bore I shall be to you with my talk about Italy when I come home.

Love and love—and ever more love from your adoring, BELLA

IV

Herbert Stafford and his sister had often talked of the pretty English girl with her fresh complexion, which made such a pleasant touch of rosy color among all those sallow faces at the Grand Hotel. The young doctor thought of her with a compassionate tenderness—her utter loneliness in that great hotel where there were so many people, her bondage to that old, old woman, where everybody else was free to think of nothing but enjoying life. It was a hard fate; and the poor child was evidently devoted to her mother, and felt the pain of separation—*only two of them, and very poor, and all the world to each other*, he thought.

Lotta told him one morning that they were to meet again at Bellaggio. "The old thing and her court are to be there before we are," she said. "I shall be charmed to have Bella again. She is so bright and gay—in spite of an occasional touch of homesickness. I never took to a girl on a short acquaintance as I did to her."

"I like her best when she is homesick," said Herbert; "for then I am sure she has a heart."

"What have you to do with hearts, except for dissection? Don't forget that Bella is an absolute pauper. She told me in confidence that her mother makes mantles for a West End shop. You can hardly have a lower depth than that."

"I shouldn't think any less of her if her mother made matchboxes."

"Not in the abstract—of course not. Matchboxes are honest labor. But you couldn't marry a girl whose mother makes mantles."

"We haven't come to the consideration of that question yet," answered Herbert, who liked to provoke his sister.

In two years' hospital practice he had seen too much of the grim realities of life to retain any prejudices about rank. Cancer, phthisis, gangrene, leave a man with little respect for the outward differences which vary the husk of humanity. The kernel is always the same—fearfully and wonderfully made—a subject for pity and terror.

Mr. Stafford and his sister arrived at Bellaggio in a fair May evening. The sun was going down as the steamer approached the pier; and all that glory of purple bloom which curtains every wall at this season of the year flushed and deepened in the glowing light. A group of ladies were standing on the pier watching the arrivals, and among them Herbert saw a pale face that startled him out of his wonted composure.

"There she is," murmured Lotta, at his elbow, "but how dreadfully changed. She looks a wreck."

They were shaking hands with her a few minutes later, and a flush had lighted up her poor pinched face in the pleasure of meeting.

"I thought you might come this evening," she said. "We have been here a week."

She did not add that she had been there every evening to watch the boat in, and a good many times during the day. The Grand Bretagne was close by, and it had been easy for her to creep to the pier when the boat bell rang. She felt a joy in meeting these people again; a sense of being with friends; a confidence which Lady Ducayne's goodness had never inspired in her.

"Oh, you poor darling, how awfully ill you must have been," exclaimed Lotta, as the two girls embraced.

Bella tried to answer, but her voice was choked with tears.

"What has been the matter, dear? That horrid influenza, I suppose?"

"No, no, I have not been ill—I have only felt a little weaker than I used to be. I don't think the air of Cap Ferrino quite agreed with me."

"It must have disagreed with you abominably. I never saw such a change in anyone. Do let Herbert doctor you. He is fully qualified, you know. He prescribed for ever so many influenza patients at the Londres. They were glad to get advice from an English doctor in a friendly way."

"I am sure he must be very clever!" faltered Bella, "but there is really nothing the matter. I am not ill, and if I were ill, Lady Ducayne's physician—"

"That dreadful man with the yellow face? I would as soon one of the Borgias prescribed for me. I hope you haven't been taking any of his medicines."

"No, dear, I have taken nothing. I have never complained of being ill."

This was said while they were all three walking to the hotel. The Staffords' rooms had been secured in advance, pretty ground-floor rooms, opening into the garden. Lady Ducayne's statelier apartments were on the floor above.

"I believe these rooms are just under ours," said Bella.

"Then it will be all the easier for you to run down to us," replied Lotta, which was not really the case, as the grand staircase was in the center of the hotel.

"Oh, I shall find it easy enough," said Bella. "I'm afraid you'll have too much of my society. Lady Ducayne sleeps away half the day in this warm weather, so I have a good deal of idle time; and I get awfully moped thinking of mother and home."

Her voice broke upon the last word. She could not have thought of that poor lodging which went by the name of home more tenderly had it been the most beautiful that art and wealth ever created. She moped and pined in this lovely garden, with the sunlit lake and the romantic hills spreading out their beauty before her. She was homesick and she had dreams: or, rather, an occasional recurrence of that one bad dream with all its strange sensations—it was more like a hallucination than dreaming— the whirring of wheels; the sinking into an abyss; the struggling back to consciousness. She had the dream shortly before she left Cap Ferrino, but not since she had come to Bellaggio, and she began to hope the air in this lake district suited her better, and that those strange sensations would never return.

Mr. Stafford wrote a prescription and had it made up at the chemist's near the hotel. It was a powerful tonic, and after two bottles, and a row or two on the lake, and some rambling over the hills and in the meadows where the spring flowers made earth seem paradise, Bella's spirits and looks improved as if by magic.

"It is a wonderful tonic," she said, but perhaps in her heart of hearts she knew that the doctor's kind voice and the friendly hand that helped her in and out of the boat, and the watchful care that went with her by land and lake, had something to do with her cure.

"I hope you don't forget that her mother makes mantles," Lotta said, warningly.

"Or matchboxes: it is just the same thing, so far as I am concerned."

"You mean that in no circumstances could you think of marrying her?"

"I mean that if ever I love a woman well enough to think of marrying her, riches or rank will count for nothing with me. But I fear—I fear your poor friend may not live to be any man's wife."

"Do you think her so very ill?"

He sighed, and left the question unanswered.

One day, while they were gathering wild hyacinths in an upland meadow, Bella told Mr. Stafford about her bad dream.

"It is curious only because it is hardly like a dream," she said. "I daresay you could find some common-sense reason for it. The position of my head on my pillow, or the atmosphere, or something."

And then she described her sensations; how in the midst of sleep there came a sudden sense of suffocation; and then those whirring wheels, so loud, so terrible; and then a blank, and then a coming back to waking consciousness.

"Have you ever had chloroform given you—by a dentist, for instance?"

"Never—Dr. Parravicini asked me that question one day."

"Lately?"

"No, long ago, when we were in the train deluxe."

"Has Dr. Parravicini prescribed for you since you began to feel weak and ill?"

"Oh, he has given me a tonic from time to time, but I hate medicine, and took very little of the stuff. And then I am not ill, only weaker than I used to be. I was ridiculously strong and well when I lived at Walworth, and used to take long walks every day. Mother made me take those tramps to Dulwich or Norwood, for fear I should suffer from too much sewing-machine; sometimes—but very seldom—she went with me. She was generally toiling at home while I was enjoying fresh air and exercise. And she was very careful about our food—that, however plain it was, it should be always nourishing and ample. I owe at to her care that I grew up such a great, strong creature."

"You don't look great or strong now, you poor dear," said Lotta.

"I'm afraid Italy doesn't agree with me."

"Perhaps it is not Italy, but being cooped up with Lady Ducayne that has made you ill."

"But I am never cooped up. Lady Ducayne is absurdly kind, and lets me roam about or sit in the balcony all day if I like. I have read more novels since I have been with her than in all the rest of my life."

"Then she is very different from the average old lady, who is usually a slave-driver," said Stafford. "I wonder why she carries a companion about with her if she has so little need of society."

"Oh, I am only part of her state. She is inordinately rich—and the salary she gives me doesn't count. *Apropos* of Dr. Parravicini, I know he is a clever doctor, for he cures my horrid mosquito bites."

"A little ammonia would do that, in the early stage of the mischief. But there are no mosquitoes to trouble you now."

"Oh, yes, there are, I had a bite just before we left Cap Ferrino." She pushed up her loose lawn sleeve, and exhibited a scar, which he scrutinized intently, with a surprised and puzzled look.

"This is no mosquito bite," he said.

"Oh, yes it is—unless there are snakes or adders at Cap Ferrino."

"It is not a bite at all. You are trifling with me. Miss Rolleston—you have allowed that wretched Italian quack to bleed you. They killed the greatest man in modern Europe that way, remember. How very foolish of you."

"I was never bled in my life, Mr. Stafford."

"Nonsense! Let me look at your other arm. Are there any more mosquito bites?"

"Yes; Dr. Parravicini says I have a bad skin for healing, and that the poison acts more virulently with me than with most people."

Stafford examined both her arms in the broad sunlight, scars new and old.

"You have been very badly bitten, Miss Rolleston," he said, "and if ever I find the mosquito I shall make him smart. But, now tell me, my dear girl, on your word of honor, tell me as you would tell a friend who is sincerely anxious for your health and happiness—as you would tell your mother if she were here to question you—have you no knowledge of any cause for these scars except mosquito bites—no suspicion even?"

"No, indeed! No, upon my honor! I have never seen a mosquito biting my arm. One never does see the horrid little fiends. But I have heard them trumpeting under the curtains, and I know that I have often had one of the pestilent wretches buzzing about me."

Later in the day Bella and her friends were sitting at tea in the garden, while Lady Ducayne took her afternoon drive with her doctor.

"How long do you mean to stop with Lady Ducayne, Miss Rolleston?" Herbert Stafford asked, after a thoughtful silence, breaking suddenly upon the trivial talk of the two girls.

"As long as she will go on paying me twenty-five pounds a quarter."

"Even if you feel your health breaking down in her service?"

"It is not the service that has injured my health. You can see that I have really nothing to do—to read aloud for an hour or so once or twice a week; to write a letter once in a way to a London tradesman. I shall never have such an easy time with anybody else. And nobody else would give me a hundred a year."

"Then you mean to go on till you break down; to die at your post?"

"Like the other two companions? No! If ever I feel seriously ill—really ill—I shall put myself in a train and go back to Walworth without stopping."

"What about the other two companions?"

"They both died. It was very unlucky for Lady Ducayne. That's why she engaged me; she chose me because I was ruddy and robust. She must feel rather disgusted at my having grown white and weak. By-the-bye, when I told her about the good your tonic had done me, she said she would like to see you and have a little talk with you about her own case."

"And I should like to see Lady Ducayne. When did she say this?"

"The day before yesterday."

"Will you ask her if she will see me this evening?"

"With pleasure I wonder what you will think of her? She looks rather terrible to a stranger; but Dr. Parravicini says she was once a famous beauty."

It was nearly ten o'clock when Mr. Stafford was summoned by message from Lady Ducayne, whose courier came to conduct him to her ladyship's salon. Bella was reading aloud when the visitor was admitted; and he noticed the languor in the low, sweet tones, the evident effort.

"Shut up the book," said the querulous old voice. "You are beginning to drawl like Miss Blandy."

Stafford saw a small, bent figure crouching over the piled-up olive logs; a shrunken old figure in a gorgeous garment of black and crimson brocade, a skinny throat emerging from a mass of old Venetian lace, clasped with diamonds that flashed like fireflies as the trembling old head turned toward him.

The eyes that looked at him out of the face were almost as bright as the diamonds—the only living feature in that narrow parchment mask. He had seen terrible faces in the hospital—faces on which disease had set dreadful marks—but he had never seen a face that impressed him so painfully as this withered countenance, with its indescribable horror of death outlived, a face that should have been hidden under a coffin-lid years and years ago.

The Italian physician was standing on the other side of the fireplace, smoking a cigarette, and looking down at the little old woman brooding over the hearth as if he were proud of her.

"Good evening, Mr. Stafford; you can go to your room, Bella, and write your everlasting letter to your mother at Walworth," said Lady Ducayne. "I believe she writes a page about every wildflower she discovers in the woods and meadows. I don't know what else she can find to write about," she added, as Bella quietly withdrew to the pretty little bedroom opening out of Lady Ducayne's spacious apartment. Here, as at Cap Ferrino, she slept in a room adjoining the old lady's.

"You are a medical man, I understand, Mr. Stafford."

"I am a qualified practitioner, but I have not begun to practice."

"You have begun upon my companion, she tells me."

"I have prescribed for her, certainly, and I am happy to find my prescription has done her good; but I look upon that improvement as temporary. Her case will require more drastic treatment."

"Never mind her case. There is nothing the matter with the girl—absolutely nothing—except girlish nonsense; too much liberty and not enough work."

"I understand that two of your ladyship's previous companions died of the same disease," said Stafford, looking first at Lady Ducayne, who gave her tremulous old head an impatient jerk, and then at Parravicini, whose yellow complexion had paled a little under Stafford's scrutiny.

"Don't bother me about my companions, sir," said Lady Ducayne. "I sent for you to consult you about myself—not about a parcel of anemic girls. You are young, and medicine is a progressive science, the newspapers tell me. Where have you studied?"

"In Edinburgh—and in Paris."

"Two good schools. And you know all the newfangled theories, the modern discoveries—that remind one of the medieval witchcraft, of Albertus Magnus, and George Ripley; you have studied hypnotism—electricity?"

"And the transfusion of blood," said Stafford, very slowly, looking at Parravicini.

"Have you made any discovery that teaches you to prolong human life—any elixir—any mode of treatment? I want my life prolonged, young man. That man there has been my physician for thirty years. He does all he can to keep me alive—after his lights. He studies all the new theories of all the scientists—but he is old; he gets older every day—his brain-power is going—he is bigoted—prejudiced—can't receive new ideas—can't grapple with new systems. He will let me die if I am not on my guard against him."

"You are of an unbelievable ingratitude, Ecclenza," said Parravicini.

"Oh, you needn't complain. I have paid you thousands to keep me alive. Every year of my life has swollen your hoards; you know there is nothing to come to you when I am gone. My whole fortune is left to endow a home for indigent women of quality who have reached their ninetieth year. Come, Mr. Stafford, I am a rich woman. Give me a few years more in the sunshine, a few years more aboveground, and I will give you the price of a fashionable London practice—I will set you up at the West End."

"How old are you, Lady Ducayne?"

"I was born the day Louis XVI was guillotined."

"Then I think you have had your share of the sunshine and the pleasures of the earth, and that you should spend your few remaining days in repenting your sins and trying to make atonement for the young lives that have been sacrificed to your love of life."

"What do you mean by that, sir?"

"Oh, Lady Ducayne, need I put your wickedness and your physician's still greater wickedness in plain words? The poor girl who is now in your employment has been reduced from robust health to a condition of absolute danger by Dr. Parravicini's experimental surgery; and I have no doubt those other two young women who broke down in your service were treated by him in the same manner. I could take upon myself to demonstrate—by most convincing evidence, to a jury of medical men—that Dr. Parravicini has been bleeding Miss Rolleston, after putting her under chloroform, at intervals, ever since she has been in your service. The deterioration in the girl's health speaks for itself; the lancet marks upon the girl's arms are unmistakable; and her description of a series of sensations, which she calls a dream, points unmistakably to the administration of chloroform while she was sleeping. A practice so nefarious, so murderous, must, if exposed, result in a sentence only less severe than the punishment of murder."

"I laugh," said Parravicini, with an airy motion of his skinny fingers; "I laugh at once at your theories and at your threats. I, Parravicini Leopold, have no fear that the law can question anything I have done."

"Take the girl away, and let me hear no more of her," cried Lady Ducayne, in the thin, old voice, which so poorly matched the energy and fire of the wicked old brain that guided its utterances. "Let her go back to her mother—I want no more girls to die in my service. There are girls enough and to spare in the world, God knows."

"If you ever engage another companion—or take another English girl into your service, Lady Ducayne, I will make all England ring with the story of your wickedness."

"I want no more girls. I don't believe in his experiments. They have been full of danger for me as well as for the girl—an air bubble, and I should be gone. I'll have no more of his dangerous quackery. I'll find some new man—a better man than you, sir, a discoverer like Pasteur, or Virchow, a genius—to keep me alive. Take your girl away, young man. Marry her if you like. I'll write her a check for a thousand pounds, and let her go and live on beef and beer, and get strong and plump again. I'll have no more such experiments. Do you hear, Parravicini?" she screamed, vindictively, the yellow, wrinkled face distorted with fury, the eyes glaring at him.

The Staffords carried Bella Rolleston off to Varese next day, she very loath to leave Lady Ducayne, whose liberal salary afforded such help for the dear mother. Herbert Stafford insisted, however, treating Bella as coolly as if he had been the family physician, and she had been given over wholly to his care.

"Do you suppose your mother would let you stop here to die?" he asked. "If Mrs. Rolleston knew how ill you are, she would come posthaste to fetch you."

"I shall never be well again till I get back to Walworth," answered Bella, who was low-spirited and inclined to tears this morning, a reaction after her good spirits of yesterday.

"We'll try a week or two at Varese first," said Stafford. "When you can walk halfway up Monte Generoso without palpitation of the heart, you shall go back to Walworth."

"Poor mother, how glad she will be to see me, and how sorry that I've lost such a good place."

This conversation took place on the boat when they were leaving Bellaggio. Lotta had gone to her friend's room at seven o'clock that morning, long before Lady Ducayne's withered eyelids had opened to the daylight, before even Francine, the French maid, was astir, and had helped to pack a Gladstone bag with essentials, and hustled Bella downstairs and out of doors before she could make any strenuous resistance.

"It's all right," Lotta assured her. "Herbert had a good talk with Lady Ducayne last night and it was settled for you to leave this morning. She doesn't like invalids, you see."

"No," sighed Bella, "she doesn't like invalids. It was very unlucky that I should break down, just like Miss Tomson and Miss Blandy."

"At any rate, you are not dead, like them," answered Lotta, "and my brother says you are not going to die."

It seemed rather a dreadful thing to be dismissed in that off-hand way, without a word of farewell from her employer.

"I wonder what Miss Torpinter will say when I go to her for another situation," Bella speculated, ruefully, while she and her friends were breakfasting onboard the steamer.

"Perhaps you may never want another situation," said Stafford.

"You mean that I may never be well enough to be useful to anybody?"

"No, I don't mean anything of the kind."

It was after dinner at Varese, when Bella had been induced to take a whole glass of Chianti, and quite sparkled after that unaccustomed stimulant, that Mr. Stafford produced a letter from his pocket.

"I forgot to give you Lady Ducayne's letter of *adieu*," he said.

"What, did she write to me? I am so glad—I hated to leave her in such a cool way; for after all she was very kind to me, and if I didn't like her it was only because she was too dreadfully old."

She tore open the envelope. The letter was short and to the point:

Goodbye, child. Go and marry your doctor. I enclose a farewell gift for your trousseau.

ADELINE DUCAYNE

"A hundred pounds, a whole year's salary—no—why, it's for a—a check for a thousand!" cried Bella. "What a generous old soul! She really is the dearest old thing."

"She just missed being very dear to you, Bella," said Stafford.

He had dropped into the use of her Christian name while they were onboard the boat. It seemed natural now that she was to be in his charge till they all three went back to England.

"I shall take upon myself the privileges of an elder brother till we land at Dover," he said; "after that—well, it must be as you please."

The question of their future relations must have been satisfactorily settled before they crossed the Channel, for Bella's next letter to her mother communicated three startling facts.

First, that the enclosed check for one thousand pounds was to be invested in debenture stock in Mrs. Rolleston's name, and was to be her very own, income and principal, for the rest of her life.

Next, that Bella was going home to Walworth immediately.

And last, that she was going to be married to Mr. Herbert Stafford in the following autumn.

And I am sure you will adore him, mother, as much as I do, wrote Bella. *It is all good Lady Ducayne's doing. I never could have married if I had not secured that little nest-egg for you. Herbert says we shall be able to add to it as the years go by, and that wherever we live there shall be always a room in our house for you. The word "mother-in-law" has no terrors for him.*

Lunch at Charon's

Melanie Tem

Melanie Tem (1949–2015) was presented with the British Fantasy Society's Icarus Award for Most Promising Newcomer in 1992. Her short fiction is collected in *The Ice Downstream* and *Singularities*, while *In Concert* and the Bram Stoker Award–winning *Imagination Box* both featured collaborations with her husband, the writer Steve Rasnic Tem.

The couple also collaborated on the multiple award–winning novella "The Man on the Ceiling," which they later expanded into a full-length work, and another novel entitled *Daughters*. Melanie Tem's solo novels include the Stoker Award–winning *Prodigal*, *Blood Moon*, *The Wilding*, *Revenant*, *Desmodus*, *Tides*, *Black River*, *Slain in the Spirit*, *The Deceiver*, *The Yellow Wood* and two collaborations with Nancy Holder, *Making Love* and *Witch-Light*.

About "Lunch at Charon's," the author explained: "My eighty-three-year-old friend is expected to be flattered when people tell her she doesn't look her age. My twenty-five-year-old friend weeps over the first crow's feet at the corner of her eye. My sixty-year-old friend says his body has betrayed him because it's slowing down. Hardly anybody wants to call death out of the shadows and make friends with it.

"All this has something to do with the vampire mythos, I think, and also something to do with the genesis of this story."

AMY ALGHIERI IS dead.

That's three out of four. Leaving only me.

I heard about Amy at the gym this morning. She didn't work out obviously—but she and my personal trainer Vonda were close; Amy'd been Vonda's physics professor in college, and a friendship had developed. "A massive stroke," she told me, keeping a critical eye on my workout. "Out of the blue. She was in the grocery store and just collapsed. The baby was in the grocery cart."

Chills raced through me, as happened whenever I heard about something like this: how could you protect yourself against lightning from a clear sky? Reminding myself that what had happened to Amy might not be as random as it seemed only made my horror more complicated.

"God," I panted, grimly maintaining the rhythm of the arm curls and the breathing that supported them, "that's awful."

"Come on, Madyson, focus. Push it."

My given name is a dowdy, old-fashioned moniker common to women of my generation. I think of Madyson as my taken name. Madyson—young, fresh, more appropriate for someone in her twenties than nearing fifty, to go with my taken body and, presumably, my taken soul. I like the sound of it, the way it looks on the page. I like the *y*. I like what it projects about me.

I obeyed Vonda's command and managed to extend my arms ten more times with the weight, heavier than any I'd pressed before, steady in my hands. The burn across my shoulders and pecs was gratifying. Between controlled inhalations and exhalations I said, "That's terrible."

Vonda said, eyeing me critically, trying to do her job but, I saw now, trembling and exhausted. By this point in the workout she would ordinarily have given me both encouragement and instruction; although I understood, of course, why she hadn't this morning, I found myself working harder, pushing harder, going a little beyond the goals she'd set for me, in hopes of catching her attention. It wasn't approval I craved from her so much as assurance—that I was strong and healthy, that I was looking good, that I was doing everything I could.

"She was dead before the paramedics got there."

"Wow." I shuddered, and added quite sincerely, "That's really tragic."

"You never think of somebody in their forties having a stroke."

"It happens," I said carefully, getting up off the mat.

Vonda gave me a quick one-armed hug, the equivalent of men swatting each other's butts. "Okay, you can go to the sauna now."

She turned to leave me for one of her other charges, but I stopped her by demanding shamelessly, "So, how'd I do?"

I had to settle for a distracted, somewhat impatient, "Fine, Madyson. You did fine." She gave me a dismissive wave and strode across the gym. I glared after her, thwarted and insulted, soothing myself with the vitriolic thought that the only interest I had in a relationship with this lithe and self-sufficient young woman was what I could get from her. In the locker room I stripped, noting with pleasure the firmness of my new breasts and the tautness of my ass, reveling in the appraising glances of the other women and thinking about the last time I'd seen Amy.

We met for lunch at Charon's to say goodbye to Kit. We didn't quite acknowledge that. We said it was because Denise was in town and the four of us hadn't been together since she'd moved to Austin. Even when Amy called me to set it up, she didn't say, "This might be the last chance we have to see Kit."

Denise and I had snagged a window table, and I saw Kit's Beemer pull up, her husband behind the wheel. He parked in the handicap space by the door and went around to help Kit out; she hadn't even opened the door. It took long minutes for her to maneuver onto her feet and, leaning on Jerry and visibly off balance, long minutes more before they made it into the restaurant. When a few days earlier I'd spent the evening at her house, she'd felt papery in my arms, like an origami flower; her fingers on my shoulders, though, had been unnervingly strong, a death grip already. Her bones had seemed about to snap under my very light massage, but she'd sighed that it felt so good; fascinated by her absolute hairlessness, I'd rubbed her legs for a long time, gently, envying their incredible smoothness, tempted to lay my cheek against her calf.

Kit had never been beautiful, but her exuberant nature had made her very attractive to a lot of people. We'd met the year we both turned forty-three. She'd just taken up skiing and was learning to clog dance. My breasts had begun to sag and more often than not my lower back hurt. We were in a yoga class together. We took to practicing between classes at her house or mine. When we helped each other with poses—her arm against the small of my back, my hands at her ankles and knees—I first marveled at, then absorbed, then siphoned off the energy I needed. I knew her heart was failing about five years before she did.

Denise had not commented on my appearance beyond a generic, "Hi, Madyson! It's so good to see you! You look great!" while we hugged hello, the kind of thing women routinely say to each other with hardly any actual referent. Most people are surprised by how young I look; Denise said nothing about it. She did not look young. She looked our age. Healthy and strong, I had to admit, but thirty pounds heavier than I'd have settled for and with wrinkles and graying hair it would have been easy to get rid of. The longer I live the less I understand women like her. They give me the creeps.

"There's Kit," I said.

"Where?"

"With the red turban."

"My God." There was a pause while we watched Kit waft the short distance to the door. She hardly seemed to be touching the ground. "She's really sick, isn't she? She's really dying." Her voice broke.

For a moment Denise hid her eyes. I noted the stubby fingernails, clean and coated with clear polish but entirely functional, the nails of a middle-aged mother and grandmother who cooked and cleaned and gardened and played and otherwise put her hands to use. Her lack of self-consciousness about her hands was disgusting, and I looked for solace to my own slim, smooth, tastefully ringed fingers on my glass of iced tea. To my horror, the polish on the right thumb had a minuscule but perfectly obvious chip, and on the left ring finger the cuticle was not perfectly smooth. For the rest of the lunch I did everything possible not to draw attention to my hands, which were usually one of my best features; I'd have to make an emergency call to my manicurist as soon as I got home, since obviously I couldn't wait for the standing weekly appointment.

"It's such a shock to see her like this," Denise said. "You've been with her all through it so you must be almost used to it, but I didn't imagine this. What am I going to say to her?"

Amy came up behind Kit and put a thick arm around her thin waist. Always on the chunky side, Amy had put on even more weight since the last time I'd seen her. Maybe she wouldn't be called obese in any clinical sense, and she certainly wasn't slovenly; her turquoise dress looked nice, and her loose chignon accentuated her flawless skin and wonderful green eyes. But she was fat. The contrast between them was breathtaking: Kit translucent, ethereal, used up; Amy substantial to a fault.

Under the table I rested my hands on my own flattened belly, murmuring to Denise, "I think I'd kill myself if I looked like that." Denise looked at me as if this were a bizarre thing to say.

When Kit and Amy approached the table, Denise sprang to her feet, smiling and overenthusiastically exclaiming, "Hi! Amy! Kit! It's so good to see you! You look great!" She hugged Kit first, very gently, and pulled out a chair for her. After Amy settled her into it, she and Denise embraced; from the stiff angle of Amy's upper body I guessed she was taking pains not to compromise her hair or makeup or clothes just for the sake of human contact, and my estimation of her rose a few notches. Denise, on the other hand, hugged her fiercely, and spent the rest of the lunch with one side of her hair sticking out. How any woman could care so little about her appearance is beyond me.

I smiled at Kit and touched her skeletal wrist. I really did care about her. "Hi," I said softly to her, under the din Denise was making. "How are you doing, sweetie?"

The others had taken their seats before Kit had gathered herself to answer, "I'm tired, Madyson. I don't have much left. I'm almost done."

Without brows or lashes, her facial expressions were all but impossible to interpret, but I thought she looked at me then as if she suspected something, unlikely as that seemed. Guilt broke through and set my stomach roiling, followed by the terror that is never far away. Mortality, which is to say death, took its place with us at the table, and I hurriedly excused myself. As I passed behind Kit, I touched the chill back of her neck, in a gesture of love and apology, gratitude and farewell.

Charon's has a truly remarkable ladies' room. In the spacious anteroom are three-way floor-length mirrors, a long vanity with tissues and cotton balls and individual mirrors, dispensers for lotions and astringent cleansers, little squirt bottles of antistatic and hairspray, nail buffers, a vending machine dispensing individual vials of various scents at a cost per ounce as exorbitant as if it were Parisian perfume. The line for Charon's ladies' room often stretch out the door.

That day only two or three other women were ahead of me, and while I waited I took stock. I'd checked myself at home, of course, as part of my morning regimen, and again at the gym, but you couldn't be too sure. Under cover of smoothing my clothes, I assured myself that the work on stomach, breasts, and buttocks was holding. Thighs below the leather miniskirt were firm and free of varicosity. There was no loose flesh on the backs of upper arms, no crow's feet at the corners of my eyes or mouth. All exposed skin, of which there was a considerable amount, was taut and moist. My hair swung nicely in the simple, youthful shoulder-length bob my hairdresser had recommended, his expert highlights creating exactly the right aura of light and lightness around my face. Although I was still not entirely satisfied with my lips and nose, my brows arched perfectly and my breasts finally were the size and shape I wanted.

But as I regarded myself in every possible mirror and combination of mirrors, I saw death encroaching. Saw my organs aging, my hair graying and thinning, the skin of my elbows wrinkling like dried fruit. Saw the crabwalk of deterioration advancing.

The effort it took to keep all this at bay—one day, one procedure, one friend at a time—was staggering. I could scarcely do anything else.

When on the way back to my friends I caught sight of Kit, faintly nodding at something Amy was saying, I realized I'd had the fantasy that in the time I was absent she'd have slipped away; at the same time, I'd been hoping she'd still be available to me for a little while. Love for her brought tears to my eyes; careful not to smudge my mascara, I dabbed them away. It was plain to see that Kit was now quite beyond my reach. So, regretfully but without hesitation, I turned my attention elsewhere.

Denise had a hefty lunch, including dessert. Amy and I had salads. We chatted stiffly; it was hard to come up with safe conversation with Kit among us. Talking about the future, even next week, seemed ghoulish. Talking about the present made Kit's illness the elephant at the table nobody could forget but nobody mentioned. Talking about our shared past reminded us of what was gone. Kit didn't take part in the conversation much and, although she ordered something, she didn't eat, just took a sip of water now and then, slowly and with great care.

Denise was into a somewhat manic recounting of her recent expedition climbing Colorado's fourteeners. "Not bad for a fifty-one-year-old grandmother, huh?" she crowed more than once. Amy was looking increasingly pained. I guessed that Denise was desperate to fill silence, to talk about anything other than the elephant, but I allowed myself to half-believe that her insensitivity justified what I was about to do.

I stopped behind her and laid my hands on her shoulders. She took it as a warning, which in part it was, and hesitated, then brought her story to a clumsy conclusion and stopped talking. Energy was racing through her body like whitewater. I pushed myself into the stream. She winced. I massaged her shoulders tenderly, employing techniques I'd learned from Vonda to loosen tight muscles and release tension, but my purpose was not to heal.

"Oh," she moaned, wriggling her shoulders sensuously. "That hurts."

"Should I stop?" But I didn't stop. I increased the pressure along her trapezius, then found a knot under her left shoulder blade and dug my knuckle in. She gasped and arched her back. I held steady. After a long moment she relaxed under my hands, I felt the underlying defenses of her body open to me, and we had the first of our exchanges. For me it was like a blood transfusion. For her, it was slow poison.

I released the pressure, swept my hands lightly over her back, and left her with a little pat of affection and regret. She said, "Wow, Madyson, you have really strong hands," and just sat there for a while.

Kit asked Amy, in a voice strong enough to make me wonder if she might have something more to offer me after all, but, tellingly, with no energy to waste on segue,

"When do you get your baby?"

Amy hesitated and looked at me, not sure she ought to go there. I shrugged. "I leave Thursday," she finally said, almost apologetically.

Denise, who'd been staring off into space, roused herself. "Baby?"

"I'm adopting a baby girl from China." Amy kept glancing at Kit and spoke with some reluctance, but the excitement that broke through was contagious. "She was a foundling so they aren't certain of her birth date, but she's about eight months old."

"A baby? At your age? At our age?" Denise shook her head in amazement and, I thought, disapproval. I disapproved, too, but not on the basis of age; while I doubted her weight was a serious health hazard, it seemed to me that one of the criteria for adoption ought to be appearance. After all, who would want a fat mother?

Amy started to defend herself, but I spoke first. "If you can climb fourteeners, *at our age*, why shouldn't Amy be able to adopt a baby?"

"Climbing a mountain takes a long spurt of energy. Raising a kid takes energy 24-7 for at least eighteen years." Denise raised her water glass in Amy's direction. "I could never do it. I'm too old. More power to you, girlfriend."

"Maybe," I said, recklessly, "this is what they mean when they talk about women discovering new power and vitality in middle age." Then, suddenly, we were all not looking at Kit, and I was ashamed of myself, and at the same time I was filing away for future reference the images of Amy's reservoir of maternal energy and—daringly, appallingly—of the raw life-force this baby would bring.

Amy asked me quietly, "Do you see Vonda?"

"Every day at the gym. I saw her this morning."

"How is she?" There was a wistfulness in her tone.

"Fine," I said. "Great."

Amy poked at the remnants of her salad with her fork. "She's stopped calling."

I didn't know what to make of this. "She's pretty busy," I tried. "Don't take it personally." This admonition had always struck me as specious, since impersonality was exactly what the complainant was objecting to. But talk of lost connections seemed cruel in the presence of Kit, who was about to lose them all, and I didn't want to encourage Amy to go on.

She went on anyway. "Vonda's going to be my daughter's godmother. She's in my will as the person to raise her if anything happened to me."

"I didn't realize you were that close."

"I thought we were. And, you know, she's young." She glanced wryly in Denise's direction.

"I'll tell her to get in touch with you."

"No!" She was adamant. "Don't do that."

"I'll tell her you said hi."

"No," she insisted, no less emphatically but lowering her voice. "Don't do that, either. If she doesn't want to see me for some reason that's up to her. I still think she'd be a good mother for Phoebe if something happened to me. My lawyer would contact her. Not that anything's going to happen to me." She gave a nervous little laugh, the way people do.

"Well," I said, "we never know." My attention had swung back to Denise and to Kit, making this comment sound more dismissive than I'd meant it to be. Amy didn't say anything more about Vonda; she didn't, in fact, say anything more to me for the rest of the lunch.

Kit died less than a week later. Her husband called me at work and said if I wanted to say goodbye I better come now. I went; how could I not?

She raised up out of the bed toward me, her face already stretched into a rictus grin, and moaned as if in warning or terrible acknowledgment. She seemed to be reaching for me, but it was easy to avoid her grasp. Kit was my friend and I longed to be of comfort, but I couldn't risk touching her now; who knew what might flow into or out of me?

There were things I might have said to her if Jerry hadn't been in the room, silently distraught and furiously protective. "Goodbye, Kit," I whispered. "Thanks for being my friend." If she heard me at all, she would know what I meant.

The memorial service was several months later. Denise came back for it, and she and Amy and I went together. Amy brought her new daughter Phoebe, who'd been malnourished in the orphanage and sickly since she came home; solemn, dwarfed by her mother's bulk, the baby fussed almost inaudibly during the service. Despite the panic that was making my skin crawl and my breath come short as the eulogies went on and on, I didn't ask to hold her; it was too soon, I wasn't quite that desperate, and her life-force, though pure and sweet because it was so new, wasn't strong enough yet to be worth much to me.

Denise was pale and noticeably thinner than she'd been at Charon's. Climbing the chapel steps, she had more trouble catching her breath than her tears would account for.

She said she hadn't been feeling right and had a doctor's appointment the next week. Probably nothing, she said, but she had a six-day, five-hundred-mile bike tour in less than a month, and she needed to be in shape for that.

I was one of the people who got up and spoke about Kit. I meant everything I said. I would miss her terribly. She'd had a profound effect on my life.

After the service there was high-intensity sort of mingling. I avoided the photo display of Kit on a lace-draped, daisy-laden table—Kit as a beaming baby, Kit in a high school cheerleader outfit leaping in a high split, Kit in a glamour shot—and made what I hoped was creditable small talk with people I knew. Phoebe got a lot of attention; it was good, someone observed, to have a baby at a funeral, to remind us all that life goes on. That the life-force is eternal and infinite, and infinitely available.

Meaning to introduce Amy to a man I'd known casually for years, I could not remember his name. The older I got the more frequently names were eluding me, but this was the most public example so far, and I was mortified. He laughed with a sort of pained graciousness, supplied the name, shook Amy's free hand, made some wry joke about losing brain cells as we get older.

I thought but did not say, *It is not going to happen to me.*

"But you're not as old as I am, are you, Madyson?" he amended, peering at me in admiration and, I thought, some bafflement, because we both knew I was.

"I don't know," I lied. "Anyway, you're only as old as you feel, right?"

People said nice things to me all afternoon, a weird but gratifying phenomenon for a memorial service. "You look great, Madyson." "You look younger every time I see you!" I thanked them lightly and tried to settle on just the right way to think about Kit.

At one point Denise said something about her grandchildren, and the woman she was chatting with affected shock and protested that she didn't look old enough to be a grandmother which was patently false, and Denise just smiled and said, "Well, I am. Twice." There was an awkward silence while both the other woman and I waited for her to express thanks. When that didn't happen, the conversation trailed off and the woman found somebody else to talk to.

"I don't know why," Denise muttered, "people assume it's a compliment to say you look younger than you are."

I was taken aback. "Well, nobody wants to look old."

"Why not? Why is young better?"

Because it's farther away from death. But saying that would have led us into a discussion I couldn't risk. I put my hand on her arm and pointedly surveyed the fine wrinkles, the graying hair, the unreconstructed breasts, and told her with only mild sarcasm, "I wish I could be like you, Denise. It must be liberating not to care about such superficial things."

She shot me a sharp glance but didn't take up the challenge. I maintained the contact between us as long as I could get away with, and felt her shudder and sway. "It's so hot," she gasped, and, indeed, her face was suddenly glistening with sweat. "I've got to get out of here."

"Are you okay? Do you need me to drive you home?" I asked boldly, hopefully.

But she shook her head and made her way out of the room, pausing only to hug Kit's husband. Refreshed, I scanned the crowd for somebody I hadn't talked to yet who would tell me, verbally or otherwise, how good I looked. I was one of the last to leave. When I embraced Jerry, he was weeping, but I also felt him having to force his gaze away from my cleavage.

A few weeks later I called Denise in Austin to find out what the doctor had said. I wanted to know, and I wasn't likely to hear through the grapevine since she lived so far away and the only mutual acquaintance we had now was Amy. "It's my heart," she told me in an affectless voice. "There's something wrong with my heart." My own heart was pounding; I laid my hand over it in a sensual caress.

"Oh, Denise, honey, I'm sorry."

"It's ironic, isn't it?" She gave a bitter laugh. "There I was thinking I was saying goodbye to Kit, and I was already sick and didn't even know it.

"It can happen to any of us," I said, lamely and disingenuously, adding silently, *not me.*

When I called her again a month or so later, there was no answer, and I have never heard from her again. Since there's nobody I know to call or who would know to call me, it's not likely I'll find out what happened to her, although certainly I can guess. It haunts me. I can only hope she had someone with her, children or grandchildren, climbing partner or a better friend than I.

After Kit's memorial service and Denise's departure, I felt great for quite a while. I increased my workouts to three hours a day, and Vonda was pleased with my progress. I started going to a spa once a month for a full-body cleansing. I had my colors done and was shocked to discover that the particular shades of blue and green I'd been favoring actually could make me look older; the recommended adjustments made a huge difference, and I replaced almost all my wardrobe. I embarked on a new relationship with a thirty-year-old man I met at the gym; he thought I was thirty-five and joked incessantly about how much better older women were in bed.

I also started doing brain exercises, crossword puzzles, and foreign language tapes and repetitions of number sequences forward and backward before I fell asleep. This was less successful than the efforts to keep my body youthful. I still seemed to be forgetting names more than I used to, if someone spoke to me while I was on the phone I'd lose both conversations, and about once a week I seriously misplaced my keys. This would not do.

Amy seemed glad to hear from me and readily agreed to meet me for a drink. I went to her office, enjoying the chance to stroll across the campus. Critically observing every young woman I passed, I repeatedly judged myself acceptable, and more than one young man barely out of adolescence glanced at me in a way I took to be admiring.

Amy was with a student. Through the half-open door she saw me and raised a hand in greeting. Her smile, I had to admit, was radiant, even within the excess flesh. She looked exhausted, though, and I worried that I might have waited too long, that the demands of her life might have used up her reserves and rendered her inaccessible to me. I took a seat in the hall outside her office, like any student in need of intellectual transfusion, and passed the next quarter hour considering my options for a contingency plan. Now and then, I caught pieces of their dialogue; the fact that it was almost completely incomprehensible to me was both frightening and reassuring.

When the student emerged, I took his measure, wondering somewhat wildly whether I'd be able to find him again if I needed him. Studying notes he must have taken during his session with Amy, he hardly glanced at me. Amy came to the office door, even bigger than when I'd seen her at the memorial service, but surprisingly graceful. She held out her hand. Breathless at my good fortune, I rose and took it. Her grip was strong. She covered my hand with her other hand. "It's so good to see you, Madyson," she told me with more fervor than I'd expected, and it crossed my mind to wonder what it was she wanted from me.

It didn't take long to figure it out. After months of single motherhood and freshman physics classes, she was craving adult conversation. But it was more than that. Amy was lonely. Having a child had made her more rather than less aware of how much she ached for a partner. She wanted us to be friends, not just friendly acquaintances; she wanted us to be lovers.

I couldn't do that. I couldn't have been close to someone who looked like that anyway, and my own circumstances made it completely unthinkable. What I had to do to survive was bad enough when love wasn't involved. Which was why, for me, love was never involved.

It was possible that I'd already got what I needed from her long hand-clasp, and I considered pleading sudden illness and making my escape. But I reminded myself of the alarming memory lapses, the decreased ability to concentrate, all the unmistakable symptoms of intellectual decline. I had to take care of myself. I had to take advantage of opportunities as they presented themselves.

Amy took my hand again as we strolled the few blocks to her house. My embarrassment at being seen holding hands with a fat person was outweighed—but only just—by the infusion of energy tingling through my palm and up my wrist. I longed to kiss her, my tongue a siphon in her mouth, although the image repulsed me. I longed to take her head in my hands.

Phoebe was asleep. We were both displeased, Amy because now the child likely wouldn't sleep through the night. After the babysitter left, Amy invited me to make myself comfortable in the living room while she went to check on her daughter, but happily agreed when I asked if I could come with her. We went into the little girl's room hand-in-hand, like proud parents who couldn't quite believe their good fortune.

I'd read that the brain development of a child in the first two years of life is so dramatic that if we could keep up that pace for the rest of our lives we'd all be mental giants. I gazed at beautiful little Phoebe in her crib. I reached to stroke her hair.

"Don't!" Amy's whisper was explosive, and she caught my hand. For a moment I thought she'd somehow divined that her child was in terrible danger from me. But she just squeezed my hand affectionately and murmured close to my ear, "Don't wake her. She'll be up all night." I nodded, and we tiptoed out of the child's room together.

Despite intense arousal—part horror, part need, and gratitude that it would be met, part a disturbing kind of joy—I could not bring myself to respond to Amy's good night kiss. I allowed it, though, another moral compromise. Her mouth lingered softly on mine. I all but sank into the billows of her body. I maintained the physical contact as long as I could stand it, absorbing so much from her that I was weak and trembling by the time I pulled away. She smiled tremulously at me and murmured, "Call me." As I left I heard Phoebe cry out for her.

I hadn't seen her since then, and now I never would. When I emerged from the steam room and had settled myself onto the massage table with my face in the terry-covered cradle and my open-pored naked body ready for Vonda's manipulations, I asked, "Where's her daughter?" I'd hoped never to have to ask this question, but it had probably been inevitable. "Phoebe," I added, gratified that I had not forgotten her name. "Where's Phoebe?"

"She's with me."

Her thumbs and then her elbow found that deep tender spot under my left shoulder blade, and she bore down. Through the exquisite pain I hoped I wasn't inadvertently taking anything from her through this kind of contact; I needed my personal trainer and massage therapist to be strong and focused. As the muscle started to loosen and warmth seeped into the pressure point, I gasped, "Are you raising her?"

"I'm her godmother and guardian. It's in Amy's will."

The massage wasn't as good as usual; Vonda's mind was obviously somewhere else, and so was mine. My various aches and pains—iliac crest, glutes, lower back, feet—seemed to have multiplied and amplified and become more resistant since the last time. I kept thinking about Amy, and Kit and Denise. I kept thinking about Phoebe, whose primal will to survive must be fierce.

"Okay," she told me after a while, without, I thought, much interest. "Flip over on your back."

I didn't draw the sheet up over my beautiful breasts. She gave no sign of noticing. Her fingers shook slightly from the pressure she was putting under the back edge of my skull, stiffened fingers relieving tension in my head and neck as if they were holes drilled into the bone, but it was the weight of my own head that generated the response rather than any direct intention on her part. She let go too soon.

"There you go, Madyson."

I lay on the table for a few minutes after her hands left me, noting with resentment and panic that my body felt neither relaxed nor supple. I was paying her good money. She owed me more than this.

"Now that I'm a mother," Vonda said, as though she were talking about the weather, "I'm not going to work here anymore. We can get by without what I make, and Phoebe needs me. She's just lost her mother."

Bereft, I managed to ask, "When are you leaving?"

"Today's my last day. You're my last client."

I could not let this happen. Vonda was a young, vital woman with plenty more to give. Carefully, raising myself on one elbow, I said, "I'll miss you."

"Thanks. I'll miss this place, too. Sort of."

"I hope we can keep in touch."

There was a pause, and I expected either no acknowledgment of my overture or one of those responses like "we'll have to get together sometime" designed to be rejecting without quite admitting it. In either case, I'd have pressed. But, to my pleasant surprise, I didn't need to. Vonda looked up at me almost shyly and said, "I hope you mean it, Madyson. I'd like that."

Heart pounding, I suggested, "Let's have lunch. Tomorrow. There's this great little place I know. Charon's. Let's meet there."

"Great." Vonda nodded happily. "I'll see if the daycare can keep Phoebe another half day."

"No!"

She raised her eyebrows at my vehemence, and I hastened to moderate it. To control and conceal how much I needed to touch that little girl, to cradle and kiss her, to stroke her baby skin and hold her against my heart and infuse myself with all that raw new energy. "No," I repeated, with great effort calming my demeanor. "I'd really love to see her. Please. Bring her along."

Forever, Amen

Elizabeth Massie

Elizabeth Massie published her first horror short story in 1984. Since then her fiction has appeared in numerous magazines and anthologies, with her novella "Stephen" winning the Bram Stoker Award and being nominated for a World Fantasy Award.

She has published such novels as the Bram Stoker Award–winning *Sineater, Welcome Back to the Night, Wire Mesh Mothers, Twisted Branch: A Novel of the Abbadon Hotel* (as "Chris Blaine"), *Homeplace, DD Murphy Secret Policeman* (with Alan M. Clark), *Brazen Bull, Desper Hollow, Hell Gate*, and the TV tie-ins *Dark Shadows: Dreams of the Dark* (with Stephen Mark Rainey) and *Buffy the Vampire Slayer: Power of Persuasion.*

In the mid-1990s she created a series of historical horror novels for young adults, including the Young Founders series and the Daughters of Liberty trilogy, and her Ameri-Scares series of regional horror novels for middle-grade readers features *Maryland: Terror in the Harbor, California: From the Pit, New York: Rips and Wrinkles, Virginia: Valley of Secrets*, and *Illinois: The Cemetery Club.*

Her short fiction is collected in *Southern Discomfort, Shadow Dreams, The Fear Report, Afraid, Sundown, Naked on the Edge*, and *A Little Magenta Book of Mean Stories*, and *It, Watching*. The first four chapters of her *Silver Slut* series of lighthearted superhero adventures were released in 2016.

"In creating 'Forever, Amen,' I considered immortality—blessing or curse?—and its various manifestations," explains Massie. "Vampirism, reincarnation, time travel. The appeal of living forever is darkened when the future is discovered to be no better than the present or the past, when progress is only technical and not humanitarian, and civil people pound their chests and boast of their foul-smelling goodness. Where is one to go then? Where is one to run?"

Then Pilate went out to the people and saith unto them, Behold, I have found no fault with this man. The chief priests and officers cried out, Crucify him!

Pilate held forth his hand toward Jesus, who bore a crown of thorns and purple robe, and saith, I may release to thee a man on this day of Feasting. Whom will ye that I release, the man Barabbas or this man Jesus?

And the crowd cried, Give us Barabbas! Jesus must die!

When Pilate saw that he could prevail nothing to save the man Jesus and that Jesus was indeed to die to please the crowd, he offered the execution of noble captives, to have the man's wrists slashed with sword and thus causing him to bleed quickly unto death. But from the crowd called up the man Andrew, son of Phinneas the shepherd, who said, Jesus must suffer for his words! Crucify Him! The crowd joined in the mocking call, He must suffer for his words!

Then Pilate went from the crowd and washed his hands, and turned Jesus to the officers and soldiers, who gave unto Him a cross and bearing such went all unto the place of the skull which is called Golgotha:

Where they crucified Him, and two others on either side with Jesus in the midst.

—Book of Trials, 7:23–28

DANIELLE STOOD AGAINST the rough wall, her red eyes turned furiously toward the shrouded figure on the gurney. Marie and Clarice were gone, spun away with dour exasperation and vanished through the small ceiling-high window of the cellar. Their words still echoed in the room like late-season flies caught in a bottle.

Marie: "He is not Alexandre. He is nothing. He is less than nothing."

Clarice: "It's done. Come with us. Sister, take my hand. It stinks in here."

Marie: "Look if you must, but be done with it, and then come."

Danielle had pressed her gloved hands to her ears and shook her head. *No.*

Marie: a sharp snapping of the fingers as if Danielle was a dog to obey her mistress, and Danielle had simply said, "Leave me be." Marie and Clarice had done just that. They thought their companion mad, not a good thing for a creature of the night. Madness could only lead to foolishness and carelessness, and with carelessness, destruction. They had left their mad friend to her own fate.

Danielle stared at the soiled sheet, the sharp protrusions beneath the cloth where the nose and chin were, the feet. Softer mounds of the shoulders, the fisted hands, the groin. Light from lanterns, hung in this subterranean room by the men who had departed here just minutes ago, sputtered from ceiling hooks. Water pipes dripped puddles onto the dirt floor. Spiders and their webs, left in corners by the hasty custodian the day before, held still as if pondering the strange and recent occurrence.

"Alexandre?" Danielle said softly, tasting the cold of her breath as it passed through her incisors, her protruding canines. "Why can that not be you?" She took several steps forward, her chin dipping down as if her face were dread to see beneath the sheet. So much she had witnessed in all these many years, so much terror and viciousness and death, yet this one was almost beyond her ken.

"Why can that not be you?" she repeated, then touched her own face. "Is this not me? Am I not still walking this squalid earth in the form of a young woman though I am one hundred seventeen years of age?"

The sheet stirred slightly. Danielle gasped and put out her hand to find that it was just a current of air passing though the damp brick room, traveling from one ill-hung door to another on the other side.

Was this world not spattered with such as her, existing in conjunction with mortals who most often believed their own reality was the sum and total? And so what incredulous magic could not happen, what damnable curse was impossible?

The room was hot and rancid, foul human scents coiling like smoke from the floor, the walls, the chairs, the gurney. The men who had been here just minutes ago had stunk at first of excitement, and then disgust. They claimed for themselves the crown of civility, yet winced and vomited at the result of their infinite goodness.

"Is this not me?" she repeated. "Look and see that flesh which you once loved." She shook her head, warding off the stench, then ripped her gloves from her hands and threw them to the floor. She clutched at the frilly bodice of her dress, and ripped it from neck to waist. Her dagger-sharp nails raked the white skin of her breast as she did, leaving long, bloodless skin-lips gaping silently in the air.

Cursed costume of the modern, nineteenth-century woman! Such prudes, such whores, tied up and trussed and playing at seduction with their prim dress, not knowing what it is to be wholly female! Ah, but she had known! Alexandre had known her femaleness and she his maleness, and have reveled in the wonder of it all.

She tossed the ripped cloth aside. Then she wrenched off the rest of her garb—the leg-of-mutton sleeves, the full muslin skirt, the petticoat, cotton stockings, garters, buttoned shoes. All were hurled away. The hat, the hair pins, the ear bobs. Her auburn hair fell free about her shoulders.

Danielle closed her eyes and caressed her cold skin. She traced the length of her arms and torso, feathering the soft hairs on her chilly stomach, strumming the already-healing skin-lips on her breasts.

She had been naked when they had taken away Alexandre from her the first time. Lying in a stall of the weanling barn they'd been, Danielle leaning gaily into the wiry hair of Alexandre's chest and laughing at the prickling straw in her hair and in her back. She had picked up a yellow stem and had ticked his chin and his nose. He had kissed the straw and then her fingers. He had wrapped his arms around her waist and nestled his chin into her neck, his tongue playing easily along the tender flesh there.

"You were tender and true," she said, her brows knotted and her lips trembling. "But only one wrong named to you, as any human would have who has lived past infancy. How, then, did this curse come to you?"

Beneath the sheet, Alexandre did not move. Danielle took several more steps, across the uneven and cold floor, and grasped the sheet which covered her beloved.

The handsome, tattered young man arrived at Bicetre on a frosty, late March morning in 1792, appearing like a specter beneath the shadows of the pear orchard behind Paris's infamous hospital and prison. The sky had rained not an hour earlier, and the rain had been cold and severe, drilling chilly puddles into the ground and knocking branch tips from the naked trees. Shivering droplets hung triumphantly to the fur of the animals in the paddocks and to the emerald leaves of the boxwood shrubs that lined the narrow dirt pathways.

The brick institution of Bicetre was large, dark, and filled with most unpleasant business—that of madness, of loneliness, of anger, desperation. Of screams. Of silence. Bright, curious doctors ministered to the sick. Hardened officers tended the miscreants.

In the shadow of the great place, flanking its west side, was a four-acre plot on which animals and vegetables were raised for the use of Bicetre's personnel, patients, and inmates. It was called appropriately the "Little Farm." Fenced paddocks monitored the cows and sheep and pigs; in a small hutch nested chickens and pigeons. Several gardens bordered with woven vine fences offered up turnips and beans in the warmer months. A tiny grove of pear trees held sentinel near the stone wall where, beyond, the citizens of Paris pounded back and forth in the rhythm of their individual and now collective lives.

Danielle, one of three young maids employed to tend the animals and gardens and assist in meal preparations, had been in the paddock on a stool, scrubbing the udder of one poorly producing cow and slapping flies from her face when she saw the man amid the naked pear trees and thought, *My God, but he is beautiful! Thank you for this gift today!* She left the stool and the muddy bovine for the orchard, stopping several yards away and drawing her wool shawl about her shoulders.

"Good morning," Danielle said. "Are you lost?"

The man raised his hand in tentative greeting—a fine, strong hand it was, a workingman's hand with dark knuckle hair and calluses—and said,

"Not now that I've beheld you." He smiled, and Danielle could see that his teeth were fine and white. Her mother, before she had died, had told Danielle that good teeth meant a good heart.

Danielle didn't back away nor did she turn her gaze to the ground as the finer of France's daughters would have done in the presence of a strange man. She was not a maid in the sense the Maid of Orleans had been; Danielle had had her lovers, most of them young doctors at Bicetre and an occasional nurse, who brought her to their private offices within the heavy walls of the institution, made over her lush body on firm, practical sofas, then laughed at her and sent her back to the barn with a slap to the ass. The Revolution stated there was to be no more class distinction, and Paris had turned nearly upside down with its fervent attention to *la chose publique*, "public things" which had to be monitored for counter-revolutionary thought and action, yet Danielle and her sister maids at the hospital farm found their lives little changed. The gnats and flies were as thick as before, the cows as dirty, the pears in the orchard as worm-ridden, and the doctors as lustful toward girls in maid garb.

The young man beneath the pear branches was quite handsome, with dark hair, a black beard, and gentle, crinkling eyes. He had obviously scaled the stone wall, and had torn the knee of his breeches.

"Are you thirsty, sir?" Danielle asked. The man nodded, and she led him past the dirty cow and the stool to the well. Here he put down his worn leather satchel and drank countless dippers-full which she supplied from the dented tin bucket. Her fingers brushed his once as she passed the dipper, and the hairs on her knuckles stood up at attention.

"What brings you here?" she pressed as he sipped. "You're not a lost patient with a simple mind, are you, to stumble back to the hospital from which you were attempting escape?"

He saw that she was joking, and he smiled broadly and shook his head.

"No," he said. "I'm from the north, and have come to Paris for work as my home and shop were burned in a fire just a week ago, leaving me without means. I am a cobbler by trade. An accident it was, with the wind knocking a lantern from the window onto the floor. Christ, such a loss." He paused to wipe stray drops from his beard. "But I cannot make it over, cannot make it right. So I brought a few things with me to the city. From the road I spied soft and browned pears, hiding in the tall grass from last autumn, and climbed the wall in hopes of plucking some without being spied. Then I saw you and was glad I'd been seen."

"Rotten pears!" Danielle raised a brow. "The third estate cannot say they eat such things now, for dire poverty is of the old time! Shush!"

"They cannot say, but they certainly can eat, yes?"

Danielle smiled, then tipped her head. "This is a hospital, and a prison. There are shoes always in need of repair. I would think you could find work here, if you would like?"

"I might like that very much," said the man.

Up the boxwood-lined path from the pigs' paddock strolled the two other maids, Marie and Clarice, each steering a waddling sow with a stick. But they only smiled at Danielle, allowing their friend her time, and trudged on to the stoop and rear door that led to Bicetre's kitchen. The pigs were poked and prodded into small wicker cages by the door, where they would await a fate their grub-fed brains could not fathom.

Danielle offered the man a place to rest in the empty weanling calves' barn and left him alone several hours until she found a spare moment between her farming and kitchen duties. She carried with her a slab of ham, some bread, and a bottle of wine beneath her skirt, pilfered from the enormous cellar beneath the kitchen. The two shared food and drink in the straw. And then kisses, caresses. She learned that he was Alexandre Demanche, twenty-two, an orphan raised in the countryside outside of Beauvais. He had been engaged but never married for the young woman had died of consumption three weeks before they were to wed. Alexandre learned that she was Danielle Boquet, born in Paris to a patient at Bicetre who expired during childbirth, leaving Danielle to be raised by various matrons about the institution who taught her to cook, garden, and manage livestock. In all her nineteen years, she had only set foot off Bicetre's property to attend weekly mass. She was, she admitted, afraid of the city and its people, but felt safe behind the stone walls of the Little Farm.

In the morning Danielle presented Alexandre to Claude LeBeque, the pudgy little man who was in charge of the massive loads of laundry produced within the thick walls of the hospital and prison. She stopped him at the hospital's front gate. Behind him on the street milk carts and fish wagons rattled back and forth in the cold spring sun, and children were tugged behind mothers with baskets on their arms and hats pinned to their hair.

LeBeque pulled at his substantial, red-splotched nose, then sniffed at being detained. "This man needs work? You're good for what, Monsieur?"

"Good with shoes," said Alexandre.

"So you say?"

"Someone must supply clothing and shoes to the inmates," said Danielle. "Who would that be?"

LeBeque pulled his nose again, then a small smile found his cracking lips. He dabbed at his fleshy forehead with a filthy handkerchief and purred, "That would be me."

Alexandre stepped forward. "I understand this place houses a good many people and therefore, I suspect, a good many shoes. I mend shoes and I make shoes. Have you a need for such as myself?"

LeBeque shrugged and raised a brow in a way that seemed to tease. "Oh, I might find a place for you. I'll send word soon. Don't go too far, sir."

With permission to stay on the premises and await hiring, Alexandre made a tidy bunk for himself in the empty barn. He used a blanket Danielle brought from her own room in the cellar and rolled his cape into a pillow. She helped rake and toss out the molded straw and pile up fresh that she'd brought in from the sheep's shed. A roost of swallows, perturbed at losing nesting space, squawked, swooped, and evacuated with a swirl of scissored tails and batting of sharp wings.

From his satchel he removed a journal, pen, ink well, and pouch of ink powder and placed them on a protruding beam. A small black volume, tied shut with a string, joined these items on the shelf.

"I will call this home for now," he said with a touch of resigned satisfaction.

Danielle linked her fingers together and said, "Take rest. I will come back to see you as soon as I am able."

Bearing a beeswax candle encased in a sooty lantern, Danielle sneaked out from the hospital to join him that evening when duties were done. Madame Duban, the head cook, demanded that the girls in her charge retire to their cots in the cellar at nine, and had always threatened dismissal at any hint of disobedience. But Danielle would not be denied, and when the old woman was snoring soundly in her spinster's bed, Danielle took several bits of bread and the light and crept outside into the tainted glow of the Paris moon. She followed the path to the barn, happy that the little building would not be needed for another few weeks when the first of the spring calves were old enough to wean and were placed in the barn to keep them from their bawling mothers.

The lantern was hung on a rusting latch on the stall door, and then Alexandre drew Danielle to himself with gentle strokes to her auburn hair. "My sweet," he said into her neck. She kissed his arms and the backs of his solid hands, then moved them across her body to the warm and secret places beneath her loose-fitting blouse and simple wool skirt. They loved until late, when she brushed off her skirt and hurried back to her cot beneath the hospital's kitchen.

Monsieur LeBeque appeared on the path near the barn the following morning. Danielle was milking one particularly ill-tempered cow and Marie was beside her, pouring milk into the churn for tomorrow's butter. The chubby man had spruced himself up since the previous morning. He had combed his thinning hair and had put rouge on his cheeks. It seemed as if the ruffled shirt he wore had seen the inside of a wash tub as recently as a week's time. He planted his cane tip into the dirt beside Danielle and demanded, "Where is the young cobbler you brought to me yesterday?"

Danielle paused in her squeezing. "You have decided to hire him?"

The man stamped his cane and frowned. "You mean to question me?"

"No, sir," said Danielle, and looked away long enough to roll her eyes in Marie's direction. Marie put her hand over her mouth so not to giggle. "He sleeps in the calves' barn, sir."

"And where is the calves' barn?"

Danielle pointed down the path.

An oily nod and the man meandered off up the path. "He shall be employed," whispered Danielle as she began squeezing again. The thin stream of milk sizzled into the bucket; the cow's tail caught her across the cheek. "He shall be able to stay here!"

"You take care, now," said Marie. "He'll be busy and so will you. He's not a doctor to make excuses for your absences. Madam Duban may be old but she can smell the scent of sex like a horse can smell fire."

Danielle grinned. "Then I'll steal some of her cheap perfume. And we'll make time. And aren't you just jealous?"

Marie put the empty bucket down by Danielle's stool and put the wooden churn lid in place. "I have my fun, don't worry about me."

The girls laughed heartily.

With the onset of April, planting time arrived. The Little Farm's plots were plowed by one of the imbecile boys from the hospital who was strong enough to guide the sharp furrowing blade behind the old sorrel gelding. The girls followed with bags of seeds on their hips, sprinkling the soil and covering up the grooves with their bare feet. It took several days to put in the rows of beets, cabbage, beans, and onions.

Yet her days were more pleasant, in spite of back-bending work and the flies, for at night she sneaked to the barn to make love with Alexandre on the blanket in the straw. Each encounter was a flurry of heat and joy, followed by the muffled of pounding hearts and the sounds of Paris's night streets. When lovemaking was done and their passions spent, Danielle lay in his arms and asked him about his day. How many shoes had he repaired, how many new pairs had been requisitioned? Had he a cobbler's shop within the institution, or did he carry with him tools from room to room? What was it like in the prison? She had seen only the kitchen and the cellar; did the men foam at the mouth and chew off their fingers?

But Alexandre gave up little detail. He had a wooden work-box with tools, purchased for him by Monsieur LeBeque, which he took around with him when he was called for repairs. Monsieur LeBeque himself had requested a new pair of boots for which he supplied the leather. "It is work I know," Alexandre said simply. "I shall do it until I must find something else."

"Why would you need to find something else?" asked Danielle. "I know your lodging is poor, but surely they shall find a room for you soon."

"I do not want a room, I want this barn and you."

It was on the fourth night that, lying against Alexandre's chest, her fingers probing his nipples, she looked at the makeshift shelf and said, "What is that book there, my dearest? The black leather?"

Alexandre wiped his mouth and then his chest, pushing Danielle's fingers away. "It's a Bible."

"You?" marveled the maid. "A God-loving man? I've yet to hear you preach to me, only to cry into my shoulder, 'Dear God, dear God!' in the height of your thrusting!"

Alexandre didn't return her laugh. His jaw tightened, drawing up the hairs on his chin. "Don't blaspheme."

"I'm not, Alex," said Danielle. Pushing up on her elbow, she took the book from its beam and brought it down to the hay. "I was raised a Catholic, I know the wages of blasphemy, at least in the eyes of the clergy."

"Put it back, please," said Alexandre. He held out his palm, and the insistence in his voice taunted Danielle and made her laugh the more. She sat abruptly and flipped open the pages. "Book of Temptations? Book of Trials? I've not seen these in a Bible. What is this, truly?"

Alexandre shoved Danielle viciously against the stall's scabby wall and snatched the book away. "I said put it back! Do you not know what to leave alone?"

Danielle blew a furious breath through her teeth. "Oh, but I do now, Monsieur Demanche! It is you I shall leave alone!" She scrambled to her feet, knocking straw dust from her breasts and arms. "I'm never worth more than a few days, anyway! Ask the doctors!"

But Alexandre's face softened, and he grabbed her suddenly by the wrist and said, "Don't leave me. I've been alone always. Please, dearest Danielle, I'm sorry." His voice broke and went silent. And she held him again then, and knew that she loved him.

The following day, a cloudy Sunday, Danielle, Marie, and Clarice attended mass under the stern supervision of Madame Duban at the Chapel of St. Matthew three blocks over, and then returned to Bicetre, for in spite of the Lord's admonition to remember the Sabbath Day to keep it holy, there were chores on Sunday as on any day of the week. Danielle had peered inside the barn before Madame had ushered them out the gate of the stone wall, hoping to convince Alexandre to join them, but the man was not there.

Surely he hasn't shoes to mend on Sunday, she thought. *Perhaps cows' udders cannot wait, but a man's bare feet can.*

They returned in the midafternoon, and the barn was still empty. "Perhaps he's gone to his own church," Danielle said to herself as she gathered her stool and buckets and settled down the pear trees. "His own peculiar Bible, perhaps his own peculiar religion. No matter." She selected the first of the four cows and brought her own for the milking. The teats were slathered in feces, and she spent a good five minutes scrubbing off what she could. Shortly afterward, Marie came out and took her by the sleeve. "Do you know what they've brought to Bicetre? Do you know what they have set up in the courtyard on the other side of the hospital?"

Danielle shook her head.

"Guess!"

"No, Marie."

"The Louisette! The beheading machine! It's been brought from the Cour du Commerce on the rue Saint-Andre-des-Arts to us this very morning. Madame Duban told me just a moment ago that as she was crossing the courtyard the wagon came in, bearing the beams and blade. They mean to test it on sheep, and on the unclaimed corpses of prisoners and patients to see if it is ready."

Danielle let go of the soft teat and brushed a loose strand of hair behind her ear. "I should like to see it," she said. "The Assembly promised the poor should have the right to a quick death as do the wealthy. No more rack or garrote for those who are covered with an honest day's filth. How can we get to see it, Marie?"

"I don't know. Unless you'd like to go as one of the corpses. I could tell Madame Duban about your trysts with Alexandre and she would choke you for certain."

"Ah!" screeched Danielle gleefully, and she flicked milk from her fingers at her friend. "You are dreadful!"

When there was no more milk to be had from this cow, Danielle led her back to the paddock to get the last of the four who were producing. She hung the bucket on the fence post and kicked at the wall-eyed creature. "Come on, you little slut," she said. "I let you have your peace until last. And don't flare those nostrils at me."

"Danielle!"

Danielle whirled about. Alexandre was there, hands on his hips, a line of sweat on his forehead.

"Dearest!" said Danielle. "I'd come for you for mass, but you weren't there. Where have you been?"

"Shoes for Monsieur LeBeque," said Alexandre. "He's been after me these past days to come measure a new pair for himself and this morning insisted I take care of that business."

"Indeed? Shoes on Sunday? God will not approve, I can tell you that."

"Nor do I," said Alexandre. "Come with me to the barn. I must speak with you." He glanced around anxiously, to the pear trees, the wall, the kitchen door up the path.

"I've got milking," said Danielle. "The cook makes a great deal of bread on Sunday afternoon to last the week, though we aren't supposed to labor on the Lord's Day. It cannot wait. But I'll come tonight as I've always . . ."

"Tonight I shall be gone."

"Gone? Beloved, no, you cannot . . ."

"And you with me, yes? Dearest Danielle, I could not leave without you, but we must be careful."

"Why? What has happened?"

"Come to the barn. I won't speak of this in the daylight. There are eyes and ears we may not see, and which we do not want to know our business."

Danielle's heart kicked, and her arms tightened. What had happened? She didn't want to know, but she had to know. She latched the gate to the cows' paddock and followed Alexandre to the barn.

Huddled in the back stall, Alexandre took Danielle's hands in his. "I've made an enemy with Monsieur LeBeque. He is furious that I've spurned his advances."

"He wanted you?" Danielle's eyes widened. "I thought the man married."

Alexandre made an exasperated sound in his throat. "Married, to show the world his respectability," he said. "The man spouts words which he feels are acceptable to those whose status at this place is above him. But then I've seen him take patients from their cells to his own room, and have seen the fear in their eyes as he closes the door. He's pulled me aside and has tried to charm me with hideous quotes from writings of Donatien-Alphonse-Francois de Sade's, thinking, perhaps, that I was as twisted a libertine as he fancies himself. This afternoon, as I sat in the laundry room nailing a sole back onto an officer's boot, LeBeque staggered in and said it was time to pay for my employment."

"Dear Lord!"

Alexandre put a finger to her lips. "Shh, my dear, don't fret. I said I would have nothing to do with a man who so cruelly and freely used others. I pushed him away, and said I would be gone by tonight, and he could keep the pay which is owed me and shove it up his own blustery dung hole."

"You didn't? Sweet Mary! You're in trouble!"

"I think if I leave quickly, the man shall forget anything about it. He's not bright, and he's got many around him who he can use much more easily."

Danielle wiped her eyes and dragged her fingers through her hair. "Yes, leave. I have little here that I need to take. I will get it right away and return before you can blink three times."

Alexandre closed his eyes, then opened them, and drew her to himself. "To have you, my only love, will make any journey a pleasure, any struggle a joy." He kissed her forehead, her ear, her cheeks. His breath on Danielle's lips made her body arch into his. Instinctively she shed her blouse and skirt and nestled into him and into the straw. "Love me quickly, dearest, most darling, for one last moment before we . . ."

The barn door was yanked open and the dusty room was filled suddenly with a swirl of dim morning light. Three men in breeches and crumpled jackets burst in, stopped short, and stared at the couple in the shadows.

"Ah, love amid the manure!" cooed one, his tone dark and ugly, his blue eyes frosty with contempt. "I remember it well when I was young."

Danielle snatched her blouse and held it before her. Alexandre jumped to his feet and grabbed the pitchfork that was leaning on the stall door.

"Get the hell out of here!" he shouted.

"Such an order from such a criminal!" laughed a second. He was a bald man with a greasy mustache and boils on his chin. "To make demands of us!"

"Criminal?" said Alexandre.

"Nearly killed LeBeque, knocked his skull and almost cracked it open," said Blue Eyes.

Danielle stared at her love, stunned. "Criminal?"

"You make a mistake," said Alexandre. "I pushed the man away, but I did not harm him in any way!"

"Pushed him away, and down against the fire grate," said the man with boils. "I found him dazed and bloody, wailing that the cobbler tried to murder him. Came up behind him and struck him what he'd hoped was a deadly blow! But you are not so lucky, my friend, and we've come for you."

The three men fell on Alexandre then, knocking the pitchfork across the stall, and in spite of his struggles, Alexandre was pinned with his arms back. Blue Eyes tied the hands with a rope. Alexandre tried to kick and knock the men off, but they wrenched the rope upward and his shoulders popped noisily. Alexandre paused in his struggling. His teeth were set against each other and his eyes wide with rage. "Monsieur LeBeque is abed now," hissed the man with boils, "tended by one of the best surgeons at the hospital. But he made demand for you to be done with and out of his sight."

Danielle saw hope. "We are leaving," she said as she slipped into her sleeves and fumbled with the hooks. "Please, do you hear me? We will be away from Bicetre in but a minute, if you just let Alexandre go!"

"No, girl, we've other plans. Plans from Monsieur LeBeque himself. They have a few corpses from the hospital morgue, but the cobbler shall be the first live one to experience the Louisette, the first to feel the kind, cold bite."

"*Dieu a la pitié!*" screamed Danielle.

Alexandre began to writhe again. Danielle saw the world swaying violently, but she held tightly to the wall so she would not fall. "No, you cannot do that! He's not been tried, nor convicted!"

"Convicted enough," said Blue Eyes. "And he should be pleased! Why, this is the method of execution provided by the Assembly. This is the humane way of putting to death those who deserve it. No rack for him. No slow, piteous strangulation in the garrote! We are a civilized society now."

"Stop!" wailed Danielle. "Sweet mercy in the name of the Lord Jesus Christ and all the saints!"

Suddenly Alexandre looked back over his shoulder at the black volume on the beam. Danielle thought he was going to ask for it, to carry it with him as a charm against harm. But he said, instead, "I remember. Oh, God. I remember now!"

The men struck out at Alexandre's heels to make him move, and tugged him from the barn. Danielle tugged on her skirt and stumbled after. "What do you remember, fool?" asked the man with the boils.

But Alexandre was addressing Danielle, as if he thought she would understand. "I remember the blade on my throat, the quick slash, the smiles of those sunburned faces. Ah, civilized, they said! We are indeed a humane society!"

"Alexandre?" cried Danielle.

"He's mad with fear," laughed Blue Eyes. "He's soft in the mind now. Maybe we should just lock him up in the hospital? But no, we've got our instructions. We should gag him, though, to keep his tongue silent."

Alexandre looked at the sky, the gray and cloudy sky which was threatening an early April rain. His eyes reflected the gray, and his teeth were barred in anguish. "I remember now! Why again? Why again? Forgive me, and no more!"

"Madman!" laughed Blue Eyes.

The third man, who had said nothing to this point, mumbled simply, "Shut your mouth," and he drove his fist into Alexandre's jaw. Alexander doubled over, groaning and spitting. Then the man pulled a handkerchief from his front jacket pocket and gagged Alexandre tightly. The man with boils pointed a finger at Danielle. "Stay here, wench. We've no patience for your whining!"

They dragged Alexandre from the Little Farm and around the north side of the huge brick building. Danielle ran after, staying back so they would not see her.

They did not notice her as she scurried through the stone archway into one of the smaller courtyards within the confines of the hospital. No one spied her as she crouched behind a two-wheeled cart in the shadows and stared, horrified, at the tall contraption erected on the barren center ground. The three men who held Alexandre drove him to his knees to watch the preliminary beheadings. First, a sheep was locked into the neck brace, and with a swift movement, the blade was dropped from the top of the wooden tower and severed the head. It flopped into a basket. From windows in the upper stories of the hospital came whoops and shouts of the prisoners. Some banged and screamed.

"Better," said the man at the control to the small gathering of witnesses—finely dressed men in hats, ruffled shirts, and heeled, buckled shoes, standing with feet planted apart and hands clasped behind their backs. "The angle of the blade, you see, makes for a cleaner cut." Heads nodded. Gentile faces, concerned with the civility of it all, clearly pleased to be part of the advancement.

Two corpses were beheaded then. One a fat, naked man with wiry red hair, the other a muscular cadaver with only one foot. The already lifeless heads popped from the lifeless necks, and spewing no blood but oozing something dark, dropped into the wicker basket.

"What have we here?" The man at the control turned to where Alexandre was held to the ground. "Who is that there? We're not using it for executions yet. We've got no papers for that man. The first is selected already, a Nicolas-Jacques Pelletier. As soon as the machine is perfected, he shall die."

Blue Eyes said simply, "Just one more test subject, sir. At the request of one of the officials here at Bicetre." He nodded toward a second-story window, where the visage of LeBeque could be seen, his head wrapped in a bandage, his arms crossed furiously.

"We've got no papers," repeated the man at the control.

"Who's to care?" said Blue Eyes. "He's a dangerous maniac who's been housed at Bicetre for years. He nearly killed the official in the window there. He'd kill you or me were we to unbind him. Who's to know, but you, these witnesses and a few babbling idiots in the windows above."

The man looked at Alexandre, then at the blade which he'd just raised back into position.

"A live one will tell you more of what you need to know," said Blue Eyes. "And then he'll merely be a third corpse."

Alexandre tried to scream around the gag, but only garglings came out. Danielle put her hands over her ears, but could not take her gaze from the dreadful sights.

"Well," said the man, whirling his hand impatiently and pursing his lips as though he had his doubts, though the temptation of a live subject was too much to pass. "All right. Quick, then. This should be our final test."

And they made quick business of Alexandre Demanche. The man was bound at the ankles and placed with much huffing and grunting upon the wooden gurney. His head was slipped through the neck trough, and then secured when the wooden slat above was brought down and locked. Alexandre, still in his gag, strained to look around as the man in charge reached out to release the heavy blade.

He spied Danielle trembling in the shade behind the wagon. His expression screamed what he had spoken back in the barn, though the words did nothing but confuse the already terrified mind of his young lover.

Why again? Why again? Forgive me, and no more!

The blade slid smoothly, an easy rush of air and steel. With a thwack, it found its rest at the bottom of the track, throwing the head neatly into the basket. But this one bled, and profusely.

Danielle covered her face with her forearms and drove her face into the ground.

She returned to the Little Farm when darkness fell. She felt her way rather than saw it, for her eyes were full of the hideous visions of the courtyard. Marie and Clarice were on the path, panicked for the loss of their friend, and when they saw her, they ran to her and held her close.

But Danielle would have nothing of it. She said simply, "I must die."

Marie shook Danielle's shoulders. "What are you saying? Where have you been?"

But then Danielle said, "But should I kill myself I go to Hell! Should I live I live in Hell!"

"Oh, sweet Mother of God," said Clarice, "what has happened to you, dear friend?"

Danielle broke away, and reached the barn to see if she'd made a mistake, to see if Alexandre was waiting for her in his stall. But the straw was kicked about, and the pitchfork dropped on the floor where Alexandre had tried to protect her. His jacket was in a tangle by the wall. Danielle wailed, picked up the jacket, and clutched it to herself. Her friends stood in the doorway, dumbfounded.

"I must die, too!" she screamed.

"Danielle!" It was Clarice. "Come out of there. Talk to us! You've got us frightened!"

Alexandre's journal was on the beam. But the Bible was gone. Danielle dug through the straw, clawing and sifting the sharp, golden bits, but the Bible was not there. Alexandre had not taken it with him. But it was no longer there. What had happened to it? She wanted it for herself, to take it with her to her death.

Danielle stood, and fled the barn. She knew the answer, as surely as she knew LeBeque and Blue Eyes and the man with boils and the man at the beheading machine would go to Hell for their civil and humane test. She shoved past the other maids, saying, "I shall go to the places where the prostitutes wander. I shall make myself available to a murderer, that's what I shall do! I will go to Heaven if I'm murdered. For I will not live without him!"

Marie and Clarice tried to grab Danielle to hold her back, but she was too fast, too mad with grief, and they were left clutching air and the first raindrops of the evening.

They followed her. Against Clarice's concerns that they'd be relieved of their duties for leaving Bicetre without permission, they scurried after Danielle, shawls drawn up around their faces. Down one narrow Parisian street after another they went, calling for their friend but not so loudly to attract undo the attention of the increasingly frightening citizenry of the streets. The rain let itself go in full force, driving some pedestrians from the roads and leaving only the determined, the tardy, and the mad.

Danielle pushed her way to the rue Leon, a small and dismal alley lined with tall, narrow whorehouses, saloons, and tenement shacks, some of which leaned precariously on poorly placed foundations. The rain blurred the lights of the lanterns which sat in splintering windowsills. Whores stood in petticoats and stockings in sagging doorways, thrusting their breasts and wiggling their tongues. Drenched clients in coats hurried for the warmth of the diseased temptresses, and vanished into the houses with low chuckles and growls. A skeletal dog limped across Danielle's pathway and wormed its way into a tenement cellar through a cracked window. In the shadows beneath rain-blackened stoops and behind rust-banded barrels lurked eyes which seemed to have no sockets. Teeth which seemed to have no mouths.

Danielle stopped in the center of the alley. She stared up at the dark, rain-sodden sky and raised her hands as if bidding some divine spirit to save her.

"Kill me!" she said above the drumming of the rain on the cobblestones and rooftops. "Come now, there is surely someone who would relish the chance to satiate a blood lust! Here I am, and there is no one to charge you for my death, for there is no one in this godforsaken town who would care I was gone!"

She closed her eyes and kept her hands aloft. She took a breath, expecting to feel a plunging knife in her ribs, or a dagger drawn across her throat. *Now,* she begged silently. *Let it be done and over.*

She heard nothing, save the giggling of the prostitutes in their houses and the cries of babies in the tenement rooms. She said again, "Here I am! A gift, for free!"

Spattering rain and muted laughter.

Then, "No, I don't want to die. God forgive me." And then again, "Yes, die I must! Release me!"

And then a hand on her forearm and a whisper, "Sister, you're soaked to the skin!"

Danielle opened her eyes to see a pair of red orbs gazing intently at her, mere inches from her own. The skin around the eyes was as white as a corpse's. Danielle gasped and floundered, but the full red mouth smiled and said, "Fear not, dear. I have what you want. You are certainly a young thing, yes?" Cold fingers gently brushed Danielle's hair from her neck and tipped her head to the side ever so slightly.

Danielle could not move her gaze from the red eyes, and she thought for the briefest moment, *This is just a painted whore. A whore who kills on the side to assuage her anxieties. That's fine. That's good. A whore may kill more kindly than a man would have.*

"I will release you to life that is not life, death that is not death. My gift to you. The gift many of us have asked for because of the dreadful state of our mortal existence as women on Earth. Hold, dear, hold now."

Danielle held her breath.

"Danielle!" The scream was from behind, and Danielle tried to look back but the whore with the white face and cold hands held her as strongly as any man.

"Danielle!" It was Marie, somewhere back at the entrance to the alley.

"Shh," cooed the whore, "Shh." The white face dipped to Danielle's bare neck. A searing pain shot through the flesh, the muscle, and into the very core of bone. Danielle screamed, but the scream was met with the whore's muffled laughter and the shifting of the rain in the wind.

Then there was warmth and numb peace, and a swirling giddiness that caught her thoughts and threw them like pebbles in the wind. She almost laughed, almost, but then she fell into herself and there was no bottom and no light and she fell and fell and thought, *This is death. I shall find you, Alexandre. In the good Lord's paradise, I shall find you!*

They settled in Buffalo, New York, in February of 1889, when Danielle insisted that the population of Sisters had grown too large in New York City. Marie was tired of moving. So was Clarice. But Danielle was always restless. No matter the availability nor the quantity of prey or the relative safety of their hideouts, she was happy in one place no more than a matter of months, then began insisting they move on. Marie and Clarice, not wanting their friend to venture off on her own, always went along.

They had stayed in Europe for over eighty years, moving from Paris to Lisbon to London and countless smaller cities and towns, taking the blood they needed to survive, meeting with other *Soeurs de la Nuit*—Sisters of the Night—and sharing their stories, their pain. Laughing with them when some memory was amusing, mourning with them when a memory was too harsh.

The Sisters were an order of the undead, much like the lone wolves of their kind but different in their need and sympathy for each other. They lived on the blood of others, most often the blood of thieves and rapists, murderers, and wife-beaters. They drank their fill, often passing the dazed man about to their fellows for a share, then killed their victims with a twist to the neck. The Sisters did they have a desire to bring such villains into eternal life with them.

On the rue Leon so many years past, a Sister had heard Danielle's pitiable cries and had come to her aid. Marie and Clarice, who had fallen at Danielle's side, were likewise brought into the world of forever.

At first they had been unable to accept their new reality, and had hidden in a whorehouse cellar for nine days, trying to go out in the morning but unable, and finding themselves nauseous when presented plates of turnips and pork yet ravenous when offered a drunk card cheat. Danielle had cried for Alexandre; Marie and Clarice had just cried. Yet with increased feedings and encouragement from the Sisters who tended them, they grew into their new selves.

They returned to Bicetre one starry evening, and while Marie and Clarice took out their rage on several doctors who had fucked them and tossed them out, Danielle had gone to the lantern-lit office of Monsieur

LeBeque and had tortured the man to near death as his champion the de Sade would have done, though she, unlike the libertine, took no orgasmic pleasure in the act. When he was reduced to an eyeless, tongueless remnant of a human, clothed in shredded flesh and pawing at the air with raw, nubbed fingers, she drank his noxious blood and twisted his neck about.

But Danielle felt no satisfaction.

For 117 years, Danielle had found no satisfaction, no peace. It was she who wandered without purpose, followed closely by her two loyal friends, watched over by them, often protected by them. Yet they knew her restlessness and her longing for what she had once had, briefly, had not drained from her even as her own life had done.

She longed for Alexandre.

She pined for him and ached for him. Her days' sleeps in random cellars and stalls, attics and storehouses, were troubled with dreams. She cried his name out and awoke herself with her cries. Sometimes she would bite her own wrists to relieve the agony of her heart, or to bring her consciousness to a close once and for all, but it could not be done.

There was nothing for Marie and Clarice but to love her, still.

Buffalo was a thriving city in the western corner of New York State. It was Clarice's suggestion once Danielle began making noises that New York City was too crowded with their kind. Not just the loners but the Sisters as well. Marie and Clarice liked the fellowship, but Danielle wore irritable with them very quickly. And so when Marie suggested Buffalo, Danielle was ready to move.

The traveled by train at night, dressed modestly as women of the time were expected to do, in prim gray dresses of wool and satin that pressed their bosoms tightly into their chests. Their undergarments that cinched their waists unmercifully. When alone, they dressed as they pleased, and often went naked, but to pass in public they played the charade.

Marie had a brochure in her lap that touted the city's finer points. "They call it the 'Electric City of the Future,'" she read, holding the paper to the light of the lamp beside her on the wall. The train jerked constantly, and she had to move her head with the tremors to keep up with the printed words. "More electric lights are in use here than in many other places in the United States. What do you think of that, Danielle?"

"That sounds fine," said Danielle. She picked at the cloth-covered buttons on her bodice, imagining her hands were Alexandre's. His hands were beautiful. She would never forget those hands. Marie continued to read and Danielle heard nothing but the tone of her voice.

Then: "Danielle?" It was Marie.

"What?"

"You've been silent for hours. It's nearly dawn and the train is still miles from Buffalo. We must find a sanctuary."

The Sisters moved gracefully from the passenger car to the storage car. It was here that luggage was stacked, and flats of tools and boxes of foodstuffs and sacks of material and paper. They curled up into within three crates filled with nails, and awakened that evening on a loading dock along the Erie Canal. Quietly, they removed themselves before the dockmen got to the crates, and wandered out to Ohio Street to the scents of filthy water and ozone. A railroad track was in the middle of the street, and in the yellow glow of street lights an engine bearing a number of freight cars clacked and rattled past.

It was easy to find the part of town that reveled in drink and sex for money. It was not unlike the seedy sections of any city, except that here the dens and whorehouses sat toe to toe with grain elevators and shipyards. The number of undead was small, Danielle estimated no more than five or six from the vibrations in the air. They were the only Sisters. They stopped outside the gate to a large, canal-side elevator and teased the lone watchman at the gate into letting them in. "We're from France," cooed Marie. "Just freshly arrived, *Monsieur*. We've never seen such a structure. It has us quite mesmerized. Please?" She touched her red lips coyly, and winked.

The man, flustered with the attention, said, "I don't do no whores. Go on 'bout your business."

Marie feigned horror at the suggestion. "Whores? *Mon Dieu!* Sir, we are ladies in the truest sense, sisters come from another land to learn what we may. But if we offend, then we shall be gone." The three turned away, and the man relinquished.

"Well, then," he said quickly. "I'm sorry, ma'ams. I meant no disrespect. Come in and I'll show you how the grain elevators work here in ole Buffalo." He unlatched the gate and the ladies came through, invited. But his brief introduction to the history of the canal was cut off as the three of them fell onto him and took his blood, then his life. They then found a comfortable hideaway in a small storeroom next to the elevator.

The following days tumbled one into the other. The Sisters slept undetected in the storeroom during the day, pressed like shadows behind old bits of furniture covered in cobwebs and many months' worth of dust. At night they walked Ohio and Erie Street, dressed like ladies, unthreatening and demur, finding human creatures on which to feed and when done, throwing the twisted bodies into the canal with the other sewage.

Things were as they had been for a long time. Until early March, when Danielle was pretending to sip coffee at a shop soon after nightfall and she spied through the grease-iced window a fruit peddler on the street pushing his cart and wiping his brow with a large and muscular hand. The man's face was not familiar—a hollow and sunken face it was—and the body thin and unspectacular. But the hands she knew. The hands were Alexandre's. She gasped.

Marie and Clarice, seated at the tiny round table with their friend, reached for her. "What is it?" whispered Clarice.

"Alexandre," said Danielle.

"You're mad!" said Marie. "What blood have you drunk last, that you would think you have seen your dead lover?"

"It's him."

"It's a fruit vendor, for Christ's sake," said Clarice. "Get your wits, and now. Don't lose your head."

Danielle tore free and raced out to the street. The vendor was gone, and she spent the rest of the night tracing his path by his scent and the scent of his rotting pears and apples. But the smells of the Electric City were strong, and mingled, woven together into a brash and stinging tapestry, and she lost track.

They retired when the darkness began to dissolve into day, and for the first time since her rebirth in Paris, Danielle felt a new hope. A new reason to embrace her immortality.

She would be with Alexandre again.

Each subsequent evening she placed herself in the same shop, at the same table, buying a cup of tea she never drank, and gazed out for the fruit peddler. Even when the shop closed at eight, she stood on the corner with her irritable friends, and studied each of the dirt-coated vendors and scraggly, mobile merchants. Surely he lived in Buffalo. Fruit peddling was not a job that took one from town to town. She only stopped in her vigil to tend to her need to feed, then returned beneath the moon or the stars or the rain or the fog to catch her love and his cart.

Several weeks later, at quarter past three in the morning, while Marie and Clarice were seated on a trolley bench comparing loose stitching in their gloves, there was the shouting of drunken men and laughter from up the street, and then a small crowd stumbled past in a makeshift parade. One man was seated in a fruit cart, another pushed, while the rest danced beside them as if they were celebrating the King of Fools. The man in the cart, nearly out with drink, was Alexandre. Danielle motioned to her friends, and they followed the mob to a rickety tenement house near the railroad station. The men dumped the cart, fruit and all, then stumbled off to the street corner and out of sight.

Danielle hurried to the drunk man's side, pushed away the squashed fruit that covered him, and took his hand in hers. "My love," she said. Her heart hammered as if it was still alive. "My love, I've found you! Alexandre, it's me, Danielle!"

Marie said sternly, "Let it be, Danielle. It is not Alexandre."

But Danielle knew they couldn't believe. It didn't matter that they didn't. She did. She helped the man to his feet, and touched his split lip with her cold finger.

And then a screech from a window above, "William Kemmler, is that you? Get your sorry ass up these steps before I come after you with this hatchet, and I'll do it, you know I will!"

"Fishwife!" screamed Danielle. "You do not know who you are talking to!"

A lantern came to the window, and then many lanterns at many windows, and there were faces peering out and down. Someone shouted, "Fishwife? Tillie ain't Kemmler's wife, just pretendin' to be so they's can fuck and still go to church on occasion!" There was a burst of raucous laughter, and then someone spit, a long, hefty hawk the color of rust that landed with a *phatt* in a puddle near Danielle's shoe.

Danielle would let it go for now. For tonight. She would come again where there was not so much attention. For to try to reclaim him now would be careless. And carelessness could bring destruction. She had found him. She would return tomorrow, quietly, as her kind was greatly talented, and speak to him.

And bring him to his senses.

And back to her bed, back to her heart. And unlike the other misfortunates who had fallen under her bite, she would raise him from the dead for herself.

The following evening was clear and cold, with a sliver moon riding above the lights of Buffalo like a jealous and forgotten toy. Marie and Clarice warned Danielle to let it go, it was insane to believe her love was reincarnated into a fruit vendor, and when she refused to hear them, they refused to go with her. "We wash our hands of this," said Marie. "We cannot endanger ourselves for your folly, as much as we love you."

Danielle said, "Then do not."

She went to the tenement house and watched from the shadows of a dwarfed maple tree as the occupants wandered in and out. Within minutes, two ragged women came out to the stoop in hats and shawls, their teeth broken and brown, and one said, "You get me some of them cigars if you can, Tillie. If you swipe 'em, we can sell 'em and make us a bit of coin, don't you think?"

Tillie, a skinny thing who could have been twenty or forty, said, "I'll swipe 'em and you can pay like the rest of 'em."

"Bitch!"

Tillie strode from the stoop and the other woman spun angrily and went in the other direction.

Danielle counted to twenty. And then she went to the door of the tenement and waited. A man opened the front door, and flinched when he saw her standing there. She kept her lids lowered so the red of her eyes would not be so obvious. "Hey, honey," he said. "What's a fine-looking wench like you doin' standing here?"

"Waiting for you to invite me inside," said Danielle simply. The man did. She broke his neck in the hall, and stuffed him under the steps. No one was outside the flats to see, and she guessed they might not have cared much, anyway.

Tillie had shouted from a third-floor window, on the left. Danielle trod softly and quickly up the flights of stairs to the flat that surely belonged to William—to Alexandre. The door was locked, but with a simple jerk to the handle it swung open freely. She stepped inside the cluttered apartment.

There were three rooms, set like boxcars one behind the other. Danielle stood in the kitchen. A door to the left led to a parlor. A door to the right led to a bedroom. There was a pot on the cast iron stove half-filled with slop. There was a bedpan on the floor by the table, filled with urine.

"Alexandre," whispered Danielle. "What has brought you to another difficult life? You suffered in Paris, and you suffer here. What, precious love, has so cursed you?"

She moved silently into the parlor. Several framed portraits sat, covered in dust, on a tiny table. The cushion of blue-upholstered settee had popped its seams, and down oozed from the splits. There was a small shelf on the wall behind the settee. On it was an ink well, a pen, several volumes, and a black leather book bound with string.

"Yes!" hissed Danielle. "It is my love, no doubt!" She took the book from the shelf and dropped onto the lumpy settee. He had not wanted her to look in this Bible, but she could not let it be. She flipped through the thin, yellowed pages and came to a place which had been thumbed to near illegibility.

It was in the Book of Trials. She read:

When Pilate saw that he could prevail nothing to save the man Jesus and that Jesus was indeed to die to please the crowd, he offered the execution of noble captives, to have the man's wrists slashed with sword and thus causing him to bleed quickly unto death. But from the crowd called up the man Andrew, son of

Phinneas the shepherd, who said, Jesus must suffer for his words! Crucify Him!
The crowd joined in the mocking call, He must suffer for his words!

"What has this to do with you, Alexandre?" Danielle wondered aloud. "I don't understand. Jesus, give me understanding so I can help my dearest lover!"

There was thumping at the door, and a woman came into the kitchen. It was Tillie. She saw Danielle through the doorway, and her lips drew back in a snarl. "Bitch!" she shrieked. "Come back to fix my shoe and what do I find here? One of William's whores, no doubt, brazen and bold as a sow, sitting on my very own sofa, she is! Waiting for him to come home, eh? Waiting to suck his little worthless worm for a few pennies, yes?"

Danielle stood slowly. There would be no contest with this woman, but she didn't care to kill her if she didn't have to. "I'm sorry," she said. "I've made a mistake. I thought this was the home of my cousin Randolph Sykes. I beg your pardon, miss."

But the woman was not to be appeased, and she reached for a hatchet that was leaning against the stove.

Danielle held out her hand. "Miss, just let me go. It would be for the best."

"What's the best is that William quit his whorin'. What's best is you die quickly and keep your trap shut about it." Tillie ran her wrist across her nose, sniffed, and stepped into the parlor, hatchet raised.

Calmly: "Put it down."

Tillie's mouth opened wide; she growled and stepped closer. "Down middle o' your head, that'd look good! Part your hair right down the middle!" And the hatchet swung out in an arc, and down toward Danielle's forehead. Danielle stepped deftly to the side and the settee received the full force of the blow. Feathers flew. "Damn it!" screamed the woman. She tugged the hatchet free and spun on Danielle again. Danielle backed into the kitchen. She would come back again, later. She'd been invited into the building so entering would be no trouble.

Suddenly there was panting on the steps, in the hall, outside the door, and she whipped about to see Alexandre standing there, clutching the doorframe and panting. He looked past Danielle to the woman with the hatchet.

"You cow!" he cried. "I could hear you wailin' from the street below! What you doin' now, gonna kill some woman who looks like she just got lost?"

"Alexandre," whispered Danielle in amazement.

But the man brushed past her and flew at Tillie, snatching for the hatchet as he clutched her hair with his other hand. "Pig! You can't be trusted with nothin' or nobody! Oughta stick you in the asylum, I oughta! Give me the damned hatchet or you'll find yourself up for murder!"

Tillie jumped away, stumbled against a straight-backed chair and fell to the floor. Alexandre—William—leapt again and grabbed for the weapon. She swung it at him and missed his face by a hair's breath.

Danielle stepped into the parlor. She could be cut, it wouldn't matter. But she would not let Alexandre be killed. Not again. She reached for the wavering hatchet just as the man snatched it from the woman on the floor.

"Get back!" he cried to Danielle.

Tillie was up on her feet in a second, and latched on to Alexandre's arm with her teeth. He screamed, and began to strike her shoulder with the blade. Again. Again.

Again.

"I'm sick of you, I'm sick of you, I'm sick of you!" he wailed.

Danielle watched in horror as the woman stumbled past her into the kitchen and fell through the door and down the stairs to the landing. Alexandre, enraged, followed, and planted a solid blow to her head. The woman on the landing stopped moving.

Every flat door seemed to open at the same moment. Screams and curses followed, with fingers pointing at Alexandre and Danielle. "Murderer!" a man cried. "Killer!" screamed a child.

Danielle, dumbfounded, retreated to the apartment and escaped through the window into the mist of the night.

William Kemmler confessed to the murder of his common-law wife, Matilda Ziegler, and was sentenced to death by the state of New York. He was transferred to the prison in Auburn, where in August of 1890 he awaited his execution.

But the execution was to be a civil and humane one, the first one in which electricity would be used to snuff out the life of the convicted. A chair had been built of oak and electrical circuits, and tested on animals to make sure the death would be humane. Though there had been arguments between the two leading moguls of electric power, Thomas Edison and George Westinghouse, as to which of the currents—Edison's "Direct Current" and Westinghouse's "Alternating Current"—it came to be through some underhanded manipulation that Edison assured that AC current would be used for the electric chair. Although Westinghouse refused to sell his equipment to the prison for the death machine, Edison arranged for some used equipment to be purchased without his competitor's knowledge and made into the chair. This, Edison knew, would seal in the minds of Americans that AC was deadly, and so DC should be used in homes. Men at Auburn prison as well as reporters in their daily and weekly newspapers began joking that a man put to death in the electric chair would be said to have been "Westinghoused," a term that horrified the developer of the alternating current.

None of this mattered to William Kemmler, however, nor to Danielle Boquet. With her charm and grace she had been able to gain welcome into the prison's main building, but had yet to be invited to enter the cold portion of the death house where her Alexandre awaited his execution. She had the power to kill the guards but did not have the power to force them to offer her entrance.

And so she waited. And she fretted. And Marie and Clarice tried to console her. She went back time and again to the tenement flat in hopes she might find a way to help her love escape yet another death by the great and humane society, but there was nothing. She took the black Bible and kept it close in her skirt's pocket, but reading it did nothing. Explained nothing.

Danielle clung to the exterior wall of the death chamber at night, and during the day slept in a closet of the prison's gasworks. Marie and Clarice stayed with her, assuring her that it was not Alexandre and once he was dead she would come to her senses.

Witnesses arrived at the prison the evening of August 6, twenty-five men, fourteen of them doctors, anxious and excited to see this new death which would not cause undo suffering. The death chamber itself was in the cellar, and Danielle lay in the steamy, bug-infested grass at one of the windows, staring through the steel bars and glass at the horrific scene playing out below. The witnesses walked in, clutching top hats and gloves, and most of them settled themselves on seats that had been arranged to face the electric chair. Other men stood. And then the warden and several guards entered, with Alexandre between them. A priest, looking bored and disinterested, followed behind in his robe, holding his Scriptures to his chest.

Alexandre glanced about the damp, stark room. His eyes were red-rimmed with lack of sleep and the terror of the impending. The guards nodded at the chair. He walked to it, but could not seem to sit down. A guard said, "You'll like this a lot better than the gallows, boy."

"I must get in," whispered Danielle to her Sisters behind her. Marie and Clarice, standing a few yards back, said, "You cannot."

Alexandre turned and lowered himself into the chair. Then he sprang up again. "I remember!" he shouted.

"Shut up and sit down," said the warden. "We'll break your arms to do it if we have to."

"No, no, hear me, I remember!" Alexandre's face twisted with dreadful knowledge. "Oh, God, I remember!"

The warden shoved Alexandre into the chair. Guards began securing the leather straps at his legs and arms. But Alexandre continued. "I remember the blade on my throat, the quick slash of the merciful Africans who said I was the first to die a civil death! I remember the blade of the Guillotine, and the assurance that the execution would be painless. I remember now! Why again?"

"He's crazed with fear," said one nervous doctor. "Let's have it done!"

"I know why! I am Sula! I am Alexandre! I am William!" said Alexandre. "But I was Andrew, by my own mouth condemning me again and again to that which I would not allow our Lord! A fair and gentle death. A courteous and mild demise!"

A strap was quickly buckled at his waist and a leather harness with electrodes was shoved down onto his head. "Enough babbling!" said the warden. "Shut your mouth, criminal!"

Danielle pressed her forehead to the tiny slit of window and screamed, "Alexandre, then do you remember me?"

All faces spun toward the window. Alexandre stared, his mouth open. "Alexandre! Let me in!"

Behind Danielle, Marie and Clarice gasped, "No, Danielle, let it be!"

Danielle banged on the steel bars. "Alexander, please, let me in!"

"Are you an angel, sent by Christ to stop this cycle?" said Alexandre. The guards fumbled with the chinstrap, and drew the leather through the buckle. Before they could seal his jaws shut with the strap, he managed, "Angel, come in!"

Marie grabbed Danielle's wrist from behind, and snarled at her, "Do not dare! They will see you for who you are. The priest has a crucifix. We will be done in, Sister!"

Danielle twisted violently, but Clarice took her other wrist and held it firmly. "We will not be destroyed by your carelessness!" Danielle bit her Sisters, and clawed. She kicked and spun, and the bones of her wrists shattered, but they would not let go.

Inside the cellar, she saw the priest raise his hand for the sign of the cross. He stepped back. A guard nodded to a man at the back of the room. "*No!*" Danielle screamed, and the witnesses ran their hands through their hair and shifted in their seats, uneasy with the spectacle this had become.

"Now," said the guard.

"No!" cried Danielle. She kicked the bars and the pane of the window. The glass shattered and sprayed the cellar floor with shards.

There was the sound of a rushing trolley, a high-pitched and whining burr that caused the entire room to vibrate. Alexandre's body convulsed and strained at the leather straps. Smoke rose from his hair, and then the hair caught fire, crackling and popping in a tongue of orange and blue.

"Jesus," said one witness.

"I pray he's dead already," said another.

The body danced within the confines of the chair, a puppet on electric strings, until the warden nodded and the current was shut off.

Danielle could not move. She lay in the grass, her fingernails dug into her forehead, her eyes staring, staring, taking it in and rejecting it at the same time. Alexandre, dead again.

And then Alexandre moaned. The witnesses gasped and put their hands to their mouths. The warden pointed urgently toward the man at the wall switch, who threw it again, and again Alexandre danced.

It was all done in six minutes. At last Alexandre was dead. Guards gingerly unstrapped him, complaining that he was boiling to the touch, and with coats over their hands for protection, they rolled the body onto a gurney that had waited at the side of the room. They covered it with a sheet. But when a doctor attempted to examine the body, he could not remove the clothing for the heat. The warden escorted the ashen-faced men from the death chamber until the body cooled.

"Half hour," the warden said. "Let it cool and let the air clear a bit. And get a guard to arrest those women in the yard!"

"I hate you," Danielle said to Marie and Clarice.

"No, you don't," said Marie.

"Oh, but I do," said Danielle. The hands loosened on her wrists, and she was at last able to transform herself to mist to move through the window and into the cellar. Her friends followed.

They stood amid the stench and the death. Danielle was silent for a moment and then said, "I'm cursed as much as he is."

"We are not cursed, Danielle," said Clarice, "we are blessed."

"What is a curse, then? That which you do not want, which you never asked for, yet which will not let you be!"

"It isn't Alexandre," Marie said again. "Come with us. Come with us."

"You don't know anything," said Danielle. And she did not go with them.

She stepped to the gurney and lifted away the sheet. Her love lay there, his sweet face charred half-away, his hair blackened and crisp. His beautiful hands cooked into claws. She held one hand and kissed it and cried her tears onto it.

"I would remove your curse if I could," she whispered. She bent to the scorched neck and bit there. The blood had the flavor of charcoal, and it made her vomit.

She heard the men's voices coming toward the chamber. Footsteps pounding the cement of the hall floor. She would go. But she would find him again. She would be keen and sharp, she would have her wits always awake, and be ready. She would follow him and perhaps, save him. Save him for what, she wasn't certain. Save him into what, she couldn't know. But she would find him.

She touched her skirt's pocket. The Bible was gone. It had gone ahead, to find her love once more.

"Until later," she said. On still-lingering tendrils of smoke, she left the cellar. Outside, Marie and Clarice were not to be found. She knew she would never see them again. That was all right. She did not want to burden them. She would do this alone.

She bought a red-eye flight ticket to Virginia from Illinois. She'd heard rumors that the Department of Corrections had decided to allow inmates on Death Row to choose the electric chair or the new, less violent, and certainly more civil method of death by lethal injection.

She did not know which condemned man was her Alexandre. She had searched for one hundred years for clues to his new life, and had found nothing. Now, though, she was close. He was there, clothed in another man's skin. She would know him by his hands.

She pushed up the plastic window curtain and stared at the moon. The moon was the same, year after year, century after century. Was it cursed?

"I come, Alexandre," she said to the night.

And if she failed, she would only have to wait again. And she had all the time there was. All the time there would be.

ΠiGHṭ LAuGHṭeR

Ellen Kushner

Ellen Kushner weaves together multiple careers as a writer, radio host, teacher, performer, and public speaker. She began her career in publishing as a fiction editor in New York City, but left to write her first novel *Swordspoint: A Melodrama of Manners*. It was followed by the World Fantasy Award– and the Mythopoeic Award–winning *Thomas the Rhymer*, *The Fall of Kings* (with Delia Sherman), and *The Privilege of the Sword*. She edited the anthology *Basilisk* and coedited *The Horns of Elfland* (with Delia Sherman and Donald G. Keller) and *Welcome to Bordertown* (with Holly Black). Her latest project is the collaborative serial *Tremontaine* (SerialBox.com and Saga Press).

Upon moving to Boston, she became a radio host for WGBH-FM. In 1996, she created Sound & Spirit, PRI's award-winning national public radio series. Her recent audio work includes narrating three of her own novels for Neil Gaiman Presents/Audible.com.

She now lives once again in New York City. In the twenty-first century, she no longer has to check the mailbox in her building lobby for rejection slips, but old habits die hard.

"Some stories just come to you whole, and this was one of them," explains the author. "I was living in New York, on the fifth floor of a building festooned with gargoyles. I walked downstairs to the mailbox to see if I'd gotten any rejection letters that day, and by the time I got back up to the apartment, I had most of this story in my head.

"I remember I was thinking, for some reason, about how vampires are always portrayed wearing evening dress, and what if that was not attributable merely to Hollywood; what if it was because they really liked to . . . ?"

THE THING IS, it's just that you start to hate the daytime. All the bad things happen during the day: rush hour, lines at the bank, unwanted phone calls, junk mail, overworked people being rotten to each other. Night is the time for lovers, for reading alone by lamplight, for dancing, for cool breezes. It doesn't matter if your blood is hot or cold; it's the time for you.

"Come on," I say, tugging at his wrist, "come on, let's have fun!" He holds back, reluctant. "Come on, let's dance!"

All over the city the lights are blinking off and on all the time. Night laughter. "Come on into the night!"

"Crazy," he says, "that's what you are." Rich nighttime laughter bubbles in me. I let a little of it show in the corners of my mouth to scare him. He's scared. He says, "You wanna dance?"

I turn away, shrug nonchalantly. "Nah, not really."

"You wanna . . . go for a ride?"

"Nah," I lick my lips, trite, unmistakable. "Let's go for a walk. In the park."

"No one's in the park at this hour."

"We'll be. Just the two of us, alone. With the long paths all to ourselves."

He rises, follows. The night is like that.

He's wearing a good suit, the best he's got. The night's the time for dressing up, dressing high, dressing fine. Your real night clothes, those are the pressed black and starched white that a gentleman wore, with maybe a touch of gold or a bright ribbon sash setting it off. And a woman was always sleek and bright, lean and clean as a new machine, streamlined as a movie queen. My dress is like that; it clings and swirls so smooth, so long. I stride along beside him in my spiky heels, like a thoroughbred horse with tiny goat's hoofs. Long ago, in Achaea, God wore goat's hoofs and played the pipes all night long. Pipes of reed, like the mouth of a saxophone, blowing long and lonely down the wind between the standing trees.

The trees of the park are sparse, hanging over us in ordered rows, dark and tall as the street lamps between them, but under the trees is shadow. The circles of light, when you come to them, are bright enough to read by. Little insects buzz and flutter against their haloes.

Bums are asleep on the benches; poor guys, don't even know if it's night or day. I always avoid them. The only thing they want is money; they never knew how to have a good time, or they've forgotten how. I knew someone once who couldn't bear the light of day, quite right. He'd get out of his white jacket and into a velvet dressing-gown, put on dark glasses and retire from the sunrise like poison, while we watched the lights going out in strings across the park, and he'd be making his jokes about what to do with the waking birds and their noise. Owl, I called him, and he called me Mouse. But finally he couldn't take it anymore, he took to sucking red life out of a wine bottle with thick glass, green as sunshades, and he lost the taste for real life altogether; now for all I know he's one of the bums on the benches. They know they're safe: we won't touch them if we don't have to.

This man I'm with, he keeps darting his eyes left and right, as if he's looking for a cop or a junkie or a mugger. I take his arm, press up against him. "You're cold," he says.

I flip my silver scarf twice around my throat. "No, I'm not."

Lights from the passing cars streak our path. I tilt my head back, eyes veiled against the glare of sky, the light bouncing off the clouds.

He says, "I think I see my office. There, over the trees."

I lead him deeper into the darkness, toward the boat pond.

He says, "Y'know it's really dangerous in here," coming all the time along with me.

I kick off my shoes, they go shooting up like silver rockets out over the old lake. My feet press the damp earth, soft and cool, perfect night feeling. Not just earth under them; there's old cigarette stubs moldering into clay and hard edges of glass and a little bird's bone.

Considerately I lean my back against a tree, unwrap my scarf, and smile one of my dream smiles.

"Cigarette?" I ask huskily. He fumbles in his pocket, holds the white stick out to me; I just lean there, holding the pose, and finally he places the end between my polished lips. I look up sultry through my eyelashes, and he produces a light.

Oh, the gorgeousness of that tiny flame, orange and strong in the darkness! You don't get orange like that by daylight. I suck it to a perfect scarlet circle on the end of my cigarette, and then I give it back to him, trailing its ghostly wisp of smoke. Automatically he smokes it.

Automatic, still too nervous. He doesn't know how to have a good time! He was a mistake, a good-looking mistake. But then, not every night is perfect. I sigh so quietly only the wind hears me. Frogs are croaking in the pond, competing with crickets for airspace over the distant traffic roar. Another good night, opening itself to me. All you have to do is want it.

"C'mere," I say in my husky dusky cigarette voice. His tie so neatly tied, his shoes so clean they catch the little light on their rounded surface . . . He walks towards me. The expression on his face is steadier, more hopeful: here at last is something he thinks he'll understand. He buries his face in my neck. My white arms glow around his shoulders.

He's all pressed into me now, I'm like sandwich filling between him and the tree. There's bubble of laughter in my throat; I'm thinking, *What would happen if I swiftly stepped aside and all his hard softness were pressing against bark?* But I just shift my weight, enjoying the way he picks up on it, shifting his body to conform to me. Now he likes the night. Now his hands have some life in them, running the maze between my dress and my skin. With my fingertips I touch his ears, his jaw, the rim of his collar, while he presses, presses, his breath playing like a brassy syncopated band, his life pulsing hard, trying to burst through his clothes. Owl always said, *Let them do that*.

He's working my dress up around my waist. His hands are hot. Ah, he's happy. He's fumbling with his buckle. I breathe on him and make him laugh.

"Fun?" I ask.

"Mm-hmm."

"You're having a good time now."

I tickle the base of his throat and he throws back his head, face joyous in the mercury-colored cloudlight. Night laughter rises in me, too strong anymore to be contained. It wells through my mouth and fixes on his throat, laughter hard and sharp as the edge of a champagne glass, wet and bright as a puddle in neon.

It's fun, it's wild, it's night-blooming orchid and splashing fountains and the fastest car you've ever been in, speeding along the coast . . . It's *life*.

He hardly weighs anything now. I leave him under the tree; the bums can have what he's got left. I take a pair of slippers out of my bag; it's after midnight, but I won't be running home barefoot, not like some unfortunate fairy-tale girl. Midnight's just the beginning for me.

In the distance a siren goes wailing by. Unsprung trucks speed across town, their trailers pounding as though they're beating the pavement to death. Moonlight and street light blend on the surface of the water.

I pass under the big statue of the hero on the horse, and walk jaunty and silent-footed among his many lamplit shadows. Around the bend I see a white gleam, too white and sharp to be anything but a pressed evening jacket. For a moment I think that it is Owl again. But his face, when he turns to look at me, is different.

His jacket is a little rumpled but not dirty, and his black bow tie is perfectly in place. He is smiling. I catch up to him.

"Cigarette?" he says.

"No thanks, I just had one."

He takes one from a gold-plated case, lights it and inhales slowly and contentedly. Where his lips touched it I see a dark stain.

"Hungry?"

"Not a bit."

"Wonderful night," I say.

He nods, still smiling. "Let's go dancing," he says.

We'll have a good time.

BOOTLEG

Christa Faust

Christa Faust grew up in New York City, in the Bronx and Hell's Kitchen. She's been making stuff up her whole life, and spent most of her teen years on endless subway rides, cutting school, and scribbling stories.

After high school finally had enough of her, she worked in the Times Square peep booths and later as a fetish model and professional dominatrix.

An avid reader and collector of vintage paperbacks, a *film noir* enthusiast, and a tattooed lady, she sold her first short story when she moved to Los Angeles in the early 1990s. Since then, her books have included two novels from Hard Case Crime, *Money Shot* and *Choke Hold*, along with *Control Freak, Hoodtown, Triads*, and *Butch Fatale: Dyke Dick: Double D Double Cross*.

Among Faust's movie and TV tie-ins are *Twilight Zone #5: Burned/One Night at Mercy, A Nightmare on Elm Street #2: Dreamspawn, Friday the 13th: The Jason Strain, Final Destination III: The Movie, Snakes on a Plane, Supernatural: Coyote's Kiss, Fringe: The Zodiac Paradox, Fringe: The Burning Man*, and *Fringe: Sins of the Fathers*.

"It's funny," reveals the author, "even though 'Bootleg' deals with blood-fetish and the cosmetic accessories of vampirism, I always thought of it as more of a ghost story or maybe even a zombie story (if you could make dead love get up and walk again), rather than a traditional vampire story.

"While I do enjoy bloodplay as a sexual indulgence, as a writer I find very little blood left to suck from that old archetype. As with my other 'vampire' story, 'Cherry' in *Love in Vein*, in this story I tried to take the idea in a slightly different direction. I wanted to get away from the whole doomed immortal thing, the romantic wish-fulfillment fantasy of being pale and thin and pretty forever and ever, and try to do something that was a little more human."

MONA CUT OFF his right hand first. It was more important to him than his penis, the source of all his brilliance, his ART (she could always hear the capital letters in his slow, jaded voice) and she took great pleasure in removing it. Then the left hand, severed just below the twisted copper bracelet she gave him last Christmas. Tattooed arms were next, lower then upper. Their swirling patterns seemed much more beautiful without him attached. She cut off his booted feet, left then right and added them to the growing pile. She sliced off his legs in thin denim sections until she reached his narrow hips. Before she detached his pelvis from the rest of his torso, she cut out his treacherous penis. (You'll never stick it in another anorexic art-school slut behind my back again, bucko.) She sliced up his belly and his stray-dog ribcage until there was nothing left but his head.

His face was serene, unaware of his own dismemberment as he was unaware of everything that did not fulfil his immediate needs. His eyes were as blue as the day Mona fell for him, a hard, pure shade of turquoise that she would forever associate with lies. She cut them out separately, left then right. She cut out his sweet, lying mouth and his angular, aristocratic nose, then tossed what remained of his head on to the pile.

"Bastard," she said softly to herself and dumped all his severed parts into the fire.

She watched him burn for a long minute, coiling flames as blue as his eyes as they devoured him. Then she set to work on the other photographs.

There weren't that many. Mostly just snapshots taken by friends. Mona and Daniel at various stuffy parties, she uncomfortable in a strappy black, thrift-store dress and he in his eternal art uniform: paint-flecked T-shirt and torn jeans and hand-rolled cigarette, too cool to dress up. Mona and Daniel in Jackson Square, posed against wrought iron and surrounded by the bright chaos of Daniel's paintings. Mona and Daniel in love, arms wound around each other, smiling and not knowing any better. She shuddered and added these to the fire.

Then the rest of Daniel by himself, photos she had taken when the angles of his face and the smooth muscles of his arms meant something to her. Daniel with streaks of cerulean and viridian across his chest and cheeks, a thick paintbrush clenched between his teeth. Daniel sleeping like a child with his fists curled up under his chin. She slashed at them with her scissors and tossed the fragments into the fire. The letters were all gone except for one, his most recent:

8/11/01

Mona,

I'm so sorry things went the way they did. I know I was an asshole and I would do anything to make it up to you if you'd let me. I know you're hurt, but you can't just shut me out after all we've been through together. Give me a chance to explain. If I could see you, talk to you, I'm sure we could work it out. This last week has been hell without you. I can't sleep. I can't eat. I can't paint. You're all I think about. I hate sleeping in this lonely studio, waking up every morning and reaching for you, only to find there's no one there. Look, I know what I did

was wrong, but don't you think I've been punished enough? I miss you so much.
Things will be different from now on I swear. Please call me, Mona. I need to
hear your voice.

I still love you.
Daniel

Mona shook her head and added the single sheet of expensive sketch paper to the fire. It was really a pathetic little fire, nothing but dark, glowing coals and pale tongues of reluctant flame in the center of the wide brick fireplace. It perked up a little with this latest addition, flaring bright and then dying down again. There was not much nourishment to be had from the leftovers of Mona's dead relationship.

All that was left was a handful of postcards from his trip to Paris. She fed them one by one to the fire, glancing only briefly at their charming little messages full of *I love you* and *I miss you* and sprawling doodles of hearts and spirals. She later found out he was fucking at least three different women during that trip. Burning these last shreds of their relationship was particularly satisfying.

As the postcards curled and blackened, their sweet lies devoured by the hungry flames, Mona felt giddy and light, buoyed up by her new freedom. Of course there had been tears and anger and broken dishes, but that seemed like a thousand years ago. Now, she felt cleansed and streamlined, stripped down to fighting weight. There was nothing left in the Magazine Street apartment that wasn't hers alone. She wandered slowly through the long rooms, touching things with strange reverence. Her curmudgeonly old word-processor, her spaceship-console stereo, bought with the unwieldy lump of money that accompanied the sale of her first novel. A glass bowl of chalky gray bone fragments gleaned from badly maintained graves in the city's many cemeteries. Tacky, colorful beads from her first Mardi Gras. Her things, her history. The uneven but sturdy shelves she constructed out of cannibalized scraps of wood and glass. A pair of spidery chairs she rescued from the trash and painted silver. Models of classic monsters, Frankenstein's creation and his bride, the tortured Wolf Man and the tragic Mummy, the Phantom of the Opera and the Creature from the Black Lagoon, all built and painted when Mona couldn't bear to look at the flashing cursor for another second. They were a habit that had horrified Daniel. He called them the most trashy, paint-by-numbers kind of non-art. But they were still here and Daniel and his ART were gone and this made Mona smile. It was as if there had never been a Mona-and-Daniel. There was only Mona, now and forever. A little wiser and a lot stronger, ready to get out there and kick the world's ass.

She stripped and showered, luxuriating under the cool spray for nearly an hour. She sang "I'm Gonna Wash That Man Right Out of My Hair" while she shaved the long, silky hair from her armpits. She only stopped shaving because Daniel thought it was sexy, so now she laughed as yet another fragment of the past went swirling down the drain.

Clean and fragrant, her skin still rosy from the shower, she sprawled across her new, post-Daniel sheets, on sale at Woolworth's for nineteen dollars and ninety-nine cents. They were dark, inky purple and smelled of innocence and fabric softener. Smiling to herself, she masturbated. She did not fantasize about anyone. Instead she dreamed of silk and water and the smell of her own skin. With each new orgasm, she felt empowered, propelled into the future.

8/17/01

Hey Mona,

You foxy bitch you. How the hell are ya? How's life in sultry New Orleans? You know I read your new book. It rules of course. Things are pretty cool here, workin hard and getting some decent sessions, but you know it's a boy's life and most guys don't trust a chick drummer (even a brilliant rhythm-goddess like myself). But I'm livin well and I got a loft in Willy-B where no one complains if I play all night. Life is good.

So anyway, my real reason for writing (besides undisguised lust for your body) is that Lulu and me are cutting a demo with this mad bass player named Nocturna and we wanna do "Blush." It was your best song and we'd really love it if you would come and sing. Come back to NYC and be Diva Demona again, just for a day, for old times sake. We'll even send you a ticket. Pretty please with sugar on top! We need to hang out and catch up. Maybe roll around with no clothes on. It's been too long, lady. I miss you.

Big love and a sloppy tongue-kiss,
Minerva

Sitting in an outdoor cafe in the Quarter with her bicycle leaning against the vine-covered brick beside her, Mona took a hot swallow of black coffee and frowned at the letter in her hand. It had been nearly ten years since she had kissed Minerva goodbye at JFK. They were never in love, only best friends and occasional, playful lovers. The night Mona fled the nightmare break-up of her live-in relationship with Victorine, Minerva had let her crash, had stayed up till dawn listening to scratchy old Kiss albums and the long and sordid tale of woe. Three days later, Minerva drove her to the airport with a single suitcase and a five-hundred-dollar loan. She picked New Orleans at random because it sounded exotic and romantic and she left her old life behind with visions of red-hot blues and chicory coffee and black-eyed Creole boys. She left everything, but most of all, she left Diva Demona.

Diva Demona, her long-lost alter ego. An apparition of ragged lace and torn velvet. Of leather and silver and dead-white flesh, of kabuki makeup and fang teeth and long black nails. She had wild black-briar hair streaked with lurid purple and a stage presence that was all blood and power, lust wrapped in razor-wire. Sometimes she wore latex, sleek and glossy like a futuristic wet dream, insectoid sexy and somehow more than human. Sometimes she wore silk, tattered gowns, and vicious corsets, like a ghost from a lost age. Men paid to watch her pose and sing, paid to feel the bite of her lash and the humiliating sting of her cruel tongue. She was a goddess and she knew it, young and arrogant and doomed. She was a burning construct with the half-life of plutonium, too volatile to live past twenty-one. So when Mona turned twenty-two, she left Diva Demona behind. The boundaries of that version of herself had become restrictive and she found she could not maintain that level of angst and theatrical rebellion without losing herself in the role. Her life had been reduced to shtick and she needed something new, something totally unexpected, to make her feel alive again.

So the idea of resurrecting that old persona was strange and even a little unpleasant, like lying down in your old crib. But even though Mona had been devoting all her time to writing over the past ten years, she hadn't lost her voice, and there was no reason why she should not go back home to see some old friends and sing some old songs. Diva Demona was dead and buried, but moderately successful writer Mona Merino was alive and well and looking for adventure. A vacation might do her good, wash the last traces of Daniel out of her system. So would have a fling with a strong, beautiful woman like Minerva, simple and sweet with no strings attached. She remembered Minerva's long, lanky body and the way her bleached and dreadlocked hair fell over her kohl-smudged eyes. She remembered long nights of conversation, of cheap red wine and Mr. Bubble baths, rock candy and stolen cigarettes. She wondered if her friend had changed as much as she had, if she still wore that smoky sandalwood perfume. Draining the rest of her coffee, Mona decided that she would go.

6/13/90

Victorine, my most exquisite slave,

I am at the dungeon, awaiting yet another repressed yuppie with a diaper fetish. Why must I endure these clowns with their desperate little pricks and their pedestrian masochism? Well, we all have to pay the bills and I'd rather be a mistress/mommy to my lame clients than slave/secretary to some misogynistic creep in the so-called "real world."

But you, my love . . .

Your delicious submission is the only thing that keeps me going on days like this. I miss you terribly, the pale, luscious curve of your upthrust ass beneath my lash, the trust in your bright eyes as I slide my last finger up inside you and curl my hand into a fist. I count the long hours until I can taste you again, the hot tang of your blood on my tongue.

Yours in Eternal Darkness, Mistress Diva Demona

Victorine pressed the yellowed letter to her lips, fingers tracing the pale scars that criss-crossed her bare chest. If she closed her eyes, she could still feel the bite of her mistress's straight razor, the heat of that hungry mouth on her burning breasts. If she opened her eyes, she could see her mistress replicated a thousand times all around her. The stark, black and white photos that were her living and her art crowded the walls with images of Diva Demona. Diva Demona on stage, sweat like diamonds in her glossy hair, black lips peeled back from acrylic fang teeth. Diva Demona poised in leather, all spike heels and attitude. Diva Demona naked and haughty, her dark bush gleaming between pale thighs. Victorine still worked shooting hopeful bands in ill-lit clubs, but her best work was of her mistress.

Beside her on the bed that she had shared with a goddess so many years ago (yesterday) was a fetishistic arrangement of love letters and memorabilia. Keys to hotel rooms and scraps of black lace. Bar napkins kissed with black lips and fragile bundles of dried roses. Rings of silver and onyx and rosaries with filigree beads. Nipple clamps and razor blades. In the dim illumination, the careful sprawl might be mistaken for a long, lanky figure reclining with one knee cocked like a dancer. On the pillow, where the figure's head would lie, Victorine had set a ragged oval of black velvet soaked in her mistress's perfume, a heady brew of cloves and roses called Night's Breath. She refreshed it every day. Its haunting aroma was the thread that bound the illusion, that gave it form. When Victorine was caught in its olfactory web, the letters and dreams became flesh and her goddess was real, the sting of her kiss and the delicious agony of her touch as true as the first time. It was as if there had never been a betrayal, and she had never been alone.

Victorine took in a deep, greedy breath, letting the fragrance transport her. The steel rings her mistress had driven through the tender flesh of Victorine's pale nipples felt cold, electric almost. Diva Demona would come again tonight. Victorine could feel it.

—

Mona gripped the grungy sink in the bathroom of a coffee shop in the East Village, panic sweat clammy in her armpits and on the back of her neck. She stared at her wide-eyed reflection in the cracked mirror. Until now, she had always thought the thick twists of early silver that had sprung up in her dark hair were striking and classy, a genetic tip of the hat to her Italian heritage. Now she wondered in a desperate frenzy if she shouldn't have had some kind of rinse. Minerva would think she was an old fart. She felt like an old fart in her plain black jeans and motorcycle boots. Yet trying to squeeze her new self into the old crushed velvet and leather would have been a joke, an exercise in infantilism.

"You look like a successful, independent thirty-one-year-old woman," she told her reflection. "You know who you are."

She fiddled with her belt buckle and slicked her mouth with an unnecessary extra coat of dark lipstick. With a deep breath, she grabbed her suitcase and yanked the door open.

Minerva had arrived while she was having her little moment in the John. Her heart froze and then revved like a Harley. She considered retreating to the bathroom but Minerva spotted her and there was nothing to do but wave and smile sheepishly.

Minerva rushed over and swept Mona up in a warm sandalwood embrace. The blonde dreadlocks were gone, shaved close to the scalp, and Minerva's tattoos seemed to have multiplied, colonizing her shoulders and the back of her neck. There were tiny lines around her dark eyes and a ring through her lower lip, but the rich scent of her skin and the mischievous curl in the corner of her wide mouth were just the way Mona remembered.

"You dirty bitch," Minerva cried, holding Mona's face between callused hands. "You look absolutely edible." She coiled a silver lock of Mona's hair around her finger. "I love the Elsa Lanchester thing. It makes you look like a real writer."

Mona pulled away, laughing. "You trying to say I look old?"

Minerva pulled her close. "I'm trying to say I missed you, you silly slit!"

Tears caressed the back of Mona's throat as she hugged Minerva back. "I missed you, too," she said.

They held each other for a good minute, content to lean into the embrace and let silent memories wash over them. Then, feeling a little wobbly, Mona let Minerva guide her to a table and order her a double espresso.

As the tide of catch-up chat flowed between them, the story of Daniel, the story of Minerva's latest butch beloved and her subsequent police-escorted departure, Mona became aware of something waiting to be said. Something important and delicate that Minerva wasn't sure if she should keep her mouth shut about. She knew her friend well in spite of ten years gone and sure enough, there came a strange break in the conversation. Mona sipped her second espresso, caffeine glittering in her veins.

"Y'know," Minerva said finally. "Not like it's my business, but I saw something really strange the other day and I thought you might like to know about it."

"Yeah, what's that?" Mona asked over the rim of her tiny cup.

"Well . . ." Minerva toyed with her napkin, folding it into chaotic origami. "Remember our new bass player, the one I told you about. Well, she lives in the building on East Ninth where you used to live. In fact, she lives in the apartment directly underneath the one you lived in. With Victorine."

The espresso in Mona's stomach gurgled, burning up the remains of her airline lunch. Just the name Victorine was enough to make her feel like eating a bottle of Rolaids.

"So anyway," Minerva continued, obviously uncomfortable, but unable to stop now. "I'm over there hanging with Nocturna and fucking with this new song when power in her place just dies. We could see lights on in other buildings outside so we figure a fuse must've blown or something. There's no light in the hallway either, so we grab a flashlight and start knocking on doors, to see if any neighbors have power. There's no one home on her floor, so we go upstairs. In the upstairs hallway, one light is on and one is off. Before I know what's happening, she's knocking on the door to your old apartment."

Minerva finished her coffee, just to have something to do.

"All the old stickers you put on the door, Siouxie and Sisters of Mercy and those weird little drawings, they were all still there. We could hear music inside so we knew there was power. Someone had to be home, but it took 'em a really long time to answer."

She paused again and Mona closed her eyes, a thin coil of nausea twisting in her stomach. She didn't want to hear it, but somehow she needed to.

"It was Victorine. She was all sweaty and she looked really nervous. She hasn't changed at all, y'know. She still wears that Cleopatra makeup and black lipstick and teases her shoe-polish hair up into this big old rat's nest, but she looks . . . I don't know. Dirty. Like she never washes all that white makeup off, just adds more. And the apartment, I mean, what I could see of it, was like a museum, a shrine to Diva Demona."

Mona turned her face away.

"Why are you telling me this?" She could feel the thick knot of a headache tightening in her skull. "I can't help it if some rejected psycho wants to keep a roadside Elvis Museum version of my past in her bedroom. That part of me is dead and buried. Why should I care what Victorine does with her wretched excuse for a life?"

"It's not that," Minerva said softly.

"Well what then?" Mona was beginning to feel sorry she came.

"When Victorine answered the door, she . . ." Minerva bit her lip. "She had some else with her."

"Great, the little leech found a new host."

"No," Minerva said. "It was you."

Mona frowned. "What?"

"Well, not you now." Minerva's eyes were dark, remembering. "It was Diva Demona."

The nausea that had been building in Mona's guts flexed like a body builder and she clenched her teeth, refusing to be sick. This was crazy. Even the thought of someone imitating her, imitating who she used to be, made her feel deeply violated, as if someone had dug up the corpse of a favorite child.

"You mean that crazy bitch has convinced someone to play the role of Diva Demona for her so she can pretend I never left?"

"It must be, although this was no bullshit dress-up. I mean, we've known each other since high school and I'm here to tell you, this chick even smelled like you. Or at least like you used to smell. If I hadn'ta known better . . ."

Mona's nausea began to curdle into slow anger in the acidic cocoon of her belly.

"I believe it," she said. "I really do."

She paused, chewing her lip. She remembered the first time she saw Victorine. Back then she was plain old Vicky, just a mousy girl with a camera at one of the shows, looking like it took all her courage to walk in the door. She was like a blank slate, an empty vessel looking for an identity. She met Diva Demona and she thought she found it.

In the beginning, it was really flattering, the way she paid such careful attention to the things Mona liked and the things she hated. She was so subtle, the way she changed herself to fit Mona's ideals.

Mona shook her head.

"She didn't know who she was before she met me," she said, half-angry, half-sick. "She worked so hard to become everything I thought I wanted, the perfect slave, wanting nothing but to make me happy. She cooked and cleaned and let me torture her in every way I could imagine. She was a pretty little vampire housewife and I was queen of her world. As long as I never changed."

Minerva nodded sympathetically.

"Christ, you don't have to tell me," she said. "She was like your own version of Frankenstein's Monster. You created her out of nothing, took a bland, blonde suburban chick and turned her into a Gothic vampire fan-girl from Hell, and when you got bored with the game, it was too late for her because the game was all she had. It's like she used up all her energy trying to be everything you ever wanted and there's nothing left for anyone else."

Mona laid her head in her hands, guilt and anger warring inside her.

"It's not my fault," she said, hating the weak sound of her voice.

"Hey, of course not."

Minerva slid her chair around the little table and put her arm around her friend. "Listen, I really didn't want to upset you with all this bullshit. I just thought you might want to know that someone is out there imitating you, that's all. Hey, look on the bright side. Maybe you can sue her for copyright infringement."

Mona smiled against Minerva's shoulder.

"Yeah, or go drive a stake through her heart!" Mona straightened up, fingers combing nervously through her silver-streaked hair. "Man, I thought I killed Diva Demona but that psycho bitch went and dug her up. Now my dead past is out there walking around and I feel like I oughta go shoot it in the head or something."

"Don't sweat it, kiddo. I'm sorry I brought it up." Minerva put her hand on her heart like a boy scout. "I swear it'll never happen again."

She leaned in and squeezed Mona's thigh.

"So, honey," she said, wiggling her eyebrows in preposterous imitation of some smooth-talking pick-up artist. "You wanna go back to my place and fool around?"

Mona laughed.

"Why, I thought you'd never ask!" she said.

Minerva had a session that night and so Mona struck out on her own, needing to move, to walk, to drink down the essence of the city, her long-lost lover. Some primal gravity drew her back to her old stomping grounds and she found herself walking the avenues of her misspent youth with a strange and clinging sense of unreality. It seemed the neighborhood had changed as much as she had. So many of the old familiar bars and clubs that had nurtured Diva Demona were gone, scabbed over with rusted metal shutters or mysteriously replaced by trendy cafés full of immaculate counter-culture acolytes. The streets all seemed fake, like a low-budget movie set of themselves.

She stood on the corner of First Avenue and Ninth Street, letting the warm ache of nostalgia wash over her. There was the Korean fruit stand where she always bought oranges and cookies and cool white roses. There was the newsstand where the old Indian man used to scowl at her choice of fetish-oriented periodicals.

In a sudden rush, she was assailed by ghosts, flickering memories of all those old endless nights sparkling with dreamy, drunken glitter and arrogant passion as she stalked these streets like a high-heeled predator, marking territory, immortal in that moment like only the young and stupid can ever really be. She remembered tumbling like a kitten through the most extreme fantasies with the utter conviction that there would never be a tomorrow.

She took a deep breath. The rich smell of hot salted dough and spiced tomatoes wafting from the steamy interior of the corner pizzeria competed with the dark thundercloud of patchouli and jasmine surrounding a vendor of essential oils and the toxic-sweet exhalations of passing buses. So many memories.

Mona shook her head. It was easy to be seduced by the past, the good times. Easy to forget the way that lifestyle had nearly swallowed her with its unrelenting embrace and narcotic bite. The armor-plated image of the Vampire Goddess, the mistress of men's fear and desire, the Queen of Pain, that exotic persona that she had worked so hard to craft had become a prison, a mask fused to the soul, with no escape, no way out. With Victorine, she had to be on stage twenty-four-seven, always performing until she began to forget who she really was. Victorine could never accept her longing for simplicity, for humanity. Everything had to be like those damn photos she always took. Gorgeous and exotic and frozen in time, immune to the entropy and inanity of everyday life.

It was Mona who had crated Diva Demona, but it was Victorine who would not let her die.

Mona bit down on the soft flesh inside her cheek. No matter what Victorine decided to do with her irretrievable leftovers, Mona had already escaped, years ago. That crazy life was forever past tense and she had grown up into a strong and unapologetic woman. A passionate writer who had mulched under the nightmares and ecstasies of the past to create fertile ground for unflinching fictions. She knew who she was.

She had missed three lights, lost in reverie. She wanted to laugh at herself, but her old apartment was less than a block away. She hustled across the street, determined to pass by that pit of hook-tipped memories without looking back. Two buildings away and then one. Her breath caught in her chest, and she cursed herself for a superstitious baby. She counted her footfalls as she walked along the coiled iron railing that fenced in the building's cluster of sad, dented garbage cans, passing the cement steps to the basement and the hot smell of fabric softener from the laundry room. Then the battered metal door with the number "3" still missing, visible only as a row of holes and an outline of older, lighter paint. She could see the ranks of mailboxes through the scratched safety glass. Her old mailbox still had the word Box written on it by Victorine as part of some obscure joke. She stepped away from the door and leaned her back against someone's car, feeling suddenly overwhelmed. Her gaze crawled up the building's brick skin toward the window of that forgotten world, that place where she had lived a thousand lifetimes ago. The black lace and velvet curtains were faded and dusty. Mona didn't know what she was expecting to see: maybe her own younger self peering down at her. Instead, she saw nothing but the still and ratty backside of those old homemade curtains that had seemed so deliciously gloomy and perfect back then when Victorine had stitched them together from balding velvet and tattered scarves out of the dollar barrel at Dizzy Dot's used clothing store.

Mona stepped away from the car and passed her hand over her eyes. When she looked back up a skinny young Asian girl on rollerblades was opening the door with a keychain sporting more toys and trinkets than keys. She looked back over her shoulder, her glitter-glossed lips twisted into a sardonic smirk.

"You coming in or what?" she said.

Mona wanted to say no, but instead she put her palm against the open door. The metal was cool and gritty, scarred with fine scratches and scribbled names nearly worn away to nothing. The girl wheeled away down the hall without another word. Mona swallowed and went inside.

1/21/91

My Beloved Slut,

One year we have been together. It was one year ago that I first held the delicate stem of your vulnerable throat between my fingers. First felt the dance of blood beneath your white skin. First tasted the luscious nectar of your submission. You are still as precious to me as you were on that first blood-kissed night. I will always love you, my exquisite slave, dark companion of my soul.

Yours in Eternal Darkness,
Mistress Demona

Victorine's lips tasted of tears and clove-sugar. She licked them repeatedly as she read the letter a third time before laying it back in place on the tattered bedspread. She stretched for the elderly tape player on her bedside table and ejected The Cure, tossing the cassette into the clutter. From the careful formation on the bed beside her, she selected a black and silver tape and slid it reverently into the machine. It was a much-played copy of the only demo Diva Demona ever cut. Its title, written in silver marker, in her mistress's own dramatic hand, was *Licking Shadows*.

The music unfurled in the aromatic dimness, swirling like incense around Victorine's naked body. Its gorgeous, hypnotic rhythms painted the inside of her closed eyelids with images of Diva Demona. When her mistress's voice slithered from the speakers, Victorine's flesh crawled with anticipation. Each visitation was stronger and longer-lasting than the one before it, and Victorine was sure that this time Diva Demona would come to stay.

She smelled her first. The exotic scent of Night's Breath, mingled with the subtle tang of passionate sweat and the secret musk of her thick, unshorn bush. She was afraid to open her eyes too soon, afraid that she might spoil it. Every tiny hair, every millimeter of skin was excruciatingly sensitive and she could feel the heat of her mistress's presence just seconds before she felt the touch.

Victorine gasped, tiny, secret muscles clenching deep inside her, and her eyes flew open.

Diva Demona stood over her, eyes burning and hungry black lips turned up in a sardonic smile. She was clad in torn black lace and a heavy leather corset, leather gloves and tall boots that laced all the way up her long white thighs. Her edges were hardly blurred at all, though her features still held a sort of soft-focus smoothness that bled out into the air around her.

"My most exquisite slave," she said. Her voice sounded slightly muddy, like a recording copied too many times.

Victorine's heart melted.

She slid to the floor and pressed her lips against the soft leather of her mistress's boots. She could almost taste the rich but vaguely unpleasant flavor of boot polish.

"My life for you, mistress," she whispered. "Anything for you."

Black-nailed fingers twined in the sticky snarls of Victorine's hair, pulling her up to the tips of her toes, yanking her head back to expose the scarred flesh of her throat. Her scalp burned and the knots of scar beneath her chin ached in curious anticipation, like track marks longing for the needle. She wanted to open her eyes, to drink in the living image of her beautiful mistress, but she was paralyzed with desperate desire. It didn't matter. Every angle, every curve of Diva Demona's fierce body and proud face was burned into her memory. She could see the lush black lips part, revealing shining canines like twin scalpels, seconds before she felt the caress of cold leather and the vicious, crushing pain of her mistress's bite.

Then, like a stiletto to the heart of her fantasy, the harsh voice of the doorbell.

Fighting for control outside the door of her old apartment, the doorway to the past, to the tomb of Diva Demona, the new Mona stood, hands opening and clenching without purpose. What the fuck did she think she was doing anyway? She had no desire to see Victorine or her new Diva knock-off. She told herself a thousand times to get out, to let dead dogs lie, but yet here she was. A film of chilly sweat coated her body. Her heart pirouetted madly. She had to piss. She could hear her own muffled voice, singing. She rang the bell again, following it up this time with her fist against the painted metal.

The door opened and in the thin slice of darkness, Victorine's narrow white face, first suspicious, then blank with shock.

The past ten years had been cruel to her former slave. Her hair and makeup was identical, but the face beneath was worn and plague thin. Her body beneath the tattered black kimono was hardly more than a skeleton, sharp bones straining against gray, unhealthy skin. She even smelled wrong. Under the heavy mask of her perfume lurked the thin, acrid stench of a skewed metabolism, of madness. Her unclean throat was smeared with blood.

"Victorine," Mona forced herself to say. "We need to talk."

Then, from over Victorine's knife-blade shoulder, a voice, her own. So young and arrogant, pretentious, real as flesh.

"Who dares to interrupt our pleasure?"

Mona would not allow the sickness in her belly to rise up and drown her. Anger was her only strength as she pushed the grimy door open all the way.

The apartment was unchanged, a meticulous shrine, just the way she remembered it.

And standing in the middle of the clutter with leather fists on her hips and black eyes blazing, was Diva Demona.

The air between them seemed to gel to a hideous thickness, skewing off into monstrously distorted perspective. Her own burning, kohl-smudged eyes stared back at her from the end of a howling tunnel. Greedy animal paws clutched at her intestines, pulling and twisting. She staggered to her knees in a pile of dirty black lace.

The stench of stale sweat seemed like the only normal thing in this mad new world, and Mona's floundering brain clung to this simple truth like a life preserver as the tips of her fingers began to split and bleed, spontaneous stigmata opening like crimson orchids, drops of blood slithering through the strange air towards a vast and gaping mouth (her mouth), pink tongue tasting, shiny black lips peeled back over fang teeth and there was blood in her mouth, just like it used to be, sweet and sickening, real as memories. She felt so weak, each beat of her heart like lifting a tremendous weight while Diva Demona stood above her, suddenly pure of outline like a living photograph superimposed on to the blue screen of the real world.

Mona's bloody hands seemed a thousand miles away, cold as moon rocks. Her flesh felt insubstantial, fading slowly, dissipating like some theoretical gaseous element. She felt so tired, but at her core was a white-hot rage slowly burning through the layers of narcotic lethargy. That thing walking around in Mona's cast-off skin was not her. It was nothing but a figment of Victorine's twisted imagination, clothed in fragments of dead love. Mona was real, flesh and blood, and she was furious.

"No," she said, forcing her numb lips to move. Heat pulsed though her body, bringing distant limbs back into focus. "You can't have this. I own who I am."

Mona closed her cold fingers into a fist and punched up through the apparition's pale chest.

The fine skin parted like rotted silk and a dull pain gripped Mona's struggling heart, but she would not flinch. Beneath the flesh of this lanky doppelgänger lay not the heat of living organs, but a strange chaos of texture that came loose beneath her fingers. There was a screeching wail that twisted up through the octaves until it lost all resemblance to Mona's voice and when she pulled her hand free, she held a fistful of crumpled letters.

The apparition before her clutched at the gaping hole in its chest, dried rose petals falling from between its fingers. The thing's face began to lose detail, its imitation of Mona's dark eyes melting into twin holes, lipsticked mouth splitting into a reptilian slash.

Grabbing a wrought-iron candelabra from a low table (Mona remembered buying it in a second-hand shop, a gift for Victorine's nineteenth birthday), she thrust the five burning candles into the monster's softening face.

A scream that was like two voices woven together and as one faded, the other swelled until Mona thought her eardrums would burst. She squeezed her eyes shut, vertigo filling the cavity of her skull and coursing through her belly. She felt as if she were suffocating, choking on the stench of burning. When she was able to open her eyes, she saw dull orange flames swathed in black smoke. The sagging old bed was burning, careful piles of letters swallowed by the greedy flames and Victorine was screaming, beating at the fire with her bare hands. Her ratted hair caught in a burst of carnival color and her screams became more frantic as she spun round and round like a flaming angel. In that moment, she was beautiful again and Mona remembered what it had been like to love her.

It must have been Mona who was screaming then when she sprang up and ripped the velvet curtains from the window. Throwing the heavy cloth over Victorine, she tackled the shrieking angel, knocking her to the floor.

The flames had begun a slow creep across the walls, tasting the photos and finding them good. All around them, the remnants of Diva Demona were being devoured one by one.

Victorine fought fiercely as Mona struggled to drag her out into the hallway, all the while ignoring the soft, reasonable voice in her head that whispered, Leave her. Let her die if she wants it. Let her die and Diva Demona will die with her.

It was all so preposterously B-movie-esque, monster and mad creator die together in the flaming ruin of the collapsing laboratory while the credits roll serenely over the destruction. But Mona knew that it could never be that simple. Diva Demona was a part of her and always would be. Victorine's patchwork version was gone, her festering obsession cauterized, cleansed and scraped clean. Letting her die now would be selfish and unnecessary, like shooting ex-lovers to avoid the uncomfortable experience of running into them at parties. Throat rough with ash and determination, Mona half carried, half dragged the girl she used to love out of the past and into the uncertain future.

There were already fire trucks outside the building when she staggered out into the street. Someone official took the struggling burden of Victorine from her arms and although she was still mostly covered by the singed velvet, Mona could see the skin that showed was shiny and lobster red, split bloodlessly in some places and charred black in others. Mona sat down on the curb, light-headed and dizzy with blood pulsing and churning in her throat. She hoped that she had done the right thing.

"One more time, Mona," the low voice of the producer suggested in the intimate space inside her headphones. She turned slightly and saw Minerva giving her the thumbs up from the board. Then the music filled her head and she listened intently, waiting for her cue.

This new version of her old song was a little slower, more muscular. Nocturna and the new guitar player had both brought their own strange twists to the familiar notes, giving it a life of its own.

Mona took a deep breath and came in soft over the driving bass, her heart beating hard in her chest.

As she sang, she found herself playing around the sounds more than she ever had before, weaving in and out of the spaces between the notes.

"Do you remember how it used to be," she sang. "When you and I were one. Come home to me, my long-lost sister, and embrace the damage done."

And somewhere between her memory and her mouth, the old words gained a kind of rich melancholy that seemed to transform the simple lyrics into a love song to a lost era. It felt so good, so cleansing. When she was through, there was a sheen of tears in her eyes.

Minerva burst into the booth and pressed a wet kiss to Mona's forehead.

"That was fucking inspired!" she said, yanking one ear of the headphones away from Mona's head and then letting it snap back.

"Ow, hey!" She pulled the headphones off and smiled. "Come on." Minerva took her chilly hand. "Don'tcha wanna hear how fabulous you are?"

Sitting in a folding chair behind the science-fiction glitter of the mixing board, Mona listened to herself. In her own ears, her voice sounded almost alien, like a living thing. There was an edge beneath the words, a rough tenderness that she had never heard before.

"There's a whole lot of living in that voice," the producer said, pushing brittle hair back from his eyes. "The old version was too pure, y'know. I don't go for that ethereal shit. You want to hear ethereal go to a fucking church. But this new version, it's meatier, more honest. I like it."

Minerva leaned in and handed Mona a pair of cassettes. One was new and unlabelled and the other was black and silver, labeled with her own handwriting.

"Why choose, when you can have both?" she said.

Mona turned the old demo over in her hands, fingers tracing the little silver roses she had drawn years ago.

"Where the hell did you dig this up?" she asked.

Minerva grinned. "You can't dig up what isn't buried, honey."

Mona slipped the tapes into her pocket, thinking of the past, of letters and lost love and the indelible images they leave behind, burned into the skin of history.

"I'll remember that," she said.

Bewitched

Edith Wharton

Edith Wharton (1862–1937) was a Pulitzer Prize–winning novelist, short story writer, and designer. She was nominated for the Nobel Prize in Literature on three occasions, and was well acquainted with many of the era's other literary and public figures, including Henry James, her closest friend and author of the classic supernatural novella, *The Turn of the Screw* (1898).

Although Wharton began inventing stories when she was six, she did not publish her first novel until she was forty. She was a productive writer, producing fifteen novels, seven novellas, and eighty-five short stories, along with poetry, books on design and travel, literary criticism, and a memoir.

Among her most famous works are the novelette *Etham Frome* (1911) and the novel *The Age of Innocence* (1920). She also wrote a number of her own supernatural stories, and these have been collected in *Ghosts* (1937), *The Ghost Stories of Edith Wharton* (1973), *The Ghost-Feeler: Stories of Terror and the Supernatural* (1996), and *The Triumph of Night* (2008).

"A classic is classic not because it conforms to certain structural rules, or fits certain definitions (of which its author had quite probably never heard)," the author explained. "It is classic because of a certain eternal and irrepressible freshness."

Which probably makes the story that follows a classic of vampire fiction . . .

I

THE SNOW WAS still falling thickly when Orrin Bosworth, who farmed the land south of Lonetop, drove up in his cutter to Saul Rutledge's gate. He was surprised to see two other cutters ahead of him. From them descended two muffled figures. Bosworth, with increasing surprise, recognized Deacon Hibben, from North Ashmore, and Sylvester Brand, the widower, from the old Bearcliff farm on the way to Lonetop.

It was not often that anybody in Hemlock County entered Saul Rutledge's gate; least of all in the dead of winter, and summoned (as Bosworth, at any rate, had been) by Mrs. Rutledge, who passed, even in that unsocial region, for a woman of cold manners and solitary character. The situation was enough to excite the curiosity of a less imaginative man than Orrin Bosworth.

As he drove in between the broken-down white gateposts topped by fluted urns the two men ahead of him were leading their horses to the adjoining shed. Bosworth followed, and hitched his horse to a post. Then the three tossed off the snow from their shoulders, clapped their numb hands together, and greeted each other.

"Hallo, Deacon."

"Well, well, Orrin—" They shook hands.

"Day, Bosworth," said Sylvester Brand, with a brief nod. He seldom put any cordiality into his manner, and on this occasion he was still busy about his horse's bridle and blanket.

Orrin Bosworth, the youngest and most communicative of the three, turned back to Deacon Hibben, whose long face, queerly blotched and moldy-looking, with blinking peering eyes, was yet less forbidding than Brand's heavily-hewn countenance.

"Queer, our all meeting here this way. Mrs. Rutledge sent me a message to come," Bosworth volunteered.

The Deacon nodded. "I got a word from her too—Andy Pond come with it yesterday noon. I hope there's no trouble here—"

He glanced through the thickening fall of snow at the desolate front of the Rutledge house, the more melancholy in its present neglected state because, like the gateposts, it kept traces of former elegance. Bosworth had often wondered how such a house had come to be built in that lonely stretch between North Ashmore and Cold Corners. People said there had once been other houses like it, forming a little township called Ashmore, a sort of mountain colony created by the caprice of an English Royalist officer, one Colonel Ashmore, who had been murdered by the Indians, with all his family, long before the Revolution. This tale was confirmed by the fact that the ruined cellars of several smaller houses were still to be discovered under the wild growth of the adjoining slopes, and that the Communion plate of the moribund Episcopal church of Cold Corners was engraved with the name of Colonel Ashmore, who had given it to the church of Ashmore in the year 1723. Of the church itself no traces remained. Doubtless it had been a modest wooden edifice, built on piles, and the conflagration which had burnt the other houses to the ground's edge had reduced it utterly to ashes. The whole place, even in summer, wore a mournful solitary air, and people wondered why Saul Rutledge's father had gone there to settle.

"I never knew a place," Deacon Hibben said, "as seemed as far away from humanity. And yet it ain't so in miles."

"Miles ain't the only distance," Orrin Bosworth answered; and the two men, followed by Sylvester Brand, walked across the drive to the front door. People in Hemlock County did not usually come and go by their front doors, but all three men seemed to feel that, on an occasion which appeared to be so exceptional, the usual and more familiar approach by the kitchen would not be suitable.

They had judged rightly; the Deacon had hardly lifted the knocker when the door opened and Mrs. Rutledge stood before them.

"Walk right in," she said in her usual dead-level tone; and Bosworth, as he followed the others, thought to himself: *Whatever's happened, she's not going to let it show in her face.*

It was doubtful, indeed, if anything unwonted could be made to show in Prudence Rutledge's face, so limited was its scope, so fixed were its features. She was dressed for the occasion in a black calico with white spots, a collar of crochet-lace fastened by a gold brooch, and a gray woolen shawl crossed under her arms and tied at the back. In her small narrow head the only marked prominence was that of the brow projecting roundly over pale spectacled eyes. Her dark hair, parted above this prominence, passed tight and flat over the tips of her ears into a small braided coil at the nape; and her contracted head looked still narrower from being perched on a long hollow neck with cord-like throat-muscles. Her eyes were of a pale cold gray, her complexion was an even white. Her age might have been anywhere from thirty-five to sixty.

The room into which she led the three men had probably been the dining-room of the Ashmore house. It was now used as a front parlor, and a black stove planted on a sheet of zinc stuck out from the delicately fluted panels of an old wooden mantel. A newly-lit fire smoldered reluctantly, and the room was at once close and bitterly cold.

"Andy Pond," Mrs. Rutledge cried to someone at the back of the house, "step out and call Mr. Rutledge. You'll likely find him in the woodshed, or round the barn somewheres." She rejoined her visitors. "Please suit yourselves to seats," she said.

The three men, with an increasing air of constraint, took the chairs she pointed out, and Mrs. Rutledge sat stiffly down upon a fourth, behind a rickety beadwork table. She glanced from one to the other of her visitors.

"I presume you folks are wondering what it is I asked you to come here for," she said in her dead-level voice. Orrin Bosworth and Deacon Hibben murmured an assent; Sylvester Brand sat silent, his eyes, under their great thicket of eyebrows, fixed on the huge boot-tip swinging before him.

"Well, I allow you didn't expect it was for a party," continued Mrs. Rutledge.

No one ventured to respond to this chill pleasantry, and she continued: "We're in trouble here, and that's the fact. And we need advice—Mr. Rutledge and myself do." She cleared her throat, and added in a lower tone, her pitilessly clear eyes looking straight before her: "There's a spell been cast over Mr. Rutledge."

The Deacon looked up sharply, an incredulous smile pinching his thin lips. "A spell?"

"That's what I said: he's bewitched."

Again the three visitors were silent; then Bosworth, more at ease or less tongue-tied than the others, asked with an attempt at humor: "Do you use the word in the strict Scripture sense, Mrs. Rutledge?"

She glanced at him before replying: "That's how *he* uses it."

The Deacon coughed and cleared his long rattling throat. "Do you care to give us more particulars before your husband joins us?"

Mrs. Rutledge looked down at her clasped hands, as if considering the question. Bosworth noticed that the inner fold of her lids was of the same uniform white as the rest of her skin, so that when she dropped them her rather prominent eyes looked like the sightless orbs of a marble statue. The impression was unpleasing, and he glanced away at the text over the mantelpiece, which read:

THE SOUL THAT SINNETH IT SHALL DIE.

"No," she said at length, "I'll wait."

At this moment Sylvester Brand suddenly stood up and pushed back his chair. "I don't know," he said, in his rough bass voice, "as I've got any particular lights on Bible mysteries; and this happens to be the day I was to go down to Starkfield to close a deal with a man."

Mrs. Rutledge lifted one of her long thin hands. Withered and wrinkled by hard work and cold, it was nevertheless of the same leaden white as her face. "You won't be kept long," she said. "Won't you be seated?"

Farmer Brand stood irresolute, his purplish underlip twitching. "The Deacon here—such things is more in his line . . ."

"I want you should stay," said Mrs. Rutledge quietly; and Brand sat down again.

A silence fell, during which the four persons present seemed all to be listening for the sound of a step; but none was heard, and after a minute or two Mrs. Rutledge began to speak again.

"It's down by that old shack on Lamer's pond; that's where they meet," she said suddenly.

Bosworth, whose eyes were on Sylvester Brand's face, fancied he saw a sort of inner flush darken the farmer's heavy leathern skin. Deacon Hibben leaned forward, a glitter of curiosity in his eyes.

"They—*who*, Mrs. Rutledge?"

"My husband, Saul Rutledge . . . and her . . ."

Sylvester Brand again stirred in his seat. "Who do you mean by *her*?" he asked abruptly, as if roused out of some far-off musing.

Mrs. Rutledge's body did not move; she simply revolved her head on her long neck and looked at him.

"Your daughter, Sylvester Brand."

The man staggered to his feet with an explosion of inarticulate sounds. "My—my daughter? What the hell are you talking about? My daughter? It's a damned lie . . . it's . . . it's . . ."

"Your daughter *Ora*, Mr. Brand," said Mrs. Rutledge slowly.

Bosworth felt an icy chill down his spine. Instinctively he turned his eyes away from Brand, and, they rested on the mildewed countenance of Deacon Hibben. Between the blotches it had become as white as Mrs. Rutledge's, and the Deacon's eyes burned in the whiteness like live embers among ashes.

Brand gave a laugh: the rusty creaking laugh of one whose springs of mirth are never moved by gaiety. "My daughter *Ora*?" he repeated.

"Yes."

"My *dead* daughter?"

"That's what he says."

"Your husband?"

"That's what Mr. Rutledge says."

Orrin Bosworth listened with a sense of suffocation; he felt as if he were wrestling with long-armed horrors in a dream. He could no longer resist letting his eyes return to Sylvester Brand's face. To his surprise it had resumed a natural imperturbable expression. Brand rose to his feet. "Is that all?" he queried contemptuously.

"All? Ain't it enough? How long is it since you folks seen Saul Rutledge, any of you?" Mrs. Rutledge flew out at them.

Bosworth, it appeared, had not seen him for nearly a year; the Deacon had only run across him once, for a minute, at the North Ashmore post office, the previous autumn, and acknowledged that he wasn't looking any too good then. Brand said nothing, but stood irresolute.

"Well, if you wait a minute you'll see with your own eyes; and he'll tell you with his own words. That's what I've got you here for—to see for yourselves what's come over him. Then you'll talk different," she added, twisting her head abruptly toward Sylvester Brand.

The Deacon raised a lean hand of interrogation.

"Does your husband know we've been sent for on this business, Mrs. Rutledge?"

Mrs. Rutledge signed assent.

"It was with his consent, then—?"

She looked coldly at her questioner. "I guess it had to be," she said. Again Bosworth felt the chill down his spine. He tried to dissipate the sensation by speaking with an affectation of energy.

"Can you tell us, Mrs. Rutledge, how this trouble you speak of shows itself . . . what makes you think . . .?"

She looked at him for a moment; then she leaned forward across the rickety beadwork table. A thin smile of disdain narrowed her colorless lips. "I don't think—I know."

"Well—but how?"

She leaned closer, both elbows on the table, her voice dropping. "I seen 'em."

In the ashen light from the veiling of snow beyond the windows the Deacon's little screwed-up eyes seemed to give out red sparks. "Him and the dead?"

"Him and the dead."

"Saul Rutledge and—and Ora Brand?"

"That's so."

Sylvester Brand's chair fell backward with a crash. He was on his feet again, crimson and cursing. "It's a God-damned fiend-begotten lie . . ."

"Friend Brand . . . friend Brand . . ." the Deacon protested.

"Here, let me get out of this. I want to see Saul Rutledge himself, and tell him—"

"Well, here he is," said Mrs. Rutledge.

The outer door had opened; they heard the familiar stamping and shaking of a man who rids his garments of their last snowflakes before penetrating to the sacred precincts of the best parlor. Then Saul Rutledge entered.

ii

As he came in he faced the light from the north window, and Bosworth's first thought was that he looked like a drowned man fished out from under the ice—"self-drowned," he added. But the snow-light plays cruel tricks with a man's color, and even with the shape of his features; it must have been partly that, Bosworth reflected, which transformed Saul Rutledge from the straight muscular fellow he had been a year before into the haggard wretch now before them.

The Deacon sought for a word to ease the horror. "Well, now, Saul—you look's if you'd ought to set right up to the stove. Had a touch of ague, maybe?"

The feeble attempt was unavailing. Rutledge neither moved nor answered. He stood among them silent, incommunicable, like one risen from the dead.

Brand grasped him roughly by the shoulder. "See here, Saul Rutledge, what's this dirty lie your wife tells us you've been putting about?"

Still Rutledge did not move. "It's no lie," he said.

Brand's hand dropped from his shoulder. In spite of the man's rough bullying power he seemed to be undefinably awed by Rutledge's look and tone.

"No lie? You've gone plumb crazy, then, have you?"

Mrs. Rutledge spoke. "My husband's not lying, nor he ain't gone crazy. Don't I tell you I seen 'em?"

Brand laughed again. "Him and the dead?"

"Yes."

"Down by the Lamer pond, you say?"

"Yes."

"And when was that, if I might ask?"

"Day before yesterday."

A silence fell on the strangely assembled group. The Deacon at length broke it to say to Mr. Brand: "Brand, in my opinion we've got to see this thing through."

Brand stood for a moment in speechless contemplation: there was something animal and primitive about him, Bosworth thought, as he hung thus, lowering and dumb, a little foam beading the corners of that heavy purplish underlip. He let himself slowly down into his chair. "I'll see it through."

The two other men and Mrs. Rutledge had remained seated. Saul Rutledge stood before them, like a prisoner at the bar, or rather like a sick man before the physicians who were to heal him. As Bosworth scrutinized that hollow face, so wan under the dark sunburn, so sucked inward and consumed by some hidden fever, there stole over the sound healthy man the thought that perhaps, after all, husband and wife spoke the truth, and that they were all at that moment really standing on the edge of some forbidden mystery. Things that the rational mind would reject without a thought seemed no longer so easy to dispose of as one looked at the actual Saul Rutledge and remembered the man he had been a year before. Yes; as the Deacon said, they would have to see it through . . .

"Sit down then, Saul; draw up to us, won't you?" the Deacon suggested, trying again for a natural tone.

Mrs. Rutledge pushed a chair forward, and her husband sat down on it. He stretched out his arms and grasped his knees in his brown bony fingers; in that attitude he remained, turning neither his head nor his eyes.

"Well, Saul," the Deacon continued, "your wife says you thought mebbe we could do something to help you through this trouble, whatever it is."

Rutledge's gray eyes widened a little. "No; I didn't think that. It was her idea to try what could be done."

"I presume, though, since you've agreed to our coming, that you don't object to our putting a few questions?"

Rutledge was silent for a moment; then he said with a visible effort: "No; I don't object."

"Well—you've heard what your wife says?"

Rutledge made a slight motion of assent.

"And—what have you got to answer? How do you explain . . .?"

Mrs. Rutledge intervened. "How can he explain? I seen 'em."

There was a silence; then Bosworth, trying to speak in an easy reassuring tone, queried: "That so, Saul?"

"That's so."

Brand lifted up his brooding head. "You mean to say you . . . you sit here before us all and say . . ."

The Deacon's hand again checked him. "Hold on, friend Brand. We're all of us trying for the facts, ain't we?" He turned to Rutledge. "We've heard what Mrs. Rutledge says. What's your answer?"

"I don't know as there's any answer. She found us."

"And you mean to tell me the person with you was . . . was what you took to be . . ." the Deacon's thin voice grew thinner: "Ora Brand?"

Saul Rutledge nodded.

"You knew . . . or thought you knew . . . you were meeting with the dead?"

Rutledge bent his head again. The snow continued to fall in a steady unwavering sheet against the window, and Bosworth felt as if a winding-sheet were descending from the sky to envelop them all in a common grave.

"Think what you're saying! It's against our religion! Ora . . . poor child! . . . died over a year ago. I saw you at her funeral, Saul. How can you make such a statement?"

"What else can he do?" thrust in Mrs. Rutledge.

There was another pause. Bosworth's resources had failed him, and Brand once more sat plunged in dark meditation. The Deacon laid his quivering fingertips together, and moistened his lips.

"Was the day before yesterday the first time?" he asked.

The movement of Rutledge's head was negative.

"Not the first? Then when . . ."

"Nigh on a year ago, I reckon."

"God! And you mean to tell us that ever since—?"

"Well . . . look at him," said his wife. The three men lowered their eyes.

After a moment Bosworth, trying to collect himself, glanced at the Deacon. "Why not ask Saul to make his own statement, if that's what we're here for?"

"That's so," the Deacon assented. He turned to Rutledge. "Will you try and give us your idea . . . of . . . of how it began?"

There was another silence. Then Rutledge tightened his grasp on his gaunt knees, and still looking straight ahead, with his curiously clear unseeing gaze: "Well," he said, "I guess it begun away back, afore even I was married to Mrs. Rutledge . . ."

He spoke in a low automatic tone, as if some invisible agent were dictating his words, or even uttering them for him. "You know," he added, "Ora and me was to have been married."

Sylvester Brand lifted his, head. "Straighten that statement out first, please," he interjected.

"What I mean is, we kept company. But Ora she was very young. Mr. Brand here he sent her away. She was gone nigh to three years, I guess. When she come back I was married."

"That's right," Brand said, relapsing once more into his sunken attitude.

"And after she came back did you meet her again?" the Deacon continued.

"Alive?" Rutledge questioned.

A perceptible shudder ran through the room.

"Well—of course," said the Deacon nervously.

Rutledge seemed to consider. "Once I did—only once. There was a lot of other people round. At Cold Corners fair it was."

"Did you talk with her then?"

"Only a minute."

"What did she say?"

His voice dropped. "She said she was sick and knew she was going to die, and when she was dead she'd come back to me."

"And what did you answer?"

"Nothing."

"Did you think anything of it at the time?"

"Well, no. Not till I heard she was dead I didn't. After that I thought of it—and I guess she drew me." He moistened his lips.

"Drew you down to that abandoned house by the pond?"

Rutledge made a faint motion of assent, and the Deacon added: "How did you know it was there she wanted you to come?"

"She . . . just drew me . . ."

There was a long pause. Bosworth felt, on himself and the other two men, the oppressive weight of the next question to be asked. Mrs. Rutledge opened and closed her narrow lips once or twice, like some beached shellfish gasping for the tide. Rutledge waited.

"Well, now, Saul, won't you go on with what you was telling us?" the Deacon at length suggested.

"That's all. There's nothing else."

The Deacon lowered his voice. "She just draws you?"

"Yes."

"Often?"

"That's as it happens . . ."

"But if it's always there she draws you, man, haven't you the strength to keep away from the place?"

For the first time, Rutledge wearily turned his head toward his questioner. A spectral smile narrowed his colorless lips. "Ain't any use. She follers after me . . ."

There was another silence. What more could they ask, then and there? Mrs. Rutledge's presence checked the next question. The Deacon seemed hopelessly to revolve the matter. At length he spoke in a more authoritative tone. "These are forbidden things. You know that, Saul. Have you tried prayer?"

Rutledge shook his head.

"Will you pray with us now?"

Rutledge cast a glance of freezing indifference on his spiritual adviser. "If you folks want to pray, I'm agreeable," he said.

But Mrs. Rutledge intervened. "Prayer ain't any good. In this kind of thing it ain't no manner of use; you know it ain't. I called you here, Deacon, because you remember the last case in this parish. Thirty years ago it was, I guess; but you remember. Lefferts Nash—did praying help him? I was a little girl then, but I used to hear my folks talk of it winter nights. Lefferts Nash and Hannah Cory. They drove a stake through her breast. That's what cured him."

"Oh—" Orrin Bosworth exclaimed.

Sylvester Brand raised his head. "You're speaking of that old story as if this was the same sort of thing?"

"Ain't it? Ain't my husband pining away the same as Lefferts Nash did? The Deacon here knows—"

The Deacon stirred anxiously in his chair. "These are forbidden things," he repeated. "Supposing your husband is quite sincere in thinking himself haunted, as you might say. Well, even then, what proof have we that the . . . the dead woman . . . is the specter of that poor girl?"

"Proof? Don't he say so? Didn't she tell him? Ain't I seen 'em?" Mrs. Rutledge almost screamed.

The three men sat silent, and suddenly the wife burst out: "A stake through the breast. That's the old way; and it's the only way. The Deacon knows it!"

"It's against our religion to disturb the dead."

"Ain't it against your religion to let the living perish as my husband is perishing?" She sprang up with one of her abrupt movements and took the family Bible from the what-not in a corner of the parlor. Putting the book on the table, and moistening a livid fingertip, she turned the pages rapidly, till she came to one on which she laid her hand like a stony paper-weight. "See here," she said, and read out in her level chanting voice:

"*Thou shalt not suffer a witch to live.* That's in Exodus, that's where it is," she added, leaving the book open as if to confirm the statement.

Bosworth continued to glance anxiously from one to the other of the four people about the table. He was younger than any of them, and had had more contact with the modern world; down in Starkfield, in the bar of the Fielding House, he could hear himself laughing with the rest of the men at such old wives' tales. But it was not for nothing that he had been born under the icy shadow of Lonetop, and had shivered and hungered as a lad through the bitter Hemlock County winters. After his parents died, and he had taken hold of the farm himself, he had got more out of it by using improved methods, and by supplying the increasing throng of summer-boarders over Stotesbury way with milk and vegetables. He had been made a selectman of North Ashmore; for so young a man he had a standing in the county. But the roots of the old life were still in him. He could remember, as a little boy, going twice a year with his mother to that bleak hill-farm out beyond Sylvester Brand's, where Mrs. Bosworth's aunt, Cressidora Cheney, had been shut up for years in a cold clean room with iron bars in the windows. When little Orrin first saw Aunt Cressidora she was a small white old woman, whom her sisters used to "make decent" for visitors the day that Orrin and his mother were expected. The child wondered why there were bars to the window. "Like a canary-bird," he said to his mother. The phrase made Mrs. Bosworth reflect. "I do believe they keep Aunt Cressidora too lonesome," she said; and the next time she went up the mountain with the little boy he carried to his great-aunt a canary in a little wooden cage. It was a great excitement; he knew it would make her happy.

The old woman's motionless face lit up when she saw the bird, and her eyes began to glitter. "It belongs to me," she said instantly, stretching her soft bony hand over the cage.

"Of course it does, Aunt Cressy," said Mrs. Bosworth, her eyes filling.

But the bird, startled by the shadow of the old woman's hand, began to flutter and beat its wings distractedly. At the sight, Aunt Cressidora's calm face suddenly became a coil of twitching features. "You she-devil, you!" she cried in a high squealing voice; and thrusting her hand into the cage she dragged out the terrified bird and wrung its neck. She was plucking the hot body, and squealing "She-devil, she-devil!" as they drew little Orrin from the room. On the way down the mountain his mother wept a great deal, and said: "You must never tell anybody that poor Auntie's crazy, or the men would come and take her down to the asylum at Starkfield, and the shame of it would kill us all. Now promise." The child promised.

He remembered the scene now, with its deep fringe of mystery, secrecy and rumor. It seemed related to a great many other things below the surface of his thoughts, things which stole up anew, making him feel that all the old people he had known, and who "believed in these things," might after all be right. Hadn't a witch been burned at North Ashmore? Didn't the summer folk still drive over in jolly buckboard loads to see the meeting-house where the trial had been held, the pond where they had ducked her and she had floated? . . . Deacon Hibben believed; Bosworth was sure of it. If he didn't, why did people from all over the place come to him when their animals had queer sicknesses, or when there was a child in the family that had to be kept shut up because it fell down flat and foamed? Yes, in spite of his religion, Deacon Hibben *knew* . . .

And Brand? Well, it came to Bosworth in a flash: that North Ashmore woman who was burned had the name of Brand. The same stock, no doubt; there had been Brands in Hemlock County ever since the white men had come there. And Orrin, when he was a child, remembered hearing his parents say that Sylvester Brand hadn't ever oughter married his own cousin, because of the blood. Yet the couple had had two healthy girls, and when Mrs. Brand pined away and died nobody suggested that anything had been wrong with her mind. And Vanessa and Ora were the handsomest girls anywhere round. Brand knew it, and scrimped and saved all he could to send Ora, the eldest, down to Starkfield to learn book-keeping. "When she's married I'll send you," he used to say to little Venny, who was his favorite. But Ora never married. She was away three years, during which Venny ran wild on the slopes of Lonetop; and when Ora came back she sickened and died—poor girl! Since then Brand had grown more savage and morose. He was a hardworking farmer, but there wasn't much to be got out of those barren Bearcliff acres. He was said to have taken to drink since his wife's death; now and then men ran across him in the "dives" of Stotesbury. But not often. And between times he labored hard on his stony acres and did his best for his daughters. In the neglected graveyard of Cold Corners there was a slanting headstone marked with his wife's name; near it, a year since, he had laid his eldest daughter. And sometimes, at dusk, in the autumn, the village people saw him walk slowly by, turn in between the graves, and stand looking down on the two stones. But he never brought a flower there, or planted a bush; nor Venny either. She was too wild and ignorant . . .

Mrs. Rutledge repeated: "That's in Exodus."

The three visitors remained silent, turning about their hats in reluctant hands. Rutledge faced them, still with that empty pellucid gaze which frightened Bosworth. What was he seeing?

"Ain't any of you folks got the grit—?" his wife burst out again, half hysterically.

Deacon Hibben held up his hand. "That's no way, Mrs. Rutledge. This ain't a question of having grit. What we want first of all is . . . proof . . ."

"That's so," said Bosworth, with an explosion of relief, as if the words had lifted something black and crouching from his breast. Involuntarily the eyes of both men had turned to Brand. He stood there smiling grimly, but did not speak.

"Ain't it so, Brand?" the Deacon prompted him.

"Proof that spooks walk?" the other sneered.

"Well—I presume you want this business settled too?"

The old farmer squared his shoulders. "Yes—I do. But I ain't a sper-ritualist. How the hell are you going to settle it?"

Deacon Hibben hesitated; then he said, in a low incisive tone: "I don't see but one way—Mrs. Rutledge's."

There was a silence.

"What?" Brand sneered again. "Spying?"

The Deacon's voice sank lower. "If the poor girl *does* walk . . . her that's your child . . . wouldn't you be the first to want her laid quiet? We all know there've been such cases . . . mysterious visitations . . . Can any one of us here deny it?"

"I seen 'em," Mrs. Rutledge interjected.

There was another heavy pause. Suddenly Brand fixed his gaze on Rutledge. "See here, Saul Rutledge, you've got to clear up this damned calumny, or I'll know why. You say my dead girl comes to you." He labored with his breath, and then jerked out: "When? You tell me that, and I'll be there."

Rutledge's head drooped a little, and his eyes wandered to the window. "Round about sunset, mostly."

"You know beforehand?"

Rutledge made a sign of assent.

"Well, then—tomorrow, will it be?"

Rutledge made the same sign.

Brand turned to the door. "I'll be there." That was all he said. He strode out between them without another glance or word.

Deacon Hibben looked at Mrs. Rutledge. "We'll be there too," he said, as if she had asked him; but she had not spoken, and Bosworth saw that her thin body was trembling all over. He was glad when he and Hibben were out again in the snow.

iii

They thought that Brand wanted to be left to himself, and to give him time to unhitch his horse they made a pretense of hanging about in the doorway while Bosworth searched his pockets for a pipe he had no mind to light.

But Brand turned back to them as they lingered. "You'll meet me down by Lamer's pond tomorrow?" he suggested. "I want witnesses. Round about sunset."

They nodded their acquiescence, and he got into his sleigh, gave the horse a cut across the flanks, and drove off under the snow-smothered hemlocks. The other two men went to the shed.

"What do you make of this business, Deacon?" Bosworth asked, to break the silence.

The Deacon shook his head. "The man's a sick man—that's sure. Something's sucking the life clean out of him."

But already, in the biting outer air, Bosworth was getting himself under better control. "Looks to me like a bad case of the ague, as you said."

"Well—ague of the mind, then. It's his brain that's sick."

Bosworth shrugged. "He ain't the first in Hemlock County."

"That's so," the Deacon agreed. "It's a worm in the brain, solitude is."

"Well, we'll know this time tomorrow, maybe," said Bosworth. He scrambled into his sleigh, and was driving off in his turn when he heard his companion calling after him. The Deacon explained that his horse had cast a shoe; would Bosworth drive him down to the forge near North Ashmore, if it wasn't too much out of his way? He didn't want the mare slipping about on the freezing snow, and he could probably get the blacksmith to drive him back and shoe her in Rutledge's shed. Bosworth made room for him under the bearskin, and the two men drove off, pursued by a puzzled whinny from the Deacon's old mare.

The road they took was not the one that Bosworth would have followed to reach his own home. But he did not mind that. The shortest way to the forge passed close by Lamer's pond, and Bosworth, since he was in for the business, was not sorry to look the ground over. They drove on in silence.

The snow had ceased, and a green sunset was spreading upward into the crystal sky. A stinging wind barbed with ice-flakes caught them in the face on the open ridges, but when they dropped down into the hollow by Lamer's pond the air was as soundless and empty as an unswung bell. They jogged along slowly, each thinking his own thoughts.

"That's the house . . . that tumble-down shack over there, I suppose?" the Deacon said, as the road drew near the edge of the frozen pond.

"Yes: that's the house. A queer hermit-fellow built it years ago, my father used to tell me. Since then I don't believe it's ever been used but by the gypsies."

Bosworth had reined in his horse, and sat looking through pine-trunks purpled by the sunset at the crumbling structure. Twilight already lay under the trees, though day lingered in the open. Between two sharply-patterned pine-boughs he saw the evening star, like a white boat in a sea of green.

His gaze dropped from that fathomless sky and followed the blue-white undulations of the snow. It gave him a curious agitated feeling to think that here, in this icy solitude, in the tumbledown house he had so often passed without heeding it, a dark mystery, too deep for thought, was being enacted. Down that very slope, coming from the graveyard at Cold Corners, the being they called "Ora" must pass toward the pond. His heart began to beat stiflingly. Suddenly he gave an exclamation: "Look!"

He had jumped out of the cutter and was stumbling up the bank toward the slope of snow. On it, turned in the direction of the house by the pond, he had detected a woman's footprints; two; then three; then more. The Deacon scrambled out after him, and they stood and stared.

"God—barefoot!" Hibben gasped. "Then it *is* . . . the dead . . ."

Bosworth said nothing. But he knew that no live woman would travel with naked feet across that freezing wilderness. Here, then, was the proof the Deacon had asked for—they held it. What should they do with it?

"Supposing we was to drive up nearer—round the turn of the pond, till we get close to the house," the Deacon proposed in a colorless voice. "Mebbe then . . ."

Postponement was a relief. They got into the sleigh and drove on. Two or three hundred yards farther the road, a mere lane under steep bushy banks, turned sharply to the right, following the bend of the pond. As they rounded the turn they saw Brand's cutter ahead of them. It was empty, the horse tied to a tree-trunk. The two men looked at each other again. This was not Brand's nearest way home.

Evidently he had been actuated by the same impulse which had made them rein in their horse by the pond-side, and then hasten on to the deserted hovel. Had he too discovered those spectral footprints? Perhaps it was for that very reason that he had left his cutter and vanished in the direction of the house. Bosworth found himself shivering all over under his bearskin. "I wish to God the dark wasn't coming on," he muttered. He tethered his own horse near Brand's, and without a word he and the Deacon ploughed through the snow, in the track of Brand's huge feet. They had only a few yards to walk to overtake him. He did not hear them following him, and when Bosworth spoke his name, and he stopped short and turned, his heavy face was dim and confused, like a darker blot on the dusk. He looked at them dully, but without surprise.

"I wanted to see the place," he merely said.

The Deacon cleared his throat. "Just take a look . . . yes . . . We thought so . . . But I guess there won't be anything to *see* . . ." He attempted a chuckle.

The other did not seem to hear him, but labored on ahead through the pines. The three men came out together in the cleared space before the house. As they emerged from beneath the trees they seemed to have left night behind. The evening star shed a luster on the speckless snow, and Brand, in that lucid circle, stopped with a jerk, and pointed to the same light footprints turned toward the house—the track of a woman in the snow. He stood still, his face working. "Bare feet . . ." he said.

The Deacon piped up in a quavering voice: "The feet of the dead."

Brand remained motionless. "The feet of the dead," he echoed.

Deacon Hibben laid a frightened hand on his arm. "Come away now, Brand; for the love of God come away."

The father hung there, gazing down at those light tracks on the snow—light as fox or squirrel trails they seemed, on the white immensity. Bosworth thought to himself, *The living couldn't walk so light—not even Ora Brand couldn't have, when she lived* . . . The cold seemed to have entered into his very marrow. His teeth were chattering.

Brand swung about on them abruptly. "*Now!*" he said, moving on as if to an assault, his head bowed forward on his bull neck.

"Now—now? Not in there?" gasped the Deacon. "What's the use? It was tomorrow he said—" He shook like a leaf.

"It's now," said Brand. He went up to the door of the crazy house, pushed it inward, and meeting with an unexpected resistance, thrust his heavy shoulder against the panel. The door collapsed like a playing card, and Brand stumbled after it into the darkness of the hut. The others, after a moment's hesitation, followed.

Bosworth was never quite sure in what order the events that succeeded took place. Coming in out of the snow-dazzle, he seemed to be plunging into total blackness. He groped his way across the threshold, caught a sharp splinter of the fallen door in his palm, seemed to see something white and wraithlike surge up out of the darkest corner of the hut, and then heard a revolver shot at his elbow, and a cry . . .

Brand had turned back, and was staggering past him out into the lingering daylight. The sunset, suddenly flushing through the trees, crimsoned his face like blood. He held a revolver in his hand and looked about him in his stupid way.

"They *do* walk, then," he said and began to laugh. He bent his head to examine his weapon. "Better here than in the churchyard. They shan't dig her up *now*," he shouted out. The two men caught him by the arms, and Bosworth got the revolver away from him.

IV

The next day Bosworth's sister Loretta, who kept house for him, asked him, when he came in for his midday dinner, if he had heard the news.

Bosworth had been sawing wood all the morning, and in spite of the cold and the driving snow, which had begun again in the night, he was covered with an icy sweat, like a man getting over a fever.

"What news?"

"Venny Brand's down sick with pneumonia. The Deacon's been there. I guess she's dying."

Bosworth looked at her with listless eyes. She seemed far off from him, miles away. "Venny Brand?" he echoed.

"You never liked her, Orrin."

"She's a child. I never knew much about her."

"Well," repeated his sister, with the guileless relish of the unimaginative for bad news, "I guess she's dying." After a pause she added: "It'll kill Sylvester Brand, all alone up there."

Bosworth got up and said: "I've got to see to poulticing the gray's fetlock." He walked out into the steadily falling snow.

Venny Brand was buried three days later. The Deacon read the service; Bosworth was one of the pallbearers. The whole countryside turned out, for the snow had stopped falling, and at any season a funeral offered an opportunity for an outing that was not to be missed. Besides, Venny Brand was young and handsome—at least some people thought her handsome, though she was so swarthy—and her dying like that, so suddenly, had the fascination of tragedy.

"They say her lungs filled right up . . . Seems she'd had bronchial troubles before . . . I always said both them girls was frail . . . Look at Ora, how she took and wasted away. And it's colder'n all outdoors up there to Brand's . . . Their mother, too, *she* pined away just the same. They don't ever make old bones on the mother's side of the family . . . There's that young Bedlow over there; they say Venny was engaged to him . . . Oh, Mrs. Rutledge, excuse *me* . . . Step right into the pew; there's a seat for you alongside of grandma . . ."

Mrs. Rutledge was advancing with deliberate step down the narrow aisle of the bleak wooden church. She had on her best bonnet, a monumental structure which no one had seen out of her trunk since old Mrs. Silsee's funeral, three years before. All the women remembered it. Under its perpendicular pile her narrow face, swaying on the long thin neck, seemed whiter than ever; but her air of fretfulness had been composed into a suitable expression of mournful immobility.

"Looks as if the stone-mason had carved her to put atop of Venny's grave," Bosworth thought as she glided past him; and then shivered at his own sepulchral fancy. When she bent over her hymn book her lowered lids reminded him again of marble eye-balls; the bony hands clasping the book were bloodless. Bosworth had never seen such hands since he had seen old Aunt Cressidora Cheney strangle the canary-bird because it fluttered.

The service was over, the coffin of Venny Brand had been lowered into her sister's grave, and the neighbors were slowly dispersing. Bosworth, as pallbearer, felt obliged to linger and say a word to the stricken father. He waited till Brand had turned from the grave with the Deacon at his side. The three men stood together for a moment; but not one of them spoke. Brand's face was the closed door of a vault, barred with wrinkles like bands of iron.

Finally the Deacon took his hand and said: "The Lord gave—"

Brand nodded and turned away toward the shed where the horses were hitched. Bosworth followed him. "Let me drive along home with you," he suggested.

Brand did not so much as turn his head. "Home? What home?" he said; and the other fell back.

Loretta Bosworth was talking with the other women while the men unblanketed their horses and backed the cutters out into the heavy snow. As Bosworth waited for her, a few feet off, he saw Mrs. Rutledge's tall bonnet lording it above the group. Andy Pond, the Rutledge farmhand, was backing out the sleigh.

"Saul ain't here today, Mrs. Rutledge, is he?" one of the village elders piped, turning a benevolent old tortoise-head about on a loose neck, and blinking up into Mrs. Rutledge's marble face.

Bosworth heard her measure out her answer in slow incisive words. "No. Mr. Rutledge he ain't here. He would 'a' come for certain, but his aunt Minorca Cummins is being buried down to Stotesbury this very day and he had to go down there. Don't it sometimes seem zif we was all walking right in the Shadow of Death?"

As she walked toward the cutter, in which Andy Pond was already seated, the Deacon went up to her with visible hesitation. Involuntarily Bosworth also moved nearer. He heard the Deacon say: "I'm glad to hear that Saul is able to be up and around."

She turned her small head on her rigid neck, and lifted the lids of marble.

"Yes, I guess he'll sleep quieter now—and her too, maybe, now she don't lay there alone any longer," she added in a low voice, with a sudden twist of her chin toward the fresh black stain in the graveyard snow. She got into the cutter, and said in a clear tone to Andy Pond: "'S long as we're down here I don't know but what I'll just call round and get a box of soap at Hiram Pringle's."

My Brother's Keeper

Pat Cadigan

Pat Cadigan is an American science fiction author who has lived in London since the mid-1990s. Often identified with the cyberpunk movement, she has won a number of awards, including the Hugo Award, the World Fantasy Award, and the Arthur C. Clarke Award twice, the latter for her novels *Synners* and *Fools*.

Her other novels include *Mindplayers*, *Tea from an Empty Cup*, and *Dervish is Digital*, and her short fiction has been collected in *Patterns: Stories*, *Home by the Sea*, and *Dirty Work: Stories*.

"Addiction really scares me," she reveals. "There are many different drugs, but addiction is addiction is addiction. It's harder to kill than a vampire and a whole lot hungrier, and it doesn't have limitations like sunlight or garlic or religious symbols."

"'My Brother's Keeper' was a story I had been writing on and off for several years before I finally finished it. It grew out of a rather unsavory experience I had back in my extreme and misspent youth, in a time before AIDS. Heroin chic, my ass."

ALL THIS HAPPENED a long time ago. Exactly when doesn't matter, not in a time when you can smoke your coke and Mommy and Daddy lock their grass in the liquor cabinet so Junior can't toke up at their expense. I used to think of it as a relevant episode, from a time when lots of things were relevant. It wasn't long before everyone got burned out on relevance. Hey, don't feel too guilty, bad, smug, perplexed. There'll be something else, you know there will. It's coming in, right along with your ship.

In those days, I was still in the midst of my triumphant rise out of the ghetto (not all white chicks are found under a suburb). I was still energized and reveling at the sight of upturned faces beaming at me, saying, "Good luck, China, you're gonna be something someday!" as I floated heavenward attached to a college scholarship. My family's pride wore out sometime after my second visit home. Higher education was one thing, high-mindedness was another. I was puffed up with delusions of better and my parents kept sticking pins in me, trying to make the swelling go down so they could see me better. I stopped going home for a while. I stopped writing, too. But my mother's letters came as frequently as ever:

Your sister Rose is pregnant again, pray God she doesn't lose this one, it could kill her; your sister Aurelia is skipping school, running around, I wish you'd come home and talk to her; and Your brother Joe . . . your brother Joe . . . your brother Joe.

My brother Joe. As though she had to identify him. I had one brother and that was Joe. My brother Joe, the original lost boy. Second oldest in the family, two years older than me, first to put a spike in his arm. Sometimes we could be close, Joe and me, squeezed between the brackets of Rose and Aurelia. He was a boner, the lone male among the daughters. Chip off the old block. Nature's middle finger to my father.

My brother Joe, the disposable man. He had no innate talents, not many learned skills other than finding a vein. He wasn't good-looking and junkies aren't known for their scintillating personalities or their sexual prowess or their kind and generous hearts. The family wasn't crazy about him; Rose wouldn't let him near her kids, Aurelia avoided him. Sometimes I wasn't sure how deep my love for him went. Junkies need love but they need a fix more. Between fixes, he could find the odd moment to wave me goodbye from the old life.

Hey, Joe, I'd say. *What the hell, huh?*

If you have to ask, babe, you don't really want to know. Already looking for another vein. Grinning with the end of a belt between his teeth.

My brother Joe was why I finally broke down and went home between semesters instead of going to suburban Connecticut with my roommate. Marlene had painted me a bright picture of scenic walks through pristine snow, leisurely shopping trips to boutiques that sold Mucha prints and glass beads, and then, hot chocolate by the hearth, each of us wrapped in an afghan crocheted by a grandmother with prematurely red hair and an awful lot of money. Marlene admitted her family was far less relevant than mine, but what were vacations for? I agreed and was packing my bag when Joe's postcard arrived.

Dear China, They threw me out for the last time. That was all, on the back of a map of Cape Cod. Words were something else not at his command. But he'd gone to the trouble of buying a stamp and sending it to the right address.

The parents had taken to throwing him out the last year I'd lived at home. There hadn't been anything I could do about it then and I didn't know what Joe thought I could do about it now but I called it off with Marlene anyway. She said she'd leave it open in case I could get away before classes started again. Just phone so Mummy could break out the extra linens. Marlene was a good sort. She survived relevance admirably. In the end, it was hedonism that got her.

I took a bus home, parked my bag in a locker in the bus station and went for a look around. I never went straight to my parents' apartment when I came back. I had to decompress before I went home to be their daughter the stuck-up college snotnose.

It was already dark and the temperature well south of freezing. Old snow lined the empty streets. You had to know where to look for the action in winter. Junkies wore coats for only as long as it took to sell them. What the hell, junkies were always cold anyway. I toured; no luck. It was late enough that anyone wanting to score already had and was nodding off somewhere. Streep's Lunch was one place to go after getting loaded, so I went there.

Streep's wasn't even half full, segregated in the usual way—straights by the windows, hopheads near the jukebox and toilets, cops and strangers at the U-shaped counter in the middle. Jake Streep didn't like the junkies but he didn't bother them unless they nodded out in the booths. The junkies tried to keep the jukebox going so they'd stay awake but apparently no one had any quarters right now. The black and purple machine (Muzik Master) stood silent, its lights flashing on and off inanely.

Joe wasn't there but some of his friends were crammed into a booth, all on the nod. They didn't notice me come in any more than they noticed Jake Streep was just about ready to throw them out. Only one of them seemed to be dressed warmly enough; I couldn't place him. I just vaguely recognized the guy he was half leaning on. I slid into the booth next to the two people sitting across from them, a lanky guy named Farmer and Stacey, who functioned more like his shadow than his girlfriend. I gave Farmer a sharp poke in the ribs and kicked one of the guys across from me. Farmer came to life with a grunt, jerking away from me and rousing Stacey.

"I'm awake, chrissakes." Farmer's head bobbed while he tried to get me in focus. A smile of realization spread across his dead face. "Oh. China. Hey, wow." He nudged Stacey. "It's China."

"Where?" Stacey leaned forward heavily. She blinked at me several times, started to nod out again and revived. "Oh. Wow. You're back. What happened?" She smeared her dark hair out of her face with one hand.

"Someone kicked me," said the guy I vaguely knew. I recognized him now. George Something-Or-Other. I'd gone to high school with him.

"Classes are out," I told Stacey.

Perplexed, she started to fade away.

"Vacation," I clarified.

"Oh. Okay." She hung on Farmer's shoulder as though they were in deep water and she couldn't swim. "You didn't quit?"

"I didn't quit."

She giggled. "That's great. Vacation. We never get vacation. We have to be us all the time."

"Shut up." Farmer made a half-hearted attempt to push her away.

"Hey. You kick me?" asked George Whoever, scratching his face.

"Sorry. It was an accident. Anyone seen Joe lately?"

Farmer scrubbed his cheek with his palm. "Ain't he in here?" He tried to look around. "I thought—" His bloodshot gaze came back to me blank. In the act of turning his head, he'd forgotten what we were talking about.

"Joe isn't here. I checked."

"You sure?" Farmer's head drooped. "Light's so bad in here, you can't see nothing, hardly."

I pulled him up against the back of the seat. "I'm sure, Farmer. Do you remember seeing him at all lately?"

His mouth opened a little. A thought was struggling through the warm ooze of his mind. "Oh. Yeah, *yeah.* Joe's been gone a couple days." He rolled his head around to Stacey. "Today Thursday?"

Stacey made a face. "Hey, do I look like a fuckin' calendar to you?"

The guy next to George woke up and smiled at nothing. "Everybody get off?" he asked. He couldn't have been more than fifteen and still looked pretty good, relatively clean and healthy. The only one with a coat. Babe in Joyland.

"When did you see Joe last, Farmer?" I asked.

"Who?" Farmer frowned with woozy suspicion.

"Joe. My brother *Joe.*"

"Joe's your brother?" said the kid, grinning like a drowsy angel. "I know Joe. He's a friend of mine."

"No, he's not," I told him. "Do you know where he is?"

"Nope." He slumped against the back of the seat and closed his eyes.

"Hey," said Stacey, "you wanna go smoke some grass? That's a college drug, ain't it? Tommy Barrow's got some. Let's all go to Tommy Barrow's and smoke grass like college kids."

"Shut *up,*" said Farmer irritably. He seemed a little more alert now. "Tommy's outa town, I'm tryin' to think here." He put a heavy hand on my shoulder. "The other day, Joe was around. With this older woman. Older, you know?"

"Where?"

"You know, around. Just around. No place special. In here. Driving around. Just around."

I yawned. Their lethargy was contagious but I hadn't started scratching my face with sympathetic quinine itch yet. "Who is she? Anyone know her?"

"His connection. His *new* connection," Stacey said in a sudden burst of lucidity. "I remember. He said she was going to set him up nice. He said she had some good sources."

"Yeah. *Yeah*," Farmer said. "That's it. She's with some distributor or something."

"What's her name?"

Farmer and Stacey looked at me. Names, sure. "Blonde," said Farmer. "Lotta money."

"And a car," George put in, sitting up and wiping his nose on his sleeve. "Like a Caddy or something."

"Caddy, shit. You think anything ain't a Volkswagen's a Caddy," Farmer said.

"It's a big white Caddy," George insisted. "I saw it."

"I saw it, too, and it ain't no Caddy."

"Where'd you see it?" I asked George.

"Seventeenth Street." He smiled dreamily. "It's gotta tape deck."

"*Where* on Seventeenth?"

"Like near Foster Circle, down there. Joe said she's got two speakers in the back. That's so cool."

"Okay, thanks. I guess I'll have a look around."

"Whoa." Farmer grabbed my arm. "It ain't there *now*. You kidding? I don't know where they are. Nobody knows."

"Farmer, I've got to find Joe. He wrote me at school. The parents threw him out and I've got to find him."

"Hey, he's okay. I told you, he's with this woman. Staying with her, probably."

I started to get up.

"Okay, *okay*," Farmer said. "Look, we're gonna see Priscilla tomorrow. She knows how to find him. Tomorrow."

I sighed. With junkies, everything was going to happen tomorrow. "When will you be seeing her?"

"Noon. You meet us here, okay?"

"Okay."

Streep glared at me as I left. At least the junkies bought coffee.

I thought about going down to Foster Circle anyway. It was a traffic island some idealistic mayor had decided to beautify with grass and flowers and park benches. Now it was just another junkie hangout the straights avoided even in daytime. It wasn't likely anyone would be hanging out there now, certainly not anyone who wanted to see me. I trudged back to the bus station, picked up my bag, and went to my parents' place.

I hadn't told my parents to expect me but they didn't seem terribly surprised when I let myself in. My father was watching TV in the living room while my mother kept busy in the kitchen. The all-American nuclear salt-of-the-earth. My father didn't look at me as I peeled off my coat and flopped down in the old green easy chair.

"Decided to come home after all, did you?" he said after a minute. There was no sign of Joe in his long, square face, which had been jammed in an expression of disgust since my sister Rose had had her first baby three months after her wedding. On the television, a woman in a fancy restaurant threw a drink in a man's face. "Thought you were going to Connecticut with your rich-bitch girlfriend."

I shrugged.

"Come back to see him, didn't you?" He reached for one of the beer cans on the end table, giving it a little shake to make sure there was something in it. "What'ud he do, call you?"

"I got a postcard." On TV the drink-throwing woman was now a corpse. A detective was frowning down at her. Women who threw drinks always ended up as corpses; if she'd watched enough TV, she'd have known that.

"A postcard. Some big deal. A postcard from a broken-down junkie. We're only your parents and we practically have to get down on our knees and beg you to come home."

I took a deep breath. "Glad to see you, too. Home sweet home."

"You watch that smart mouth on you. You coulda phoned. I'd a picked you up at the bus station. It ain't like it used to be around here." My father finished the can and parked it with the other empties. "There's a new element coming in. You don't know them and they don't know you and they don't care whose sister you are. Girl on the next block, lived here all her life—raped. On the street and it wasn't hardly dark out."

"Who was it?"

"How the hell should I know, goddamit, what am I, the Census Bureau? I don't keep track of every urchin around here."

"Then how do you know she lived here all her life?"

My father was about to bellow at me when my mother appeared in the doorway to the kitchen. "China. Come in here. I'll fix you something to eat."

"I'm not hungry."

Her face didn't change expression. "We got salami and Swiss cheese. I'll make you a sandwich."

Why not. She could make me a sandwich, I wouldn't eat it, and we could keep the enmity level up where it belonged. I heaved myself up out of the chair and went into the kitchen.

"*Did* you come home on his account?" my mother asked as I sat down at the kitchen table.

"I got a postcard from him."

"Did you." She kept her back to me while she worked at the counter. Always a soft doughy woman, my mother seemed softer and doughier than ever, as though a release had been sprung somewhere inside her, loosening everything. After a bit, she turned around holding a plate with a sandwich on it. Motherhood magic, culinary prestidigitation with ordinary salami, Swiss cheese, and white bread. Behold, the family life. Too many *Leave It to Beaver* reruns. She set the plate down in front of me.

"I did it," she said. "I threw him out."

"I figured."

She poured me a cup of coffee. "First I broke all his needles and threw them in the trash."

"Good, Ma. You know the police sometimes go through the trash where junkies are known to live?"

"So what are they going to do, bust me and your father? Joe doesn't live here anymore. I wouldn't stand for him using this place as a shooting gallery. He stole. Took money out of my purse, took things and sold them. Like we don't work hard enough for anything that we can just let a junkie steal from us."

I didn't say anything. It would have been the same if he'd been staying with me. "I know, Ma."

"So?" She was gripping the back of a chair as though she didn't know whether she wanted to throw it or pull it out and sit down.

"So what," I said.

"So what do you want with him?"

"He asked for me, Ma."

"Oh, he asked for you. Great. What are you going to do, take him to live with you in your dorm room? Won't that be cozy."

I had an absurd picture of it. He'd have had a field day with all of Marlene's small valuables. "Where's Aurelia?"

"How should I know? We're on notice here—she does what she wants. I asked you to come home and talk to her. You wouldn't even answer my letters."

"What do you think I can do about her? I'm not her mother."

She gave me a dirty look. "Eat your sandwich."

I forced a bite and shoved the plate away. "I'm just not hungry."

"Suit yourself. You should have told me if you wanted something else."

"I didn't want something else. I didn't want anything." I helped myself to a cigarette. My mother's eyebrows went up but she said nothing. "When Aurelia comes home, I'll talk to her, okay?"

"*If* she comes home. Sometimes she doesn't. I don't know where she stays. I don't know if she even bothers to go to school sometimes."

I tapped ashes into the ashtray. "*I* was never able to get away with anything like that."

The look she gave me was unidentifiable. Her eyelids lowered, one corner of her mouth pulling down. For a few moments I saw her as a stranger, some woman I'd never seen before who was waiting for me to figure something out but who was pretty sure I was too stupid to do it."

"Okay, *if* she comes home, I'll talk to her."

"Don't do me any favors. Anyway, you'll probably be out looking for *him*."

"I've always been closer to him than anyone else in the family was."

My mother made a disgusted noise. "Isn't that sweet?"

"He's still a human being, Ma. And he's still my brother."

"Don't lecture to *me* about family, you. What do you think I am, the custodian here? Maybe when you back to college, you'd like to take Joe and Aurelia with you. Maybe you'd do better at making her come home at night and keeping him off the heroin. Go ahead. You're welcome to do your best."

"I'm not their mother or father."

"Yeah, yeah, yeah." My mother took a cigarette from the pack on the table and lit it. "They're still human beings, still your brother and sister. So what does that make me?"

I put my own cigarette out, picked my bag up in the living room and went to the bedroom I shared with Aurelia. She had started to spread out a little in it, though the division between her side and my side was still fairly evident. Mainly because she obviously wasn't spending a lot of time here.

For a long time, I sat on my bed fully clothed, just staring out the window. The street below was empty and dark and there was nothing to look at. I kept looking at it until I heard my parents go to bed. A little later, when I thought they were asleep, I opened the window a crack and rolled a joint from the stuff in the bottom drawer of my bureau. Most of the lid was still there, which meant Aurelia hadn't found it. I'd never liked grass that much after the novelty wore off, but I wanted something to blot out the bad taste the evening had left in my brain.

A whole joint to myself was a lot more than I was used to and the buzz was thick and debilitating. The smoke coiled into unreadable symbols and patterns before it was sucked out the window into the cold and dark. I thought of ragged ghosts fleeing a house like rats jumping off a sinking ship. It was the kind of dopey thought that occupies your mind for hours when you're stoned, which was fine with me. I didn't want to have to think about anything that mattered.

Eventually, I became aware that I was cold. When I could move, I reached over to shut the window and something down on the street caught my eye. It was too much in the shadows close to the building to see very well if it was even there at all. Hasher's delirium, or in this case. Grasser's delirium. I tried to watch it anyway. There was a certain strength of definition and independence from the general fuzziness of my stoned eyesight, something that suggested there was more to it than the dope in my brain. Whatever it was—a dope exaggeration of a cat or a dog or a big rat—I didn't like it. Unbidden, my father's words about a new element moving in slide into my head. Something about the thing made me think of a reptile, stunted evolution or evolution reversed, and a sort of evil that might have lain thickly in pools of decay millions of years ago, predating warm-blooded life. Which was ridiculous, I thought, because human beings brought the distinction between good and evil into the world. Good and evil, and stoned and not stoned. I was stoned. I went to bed.

But remember, said my still-buzzing mind as I was drifting into stupor-sleep, in order to make distinctions between any two things like good and evil, they first have to exist, don't they.

This is what happens when would-be intellectuals get stoned, I thought and passed out.

The sound of my father leaving for work woke me. I lay listening to my mother in the kitchen, waiting for the sound of bacon and eggs frying and her summons to get up and have a good breakfast. Instead, I heard water running briefly in the sink and then her footsteps going back to the bedroom and the door closing. That was new—my mother going back to bed after my father went to work in spite of the fact that the college kid was home. I hadn't particularly wanted to talk to her anyway, especially if it were just going to be a continuation of the previous night but it still made me feel funny.

I washed and dressed, taking my time, but my mother never reemerged. Apparently she was just not going to be part of my day. I left the house far earlier than I'd intended to, figuring I'd go find something to do with myself until it was time to meet Farmer and the others.

In the front vestibule of the apartment building, I nearly collided with my sister Rose, who seemed about ready to have her baby at any moment. She had dyed her hair blonde again, a cornsilk yellow color already brassing at the ends and showing dark roots.

"What are you doing home?" she asked, putting her hands protectively over her belly, protruding so much she couldn't button her coat.

"Vacation," I said. "How are you?"

"How am I ever? Pregnant."

"There *is* such a thing as birth control."

"Yeah, and there is such a thing as it not working. So?"

"Well. This is number five, isn't it?"

"I didn't know *you* were keeping score." She tried pulling her coat around her front but it wouldn't go. "It's cold down here. I'm going up to Ma."

"She went back to bed."

"She'll get up for me."

"Should you be climbing all those stairs in your condition?"

Rose lifted her plucked-to-nothing eyebrows. "You wanna carry me?" She pushed past me and slowly started up the first flight of steps.

"Come on, Rose," I called after her, "what'll happen if your bag of waters breaks or something while you're on the stairs?"

She turned to look at me from seven steps up. "I'll scream, what do you think I'll do?" She resumed her climb.

"Well, do you want me to walk up with you?" I asked, starting after her. She just waved a hand at me and kept going. Annoyed and amused, I waited until she had made the first landing and begun the next flight, wondering if I shouldn't run up after her anyway or at least stay there until I heard my mother let her in. Then I decided Rose probably knew what she was doing, in a half-assed way. My theory was that she had been born pregnant and waited sixteen years until she found someone to act as father. She hadn't been much smaller than she was now when she and Roger had gotten married, much to my parents' dismay. It hadn't bothered Rose in the least.

The sun was shining brightly but there was no warmth to it. The snow lining the curb was dirtier than ever, pitted and brittle. Here and there on the sidewalk, old patches of ice clung to the pavement like frozen jellyfish left after a receding tide. It wasn't even 10:30 but I went over to Streep's Lunch, in case anyone put in an early appearance. That wasn't very likely but there wasn't much else to do.

Streep had the place to himself except for a couple of old people sitting near the windows. I took a seat at the counter and ordered breakfast to make up for the night before. My atonement didn't exactly impress him but surprised me by actually speaking to me as he poured my coffee. "You home on vacation?"

"That's right," I said, feeling a little wary as I added cream from an aluminum pitcher.

"You like college?"

"It would be heaven if it weren't for the classes."

Streep's rubbery mouth twitched, shaking his jowls. "I thought that was what you went for, to go to classes and get smart."

I shrugged.

"Maybe you think you're already smart."

"Some people would say so." I smiled, thinking he should have asked my father.

"You think it's smart to keep coming around here and hanging out with junkies?"

I blinked at him. "I didn't know you cared."

"Just askin' a question."

"You haven't seen my brother Joe lately, have you?"

Streep made a fast little noise that was less than a laugh and walked away. Someone had left a newspaper on one of the stools to my right. I picked it up and read it over breakfast just for something to do. An hour passed, with Streep coming back every so often to refill my cup without any more conversation. I bought a pack of cigarettes from the machine just to have something else to do and noticed one of the old people had gone to sleep before finishing breakfast. She was very old, with frizzy gray hair and a sagging hawk nose. Her mouth had dropped open to show a few long, stained teeth. I had a half-baked idea of waking her when she gave an enormous snore. Streep didn't even look at her. What the hell, her hash browns were probably stone cold anyway. I went back to my newspaper.

When the clock over the grill said 12:10, I left some money on the counter and went outside. I should have known they'd be late, I thought. I'd probably have to stand around until close to dark, when they'd finally remember they were supposed to meet me here and not show, figuring I'd split.

A horn honked several times. George poked his head out the driver's side window of a car parked across the street. I hurried over as the back door swung open.

"Christ, we been waiting for you," Farmer said irritably as I climbed in. "You been in there the whole time?"

"I thought you were meeting Priscilla here."

"Change of venue, you should pardon the expression," Farmer said. "Streep won't give you a cup of water to go." He was in the front with George. Stacey and the kid were in the back with me. The kid didn't look so good today. He had dark circles under his eyes and wherever he'd spent the night hadn't had a washroom.

"Why aren't you in school?" I asked him.

"Screw it, what's it to you?" he said flippantly.

"Haven't been home yet, have you?"

"Chrissakes, what are you, his probation officer?" said Farmer. "Let's go, she's waiting."

The car pulled away from the curb with a jerk. George swore as he eased it into the light noontime traffic. "I ain't used to automatics," he complained to no one.

Farmer was rummaging in the glove compartment. "Hey, there's no works in here. You got any?"

"I got them, don't worry. Just wait till we pick up Priscilla, okay?"

"Just tell me where they are."

"Don't sweat it, I told you I got them."

"I just want to know where."

"Up my ass, all right? Now let me drive."

"I'll give you up your ass," Farmer said darkly.

Stacey tapped him on the back of the head. "Come on, take it easy, Farmer. Everybody's gonna get what they need from Priscilla."

"Does Priscilla know where Joe is?" I asked.

"Priscilla knows everything," said Stacey, believing it.

Priscilla herself was standing on the sidewalk in front of a beauty parlor, holding a big Styrofoam cup. She barely waited for the car to stop before she yanked the door open and got into the front seat next to Farmer.

"You got works?" he asked as she handed him the cup. "This asshole won't tell me if he's got any."

"In a minute, Farmer. I have to say hello to China." She knelt on the front seat and held her arms out to me. Obediently, I leaned forward over the kid so she could hug me. She was as bizarre-looking as ever, with her pale pancake makeup, frosted pink lipstick, heavily outlined eyes, and flat-black hair. The junkie version of Elizabeth Taylor. She was a strange little girl in a puffy woman's body and she ran hot and cold with me, sometimes playing my older sister, then snubbing me outright, depending on Joe. They'd been on and off for as long as he'd been shooting, with her as the pursuer unless Joe knew for sure that she had a good connection.

Today she surprised me by kissing me lightly on the lips. It was like being kissed by a crayon. "How's our college kid?" she asked tenderly.

"Fine, Priscilla. Have you—"

"I haven't seen you since the fall," she went on, gripping the back of the seat as George pulled into the street again. "How do you like school? Are you doing real well?"

Farmer pulled her around. "This is very sweet, old home week and all, but do you have anything?"

"No, Farmer, I always stand around on the street with a cup of water. Don't spill it."

"I've got a spoon," said the kid, holding one up. Stacey took it from him.

"Me first?" she asked hopefully.

Priscilla turned around and stared down her nose at her, junkie aristocracy surveying the rabble. "I understand I'm not the only one in this car with works?"

George was patting himself down awkwardly as he drove, muttering, "Shit, shit, shit."

"Asshole," said Farmer. "I knew you didn't have any."

"I *had* some, but I don't know where they are now."

"Try looking up your ass. Priscilla?"

Priscilla let out a noisy sigh. "I'm not going to do this anymore. Someday we're all going to get hep and die."

"Well, *I'm* clean," the kid announced proudly.

"Keep borrowing works, you'll get a nice case of hepatitis," I said. "Joe got the clap once, using someone else's."

"Bullshit."

"Tell him whose spike it was, Stacey," I said, feeling mean. Stacey flushed.

"And you want to go first?" Priscilla said. "No way."

"That was last year. I'm cured now, honest. I don't even have a cold." She glared at me. "Please, Priscilla. Please."

Priscilla sighed again and passed her a small square of foil and a plastic syringe. "You give me anything and I'll fucking kill you, I swear."

"Here, hold this." Stacey dumped everything in the kid's lap and took the water from Farmer. "Who's got a belt?"

Somehow, everyone looked at everyone else and ended up looking at me.

"Shit," I said and slipped it off. Stacey reached for it and I held it back. "Somebody tell me where Joe is or I'll throw this out the window right now."

"China, don't be like that. You're holding things up," said Priscilla chidingly, as though I were a bratty younger sister.

"I just want to know where Joe is."

"Just let us fix first, okay? Now give Stacey your belt."

Stacey snatched the belt away from me before I could say anything else and shoved her shirt and sweater sleeves high up on her arm. "Wrap it on me," she said to the kid. Her voice was getting shaky. The kid got the belt around her upper arm and pulled it snug. He had to pour a little water into the bowl of the spoon for her, too, and shake the heroin out of the foil. Someone had a ragged piece of something that had to pass for cheesecloth. Stacey fidgeted with it while the kid held a match under the spoon. When the mix in the bowl started to bubble, Stacey laid the cloth over the surface and drew some solution into the syringe. Her hands were very steady now. She held the syringe up and flicked it with her finger.

"Will you hurry it up?" Farmer snapped. "There's other people besides you."

"Keep your shirt on, I'm trying to lose some bubbles. Help me," Stacey said. "Tighten that belt."

The kid pulled the belt tighter for her as she straightened her arm. She felt in the fold of her elbow with her pinky. "There he is. Old Faithful. He shoulda collapsed long ago but he just keeps on truckin'. I heard about this guy, you know? Who shot an air bubble and he saw it in his vein just as he was nodding out, you know?" She probed with the needle, drew back the plunger and found blood. "That poor guy just kept stroking it down and stroking it down and would you believe—" Her eyelids fluttered. I reached over the kid to loosen the belt on her arm. "He actually got rid of it. He's still shooting." She started to say something else and passed out.

"Jesus, Priscilla." I took the needle out of Stacey's arm. "What kind of stuff have you got?"

"Only the best. Joe's new connection. You next?" she asked the kid.

"He's not an addict yet," I said. "He can pass this time."

"Who asked you?" said the kid. "You're not my fucking mother."

"You have to mainline for two weeks straight to get a habit," I said. "Take the day off."

But he already had the belt around his arm. "No. Give me the needle."

I plunged the syringe into the cup he was holding. "You have to clean it first, jerk-off." I cranked down the window and squirted a thin stream of water into the air. "If you're going to do this anyway, you might as well do it right."

Suddenly he looked unsure of himself. "I never shot myself up before. Stacey always did me."

I looked at her, sprawled out on his other side. "She's a big help, that girl. Looks like you're on your own. I don't give injections."

But I flicked the bubbles out of the syringe for him. It was better than watching him shoot an air bubble. He had veins like power cables.

Priscilla went next. I barely had time to clean the needle and spoon for her. Farmer fixed after her. The spoon was looking bad. I was scrubbing the mess out of it with a corner of my shirt when I noticed it was real silver. The kid's spoon. Probably stolen out of his mother's service for eight. Or maybe it was the one they'd found lodged in his mouth when he'd been born. I looked at him slumped next to Stacey, eyes half-closed, too ecstatic to smile. Was this part of the new element moving in that my father had mentioned, a pampered high school kid?

"Priscilla, are you awake?" I asked, squirting water from the needle out the window while Farmer cooked his load.

"Mmm," she said, lazily.

"Do you really know where Joe is?"

She didn't answer. I dipped the needle into the water one last time and squirted a stream out the window again. It arched gracefully into the air and splattered against the passenger side window of the police car that had pulled up even with us. I froze, still holding the needle up in plain sight. Farmer was telling me to hand him the fucking spike but his voice seemed to be coming through miles of cotton batting. I was back in the buzz of the night before, the world doing a slow-motion underwater ballet of the macabre while I watched my future dribble down the window along with the water. The cop at the wheel turned his head for a year before his eyes met mine. Riding all alone, must be budget-cutting time, my mind babbled. His face was flat and I could see through the dirty glass that his skin was rough and leathery. His tongue flicked out and ran over his lips as we stared at each other. He blinked once, in a funny way, as though the lower lids of his colorless eyes had risen to meet the upper ones. A kind of recognition passed between us. Then he turned away and the police car accelerated, passing us.

"Did you see that?" I gave the needle to Farmer, who was calling me nine kinds of bastard.

"Nope," George said grimly. "And he didn't see us, neither."

I tried to laugh, as though I were in on the joke. "Oh, man. I thought for sure we were all busted."

"Times are changing."

"Don't tell me the junkies are pooling their money to buy off the cops."

Priscilla came to and sighed happily. "Somebody is. We got all the conveniences. Good dope, bad cops. Things ain't so bad around here these days."

The kid was pulling himself up on me. I sat him up without thinking about it. "Priscilla? Do you know where Joe is? Priscilla?"

"Joe? Oh, yeah. He's at my place."

"I thought he was going around with his connection."

"He's at my place. Or he was."

George pulled the car over again as Farmer woozily began cooking his shot for him. "Let me fix and I'll drive you over there, okay?" he said, smiling thinly over his shoulder at me.

The kid threw himself over my lap and fumbled the car door open. "Wanna go for a walk," he mumbled, crawling over my legs and hauling himself upright on the door. He stood swaying and tried a few tentative steps. "Can't make it. Too loaded." I caught him and pulled him back in, shoving him over next to Stacey. He smiled at me. "You're a real nice girl, you know that? You're a real nice girl."

"Shit!" George slammed his hand against the steering wheel. "It broke, the fucking needle broke!"

"Did you fix?" asked Farmer.

"Yeah, just in time. Sorry, Priscilla." George turned to look at her and nearly fell across Farmer. "I'll find mine and give it to you. Never been used, I swear."

Priscilla made a disgusted noise.

"Hey, if everybody's happy, let's go over to Priscilla's place now," I said.

George wagged his head. "Not yet. Can't get that far, stuff was too strong. I gotta let it wear off some first. Where are we?" He opened his door and nearly fell out. "Hey, we're back near Streep's. Go there for a while, okay?" No one answered. "Okay? Go to Streep's, get some coffee, listen to some music. Okay?" He nudged Farmer. "Okay?"

"Shit." I got out, hauled the kid out after me and left him leaning on the door while I dragged Stacey out. She woke up enough to smile at me. Farmer and Priscilla found their way around the car, stumbling over each other. I looked around. A few cars passed, no one paying any attention. Here we are in scenic Junk City in the Land of Nod, where five loaded hopheads can attract no interest. What's wrong with this picture?

George reeled past me and I grabbed him, patting his pants pockets.

"What?" he said dreamily.

"Let me borrow your car."

"It's not my car. It's—" His voice trailed off as head drooped.

"That's okay," I said, shaking him, "just give me the keys." I dug them out of his right pants pocket, giving him a thrill he was too far gone to appreciate. George wasn't wearing any underwear. "Priscilla."

She had managed to go nearly half a block unassisted. At the sound of her name, she swiveled around, hugging herself against a cold she probably wasn't really feeling.

"Is Joe really at your place?"

She shrugged elaborately. "Hurry, you might catch him." Farmer went by and yanked her along with him. I watched them all weaving and staggering away from me, a ragged little group minus one, who was still leaning against the car.

"My name's Tad," he said. Probably short for tadpole, I thought. "Take me with you."

I went to call out to Farmer and the rest of them but they had already turned the corner. I was stuck with their new friend unless I chose to leave him in some doorway. He was grinning at me as he swayed from side to side. The coat was dirty now but it was still pretty nice. His gloves looked like kidskin and the boots were brand new. If I left him, I'd come back and find him up on blocks, nude. I shoved him into the back seat.

"Lie down, pass out, and don't give me any trouble."

"You're a real nice girl," he mumbled.

"Yeah, we could go to the prom together in a couple of years."

The front seat was too far back for me and wouldn't move up. I perched on the edge of the broken-down cushion and just managed to reach the pedals. I got the car started but pulling out was the tricky part. I'd never learned to drive. The car itself wasn't in terrific running condition—it wanted either to stall or race. I eased it down the street in half a dozen jerks that pushed me against the steering wheel and sent the kid in back off the seat and onto the floor. He didn't complain.

Priscilla had an apartment in one of the tenements near the railroad yard. The buildings looked abandoned at first glance; at second glance, they still looked abandoned. I steered the car off the road into an unpaved area that served as a parking lot and pulled up in front of the building nearest to the tracks. In the back, my companion pulled himself up on the seat, rubbing his eyes. "Where are we?"

"Wait here," I said, getting out of the car.

He shook his head emphatically. "No, I was here last night. This is Priscilla's. It ain't safe. I should go with you." He stumbled out of the car and leaned against it, trying to look sober. "I'm okay now. I'm just high."

"I'm not going to wait for you." I headed toward the building with him staggering after me. The heroin in his system had stabilized somewhat and he fell only three times. I kept going.

He gave up on the first flight. I left him hanging on the railing muttering to himself while I trotted up to Priscilla's place on the second floor. The door was unlocked, I knew—the lock had been broken ages ago and Priscilla wasn't about to spend good junk money on getting it fixed—but the sagging screen door was latched. I found a torn place in the screen and reached in to unhook it.

"Joe?" I called, stepping into the filthy kitchen. An odor of something long dead hit me square in the face, making me gag. "Joe?" I tiptoed across the room. On the sink was a package of hamburger Priscilla had probably left out to thaw then forgotten about, three weeks before, it seemed like. I wondered how she could stand it and then remembered how she liked to brag that coke had destroyed her nose. The rest of them wouldn't care as long as they could get fixed. My stomach leaped and I heaved on the floor. It was just a bit of bile in spite of the breakfast I'd eaten but I couldn't take any more and headed for the porch.

"Whaddaya want?"

I whirled, holding my hand over my mouth and nose as my gag reflex went into action again. A large black man wearing only a pair of pajama bottoms was standing in the doorway to the bedroom. We stared at each other curiously.

"Whaddaya want?" he asked me again.

"I'm looking for Joe," I said from behind my hand.

"I'm Joe." He scratched his face and I saw a thin line of blood trickling from the corner of his mouth.

"Wrong Joe," I said, cursing Priscilla. She knew goddamn well, the con artist. What did she think, that I'd forget about finding Joe and curl up with this guy instead? Yeah, that was Priscilla all over. A Joe for a Joe, fair deal. "The Joe I'm looking for is my brother."

"I'm a brother."

"Yeah. You're bleeding."

He touched his mouth and looked dully at his fingers. "I'm blood."

I nodded. "Well, if you see a white guy named Joe, he's *my* brother. Tell him China was looking for him."

"China."

"Right. China."

"China's something real fragile. Could break." His expression altered slightly and that same kind of recognition that had passed between me and the cop in the patrol car seemed to pass between us now in Priscilla's stinking kitchen.

I glanced at the rotting hamburger on the counter and suddenly it didn't look like rotting meat any more than the man standing in the doorway of Priscilla's bedroom looked like another junkie, or even a human being. He tilted his head and studied me, his eyes narrowing, and it all seemed to be going in slow motion, that underwater feeling again.

"If you ain't in some kinda big hurry, why don't you hang around," he said. "Here all by myself. Not too interesting, nobody to rap with. Bet you got a lot of stuff you could rap about."

Yeah, he was probably craving to find out if I'd read any good books lately. I opened my mouth to say something and the stink hit me again in the back of the throat.

"Whaddaya say, you stick around here for a while. I don't bite. 'Less I'm invited to."

I wanted to ask him what he'd bitten just recently. He touched his lip as though he'd been reading my mind and shrugged. I took a step back. He didn't seem too awfully junked up anymore and it occurred to me that it was strange that he wasn't with Priscilla instead of here, all by himself.

Maybe, I thought suddenly, he was waiting for someone. Maybe Joe was supposed to be here after all, maybe he was supposed to come here for some reason and I'd just arrived ahead of him.

I swallowed against the stink, almost choked again, and said, "He, did Priscilla tell you she had a friend coming by, a guy named Joe, or just a guy maybe? I mean, have you been waiting for someone?"

"Just you, babe."

I'd heard that line once or twice but it never sounded so true as it did just then. The kid's words suddenly came back to me. *This is Priscilla's. I was here last night.* Farmer must have run right over after I'd seen him, to tell her I was looking g for Joe. So she decided to send me on a trip to nowhere, with Farmer and the rest of them in on it, playing out the little charade of meeting her today so I could ask her about Joe and she could run this ramadoola on me. But why? What was the point?

"No, man," I said, taking another step back. "Not me."

"You sure about that?" The voice was smooth enough to slip on, like glare ice. Ice. It was chilly in the apartment, but he didn't seem to feel it. "Must be something I can . . . help you with."

Outside there was the sound of a train approaching in the distance. In a few moments, you wouldn't be able to hear anything for the roar of the train passing.

I turned and fled out to the porch. The dead-meat smell seemed to follow me as I galloped back down the stairs and woke the kid still hanging in the banister. "Let's go, let's get out of here."

The train was thundering past as I shoved him back into the car and pulled out.

"You find Joe?" he shouted as we bounced across the parking lot.

"Yeah, I found him. I found the wrong fucking Joe."

The kid giggled a little. "There's lots of guys named Joe."

"Thanks for the information, I'll keep it in mind." I steered the car onto the street again, unsure of what to do next. Maybe just cruise around, stopping random junkies and asking them if they'd seen Joe, or look for the white Caddy or whatever it was. A white luxury car would stand out, especially if a pretty blonde woman were driving it.

The junkies were starting to come out in force now, appearing on the sidewalks and street corners. A few of them waved at the car and then looked confused when they me at the wheel. It seemed to me there were more new faces among the familiar ones, people I didn't even know by sight. But that would figure, I thought—had I really expected the junkie population to go into some kind of stasis while I was away at college. Every junkie's got a friend and eventually the friend's got a habit. Like the jailbait in the back seat.

I glanced in the rearview mirror at him. He was sitting up with his head thrown back, almost conscious. If I were going to find Joe or at least his lady friend, I'd have to dump the kid.

"Wake up," I said, making a right turn onto the street that would take me past Foster Circle and down to Streep's. "I'm going to leave you off at the restaurant with everyone else. Can you handle that?"

He struggled forward and leaned over the front seat. "But we ain't found Joe yet."

"'Haven't found Joe yet.' What's the matter, do you just nod out in English class?"

He giggled. "Yeah. Don't everyone?"

"Maybe. I can't be hauling your ass all over with me. There's no end-of-class bell around here. You're on your own." I took another look at him as he hung over the seat, grinning at me like God's own fool. "You don't know that, do you?"

"Know what." He ruffled my hair clumsily.

"Quit that. You don't know that you're on your own."

"Shit, I got *lots* of friends."

"You've got junkies is what you've got. Don't confuse them with friends."

"Yeah?" He ruffled my hair again and I slapped his hand away. "So why are you so hot to find Joe?"

"Joe isn't my friend, he's my brother."

"Jeez, no kidding? I thought you were like his old lady or something."

How quickly they forget, junkies. I was about to answer him when I saw it, gleaming like fresh snow in the afternoon sunlight, impossibly clean, illegally parked right at the curb at Foster Circle. George had been right—it was a Caddy after all. I looked for a place to pull over and found one in front of a fire hydrant.

"Wait here," I said, killing the engine. "If I'm not back in ten minutes, you're free to go."

"Unh-unh," the kid said, falling back and fumbling for the door handle. "I'm coming with you."

"Fuck off." I jumped out of the car and darted across two lanes of oncoming traffic, hoping the kid would pass out again before he solved the mystery of the door handle. The Caddy was unoccupied; I stepped over the low thorny bushes the ex-mayor had chosen for their red summer blooms and look around wildly.

At the time, it didn't seem strange that I almost didn't see her. She was sitting on a bench fifty feet away looking as immaculate as her car in a thick brown coat and spike-heeled boots. Her pale blonde hair curved over her scarf in a simple, classy pageboy, like a fashion model. More like an ex-fashion model, from the careful, composed way she was sitting with her ankles crossed and her tidy purse resting on her knees, except the guy on the bench next to her wasn't material for the Brut ad campaign. It was Farmer. He still looked pretty bleary but he raised one arm and pointed at me. She turned to look and her elegantly made-up face broke into that sort of cheery smile some stewardesses reserve for men who drink heavily in First Class.

She beckoned with a gloved hand and I went over to them.

"Hello," she said in a warm contralto. "We've been waiting for you."

"Oh, yeah?" I said casually. "Seems like there's always someone waiting for me these days. Right, Farmer?" He was too busy staring at the woman to answer. "I thought you didn't know how to find her."

"I don't," Farmer said and smiled moonily at the woman, which pissed me off. "She found me. Kind of."

"At *Streep's*?" I didn't look right at her but I could see she was following the exchange with that same cheery smile, completely unoffended that we were talking about her in the third person.

"Nah. After you left us off, I left everybody at Streep's and came down here, figuring maybe I could find somebody who'd get in touch with Joe for you."

"Sure. Except Priscilla told me Joe was at her place. Only he wasn't. What about that, Farmer? You wanna talk about that a little? Like how you were there last night?"

Farmer could have cared less, though it was hard to see how. "Yeah, we was there. She wouldn't let us in, said she'd meet us today like we planned." He shrugged. "Anyway, I came down here and there was her car going down the street, so I flagged her down and told you you were looking for Joe. So then we came here. I figured you'd look here sooner or later because this was there I told you I saw her and Joe. And, you know, Streep's, shit, it's not a good place."

Sure wasn't, especially if you thought you could make your own connection and not have to let the rest of your junkie pals in on it directly. "So you decided to sit out in the cold instead." I blew out a short, disgusted breath. "I'd have gone back to Streep's eventually."

"Well, if it got too cold, we was gonna get in the car." Farmer looked uncomfortable. "Hey, what are you bitching at me for? I found her, didn't I?"

I turned to the woman. "Where's Joe?"

Her eyes were deep blue, almost navy. "He's at my place. I understand you're his sister, China?" She tilted her head like game show women do when they're showing you the year's supply of Turtle Wax behind the door number three. "I had no idea Joe had a sister in college. But I see the resemblance, you have the same eyes, the same mouth. You're very close to Joe?"

"I'd like to see him."

She spread her hands. "Then we'll go see him. All of us." She smiled past me and I turned around. The kid was standing several feet behind me, still doped up and a little unsteady but looking eager and interested in that way junkies have when they smell a possibility of more heroin. Fuck the two weeks; he'd been a junkie all his life, just like Joe.

I turned back to the woman, intending to tell her the kid was only fifteen and surely she didn't want that kind of trouble but she was already on her feet, helping Farmer up, her expensive gloves shining incongruously against his worn, dirty denim jacket.

But then again, she didn't have to touch him with her bare hands.

She made no objection when I got into the front seat with her and jerked my thumb over my shoulder instead of moving over so Farmer could get in next to me. He piled into the back with the kid and we drove off just as a meter maid pulled up next to George's car. I looked over my shoulder at the Cushman.

"Looks like we're leaving just in time," I said.

"They never ticket my car." She pushed a Grateful Dead eight-track into the tape deck and adjusted the volume on the rear speakers.

"That's funny," I said, "you don't seem like the Grateful Dead type. I'd have thought you were more of a Sinatra fan. Or maybe Tony Bennett."

"Actually, my own taste runs to chamber music," she said smoothly. "But it has a very limited appeal with most of our clients. The Grateful Dead have a certain rough charm, especially in their ballads, though I will never have the appreciation for them that so many young people do. I understand they're quite popular among college students."

"Yeah, St. Stephen with a rose," I said. "Have another hit and all that. Except that's Quicksilver Messenger Service."

"I have one of their tapes, too, if you'd prefer to hear that instead."

"No, the Dead will do."

She almost looked at me. Then Farmer called out, "This is *such* a great *car!*" and she turned up the volume slightly.

"They can't hear us," she said.

"They sure can't."

Her face should have been tired from smiling so much but she was a true professional. Don't try this at home. Suddenly I wished I hadn't. My father was right; cocky snot-nosed college know-it-all. I hadn't had the first idea of what I'd gotten into here with this white Cadillac and this ex-fashion model who referred to junkies as clients, but I was beginning to get a clue. We were heading for the toll bridge over the river. The thing to do was jump out as soon as she stopped, jump out and run like hell and hope that would be fast enough.

There was soft, metallic click. Power locks.

"Such a bad area," she said. "Must always keep the doors secure when you drive through."

And then, of course, she blinked. Even with her in profile, I could see her lower eyelid rise to meet the upper one.

She used the exact change lane, barely slowing as she lowered the window and reached toward the basket. For my benefit only, I guessed; her hand was empty.

She took us to a warehouse just on the other side of the river, one of several in an industrial cluster. Some seemed to be abandoned, some not. It wasn't quite evening yet but the place was shadowy. Still, I was willing to make a run for it as soon as we stopped and fuck whatever was in the shadows, I'd take my chances that I'd be able to get away, maybe come back with the cops. After I'd given them a blink test. But she had some arrangement; no stops. While the Dead kept on trucking, she drove us right up a ramp to a garage door, which automatically rumbled upward. We drove onto a platform that had chicken wire fencing on either side. Two bright lamps hanging on the chicken wire went on. After a moment, there was a jerk and the platform began to lift slowly. Really some arrangement.

"Such a bad area," she said. "You take your life in your hands if you get out of the car."

Yeah, I thought, I just bet you did.

After a long minute, the elevator thumped to a stop and the doors in front of us slid open. We were looking into a huge, elegantly furnished living room. *House and Garden* conquers the universe.

"This is it," she said gaily, killing the engine and the Dead. "Everybody out. Careful when you open the door, don't scratch the paint. Such a pain getting it touched up."

I waited for her to release the locks and then I banged my door loudly against the chicken wire. What the hell, I figured; I'd had it anyway. Only a cocky snot-nosed college know-it-all would think like that.

But she didn't say anything to me about it, or even give me a look. She led the way into the living room and gestured at the long beige sofa facing the elevator doors, which slid closed just as Farmer and the kid staggered across the threshold.

"Make yourselves, comfortable," she said. "Plenty of refreshments on the table."

"Oh, man," said Farmer, plumping down on the couch. "Can we play some more music, maybe some more Dead?"

"Patience, Farmer," she said as she took of her coat and laid it on one of the stools in front of a large mahogany wet bar. It had a mirror behind it and, above that, an old-fashioned picture of a plump woman in bloomers and corset lounging on her side eating chocolates from a box. It was like a stage set. She watched me staring at it.

"Drink?" she said. "I didn't think people your age partook in that very much nowadays but we have a complete stock for those who can appreciate vats and vintages and whatnot."

"I'll take a shot of twenty-year-old Scotch right after you show me where Joe is."

The woman chuckled indulgently. "Wouldn't you prefer a nice cognac?"

"Whatever you think is best," I said.

"I'll be right back." She didn't move her hips much when she walked, but in that cream-colored cashmere dress, she didn't have to. This was real refinement, real class and taste. Smiling at me over her shoulder one more time, she slipped through a heavy wooden door at the far end of the room next to an enormous antique secretary.

I looked at Farmer and the kid, who were collapsed on the sofa like junkie versions of Raggedy Andy.

"Oh, *man*," said Farmer, "this is *such* a *great place*! I never been in such a *great place*!"

"Yeah," said the kid, "it's so far out."

There were three silver boxes on the coffee table in front of them. I went over and opened one; there were several syringes in it, all clean and new. The box next to it held teaspoons and the one next to that, white powder. That one was next to the table lighter. I picked it up. It was an elaborately carved silver dragon coiled around a rock or a monolith or something, its wings pulled in close to its scaly body. You flicked the wheel in the middle of its back and the flame came out of its mouth. All I needed was a can of aerosol deodorant and I'd have had a flame-thrower. Maybe I'd have been able to get out with a flame-thrower. I doubted it.

"Jeez, will you look at that!" said the kid, sitting up in delayed reaction to the boxes. "What a setup!"

"This is such a *great place!*" Farmer said, picking up the box of heroin.

"Yeah, a real junkie heaven," I said. "It's been nice knowing you."

Farmer squinted up at me. "You going?"

"We're all going."

He sat back, still holding the box while the kid eyed him nervously. "You go ahead. I mean, this isn't exactly your scene anyway. But I'm hanging in."

"You just don't get it, do you? You think Blondie is just going to let you wander back out across the river with all the horse you can carry?"

Farmer smiled. "Shit, maybe she wants me to move in. I think she likes me. I get that very definite feeling."

"Yeah, and the two of you could adopt Tadpole here, and Stacey and Priscilla and George can come over for Sunday roast."

The kid shot me a dirty look. Farmer shrugged. "Hey, somebody's got to be out there, takin' care of the distribution."

"And she throws out Joe to make room for you, right?" I said.

"Oh, yeah, Joe." Farmer tried to think. "Well, hell, this is a big place. There's room for three. More, even." He giggled again.

"*Farmer.* I don't think many people see this place and live."

He yawned widely, showing his coated tongue. "Hey, ain't we all lucky, then."

"No. We're not lucky."

Farmer stared at me for a long moment. Then he laughed. "Shit. You're crazy."

The door at the far end of the room opened again and the woman came out. "Here he is!" she announced cheerfully and pulled Joe into the room.

My brother Joe, the original lost boy, the disposable man in an ankle-length bathrobe knotting loosely at the waist, showing his bony chest. The curly brown hair was cleaner than it had been the last time I'd seen him but duller and thinner, too. His eyes seemed to be sunk deep in the sockets and his skin looked dry and flaky. But he was steady on his bare feet as he came toward me.

"Joe," I said. "It's me, Chi—"

"I know, babe, I know." He didn't even change expression. "What the fuck?"

"I got your card."

"Shit. I told you, it was for the last time."

I blinked at him. "I came home because I thought—" I stopped, looking at the woman who was still smiling as she moved behind the bar and poured a little cognac into a glass.

"Well, go on," she said. "Tell him what you thought. And have your cognac. You should warm the bowl between your hands."

I shook my head slightly, looking down at the plush carpet. It was also beige. Not much foot traffic around here. "I thought you needed me to do something. Help you or something."

"I was saying goodbye, babe. That's all. I thought I should, you know, after everything you've seen me through. I figured, what the hell, one person in the world who ever cared what happened to me, I'd say goodbye. Fucking parents don't care if they never see me again. Rose, Aurelia—like, forget it."

I looked up at him. He still hadn't changed expression. He might have been telling me it was going to snow again this winter.

"Have your cognac," the woman said to me again. "You warm the bowl between your hands like this." She demonstrated and then held the glass out to me. When I didn't move to take it, she put it down on the bar. "Perhaps you'll feel like it later." She hurried over to the couch where Farmer and the kid were rifling the syringes and the spoons. Joe took a deep breath and let it out in a not-quite sigh.

"I can tell her to let you go," he said. "She'll probably do it."

"*Probably?*" I said.

He made a helpless, impotent gesture with one hand. "What the fuck did you come here for?"

"For you, asshole. What the fuck did *you* come here for?"

Bending over the coffee table, the woman looked back at us. "Are you going to answer that, Joe? Or shall I?"

Joe turned toward her slightly and gave a little shrug. "Will you let her go?"

That smile. "Probably."

Farmer was holding up a syringe. "Hey, I need some water. And a cooker. You got a spoon? And some cloth."

"Little early for your next fix, isn't it?" I said.

"Why wait?" He patted the box of junk cuddled in his lap.

The woman took the syringe from him and set it on the table. "You won't need any of that. We kept it around for those who have to be else-where—say, if you had an appointment to keep or if Joe were running an errand—but here we do it differently."

"Snort?" Farmer was disgusted. "Lady, I'm way past the snort stage."

She gave a refined little laugh and moved around the coffee table to sit down beside him. "Snort. How revolting. There's no snorting here. Take off your jacket."

Farmer obeyed, tossing his jacket over the back of the couch. She pushed up his left shirtsleeve and studied his arm.

"Hey, China," Farmer said, watching the woman with junkie avidity, "gimme your belt."

"No belt," said the woman. "Sit back, relax. I'll take care of everything." She touched the inside of his elbow with two fingers and then ran her hand up to his neck. "Here is actually a lot better."

Farmer looked nervous. "In the neck? You sure you know what you're doing? Nobody does it in the neck."

"It's not an easy technique to master but it's far superior to your present methods. Not to mention faster and far more potent."

"Well, hey." Farmer laughed, still nervous. "More potent, sure, I'm for that."

"*Relax,*" the woman said, pushing his head back against the couch. "Joe's done it this way a lot of times, haven't you, Joe?"

I looked at his neck but I didn't see anything, not even dirt.

The woman loosened Farmer's collar and pushed his hair back, ignoring the fact that it was badly in need of washing. She stroked his skin with her fingertips, making a low, crooning noise, the kind of sound you'd use to calm a scared puppy. "There, now," she murmured, close to Farmer's neck. "There it is, there's our baby. All nice and strong. That's a good one."

Farmer moaned pleasurably and reached for her but she caught his hand and held it firmly on his thigh.

"Don't squirm around now," she said. "This won't take long. Not very long."

She licked his neck.

I couldn't believe it. Farmer's dirty old neck. I'd have licked the sidewalk first. And *this* woman—I looked at Joe but he was watching the woman run her tongue up Farmer's neck and still no expression on him, as though he were watching a dull TV program he'd already seen.

Farmer's eyelids were at half-mast. He gave a small laugh. "Tickles a little."

The woman pulled back and then blew on the spot gently. "There now. We're almost ready." She took the box of heroin from his lap.

I didn't want to see this. I looked at Joe again. He shook his head slightly, keeping his gaze on the woman. She smiled at me, scooped up a small amount of heroin and put it in her mouth.

"Fucking lowlife," I said, but my voice sounded far away. The woman nodded, as if to tell me I had it right and then, fast, like a snake striking, she clamped her mouth on Farmer's neck.

Farmer jumped slightly, his eyes widening. Then he went completely slack, only the woman's mouth on him holding him up.

I opened my mouth to yell, but nothing came out. As though there was a field around me and Joe that kept us still.

She seemed to stay like that on Farmer's neck forever. I stood there, unable to look away. I'd watched Farmer and Joe and the rest of them fix countless times. The scene played in my brain, the needle sliding into skin, probing, finding the vein and the blood tendriling in the syringe when it hit. Going for the boot because it made the rush better. Maybe this made the rush better for both of them.

Time passed and left us all behind. I'd thought it was too soon to fix again, but yeah, it would figure that she'd have to get them while they were still fucked up, so they'd just sit there and take it. Hey, was that last fix a little strange? —Strange? What's strange? Nod.

Then the woman drew her head back a little and I saw it. A living needle, like a stinger. I wished I were a fainter so I could have passed out, shut the picture off, but she held my gaze as strongly as she held Farmer. I'd come to see Joe and this was part of it, package deal. In another part of my mind, I was screaming and yelling and begging Joe to take us both out of there, but that place was too far away, in some other world where none of this was possible.

She brought her mouth down to Farmer's neck again, paused, and lifted her head. There was a small red mark on Farmer's skin, like a vaccination. She swallowed and gave me that professional smile.

"That's what he came here for," she said. "Now, shall I do the next one, Joe, or would you like to?"

"Oh, Jesus, Joe," I said. "Oh, *Jesus.*"

"I don't like boys," he said. And blinked.

"Oh, *Jesus*—"

"Well, there's only one girl here for you." She actually crinkled her nose.

"No. *No*, oh, Jesus, *Joe*—" I grabbed two fistfuls of his bathrobe and shook him. He swayed in my grasp and it felt like I was shaking a store mannequin. Even in his deepest junked-out stupor, he'd been a million times more alive than he was now. My late brother, Joe, the original lost boy now lost for all time, the disposable man finally disposed of.

He waited until I stopped shaking him and looked down at me. I took a step back. A dull television program he'd already seen. "Let her go, okay?"

"Now, Joe," she said, admonishing.

I bolted for the elevator but the doors didn't open. She had the power over them, over everything, junkies, me, even tollbooths. I just stood there until I felt Joe's hands on my shoulders.

"China—"

I jumped away from him and backed up against the elevator doors. There was a buzzing in my ears. Hyperventilating. In a moment, I was going to pass out and they could do whatever they liked. Standing between Farmer comatose on the couch and the kid, who was sitting like a junked-up lump, the woman looked bored.

"China," my brother repeated, but he didn't reach for me again.

I forced myself to breathe more slowly. The buzzing in my ears receded and I was almost steady again. "Oh, Jesus, Joe, where did you *find* these—these whatever-they-are. They're not people."

"I didn't really find them," he said. "One day I looked around and they were just there. Where they've always been."

"I never saw them before."

"You never had to. People like me and Farmer and whatsisname over there, the kid, we're the ones they come for. Not for you."

"Then why did *I* find them?"

"I don't like to think about that. It's—" he fumbled for a moment. "I don't know. Contagious, I guess. Maybe someday they'll come for everyone."

"Well, that *is* in the plan," the woman said. "There are only so many Joes and Farmers in the world. Then you have to branch out. Fortunately, it's not hard to find new ways to reach new receptors." She ran a finger along the collar of her dress. "The damnedest things come into fashion and you know how that is. Something can just sweep the country."

"Let her go now," Joe said.

"But it's close to time for you, dear one."

"Take her back to Streep's. Stacey and George'll be there, maybe Priscilla. You can bring them here, leave her there."

"But, *Joe*," she said insistently, "she's *seen* us."

"So you can get her later."

I began to shake.

"*Joe.*" The stewardess smile went away. "There are *rules*. And they're not just arbitrary instructions designed to keep the unwashed multitude moving smoothly through intersections during rush hour." She came around the coffee table to him and put her hand on his arm. I saw her thumb sink deeply into the material of his bathrobe. "You *chose* this, Joe. You *asked* for it, and when we gave it to you, you agreed. And this is part of the deal."

He pried her hand off his arm and shoved it away. "No, it's not. My sister isn't a junkie. It wouldn't go right, not now. You know it wouldn't. You'd just end up with a troublesome body to dispose of and the trail would lead directly to me. Here. Because everyone probably knows she's been looking for me. She's probably asked half the city if they've seen me. Isn't that right, China."

I nodded, unable to speak.

"You know we've got the cops."

"Not all of them. Not even enough of them."

The woman considered it. Then she shook her head at him as though he were a favored, spoiled pet. "I wouldn't do this for anyone else, I hope you know that."

"I know it," said Joe.

"I mean, in spite of everything you said. I might have decided just to work around the difficulties. It's just that I like you so much. You fit in so well. You're just so—*appropriate*." She glanced back at the kid on the couch. "Well, I hope this can wait until I take care of our other matter."

"Whatever you like," Joe said.

She turned her smile on me again but there was a fair amount of sneer in it. "I'll be with you shortly."

I turned away as she went back to the couch so I wouldn't have to see her do the kid. Joe just stood there the whole time, making no move toward me or away from me. I was still shaking a little; I could see my frizzy bangs trembling in front of my eyes. The absurd things you noticed, I thought, and concentrated on them, out of focus against the background of the fabulous antique bar, trying to make them hold still. If they stopped trembling, then I would have stopped shaking. The kid on the couch made a small noise, pleasure or pain or both, and I looked up at Joe, wanting to scream at him to make her stop it but there was nothing there to hear that kind of scream. The kid was on his own; *I* was the one who really hadn't known that. We were all on our own, now.

The dead eyes stared at me, the gaze as flat as an animal's. I tried to will one last spark of life to appear, even just that greedy, gotta-score look he used to get, but it wouldn't come. Whatever he'd had left had been used up when he'd gotten her to let me go. Maybe it hadn't even been there then; maybe he'd been genuinely concerned about the problem of getting rid of my corpse. Junkies need love but they need a fix more.

Eventually, I heard the kid slump over on the couch.

"Well, come on," the woman said, going over to the bar to pick up her coat. The elevator doors slid open.

"Wait," Joe said.

I paused in the act of going toward the car and turned back to him.

"She goes back to Streep's," Joe said. "Just like I told you. And you pick up Stacey and George and Priscilla and whoever else is around if you want. But you fucking leave her off. Because I'll know if you don't."

I wanted to say his name but I still couldn't make a sound.

Hey, Joe. What the hell.

If you have to ask, babe, you don't really want to know.

"All right, Joe," the woman said amiably. "I told you I'd do it your way."

His lower lids rose up and stayed shut. *Good-bye Joe.*

"Too bad you never got to drink your cognac," the woman said to me as she put on her coat. She nodded at the snifter where it still stood on the bar. "It's VSOP, you know."

Night was already falling as she took me back across the river. She put on the Quicksilver Messenger Service tape for me. Have another hit. Neither of us said anything until she pulled up in front of Streep's.

"Run in and tell them I'm waiting, will you?" she asked cheerfully.

I looked over at her. "What should I say?"

"Tell them Joe and I are having a party. They'll like that."

"You and Joe, huh? Think you'll be able to handle such an embarrassment of riches, just the two of you?"

"Oh, there'll be a few others by the time I get back. You don't think we need all that space for just the two of us, do you?"

I shrugged. "What do I know?"

"You know enough." We stared at each other in the faint light from the dashboard. "Sure you don't want to ride back?" Priscilla's friend will undoubtedly have arrived by the time we get there."

I took a deep breath. "I don't know what she told him about me, but it wasn't even close."

"Are you sure about that?"

"Real sure."

She stared at me a moment longer, as though she were measuring me for something. "Then I'll see you later, China."

I got out of the car and went into Streep's.

After that I went home just long enough to pack my bag again while my father bellowed at me and my mother watched. I phoned Marlene from the bus station. She was out but her grandmother sounded happy to hear from me and told me to come ahead, she'd send Marlene out with the car.

So that was all. I went home even less after that, so I never saw Joe again. But I saw them. Not her, not Joe's blonde or the cop or the guy from Priscilla's apartment, but others. Apparently once you'd seen them, you couldn't not see them. They were around. Sometimes they would give me a nod, like they knew me. I kept on trucking, got my degree, got a job, got a life, and saw them some more.

I don't see them any more frequently but no less, either. They're around. If I don't see them, I see where they've been. A lot of the same places I've been. Sometimes I don't think about them and it's like a small intermission of freedom, but it doesn't last, of course. I see them and they see me and someday they'll find the time to come for me. So far, I've survived relevance and hedonism and I'm not a Yuppie. Nor my brother's keeper.

But I'm something. I was always going to be something someday. And eventually, they're going to find out what it is.

So Runs the World Away

Caitlín R. Kiernan

Caitlín R. Kiernan is the author of the novels *Silk*, *Threshold*, *Low Red Moon*, *Murder of Angels*, *Daughter of Hounds*, *The Red Tree*, and *The Drowning Girl: A Memoir*. She also wrote the movie novelization of *Beowulf* and, more recently, she has published the Siobhan Quinn series of urban fantasies (*Blood Oranges*, *Red Delicious*, and *Cherry Bomb*) under the pseudonym "Kathleen Tierney."

Her shorter tales of the weird, fantastic, and macabre have been collected in a number of volumes, including *Tales of Pain and Wonder*; *From Weird and Distant Shores*; *To Charles Fort, with Love*; *Alabaster*; *A is for Alien*; *The Ammonite Violin & Others*; *Two Worlds and In Between: The Best of Caitlín R. Kiernan (Volume One)*; *Confessions of a Five-Chambered Heart*; *The Ape's Wife and Other Tales*; *Beneath an Oil-Dark Sea: The Best of Caitlín R. Kiernan (Volume Two)*; and *Dear Sweet Filthy World*.

Kiernan is a multiple recipient of the World Fantasy Award, the Bram Stoker Award, the International Horror Guild Award, and the Shirley Jackson Award, as well as a winner of the Nebula Award, the British Fantasy Award, and the Mythopoeic Award.

"Sometime in 1995," reveals the author, "I publicly vowed to stop writing stories about vampires for at least six years and also encouraged other writers to do the same. Though I am a great admirer of good vampire fiction, a commodity almost as scarce as hens' teeth, and although I'd written and sold a vampire novel of my own (*The Five of Cups*), I could see very little sense in fantasy writers continuing to grind out mediocre tales of bloodsucking fiends when the shelves were already hemorrhaging with the things.

"So I did stop. I wrote no new vampire stories for five years (that's almost six, I tell myself). And then I got an idea, which actually had a lot more to do with ghouls, originally; but, somehow, vampires ended up worming their way in and taking over. I suppose that's what vampires do. Anyway, that's how I came to write 'So Runs the World Away.'

"Now, if I can only make it another five years . . ."

"A FALLING STAR for your thoughts," she says and Gable, the girl with foil-silver eyes and teeth like the last day of winter, points at the night sky draped high above Providence and the wide Seekonk River.

Night-secret New England sky, and a few miles farther north you have to call it the Pawtucket River, but down here, where it laps fishy against Swan Point and the steep cemetery slopes, down here it's still the Seekonk and way over there are the orange, industrial lights of Phillipsdale; Dead Girl blinks once or twice to get the taste out of her mouth, and then she follows Gable's grimy finger all the way up to Heaven and there's the briefest streak of white light drawn quick across the eastern sky.

"That's very nice, but they aren't really, you know," she says and Gable makes a face, pale face squinched up like a very old woman, dried-apple face to say she doesn't understand and "Aren't really *what*?" she asks.

"Stars," says Dead Girl. "They're only meteorites. Just chunks of rock and metal flying around through space and burning up if they get too close. But they aren't stars. Not if they fall like that."

"Or angels," Bobby whispers and then goes right back to eating from the handful of blackberries he's picked from the brambles growing along the water's edge.

"I never said anything about angels," Gable growls at the boy, and he throws a blackberry at her. "There are *lots* of different words for angels."

"And for falling stars," Dead Girl says with a stony finality so they'll know that's all she wants to hear about it; meteorites that stop being meteors, Seekonk changing into Pawtucket, and in the end it's nothing but the distance between this point and that. As arbitrary as any change, and so she presses her lips against the jogging lady's left wrist again. Not even the sheet-thin ghost of a pulse left in there, cooling meat against her teeth, flesh that might as well be clay except there are still a few red mouthfuls and the sound of her busy lips isn't all that different from the sound of the waves against the shore.

"I know seven words for gray," Bobby says, talking through a mouthful of seeds and pulp and the dark juice dribbling down his bloodstained chin. "I got them out of a dictionary."

"You're a little faggot," Gable snarls at the boy, those narrow mercury eyes and her lower lip stuck way out like maybe someone's been beating her again, and Dead Girl knows she shouldn't have argued with Gable about falling stars and angels. Next time, she thinks, I'll remember that. Next time I'll smile and say whatever she wants me to say. And when she's finally finished with the jogging lady, Dead Girl's the first one to slip quiet as a mousey in silk bedroom slippers across the mud and pebbles and the river is as cold as the unfalling stars speckling the August night.

An hour and four minutes past midnight in the big house on Benefit Street and the ghouls are still picking at the corpses in the basement.

Dead Girl sits with Bobby on the stairs that lead back up to the music and conversation overhead, the electric lights and acrid-sweet clouds of opium smoke; down here there are only candles and the air smells like bare dirt walls and mildew, like the embalmed meat spread out on the ghouls' long carving table. When they work like this, the ghouls stand up on their crooked hind legs and press their canine faces close together. The very thin one named Barnaby (his nervous ears alert to every footfall overhead, every creaking door, as if anyone up there even cares what they're up to down here) picks up a rusty boning knife and uses it to lift a strip of dry flesh the color of old chewing gum.

"That's the gastrocnemius," he says and the yellow-orange iris of his left eye drifts nervously toward the others, toward Madam Terpsichore, especially, who shakes her head and laughs the way that all ghouls laugh. The way starving dogs would laugh, Dead Girl thinks, if they ever dared, and she's starting to wish she and Bobby had gone down to Warwick with Gable and The Bailiff after all.

"No, that's the soleus, dear," Madam Terpsichore says, and sneers at Barnaby, that practiced curl of black lips to flash her jaundiced teeth like sharpened piano keys, a pink-red flick of her long tongue along the edge of her muzzle, and "*That's* the gastrocnemius, there," she says. "You haven't been paying attention."

Barnaby frowns and scratches at his head. "Well, if we ever got anything fresh, maybe I could keep them straight," he grumbles, making excuses again, and Dead Girl knows the dissection is beginning to bore Bobby. He's staring over his shoulder at the basement door, the warm sliver of light getting in around the edges.

"Now, show me the lower terminus of the long peroneal," Madam Terpsichore says, her professorial litany and the impatient clatter of Barnaby digging about in his kit for a pair of poultry shears or an oyster fork, one or the other or something else entirely.

"You want to go back upstairs for a while?" Dead Girl asks the boy and he shrugs, but doesn't take his eyes off the basement door, doesn't turn back around to watch the ghouls.

"Well come on then," and she stands up, takes his hand, and that's when Madam Terpsichore finally notices them.

"Please don't go, dear," she says. "It's always better with an audience, and if Master Barnaby ever finds the proper instrument, there may be a flensing yet," and the other ghouls snicker and laugh.

"I don't think I like them very much," Bobby whispers very quietly and Dead Girl only nods and leads him back up the stairs to the party.

—

Bobby says he wants something to drink, so they go to the kitchen first, to the noisy antique refrigerator, and he has a Coke and Dead Girl takes out a Heineken for herself. One chilly, apple-green bottle and she twists the cap off and sips the bitter, German beer; she never liked the taste of beer, before, but sometimes it seems like there were an awful lot of things she didn't like before. The beer is very, very cold and washes away the last rags of the basement air lingering stale in her mouth like a dusty patch of mushrooms, basement-dry earth and a billion microscopic spores looking for a place to grow.

"I don't think I like them at all," Bobby says, still whispering even though they're upstairs. Dead Girl starts to tell him that he doesn't have to whisper anymore, but then she remembers Barnaby, his inquisitive, dog-cocked ears, and she doesn't say anything at all.

Almost everyone else is sitting together in the front parlor, the spacious, booklined room with its stained-glass lampshades in all the sweet and sour colors of hard candy, sugar-filtered light that hurts her eyes. The first time she was allowed into the house on Benefit Street, Gable showed her all the lamps, all the books, all the rooms, like they were hers. Like she belonged here, instead of the muddy bottom of the Seekonk River, another pretty, broken thing in a house filled up with things that are pretty or broken or both. Filled up with antiques, and some of them breathe and some of them don't. Some, like Miss Josephine, have forgotten how or why to breathe, except to talk.

They sit around her in their black funeral clothes and the chairs carved in 1754 or 1773, rough circle of men and women that always makes Dead Girl think of ravens gathered around carrion, blackbirds about a raccoon's corpse, jostling each other for all the best bits; sharp beaks for her bright and sapphire eyes, for the porcelain tips of her fingers, or that silent, unbeating heart. The empress as summer roadkill, Dead Girl thinks, and doesn't laugh out loud, even though she wants to, wants to laugh at these stiff and obsolescent beings, these tragic, waxwork shades sipping absinthe and hanging on Miss Josephine's every word like gospel, like salvation. Better to slip in quiet, unnoticed, and find some place for her and Bobby to sit where they won't be in the way.

"Have you ever seen a firestorm, Signior Garzarek?" Miss Josephine asks and she looks down at a book lying open in her lap, a green book like Dead Girl's green beer bottle.

"No, I never have," one of the waxworks says, tall man with slippery hair and ears that are too big for his head and almost come to points. "I dislike such things."

"But it was beautiful," Miss Josephine says and then she pauses, still looking at the green book in her lap and Dead Girl can tell from the way her eyes move back and forth, back and forth, that she's reading whatever's on the pages. "No, that's not the right word," she says, "That's not the right word at all."

"I was at Dresden," one of the women volunteers and Josephine looks up, blinks at the woman as if she can't quite remember what this particular waxwork is called.

"No, no, Addie, it wasn't like that at all. Oh, I'm sure Dresden was exquisite, too, yes. But this wasn't something man did. This was something that was done to men. And that's the thing that makes it truly transcendent, the thing that makes it . . ." and she trails off and glances back down at the book as if the word she's missing is in there somewhere.

"Well, then, read some of it to us," Signior Garzarek says and he points a gloved hand at the green book and Miss Josephine looks up at him with her blue-brilliant eyes, eyes that seem grateful and malicious at the same time.

"Are you sure?" she asks them all. "I wouldn't want to bore any of you."

"Please," says the man who hasn't taken off his bowler, and Dead Girl thinks his name is Nathaniel. "We always like to hear you read."

"Well, only if you're sure," Miss Josephine says and she sits up a little straighter on her divan, clears her throat, and fusses with the shiny folds of her black, satin skirt, the dress that only looks as old as the chairs, before she begins to read.

"*That* was what came next—the fire,'" she says, and this is her reading voice now and Dead Girl closes her eyes and listens. "'It shot up everywhere. The fierce wave of destruction had carried a flaming torch with it—agony, death and a flaming torch. It was just as if some fire demon was rushing from place to place with such a torch. Flames streamed out of half-shattered buildings all along Market Street.

"'I sat down on the sidewalk and picked the broken glass out of the soles of my feet and put on my clothes.

"'All wires down, all wires down!'"

And that's the way it goes for the next twenty minutes or so, the kindly half-dark behind Dead Girl's eyes and Miss Josephine reading from her green book while Bobby slurps at his Coke and the waxwork ravens make no sound at all. She loves the rhythm of Miss Josephine's reading voice, the cadence like rain on a hot day or ice cream, that sort of a voice. But it would be better if she were reading something else, "The Rime of the Ancient Mariner," maybe, or Keats or Tennyson. But this is better than nothing at all, so Dead Girl listens, content enough and never mind that it's only earthquakes and conflagration, smoke and the screams of dying men and horses. It's the *sound* of the voice that matters, not the words or anything they mean, and if that's true for her it's just as true for the silent waxworks in their stiff, colonial chairs.

When she's finished, Miss Josephine closes the book and smiles, showing them all the stingiest glimpse of her sharp, white teeth.

"Superb," says Nathaniel, and "Oh yes, superb," says Addie Goodwine.

"You are indeed a wicked creature, Josephine," says the Signior and he lights a fat cigar and exhales a billowing phantom from his mouth. "Such delicious perversity wrapped up in such a comely package."

"I was writing as James Russell Williams, then," Miss Josephine says proudly. "They even paid me."

Dead Girl opens her eyes and Bobby's finished his Coke, is rolling the empty bottle back and forth across the rug like a wooden rolling pin on cookie dough. "Did you like it?" she asks him and he shrugs.

"Not at all?"

"Well, it wasn't as bad as the ghouls," he says, but he doesn't look at her, hardly ever looks directly at her or anyone else these days.

A few more minutes and then Miss Josephine suddenly remembers something in another room that she wants the waxworks to see, something they *must* see, an urn or a brass sundial, the latest knick-knack hidden somewhere in the bowels of the great, cluttered house. They follow her out of the parlor, into the hallway, chattering and trailing cigarette smoke, and if anyone even notices Bobby and Dead Girl sitting on the floor, they pretend that they haven't. Which is fine by Dead Girl; she dislikes them, the lifeless smell of them, the guarded desperation in their eyes.

Miss Josephine has left her book on the cranberry divan and when the last of the vampires has gone, Dead Girl gets up and steps inside the circle of chairs, stands staring down at the cover.

"What does it say?" Bobby asks and so she reads the title to him.

"*San Francisco's Horror of Earthquake, Fire, and Famine,*" she reads, and then Dead Girl picks the book up and shows him the cover, the letters stamped into the green cloth in faded gold ink. And underneath, a woman in dark-colored robes, her feet in fire and water, chaos wrapped about her ankles, and she seems to be bowing to a shattered row of marble columns and a cornerstone with the words In Memoriam of California's Dead—April 18th, 1906.

"That was a long time ago, wasn't it?" Bobby asks and Dead Girl sets the book down again. "Not if you're Miss Josephine, it isn't," she says. If you're Miss Josephine, that was only yesterday, the day before yesterday.

If you're her—but that's the sort of thought it's best not to finish, better if she'd never thought it at all.

"We don't have to go back to the basement, do we?" Bobby asks and Dead Girl shakes her head. "Not if you don't want to," she says. And then she goes to the window and stares out at Benefit Street, at the passing cars and the living people with their smaller, petty reasons for hating time. In a moment, Bobby comes and stands beside her and he holds her hand.

Dead Girl keeps her secrets in an old Hav-A-Tampa cigar box, the few she can't just keep inside her head, and she keeps the old cigar box on a shelf inside a mausoleum at Swan Point. This manicured hillside that rises up so sharp from the river's edge, steep and dead-adorned hill, green grass in the summer and the wind-rustling branches of the trees, and only Bobby knows about the box and she thinks he'll keep it to himself. He rarely says anything to anyone, especially Gable; Dead Girl knows what Gable would do if she found out about the box, *thinks* she knows and that's good enough, bad enough, that she keeps it hidden in the mausoleum.

The caretakers bricked up the front of the vault years and years ago, but they left a small cast-iron grate set into the masonry just below the marble keystone and the verdigris-streaked plaque with the name STANTON on it, though Dead Girl can't imagine why. Maybe it's there so the bugs can come in and out, or so all those dead

Stantons can get a breath of fresh air now and then, but not even enough room for bats to squeeze in, or the swifts, or rats. But plenty of space between the bars for her and Bobby to slip inside whenever she wants to look at the things she keeps inside the old cigar box.

Nights like tonight, after the long parties, after Miss Josephine finally loses interest in her waxwork ravens and chases them all away (everyone except the ghouls, of course, who come and go as they please through the tunnels in the basement); still a coal-gray hour left until dawn and she knows that Gable is probably already waiting for them in the river, but she can wait a few minutes more.

"She might come looking for us," Bobby says when they're inside the mausoleum and he's standing on tiptoes to see out but the grate is still a foot above his head.

"No, she won't," Dead Girl tells him, tells herself that it's true, that Gable's too glad to be back down there in the dark to be bothered. "She's probably already asleep by now."

"Maybe so," Bobby says, not sounding even the least bit convinced, and then he sits down on the concrete floor and watches Dead Girl with his quicksilver eyes, mirror eyes so full of light they'll still see when the last star in the whole goddamned universe has burned itself down to a spinning cinder.

"You let me worry about Gable," she says and opens the box and everything's still inside, just the way she left it. The newspaper clippings and a handful of coins, a pewter St. Christopher's medal and a doll's plastic right arm. Three keys and a ragged swatch of indigo velvet stained maroon around the edges. Things that mean nothing to anyone but Dead Girl, her puzzle and no one else knows the way that all these pieces fit together. Or even *if* they all fit together; sometimes even she can't remember, but it makes her feel better to see them, anyway, to lay her white hands on these trinkets and scraps, to hold them.

Bobby is tapping his fingers restlessly against the floor, and when she looks at him he frowns and stares up at the ceiling. "Read me the one about Mercy," he says and she looks back down at the Hav-A-Tampa box.

"It's getting late, Bobby. Someone might hear me."

And he doesn't ask her again, keeps his eyes on the ceiling directly above her head and taps his fingers on the floor.

"It's not even a story," she says, and fishes one of the newspaper clippings from the box. Nut-brown paper gone almost as brittle as she feels inside and the words printed there more than a century ago, and "It's almost like a story, when you read it," Bobby replies.

For a moment, Dead Girl stands very still, listening to the last of the night sounds fading slowly away and the stranger sounds that come just before sunrise; birds and the blind, burrowing progress of earthworms, insects and a ship's bell somewhere down in Providence Harbor, and Bobby's fingers drumming on the concrete. She thinks about Miss Josephine and the comfort in her voice, her ice-cream voice against every vacant moment of eternity. And, in a moment, she begins to read.

Letter from the *Pawtuxet Valley Gleaner*, dated March 1892:

"Exeter Hill"

Mr. Editor,

As considerable notoriety has resulted from the exhuming of three bodies in Exeter cemetery on the 17th inst., I will give the main facts as I have received them for the benefit of such of your readers as "have not taken the papers" containing the same. To begin, we will say that our neighbor, a good and respectable citizen, George T. Brown, has been bereft of his wife and two grown-up daughters by consumption, the wife and mother about eight years ago, and the eldest daughter, Olive, two years or no later, while the other daughter, Mercy Lena, died about two months since, after nearly one year's illness from the same dread disease. About two years ago Mr. Brown's only son Edwin A., a young married man of good habits, began to give evidence of lung trouble, which increased, until in hopes of checking and curing the same, he was induced to visit the famous Colorado Springs, where his wife followed him later on and though for a time he seemed to improve, it soon became evident that there was no real benefit derived, and this coupled with a strong desire on the part of both husband and wife to see their Rhode Island friends, decided them to return east after an absence of about 18 months and are staying with Mrs. Brown's parents, Willet Himes. We are sorry to say that Eddie's health is not encouraging at this time. And now comes in the queer part, viz: The revival of a pagan or other superstition regarding the feeding of the dead upon a living relative where consumption was the cause of death and now bringing the living person soon into a similar condition, etc. and to avoid this result, according to the same high authority, the "vampire" in question which is said to inhabit the heart of a dead consumptive while any blood remains in that organ, must be cremated and the ashes carefully preserved and administered in some form to the living victim, when a speedy cure may (un) reasonably be expected. I will here say that the husband and father of the deceased ones, from the first, disclaimed any faith at all in the vampire theory but being urged, he allowed other, if not wiser, counsel to prevail, and on the 17th inst., as before stated the three bodies alluded to were exhumed and then examined by Doctor Metcalt of Wickford (under protest, as it were, being an unbeliever). The two bodies longest buried were found decayed and bloodless, while the last one who has been only about two months buried showed some blood in the heart as a matter of course, and as the doctor expected but to carry out what was a forgone conclusion, the heart and lungs of the last named (M. Lena) were then and there duly cremated, but deponent saith not how the ashes were disposed of. Not many persons were present, Mr. Brown being among the absent ones. While we do not blame anyone for these proceedings as they were intended without doubt to relieve the anxiety of the living, still, it seems incredible that anyone can attach the least importance to the subject, being so entirely incompatible with reason and conflicts also with scripture, which requires us "to give a reason for the hope that is in us," or the why and wherefore which certainly cannot be done as applied to the foregoing.

With the silt and fish shit settling gentle on her eyelids and lungs filled up with cold river water, Dead Girl sleeps, the soot-black ooze for her blanket, her cocoon, and Bobby safe in her arms. Gable is there, too, lying somewhere nearby, coiled like an eel in the roots of a drowned willow.

And in her dreams Dead Girl counts the boats passing overhead, their prows to split the day-drenched sky, their wakes the roil and swirl of thunderstorm clouds. Crabs and tiny snails nest in her hair and her wet thoughts slip by as smooth and capricious as the Seekonk, one instant or memory flowing seamlessly into the next. And *this* moment, this one here, is the last night that she was still a living girl. Last frosty night before Halloween and she's stoned and sneaking into Swan Point Cemetery with a boy named Adrian that she only met a few hours ago in the loud and smoky confusion of a Throwing Muses show, Adrian Mobley and his long yellow hair like strands of the sun or purest, spun gold.

Adrian won't or can't stop giggling, a joke or just all the pot they've been smoking, and she leads him straight down Holly Avenue, the long-paved drive to carry them across The Old Road and into the vast maze of the cemetery's slate and granite intestines. Headstones and more ambitious monuments lined up neat or scattered wild among the trees, reflecting pools to catch and hold the high, white moon, and she's only having a little trouble finding her way in the dark.

"Shut up," she hisses, casts anxious serpent sounds from her chapped lips, across her chattering teeth, and "Someone's going to fucking hear us," she says. She can see her breath, her soul escaping mouthful by steaming mouthful.

Then Adrian puts his arm around her, sweater wool and warm flesh around warm flesh, and he whispers something in her ear, something she should have always remembered but doesn't. Something forgotten the way she's forgotten the smell of a late summer afternoon, or sunlight on sand, and he kisses her.

And for a kiss she shows him the place where Lovecraft is buried, the quiet place she comes when she only wants to be alone, no company but her thoughts and the considerate, sleeping bodies underground. The Phillips family obelisk and then his own little headstone; she takes a plastic cigarette lighter from the front pocket of her jeans and holds the flame close to the ground so that Adrian can read the marker: AUGUST 20, 1890–MARCH 15, 1937, "I AM PROVIDENCE," and she shows him all the offerings that odd pilgrims leave behind. A handful of pencils and one rusty screw, two nickels, a small rubber octopus and a handwritten letter folded neat and weighted with a rock so the wind won't blow it away. The letter begins *Dear Howard*, but she doesn't read any farther, nothing there written for her, and then Adrian tries to kiss her again.

"No, wait. You haven't seen the tree," she says, wriggling free of Adrian Mobley's skinny arms, dragging him roughly away from the obelisk; two steps, three, and they're both swallowed by the shadow of an enormous, ancient birch, this tree that must have been old when her great grandfather was a boy. Its sprawling branches are still shaggy with autumn-painted leaves, its roots like the scabby knuckles of some sky-bound giant, clutching at the earth for fear that he will fall and tumble forever toward the stars.

"Yeah, so it's a tree," Adrian mumbles, not understanding, not even trying to understand, and now she knows that it was a mistake to bring him here.

"People have carved things," she says, and strikes the lighter again, holds the flickering, orange flame so that Adrian can see all the pocket-knife graffiti worked into the smooth, pale bark of the tree. The unpronounceable names of dark, fictitious gods and entire passages from Lovecraft, razor steel for ink to tattoo these occult wounds and lonely messages to a dead man, and she runs an index finger across a scar in the shape of a tentacle-headed fish.

"Isn't it beautiful?" she whispers and that's when Dead Girl sees the eyes watching them from the lowest limbs of the tree, *their* shimmering, silver eyes like spiteful coins hanging in the night, strange fruit.

"This shit isn't the way it happened at all," Gable says. "These aren't even *your* memories. This is just some bitch we killed."

"Oh, I think she knows that." The Bailiff laughs and it's worse than the ghouls snickering for Madam Terpsichore.

"I only wanted him to see the tree," Dead Girl says. "I wanted to show him something carved into the Lovecraft tree."

"Liar," Gable sneers and that makes The Bailiff laugh again. He squats in the dust and fallen leaves and begins to pick something stringy from his teeth.

And she would run, but the river has almost washed the world away, nothing left now but the tree and the moon and the thing that clambers down its trunk on spider-long legs and arms the color of chalk dust.

Is that a Death? And are there two?

"We know you would forget us," Gable says, "If we ever let you. You would pretend you were an innocent, a victim." Her dry tongue feels as rough as sandpaper against Dead Girl's wrist, dead cat's tongue, and above them the constellations swirl in a mad, kaleidoscope dance about the moon; the tree moans and raises its swaying branches to Heaven, praying for dawn, for light and mercy from everything it's seen and will ever see again.

Is Death that woman's mate?

And at the muddy bottom of the Seekonk River, in the lee of the Henderson Bridge, Dead Girl's eyelids flutter as she stirs uneasily, frightening fish, fighting sleep and her dreams. But the night is still hours away, waiting on the far side of the scalding day, and so she holds Bobby tighter and he sighs and makes a small, lost sound that the river snatches and drags away toward the sea.

Dead Girl sits alone on the floor in the parlor of the house on Benefit Street, alone because Gable has Bobby with her tonight; Dead Girl drinks her Heineken and watches the yellow and aubergine circles that their voices trace in the stagnant, smoky air, and she tries to recall what it was like before she knew the colors of sound.

Miss Josephine raises the carafe and carefully pours tap water over the sugar cube on her slotted spoon; the water and dissolved sugar sink to the bottom of her glass and at once the liqueur begins to louche, the clear and emerald bright mix of alcohol and herbs clouding quickly to a milky, opaque green.

"Oh, of course," she says to the attentive circle of waxwork ravens. "I remember Mercy Brown, and Nellie Vaughn, too, and that man in Connecticut. What was his name?"

"William Rose," Signior Garzarek suggests, but Miss Josephine frowns and shakes her head. "No, no. Not Rose. He was that peculiar fellow in Peace Dale, remember? No, the man in Connecticut had a different name."

"They were maniacs, every one of them," Addie Goodwine says nervously and sips from her own glass of absinthe. "Cutting the hearts and livers out of corpses and burning them, eating the ashes. It's ridiculous. It's even worse than what *they* do," and she points confidentially at the floor.

"Of course it is, dear," Miss Josephine says.

"But the little Vaughn girl, Nellie, I understand she's still something of a sensation among the local high school crowd," Signior Garzarek says and smiles, dabs at his wet, red lips with a lace handkerchief. "They do love their ghost stories, you know. They must find the epitaph on her tombstone an endless source of delight."

"What does it say?" Addie asks and when Miss Josephine turns and stares at her, Addie Goodwine flinches and almost drops her glass.

"You really should get out more often, dear," Miss Josephine says and "Yes," Addie stammers. "Yes, I know. I should."

The waxwork named Nathaniel fumbles with the brim of his black bowler and, "I remember," he says. "'I am watching and waiting for you.' That's what it says, isn't it?"

"Delightful, I tell you," Signior Garzarek chuckles and then he drains his glass and reaches for the absinthe bottle on its silver serving tray.

"What do you see out there?"

The boy that Dead Girl calls Bobby is standing at the window in Miss Josephine's parlor, standing there with the sash up and snow blowing in, small drift of snow at his bare feet and he turns around when she says his name.

"There was a bear on the street," he says and puts the glass paperweight in her hands; glass dome filled with water and when she shakes it all the tiny white flakes inside swirl around and around, a miniature blizzard trapped in her palm, plastic snow to settle slow across the frozen field, the barn, the dark and winter-bare line of trees in the distance.

"I saw a bear," he says again, more insistent than before, and points at the open window.

"You did *not* see a bear," Dead Girl says, but she doesn't look to see for herself, doesn't take her silver eyes off the paperweight; she'd almost forgotten about the barn, that day and the storm, January or February or March, more years ago than she'd have ever guessed and the wind howling like hungry wolves.

"I *did*," Bobby says. "I saw a big black bear dancing in the street. I know a bear when I see one."

And Dead Girl closes her eyes and lets the globe fall from her fingers, lets it roll from her hand and she knows that when it hits the floor it will shatter into a thousand pieces. World shatter, watersky shatter to bleed Heaven away across the floor, and so there isn't much time if she's going to make it all the way to the barn.

"I think it knew our names," the boy says and he sounds afraid, but when she looks back she can't see him anymore. Nothing behind her now but the little stone wall to divide this field from the next, the slate and sandstone boulders already half buried by the storm, and the wind pricks her skin with icing needle teeth. The snow spirals down from the leaden clouds and the wind sends it spinning and dancing in dervish crystal curtains.

"We forget for a reason, child," The Bailiff says, his rust-crimson voice woven tight between the air and every snowflake. "Time is too heavy to carry so much of it strung about our necks."

"I don't hear you," she lies, and it doesn't matter anyway, whatever he says, because Dead Girl is already at the barn door; both the doors left standing open and her father will be angry, will be furious if he finds out.

The horses could catch cold, he will say to her. The cows, he will say, the cows are already giving sour milk, as it is.

Shut the doors and don't look inside. Shut the doors and run all the way home.

"It fell from the sky," he said, the night before. "It fell screaming from a clear, blue sky. No one's gone looking for it. I don't think they will."

"It was only a bird," her mother said.

"No," her father said. "It wasn't a bird."

Shut the doors and run . . .

But she doesn't do either, because that isn't the way this happened, the way it happens, and the naked thing crouched there in the straw and the blood looks up at her with Gable's pretty face. Takes its mouth away from the mare's mangled throat and blood spills out between clenched teeth and runs down its chin.

"The bear was singing our names."

And then the paperweight hits the floor and bursts in a sudden, merciful spray of glass and water that tears the winter day apart around her. "Wake up," Miss Josephine says, spits out impatient words that smell like anise and dust, and she shakes Dead Girl again.

"I expect Madam Terpsichore is finishing up downstairs. And the Bailiff will be back soon. You can't sleep here."

Dead Girl blinks and squints past Miss Josephine and all the colorful, candy-shaded lamps. And the summer night outside the parlor window, the night that carries her rotten soul beneath its tongue, stares back with eyes as black and secret as the bottom of a river.

In the basement, Madam Terpsichore, lady of rib spreaders and carving knives, has already gone, has crept away down one of the damp and brick-throated tunnels with her snuffling entourage in tow. Their bellies full and all their entrail curiosities sated for another night, and only Barnaby is left behind to tidy up; part of his modest punishment for slicing too deeply through a sclera and ruining a violet eye meant for some graveyard potentate or another, the precious vitreous humor spilled by his hand, and there's a fresh notch in his left ear where Madam Terpsichore bit him for ruining such a delicacy. Dead Girl is sitting on an old produce crate, watching while he scrubs bile from the stainless steel tabletop.

"I'm not very good with dreams, I'm afraid," he says to her and wrinkles his wet black nose.

"Or eyes," Dead Girl says and Barnaby nods his head.

"Or eyes," he agrees.

"I just thought you might listen, that's all. It's not the sort of thing I can tell Gable, and Bobby, well . . ."

"He's a sweet child, though," Barnaby says, and then he frowns and scrubs harder at a stubborn smear the color of scorched chestnuts.

"But I can't tell anyone else," Dead Girl says; she sighs and Barnaby dips his pig-bristle brush into a pail of soapy water and goes back to work on the stain.

"I don't suppose I can do *very* much damage, if all I do is listen," and the ghoul smiles a crooked smile for her and touches a claw to the bloody place where Madam Terpsichore nicked the base of his right ear with her sharp incisors.

"Thank you, Barnaby," she says and draws a thoughtless half-circle on the dirt floor with the scuffed toe of one shoe. "It isn't a very long dream. It won't take but a minute," and what she tells him, then, isn't the dream of Adrian Mobley and the Lovecraft tree and it isn't the barn and the blizzard, the white thing waiting for her inside the barn. This is another dream, a moonless night at Swan Point and someone's built a great, roaring bonfire near the river's edge. Dead Girl's watching the flames reflected in the water, the air heavy with wood smoke and the hungry sound of fire; and Bobby and Gable are lying on the rocky beach, laid out neat as an undertaker's work, their arms at their sides, pennies on their eyes. And they're both slit open from collarbones to crotch, stem to stern, ragged Y-incisions and their innards glint wetly in the light of the bonfire.

"No, I don't think it was me," Dead Girl says, even though it isn't true, and draws another half-circle on the floor to keep the first one company. Barnaby has stopped scrubbing at the table and is watching her uneasily with his distrustful, scavenger eyes.

"Their hearts are lying there together on a boulder," and she's speaking very quietly now, almost whispering as if she's afraid someone upstairs might be listening, too, and Barnaby perks up his ears and leans toward her. Their hearts on a stone, and their livers, and she burns the organs in a brass bowl until there's nothing left but a handful of greasy ashes.

"I think I eat them," Dead Girl says. "But there are blackbirds then, a whole flock of blackbirds, and all I can hear are their wings. Their wings bruise the sky."

And Barnaby shakes his head, makes a rumbling, anxious sound deep in his throat, and he starts scrubbing at the table again. "I should learn to quit while I'm only a little ways behind," he snorts. "I should learn what's none of my goddamn business."

"Why, Barnaby? What does it mean?" and at first he doesn't answer her, only grumbles to himself and the pig bristle brush flies back and forth across the surgical table even though there are no stains left to scrub, nothing but a few soap suds and the candlelight reflected in the scratched and dented silver surface.

"The Bailiff would have my balls in a bottle of brine if I told you that," he says. "Go away. Go back upstairs where you belong and leave me alone. I'm busy."

"But you do know, don't you? I heard a story, Barnaby, about another dead girl named Mercy Brown. They burned *her* heart—"

And the ghoul opens his jaws wide and roars like a caged lion, hurls his brush at Dead Girl, but it sails over her head and smashes into a shelf of Ball mason jars behind her. Broken glass and the sudden stink of vinegar and pickled kidneys, and she runs for the stairs.

"Go pester someone else, *corpse*," Barnaby snarls at her back. "Tell your blasphemous dreams to those effete cadavers upstairs. Ask one of *those* snotty fuckers to cross him," and then he throws something else, something shiny and sharp that whizzes past her face and sticks in the wall. Dead Girl takes the stairs two at a time, slams the basement door behind her and turns the lock. And if anyone's heard, if Miss Josephine or Signior Garzarek or anyone else even notices her reckless dash out the front doors and down the steps of the big, old house on Benefit Street, they know better than Barnaby and keep it to themselves.

In the east, there's the thinnest blue-white sliver of dawn to mark the horizon, the light a pearl would make, and Bobby hands Dead Girl another stone. "That should be enough," she says and so he sits down in the grass at the edge of the narrow beach to watch as she stuffs this last rock inside the hole where Gable's heart used to be. Twelve big rocks shoved inside her now, granite-cobble viscera to carry the vampire's body straight to the bottom of the Seekonk and this time that's where it will stay. Dead Girl has a fat roll of gray duct tape to seal the wound.

"Will they come after us?" Bobby asks and the question takes her by surprise, not the sort of thing she would ever have expected from him. She stops wrapping Gable's abdomen with the duct tape and stares silently at him for a moment, but he doesn't look back at her, keeps his eyes on that distant, jagged rind of daylight.

"They might," she tells him. "I don't know for sure. Are you afraid, Bobby?"

"I'll miss Miss Josephine," he says. "I'll miss the way she read us stories," and Dead Girl nods her head and "Yes," she says. "Me too. But I'll always read you stories," and he smiles when she says that.

When Dead Girl is finally finished, they push Gable's body out into the water and follow it all the way down, wedge it tight between the roots of the sunken willow tree below Henderson Bridge. And then Bobby nestles close to Dead Girl and in a moment he's asleep, lost in his own dreams, and she closes her eyes and waits for the world to turn itself around again.

The Night Stair

Angela Slatter

Angela Slatter has won a World Fantasy Award and six Aurealis Awards, and she was the first Australian to win a British Fantasy Award. She's published a number of short story collections (including *Sourdough and Other Stories* and *The Bitterwood Bible and Other Recountings* from Tartarus Press), has a PhD, and occasionally teaches creative writing.

Jo Fletcher Books published her debut novel, *Vigil*, in 2016, followed by the sequels *Corpselight* and *Restoration*.

"Like many of my disposition and vintage I grew up watching Hammer Horror Films," recalls the author, "and a lot of those were vampire movies, so the imagery of the bloodsucker as a weird dichotomy of upper-class sensitivity and vicious murdering instinct always stayed with me—although, on further consideration, perhaps those two things aren't natural oppositions.

"*Dracula, The Vampire Lovers, Twins of Evil, Countess Dracula*, I loved—love—the aesthetic of those movies, the wondrous mix of lush set-dressing, fantastic frocks and frock-coats, and all the gore one could desire! The vampire is the best warning to us that the dead envy the living.

"It might seem strange then that I didn't actually read Stoker's *Dracula* until I was fourteen, nor 'Carmilla' until about twenty. I remember both giving me nightmares, but that not being enough to turn me away. Over the years I have read a lot of vampire lit, and my favorites include Kim Newman's magnificent Anno Dracula series and Barbara Hambly's James Asher series; what I think I love most about those two bodies of work is that the vampires aren't simply mindless creatures. They live longer than anyone, some suffer for it, some revel in their immortality, but none of them remain untouched by the drawbacks of existing so long, and it's up for debate as to whether or not the likes of Geneviève Dieudonné or Don Simon Ysidro are lacking in souls.

"'The Night Stair' is one of those stories that started as no more than a title in search of a story. In 2012, I visited Battle Abbey where the Battle of Hastings had taken place, and one of the signs directing you around the ruins pointed out the night stair that the monks had taken when going to early services. I just loved that name and thought it sounded positively sinister. Where might it really lead?

"I carried that around in my head as a title for the better part of a year until I started thinking about a vampire tale for *The Bitterwood Bible and Other Recountings* collection. I could see Adlisa standing in the selection line, waiting, hoping to be chosen, not for a perceived better life, but so she could act, find the truth, and, with any luck at all, get revenge. But, as always, there's a sting in the tale. She's another character I want to revisit later, as Adlisa the Bloodless—she's already got a mention in a new collection, *The Tallow-Wife and Other Tales*, and I hope to expand on that some time in the future.

"For a long while I chose not to write vampire fiction because it felt as if it had all been done, but then Adlisa came into my imagination. I hope she adds something to an impressive body of work."

THE STEWARD IS a tall man, entirely bald, gaunt in the face, yet rotund in the belly. His legs in their loose fawn linen trews look like a scarecrow's, sticking out under the awning of his gut—perpetually in shade, perhaps they don't get enough light to grow. His tunic of padded green silk, his sable wool coat with its thick fur collar, are too warm even for the end of summer, but as marks of his office, must be *seen*, just like the yellow crystal hanging about his neck.

Called the "Steward's Gaze," it's the size of the top joint of a man's thumb, and has passed from incumbent to incumbent for as long as any-one has the will to recall. He puts it in his mouth and sucks hard when he thinks no one is watching. It's worth a king's ransom, and I'll warrant the gold chatelaine belt around his waist could buy the city's food for half a year.

His finery makes me aware of the state of my black dress—not that it's poor or made shiny by age, but it belonged to others before me. Both my sisters—my only full-blood siblings—wore it to their own choosing. I am certain I can smell them, their scents imprinted into the warp and weft of the fabric despite washing. The color makes my skin paler, my eyes bluer, provides the perfect background for the tresses, which pour down my back like gold fresh from the smelter.

I was careful, so careful with my toilette: brushing my hair, one hun-dred strokes; rubbing the cream that was my mother's (comfrey and rose to soften and plump, a little lemon balm for lightening) into my skin; drops of eyebright to ensure my gaze is clear. I refrained from pinching my cheeks—pale is best—but I did nip gently at my lips, to carmine them a little, so it seems as if all life is concentrated there. I will not be found wanting.

I stand in line with seven other girls who have been presented this day. We are of an age, none more than sixteen springs, and there is only one of them, perhaps two, who *might* outdo me. To my right is Essa, with her milky skin and eyes like the sky reflected in ice, hair bright platinum; even her nails seem to have a silvery sheen. She watches me from the corner of her eye, just as I watch her.

To my left is Dimity, whose eyes are bright green, her cheeks with the tiniest hint of pink. She keeps her regard firmly fixed upon her own feet. Our Lady best likes girls who resemble herself; that is not Dimity for all her snow-washed whiteness—the eyes are all wrong and the eyes count.

So, Essa. Essa is the one to beat—the Steward will surely select between the two of us.

Filling this large room in the city hall are parents, including my father, who's left the running of the mine's smelter to his deputies so he can see what deals might be struck. Behind him are three of my younger half-siblings, those not yet old enough to be exhibited, but deemed mature enough to watch proceedings in order to learn how to behave when—if—their time comes. Another ten still wait at home; not all will be offered, only those whose appearance is *right*, those whose behavior does not mark them out as more trouble than they're worth.

My father has twice made a small fortune from this process, and I imagine he hopes to again—his tendency for taking new wives, sometimes before the old one is done, and his proclivity for procreation, his personal fecundity, constantly require more funds than his well-paid position provides.

Steward Oswain walks slowly up and down our line, as if inspecting troops. His brown eyes are considering, patient, although a little uncertain, as if offered several courses at a banquet and told he might only have one. He stops in front of the Toop girl and shakes his head (anyone can see she's too fat), then the Ansible twins (hair too dark), and then Mistress Garran's girl (whose neck is smudged by a red birthmark); a dismissal for each. At the back of the crowd I hear a woman crying; she is shushed and hustled out—I cannot tell if her weeping was of relief or despair. The desperate whirring of my own thoughts is far too loud.

I straighten my shoulders, lift my head a little higher, blink quickly so that tears of fear do not start and cause the coal-mascara on my lashes to run. The Steward takes one more pass; another. He stops in front of Dimity—Dimity!—puts a finger under her chin and makes her look at him. Her lips tremble; he smiles kindly and nods. Essa makes a noise, and this one I know for relief. The Steward steps back, turns away. All scrutiny has left us.

Parents mill around the tall stork of a man to strike bargains; Dimity's mother to get the highest price, the others to find out when there might be another choosing—as if the Steward can predict Our Lady's moods to a day and date! Only my siblings still watch, their eyes fastened onto me as if by hooks.

Dimity takes her first step forward as a chosen girl and I trip her. Essa's intake of breath is sharp. The green-eyed maiden falls so fast, is so surprised, that she does not put her hands out to save herself. Her face meets the floor with a satisfying *crunch* of bone and cartilage. There is that tiny broken moment when nothing happens, no one moves, when time is divided into *before* and *after*, then, as if a clock's hands click over, everything starts again, and the girl on the floor wails. I do not move.

Dimity sits up, blood pouring from her ruined nose. She stares at me all uncomprehending, hands twitching as if to point me out, but she catches my glance and I can see her crumple inside. She sobs a little more quietly and when an adult asks what happened, she answers with "I fell."

She will thank me; or rather, she would if she thought about it.

The Steward is displeased—she is no longer *acceptable*. He turns to Essa, and I glare for a few moments until her nerve breaks and she steps backward, in effect removing herself from the field. I am thankful for I have no more tricks.

"You then," says the Steward, giving me a calculating glance. He looks at my father, who nods approvingly (what kind of fool thinks I do this for him?). "Perhaps you will do best. Your father's blood runs strong."

It is not the sort of compliment I wished for, but I duck my head in assent, then notice that my half-siblings still watch, mouths agape.

Never let it be said I've taught them nothing.

"Never speak first."

The Steward had continued his litany of rules as we made our way from Caulder's city hall to the hostelry where he'd left his tall gray horse. He mounted, then pulled me up to sit in front of him, perched uncomfortably on the saddle. "Do not ask questions that are not invited."

Wear only the clothing you are assigned.
Eat and drink only that which is offered to you.
Always answer when Our Lady calls you "daughter."
Do not enter the undercroft.
Do not enter our Lord and Lady's chambers without invitation.
Do not correct our Lord and Lady.
Do not run along the corridors.
Do not take anything that has not been given to you.
Do not investigate locked doors.
Do not wish for more than is given.

Do not ask them to make you as they are.
Do not.
Do not.
Do not.

My head buzzed by the time we'd left behind the cobbled streets and begun to traverse fields yellow with wheat, pastures thick with cattle and sheep, enormous garden beds sown with all the things that can be stored in root cellars to tide the city over during winter.

By the time we'd ridden to the far end of the horseshoe-shaped valley, to the sweet spot where the manor house with its great hall and single lofty tower rested in the curve of the "u" . . . by the time we'd left the horse to the lad at the stables and entered the house . . . by the time I'd been led up to this very room . . . well, by then my head ached.

This bedchamber has windows that do not open, the shutters are nailed in place to keep the light out. If I feel the need for sun, I have been told, I may walk in the gardens, but for my own sake I should wear one of the muslin visages and a pair of gloves to protect my complexion, for even a light bronzing will ruin everything.

"That was your sister's sin," says the Steward.

"Which one?"

"The first one."

Sophie always did like to play outside. She'd have darkened so fast.

The bed is enormous, with a mattress thick and high, a satin canopy of deepest crimson, a matching coverlet, and so many pillows I may well suffocate if I don't remove them before I sleep. I think back to the bed I shared with my sisters when our mother would read to us in the evenings—before everything changed. It was barely big enough for all of us, sleeping like pups pressed against each other, breaths mingling, hearts beating in time; here we would lose each other. We shared a wardrobe, a washstand, a mirror, our clothes; we fought over hairbrushes and ribbons. Hardly a year apart, we were more like triplets, close enough to finish each other's sentences, to know the others' thoughts before they were spoken.

Here, there is a desk with a roll-top, a tall wardrobe, a long sofa with scarlet velvet bolsters, a tiny round table with mother-of-pearl inlay in a bird-and-girl pattern, and two wingback chairs set either side of it; all the furniture is a burnished mahogany. Through a door concealed by a *trompe l'oeil* design of a sunny sandstone courtyard packed with fruit trees and climbing vines, is a marble-floored bathroom, almost as big as the bedroom. There is a sunken pool, golden wash basins, and a corner where water flows in a continuous shower then runs out a cleverly decorated drain that looks like a posy of roses.

I was delighted when I saw it. All this space just for me, but there are no bookshelves and no books. It is said that all manner of tomes are kept in the tower. I wonder if I will be allowed there—I do not ask, for then I cannot be refused.

"And April?" I ask and he gives me a look so blank my heart aches. By the time her body was returned to us she'd had a good run compared to others, such as Sophie, who'd lasted but a month. "My other sister; she stayed here eighteen months."

He shakes his head, quite sadly. "I cannot remember them all. Some infraction, some upset to Our Lady. Let it serve as a lesson to you, Adlisa, let all your steps be careful ones." He plays with the crystal, almost popping it into his mouth—but he catches himself first and the slip makes him brusque. "Now, I suggest you bathe—I will send one of the women to do your hair. There is a selection of dresses so you will surely find one to fit; fold your old one up and leave it at the foot of the bed. It will be returned to your family. And have a nap if you can manage—from this day onward you live half in light and half in shadow. And I'm sure your mind is moving apace after the other candidate's misfortune."

I meet his eye steadily, do not flinch. The Steward grips my arm and whispers, "I have been here thirty years, girl. I have seen your kind come and go, the ambitious and the unassuming. None of them has survived."

My expression does not change for I am neither one nor the other, although I am sure he must hear my heart clattering in my rib cage like one of the machines in the smelter that crushes chunks of rock and ore into smaller pieces. I raise my chin, just a fraction and he lets me go, straightening his coat before he leaves this room, which is mine however ephemerally.

"Call me 'Mother,' child," says the alabaster woman.

Her voice is soft but the tone brooks no refusal. We are in the circular chamber that serves as her solar, its skylight open only at night. On her lap is a piece of embroidery, a fine stitching of black silk roses on snowy cambric.

That word has not crossed my lips in some years, not since my own mother disappeared in a night of shouting and rage after which my father ceased to speak of her. It was a title I'd refused to accord to any of Father's subsequent wives or concubines, despite all the slaps and bruises that defiance brought. The term conjures a shadowy, slippery, precious memory—an ache—but that isn't why I do not give it lightly. I keep it close, pristine and unused, for it has power; power for both she who gives and she who receives, and I must be careful about bestowing such potential. It is tricksy and dangerous, it can make one party think they are stronger than they are, when really it is a key to their heart. Our Lady would like to think it gains her the upper hand, but in this conferral *I* alone acquire the advantage.

"Mother," I say. It slides the across my lips with barely a hiccup. And I smile, meeting her glacial blue gaze for the first time; I have kept my eyes downcast as a polite and chaste child should, addressing My Lady respectfully and shyly.

"Come closer, Adlisa," she says and I step forward to where she reclines on a *chaise longue*; her watered silk gown in shades of oyster pink and dove gray drapes beautifully about her slender form, but she must lie on a slight angle to accommodate the beribboned bustle. Her hair is the same shade as mine, a good sign, gilded as the statues that stare down from the portico of the city hall. Her skin is so pale it's almost transparent—I wonder if I stare hard enough might I see the skull beneath this bleached canvas?—and her forehead high and domed, eyebrows fine as golden pin feathers, cheekbones sharp, lips a petulant pout even in repose. Her chin is a little weak and it appears she is aware of this, for the tilt of her head seems a conscious combat against it. A thin hand with long digits reaches out and turns my head this way and that, not cruelly or painfully, but in a determined grip I could not break. If she wanted, she could shatter my jaw with the snap of her fingers.

"My, you are lovely. You do remind me of someone else, but I cannot think who." Her lips lift at their corners. Her fingers toy with the soft curls the old woman Rikke left dangling by my cheeks when she swept the rest up in a great loose bun on top of my head.

I think of my sisters, wonder if she genuinely remembers them, but I do not say *My Lady, you ate them*. April and Sophie would have been afraid of her. They would have been scared and it would have finally got the better of them. At some point, she'd have called them to her and they would have shown reluctance; she with her predator's instinct would have smelled their terror, and that would have meant death. Our mad Lady, who has sought across so many years, in the faces of so many others, a replacement for her lost daughter, and found them all wanting.

Sophie's tanning would not have offended nearly so much as the sight of her nerve fracturing. The shaking and shattering of Our Lady's happy illusions would have broken her mother's heart anew. Like most folk, she loathes and destroys the things that make her see the truth, has done for three centuries or more. There is barely a family in Caulder that has been untouched; barely a family that hasn't had an inert, empty body delivered back to them.

"Mother, will you show me how?" I point shyly at the embroidery in her bloodless hands and she beams, patting the seat next to her. Her delight in my interest is childlike, unalloyed. I know that my survival depends on the illusion I create for her being flawless. I am careful not to prick myself with the sharp golden needle—it would not do to either ruin this piece of work or tempt her with blood. We are there long enough that I am able to finish one black petal under her instruction.

"Shall I begin another, Mother?" I ask.

She looks at the elaborate timepiece on the mantle—a thing of porcelain and bronze, which disgorges three dancing maids on the hour—and shakes her head. "No, no, I have let our time fly. Where is my sense? Come, we must to dinner."

I walk a step behind her, but slip my fingers into the cold cocoon of her palm. She smiles down at me and leads me along corridors until we reach a narrow formal dining room with an extravagant fireplace, two magnificent chandeliers in crystal and gilt, and a terribly long table in polished ebony, with padded seats for fifty people—although how they would ever manage to find so many willing guests is anyone's guess. At the far end, are three place settings and one man sitting at the head. He looks up and smiles at us, but his stare is cool—we are late. Behind him stand two plump girls with ruddy complexions and gowns of a better quality than the housemaids': winepresses, these, being fed on one night, then rested for six while they themselves drink strong red wines and eat rare meats to build up their blood once again. They look at me with wary boredom. How many day-daughters have they seen come and go? How many girls whose privileges hardly seem worth the price they all ultimately pay? How much better to be one of these, these valued *cattle*—kept and preserved, not drained and thrown away on a whim, like an empty Jeroboam.

I can see they think themselves better than me, more permanent; there's an arrogance yet a wariness, for the day-daughters are still favored if only for a short time. The day-daughters are *family* and no insolence will be tolerated from anyone, not even these precious casks.

So as we approach, the two ruddy girls bob curtsies, eyes hooded.

"Edward, my love. This is Adlisa."

Our Lady hands me forward as the Lord pushes back his chair, but does not rise. He surveys me and I drop into a deep curtsey, mirroring that of the drinking vessels. I do not look up until he says, after proper pause, "Good evening, Adlisa."

In his green gaze I see the same weariness as that of the winepresses; how many day-daughters has *he* seen? How many times has he indulged his wife's madness? He must love her a great deal to repeat this scene over and over.

He is very handsome, with chiseled features, thin lips, and dark red hair. Any freckles that might have marred his complexion in life have been long-since faded by his death years.

He nods toward the only place that is set with food—roasted meats, piles of steaming vegetables, a platter of white bread with delicate curls of butter in a small dish by its side. "Sit, it is well past time to eat."

Our Lady ignores the gibe and seats herself, gaily chattering about how she taught me to embroider and what an apt pupil I am, learning so terribly quickly—it does not seem to occur to her that perhaps I learned well before I was chosen. But then, that is part of her fantasy—refusing to believe that there was any life for me before becoming a day-daughter. I play my part. "Thank you for teaching me, Mother."

She positively glows. Our Lord gives me a sideways glance, which I answer with a guileless smile and an innocent gaze. After a pause he nods toward my meal, and I carefully serve myself ladylike portions although I ache to scoff down as much sustenance as I can. I'm starving, but eating like a peasant will not make a good impression. There is no servant to attend me—as few witnesses as possible to see them feed, I suppose. A strange delicacy.

The girls move into position, one beside the Lord, the other beside the Lady, both of whom carefully flutter embroidered serviettes into their laps before taking the chubby wrists offered and fastidiously biting through the skin as one might a peach. I glimpse trickles of blood that are swiftly licked away and I concentrate on my own dinner, forcing myself to eat despite a sudden loss of appetite. There is no more conversation until the repast is finished and the winepresses are swooning dreamily, then our Lord says, "Adlisa, as this is your first night, you will be tired. You may retire."

His inflection tells me this is not a suggestion and, despite the Lady's disappointed moue, I nod and stand, curtsey, and leave the room. The Steward is waiting outside the door and nods approvingly, but says nothing. It makes me wonder how badly other first nights have gone, that he thinks this meal a triumph.

Out in the garden, the small one behind the manor, between the kitchen door, the stables and the upward slope of the mountainside, I am sketching meadowsweet into the small leather-bound herbal that was my mother's—the only thing I brought with me, tucked deep into the pocket of my black dress. I run my fingers along the spine, feeling the outline of what has lain hidden there for decades. I carefully reproduce the plant's appearance and label all its parts; I jot down what I know of its properties, whether it may heal or hurt (it will assuage vomiting, fluxes, and the pain of women's courses). I leave enough space to make new notes that reflect what I might learn of it in my lifetime (however long or short that might be), just as my mother did and hers before her. I wonder who will have it when I am gone, who will fill the empty pages at the back? I adjust the muslin visage, surreptitiously using it to mop the sweat from my face.

This is my time to myself, before the Lord and Lady rise at nightfall and after I have spent some hours helping the Steward with the tasks needed to keep the manor and the city—the whole demesne—running smoothly. I awaken late, past midday, in order to straddle day and night, eat, then present myself at Oswain's office, which is a chamber of middling size. I have been put to copying, neatly and tidily, invoices and payment advices into the huge account book that is chained to the broad desk, the record of all the Lord and Lady's incomings and outgoings during Oswain's tenure.

Against the opposite wall are shelves lined with other books like it— those to the left are filled with the scribblings of Stewards past; those to the right are blank, awaiting the day when this one is full and the stroke of a pen will begin the process of recording anew.

There are two doors to this room, the one I use daily to enter and exit, and the other of black oak, which I spent most of my time studiously ignoring. It is, I was told severely, the entrance to the undercroft—beyond it lies the night stair leading to our Lord and Lady's crypt, where they sleep during the day. I shall never see it, I am told.

Sometimes, when I finish my duties early, I go to the far end of the manor house, to where the stone tower of the library sits. I read the history books, the tales of how the estate grew into a village that grew into a town and finally a city. I read the stories of how the Lord and Lady *became*, of the dark man who passed through Caulder and left his mark in their blood, taking their only child and leaving them to wander forever. I read the diaries of the long-dead Stewards, the lists of the very first orders given to ensure the safety of the newly reborn Lord and Lady—such as the scouring of the hawthorn trees and the garlic plants, the burning of the tiny wooden church and how the priest was thrown on the pyre as extra kindling. How the system of pricing was established so that people were properly compensated for the service they paid to their overlords. Our Lord and Lady have long understood that a gentle hand and a slow corruption will keep them in position much longer than repression and tyranny; that ensuring the population is contented, compliant—bovine— is the way to retain power.

Make lives, for the most part, enjoyable; all it costs is a little blood. And if any should question, if any should complain too loudly, or say "I do not wish to make this bargain for my child's life," then their voice is silenced. But cunningly—an outspoken individual can be made to seem a thief, a law-breaker, a disturber of the peace, so that when they are taken away, it is in broad daylight and all might see that this is not some secretive retribution, but an open and honest operation of the law of the land. The punishment is delivered not by the Lord and Lady, no, but by the council of our fair city, so we might think ourselves self-determining, living and thriving under a system fair and equitable.

Other times, all this reading hurts my head, all the knowledge I gain of consequences and injustices, of loss and mourning disguised as justice, of my sisters fed to an unnatural hunger, settles in my chest and swells there, making it hard to breathe. Those are times when I take to the herb garden and let myself think on nothing but the plants, on keeping my hand steady and my drawings accurate. As I add a few more veins to a leaf my fingers, too long clenched, spasm and I drop the pencil. It rolls under the meadowsweet and I kneel to locate it below the lush foliage.

At the base of the bush, quite well hidden, I find a tiny white flower, which I recognize but have never seen, at least not in its true form. I flick to a page in the back of the herbal, one that's folded in on itself and tucked behind the endpaper so only a sharp eye will see it. My grandmother's etchings of the garlic plant. Her notes tell me there will be bulbs beneath the earth. The flower is shrouded by the meadowsweet; no one will expect it, no one will know. It makes me lightheaded with possibilities. All the time spent planning to gain a place in this manor house, all the recent weeks looking for weaknesses, for some idea of how I might take my revenge and here is this unlooked-for boon, something for which I'd never thought to hope.

"Will you help?" A soft voice almost scares me to death and I look up, stricken. Rikke's gentle smile fades. She kneels beside me before I can rise, distract her, turn her attention elsewhere. "What is it, Adlisa?"

And she catches sight of the tiny white flowers and the pupils of her gray eyes dilate as if she's taken a dose of belladonna. And I see that *she* knows what it is as no one from this city should. My heart hammers, then she climbs slowly to her feet, knees cracking and creaking, her white hair lifted by the breeze that seems to have started just for us. She makes sure the stalks of the meadowsweet cover the nascent blossoms, then offers her hand to me, and repeats, "Will you help?"

I nod, scramble up.

"Another set of hands on Our Lady's new dress will make the work go faster. And then you may help with dinner if you wish," she says. As we move toward the kitchen door, she lowers her voice and adds, "Be careful, Adlisa."

And I wonder at her. She can't have been born here, recognizing a plant that has not been seen in this area for hundreds of years. Do I perhaps remember she arrived here some years since and the Steward claimed her as his cousin? Our visitors are few and far between, and none come without invitation. Will she tell Oswain what she has seen?

In the library, on the third floor, there are many books of strategy and philosophy, well-read, their pages thumbed, markings made in the margins, all by the Lord's hand. After the first few weeks as a day-daughter, I settled myself at the desk opposite the arched window, the one that looks out across the valley, and piled tomes in front of me—where the Lord might find me. He'd raised his brows and asked if I understood what I was reading; it was the first time he showed any interest in me beyond a polite "Good evening, Adlisa" and "Good night, Adlisa," beyond humoring his Lady.

"Some of it—the strategies mostly. I enjoyed *Deor's Art of War* best so far. The philosophy, though—it's beyond me." I shrugged, fingers resting on the cover of the Angelic Bergevilde's *Philosophies and Mores*.

He questioned me about the *Deor*, trying to trip me up—but I have studied the book, more than once. My father had a copy—old, tattered, inherited from a grandparent I never knew—and I've read it cover to cover and back again. I particularly liked how it speaks of infiltrating the enemy's camp, sowing trust in order to reap revenge; how to make your adversary expect a warm hand in the dark, but find only cold steel. Oh, I know my *Deor*.

Tonight we discuss *Leofgod's Military Tactics* and the Lord shows his age—the book is three hundred years old if it's a day and it was ancient before the Lord himself became what he is. He is of a generation that believes battles are won on fields watered with blood and filled with men soon to become corpses, with weapons that catch the sun, while monumental music provided by drummers and buglers thickens the air. That land must be gained and lost several times before a victor is named. That all war should be out in the open, frank and honest. Deor's advices have passed him by—he has read them but finds them . . . ungentlemanly, and as such he has let them slip away like lightly held thoughts.

We debate the relative merits of the tacticians and I do not let him win. We argue to a stalemate and he sits back in his armchair with a satisfied air. He sees me, at last, as something other than an ephemeral day-daughter, a creature whose lifespan is determined entirely by how long

Our Lady remains fixated on me. I smile brightly, thinking only that he is one of those men who have never had to ride to war and cannot know that strategy survives only so long as one has no contact with the enemy.

He offers me his arm to go to dinner and I think, foolishly, how pleased My Lady will be to see that at last we are friends, for she has spent so much time trying to encourage him to pay attention to me.

"You're late," snaps she when we enter the dining room. The wine-presses—the same ones who witnessed my first triumphant meal here—cover their smirking smiles with raised hands. I can see the tiny scars around their wrists, cicatrices like bracelets.

"My apologies, my love," says the Lord smoothly. "Our daughter and I lost ourselves in the heat of intellectual intercourse."

The hairs on the back of my neck stand to attention as he leads me to my seat before taking his own at the head of the table. My Lady looks daggers at me from across the silver filigree candle tree; she seems thinner, whiter, not quite well. Her eyes catch the tips of the flames and flash red. My Lord reaches out and strokes my hand—I pull away without thought. I fear it's too late to appease My Lady, for something has begun here that I had not foreseen. So smug I have been, that I too have forgotten that *a strategy survives only so long as one has no contact with the enemy*. I see now that I was merely her mouse to be dangled in front of the cat to torment it—not to make friends with it.

"Your hair," she begins, "is ghastly, Adlisa, all dressed and pomaded like a harlot."

No matter that the coiffure is one she herself has asked me to wear.

"And your skin is looking . . . golden," she says with distaste. "You have been outdoors without your visage."

I have not—I am as anemic-pale as I ever was.

"And that dress is ugly. The color does not suit you, it makes you look jaundiced." That the dress was an especial present from her, seems to make no mind as she warms to her topic. I am lazy and tardy, selfish and slatternly in my person, ignorant and ungrateful, and I do not truly love her.

My Lord says nothing, merely smiling slyly and affixing himself to the wrist of this evening's fat girl—they have favorites, he and the Lady. I've noticed that they do not share, do not swap; always the same seven girls each, in the same order each week. He watches us over the barrier of porky pink flesh, and I rethink my opinion of him. Perhaps he has not dismissed all of Deor's lessons out of hand.

Answering back, trying to defend myself, will do no good. My only choice is to burst into tears, which I summon by thinking of my lost sisters. My Lord, overthrown by a woman's weeping—our surest weapon against which no man has a defense—tidily finishes his meal and leaves the room. Out of his presence and shocked by my sobbing, Our Lady is contrite, tender, motherly.

"Oh, Adlisa, come here," she cries, pushing back her chair so I may sit at her feet, my head in her lap. She caresses my hair. "I'm so sorry, my darling—I'm a terrible mother. A terrible person. How can I say such things, such cruel things?"

"No, no Mother, you are the kindest, sweetest woman. I give thanks every day that you chose me," I aver, words sticking my throat. "I did not mean to displease you, only I thought you would be happy, to see Father and I as friends."

She slips to the floor, her silken apricot skirts pooling around her, and holds my face close to hers. As she speaks I catch the rankness of old blood seeping up from her stomach. She has not fed yet—she is paler than usual, and she would smell differently if she had—meatier, wetter. "You must not trust him, Adlisa. You must not. That was the mistake the others made, thinking him harmless, a kind father. But if you trust him, he will . . . then I will . . ." She does not finish the thought, but rocks me back and forth as if I am a child and not almost a woman grown. She emits little moaning sounds that make the skin on my spine shiver and pucker. In the end, I gently pull away and call to the untapped winepress.

"Our Lady is thirsty. Our Lady hungers. My Mother must be fed," I say and there is a grudging admiration in the girl's eyes, to see that I have salvaged myself at least for this night. She comes close and the scent coming off her skin is faint but I can detect it because I am looking for it. She offers her wrist, and Our Lady bites into it as if she is starving.

I stay until she is sated and the drinking vessel has all but passed out. Our Lady, despite her repletion, does not seem any stronger. I help her up and take her to lie on the *chaise* in her solar, where she drifts into an uneasy sleep until such time as Rikke or one of the lesser maids will wake her and escort her to the night stair before the day dawns.

"A visitor arrived for you this afternoon, My Lord. He has conducted previous correspondence with your good self, I believe." The Steward's tone tells precisely what he thinks of this visitor, a blond man perhaps in his mid-forties—vain, I can tell, for he wears makeup as women do to try and fill the furrows time has made in his face. I watched him, surreptitiously, from the kitchen while I was helping Rikke prepare for the evening meal.

Some of the day-daughters, she has told me, have determinedly refused to undertake such tasks, acting as if they're born porcelain ladies and not temporarily elevated earthenware, but I have ever been willing to assist with meals for the entire household, taking it on myself to season the rich, meaty stews and roasts for the winepresses.

The sound of smashing drew my attention away from the visitor—Rikke, standing behind me, eyes wide, expression disbelieving. When I asked her what was wrong, she stooped to pick up the shards of the terracotta jar, shook her head.

"I thought . . ." she began and shook her head again, summoned a smile. "I thought I knew him, from a long time ago. But that's not possible, is it, with him unchanged?"

We gave each other a shaky grin—do we not live in the shadow of the unchanging?

The man was very handsome, his eyes terribly blue as they watched the slow spin of the Steward's Gaze at Oswain's chest, but lacking in warmth, cold as the depths of a sapphire are cold, and his lips were very full, over-ripe, and I did not trust his mouth. Everything he is resides there, in its petulance, its greed, its formation of want. I do not think him a friend to the Lord, but rather someone who wants something—and who resents having to ask for it. He does not wear the cloak of a supplicant well. Oswain gave him a guest room, for it is winter now and the Lord has been rising late—the Lady later still—and left him there to wait until someone came to lead him to the library for an audience.

I had not heard My Lord enter the Steward's office, but then one seldom hears either of them if they do not wish it so—although the Lady has become slow, more heavy-footed of late, liable to send vases and suits of armor crashing to the floor without any effort at all. Lord Edward stands in front of the great desk where Oswain sits hunched over one of his ledgers, while I sort a stack of invoices into their proper order at a smaller desk in one corner. I have been avoiding him, this strange father-figure, since that night when all my intricate planning seemed to go astray, when my steps appeared to leave the sure path I'd been so careful to stay on, and I could not divine the *why* of it.

The library at night has been off-limits by my own design, and each evening I wait in the Lady's solar until she rises, then help her to the dining room. She is weakest and most disoriented after waking, so when I've seen her safely to her seat, I take a small sharp knife and tap the veins of her winepress, letting the thick rich red trickle into a crystal glass. It is still warm with an echo of life vibrating through, enough to give her some strength, but one must be quick for the heartbeat rapidly fades. Her mystery ailment has made her too feeble to feed straight from the source until she has had a little taste to energize her, to remind her that the *claret* is what she craves. And as I render this service, our Lord eyes me with displeasure but says nothing; his mood has deteriorated with Our Lady's health. He no longer addresses me directly, but follows me with a gaze that broods and promises punishment.

For the moment, though, I am of no interest to him and our Lord fixes the Steward with a glare, ignoring mention of the guest, and jerks a thumb behind him as if to signify the rows of covered baskets in the hall.

"And what is all *this*, Oswain?"

"My Lord, there was a cave-in at the mine; three families lost sons and fathers. I have taken the liberty of having these supplies prepared to help tide the broods over until arrangements can be made for new husbands." More than one woman has found herself widowed by the black rock of the mountain, then newly married a few days later to ensure no impoverished relicts mar our streets.

"You coddle them, Oswain! Surely they should be able to care for themselves without your constant attention?" The undertone is mean, petty, and I can see the Steward stiffen. His lips tighten, blanch.

"My Lord, I and my kind have kept your *cattle* alive, healthy and contented in the interests of keeping you and your Lady contented and healthy and . . . alive," he stumbles, just a little, over that word. "Few things will disturb your pleasant existence more than an untended populous, but if you truly wish me to change how I discharge my duty then the choice is yours."

The Steward's tone is steely, and I hold my breath, fearful—I have become fond of him in these past months. He is stern but kind, and I have never seen him commit an act of cruelty. The moments stretch, scraping my nerves like a knife's edge on ligaments. Then the Lord grins ruefully.

"Oswain, you have the right of it, old friend. But be careful you do not overstep."

"I am ever mindful of your well-being, My Lord." Oswain bows his head, relief palpable. I sense that the Lord, too, did not wish a confrontation—did not wish to push against a limit, a barrier that might crack and break too easily.

"Add some bottles of tokay from the cellar to the baskets, as many as we can spare. And to send the visitor to the library—there will be no formal meal tonight, so make sure he is fed in his room."

Oswain raises an eyebrow. "My Lord?"

"Tonight, My Lady and I shall hunt," he says, smiling and raising his hand to forestall the Steward's protests. "Do not fear, Oswain, we will take the carriage and go beyond the boundaries of our demesne. None of your charges will be harmed."

Oswain nods slowly. "Make sure you choose an isolated farm so no one might raise an alarm. Leave no trace of yourself or your . . . meal."

"I recall how to hunt, Oswain, though it has been an age." He drops his voice. "I fear for My Lady, Marcella. I hope this—excursion—will help to heal her. Perhaps we have been too long sedentary, too long content to be fed; we have forgotten how to take something of the prey into us." His eyes glitter and for a moment he looks like a feral thing, dangerous, struggling against the bonds he's put on himself. Then his face relaxes and the moment is passed.

But I cannot forget that expression, even when he smiles at me, seemingly once again the doting father who had indulged in mock argument with me, testing me and finding himself pleased. He turns his back and leaves.

After interminable seconds, Oswain stands and closes the door. I can see a fine beading of sweat on his bald pate.

"Why do you serve them?" I say, the words out before I can think better of it. For a moment I doubt he will answer.

"Because without them, there will be a vacuum and a vacuum must be filled. And we can never know that what might come along isn't worse than this pair." He hides his face in his hands. "I do what I can as did my father and his before him and his before him. This is a *business* upon which an entire city depends, and as long as we remain clever and careful, we will survive."

"Why Dimity?" I ask. It's been bothering me for so long now and he seems inclined to talk. "She doesn't look like Our Lady."

He shakes his head. "No. She looks a little like our Lord, though. But it was . . . I thought it might preserve a life. She would not interest Our Lady much, and consequently nor our Lord. She might have simply faded into the domestic staff or become a winepress . . . anything's better than me having to deliver another hollow body to parents who had higher hopes for their child."

I had not thought about it that way—I had not thought the choice of Dimity might be calculated. Steward Oswain is a good man doing his best under a mighty burden. I respect him and I pity him. Once I'd thought to take revenge on him, for it was he who chose my sisters. But now, having seen how he aches . . . I cannot raise my hand against him.

"What is wrong with Our Lady?" I ask.

He shrugs. "They are *old*, Adlisa. Nothing is meant to live that long. Perhaps it is simply death catching up with them."

"Are there others of their kind?"

Again, a shrug. "Somewhere, I suppose, but I've not heard of any for the length of my life. My grandfather said the man who made them was not like them, not the same thing he turned them into. He—it—cursed them and stole their child. They've been changeless for so many centuries, but perhaps the curse is coming to its end and so are their lives?" Again he rubs his hands over his face, the sound of skin against stubble is loud. "They were never bad rulers, Adlisa—if you've spent your time wisely in the library you will know that. And as they are now, they are nowhere near as bad as they could be. Time has made them strange."

Silence falls and reigns, broken only by the ticking of the timepiece on the desk, a thing with a bird that coos the hours. I think we will stay there forever if I do not speak. "Shall I have the baskets delivered?"

"No, I'll organize that. You go and collect the guest and take him to the library. After that, I think you might be best keeping to your room tonight."

I pass through the kitchen and, from the small wooden box I've concealed behind the sacks of potatoes, I take three bulbs. I crush them quickly against the bricks of the fireplace while no one's looking and drop the garlic fragments into the thick, meaty pottage bubbling over the fire. The taste will be disguised by that of the leeks, chives and onions already in the mix. I scrub my hands carefully at the stone sink with lye soap, then splash some of the lemon juice wash Rikke keeps there for when she has been handling fish and needs to get rid of the smell.

The guest has been given a room three doors along from mine, an elaborate decor in greens and golds and bronze. When I knock, he is slow in answering, then makes me wait after I tell him why I am there—although he surely must know—but he takes his time putting on his seemingly brand new velvet frock coat with its intricate enamel buttons, teasing the lace cuffs of his shirt sleeves out so they might be seen and admired. He pushes at his hair, this way and that, in front of the large gaudy *cloisonné* mirror over the fireplace, vain as a woman, as if such fussing might help his cause.

He does not engage me in conversation, but I can feel his eyes boring into the back of me as I lead him along corridors, down staircases, through smaller rooms until at last we reach the library.

"Thank you, Adlisa," says My Lord when I introduce his guest. He grabs my upper arm without seeming to offer me violence, and strokes my face and curls. It is not the act of a father, and it makes me afraid, as if I'm being pulled toward something I cannot escape, a whirlpool, a drowning wave. As his wife fades, he grows more predatory. As she gives in, he fights against whatever is happening. He lets me go as if dropping me from a height. "Off you go."

"Pretty girl," I hear the blond man say as I close the door. "Rather reminds me of my sister . . ."

I waited until I heard the carriage rattle away; the Lord and Lady would be gone for hours. I waited until the house had quietened as the staff took the rare opportunity to rest earlier in the evening than was their wont. When all is quiet, I slip from my room and tiptoe along the corridor, carefully past the guest's room, then down one set of stairs and up another. Along a long landing; the door I'm seeking is at its end and I try the handle, find it unlocked, press my ear against the thick wood and listen intently, then push it open, quiet as can be.

There is a snuffle and a snort, a contented sleeper's noise, from the large bed beneath the window. In the winter moonlight, the thin form of the Steward is curled about Rikke's naked roundness. Not cousins, then. On the chest of drawers beside the door, right next to me, is the gleaming eye of the Steward's Gaze, and beside it the great golden pile of the chatelaine and keys, carelessly discarded for the night when he keeps it so carefully during the daylight hours. The cold radiates off it as I clasp it tightly.

Oswain gives a tremendous snore, fit to wake the household. I freeze, will myself invisible, wait to see if he rouses himself. He subsides into shallow breaths and sighs, and I slip out. Bouncing with nerves on my bare tiptoes, holding the chatelaine with both hands so it does not jingle and give me away, I scurry along the thin hallway rugs laid end to end; they muffle the sounds of my passage. I am so keyed up, listening so hard to the silent house that I almost overshoot my destination.

I unlock the office, and step inside. The room is dark except for the weak embers of the banked fire, but these weeks as a daughter in a house which comes alive at night have made my eyes sensitive to the darkness, as if I've become a cat. There it is: the black door, the locked door, the door that leads *down*.

I have no reason to go there, merely curiosity as hot and intense as flame. A desire to see a place where my sisters might have met their fate, where I might yet meet mine. I take a taper from the top drawer of the great desk, hold it to the glowing coals and let the wick catch. It glimmers weakly.

Five paces and the key is sliding into the lock easily, then the Stygian wood is pushed back to reveal the night stair. There is no illumination here. The cold stone steps beneath my naked feet answer back a quiet *shhh* as I descend into the earth. The walls are pocked with burial niches, some with moldering bones huddling sadly in corners, others with intact skeletons lying fully prone and relaxed in death. When I reach the bottom, I blink and stare into the deeper darkness.

There are two empty biers made of marble. I step forward, tiptoeing although I know no one is here; I catch my foot on something frail and friable. There is the faintest *crack*. I look down and see I have stepped on a doll, swaddled in sepia cloth and wearing a lace bonnet of ancient style. I bend and sweep it up, hold it close to my frail taper, look into its face to find it is in fact a mummified baby, empty-eyed, hollow-cheeked, hungry-mouthed. Beneath the swaddling I can feel where I snapped one of its ribs. I look about for a place to hide it and notice at last the pile—mound—of more of the same, all dressed so sweetly in styles of different ages, all as dead as dust, all with that same expression.

I carefully bury the one I broke beneath its fellows and hope that My Lady does not go looking for it. A quick survey of the space yields nothing, and I am about to return to the Steward's office when there is the sound of scuffing, of shoes hastily making contact with stone. I am frozen, unable to blow out the taper, to hide. What good would it do me?

"Adlisa?" It is Rikke's voice, taut with fear. Rikke, who has been so kind. Rikke, who has kept my secret. Rikke, who asked if she might create a facsimile of my herbal so there might be more than one copy in the world. Gentle Rikke, who has followed me down into this hell. "Adlisa, what are you doing? Come, you must leave now. They have returned—I heard the carriage."

We fly up the stairs. My hands shake too much and she must take the chatelaine from me and lock the black door, then the office too. She slips the heavy golden thing into the pocket of her brown woolen dressing-robe. We are waiting in the entrance hall when the main doors are thrown open and the Lord, Our Lady in his arms, charges in, both of them pale as the winter moon, but streaked with blood. The Lord's gaze is wild, the Lady's eyes are firmly closed.

"Drink this. Our Lady needs you," I say to the plump winepress. She is still befuddled by slumber and does not question me, merely lifts the goblet I put in her hand, chugging down the red wine, not commenting on the taste. Ah, bless these gluttonous girls.

I don't not let her dress, lest the Lord think I did not fetch her swiftly enough, and lead her to Our Lady's chamber. As I walk, in my pocket I can feel the weight of the item I've kept hidden inside the fat mattress of my bed ever since I lent Rikke my herbal. It hits against my thigh with each step, not heavy but still solid. *Tap-tap-tap. Tap-tap-tap.*

In the solar, Our Lady is draped across the *chaise* seemingly in a faint, but her eyelids flutter when she hears my voice. "My Lord, here is the girl."

He, in all his blood-streaked glory, grabs the winepress's forearm and drags her over to his wife. He forces her to her knees and presses her wrist to Our Lady's mouth. The wine-girl yelps in surprise; this is the roughest handling she's ever had. The first time she's seen the Lord's true nature, which he has subsumed for so many, many years. Our Lady grimaces and turns her face away, batting the air weakly with hands grown skeletal. The Lord, seeing this, raises the girl's wrist to his own mouth and his teeth—those canines they've gone to such trouble to carefully cover, speaking with lips close together so only the barest tips can be seen—those teeth seem to lengthen, sharpen, and he tears at the girl's flesh with them. He offers the limb once again to his wife and this time she opens her mouth, roused by the rich scent, latching on like a leech.

Her lids flutter up, eyes widen as she watches me. Her throat convulses with each gulp, each swallow, the marble flesh undulating painfully. I wonder if she knows what is happening.

The Lord, now certain she is drinking, strides around the room.

"The hunt did not go well?" I ask quietly and he hisses at me.

"No! Fool child, it did not. We found a farm, but there were too many—we did not know. Once I could have counted the heartbeats in this entire city, but now . . . they came from nowhere and we . . . we have grown sluggish and lazy, feeding on these thin-veined, fat-arsed bitches." His movements are jerky, graceless; his control is slipping. He paces past the drowsing winepress and offers her ample backside a kick, then changes direction. He has been less affected than his wife; perhaps his vessels have drunk less deeply or eaten less heartily of what I've prepared for them, or perhaps he is simply stronger. But now his face is thinner and his eyes stare, protrude just a little, the skin around his throat looser, perhaps. "We will feed on you all—it will make her well. You see? You see how she is after feeding on one of them? Before they woke and turned on us, before one of them fetched her a blow to her poor head. You see?"

At this we both turn and look at Our Lady.

The winepress lies on the floor, insensible; her wrist, beribboned in red, drops slowly to the carpet as its captor looses it. Marcella, her mouth a ravening hole, has tried hard, so terribly hard to get all the sustenance she needs, but the blood of the wine-girls has been tainted for weeks now with garlic and belladonna, just small amounts in their own food and wine. It makes them terrible sleepy—although it does protect them against colds—and it's been building up slowly in them and then in My

Lord and Lady—whose bodily functions no longer function, have neither excreted nor sweated nor vomited the poison out. The extra dose I put in the girl's wine before bringing her here finally had the desired effect.

I've watched as My Lady's grown weaker, more tired. I've stroked her lovely hair as she's clung to me like a child to a doll. I've whispered promises that she would grow well again soon and be strong. I've told her she would find peace. A thin shiver of guilt ripples through me until I think of all those tiny babies down in the undercroft, all those dried-up little creatures deprived of life and all their chances.

And now . . . and now, My Lady Mother lies there, replete, finished. Before our very eyes, her skin wrinkles like lace left too close to a fire. Her locks turn white faster than I can think, then drop away from the skull that is shrinking as its true age catches up with it. The body beneath her glorious burgundy evening gown diminishes, leave the dress too large, a hulking shell for a withering creature. The pale eyes glaze over, then shrink to tiny marbles, then disappear completely, and then . . . and then, she is nothing but brittle bones, then dust on a velvet couch, an empty dress, and discarded tresses shining like forgotten gold in the lambent light of the candles.

The Lord rushes toward the remains of his wife, stops, spreads his hands wide, but does not touch her—there is nothing, really, to touch. His howl is like that of a wolf, only worse, darker, deeper, blacker.

I step back, although I know I should use this moment when his attention is turned away from me. But I am so afraid, so afraid that my heart is a leaden thing in my chest; so afraid that it seems to have ceased to beat; so afraid that I fumble when I draw the wooden dagger from my pocket and drop it on the carpet between us.

It is so slim and simple, nothing to excite the interest, not especially beautifully or elegantly made, but it is compact enough to lie hidden in the spine of my herbal, its blade is honed to a fine sharp edge, and it is carved of hawthorn, one of the last of its kind, and, now, it seems so small and inadequate. But I cannot falter, I cannot fail. If I do not remove this creature then our whole city will suffer; all lives will change, and not for the better.

I fall over myself to get to it, scrambling on hands and knees, my fingers touching, clutching the haft, just as the Lord wheels around and sees me. In the shortest of moments, he knows, he understands that somehow this has all been me, the viper in the nest of vipers. His expression is a swirling vortex of shock, bitter amusement, rage, and hatred. He moves, fast, so fast, his right hand closing in on itself, all the nails becoming talons and gathered together like a spearhead. He draws his arm back and then drives the point through my chest and into my heart. All I have time to do is to bring my dagger, my tiny dagger up and across to slice through the skin and flesh of his throat. The cut itself cannot be mortal, but the substance of the knife—ah, now therein lies *cessation*.

I cannot look at him for there is blood pouring over me, in my eyes, my mouth, down my wounded chest, then there is a shower of grave dust. The rug beneath me is thick and soft as I draw my dying breaths. There is the sound of running footsteps and doors opening and closing, but all is muted to me. I'm not cold, but warm as death reaches for me.

But I don't mind. I don't mind dying with all my deeds done.

In front of me I think I see beacons, my sisters burning before me, April and Sophie, smiling. I think I see all the other girls, the day-daughters who have come and gone, the great rolling tally of years. I see them all though I do not know their names.

Then there is darkness and they fade from sight, and I see no more.

I did not expect to wake, and when I realize *why* I have, I want to weep.

The dark lies on me like a blanket, but I can see through it as if it's pure daylight down here. My throat hurts and my mouth is dry. My chest aches where it was pierced, but when I put my hand to the torn place, feel through the ragged rips in the fabric of my dress, I find no holes, no rents in my torso, just smooth cold skin.

A tiny glimmer catches my attention, bobbing as it slowly descends the night stair. I am in the undercroft. I lie on a bed of marble.

Oswain's kind face looms over me; beside him is Rikke, her eyes sad and silver in the strange light. They seem reluctant to speak. Oswain offers a hand and helps me sit up. I can smell them both; they are *warm* and full of life. I push the thought aside, as hunger buzzes nastily in my head.

"The blood," I say. "His blood?"

Oswain nods. "Entered your wounds. Healed you inside out. Changed you."

I look around the undercroft so I do not need to see the pity in their eyes. My gaze comes to rest on the mound of mummified children.

"The babies?" I ask. The Steward glances away, blinking. Rikke peers at him, perhaps thinking it is his tale to tell, but when he opens and closes his mouth, once, twice, and no words come out, she explains.

"The Lord and Lady played games with each other—being as they were, all that time, anyone would begin to hate the other. The Lord tolerated his wife's obsession only so long. The fonder Our Lady became of her day-daughters, the more perverse grew the Lord. He would begin to woo girls until finally he bedded them. Those that became pregnant thought themselves safe—he told them he loved them, that he wanted only them, that his Lady was old and desiccated." She takes a breath, glances at Oswain, who is now sobbing quietly, his shoulders quaking.

"But as they grew great, as the evidence of what had been done came clear, the Lady knew herself betrayed and found her love diminishing; her daughters had failed her. When they gave birth, she took their children away and the Lord . . . the Lord dealt with the day-daughters. The Lady thought the babies adorable for a time, but they cry as babies do, then she found them too much trouble. Eventually, she would stop their crying the only way she knew how, but she still didn't like to part with them so she kept them here."

We are silent for a while. I wonder which of the tiny dead dolls belonged to April. Sophie was not here long enough. I have a tiny niece or a nephew, lying there amongst the dead.

"You should kill me, Oswain," I say gently. "I do not wish to live like this. Even now I can smell you—your blood. Kill me and I will not fight you. There are garlic bulbs aplenty beneath the meadowsweet. And my knife—where is my knife?"

"Adlisa, we are a city of many souls. Do you remember when I spoke to you of vacuums? Who do you think might fill the one you've created? Hmmm?" I notice he does not answer me about the hawthorn dagger.

"You could. You are kind and wise," I say, stretching my arms above my head, expecting to be stiff and sore but finding my cold limbs strangely limber, pliable, although my flesh is marble.

He shakes his head. "My power derives only from being the representative of the manor house. Without a Lord and Lady, there is no figurehead, no sense of order from above. You have created this situation, Adlisa, you must fix it."

I blink hard, thinking if I close my eyes for long enough everything will go away. Then a thought. "The visitor? Our Lord's supplicant?"

Oswain's hand goes to where the Steward's Gaze usually hangs and I notice at last the jewel's absence. His fingers jerk, spider-like, seeking a phantom limb. He does not need to tell me that in the chaos of my making, the guest sneaked into the Steward's room much as I did earlier, that the gem is by now far away from Caulder.

Rikke looks at her feet, then into my eyes. "You must feed, Adlisa. One of the winepresses?"

"You will need to find a new one. I fed them all on garlic and belladonna."

Oswain nods. "I'd wondered what you'd done. You terrible, clever girl."

"I don't want to live like this," I repeat, and there is a break in my voice and I wonder if I can cry now that I am *like this*. Or is it merely the echoes of the pity a dead thing feels for itself? Could I walk out into the sun or is the sleep that comes with the daylight too profound? Or is it simply that I am starting to feel what the Lord and Lady felt for so long: a desperation to hold onto life. A refusal, a denial of true death, a determined clinging to some sort of existence.

"Adlisa, we will find a cure," says Rikke, and Oswain gives her a warning look. I know what he is thinking: *The girl is dead, make her no false promises.* She ignores him. "There is a great library far from here, at Cwen's Reach, a repository such as few can imagine. The women of St. Florian's gather rare and arcane books, copy them to make sure the knowledge never passes from the world. I am sure, Adlisa, that in one of those books is the secret to curing you. I will write to my sisters, some will remember me there. You are not without hope."

Her voice is so sincere, so filled with faith that I want to believe her. I want to believe her the way children believe the fairy tales they're told at their mother's knee. And I see how it will be for me for some years, listening to the stories she tells me of this place, of her time there, of how she came there and why she left, of how the answer to my *unfortunate condition* lies there, and how, one day, we will find it.

Until then, my life will be darkness and blood.

A North Light

Gwyneth Jones

Gwyneth Jones is an author and critic of science fiction and fantasy, and a writer of teenage fiction under the pseudonym "Ann Halam." Recent credits include *The Grasshopper's Child*, book six in the Bold as Love cycle, and the young adult novels *Siberia* and *Snakehead*.

Her short fiction has been collected in *Seven Tales and a Fable*, *Grazing the Long Acre*, *The Buonarotti Quartet*, and *The Universe of Things*, and she is a winner of two World Fantasy Awards, the James Tiptree, Jr. Award, the Arthur C. Clarke Award, the Philip K. Dick Award, and the SFRA Pilgrim Award for Lifetime Achievement in science fiction criticism.

"Maybe every writer of fantasy fiction has a vampire story in them," says Jones. "This is my second foray. My teenage vampire novel (*The Fear Man*) won the Dracula Society's Children of the Night Award in 1995; but that was a pro-vampire version, in which the children of the night were aliens among us, and some of them at least were capable of virtue.

"'A North Light' takes a harsher view. It's sort of a modern version of the J. Sheridan Le Fanu story 'Carmilla' (note the coincidence in names), and treats of the vampire as tourist and tourist as vampire. I think there's a lot to be said for the analogy. But from personal experience, I am convinced that there are Bed and Breakfast landladies (in Erin's green isle and elsewhere!) who would be the match for any sophisticated undead bloodsucker.

"Poor Camilla! Redemption is such a humiliating fate."

A CAREFREE TRAVELER'S life is full of evenings like this one. You have the money, you have the looks, you have the style; you even have what used to be called the *letters of introduction*, in the old days. Yet still you find yourself winding along the disturbingly narrow lanes, livid green pasture on either side, a voluptuous sunset overhead, and nowhere to spend the night. The grass, growing in a stiff Mohican strip down the middle of the asphalt, confesses that this is a route only used by those high-slung, soot-belching, infuriating tractors. The desk staff at the quaint, olde-worlde (but surprisingly expensive) little inn that just turned you away—with the offensive smugness of a fully-booked hostelry in high season—obviously sent you on a wild goose chase.

Never again! you say to yourself.

But the lure of the open road will prevail. Wanderlust.

"My God, here it is," breathed Camilla.

The house stood foursquare and somewhat sinister in its bulk of yellow stone, at the top of one of those endless rank pastures. No trace of a garden, except for a bizarrely suburban machicolation of cypress hedge. The gate at the road announced the services of JONAS O'DROSCOLL, BUILDER. Also, VACANCIES. But VACANCIES cannot be trusted.

"*Should* be okay," said Sheridan, scanning the whereabouts and liking the isolation. "It's fucking huge for a B&B. Unreal!"

"Not at all," she corrected him. Camilla was always wise to the local ways. "Traditional Irish rural industry needs bedrooms. The only crop that thrives in this country is babies. Breed them up for emigration, ship them out and look forward to a comfortable retirement on their earnings."

"That's cold-blooded, isn't it?"

She laughed. "I like it. It shows a fine ruthlessness. Children as a business venture, why not?" She was childless herself.

"Bring me tangle-curled barefoot peasant girls," groaned Sheridan. "Bring me a reeking cottage with a pig looking out—"

Mine hostess was at the door, a young woman with mouse-brown hair cropped short as a boy's, her large behind embraced in boyish dark blue jeans; pink cheeks, naïve round hazel eyes and a cute, piggy turned-up nose. The tourists smothered their giggles as she welcomed them in to a stark, tiled hallway with a huge varnished pine dresser and varnished pine umbrella-stand. Pokerwork signs hung on the walls, inscribed with the rules of the B&B (ALL CREDIT CARDS; ROOMS MUST BE VACATED, etc). Miniature warming pans, decorative teacloths, china donkeys on a knick-knack shelf. Everything excruciatingly new. The travelers caught each other's eyes and sighed. Their hostess was Noreen O'Driscoll. She'd had a phone call from the inn, and she could show them to an *en suite* room. She beamed naïvely when they accepted the astonishing price of a night's lodging; displayed flushed puzzlement when they insisted on shaking hands.

Camilla and Sheridan liked to shake hands with the natives. They followed her round denim bottom up the varnished pine stairs, savoring the touch of that scrubbed peasant skin—already worn down (she can't be more than twenty-five or so, poor girl) to the texture of spongy sandpaper.

Room number four, *en suite*. How many rooms are there? Maybe six, maybe eight. Maybe it goes on forever, into the antechambers of Hell. Thick yellowy varnished pine, brass number plates. The wallpaper in number four is the same as in the stairwell: strawberries and strawberry flowers, in shades of pastel brown and pastel apricot. The bed takes up most of the space. The bedding is . . . pastel apricot, poly-something, with the same debased, dreary strawberries and strawberry flowers. There's a fitted wardrobe, a vanity unit. A window with meager flimsy curtains provides a magnificent sea view. As they stare at the room, Noreen frankly stares at *them*, these two exotic birds of passage, tall and slender, blonde and sophisticated (he is tall, she is blonde). Her round, bright eyes are filled with a peasant's ingenuous hunger for sensation.

"This is fine," says Sheridan briskly. "We'll take it."

Noreen looks at Cam, a little puzzled (Camilla must remind Sher that he's in a country where menfolk do not make domestic decisions. It's his place to be silent!). But she also looks very happy. They are welcome, they are accepted, they are fascinating: all is as it should be.

When they were alone, Camilla sniffed the towels and moaned softly. The polyester sheets, cheap enough to start with, are worn to a grisly fungoid sheen; and why in the world, in a house so big, does this "double room" have to be so mean and cramped? It's a battery cage for tourists. "I can't stand these places," muttered Camilla. "I cannot *bear* them. The sheer effrontery! I thought Ireland was supposed to be romantic."

"That's *my* line," said Sheridan. He had to stoop a little to look out of the window. Beyond the pasture, a wide sea shore under a fabulous sweep of sky, but the back of the house is like a builders' yard. A heap of sand under a tarpaulin, a stack of roof tiles. The children are playing: two boys of that touching age between childhood and adolescence, trying to humiliate each other with BMX bike tricks. A girl a little older, chivvying a terrier puppy. A couple of infants. Unseen, above, he smiled on them benignly.

"The light is wonderful."

She could hear the children's voices. "How can you tell? It's nearly dark."

"Exactly." He turned with a knowing grin. "I'm sure you'll find something to do."

Camilla went on grumbling as they carried up their bags, unpacked, and made futile efforts to render the battery cage habitable. But when they ventured into the lower regions, in search of advice about an evening meal, she was the one who accepted the offer of a cup of tea—condemning them to a *tête à tête* with Noreen in the Guests' Lounge and TV Room. Mine hostess brought tea and fairy cakes (one per guest). Later she brought the baby, eight-month-old Roisin, suffering from the colic; told Camilla the names of her other children; confided the state of her husband's business. Camilla tasted the admiration in Noreen's eyes, and drew more of it to herself insensately, out of habit, like a pianist running over her scales: she couldn't help it. She really meant no harm. *Why are you dressed as a boy?* she wondered. *Wouldn't you be more* comfortable *in a nice print frock and an apron?* Thus the wheel of fashion turns, and it gets harder and harder to find the true wilderness experience. Peasants the world over have Coca Cola and Internet access. But their lives (sadly enough, agreeably enough) are no less empty. An attractive stranger is still fascinating, same as she ever was.

Noreen jigged the grizzling baby with businesslike indifference. Camilla admired the family photographs (Noreen in a huge white dress that would have looked better on a pickup truck, clasping her red-faced builder to her side). Sheridan sat there in his black biker jacket and his black jeans, one long leg crossed over the other, saying little, grinning secretly. "Jaysus," remarked Noreen, in astonishment. "It seems like we've been friends forever! And will you look at the time. Jonas'll be home and no dinner cooked!"

They went out to eat at a roadhouse with pretensions (Noreen exhorting them from the doorstep to be careful of "the drunk driving"). In the morning Camilla declined to rise for the Full Irish Breakfast. Folded between sickly polyester surfaces, the smell of bad laundry in her nostrils, she listened to middle-aged Americans tramping heavily down the stairs. She could tell by the sound of their voices that there was nothing worth getting up for in that dining room. *I won't stay another night*, she thought. *I won't.* A quarter-hour later, a tap on the door: Noreen with a tray of tea and wheaten bread. "Are yez poorly?" asked the young housewife, gravely concerned. "He says I'm to tell you he's gone out to take a look around the possibilities. He says you'll know what he means."

"Sheridan's a photographer," said Camilla. "He loves the light here. How nice of you to bring me the tea. You shouldn't have. I'm so sorry to be a nuisance."

So Noreen stayed, and talked, and stayed, and told terrible stories about rude unreasonable tourists. (Camilla having deftly established that she and Sheridan were actually neither English nor American). Downstairs baby Roisin's grizzling rose to a roar. Camilla heard her, but Noreen didn't. When she left at last, her round eyes were bright as stars, she turned at the door for a lingering glance: came back and patted Camilla's toned and slender forearm with shy, blundering tenderness.

"You have a good lie-in, Camilla. Ye'll be right as rain."

It's so simple, so harmless, such a breeze, to elicit the kindness of strangers. The wheaten bread, poisonously tainted with an overdose of soda, was crumbled, uneaten. Camilla sat up in bed, licking her lips and smiling. She negotiated the battery cage to reach the tiny *en suite*, and crouched on the edge of the bath that doubled for a shower-stall, which was the only way to get a good look in the mirror above the basin.

"I'm not a *bad* person," she murmured.

Whatever possesses anyone to build a bathroom with a light from the north? An unkind light, clear and shadowless, that picks out every tiny pore. But this is not a luxury hotel. An Irish B&B is not designed to coddle the guest's sensitive *amour propre*. Passing trade, never passing this way again, too much attention to detail would not be cost effective. *A fine ruthlessness*, thought Camilla, indulgently, as she applied her makeup. She could afford to be indulgent. She was feeling much better, all the draining little experiences of yesterday soothed.

Outdoors, in the clear light that had painted a disquieting picture on Camilla's mirror, Sheridan walked around the shore of the sea-lough. He stopped on a rocky outcrop above the water and sat cross-legged, taking camera lenses out of his bag. A boy of twelve or thirteen came sailing along on a bicycle. The tall man had seen the boy coming from a long way off. Without appearing to do so, he was displaying his wares. The bike swerved to a halt, leaving an impressive skid mark on the gravel track. Sherdian grinned at the sound, and went on thoughtfully laying out his big black truncheons of lenses, his electronic light meters, his tripod. Here comes the boy, the last, late beauty of childhood wrecked by a bullet-headed haircut, magnetically attracted to the stranger: a dignified scowl on his face.

"What'r ye doing?"

"I'm going to take some pictures."

The boy comes closer. Sheridan is an adult, and therefore of no account, but he's dressed like a big teenager, and big teenagers are gods.

"There's seals in the lough. But yez won't see them."

Sheridan shrugged, indifferent to the kind of wildlife that most tourists pursue. "There are seals in a zoo. I'll take pictures of the light and the water." He grinned, as the boy came closer still. "Maybe I'll take pictures of you."

Sheridan drove an ancient Bentley, 1940s vintage, British racing green, a fabulous monster. The car suffered some kind of mechanical failure. It had to be nursed to the town beyond the pretentious roadhouse and left there for diagnosis and treatment. Camilla was not exactly ill, but she was tired out by weeks of travel. She took to her bed in Number Four, and soon had Noreen waiting on her hand and foot. The passing trade of heavy Americans would have been astonished at this unheard-of behavior, but they never heard anything about it. Short shrift, in and out, was Noreen's usual way. Her conversation was all reserved for the beautiful stranger. She was in and out of Number Four all day, sometimes jigging baby Roisin on her arm, very concerned at Camilla's bird-like appetite. "Sure, yez don't eat enough to keep a sparrow alive," she sighed, stroking back Camilla's lovely blonde hair. A little physical intimacy had become natural: a touch here, and arm around the shoulders there, nothing shocking, just like sisters.

"I'm eating very well," protested Camilla, with a gentle smile. "You look after me wonderfully." The mirror in that apology for a bathroom obstinately showed a face more worn and wan than Camilla liked to see, but it was deceptive. She had been at a low ebb, running on empty: she was feeling stronger every day.

"Is the photography a living, then?" asked Noreen curiously, lifting a tray with a soup bowl that had barely been tasted, glancing admiringly at the food refused, that mark of true sophistication. Roisin on her arm in a sick-stained pajama suit.

"Oh yes. A very good living."

"And you?"

Camilla said she didn't have a job. She didn't need one.

"So ye're like . . . a kept woman?" said Noreen, round eyed. "Jayus, I couldn't do that. I'd be afraid to do that."

Slightly needled, Camilla laughed. "Oh, no. No, no. What I mean is we work together. He takes the pictures, I write the text, we make beautiful books." Neither of them needs a job. They are financially independent, but it's better not to say so. And it's very true that Sheridan makes a living for himself out of his photography. Very true.

Thumps and yells from downstairs. The children are indoors. There's "a bug going around" which has robbed the oldest boy of his playmates, so he's at home watching television. The girl has stayed in too, for some reason, and therefore also the younger mites. "I hope to God they don't get sick," mutters Noreen bitterly. "It would be like their awkwardness, in August when I have me hands full with the plaguey tourists."

Camilla murmurs something apologetic. But no! Noreen won't hear a word. No! She's *loving* having Camilla here. Looking after Camilla is like a big treat, like going to the pictures. Like going to the hairdresser's she adds, dreamily; and sitting there reading a magazine . . . The height of Noreen's notions of idle splendor.

Sheridan takes a walk in the lichen-gnarled oak wood by the shore, in the company of a ten-year-old girl. Not the daughter of the B&B, another little girl. He shows her things that she has never known, and tells her the names of flowers and trees which have merely been *flowers, trees,* to the barren little mind of the modern peasant. Here's a wood ants' nest, a treacle brown heap of sifted soil that looks like a small grave: but when you take a second glance the grave is heaving. "Did you know," says Sheridan, "that ants are farmers?" They lie down together, the tall man and the little girl, in the leaf-litter and watch an ant-shepherd teasing a drop of nectar from the pointed belly of one of its aphid charges. "Holy Jesus God," says the little girl. "It's like a science fiction film."

"The weak are here to justify the strong," says Sheridan, stroking a drop from another insect with a pointed grass-blade, to show how easy it is to milk this crop.

"Jesus," says the little girl, peering intently. "If they were bigger, it would be like a horror movie." She sighed. "Yez knows a lot. It's like talking to the Internet."

"Shall I take your picture now?"

The little girl thinks maybe she ought to run. But she doesn't.

Camilla and Noreen walk by the shore, Noreen pushing a stoutly built tartan upholstered buggy ahead of her. It's what passes for a fine summer day on the west coast of Ireland. There are cars ranked in the car park, battalions of windbreaks; very few foreign tourists. Camilla's thinking of her glimpses of native life before this providential halt. Shovel-faced young women marching along lanes where only tractors and tourists ply, with the baby in the buggy: and you wonder where is she going? You wonder what kind of life is it she leads. You want to touch her. Now Camilla is *in the picture*. She has penetrated to the heart of the alien world. It's always a thrill, however often repeated.

She has seen Noreen's husband briefly. A kitchen monster, sitting at the table, knife and fork in either fist, red impassive slab of a face. My God, to lie under that, while it silently prods children into you . . .! But she keeps such thoughts to herself, tucks her arm in Noreen's arm and recounts her adventures as a world traveler, long-haul traveler. The pyramids at Giza, the restaurants of New York. Wise insights. "In West Africa, in the market in Foumban, beside the earth-walled palace of the sultans, did you know you will only find Dutch printed cotton?"

"Is that a fact. Would there not be any native handicrafts there?"

"Noreen, it's a big lie that the colonial powers went to Africa and Asia to plunder the natural resources. That was an afterthought. They went to force new markets for their goods. To sell, not to buy. It's the same with tourists, did you ever think of that? They don't come to see, they come to be looked at. Did you ever think of that?"

"I did not!" said Noreen, blinking in bewilderment. "Oh, but I could never call you a *tourist*, Cam. Ye're much more than that to me." Shyly, she clasped Camilla's arm to her well-nourished flank. (The pleasure lies in knowing that it will *go no further*. There will be no consequences, because Camilla isn't staying. Tastes and smells, moments of intensity, never a bill presented.) They walked on, Noreen silenced for a little by her own outburst. "You know," she said, after a moment or two, "I'm worried about this bug that's going round. Some folk are keeping the children in. D'ye think I should keep them indoors?"

"Them?"

"The kids?"

"Ah." Camilla frowned, and looked away. "Don't worry. *Your* kids are safe." She didn't explain the emphasis.

The steel-blue waves rushed in and out, the mothers sat behind the windbreaks, a somewhat depleted cohort of local boys and girls jumped and splashed in the water. "I suppose all your children are grown up and gone," sighed Noreen, shoving the buggy over recalcitrant tidewrack . . . and compounded this *faux-pas* by adding hurriedly, "Och, I mean, you must have been married very young!"

"Married?" Camilla dispelled the idea with a laugh, slightly put out that her dark hint has been ignored. "Sheridan and I have been together so long we're almost like brother and sister, but we've never been, ah, officially *married*."

"Not married?" gulped Noreen.

"I've never been married. I like my independence."

"But yez said, you was like, a . . . a kept woman?"

"That was my joke."

Never married! The buggy gave a jolt that made Roisin wail. Among the family portraits so readily on display in the Guests' Lounge and TV Room, there are several women who have never married, holding ugly babies against their bolster chests. Noreen's astonished gaze is comparing Camilla with those crewel-working great aunts, finding a place for her among the failed huntresses, old maids . . .

"You look so young!" she gasped, as if unmarried bliss was in her mind inextricably linked with spinster middle age. "You look like a fashion model!"

Camilla squeezed the housewife's arm more tightly, and leaned close to rub her cool pale cheek against Noreen's warm, rosy one. "I've been young for so long," she murmured, "I can't remember being anything else."

"Ah!" sighed Noreen. "For two pins I'd—"

What would she do? Take Camilla away from all this? The blushing ploughboy, the sophisticated older woman, the configurations are endless; and pity may play a part. It's all grist to Camilla's mill. It's like a transfusion of fresh blood, without any of those ugly, depressing emergency-room details.

Love is the hunger on which we feed.

Sheridan prowled the woods and the shore. Camilla, no longer poorly, haunted the kitchen of the B&B, where Noreen was penned for most of her life, incessantly cooking, stowing the washing machine, ironing dank sheets. Noreen relayed tales of the disastrous epidemic. The boy with the nightmares, and no one in that house gets a wink of sleep. The girl that they rushed to hospital: but then the doctors couldn't find anything wrong. So that was a whole day gone for nothing, with the driving her there and the waiting in the waiting room, and the driving her back. In August, too. Jesus God. *Schadenfreude*. Noreen is miraculously preserved.

Camilla changes the subject. We are all *kept women*, she says. (Noreen has confided that romance is long out of the window, with her Jonas.) We can't do without them, can we. We may look like the perfect couple, but the truth is . . . there are things I . . . She breaks off, and will say no more.

One day Sheridan came home from his adventures in a thoughtful mood, laid out digital prints on the tired candlewick bedspread, and pondered them with a happy smile. "Time to get the hell out of here," he said. "I'm done."

"The hell is right," said Camilla, glancing and averting her eyes.

"Why so squeamish? I have to live, don't I?"

"I can see why you want to leave!"

He put on his sunglasses, and grinned at her. "No one ever knows. I'm careful."

"Good, because I'm not done. I haven't finished. Not yet."

The dark lenses gave back a double image of her face, so richly shadowed, it's a shame she needs another partner. But two predators can't feed on each other. This is their eroticism, these tastes and smells, this contact at a remove: and it still thrills her. Sheridan always comes first, true. But Camilla likes it that way.

"Go, sister," says Sheridan, the big teenager. "You look like you need a fix."

The car had been repaired. It arrived back at the B&B that evening. They announced their departure the next morning, and settled the bill. Noreen was very sorry to see them go, but she made no fond farewells in front of Camilla's *ersatz* husband. Camilla conveyed, by a sad glance or two, that the sudden decision was not her own; and that she wished they could say goodbye more warmly. She got up about an hour after midnight, Sheridan peacefully unconscious. The sheets, although freshly changed, still had that bad-laundry smell. *How does she do it?* wondered Camilla, wrapping herself in an elegant blue and white kimono. Poor Noreen is a genius of poor housekeeping, of meager portions . . . She went into the *en suite* and checked her face. Good God, even the electricity in the mean fluorescent tube seems to come straight from the North Pole. Tiny crow's feet around her eyes, lines between her brows, is that a *broken vein?* Can't be! Never mind. Soon, soon this washed-out hag will disappear. The mirrors of civilization will restore Camilla's beauty, infused with fresh magic. For a last thrill, she walked the immeasurably ugly, pine-varnished, passageways of the big lumpen house, possessing it like a ghost. American couples snore peacefully behind their brass number-plates, dreaming of Blarney Castle and the Rock of Cashel. Noreen shares a room and a bed with Jonas, with baby Roisin in her cot. The baby, for a wonder, is not grizzling. But the house is unquiet.

Camilla followed a trail of sound—buzzes and clicks and muted thunderclaps. Silently, she opened a door and saw the BMX boy there in the shadows, with his back to her, lost in contemplation of the graphics on his TV screen. His little hands were moving incessantly, *clickety clickety clickety*. Camilla knew the names of all the children. This one was Declan, the ten-year-old, fortunately immune to the virus that's going round. He's actually a little young for that virus: the bud not quite bursting, the sap not yet on the rise, but he'd be immune anyway. There are rules. She slipped into the room and stood behind him, wondering about passions that she did not share. She was standing so close, it was amazing that the child didn't turn around. Over his shoulder she could see her own face reflected on the screen, clearly visible within the racetrack image.

Declan turned and saw nothing (an adult woman, a mother, a featureless conduit). Without changing expression, he turned back and resumed his game.

Shuddering with horror, Camilla retreated: and that's Noreen's diet. That's all the feeding her poor starved soul ever gets.

She went down to the TV Lounge, feeling morally justified. I'm not a bad person. Not entirely greedy. I give as well as take! A quarter of an hour, and Noreen appeared, red-faced with sleep, her crop-head tousled, bundled up in a dreadful dressing gown. "I thought I heard . . . Ough, Camilla *what is it?*"

Camilla was weeping, stifling her sobs with fists clenched against her teeth.

She was beside herself. It was some time before she could be persuaded to talk. In choked, half sentences, covering her face, she told the story.

Her suspicions. Her certainty. The terrible burden.

"I can't prove it," she explained. "But I know, more surely every time it happens. *He steals something from them* . . . How can I say it? They surrender to him."

"Jesus God. Ye're saying he interferes with them."

"No!" wailed Camilla. "That's *nothing*. I'm saying he takes the life out of them."

"But Camilla, nobody's died!"

"No! He doesn't kill them, he's too clever for that. They die later, of something else, an accident, the flu; I've kept track. I know it happens. But he never gets the blame. What's worse is when they live, but it would be better if they didn't, *because they're like him*. I've known that happen, too."

The harshly furnished room listened in shock. The big TV screen gazed somberly.

Camilla showed Noreen the photographs. The young housewife trembled. She babbled of "the polis." Camilla said, *then he'd kill me*. Oh God, I don't want to die!

"I had to tell you," she wept. "I just had to tell. Oh, Noreen, *the things I know—*"

And then the broken whispers, the breath coming fast. The last protests, the surrender. Noreen agrees abjectly that she will not raise the alarm. Shivering, sickened, she is deflowered, degraded, made complicit in something monstrous . . . and she loves it.

For Camilla too, the experience was deeply satisfying.

She left the room, and crept back to Number Four.

A flash caught her as she opened the door, her lips still wet, features softened and eyes blind with afterglow. "Gotcha!" cried Sheridan, brandishing the camera, grinning; and she laughed. It was almost as if he'd kissed her. He turned away, and checked the preview screen. "Hmm." He sounded disappointed; or maybe puzzled.

"What is it?"

"Oh, nothing."

They left the big, stark yellow house early in the morning. Camilla found the moment of departure oddly disappointing. She would have liked to see Noreen again. She would have liked to see some consciousness, a touch of pallor; some shamed disquiet in the young housewife's eyes. But it's time to make a clean getaway. Noreen will wake up unsure that anything really happened in the night (she'll probably never miss what Camilla took from her): and that's the way it's supposed to be. In and out without a trace, love them and leave them.

She went into the kitchen for a moment, and stood looking around. The smells of kippers, blood-pudding, and laundry that's been dried indoors mingled sickeningly. Camilla felt suddenly, deeply disoriented. The *taste* of Noreen's life was in her throat, she had a horrible, momentary vision of somehow staying here, *being trapped here*, with the slab of a husband, the indifferent children, the sonorous Americans chewing overcooked bacon in that drear, meager dining room. She felt she had become transparent, suffocated . . .

Sheridan tooted on the Bentley's horn.

"Sssh!" muttered Camilla, and hurried out to join him.

The big car drove away.

Noreen was up in time to hear them go. She'd had a sleepless night, but no staying in bed for Noreen. No one to bring her a tray. She had the breakfast for the guests to cook, Jonas in a poor temper, the children giving her hell and the baby fretful. But she was smiling. She stood in the porch and listened to the deep purr of the big car's engine. There they go, the beautiful people. She was fingering a rectangle of chaste cream pasteboard, simply inscribed CAMILLA SIIBU. Nothing else, no address, no phone number: that's arrogance, isn't it? But it doesn't matter. You never do see them again, the passing trade. She tucked the card into the drawer, where she kept a select collection of such trophies.

"I have *lovely* guests, sometimes," she murmured. "It's *lovely* to have them."

And she returned to her domestic servitude, with a gleam of secret triumph in that beaming, rapacious smile; her naïve hazel eyes no longer hungry, but replete.

They called ahead and booked a room in a place as far removed from that primitive B&B as money could buy. The country house hotel set in its own lush grounds, now this is more like it. Sheridan handed over the keys to the Bentley. Camilla flashed an automatically dazzling smile at the boy who took their luggage, and was faintly surprised to receive no eye-kick of appreciation in return.

They walked into the hotel, and how wide the lobby seemed. It was not crowded but full of people. No one glanced her way. Or if they did, by chance, happen to look in Camilla's direction, they appeared to see nothing. By the time they reached the desk, she was feeling disquieted, and strangely weary, as if that short walk had been a long trek across empty tundra. Camilla's progress through the human world has been, for so long, a continuous *sip*, *sip*, at the nectar of attention. Full-blown seduction is an occasional indulgence (she's not an addict, like Sheridan!). Her eternal beauty, everlasting youth, is nourished by subtler means. She doesn't even have to think about it, she is so used to eliciting the response. The admiration that comes back to her, from almost any human being, male or female, young or old, is her daily bread, the air she breathes. Beautiful people feed like this. The rest are there to be fed upon. That's the law of nature.

All the way up to their room, Sheridan placidly silent and indifferent beside her, she could not stop herself from peering at the glass walls of the lift, at a passing chambermaid, at the bellboy waiting for his tip. Nothing. She might as well be invisible. *What's happened to me?*

"What's wrong with you, Cam?"

"Nothing," she says, sitting in the middle of the vast acreage of their room, on the king-sized bed, sumptuous with pillows; the white sheets crisp and fragrant. But where's Noreen, with her humble, hungry eyes? "I think I'll have a shower."

She went into the bathroom.

As long as you can look at yourself in the mirror, you're not too far gone. That's what Sheridan says. One day all the mirrors will be empty, and sometimes, tired of the endless repetitive toil of her delicate feeding, she has looked forward to the day when there will be no more subtlety, when they will have no choice but to be monsters. Really, neither of them wants to cross that borderline. It will be a kind of death. It's a fate they prefer to put off as long as possible. But this is something else.

A fair-haired woman's face looks back at her, naked and weary: a little pale, a few fine lines, a few faint broken veins in the cheeks. There's nothing unusual about this reflection. It's neither old or very young, neither beautiful nor ugly: there's certainly no mark of immortal evil. Oh God, she whispers—the redeemed, the newly mortal. What's happened to me? She turns her face, she turns her face. It's no use. Wherever she looks, every light is coming, pure and clear, straight from the north.

JACK

Connie Willis

Connie Willis made her fiction debut in 1971 in the magazine *Worlds of Fantasy*, but only began appearing regularly in the genre in the early 1980s. The author of such recent novels as *Blackout* and *Crosstalk*, some of her finest short fiction can be found in *The Best of Connie Willis: Award-Winning Stories*.

She has won more major awards than any writer, including multiple Hugo Awards and Nebula Awards, and she was inducted into the Science Fiction Hall of Fame in 2009 and named as a Grand Master by the Science Fiction & Fantasy Writers of America two years later.

About the following novella, she reveals: "I became fascinated by the Blitz the first time I went to St. Paul's in London. It seemed impossible to me that the cathedral hadn't burned down that night in December (it still seems impossible), and I began doing research for the story that eventually became 'Fire Watch' (1982).

"In the course of my reading, I kept seeing references to 'body-sniffers,' people who worked on the rescue squads who had an unusual knack for finding bodies. On a rational level, I knew that this was probably because they had exceptional hearing (everybody was practically deaf from the continuous din) or were good guessers, or else were exceptionally lucky. It did occur to me, though, that there might be another, more sinister reason . . ."

THE NIGHT JACK joined our post, Vi was late. So was the Luftwaffe. The sirens still hadn't gone by eight o'clock.

"Perhaps our Violet's tired of the RAF and begun on the aircraft spotters," Morris said, "and they're so taken by her charms they've forgotten to wind the sirens."

"You'd best watch out then," Swales said, taking off his tin warden's hat. He'd just come back from patrol. We made room for him at the linoleum-covered table, moving our tea cups and the litter of gas masks and pocket torches. Twickenham shuffled his papers into one pile next to his typewriter and went on typing.

Swales sat down and poured himself a cup of tea. "She'll set her cap for the ARP next," he said, reaching for the milk. Morris pushed it toward him. "And none of us will be safe." He grinned at me. "Especially the young ones, Jack."

"I'm safe," I said. "I'm being called up soon. Twickenham's the one who should be worrying."

Twickenham looked up from his typing at the sound of his name. "Worrying about what?" he asked, his hands poised over the keyboard.

"Our Violet setting her cap for you," Swales said. 'Girls always go for poets."

"I'm a journalist, not a poet. What about Renfrew?" He nodded his head toward the cots in the other room.

"Renfrew!" Swales boomed, pushing his chair back and starting into the room.

"Shh," I said. "Don't wake him. He hasn't slept all week."

"You're right. It wouldn't be fair in his weakened condition." He sat back down. "And Morris is married. What about your son, Morris? He's a pilot, isn't he? Stationed in London?"

Morris shook his head. "Quincy's up at North Weald."

"Lucky, that," Swales said. "Looks as if that leaves you, Twickenham."

"Sorry," Twickenham said, typing. "She's not my type."

"She's not anyone's type, is she?" Swales said.

"The RAF's," Morris said, and we all fell silent, thinking of Vi and her bewildering popularity with the RAF pilots in and around London. She had pale eyelashes and colorless brown hair she put up in flat little pin-curls while she was on duty, which was against regulations, though Mrs. Lucy didn't say anything to her about them. Vi was dumpy and rather stupid, and yet she was out constantly with one pilot after another, going to dances and parties.

"I still say she makes it all up," Swales said. "She buys all those things she says they give her herself, all those oranges and chocolate. She buys them on the black market."

"On a full-time's salary?" I said. We only made two pounds a week, and the things she brought home to the post—sweets and sherry and ciga-rettes—couldn't be bought on that. Vi shared them round freely, though liquor and cigarettes were against regulations as well. Mrs. Lucy didn't say anything about them either.

She never reprimanded her wardens about anything, except being mali-cious about Vi, and we never gossiped in her presence. I wondered where she was. I hadn't seen her since I came in.

"Where's Mrs. Lucy?" I asked. "She's not late as well, is she?"

Morris nodded toward the pantry door. "She's in her office. Olmwood's replacement is here. She's filling him in."

Olmwood had been our best part-time, a huge out-of-work collier who could lift a house beam by himself, which was why Nelson, using his authority as district warden, had had him transferred to his own post.

"I hope the new man's not any good," Swales said. "Or Nelson will steal *him*."

"I saw Olmwood yesterday," Morris said. "He looked like Renfrew, only worse. He told me Nelson keeps them out the whole night patrolling and looking for incendiaries."

There was no point in that. You couldn't see where the incendiaries were falling from the street, and if there was an incident, nobody was anywhere to be found. Mrs. Lucy had assigned patrols at the beginning of the Blitz, but within a week she'd stopped them at midnight so we could get some sleep. Mrs. Lucy said she saw no point in our getting killed when everyone was already in bed anyway.

"Olmwood says Nelson makes them wear their gas masks the entire time they're on duty and holds stirrup pump drills twice a shift," Morris said.

"Stirrup pump drills!" Swales exploded. "How difficult does he think it is to learn to use one? Nelson's not getting me on his post, I don't care if Churchill himself signs the transfer papers."

The pantry door opened. Mrs. Lucy poked her head out. "It's half-past eight. The spotter'd better go upstairs even if the sirens haven't gone," she said. "Who's on duty tonight?"

"Vi," I said, "but she hasn't come in yet."

"Oh, dear," she said. "Perhaps someone had better go look for her."

"I'll go," I said, and started pulling on my boots.

"Thank you, Jack," she said. She shut the door.

I stood up and tucked my pocket torch into my belt. I picked up my gas mask and slung it over my arm in case I ran into Nelson. The regulations said they were to be worn while patrolling, but Mrs. Lucy had realized early on that you couldn't see anything with them on. Which is why, I thought, she has the best post in the district, including Admiral Nelson's.

Mrs. Lucy opened the door again and leaned out for a moment. "She usually comes by Underground. Sloane Square," she said.

"Take care."

"Right," Swales said. "Vi might be lurking outside in the dark, waiting to pounce!" He grabbed Twickenham round the neck and hugged him to his chest.

"I'll be careful," I said and went up the basement stairs and out onto the street.

I went the way Vi usually came from Sloane Square Station, but there was no one in the blacked-out streets except a girl hurrying to the Underground station, carrying a blanket, a pillow, and a dress on a hanger.

I walked the rest of the way to the tube station with her to make sure she found her way, though it wasn't that dark. The nearly full moon was up, and there was a fire still burning down by the docks from the raid of the night before.

"Thanks awfully," the girl said, switching the hanger to her other hand so she could shake hands with me. She was much nicer-looking than Vi, with blonde, very curly hair. "I work for this old stewpot at John Lewis's, and she won't let me leave even a minute before closing, will she, even if the sirens have gone."

I waited outside the station for a few minutes and then walked up to the Brompton Road, thinking Vi might have come in at South Kensington instead, but I didn't see her, and she still wasn't at the post when I got back.

"We've a new theory for why the sirens haven't gone," Swales said. "We've decided our Vi's set her cap for the Luftwaffe, and they've surrendered."

"Where's Mrs. Lucy?" I asked.

"Still in with the new man," Twickenham said.

"I'd better tell Mrs. Lucy I couldn't find her," I said and started for the pantry.

Halfway there the door opened, and Mrs. Lucy and the new man came out. He was scarcely a replacement for the burly Olmwood. He was not much older than I was, slightly built, hardly the sort to lift house beams. His face was thin and rather pale, and I wondered if he was a student.

"This is our new part-time, Mr. Settle," Mrs. Lucy said. She pointed to each of us in turn. "Mr. Morris, Mr. Twickenham, Mr. Swales, Mr. Harker." She smiled at the part-time and then at me. "Mr. Harker's name is Jack, too," she said. "I shall have to work at keeping you straight."

"A pair of jacks," Swales said. "Not a bad hand."

The part-time smiled.

"Cots are in there if you'd like to have a lie-down," Mrs. Lucy said, "and if the raids are close, the coal cellar's reinforced. I'm afraid the rest of the basement isn't, but I'm attempting to rectify that." She waved the papers in her hand. "I've applied to the district warden for reinforcing beams. Gas masks are in there," she said, pointing at a wooden chest, "batteries for the torches are in here," she pulled a drawer open, "and the duty roster's posted on this wall." She pointed at the neat columns. "Patrols here and watches here. As you can see, Miss Westen has the first watch for tonight."

"She's still not here," Twickenham said, not even pausing in his typing.

"I couldn't find her," I said.

"Oh, dear," she said. "I do hope she's all right. Mr. Twickenham, would you mind terribly taking Vi's watch?"

"I'll take it," Jack said. "Where do I go?"

"I'll show him," I said, starting for the stairs.

"No, wait," Mrs. Lucy said. "Mr. Settle, I hate to put you to work before you've even had a chance to become acquainted with everyone, and there really isn't any need to go up till after the sirens have gone. Come and sit down, both of you." She took the flowered cozy off the teapot. "Would you like a cup of tea, Mr. Settle?"

"No, thank you," he said.

She put the cozy back on and smiled at him. "You're from Yorkshire, Mr. Settle," she said as if we were all at a tea party. "Whereabouts?"

"Scarborough," he said politely.

"What brings you to London?" Morris said.

"The war," he said, still politely.

"Wanted to do your bit, eh?"

"Yes."

"That's what my son Quincy said. 'Dad,' he says. 'I want to do my bit for England. I'm going to be a pilot.' Downed twenty-one planes, he has, my Quincy," Morris told Jack, "and been shot down twice himself. Oh, he's had some scrapes, I could tell you, but it's all top-secret."

Jack nodded.

There were times I wondered whether Morris, like Violet with her RAF pilots, had invented his son's exploits. Sometimes I even wondered if he had invented the son, though if that were the case he might surely have made up a better name than Quincy.

"'Dad,' he says to me out of the blue, 'I've got to do my bit,' and he shows me his enlistment papers. You could've knocked me over with a feather. Not that he's not patriotic, you understand, but he'd had his little difficulties at school, sowed his wild oats, so to speak, and here he was, saying, 'Dad, I want to do my bit.'"

The sirens went, taking up one after the other. Mrs. Lucy said, "Ah, well, here they are now," as if the last guest had finally arrived at her tea party, and Jack stood up.

"If you'll just show me where the spotter's post is, Mr. Harker," he said.

"Jack," I said. "It's a name that should be easy for you to remember."

I took him upstairs to what had been Mrs. Lucy's cook's garret bedroom, unlike the street a perfect place to watch for incendiaries. It was on the fourth floor, higher than most of the buildings on the street so one could see anything that fell on the roofs around. One could see the

Thames, too, between the chimneypots, and in the other direction the searchlights in Hyde Park.

Mrs. Lucy had set a wing-backed chair by the window, from which the glass had been removed, and the narrow landing at the head of the stairs had been reinforced with heavy oak beams that even Olmwood couldn't have lifted.

"One ducks out here when the bombs get close," I said, shining the torch on the beams. "It'll be a swish and then a sort of rising whine." I led him into the bedroom. "If you see incendiaries, call out and try to mark exactly where they fall on the roofs." I showed him how to use the gun-sight mounted on a wooden base that we used for a sextant and handed him the binoculars. "Anything else you need?" I asked.

"No," he said soberly. "Thank you."

I left him and went back downstairs. They were still discussing Violet.

"I'm really becoming worried about her," Mrs. Lucy said. One of the ack-ack guns started up, and there was the dull crump of bombs far away, and we all stopped to listen.

"ME 109's," Morris said. "They're coming in from the south again."

"I do hope she has the sense to get to a shelter." Mrs. Lucy said, and Vi burst in the door.

"Sorry I'm late," she said, setting a box tied with string on the table next to Twickenham's typewriter. She was out of breath and her face was suffused with blood. "I know I'm supposed to be on watch, but Harry took me out to see his plane this afternoon, and I had a horrid time getting back." She heaved herself out of her coat and hung it over the back of Jack's chair. "You'll never believe what he's named it! The Sweet Violet!" She untied the string on the box. "We were so late we hadn't time for tea, and he said, 'You take this to your post and have a good tea, and I'll keep the Jerries busy till you've finished.'" She reached in the box and lifted out a torte with sugar icing. "He's painted the name on the nose and put little violets in purple all round it," she said, setting it on the table. "One for every Jerry he's shot down."

We stared at the cake. Eggs and sugar had been rationed since the beginning of the year and they'd been in short supply even before that. I hadn't seen a fancy torte like this in over a year.

"It's raspberry filling," she said, slicing through the cake with a knife. "They hadn't any chocolate." She held the knife up, dripping jam. "Now, who wants some then?"

"I do," I said. I had been hungry since the beginning of the war and ravenous since I'd joined the ARP, especially for sweets, and I had my piece eaten before she'd finished setting slices on Mrs. Lucy's Wedgwood plates and passing them round.

There was still a quarter left. "Who's upstairs taking my watch?" she said, sucking a bit of raspberry jam off her finger.

"The new part-time," I said. "I'll take it up to him."

She cut a slice and eased it off the knife and onto the plate. "What's he like?" she asked.

"He's from Yorkshire," Twickenham said, looking at Mrs. Lucy. "What did he do up there before the war?"

Mrs. Lucy looked at her cake, as if surprised that it was nearly eaten. "He didn't say," she said.

"I meant, is he handsome?" Vi said, putting a fork on the plate with the slice of cake. "Perhaps I should take it up to him myself."

"He's puny. Pale," Swales said, his mouth full of cake. "Looks as if he's got consumption."

"Nelson won't steal him any time soon, that's certain," Morris said.

"Oh, well, then," Vi said, and handed the plate to me.

I took it and went upstairs, stopping on the second-floor landing to shift it to my left hand and switch on my pocket torch.

Jack was standing by the window, the binoculars dangling from his neck, looking out past the rooftops toward the river. The moon was up, reflecting whitely off the water like one of the German flares, lighting the bombers' way.

"Anything in our sector yet?" I said.

"No," he said, without turning round. "They're still to the east."

"I've brought you some raspberry cake," I said.

He turned and looked at me.

I held the cake out. "Violet's young man in the RAF sent it."

"No, thank you," he said. "I'm not fond of cake."

I looked at him with the same disbelief I had felt for Violet's name emblazoned on a Spitfire. "There's plenty," I said. "She brought a whole torte."

"I'm not hungry, thanks. You eat it."

"Are you sure? One can't get this sort of thing these days."

"I'm certain," he said and turned back to the window.

I looked hesitantly at the slice of cake, guilty about my greed but hating to see it go to waste and still hungry. At the least I should stay up and keep him company.

"Violet's the warden whose watch you took, the one who was late," I said. I sat down on the floor, my back to the painted baseboard, and started to eat. "She's full-time. We've got five full-timers. Violet and I and Renfrew—you haven't met him yet, he was asleep. He's had rather a bad time. Can't sleep in the day—and Morris and Twickenham. And then there's Petersby. He's part-time like you."

He didn't turn around while I was talking or say anything, only continued looking out the window. A scattering of flares drifted down, lighting the room.

"They're a nice lot," I said, cutting a bite of cake with my fork. In the odd light from the flares the jam filling looked black. "Swales can be rather a nuisance with his teasing sometimes, and Twickenham will ask you all sorts of questions, but they're good men on an incident."

He turned around. "Questions?"

"For the post newspaper. Notice sheet, really, information on new sorts of bombs, ARP regulations, that sort of thing. All Twickenham's supposed to do is type it and send it round to the other posts, but I think he's always fancied himself an author, and now he's got his chance. He's named the notice sheet *Twickenham's Twitterings*, and he adds all sorts of things—drawings, news, gossip, interviews."

While I had been talking, the drone of engines overhead had been growing steadily louder. It passed, there was a sighing whoosh and then a whistle that turned into a whine.

"Stairs," I said, dropping my plate. I grabbed his arm, and yanked him into the shelter of the landing. We crouched against the blast, my hands over my head, but nothing happened. The whine became a scream and then sounded suddenly farther off. I peeked round the reinforcing beam at the open window. Light flashed and then the *crump* came, at least three sectors away. "Lees," I said, going over to the window to see if I could tell exactly where it was. "High explosive bomb." Jack focused the binoculars where I was pointing.

I went out to the landing, cupped my hands, and shouted down the stairs, "HE. Lees." The planes were still too close to bother sitting down again. "Twickenham's done interviews with all the wardens," I said, leaning against the wall. "He'll want to know what you did before the war, why you became a warden, that sort of thing. He wrote up a piece on Vi last week."

Jack had lowered the binoculars and was watching where I had pointed. The fires didn't start right away with a high explosive bomb. It took a bit for the ruptured gas mains and scattered coal fires to catch. "What was she before the war?" he asked.

"Vi? A stenographer," I said. "And something of a wallflower, I should think. The war's been rather a blessing for our Vi."

"A blessing," Jack said, looking out at the high explosive in Lees. From where I was sitting, I couldn't see his face except in silhouette, and I couldn't tell whether he disapproved of the word or was merely bemused by it.

"I didn't mean a blessing exactly. One can scarcely call something as dreadful as this a blessing. But the war's given Vi a chance she wouldn't have had otherwise. Morris says without it she'd have died an old maid, and now she's got all sorts of beaux." A flare drifted down, white and then red. "Morris says the war's the best thing that ever happened to her."

"Morris," he said, as if he didn't know which one that was.

"Sandy hair, toothbrush mustache," I said. "His son's a pilot."

"Doing his bit," he said, and I could see his face clearly in the reddish light, but I still couldn't read his expression.

A stick of incendiaries came down over the river, glittering like sparklers, and fires sprang up everywhere.

The next night there was a bad incident off Old Church Street, two HE's. Mrs. Lucy sent Jack and me over to see if we could help. It was completely overcast, which was supposed to stop the Luftwaffe but obviously hadn't, and very dark. By the time we reached Kings Road I had completely lost my bearings.

I knew the incident had to be close, though, because I could smell it. It wasn't truly a smell; it was a painful sharpness in the nose from the plaster dust and smoke and whatever explosive the Germans put in their bombs. It always made Vi sneeze.

I tried to make out landmarks, but all I could see was the slightly darker outline of a hill on my left. I thought blankly, *We must be lost. There aren't any hills in Chelsea*, and then realized it must be the incident.

"The first thing we do is find the incident officer," I told Jack. I looked round for the officer's blue light, but I couldn't see it. It must be behind the hill.

I scrabbled up it with Jack behind me, trying not to slip on the uncertain slope. The light was on the far side of another, lower hill, a ghostly bluish blur off to the left. "It's over there," I said. "We must report in. Nelson's likely to be the incident officer, and he's a stickler for procedure."

I started down, skidding on the broken bricks and plaster. "Be careful," I called back to Jack. "There are all sorts of jagged pieces of wood and glass."

"Jack," he said.

I turned around. He had stopped halfway down the hill and was looking up, as if he had heard something. I glanced up, afraid the bombers were coming back, but couldn't hear anything over the antiaircraft guns. Jack stood motionless, his head down now, looking at the rubble.

"What is it?" I said.

He didn't answer. He snatched his torch out of his pocket and swung it wildly round.

"You can't do that!" I shouted. "There's a blackout on!"

He snapped it off. "Go and find something to dig with," he said and dropped to his knees. "There's someone alive under here."

He wrenched the banister free and began stabbing into the rubble with its broken end.

I looked stupidly at him. "How do you know?"

He jabbed viciously at the mess. "Get a pickaxe. This stuff's hard as rock." He looked up at me impatiently. "Hurry!"

The incident officer was someone I didn't know. I was glad. Nelson would have refused to give me a pickaxe without the necessary authorization and lectured me instead on departmentalization of duties. This officer, who was younger than me and broken out in spots under his powdering of brick dust, didn't have a pickaxe, but he gave me two shovels without any argument.

The dust and smoke were clearing a bit by the time I started back across the mounds, and a shower of flares drifted down over by the river, lighting everything in a fuzzy, overbright light like headlights in a fog. I could see Jack on his hands and knees halfway down the mound, stabbing with the banister. He looked like he was murdering someone with a knife, plunging it in again and again.

Another shower of flares came down, much closer. I ducked and hurried across to Jack, offering him one of the shovels.

"That's no good," he said, waving it away.

"What's wrong? Can't you hear the voice anymore?"

He went on jabbing with the banister. "What?" he said, and looked in the flare's dazzling light like he had no idea what I was talking about.

"The voice you heard," I said. "Has it stopped calling?"

"It's this stuff," he said. "There's no way to get a shovel into it. Did you bring any baskets?"

I hadn't, but farther down the mound I had seen a large tin saucepan. I fetched it for him and began digging. He was right, of course. I got one good shovelful and then struck an end of a floor joist and bent the blade of the shovel. I tried to get it under the joist so I could pry it upward, but it was wedged under a large section of beam farther on. I gave it up, broke off another of the banisters, and got down beside Jack.

The beam was not the only thing holding the joist down. The rubble looked loose—bricks and chunks of plaster and pieces of wood—but it was as solid as cement. Swales, who showed up out of nowhere when we were three feet down, said, "It's the clay. All London's built on it. Hard as statues." He had brought two buckets with him and the news that Nelson had shown up and had had a fight with the spotty officer over whose incident it was.

"'It's *my* incident,' Nelson says, and gets out the map to show him how this side of King's Road is in his district," Swales said gleefully, "and the incident officer says, 'Your *incident*? Who wants the bloody thing, I say,' he says."

Even with Swales helping, the going was so slow whoever was under there would probably have suffocated or bled to death before we could get to him. Jack didn't stop at all, even when the bombs were directly overhead. He seemed to know exactly where he was going, though none of us heard anything in those brief intervals of silence and Jack seemed scarcely to listen.

The banister he was using broke off in the iron-hard clay, and he took mine and kept digging. A broken clock came up, and an egg cup. Morris arrived. He had been evacuating people from two streets over where a bomb had buried itself in the middle of the street without exploding. Swales told him the story of Nelson and the spotty young officer and then went off to see what he could find out about the inhabitants of the house.

Jack came up out of the hole. "I need braces," he said. "The sides are collapsing."

I found some unbroken bed slats at the base of the mound. One of the slats was too long for the shaft. Jack sawed it halfway through and then broke it off.

Swales came back. "Nobody in the house," he shouted down the hole. "The Colonel and Mrs. Godalming went to Surrey this morning." The all-clear sounded, drowning out his words.

"Jack," Jack said from the hole, and I turned around to see if the rescue squad had brought it down with them.

"Jack," he said again, more urgently.

I leaned over the tunnel.

"What time is it?" he said.

"About five," I said. "The all-clear just went."

"Is it getting light?"

"Not yet," I said. "Have you found anything?"

"Yes," he said. "Give us a hand."

I eased myself into the hole. I could understand his question; it was pitch dark down here. I switched my torch on. It lit up our faces from beneath like specters.

"In there," he said, and reached for a banister just like the one he'd been digging with.

"Is he under a stairway?" I said and the banister clutched at his hand.

It only took a minute or two to get him out. Jack pulled on the arm I had mistaken for a banister, and I scrabbled through the last few inches of plaster and clay to the little cave he was in, formed by an icebox and a door leaning against each other.

"Colonel Godalming?" I said, reaching for him.

He shook off my hand. "Where the bleeding hell have you people been?" he said. "Taking a tea break?"

He was in full evening dress, and his big mustache was covered with plaster dust. "What sort of country is this, leave a man to dig himself out?" he shouted, brandishing a serving spoon full of plaster in Jack's face. "I could have dug all the way to China in the time it took you blighters to get me out!"

Hands came down into the hole and hoisted him up. "Blasted incompetents!" he yelled. We pushed on the seat of his elegant trousers. "Slackers, the lot of you! Couldn't find the nose in front of your own face!"

Colonel Godalming had in fact left for Surrey the day before but had decided to come back for his hunting rifle, in case of invasion. "Can't rely on the blasted Civil Defense to stop the Jerries," he had said as I led him down the ambulance.

It was starting to get light. The incident was smaller than I'd thought, not much more than two blocks square. What I had taken for a mound to the south was actually a squat office block, and beyond it the row houses hadn't even had their windows blown out.

The ambulance had pulled up as near as possible to the mound. I helped him over to it. "What's your name?" he said, ignoring the doors I'd opened. "I intend to report you to your superiors. And the other one. Practically pulled my arm out of its socket. Where's he got to?"

"He had to go to his day job," I said. As soon as we had Godalming out, Jack had switched on his pocket torch again to glance at his watch and said, "I've got to leave."

I told him I'd check him out with the incident officer and started to help Godalming down the mound. Now I was sorry I hadn't gone with him.

"Day job!" Godalming snorted. "Gone off to take a nap is more like it. Lazy slacker. Nearly breaks my arm and then goes off and leaves me to die. I'll have his job!"

"Without him, we'd never even have found you," I said angrily. "He's the one who heard your cries for help."

"Cries for help!" the colonel said, going red in the face. "Cries for help! Why would I cry out to a lot of damned slackers!"

The ambulance driver got out of the car and came round to see what the delay was.

"Accused me of crying out like a damned coward!" he blustered to her. "I didn't make a sound. Knew it wouldn't do any good. Knew if I didn't dig myself out, I'd be there till Kingdom Come! Nearly had myself out, too, and then he comes along and accuses me of blubbering like a baby! It's monstrous, that's what it is! Monstrous!"

She took hold of his arm.

"What do you think you're doing, young woman? You should be at home instead of out running round in short skirts! It's indecent, that's what it is!"

She shoved him, still protesting, onto a bunk, and covered him up with a blanket. I slammed the doors to, watched her off, and then made a circuit of the incident, looking for Swales and Morris. The rising sun appeared between two bands of cloud, reddening the mounds and glinting off a broken mirror.

I couldn't find either of them, so I reported in to Nelson, who was talking angrily on a field telephone and who nodded and waved me off when I tried to tell him about Jack, and then went back to the post.

Swales was already regaling Morris and Vi, who were eating breakfast, with an imitation of Colonel Godalming. Mrs. Lucy was still filling out papers, apparently the same form as when we'd left.

"Huge mustaches," Swales was saying, his hands two feet apart to illustrate their size, "like a walrus's, and tails, if you please. 'Oi siy, this is disgriceful!'" he sputtered, his right hand squinted shut with an imaginary monocle, "'Wot's the Impire coming to when a man cahn't even be rescued!'" He dropped into his natural voice. "I thought he was going to have our two Jacks court-martialed on the spot." He peered round me. "Where's Settle?"

"He had to go to his day job," I said.

"Just as well," he said, screwing the monocle back in. "The colonel looked like he was coming back with the Royal Lancers." He raised his arm, gripping an imaginary sword. "Charge!"

Vi tittered. Mrs. Lucy looked up and said, "Violet, make Jack some toast. Sit down, Jack. You look done in."

I took my helmet off and started to set it on the table. It was caked with plaster dust, so thick it was impossible to see the red W through it. I hung it on my chair and sat down.

Morris shoved a plate of kippers at me. "You never know what they're going to do when you get them out," he said. "Some of them fall all over you, sobbing, and some act like they're doing you a favor. I had one old woman acted all offended, claimed I made an improper advance when I was working her leg free."

Renfrew came in from the other room, wrapped in a blanket. He looked as bad as I thought I must, his face slack and gray with fatigue. "Where was the incident?" he asked anxiously.

"Just off Old Church Street. In Nelson's sector," I added to reassure him.

But he said nervously, "They're coming closer every night. Have you noticed that?"

"No, they aren't," Vi said. "We haven't had anything in our sector all week."

Renfrew ignored her. "First Gloucester Road and then Ixworth Place and now Old Church Street. It's as if they're circling, searching for something."

"London," Mrs. Lucy said briskly. "And if we don't enforce the blackout, they're likely to find it." She handed Morris a typed list. "Reported infractions from last night. Go round and reprimand them." She put her hand on Renfrew's shoulder. "Why don't you go have a nice lie-down, Mr. Renfrew, while I cook you breakfast?"

"I'm not hungry," he said, but he let her lead him, clutching his blanket, back to the cot.

We watched Mrs. Lucy spread the blanket over him and then lean down and tuck it in around his shoulders, and then Swales said, "You know who this Godalming fellow reminds me of? A lady we rescued over in Gower Street," he said, yawning. "Hauled her out and asked her if her husband was in there with her. 'No,' she says, 'the bleedin' coward's at the front.'"

We all laughed.

"People like this colonel person don't deserve to be rescued," Vi said, spreading oleo on a slice of toast. "You should have left him there awhile and seen how he liked that."

"He was lucky they didn't leave him there altogether," Morris said. "The register had him in Surrey with his wife."

"Lucky he had such a loud voice," Swales said. He twirled the end of an enormous mustache. "Oi siy," he boomed. "Get me out of her immeejutly, you slackers!"

But he said he didn't call out, I thought, and could hear Jack shouting over the din of the antiaircraft guns, the drone of the planes, "There's someone under here."

Mrs. Lucy came back to the table. "I've applied for reinforcements for the post," she said, standing her papers on end and tamping them into an even stack. "Someone from the Town Hall will be coming to inspect in the next few days." She picked up two bottles of ale and an ashtray and carried them over to the dustbin.

"Applied for reinforcements?" Swales asked. "Why? Afraid Colonel Godalming'll be back with the heavy artillery?"

There was a loud banging on the door.

"Oi siy," Swales said. "Here he is now, and he's brought his hounds."

Mrs. Lucy opened the door. "Worse," Vi whispered, diving for the last bottle of ale. "It's Nelson." She passed the bottle to me under the table, and I passed it to Renfield, who tucked it under his blanket.

"Mr. Nelson," Mrs. Lucy said as if she were delighted to see him, "do come in. And how are things over your way?"

"We took a beating last night," he said, glaring at us as though we were responsible.

"He's had a complaint from the colonel," Swales whispered to me. "You're done for, mate."

"Oh, I'm so sorry to hear that," Mrs. Lucy said. "Now, how may I help you?"

He pulled a folded paper from the pocket of his uniform and carefully opened it out. "This was forwarded to me from the City Engineer," he said. "All requests for material improvements are to be sent to the district warden, *not* over his head to the Town Hall."

"Oh, I'm so *glad*," Mrs. Lucy said, leading him into the pantry. "It is such a comfort to deal with someone one knows, rather than a faceless bureaucracy. If I had realized you were the proper person to appeal to, I should have contacted you *immediately*." She shut the door.

Renfield took the ale bottle out from under his blanket and buried it in the dustbin. Violet began taking out her bobby pins.

"We'll never get our reinforcements now," Swales said. "Not with Adolf von Nelson in charge."

"Shh," Vi said, yanking at her snail-like curls. "You don't want him to hear you." "Olmwood told me he makes them keep working at an incident, even when the bombs are right overhead. Thinks all the posts should do it."

"Shh!" Vi said.

"He's a bleeding Nazi!" Swales said, but he lowered his voice. "Got two of his wardens killed that way. You better not let him find out you and Jack are good at finding bodies or you'll be out there dodging shrapnel, too."

Good at finding bodies. I thought of Jack, standing motionless, looking at the rubble and saying, "There's someone alive under here. Hurry."

"That's why Nelson steals from the other posts," Vi said, scooping her bobby pins off the table and into her haversack.

"Because he does his own in." She pulled out a comb and began yanking it through her snarled curls.

The pantry door opened and Nelson and Mrs. Lucy came out, Nelson still holding the unfolded paper. She was still wearing her tea-party smile, but it was a bit thin. "I'm sure you can see it's unrealistic to expect nine people to huddle in a coal cellar for hours at a time," she said.

"There are people all over London 'huddling in coal cellars for hours at a time,' as you put it," Nelson said coldly, "who do not wish their Civil Defense funds spent on frivolities."

"I do not consider the safety of my wardens a frivolity," she said, "though it is clear to me that you do, as witnessed by your very poor record."

Nelson stared for a full minute at Mrs. Lucy, trying to think of a retort, and then turned on me. "Your uniform is a disgrace, warden," he said and stomped out.

Whatever it was Jack had used to find Colonel Godalming, it didn't work on incendiaries. He searched as haphazardly for them as the rest of us, Vi, who had been on spotter duty, shouting directions: "No, farther down Fulham Road. In the grocer's."

She had apparently been daydreaming about her pilots, instead of spotting. The incendiary was not in the grocer's but in the butcher's three doors down, and by the time Jack and I got to it, the meat locker was on fire. It wasn't hard to put out, there were no furniture or curtains to catch and the cold kept the wooden shelves from catching, but the butcher was extravagantly grateful. He insisted on wrapping up five pounds of lamb chops in white paper and thrusting them into Jack's arms.

"Did you really have to be at your day job so early or were you only trying to escape the colonel?" I asked Jack on the way back to the post.

"Was he that bad?" he said, handing me the parcel of lamb chops.

"He nearly took my head off when I said you'd heard him shouting. Said he didn't call for help. Said he was digging himself out." The white butcher's paper was so bright the Luftwaffe would think it was a searchlight. I tucked the parcel inside my overalls so it wouldn't show. "What sort of work is it, your day job?" I asked.

"War work," he said.

"Did they transfer you? Is that why you came to London?"

"No," he said. "I wanted to come." We turned into Mrs. Lucy's street. "Why did you join the ARP?"

"I'm waiting to be called up," I said, "so no one would hire me."

"And you wanted to do your bit."

"Yes," I said, wishing I could see his face.

"What about Mrs. Lucy? Why did she become a warden?"

"Mrs. Lucy?" I said blankly. The question had never even occurred to me. She was the best warden in London. It was her natural calling, and I'd thought of her as always having been one. "I've no idea," I said. "It's her house, she's a widow. Perhaps the Civil Defense commandeered it, and she had to become one. It's the tallest in the street." I tried to remember what Twickenham had written about her in his interview. "Before the war she was something to do with a church."

"A church," he said, and I wished again I could see his face. I couldn't tell in the dark whether he spoke in contempt or longing.

"She was a deaconess or something," I said. "What sort of war work is it? Munitions?"

"No," he said and walked on ahead.

Mrs. Lucy met us at the door of the post. I gave her the packages of lamb chops, and Jack went upstairs to replace Vi as spotter. Mrs. Lucy cooked the chops up immediately, running upstairs to the kitchen during a lull in the raids for salt and a jar of mint sauce, standing over the gas ring at the end of the table and turning them for what seemed an eternity. They smelled wonderful.

Twickenham passed round newly run-off copies of *Twickenham's Twitterings*. "Something for you to read while you wait for your dinner," he said proudly.

The lead article was about the change in address of Sub-Post D, which had taken a partial hit that broke the water mains.

"Had Nelson refused them reinforcements, too?" Swales asked.

"Listen to this," Petersby said. He read aloud from the news-sheet. "'The crime rate in London has risen twenty-eight percent since the beginning of the blackout.'"

"And no wonder," Vi said, coming down from upstairs. "You can't see your nose in front of your face at night, let alone someone lurking in an alley. I'm always afraid someone's going to jump out at me while I'm on patrol."

"All those houses standing empty, and half of London sleeping in the shelters," Swales said. "It's easy pickings. If I was a bad'un, I'd come straight to London."

"It's disgusting," Morris said indignantly. "The idea of someone taking advantage of there being a war like that to commit crimes."

"Oh, Mr. Morris, that reminds me. Your son telephoned," Mrs. Lucy said, cutting into a chop to see if it was done. Blood welled up. "He said he'd a surprise for you, and you were to come out to—" She switched the fork to her left hand and rummaged in her overall pocket till she found a slip of paper, "—North Weald on Monday, I think. His commanding officer's made the necessary travel arrangements for you. I wrote it all down."

She handed it to him and went back to turning the chops.

"A surprise?" Morris said, sounding worried. "He's not in trouble, is he? His commanding officer wants to see me?"

"I don't know. He didn't say what it was about. Only that he wanted you to come."

Vi went over to Mrs. Lucy and peered into the skillet. "I'm glad it was the butcher's and not the grocer's," she said. "Rutabagas wouldn't have cooked up half so nice."

Mrs. Lucy speared a chop, put it on a plate, and handed it to Vi. "Take this up to Jack," she said.

"He doesn't want any," Vi said. She took the plate and sat down at the table.

"Did he say why he didn't?" I asked.

She looked curiously at me. "I suppose he's not hungry," she said. "Or perhaps he doesn't like lamb chops."

"I do hope he's not in any trouble," Morris said, and it took me a minute to realize he was talking about his son. "He's not a bad boy, but he does things without thinking. Youthful high spirits, that's all it is."

"He didn't eat the cake either," I said. "Did he say why he didn't want the lamb chop?"

"If Mr. Settle doesn't want it, then take it to Mr. Renfrew," Mrs. Lucy said sharply. She snatched the plate away from Vi. "And don't let him tell you he's not hungry. He must eat. He's getting very run-down."

Vi sighed and stood up. Mrs. Lucy handed her back the plate and she went into the other room.

"We all need to eat plenty of good food and get lots of sleep," Mrs. Lucy said reprovingly. "To keep our strength up."

"I've written an article about it in the *Twitterings*," Twickenham said, beaming. "It's known as 'walking death.' It's brought about by lack of sleep and poor nutrition, with the anxiety of the raids. The walking dead exhibit slowed reaction time and impaired judgment which resulted in increased accidents on the job."

"Well, I won't have any walking dead among *my* wardens," Mrs. Lucy said, dishing up the rest of the chops. "As soon as you've had these, I want you all to go to bed."

The chops tasted even better than they had smelled. I ate mine, reading Twickenham's article on the walking dead. It said that loss of appetite was a common reaction to the raids. It also said that lack of sleep could cause compulsive behavior and odd fixations. "The walking dead may become convinced that they are being poisoned or that a friend or relative is a German agent. They may hallucinate, hearing voices, seeing visions or believing fantastical things."

"He was in trouble at school, before the war, but he's steadied down since he joined up," Morris said. "I wonder what he's done."

At three the next morning a land mine exploded in almost the same spot off Old Church Street as the HE's. Nelson sent Olmwood to ask for help, and Mrs. Lucy ordered Swales, Jack, and me to go with him.

"The mine didn't land more'n two houses away from the first crater," Olmwood said while we were getting on our gear. "The Jerries couldn't have come closer if they'd been aiming at it."

"I know what they're aiming at," Renfrew said from the doorway. He looked terrible, pale and drawn as a ghost. "And I know why you've applied for reinforcements for the post. It's me, isn't it? They're after me."

"They're not after any of us," Mrs. Lucy said firmly.

"They're two miles up. They're not aiming at anything."

"Why would Hitler want to bomb you more than the rest of us?" Swales said.

"I don't know." He sank down on one of the chairs and put his head in his hands. "I don't *know*. But they're after me. I can feel it."

Mrs. Lucy had sent Swales, Jack, and me to the incident because "you've been there before. You'll know the terrain," but that was a fond hope. Since they explode above ground, land mines do considerably more damage than HE's. There was now a hill where the incident officer's tent had been, and three more beyond it, a mountain range in the middle of London. Swales started up the nearest peak to look for the incident officer's light.

"Jack, over here!" somebody called from the hill behind us, and both of us scrambled up a slope toward the voice.

A group of five men were halfway up the hill looking down into a hole.

"Jack!" the man yelled again. He was wearing a blue foreman's arm-band, and he was looking straight past us at someone toiling up the slope with what looked like a stirrup pump. I thought, surely they're not trying to fight a fire down that shaft, and then saw it wasn't a pump. It was, in fact, an automobile jack, and the man with the blue armband reached between us for it, lowered it down the hole, and scrambled in after it.

The rest of the rescue squad stood looking down into the blackness as if they could actually see something. After awhile they began handing empty buckets down into the hole and pulling them out heaped full of broken bricks and pieces of splintered wood. None of them took any notice of us, even when Jack held out his hands to take one of the buckets.

"We're from Chelsea," I shouted to the foreman over the din of the planes and bombs. "What can we do to help?"

They went on bucket-brigading. A china teapot came up on the top of one load, covered with dust but not even chipped.

I tried again. "Who is it down there?"

"Two of 'em," the man nearest me said. He plucked the teapot off the heap and handed it to a man wearing a balaclava under his helmet. "Man and a woman."

"We're from Chelsea," I shouted over a burst of antiaircraft fire. "What do you want us to do?"

He took the teapot away from the man with the balaclava and handed it to me. "Take this down to the pavement with the other valuables."

It took me a long while to get down the slope, holding the teapot in one hand and the lid on with the other and trying to keep my footing among the broken bricks, and even longer to find any pavement. The land mine had heaved most of it up, and the street with it.

I finally found it, a square of unbroken pavement in front of a blown-out bakery, with the "valuables" neatly lined up against it: a radio, a boot, two serving spoons like the one Colonel Godalming had threatened me with, a lady's beaded evening bag. A rescue worker was standing guard next to them.

"Halt!" he said, stepping in front of them as I came up, holding a pocket torch or a gun. "No one's allowed inside the incident perimeter."

"I'm ARP," I said hastily. "Jack Harker. Chelsea." I held up the teapot. "They sent me down with this."

It was a torch. He flicked it on and off, an eyeblink. "Sorry," he said. "We've had a good deal of looting recently." He took the teapot and placed it at the end of the line next to the evening bag. "Caught a man last week going through the pockets of the bodies laid out in the street waiting for the mortuary van. Terrible how some people will take advantage of something like this."

I went back up to where the rescue workers were digging. Jack was at the mouth of the shaft, hauling buckets up and handing them back. I got in line behind him.

"Have they found them yet?" I asked him as soon as there was a lull in the bombing.

"Quiet!" a voice shouted from the hole, and the man in the balaclava repeated, "Quiet, everyone! We must have absolute quiet!"

Everyone stopped working and listened. Jack had handed me a bucket full of bricks, and the handle cut into my hands. For a second there was absolute silence, and then the drone of a plane and the distant swish and crump of a HE.

"Don't worry," the voice from the hole shouted, "we're nearly there." The buckets began coming up out of the hole again.

I hadn't heard anything, but apparently down in the shaft they had, a voice or the sound of tapping, and I felt relieved, both that one of them at least was still alive, and that the diggers were on course. I'd been on an incident in October where we'd had to stop halfway down and sink a new shaft because the rubble kept distorting and displacing the sound. Even if the shaft was directly above the victim, it tended to go crooked in working past obstacles, and the only way to keep it straight was with frequent soundings. I thought of Jack digging for Colonel Godalming with the banister. He hadn't taken any soundings at all. He had seemed to know exactly where he was going.

The men in the shaft called for the jack again, and Jack and I lowered it down to them. As the man below it reached up to take it, Jack stopped. He raised his head, as if he were listening.

"What is it?" I said. I couldn't hear anything but the ack-ack guns in Hyde Park. "Did you hear someone calling?"

"Where's the bloody jack?" the foreman shouted.

"It's too late," Jack said to me. "They're dead."

"Come along, get it down here," the foreman shouted. "We haven't got all day."

He handed the jack down.

"Quiet," the foreman shouted, and above us, like a ghostly echo, we could hear the balaclava call, "Quiet, please everyone."

A church clock began to chime and I could hear the balaclava say irritably, "We must have absolute quiet."

The clock chimed four and stopped, and there was a skittering sound of dirt falling on metal. Then silence, and a faint sound.

"Quiet!" the foreman called again, and there was another silence, and the sound again. A whimper. Or a moan. "We hear you," he shouted. "Don't be afraid."

"One of them's still alive," I said.

Jack didn't say anything.

"We just *heard* them," I said angrily.

Jack shook his head.

"We'll need lumber for bracing," the man in the balaclava said to Jack, and I expected him to tell him it was no use, but he went off immediately and came back dragging a white-painted bookcase.

It still had three books in it. I helped Jack and the balaclava knock the shelves out of the case and then took the books down to the store of "valuables." The guard was sitting on the pavement going through the beaded evening bag.

"Taking inventory," he said, scrambling up hastily. He jammed a lipstick and a handkerchief into the bag. "So's to make certain nothing gets stolen."

"I've brought you something to read," I said, and laid the books next to the teapot. "*Crime and Punishment.*"

I toiled back up the hill and helped Jack lover the bookshelves down the shaft and after a few minutes buckets began coming up again. We reformed our scraggly bucket brigade, the balaclava at the head of it and me and then Jack at its end.

The all-clear went. As soon as it wound down, the foreman took another sounding. This time we didn't hear anything, and when the buckets started again I handed them to Jack without looking at him.

It began to get light in the east, a slow graying of the hills above us. Two of them, several stories high, stood where the row houses that had escaped the night before had been, and we were still in their shadow, though I could see the shaft now, with the end of one of the white bookshelves sticking up from it like a gravestone.

The buckets began to come more slowly.

"Put out your cigarettes!" the foreman called up, and we all stopped, trying to catch the smell of gas. If they were dead, as Jack had said, it was most likely gas leaking in from the broken mains that had killed them, and not internal injuries. The week before we had brought up a boy and his dog, not a scratch on them. The dog had barked and whimpered almost up to when we found them, and the ambulance driver said she thought they'd only been dead a few minutes.

I couldn't smell any gas and after a minute the foreman said excitedly, "I see them!"

The balaclava leaned over the shaft, his hands on his knees. "Are they alive?"

"Yes! Fetch an ambulance!"

The balaclava went leaping down the hill, skidding on broken bricks that skittered down in a minor avalanche.

I knelt over the shaft. "Will they need a stretcher?" I called down.

"No," the foreman said, and I knew by the sound of his voice they were dead.

"Both of them?" I said.

"Yes."

I stood up. "How did you know they were dead?" I said, turning to look at Jack. "How did—"

He wasn't there. I looked down the hill. The balaclava was nearly to the bottom—grabbing at a broken window sash to stop his headlong descent, his wake a smoky cloud of brick dust—but Jack was nowhere to be seen.

It was nearly dawn. I could see the gray hills and at the far end of them the warden and his "valuables." There was another rescue party on the third hill over, still digging. I could see Swales handing down a bucket.

"Give a hand here," the foreman said impatiently and hoisted the jack up to me. I hauled it over to the side and then came back and helped the foreman out of the shaft. His hands were filthy, covered in reddish-brown mud.

"Was it the gas that killed them?" I asked, even though he was already pulling out a packet of cigarettes.

"No," he said, shaking a cigarette out and taking it between his teeth. He patted the front of his coverall, leaving red stains.

"How long have they been dead?" I asked.

He found his matches, struck one, and lit the cigarette. "Shortly after we last heard them, I should say," he said, and I thought, *but they were already dead by then*. And Jack knew it. "They've been dead at least two hours."

I looked at my watch. I read a little past six. "But the mine didn't kill them?"

He took the cigarette between his fingers and blew a long puff of smoke. When he put the cigarette back in his mouth there was a red smear on it. "Loss of blood."

The next night the Luftwaffe was early. I hadn't gotten much sleep after the incident. Morris had fretted about his son the whole day and Swales had teased Renfrew mercilessly. "Goering's found out about your spying," he said, "And now he's sent his Stukas after you."

I finally went up to the third floor and tried to sleep in the spotter's chair, but it was too light. The afternoon was cloudy, and the fires burning in the East End gave the sky a nasty reddish cast.

Someone had left a copy of *Twickenham's Twitterings* on the floor. I read the article on the walking dead again, and then, still unable to sleep, the rest of the news-sheet. There was an account of Hitler's invasion of Transylvania, and a recipe for butterless strawberry tart, and the account of the crime rate. "London is currently the perfect place for the criminal element," Nelson was quoted as saying. "We must constantly be on the lookout for wrongdoing."

Below the recipe was a story about a Scottish terrier named Bonny Charlie who had barked and scrabbled wildly at the ruins of a collapsed house till wardens heeded his cries, dug down, and discovered two unharmed children.

I must have fallen asleep reading that because the next thing I knew Morris was shaking me and telling me the sirens had gone. It was only five o'clock.

At half-past we had a HE in our sector. It was just three blocks from the post, and the walls shook and plaster rained down on Twickenham's typewriter and on Renfrew, lying awake in his cot.

"Frivolities, my foot," Mrs. Lucy muttered as we dived for our tin hats. "We need those reinforcing beams."

The part-times hadn't come on duty yet. Mrs. Lucy left Renfrew to send them on. We knew exactly where the incident was—Morris had been looking in that direction when it went—but we still had difficulty finding it. It was still evening, but by the time we had gone half a street, it was pitch black.

The first time that had happened, I thought it was some sort of after-blindness from the blast, but it's only the brick and plaster dust from the collapsed buildings. It rises up in a haze that's darker than any blackout curtain, obscuring everything. When Mrs. Lucy set up shop on a stretch of pavement and switched on the blue incident light it glowed spectrally in the man-made fog.

"Only two families still in the street," she said, holding the register up to the light. "The Kirkcuddy family and the Hodgsons."

"Are they an old couple?" Morris asked, appearing suddenly out of the fog.

She peered at the register. "Yes. Pensioners."

"I found them," he said in that flat voice that meant they were dead. "Blast."

"Oh, dear," she said. "The Kirkcuddys are a mother and two children. They've an Anderson shelter." She held the register closer to the blue light. "Everyone else has been using the tube shelter." She unfolded a map and showed us where the Kirkcuddys' backyard had been, but it was no help. We spent the next hour wandering blindly over the mounds, listening for sounds that were impossible to hear over the Luftwaffe's comments and the ack-ack's replies.

Petersby showed up a little past eight and Jack a few minutes later, and Mrs. Lucy set them to wandering in the fog, too.

"Over here," Jack shouted almost immediately, and my heart gave an odd jerk.

"Oh, good, he's heard them," Mrs. Lucy said. "Jack, go and find him."

"Over here," he called again, and I started off in the direction of his voice, almost afraid of what I would find, but I hadn't gone ten steps before I could hear it, too. A baby crying, and a hollow, echoing sound like someone banging a fist against tin.

"Don't stop," Vi shouted. She was kneeling next to Jack in a shallow crater. "Keep making noise. We're coming." She looked up at me. "Tell Mrs. Lucy to ring the rescue squad."

I blundered my way back to Mrs. Lucy through the darkness. She had already rung up the rescue squad. She sent me to Sloane Square to make sure the rest of the inhabitants of the block were safely there.

The dust had lifted a little but not enough for me to see where I was going. I pitched off a curb into the street and tripped over a pile of debris and then a body. When I shone my torch on it, I saw it was the girl I had walked to the shelter two nights before.

She was sitting against the tiled entrance to the station, still holding a dress on a hanger in her limp hand. The old stewpot at John Lewis's never let her off even a minute before closing, and the Luftwaffe had been early. She had been killed by blast, or by flying glass. Her face and neck and hands were covered with tiny cuts, and glass crunched underfoot when I moved her legs together.

I went back to the incident and waited for the mortuary van and went with them to the shelter. It took me three hours to find the families on my list. By the time I got back to the incident, the rescue squad was five feet down.

"They're nearly there," Vi said, dumping a basket on the far side of the crater. "All that's coming up now is dirt and the occasional rosebush."

"Where's Jack?" I said.

"He went for a saw." She took the basket back and handed it to one of the rescue squad, who had to put his cigarette into his mouth to free his hands before he could take it. "There was a board, but they dug past it."

I leaned over the hole. I could hear the sound of banging but not the baby. "Are they still alive?"

She shook her head. "We haven't heard the baby for an hour or so. We keep calling, but there's no answer. We're afraid the banging may be something mechanical."

I wondered if they were dead and Jack, knowing it, had not gone for a saw at all but off to that day job of his.

Swales came up. "Guess who's in hospital?" he said.

"Who?" Vi said.

"Olmwood. Nelson had his wardens out walking patrols during a raid, and he caught a piece of shrapnel from one of the ack-acks in the leg. Nearly took it off."

The rescue worker with the cigarette handed a heaping basket to Vi. She took it, staggering a little under the weight, and carried it off.

"You'd better not let Nelson see you working like that," Swales called after her, "or he'll have you transferred to his sector. Where's Morris?" he said and went off, presumably to tell him and whoever else he could find about Olmwood.

Jack came up, carrying the saw.

"They don't need it," the rescue worker said, the cigarette dangling from the side of his mouth. "Mobile's here," he said and went off for a cup of tea.

Jack knelt and handed the saw down the hole.

"Are they still alive?" I asked.

Jack leaned over the hole, his hands clutching the edges. The banging was incredibly loud. It must have been deafening inside the Anderson. Jack stared into the hole as if he heard neither the banging nor my voice.

He stood up, still looking into the hole. "They're farther to the left," he said.

How can they be farther to the left? I thought. *We can hear them. They're directly under us.* "Are they alive?" I said.

"Yes."

Swales came back. "He's a spy, that's what he is," he said. "Hitler sent him here to kill off our best men one by one. I told you his name was Adolf Von Nelson."

The Kirkcuddys were farther to the left. The rescue squad had to widen the tunnel, cut the top of the Anderson open and pry it back, like opening a can of tomatoes. It took till nine o'clock in the morning, but they were all alive.

Jack left sometime before it got light. I didn't see him go. Swales was telling me about Olmwood's injury, and when I turned around, Jack was gone.

"Has Jack told you where this job of his is that he has to leave so early for?" I asked Vi when I got back to the post.

She had propped a mirror against one of the gas masks and was putting her hair up in pincurls. "No," she said, dipping a comb in a glass of water and wetting a lock of her hair. "Jack, could you pass me my bobby pins? I've a date this afternoon, and I want to look my best."

I pushed the pins across to her. "What sort of job is it? Did Jack say?"

"No. Some sort of war work, I should think." She wound a lock of hair around her finger. "He's had ten kills. Four Stukas and six 109's."

I sat down next to Twickenham, who was typing up the incident report. "Have you interviewed Jack yet?"

"When would I have had time?" Twickenham asked. "We haven't had a quiet night since he came."

Renfrew shuffled in from the other room. He had a blanket wrapped round him Indian-style and a bedspread over his shoulders. He looked terrible, pale and drawn as a ghost.

"Would you like some breakfast?" Vi asked, prying a pin open with her teeth.

He shook his head. "Did Nelson approve the reinforcements?"

"No," Twickenham said in spite of Vi's signaling him not to.

"You must tell Nelson it's an emergency," he said, hugging the blanket to him as if he were cold. "I know why they're after me. It was before the war. When Hitler invaded Czechoslovakia.

"I wrote a letter to *The Times*."

I was grateful Swales wasn't there. A letter to *The Times*.

"Come, now, why don't you go and lie down for a bit?" Vi said, securing a curl with a bobby pin as she stood up. "You're tired, that's all, and that's what's getting you so worried.

"They don't even get *The Times* over there."

She took his arm, and he went docilely with her into the other room. I heard him say, "I called him a lowland bully. In the letter." *The person suffering from severe sleep loss, hearing voices, seeing visions, or believing fantastical things.*

"Has he mentioned what sort of day job he has?" I asked Twickenham.

"Who?" he asked, still typing.

"Jack."

"No, but whatever it is, let's hope he's as good at it as he is at finding bodies." He stopped and peered at what he'd just typed. "This makes five, doesn't it?"

Vi came back. "And we'd best not let von Nelson find out about it," she said. She sat down and dipped the comb into the glass of water. "He'd take him like he took Olmwood, and we're already shorthanded, with Renfrew the way he is."

Mrs. Lucy came in carrying the incident light, disappeared into the pantry with it, and came out again carrying an application form. "Might I use the typewriter, Mr. Twickenham?" she asked.

He pulled his sheet of paper out of the typewriter and stood up. Mrs. Lucy sat down, rolled in the form, and began typing. "I've decided to apply directly to Civil Defense for reinforcements," she said.

"What sort of day job does Jack have?" I asked her.

"War work," she said. She pulled the application out, turned it over, rolled it back in. "Jack, would you mind taking this over to headquarters?"

"Works days," Vi said, making a pin curl on the back of her head. "Raids every night. When does he sleep?"

"I don't know," I said.

"He'd best be careful," she said. "Or he'll turn into one of the walking dead, like Renfrew."

Mrs. Lucy signed the application form, folded it in half, and gave it to me. I took it to Civil Defense headquarters and spent half a day trying to find the right office to give it to.

"It's not the correct form," the sixth girl said. "She needs to file an A-114, Exterior Improvements."

"It's not exterior," I said. "The post is applying for reinforcing beams for the cellar." "Reinforcements are classified as exterior improvements," she said. She handed me the form, which looked identical to the one Mrs. Lucy had already filled out, and I left.

On the way out, Nelson stopped me. I thought he was going to tell me my uniform was a disgrace again, but instead he pointed to my tin hat and demanded, "Why aren't you wearing a regulation helmet, warden? 'All ARP wardens shall wear a helmet with the letter W in red on the front,'" he quoted.

I took my hat off and looked at it. The red W had partly chipped away so that it looked like a V.

"What post are you?" he barked.

"Forty-eight. Chelsea," I said and wondered if he expected me to salute.

"Mrs. Lucy is your warden," he said disgustedly, and I expected his next question to be what I was doing at Civil Defense, but instead he said, "I heard about Colonel Godalming. Your post has been having good luck locating casualties these last few raids."

"Yes, sir," was obviously the wrong answer, and "no, sir," would make him suspicious. "We found three people in an Anderson last night," I said. "One of the children had the wits to bang on the roof with a pair of pliers."

"I've heard that the person finding them is a new man, Settle." He sounded friendly, almost jovial. Like Hitler at Munich.

"Settle?" I said blankly. "Mrs. Lucy was the one who found the Anderson."

Morris's son Quincy's surprise was the Victoria Cross. "A medal," he said over and over. "Who'd have thought it, my Quincy with a medal? Fifteen planes he shot down."

It had been presented at a special ceremony at Quincy's commanding officer's headquarters, and the Duchess of York herself had been there. Morris had pinned the medal on himself.

"I wore my suit," he told us for the hundredth time, "in case he was in trouble I wanted to make a good impression, and a good thing, too. What would the Duchess of York have thought if I'd gone looking like this?"

He looked pretty bad. We all did. We'd had two breadbaskets of incendiaries, one right after the other, and Vi had been on watch. We had had to save the butcher's again, and a baker's two blocks farther down, and a 13th century crucifix.

"I *told* him it went through the altar roof," Vi had said disgustedly when she and I finally got it out. "Your friend Jack couldn't find an incendiary if it fell on him."

"You told Jack the incendiary came down on the church?" I said, looking up at the carved wooden figure. The bottom of the cross was blackened, and Christ's nailed feet, as if he had been burned at the stake instead of crucified.

"Yes," she said. "I even told him it was the altar." She looked back up the nave. "And he could have seen it as soon as he came into the church."

"What did he say? That it wasn't there?"

Vi was looking speculatively up at the roof. "It could have been caught in the rafters and come down after. It hardly matters, does it? We put it out. Come on, let's get back to the post," she said, shivering. "I'm freezing."

I was freezing, too. We were both sopping wet. The AFS had stormed up after we had the fire under control and sprayed everything in sight with icy water.

"Pinned it on myself, I did," Morris said. "The Duchess of York kissed him on both cheeks and said he was the pride of England." He had brought a bottle of wine to celebrate the Cross. He got Renfrew up and brought him to the table, draped in his blankets, and ordered Twickenham to put his typewriter away.

Petersby brought in extra chairs, and Mrs. Lucy went upstairs to get her crystal.

"Only eight, I'm afraid," she said, coming down with the stemmed goblets in her blackened hands. "The Germans have broken the rest. Who's willing to make do with the tooth glass?"

"I don't care for any, thank you," Jack said. "I don't drink."

"What's that?" Morris said jovially. He had taken off his tin helmet, and below the white line it left he looked like he was wearing blackface in a music-hall show. "You've got to toast my boy at least. Just imagine. My Quincy with a medal."

Mrs. Lucy rinsed out the porcelain tooth glass and handed it to Vi, who was pouring out the wine. They passed the goblets round. Jack took the tooth glass.

"To my son Quincy, the best pilot in the RAF!" Morris said, raising his goblet.

"May he shoot down the entire Luftwaffe!" Swales shouted, "and put an end to this bloody war!"

"So a man can get a decent night's sleep!" Renfrew said, and everyone laughed.

We drank. Jack raised his glass with the others but when Vi took the bottle round again, he put his hand over the mouth of it.

"Just think of it," Morris said. "My son Quincy with a medal. He had his troubles in school, in with a bad lot, problems with the police. I worried about him, I did, wondered what he'd come to, and then this war comes along and here he is a hero."

"To heroes!" Petersby said.

We drank again, and Vi dribbled out the last of the wine into Morris's glass. "That's the lot, I'm afraid." She brightened. "I've a bottle of cherry cordial Charlie gave me."

Mrs. Lucy made a face. "Just a minute," she said, disappeared into the pantry, and came back with two cobwebbed bottles of port, which she poured out generously and a little sloppily.

"The presence of intoxicating beverages on post is strictly forbidden," she said. "A fine of five shillings will be imposed for a first offence, one pound for subsequent offences." She took out a pound note and laid it on the table. "I wonder what Nelson was before the war?"

"A monster," Vi said.

I looked across at Jack. He still had his hand over his glass.

"A headmaster," Swales said. "No, I've got it. An Inland Revenue collector!"

Everyone laughed.

"I was a horrid person before the war," Mrs. Lucy said.

Vi giggled.

"I was a deaconess, one of those dreadful women who arranges the flowers in the sanctuary and gets up jumble sales and bullies the rector.

'The Terror of the Churchwardens,' that's what I used to be. I was determined that they should put the hymnals front side out on the backs of the pews. Morris knows. He sang in the choir."

"It's true," Morris said. "She used to instruct the choir on the proper way to line up."

I tried to imagine her as a stickler, as a petty tyrant like Nelson, and failed.

"Sometimes it takes something dreadful like a war for one to find one's proper job," she said, staring at her glass.

"To the war!" Swales said gaily.

"I'm not sure we should toast something so terrible as that," Twickenham said doubtfully.

"It isn't all that terrible," Vi said. "I mean, without it, we wouldn't all be here together, would we?"

"And you'd never have met all those pilots of yours, would you, Vi?" Swales said.

"There's nothing wrong with making the best of a bad job," Vi said, miffed.

"Some people do more than that," Swales said. "Some people take positive advantage of the war. Like Colonel Godalming. I had a word with one of the AFS volunteers. Seems the Colonel didn't come back for his hunting rifle after all." He leaned forward confidingly. "Seems he was having a bit on with a blonde dancer from the Windmill. *Seems* his wife thought he was out shooting grouse in Surrey and now she's asking all sorts of unpleasant questions."

"He's not the only one taking advantage," Morris said. "That night you got the Kirkcuddys out, Jack, I found an old couple killed by blast. I put them by the road for the mortuary van, and later I saw somebody over there, bending over the bodies, doing something to them. I thought, he must be straightening them out before the rigor set in, but then it comes to me. He's robbing them. Dead bodies."

"And who's to say they were killed by blast?" Swales said. "Who's to say they weren't murdered? There's lots of bodies, aren't there, and nobody looks close at them? Who's to say they were all killed by the Germans?"

"How did we get on to this?" Petersby said. "We're supposed to be celebrating Quincy Morris's medal, not talking about murderers." He raised his glass. "To Quincy Morris!"

"And the RAF!" Vi said.

"To making the best of a bad job," Mrs. Lucy said.

"Hear, hear," Jack said softly and raised his glass, but he still didn't drink.

Jack found four people in the next three days. I did not hear any of them until well after we had started digging, and the last one, a fat woman in striped pajamas and a pink hairnet, I never did hear, though she said when we brought her up that she had "called and called between prayers."

Twickenham wrote it all up for the *Twitterings*, tossing out the article on Quincy Morris's medal and typing up a new master's. When Mrs. Lucy borrowed the typewriter to fill out the A-114, she said, "What's this?"

"My lead story," he said. "'Settle Finds Four in Rubble.'" He handed her the master's.

"'Jack Settle, the newest addition to Post Forty-Eight,'" she read, "'located four air-raid victims last night. "I wanted to be useful," says the modest Mr. Settle when asked why he came to London from Yorkshire. And he's been useful since his very first night on the job when he—'" She handed it back to him. "Sorry. You can't print that. Nelson's been nosing about, asking questions. He's already taken one of my wardens and nearly gotten him killed. I won't let him have another."

"That's censorship!" Twickenham said, outraged.

"There's a war on," Mrs. Lucy said, "and we're shorthanded. I've relieved Mr. Renfrew of duty. He's going to stay with his sister in Birmingham. And I wouldn't let Nelson have another one of my wardens if we were overstaffed. He's already gotten Olmwood nearly killed."

She handed me the A-114 and asked me to take it to Civil Defense. I did. The girl I had spoken to wasn't there, and the girl who was said, "This is for *interior* improvements. You need to fill out a D-268."

"I did," I said, "and I was told that reinforcements qualified as exterior improvements."

"Only if they're on the outside." She handed me a D-268.

"Sorry," she said apologetically. "I'd help you if I could, but my boss is a stickler for the correct forms."

"There's something else you can do for me," I said. "I was supposed to take one of our part-times a message at his day job, but I've lost the address. If you could look it up for me. Jack Settle? If not, I've got to go all the way back to Chelsea to get it."

She looked back over her shoulder and then said, "Wait a mo," and darted down the hall. She came back with a sheet of paper.

"Settle?" she said. "Post Forty Eight, Chelsea?"

"That's the one," I said. "I need his work address."

"He hasn't got one."

He had left the incident while we were still getting the fat woman out. It was starting to get light. We had a rope under her, and a makeshift winch, and he had abruptly handed his end to Swales and said, "I've got to leave for my day job."

"You're certain?" I said.

"I'm certain." She handed me the sheet of paper. It was Jack's approval for employment as a part-time warden, signed by Mrs. Lucy. The spaces for work and home addresses had been left blank. "This is all there was in the file," she said. "No work permit, no identity card, not even a ration card. We keep copies of all that, so he must not have a job."

I took the D-268 back to the post, but Mrs. Lucy wasn't there. "One of Nelson's wardens came round with a new regulation," Twickenham said, running off copies on the duplicating machine. "All wardens will be out on patrol unless on telephone or spotter duty. *All* wardens. She went off to give him what-for," he said, sounding pleased. He was apparently over his anger at her for censoring his story on Jack.

I picked up one of the still-wet copies of the news-sheet. The lead story was about Hitler's invasion of Greece. He had put the article about Quincy Morris's medal down in the right-hand corner under a list of "What the War Has Done For Us." Number one was, "It's made us discover capabilities we didn't know we had."

"She called him a murderer," Twickenham said.

A murderer.

"What did you want to tell her?" Twickenham said.

That Jack doesn't have a job, I thought. *Or a ration card. That he didn't put out the incendiary in the church even though Vi told him it had gone through the altar roof. That he knew the Anderson was farther to the left.*

"It's still the wrong form," I said, taking out the D-268.

"That's easily remedied," he said. He rolled the application into the typewriter, typed for a few minutes, handed it back to me.

"Mrs. Lucy has to sign it," I said, and he snatched it back, whipped out a fountain pen, and signed her name.

"What were you before the war?" I asked. "A forger?"

"You'd be surprised." He handed the form back to me. "You look dreadful, Jack. Have you gotten any sleep this last week?"

"When would I have had the chance?"

"Why don't you lie down now while no one's here?" he said, reaching for my arm the way Vi had reached for Renfrew's. "I'll take the form back to Civil Defense for you."

I shook off his arm. "I'm all right."

I walked back to Civil Defense. The girl who had tried to find Jack's file wasn't there, and the first girl was. I was sorry I hadn't brought the A-114 along as well, but she scrutinized the form without comment and stamped the back. "It will take approximately six weeks to process," she said.

"Six weeks!" I said. "Hitler could have invaded the entire Empire by then."

"In that case, you'll very likely have to file a different form."

I didn't go back to the post. Mrs. Lucy would doubtless be back by the time I returned, but what could I say to her? I suspect Jack. Of what? Of not liking lamb chops and cake? Of having to leave early for work? Of rescuing children from the rubble?

He had said he had a job and the girl couldn't find his work permit, but it took the Civil Defense six weeks to process a request for a few beams. It would probably take them till the end of the war to file the work permits. Or perhaps his had been in the file, and the girl had missed it. Loss of sleep can result in mistakes on the job. And odd fixations.

I walked to Sloane Square Station. There was no sign of where the young woman had been. They had even swept the glass up. Her stewpot of a boss at John Lewis never let her go till closing time, even if the sirens had gone, even if it was dark. She had had to hurry through the blacked-out streets all alone, carrying her dress for the next day on a hanger, listening to the guns and trying to make out how far off the planes were. If someone had been stalking her, she would never have heard him, never have seen him in the darkness. Whoever found her would think she had been killed by flying glass.

He doesn't eat, I would say to Mrs. Lucy. *He didn't put out an incendiary in a church. He always leaves the incidents before dawn, even when we don't have the casualties up. The Luftwaffe is trying to kill me. It was a letter I wrote to* The Times. *The walking dead may hallucinate, hearing voices, seeing visions, or believing fantastical things.*

The sirens went. I must have been standing there for hours, staring at the pavement. I went back to the post. Mrs. Lucy was there. "You look dreadful, Jack. How long's it been since you've slept?"

"I don't know," I said. "Where's Jack?"

"On watch," Mrs. Lucy said.

"You'd best be careful," Vi said, setting chocolates on a plate. "Or you'll turn into one of the walking dead. Would you like a sweet? Eddie gave them to me."

The telephone pipped. Mrs. Lucy answered it, spoke a minute, hung up. "Slaney needs help on an incident," she said. "They've asked for Jack."

She sent both of us. We found the incident without any trouble. There was no dust cloud, no smell except from a fire burning off to one side. "This didn't just happen," I said. "It's a day old at least."

I was wrong. It was two days old. The rescue squads had been working straight through, and there were still at least thirty people unaccounted for. Some of the rescue squad was digging half-heartedly halfway up a mound, but most of them were standing about, smoking and looking like they were casualties themselves. Jack went up to where the men were digging, shook his head, and set off across the mound.

"Heard you had a body-sniffer," one of the smokers said to me. "They've got one in Whitechapel, too. Crawls round the incident on his hands and knees, sniffing like a bloodhound. Yours do that?"

"No," I said.

"Over here," Jack said.

"Says he can read their minds, the one in Whitechapel does," he said, putting out his cigarette and taking up a pickaxe. He clambered up the slope to where Jack was already digging.

It was easy to see because of the fire, and fairly easy to dig, but halfway down we struck the massive headboard of a bed.

"We'll have to go in from the side," Jack said.

"The hell with that," the man who'd told me about the body-sniffer said. "How do you know somebody's down there? I don't hear anything."

Jack didn't answer him. He moved down the slope and began digging into its side.

"They've been in there two days," the man said. "They're dead and I'm not getting overtime." He flung down the pickaxe and stalked off to the mobile canteen. Jack didn't even notice he was gone. He handed me baskets, and I emptied them, and occasionally Jack said, "Saw," or "Tin-snips," and I handed them to him. I was off getting the stretcher when he brought her out. She was perhaps thirteen. She was wearing a white nightgown, or perhaps it only looked white because of the plaster dust. Jack's face was ghastly with it. He had picked her up in his arms, and she had fastened her arms about his neck and buried her face against his shoulder. They were both outlined by the fire.

I brought the stretcher up, and Jack knelt down and tried to lay her on it, but she would not let go of his neck. "It's all right," he said gently. "You're safe now."

He unclasped her hands and folded them on her chest. Her nightgown was streaked with dried blood, but it didn't seem to be hers. I wondered who else had been in there with her. "What's your name?" Jack said.

"Mina," she said. It was no more than a whisper.

"My name's Jack," he said. He nodded at me. "So's his. We're going to carry you down to the ambulance now. Don't be afraid. You're safe now."

The ambulance wasn't there yet. We laid the stretcher on the pavement, and I went over to the incident officer to see if it was on its way. Before I could get back, somebody shouted, "Here's another," and I went and helped dig out a hand that the foreman had found, and then the body all the blood had come from. When I looked down the hill the girl was still lying there on the stretcher, and Jack was bending over it.

I went out to Whitechapel to see the body-sniffer the next day. He wasn't there. "He's a part-time," the post warden told me, clearing off a chair so I could sit down. The post was a mess, dirty clothes and dishes everywhere.

An old woman in a print wrapper was frying up kidneys in a skillet. "Works days in munitions out to Dorking," she said.

"How exactly is he able to locate the bodies?" I asked. "I heard—"

"That he reads their minds?" the woman said. She scraped the kidneys onto a plate and handed it to the post warden. "He's heard it, too, more's the pity, and it's gone straight to his head. 'I can feel them under here,' he says to the rescue squads, like he was Houdini or something, and points to where they're supposed to start digging."

"Then how does he find them?"

"Luck," the warden said.

"*I* think he smells 'em," the woman said. "That's why they call 'em body-sniffers."

The warden snorted. "Over the stink the Jerries put in the bombs and the gas and all the rest of it?"

"If he were a—" I said and didn't finish it. "If he had an acute sense of smell, perhaps he could smell the blood."

"You can't even smell the bodies when they've been dead a week," the warden said, his mouth full of kidneys. "He hears them screaming, same as us."

"He's got better hearing than us," the woman said, switching happily to his theory. "Most of us are half-deaf from the guns, and he isn't."

I hadn't been able to hear the fat woman in the pink hairnet, although she'd said she had called for help. But Jack, just down from Yorkshire, where they hadn't been deafened by antiaircraft guns for weeks, could. There was nothing sinister about it. Some people had better hearing than others.

"We pulled an army colonel out last week who claimed he didn't cry out," I said.

"He's lying," the warden said, sawing at a kidney. "We had a nanny, two days ago, prim and proper as you please, swore the whole time we was getting her out, words to make a sailor blush, and then claimed she didn't. 'Unclean words have *never* crossed my lips and never will,' she says to me." He brandished his fork at me. 'Your colonel cried out, all right. He just won't admit it."

"I didn't make a sound," Colonel Godalming had said, brandishing his serving spoon. "Knew it wouldn't do any good," and perhaps the warden was right, and it was only bluster. But he hadn't wanted his wife to know he was in London, to find out about the dancer at the Windmill. He had had good reason to keep silent, to try to dig himself out.

I went home and rang up a girl I knew in the ambulance service and asked her to find out where they had taken Mina. She rang me back with the answer in a few minutes, and I took the tube over to St. George's Hospital. The others had all cried out, or banged on the roof of the Anderson, except Mina. She had been so frightened when Jack got her out she couldn't speak above a whisper, but that didn't mean she hadn't cried or whimpered.

"When you were buried last night, did you call for help?" I would ask her, and she would answer me in her mouse voice, "I called and called between prayers. Why?" And I would say, "It's nothing, an odd fixation brought on by lack of sleep. Jack spends his days in Dorking, at a munitions plant, and has exceptionally acute hearing." And there is no more truth to my theory than to Renfrew's belief that the raids were brought on by a letter to *The Times*.

St. George's had an entrance marked Casualty Clearing Station. I asked the nursing sister behind the desk if I could see Mina.

"She was brought in last night. The James Street incident."

She looked at a penciled and crossed-over roster. "I don't show an admission by that name."

"I'm certain she was brought here," I said, twisting my head round to read the list. "There isn't another St. George's, is there?"

She shook her head and lifted up the roster to look at a second sheet.

"Here she is," she said, and I had heard the rescue squads use that tone of voice often enough to know what it meant, but that was impossible. She had been under that headboard. The blood on her nightgown hadn't even been hers.

"I'm so sorry," the sister said.

"When did she die?" I said.

"This morning," she said, checking the second list, which was much longer than the first.

"Did anyone else come to see her?"

"I don't know. I've just been on since eleven."

"What did she die of?"

She looked at me as if I was insane.

"What was the listed cause of death?" I said.

She had to find Mina's name on the roster again. "Shock due to loss of blood," she said, and I thanked her and went to find Jack.

He found me. I had gone back to the post and waited till everyone was asleep and Mrs. Lucy had gone upstairs and then sneaked into the pantry to look up Jack's address in Mrs. Lucy's files. It had not been there, as I had known it wouldn't. And if there had been an address, what would it have turned out to be when I went to find it? A gutted house? A mound of rubble?

I had gone to Sloane Square Station, knowing he wouldn't be there, but having no other place to look. He could have been anywhere. London was full of empty houses, bombed-out cellars, secret places to hide until it got dark. That was why he had come here.

"If I was a bad'n, I'd head straight for London," Swales had said. But the criminal element weren't the only ones who had come, drawn by the blackout and the easy pickings and the bodies. Drawn by the blood.

I stood there until it started to get dark, watching two boys scrabble in the gutter for sweets that had been blown out of a newsagent's front window, and then walked back to a doorway down the street from the post, where I could see the door, and waited. The sirens went. Swales left on patrol. Petersby went in. Morris came out, stopping to peer at the sky as if he were looking for his son Quincy. Mrs. Lucy must not have managed to talk Nelson out of the patrols.

It got dark. The searchlights began to criss-cross the sky, catching the silver of the barrage balloons. The planes started coming in from the east, a low hum. Vi hurried in, wearing high heels and carrying a box tied with string. Petersby and Twickenham left on patrol. Vi came out, fastening her helmet strap under her chin and eating something.

"I've been looking for you everywhere," Jack said.

I turned around. He had driven up in a lorry marked ATS. He had left the door open and the motor running. "I've got the beams," he said. "For reinforcing the post. The incident we were on last night, all these beams were lying on top, and I asked the owner of the house if I could buy them from him."

He gestured to the back of the lorry, where jagged ends of wood were sticking out. "Come along then, we can get them up tonight if we hurry." He started toward the truck. "Where were you? I've looked everywhere for you."

"I went to St. George's Hospital," I said.

He stopped, his hand on the open door of the truck.

"Mina's dead," I said, "but you knew that, didn't you?"

He didn't say anything.

"The nurse said she died of loss of blood," I said. A flare drifted down, lighting his face with a deadly whiteness. "I know what you are."

"If we hurry, we can get the reinforcements up before the raid starts," he said. He started to pull the door to.

I put my hand on it to keep him from closing it. "War work," I said bitterly. "What do you do, make sure you're alone in the tunnel with them or go to see them in hospital afterward?"

He let go of the door.

"Brilliant stroke, volunteering for the ARP," I said. "Nobody's going to suspect the noble air-raid warden, especially when he's so good at locating casualties. And if some of those casualties die later, if somebody's found dead on the street after a raid, well, it's only to be expected. There's a war on."

The drone overhead got suddenly louder, and a whole shower of flares came down. The searchlights wheeled, trying to find the planes. Jack took hold of my arm.

"Get down," he said, and tried to drag me into the doorway.

I shook his arm off. "I'd kill you if I could," I said. "But I can't, can I?" I waved my hand at the sky. "And neither can they. Your sort don't die, do they?"

There was a long swish, and the rising scream. "I *will* kill you, though," I shouted over it. "If you touch Vi or Mrs. Lucy."

"Mrs. Lucy," he said, and I couldn't tell if he said it with astonishment or contempt.

"Or Vi or any of the rest of them. I'll drive a stake through your heart or whatever it takes," I said, and the air fell apart.

There was a long sound like an enormous monster growling. It seemed to go on and on. I tried to put my hands over my ears, but I had to hang onto the road to keep from falling. The roar became a scream, and the pavement shook itself sharply, and I fell off.

"Are you all right?" Jack said.

I was sitting next to the lorry, which was on its side. The beams had spilled out the back. "Were we hit?" I said.

"No," he said, but I already knew that, and before he had finished pulling me to my feet, I was running toward the post that we couldn't see for the dust.

Mrs. Lucy had told Nelson having everyone out on patrol would mean no one could be found in an emergency, but that was not true. They were all there within minutes, Swales and Morris and Violet, clattering up in her high heels, and Petersby. They ran up, one after the other, and then stopped and looked stupidly at the space that had been Mrs. Lucy's house, as if they couldn't make out what it was.

"Where's Renfrew?" Jack said.

"In Birmingham," Vi said.

"He wasn't here," I explained. "He's on sick leave." I peered through the smoke and dust, trying to see their faces.

"Where's Twickenham?"

"Here," he said.

"Where's Mrs. Lucy?" I said.

"Over here," Jack said, and pointed down into the rubble. We dug all night. Two different rescue squads came to help. They called down every half-hour, but there was no answer. Vi borrowed a light from somewhere, draped a blue headscarf over it, and set up as incident officer. An ambulance came, sat awhile, left to go to another incident, came back. Nelson took over as incident officer, and Vi came back up to help. "Is she alive?" she asked.

"She'd better be," I said, looking at Jack.

It began to mist. The planes came over again, dropping flares and incendiaries, but no one stopped work. Twickenham's typewriter came up in the baskets, and one of Mrs. Lucy's wine glasses. It began to get light. Jack looked vaguely up at the sky.

"Don't even think about it," I said. "You're not going anywhere."

At around three Morris thought he heard something, and we stopped and called down, but there was no answer. The mist turned into a drizzle. At half-past four I shouted to Mrs. Lucy, and she called back, from far underground, "I'm here."

"Are you all right?" I shouted.

"My leg's hurt. I think it's broken," she shouted, her voice calm. "I seem to be under the table."

"Don't worry," I shouted. "We're nearly there."

The drizzle turned the plaster dust into a slippery, disgusting mess. We had to brace the tunnel repeatedly and cover it with a tarpaulin, and then it was too dark to see to dig. Swales lay above us, holding a pocket torch over our heads so we could see. The all-clear went.

"Jack!" Mrs. Lucy called up.

"Yes!" I shouted.

"Was that the all-clear?"

"Yes," I shouted. "Don't worry. We'll have you out soon now."

"What time is it?"

It was too dark in the tunnel to see my watch. I made a guess. "A little after five."

"Is Jack there?"

"Yes."

"He mustn't stay," she said. "Tell him to go home."

The rain stopped. We ran into one and then another of the oak beams that had reinforced the landing on the fourth floor and had to saw through them. Swales reported that Morris had called Nelson "a bloody murderer." Vi brought us paper cups of tea.

We called down to Mrs. Lucy, but there wasn't any answer. "She's probably dozed off," Twickenham said, and the others nodded as if they believed him.

We could smell the gas long before we got to her, but Jack kept on digging, and like the others, I told myself that she was all right, that we would get to her in time.

She was not under the table after all, but under part of the pantry door. We had to call for a jack to get it off her. It took Morris a long time to come back with it, but it didn't matter. She was lying perfectly straight, her arms folded across her chest and her eyes closed as if she were asleep. Her left leg had been taken off at the knee. Jack knelt beside her and cradled her head.

"Keep your hands off her," I said.

I made Swales come down and help get her out. Vi and Twickenham put her on the stretcher. Petersby went for the ambulance. "She was never a horrid person, you know," Morris said. "Never."

It began to rain again, the sky so dark it was impossible to tell whether the sun had come up yet or not. Swales brought a tarp to cover Mrs. Lucy.

Petersby came back. "The ambulance has gone off again," he said. "I've sent for the mortuary van, but they said they doubt they can be here before half past eight."

I looked at Jack. He was standing over the tarp, his hands slackly at his sides. He looked worse than Renfrew ever had, impossibly tired, his face gray with wet plaster dust. "We'll wait," I said.

"There's no point in all of us standing here in the rain for two hours," Morris said. "I'll wait here with the . . . I'll wait here. Jack," he turned to him, "go and report to Nelson."

"I'll do it," Vi said. "Jack needs to get to his day job."

"Is she up?" Nelson said. He clambered over the fourth-floor beams to where we were standing. "Is she dead?" He glared at Morris and then at my hat, and I wondered if he were going to reprimand me for the condition of my uniform.

554 / *Connie Willis*

"Which of you found her?" he demanded.

I looked at Jack. "Settle did," I said. "He's a regular wonder. He's found six this week alone."

Two days after Mrs. Lucy's funeral, a memo came through from Civil Defense transferring Jack to Nelson's post, and I got my official notice to report for duty. I was sent to basic training and then on to Portsmouth. Vi sent me food packets, and Twickenham posted me copies of his *Twitterings*.

The post had relocated across the street from the butcher's in a house belonging to a Miss Arthur, who had subsequently joined the post. "Miss Arthur loves knitting and flower arranging and will make a valuable addition to our brave little band," Twickenham had written. Vi had got engaged to a pilot in the RAF. Hitler had bombed Birmingham. Jack, in Nelson's post now, had saved sixteen people in one week, a record for the ARP.

After two weeks I was shipped to North Africa, out of the reach of the mails. When I finally got Morris's letter, it was three months old. Jack had been killed while rescuing a child at an incident. A delayed-action bomb had fallen nearby, but "that bloody murderer Nelson" had refused to allow the rescue squad to evacuate. The DA had gone off, the tunnel Jack was working in had collapsed, and he'd been killed. They had gotten the child out, though, and she was unhurt except for a few cuts.

But he isn't dead, I thought. *It's impossible to kill him.* I had tried, but even betraying him to von Nelson hadn't worked, and he was still somewhere in London, hidden by the blackout and the noise of the bombs and the number of dead bodies, and who would notice a few more?

In January I helped take out a tank battalion at Tobruk. I killed nine Germans before I caught a piece of shrapnel. I was shipped to Gibraltar to hospital, where the rest of my mail caught up with me. Vi had got married, the raids had let up considerably, Jack had been awarded the George Cross posthumously.

In March I was sent back to hospital in England for surgery. It was near North Weald, where Morris's son Quincy was stationed. He came to see me after the surgery. He looked the very picture of a RAF pilot, firm-jawed, steely-eyed, rakish grin, not at all like a delinquent minor. He was flying nightly bombing missions over Germany, he told me, "giving Hitler a bit of our own back."

"I hear you're to get a medal," he said, looking at the wall above my head as if he expected to see violets painted there, nine of them, one for each kill.

I asked him about his father. He was fine, he told me. He'd been appointed Senior Warden. "I admire you ARP people," he said, "saving lives and all that."

He meant it. He was flying nightly bombing missions over Germany, reducing their cities to rubble, creating incidents for their air-raid wardens to scrabble through looking for dead children. I wondered if they had body-sniffers there, too, and if they were monsters like Jack.

"Dad wrote to me about your friend Jack," Quincy said. "It must have been rough, hearing so far away from home and all."

He looked genuinely sympathetic, and I supposed he was. He had shot down twenty-eight planes and killed who knows how many fat women in hairnets and thirteen-year-old girls, but no one had ever thought to call him a monster. The Duchess of York had called him the pride of England and kissed him on both cheeks.

"I went with Dad to Vi Westren's wedding," he said. "Pretty as a picture she was."

I thought of Vi, with her pincurls and her plain face. It was as though the war had transformed her into someone completely different, someone pretty and sought-after.

"There were strawberries and two kinds of cake," he said. "One of the wardens—Tottenham?—read a poem in honor of the happy couple. Wrote it himself."

It was as if the war had transformed Twickenham as well, and Mrs. Lucy, who had been the terror of the churchwardens. What the War Has Done for Us. But it hadn't transformed them. All that was wanted was for someone to give Vi a bit of attention for all her latent sweetness to blossom. Every girl is pretty when she knows she's sought after.

Twickenham had always longed to be a writer. Nelson had always been a bully and a stickler, and Mrs. Lucy, in spite of what she said, had never been either. "Sometimes it takes something dreadful like a war for one to find one's proper job," she'd said.

Like Quincy, who had been, in spite of what Morris said, a bad boy, headed for a life of petty crime or worse, when the war came along. And suddenly his wildness and daring and "high spirits" were virtues, were just what was needed.

What the War Has Done For Us. Number Two. It has made jobs that didn't exist before. Like RAF pilot. Like post warden. Like body-sniffer.

"Did they find Jack's body?" I asked, though I knew the answer. *No*, Quincy would say, *we couldn't find it*, or *there was nothing left*.

"Didn't Dad tell you?" Quincy said with an anxious look at the transfusion bag hanging above the bed. "They had to dig past him to get to the little girl. It was pretty bad, Dad said. The blast from the DA had driven the leg of a chair straight through his chest."

So I had killed him after all. Nelson and Hitler and I.

"I shouldn't have told you that," Quincy said, watching the blood drip from the bag into my veins as if it were a bad sign. "I know he was a friend of yours. I wouldn't have told you only Dad said to tell you yours was the last name he said before he died. Just before the DA went up. 'Jack,' he said, like he knew what was going to happen, Dad said, and called out your name."

He didn't though, I thought. And "that bloody murderer Nelson" hadn't refused to evacuate him. Jack had just gone on working, oblivious to Nelson and the DA, stabbing at the rubble as though he were trying to murder it, calling out "saw" and "wire cutters" and "braces." Calling out "jack." Oblivious to everything except getting them out before the gas killed them, before they bled to death. Oblivious to everything but his job.

I had been wrong about why he had joined the ARP, about why he had come to London. He must have lived a terrible life up there in Yorkshire, full of darkness and self-hatred and killing. When the war came, when he began reading of people buried in the rubble, of rescue wardens searching blindly for them, it must have seemed a godsend. A blessing.

It wasn't, I think, that he was trying to atone for what he'd done, for what he was. It's impossible, at any rate. I had only killed ten people, counting Jack, and had helped rescue nearly twenty, but it doesn't cancel out. And I don't think that was what he wanted. What he had wanted was to be useful.

"Here's to making the best of a bad job," Mrs. Lucy had said, and that was all any of them had been doing: Swales with his jokes and gossip, and Twickenham, and Jack, and if they found friendship or love or atonement as well, it was no less than they deserved. And it was still a bad job.

"I should be going," Quincy said, looking worriedly at me. "You need your rest, and I need to be getting back to work. The German army's halfway to Cairo, and Yugoslavia's joined the Axis." He looked excited, happy. "You must rest, and get well. We need you back in this war."

"I'm glad you came," I said.

"Yes, well, Dad wanted me to tell you that about Jack calling for you." He stood up. "Tough luck, your getting it in the neck like this." He slapped his flight cap against his leg. "I hate this war," he said, but he was lying.

"So do I," I said.

"They'll have you back killing Jerries in no time," he said.

"Yes."

He put his cap on at a rakish angle and went off to bomb lecherous retired colonels and children and widows who had not yet managed to get reinforcing beams out of the Hamburg Civil Defense and paint violets on his plane. Doing his bit.

A sister brought in a tray. She had a large red cross sewn to the bib of her apron.

"No, thanks, I'm not hungry," I said.

"You must keep your strength up," she said. She set the tray beside the bed and went out.

"The war's been rather a blessing for our Vi," I had told Jack, and perhaps it was. But not for most people. Not for girls who worked at John Lewis for old stewpots who never let them leave early even when the sirens had gone. Not for those people who discovered hidden capabilities for insanity or betrayal or bleeding to death. Or murder.

The sirens went. The nurse came in to check my transfusion and take the tray away. I lay there for a long time, watching the blood come down into my arm.

"Jack," I said, and didn't know who I called out to, or if I had made a sound.

Vampyr

Jane Yolen

Jane Yolen has been called "America's Hans Christian Andersen" (*Newsweek*) and "the Aesop of the 20th Century" (*New York Times*). With more than 360 books to her credit, she is a two-time Nebula Award winner and a recipient of the Caldecott Medal, The Catholic Library Association's Regina Medal (for her contribution to children's literature), the World Fantasy Award for Life Achievement, and the Science Fiction Grand Master of Poetry, as well as the 2017 recipient of SFWA's Damon Knight Grand Master award.

In 1991 she coedited the anthology *Vampires* with Martin H. Greenberg, and she has contributed tales of the undead to other anthologies such as *Blood Muse* and *Sisters of the Night*, as well as a vampire story in *Asimov's Science Fiction* magazine (in collaboration with Robert J. Harris). Among her more recent titles are the young adult novels *The Seelie King's War* and graphic novel *Stone Cold*, both written in collaboration with her musician son, Adam Stemple.

"My only insight about vampires is that they suck," explains the writer. "This poem was written with a melody in my head (I was writing songs for Boiled in Lead at the time, as well as for the Flash Girls and Lui Collins), but the melody has gone away."

We stalk the dark,
Live in the flood.
We take the madness
In the blood.

A moment's prick,
A minute's pain
And then we live
To Love Again.

Drink the night.
Rue the day.

We hear the beat
Beneath the breast.
We sip the wine
That fills the chest.

A moment's prick,
A minute's pain.
Our living is not
Just in vein.

    Drink the night,
    Rue the day.

We do not shrink
From blood's dark feast.
We take the man,
We leave the beast.

A moment's prick,
A minute's pain.
We live to love
To live again.

    Drink the night,
    Rue the day.

Acknowledgments

Special thanks for their help and support in compiling this volume to Herman Graf, Kim Lim, Tina Rath, Stefan Dziemianowicz, Sara Broecker, Kim Newman, Ellen Datlow, The Author's Guild, Mandy Slater, Ellen Datlow, Jo Fletcher, Roger MacBride Allen, John Clute, Robert L. Fleck, Krystyna Green, Nick Robinson, and, of course, the incomparable Ingrid Pitt.

About the Editor

Stephen Jones lives in London, England. A Hugo Award nominee, he is the winner of four World Fantasy Awards, three International Horror Guild Awards, five Bram Stoker Awards, twenty-one British Fantasy Awards, and a Lifetime Achievement Award from the Horror Writers Association. One of Britain's most acclaimed horror and dark fantasy writers and editors, he has more than 140 books to his credit, including *The Art of Horror Movies: An Illustrated History*, the film books of Neil Gaiman's *Coraline* and *Stardust*, *The Illustrated Monster Movie Guide* and *The Hellraiser Chronicles*; the non-fiction studies *Horror: 100 Best Books* and *Horror: Another 100 Best Books* (both with Kim Newman); the single-author collections *Necronomicon* and *Eldritch Tales* by H. P. Lovecraft, *The Complete Chronicles of Conan* and *Conan's Brethren* by Robert E. Howard, and *Curious Warnings: The Great Ghost Stories of M.R. James*; plus such anthologies as *Horrorology: The Lexicon of Fear*, *Fearie Tales: Stories of the Grimm and Gruesome*, *A Book of Horrors*, *The Mammoth Book of Vampires*, *The Lovecraft Squad*, and *Zombie Apocalypse!* series, and twenty-eight volumes of *Best New Horror*. You can visit his web site at www.stephenjoneseditor.com or follow him on Facebook at "Stephen Jones-Editor."